A DANCE in BLOOD VELVET

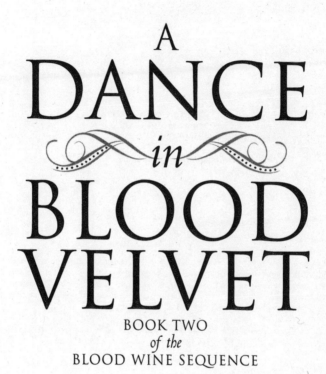

BOOK TWO
of the
BLOOD WINE SEQUENCE

FREDA WARRINGTON

TITAN BOOKS

A Dance in Blood Velvet
Print edition ISBN: 9781781167069
E-book edition ISBN: 9781781167267

Published by Titan Books
A division of Titan Publishing Group Ltd
144 Southwark Street, London SE1 0UP
www.titanbooks.com

First edition: April 2014

1 3 5 7 9 10 8 6 4 2

Did you enjoy this book? We love to hear from our readers.
Please email us at: readerfeedback@titanemail.com

To receive advance information, news, competitions, and exclusive
offers online, please sign up for the Titan newsletter on our website:
TITANBOOKS.COM

A
DANCE
in
BLOOD
VELVET

BOOK TWO
of the
BLOOD WINE SEQUENCE

CONTENTS

This book is dedicated to all our friends in Canada, old and new, with love and thanks for wonderful times.

CARNIVAL OF ICE

A vampire woke, not knowing where or who he was.

He was lying in a blazing white tomb. Yet the tomb seemed infinite... an endless drift of snow roofed by the heavens. A gale lifted ice crystals, sweeping them in shimmering ribbons towards the blurred fringes of the plain. Arms of white mist enfolded him. The cold was absolute, but the vampire barely felt it. He was sure he'd been there forever.

Beneath a crust of ice, his body was a dark, papery husk, burned black not by fire, but by the cold itself.

Why was he suddenly aware? What was this place?

Panic. Something had disturbed him. A command, a voice in his mind. "*Wake, wake.*"

Must obey... The vampire feared that if he moved, he would shatter into ash, but the demand was imperative. Someone was willing him awake with their last wisp of strength, their dying breath.

And the voice said, "*Wake. Take revenge. Don't let them forget me. You are my children. I commanded you to sleep and now I command you to wake!*"

A shiver of terror went through the vampire. Against his own judgment, he flexed his arms. Excruciating pain cracked his limbs. He convulsed with shock, bringing more pain. His whole body was shattering...

No. It was only the carapace of ice falling away. The vampire examined his naked body in disbelief. Dusty black, dragonfly-fragile, draped with false wings like torn cobwebs: he was a scrap of black lace on snow.

The sun, a bleached coin, seared him with its frigid light. The sky was a blue-black shell, pricked by fire. He saw the whorls of countless galaxies, huge ringed planets. The vampire opened his mouth and cried with awe.

How did I come to be here? Help help help…

Crystals scratched his skin like grit as he began to crawl forwards. The pain of returning to life was unbearable. An image flashed in his mind… A dark-haired woman watched a man pacing around a room in agitation… the scene must have been significant but he couldn't grasp its meaning. He sobbed and crawled on.

No concept of time. His tortuous progress across the snow was eternal. *Nightmare… Help… I'm dead and in hell…* Then another memory-fragment.

A book of poetry lay open in front of him. A large hand slammed down on the page and a portentous voice declaimed, "Human poetry? Worthless, Andreas. Look on the face of God!"

Gone. But the vampire clung to the name. *Andreas, I'm Andreas…*

Then the snow crust gave way and he fell.

Beneath him was… nothingness. An infinite sky. He flailed in terror, but his torn-cobweb wings were useless.

Tumbling through clouds of ice-flakes, Andreas had the impression of other vampires around him. Faint shadow-crosses on the mist, spiralling along their own paths. Illusion? Even if they were real, he couldn't reach them. Each one was alone in this strange, dense ocean of air.

This isn't the world… but where am I? Heaven or hell, or…

As he left the white plains far above, the light dimmed to rich blue, then to stormy violet brushed with red flame… Andreas gasped, distracted from fear. The sky was full of gorgeous colours. Cloud-mountains sailed through the air below him. His descent slowed. A current took his weightless body, and he floated face down above peaks that rolled like slow ocean-waves. Their valleys were bottomless, painted crimson by fire. Hell lay below him. His skin – fossil-cold for an eternity – began to prickle with unbearable heat.

Silent scream. *Help help help...*

Another fragment, without context.

A parlour, all fine furniture and oriental rugs. The same two figures were dark against the firelight. Yet how pale was their skin, how radiant! Vampires. And he knew them, hated and loved them... if he could only remember who they were...

"I can't endure this!" said the man. "Kristian killed my wife and expects me to love him for it!"

Andreas was present, part of the scene. He heard himself say, "Karl, take the easy way. Pretend you love him, as we do."

"You're frightened of him," Karl said darkly – *that's it, this was Karl, beloved Karl...*

"No," lied Andreas. "I'm lazy."

Then the woman spoke. *Dear God, what was her name, this chestnut-haired enchantress?*

"If you disobey Kristian, he'll put you in the *Weisskalt*."

Weisskalt... a place of hideous winter and everlasting sleep.

She went to Karl and touched his arm. "Karl, if Andrei and I defy Kristian and stay with you, he's sure to find out."

"Well?" said Karl. "What will you do? You could reject me, as Ilona has. Make Kristian believe you hate me. I'd rather you and Andrei saved yourselves, Katti, than –"

"Never." The woman embraced Karl, holding him tight. "Never."

That was her name! Katerina. The vampire clutched at the scene but it vanished, leaving the merest shimmer of understanding.

Kristian had found them out, and punished them. That was the last Andreas could recall... Kristian's huge silhouette. *Kristian, who gave me immortality then took it away – twice, because I wrote no more poetry after the transformation. Took me away and imprisoned me in the* Weisskalt.

He remembered Katti's screams. Helpless despair.

Strangely, the pain of the *Weisskalt* had not lasted long. Once the cold bit into his brain, Andreas felt nothing... only faintly aware as he lay beneath the pitiless Eye of God for years...

Years. His teeth chattered with horror. He almost laughed.

Kristian put me to sleep, so it follows that Kristian woke me... Again, the voice vibrated in Andreas's head. *"Wake! I send you as the envoys of Almighty God to avenge me!"*

11

Andreas drifted on through the firmament. Panic remained a dull whine within him. He wished to die, but his consciousness persisted.

The call came like a butterfly-shiver of the ether. It wasn't Kristian's harsh tone but a different pull, tentative yet insistent. Andreas felt the vibration catch him and draw him downwards towards the ruby fires of hell. Although the summons was weak, he had no strength to resist.

Cloud-mountains swallowed him. Grim twilight rushed up. He strained his tormented eyes, but all was as dense as soot. Then, with a wrench, he felt the very world turn inside out.

Oh God, Katti, where are you? Help, help...

He became aware of a ghastly change in his body. No longer weightless, he felt heavy, cumbersome, malformed inside his skin.

Darts of memory pierced the chaos. Something pale twitched in the darkness. His own hands! No longer black and ethereal, they were corpse-white and heavy.

God. Human hands!

Andreas was lying on a hard surface in thick, hot darkness. His eyelids flickered as he strained to see, discovering that this place made no more sense than the realm from which he'd materialised. Corridors of mirrors stretched in every direction, endlessly reflecting a purple splash of light.

Pungent smoke shocked his senses.

But through the incense wove a richer scent that set his frozen form burning with need.... He had to reach the source of the aroma, had to seize and bite and drink...

"It worked!" hissed a stupefied male voice. "Great God Almighty, I don't believe it! Holly –"

Two figures in hooded lavender robes stood before him. Their reflections stretched away through the limbo of mirrors. The smaller figure craned forwards, staring down at Andreas through the eyeholes of a mask.

"It looks dead." The woman's voice was thick with revulsion. "Get rid of it, Ben."

"Not yet." The man sounded both horrified and madly excited. "We did it! We brought something through."

"But this isn't what we wanted!"

Ignoring her, the man took a step towards Andreas. The

blood-scent became unbearable. A thin dry groan filled the air... the vampire wished it would stop, not realising it came from his own throat.

"Can you hear me?" said the man. "I am Benedict. Do you understand? Can you speak?"

The vampire was confused. The man had an incredible aura of power... yet he was only a mortal, the source of the delicious salty heat. With effort, Andreas pushed himself up onto his hands. The man and woman both gasped, caught between fascination and fear.

The vampire did not see them as *people*, full of passions and hopes; he saw them only as swollen vessels of blood. They drew him with an urgent promise of warmth, nourishment, everything he craved...

"Banish it, Ben!" the woman cried. "Now!"

Propelled by unnatural strength, the vampire leapt.

The man raised his hands in self-defence – and vanished. Another realm rushed in, throwing Andreas through dizzying tunnels. At last he came to rest, paralysed, his mind blank within a screaming tornado of thirst.

Dull shapes leaned over him like a nightmare forest. He was in the otherworld again, while the world of humans hovered a breath away, just out of his reach. *That man Benedict did this to me,* he thought. *Tortured me with the scent of his blood, then pushed me back into this half-death! Katerina, Karl, help me...*

There was no one to hear him. No one to care if he lay on the edge of death forever. But now his fear had two companions. Burning thirst, and rage.

PART ONE

In my dreams I see a carnival of ice
You're wearing white and pirouette so nice
When I stop to ask the nature of surprise
A veil of contradiction is slipped before my eyes

Death is a ring-a-ring-a-rosey
You never reach the end
Ring-a-ring-a-rosary
I'll pray for you, my friend

HORSLIPS, "RING-A-ROSEY"

CHAPTER ONE

THE BLOOD-CRYSTAL RING

He knew only her first name: Charlotte.

When he'd first met her at the concert, she seemed an averagely pretty young woman; medium height, slim rather than fashionably thin, nothing extraordinary. Her hair colour was difficult to define; a warm brown in shadow, the slightest ray of light drew out gleams of pure gold. And then she'd smiled, and her subtle beauty had first begun to enchant, then to obsess him.

Her name, the face in the photograph he carried: too much of a coincidence. Milner was convinced she was the woman he'd been sent to find.

And now – one week since their first meeting – he was alone with her in the moonlight, walking up a long, steep forest path to her house. They'd had to leave his car at the bottom of the hill. Although he considered himself fit for a man in his thirties, he was perspiring long before they reached the top.

"My goodness, you have this walk every time you go out?" he gasped, wiping his forehead.

Charlotte looked cool and not at all breathless, despite her evening coat and fur stole. "It's impossible to get a motor up here. We don't mind; we like the solitude. I'm only sorry that it's inconvenient for our guests... Not that we have many. Do you want to rest a moment?"

Looking up, he saw a chalet through the pines, a shadowy-black structure with overhanging eaves, white window-frames and flowers along the balconies.

"No, no, I'm fine," he insisted.

"Well, we're almost there," she said, striding on without effort. She led him inside, hung up his coat with hers and lit a lamp. Even in these simple actions she was magically graceful. Milner found it impossible not to appreciate the way her silky dress clung to her hips. The soft warm colours suited her; creamy-gold and clover shades, trimmed with old gold lace and tiny beads of bronze glass.

The chalet's dark-wood interior was full of unlit alcoves. No electric lights, only golden-dim lamps and candles that she lit as she went. She led him to a reception room, where he stood trying to recover his breath while she rekindled the fire.

The house felt still and quiet. Fire-glow licked the dull-pink roses of the wallpaper – a cosy English touch – but failed to reach the rustic beamed ceiling. He noted French doors onto a balcony, and, near the fireplace, an archway to a darkened library. Milner found himself repeatedly glancing in there, like a child waiting for some monster to leap from behind the bookshelves.

He had no idea why he was so jumpy, so feverishly excited.

Charlotte was moving around the room, drawing curtains, winding up a gramophone. No servants? The mournful tones of *Death and the Maiden* wound softly around them as she came to him and placed a glass of whisky in his hand.

"Would you like a cigarette?" she asked.

He had noticed she didn't smoke. He needed one to relax him, but was worried she mightn't like the smell – why did that matter?

"No, no thank you."

"Won't you sit down, Mr Milner?"

He sat where she indicated, in a chair by the fire. He couldn't take his eyes off her. She looked girlish and innocent, but solemn, haunted.

"This is too kind of you, Mrs – or should I say Frau –"

"Just Charlotte," she said with a brief smile. How her face lit up when she smiled.

Ah, embarrassment over her marital status, he thought. *She's choosing to be discreet, rather than lie.*

"Well, then, you mustn't call me 'Mr'. It's John," he said, feeling awkward. "Isn't your – er – the gentleman at home?"

"Not at the moment. I don't expect Karl back for quite some time."

The way she looked at him sent a rush of heat to his face. *My God, would she really proposition me while her lover is off the scene?* Though her morals appalled him, he turned dizzy with excitement.

She knelt and prodded the fire. Sparks roared up, outlining her with liquid red-gold light. *God, she is so lovely.* He gripped the whisky glass hard on his thigh to stop his hand shaking.

He said, "So, er, I trust you enjoyed the opera tonight?"

"Very much. And it's so kind of you to escort me while Karl is away. But I have a confession to make."

"Yes?" Milner swallowed.

She turned with the poker in her hand. "I prefer the ballet."

At last, a safe topic of conversation; she left him damned near speechless. "You've seen the Ballets Russes? Pavlova?"

"Yes, at every chance." He found her manner strange, almost abrupt, as if she disliked making small talk for the sake of it.

"And Ballet Janacek?"

"Not yet."

"Well, you simply must. Their *Giselle* is on a par with anything of the Ballets Russes. Wonderful prima ballerina."

She didn't respond. The silence purred like static. *I never dreamed this would be so difficult!* he thought. *Must say something.* "It's most kind of you to invite me here, Frau – Charlotte, but –"

"You expressed interest in seeing Karl's Stradivarius cello," she said. "Don't you wish to see it?"

"Good God, yes, of course," he said too enthusiastically, sitting forward. "I should say so. It's so good of you to –"

He broke off, because of the way she was gazing at him. Challenging him with wide, clear eyes.

"Well, it isn't why I asked you here," she said. "And it's not really why you came, is it?"

He gulped a mouthful of whisky and nearly choked as it burned its way down.

"What do you mean?"

"There is something on your mind, but it isn't music, or art, or anything in which you professed to share our interest when Karl and I met you last week. You are too friendly, then, when you think no one's watching, your face changes and your eyes go cold. Taking everything in, like a policeman."

Her words were so close to the truth that he couldn't gloss over them. The scene he'd envisaged was falling apart. She saw through him, and his desire for her was clouding his judgment. *A story, quick, think of a story. Then, maybe… well, why did she invite me here, alone?*

He cleared his throat. "Can you read my mind?" he said lightly.

"No, or I wouldn't be asking." Her voice was low and serious.

His imagination, never powerful, deserted him. The way Charlotte's large, deep-lidded eyes bore into him made him feel guilty, as if he were trying to deceive a child whose perception and intelligence were greater than his own.

And she was armed with a red-hot poker. There was nothing for it but the truth.

"Is your name Charlotte Millward?"

She stiffened visibly as he spoke. "No. I never use that name."

"Then do you use the name Neville, or von Wultendorf?"

The look in her eyes showed he was not mistaken. How was it possible for her sweet face to fill him with such unease?

"You had better tell me who in hell you are," she said.

John Milner reached into his pocket and took out the letter. He hadn't sealed the envelope because he'd intended to write more after this encounter. With a resigned sigh he passed her the top page. Still kneeling, she replaced the poker in its stand and read aloud, her voice soft and puzzled,

Dear David,

Wonderful news at last! I am ninety-nine per cent certain that I've found your sister. Can't claim brilliant detective work, just hard slog. I located her through a mixture of educated guesswork and luck.

No joy in Vienna; as we thought, the chap wouldn't be so obvious as to go back to his hometown. Still, I had a feeling he wouldn't stray far. I tried Prague, Budapesth, Rome. You said he claimed to have been a cellist, and that they both liked music, so I've been to concerts until the damned stuff is coming out of my ears. Finally, in Switzerland, eureka! Concert in Berne last week, I saw a girl in the foyer who was the image of the photograph you gave me. Your description of her companion clinched it; striking fellow, had all the ladies turning their heads. It was remarkably easy to get talking to them. No apparent attempt at hiding their identities; they gave no surname, very little personal information – hence the tiny doubt – but they openly called each other Karl and Charlotte and gave the impression they lived in the locality.

So, to answer your first question, yes, they are still together. Your sister is charming. So is the man, though I confess he's also oddly unnerving. Difficult to explain, but I now understand why you warned me to be careful. However, your sister showed no fear of him. Seemed quite the perfect couple. That might not be what you hoped to hear, but it may at least set your mind at rest.

I dared not appear too pushy in case they grew suspicious, but as we parted, I invited them to an opera this coming Saturday. Charlotte expressed interest. Karl said he'd be otherwise occupied, yet seemed happy for Charlotte to be escorted by me – a man they'd only just met! Odd. Still, fingers crossed she'll turn up and I'll have more to share with you.

While I know you didn't intend to tell –

Charlotte stopped. She'd reached the bottom of the page. "Where is the rest?"

Milner waved the second page uneasily. "I was going to finish after I'd spoken to you."

She looked stunned, and he was desperately sorry he'd distressed her so much. *God, if only things were different and I could draw her down onto the Persian carpet...* But her face was like ice.

"I can't believe it. I thought David had accepted this and let me go. Why – why would he hire a stranger to look for me?"

"I'm not a stranger. I've known your brother for years. I was with his regiment in the War. Afterwards, through a set of circumstances I won't bore you with, I became a private detective; nothing glamorous, just finding errant spouses, hanging around boarding houses in Brighton for evidence in adultery cases – you know the sort of thing?"

"No, I don't," Charlotte said thinly. "What in God's name did David tell you about me?"

"He got in touch out of the blue last year. He said that you'd left your husband – well, it would be eighteen months ago by now – and run off with another man whom he didn't seem to think at all suitable. He wanted me to find you."

"Why? To bring me back? He knows that's impossible." She leaned anxiously towards him, making his heart leap. "Is there news of my family? Bad news?"

"None that I know of. Your father isn't well, but I gather you knew that when you left. David didn't tell me much at all, to be honest. One shouldn't make assumptions, but it may be that your husband wants to initiate divorce proceedings…"

She sat back on her heels, staring at the fire. "That's in the past. I have no husband except Karl."

He continued gently, "Or it may be that David was simply worried and wanted to know you were safe."

Charlotte fell silent. He studied her neat profile, the enticing pink sheen of her mouth. Then she said, "He doesn't need to know. As far as he's concerned, I'm dead."

She rose fluidly to her feet, walked to the doors and went out onto the balcony.

Milner drained his whisky glass and set it down. It wasn't drink that made him light-headed. He was unreasonably glad that her "husband" wasn't here. For no rational reason, he dreaded meeting Karl again. At least his absence gave Milner a chance to mend things with Charlotte.

He followed her and stood in the doorway. "I'm sorry you've taken this so badly. You must be furious at me."

A gorgeous smell of pine filled the spring air. Light from inside outlined her form; the Alps and forest were iron-blue behind her. Charlotte was an indistinct yet perfect, elegant figure of the modern age. Thin straps on creamy shoulders, long pearls, her beaded dress sashed low across her hips, the casual drape of silk emphasising the allure of her breasts. Her long hair was gathered loosely at the nape of her neck.

Milner loved long hair. He hated the fashion for cropping it short. And Charlotte's hair was so beautiful, the glossy russet waves sprinkled with gold. Under a sequinned bandeau, her forehead was broad and pale, her eyes sea-grey.

"Why should I be angry with you?" she said.

"For deceiving you."

"You didn't deceive me. You aren't good enough at it. I like you, actually; I can see why David trusts you."

Her expression captivated him. She looked solemn, her deep-rose mouth turned down at the corners, her glorious eyes smouldering like those of an actress on film.

"I wish I could have bluffed it out," he said. "You don't want to be found, do you?"

"How perceptive," she murmured. Milner smiled. He felt a growing rapport between them, warmth swelling into magnetism. "And I won't be found. Come here."

She turned towards him, one hand on the balcony; open, receptive. So she had married one man, run off with another, and now while her lover was out she was trying to buy his silence with seduction! So what? She was lovely.

He went to her, drawn by the curve of her arms. More amethyst than grey, her eyes were expanding to fill his vision. Glittering. Was she crying?

"John," she said.

He put his arms around her. Christ, she was cold! "You don't have to do this," he said.

"But I want to."

"Come inside. You're freezing."

"Then warm me." Suddenly her voice trembled. "Warm me."

He bent to kiss her but she drew back, avoiding his lips. She opened her mouth as if in pain, and he saw how long and sharp her canine teeth were, seeming to lengthen as he watched. Even then he was too slow to understand.

"This is why he mustn't find me," she whispered. She dropped her face onto his shoulder and he felt her lips move against his neck. "This is why!" She was shuddering. The faintest groan came from her throat. "*Ohh...*"

And she bit him. Not playfully, not even in anger, but with an awful, hungry determination. Her teeth broke through the skin, piercing flesh and muscle and blood vessels. The pain was vicious, frightening, nightmarishly weird. Her mouth was a steel trap on his throat... A sick feeling spread from his stomach to fill his whole body with pins and needles. He was floating and the sensation was unbearable. He was dying.

Lights spun around him, dazzling and blinding. There was a deep, throaty roar all around him, the roar of the Devil as it came to claim his soul. The whole world slopped around him like floodwater. Only one thing remained clear and steady: the woman's face.

As lovely as the moon, her lips red with his blood, she looked sadly down at him. He clutched at her, but she pushed his hand away.

"I'll die..." he rasped.

"No, you won't," she said calmly.

"I'll die if I don't see you again."

She blinked, her eyes briefly shaded by her smoky lids and luxurious eyelashes. Then she whispered, "You will never see me again. You have never seen me at all. Forget me. Because if you ever tell David, or if you ever cross my path again, I'll kill you. I promise."

Who's David?

He couldn't even remember the woman's name. Who was she? She couldn't abandon him to the Devil who was storming through the night to take him.

"No. Don't go!" he cried, terrified.

She touched a luminous hand to his hair and said, "I'm sorry."

She drew away, watching him with sad affection. Then, like the moon passing behind a cloud, she vanished.

Sometimes Karl would drift through the Crystal Ring at ground level, lost in fascination that another dimension, fitting the Earth like a glove, could exist. A dream-realm that only vampires could enter. To vanish from mortal eyes, and walk unseen through their dwellings... Irresistible, even though reality became a warped ghost of itself, and the only light was a sinister, luminous twilight.

Houses, trees, every barrier gave like cobwebs to Karl's unearthly body. Even the mountains above the quiet town were like a crust of ash over a dead fire. Nothing was solid here.

Nothing could be trusted. At times Karl loathed the Crystal Ring, because it was terrifying, impossible to understand, and yet part of him. Part of the incomprehensible, twisted darkness that had made him a vampire.

For all the freedom the Ring gives us, he thought, *it exacts payment. No certainty, no comfort, no rest. I resent it because it demands love; and I love its wildness, its refusal to conform to any theory. Perhaps it is God. Perhaps the Devil. Or, as Charlotte asserts, the human subconscious made tangible.*

Karl, an eternal cynic, was more inclined to believe Charlotte than anyone.

It was painful to think too deeply, and unwise to keep asking, after all this time, why he'd been chosen to become undead: a creature who stood apart from humanity but needed them to feed his dark appetite. Pointless to worry what the same metamorphosis had done to Charlotte. They'd both known the cost of staying together.

Karl smiled, thinking of her. Hadn't their glorious, destructive love made any sacrifice worthwhile? Even the sacrifice of the victims Charlotte now needed? In truth, any vampire claiming a conscience was a hypocrite.

The strangest thing, he thought, *is that she hardly seems changed at all. She insists she's always been the same inside: amoral. It took only the vampire's kiss to bring her home. Yet I know she has changed, is still changing… how could it be otherwise? The look in her eyes, the way she is with her victims…*

Charlotte had wanted to meet the stranger, John Milner, again. Karl had not. *Was I wrong to let her go alone? To find out what he really wanted,* she said. *Only that.*

Karl moved slowly, thinking of Charlotte and taking little notice of his surroundings. He saw a human walking towards him through the real world; not solid, but a bright corona against the dim folds of the Ring. A signature of life written in crackling energy.

A second later, Karl knew he was being followed.

Held still by a rush of life-or-death peril, he was aware of some *thing* that seemed distant, but at the same time close and threatening. He felt presences, an impression of tall shadows watching him. Their gaze struck through his defences to stir a primeval fear that he thought had died with his humanity.

Instinct took over. Karl stepped out of the Ring, felt the world snap into solidity. He found himself in a narrow medieval street. A human cannoned into him and reeled away with a cry of shock.

A young man with spectacles, oiled hair, the dull look of a clerk about him, stood gaping at Karl, frozen.

Karl's fear dissipated as he cursed his own carelessness. Normally he would never step from the Ring in clear view of a mortal. It was unlike him to be alarmed by his own imagination, but the wretched man had a worse fright as he took in the vampire's gleaming skin and uncanny stillness with flat panic in his eyes. Karl regretted the situation, while still finding it faintly, horribly amusing.

The young clerk was backing up, angry now. Also embarrassed, as if caught slipping away from a guilty tryst. He said in Swiss German, "Good God, sir, you frightened the life out of me!"

Karl did not reply. He simply watched the man without emotion, as if watching a bird in a cage. He saw him as a core of frantic life, smelled his salty heat, heard the blood pulsing through his heart.

Karl's hands shot out and seized the clerk's shoulders. His coat felt rough, releasing scents of camphor and dust. He struggled ineffectually, without sound, like a comic actor in a film. At the same time, Karl was aware of lighted windows in the old houses, the babble of voices, the banal struggle of life continuing everywhere. Drizzle fell from a strip of wet, slaty sky. But through the soft rain of impressions, the only reality was the ruthless, throbbing heat of his thirst.

Charlotte spent an hour helping Mr Milner down the forest path and into his car, then driving him to a quiet street near his hotel in Interlaken. Returning to the chalet took minutes. She simply stepped into the Crystal Ring and arrowed back as if winged.

The drawing room coalesced around her. The fire still crackled and lights burned under their Tiffany shades. The man's smell lingered; a trace of tobacco, hair oil, whisky. And blood. Red stains dotted the carpet by the balcony doors.

She stared at the spots as if in a trance. Although his delicious blood-heat filled her, she couldn't bear to recall the way he'd looked at her afterwards: with a mixture of terror and obsession, as if she'd become his entire world.

Charlotte wondered how long his madness would last. She had liked him – almost loved him, as she took long exquisite sips of his blood. Although her bite had unhinged his mind, as a vampire's bite usually did, this didn't seem to matter. How was it possible to feel both tenderness and indifference, at the same time?

She went to the chair where he'd sat, and picked up both pages of the letter. Kneeling by the fire again, she read the rest.

While I know you didn't intend to tell your family of your search attempt, I've a feeling you might change your mind once I reassure you that she is (to all appearances) well and happy. Even if Dr Neville won't relent his decision to disown her, it may still have a beneficial effect on his health to know. Even if – from what you tell me of your father! – he won't admit it.

Anyway, my friend, it's your decision. I feel I'm very close to bringing you the good news you want to hear.

The letter ended there, halfway down the page.

Charlotte's hands fell to her lap with the letter held tight. She bowed her head and wept.

In heaven's name, David, why did you do this? You know what Karl is, and what he made me. You know I can never go back.

Her family had adored Karl, until they discovered the unholy truth of his nature. And for continuing to love him, for consenting to become like him, Charlotte had earned their rejection. She couldn't blame them, but it was against her will that she'd had to reject them in turn. Now to learn that David was trying to find her, that he still couldn't bear to give up, caused her anguish. News of her father's ill health was worse. She was partly, if not wholly, responsible. *How would it help him recover*, she thought, *to hear that I'm still with Karl?*

The price of being with Karl was to leave my human life behind. Oh, David, what good could come of you or Anne or Father seeing me again? Gods, why can't you let go... and why can't I?

But I can. I must.

She crumpled the letter and pushed it into the fire. Flames leapt. With the poker she worried at the paper until it was ash, black flakes spiralling up the chimney. Searing away another link with her family, as she must destroy every link until they were all gone.

Tears blurred the gleam of the red garnet on her wedding finger; the ring Karl had given her. "For eternity," he'd said. The blood-crystal ring that held her.

A year and a half they'd been together, though their mutual obsession had yet to fade into comfortable familiarity. How could it? The first time she had truly *seen* him, seen the incandescent beauty of danger – that moment sang in her mind forever. And she'd nearly lost him so many times. Now, whenever they were apart, there was always a tug of fear whispering, *you may never see him again.*

Then, blessedly, she realised she was not alone.

She sensed Karl's presence; not warm and messily radiant like a human, but night-dark and self-contained. He placed a hand on her hair.

"Charlotte," he said. "What is it?"

She sighed. Her tears had ended. Now she felt hollow. "It doesn't matter."

"Yes, it does. How can a piece of paper upset you so much that you burn it? Tell me."

Not a demand, only gentle concern. Karl had always been like this with her, before she knew he was a vampire and after. Incongruous, that he could be so kind. Part of his fascination, of course.

"A letter I couldn't allow to be sent." She rose to her feet, brushing crumbs of ash from her dress. They left grey trails, like tearstains. Not wanting to confess, she made to walk past, but he placed his hand on her shoulder. His fine, long fingers felt warm with stolen blood.

"Did you bring him here?"

A dart of apprehension. She wanted to forget everything in the warmth of Karl's arms, the ravenous pleasure of kisses. Instead she told him about John Milner and the letter.

As she spoke, Karl took pins from her hair and loosened the waves over her shoulders. She loved the touch of his hands. But he did so almost absently, his expression dark. His disapproval infuriated and distressed her. So lovely, his face; the fine bones of an aristocrat, the beauty of a renaissance saint, large, deep-amber eyes under dark brows. To see anything but love there was a knife through her heart. And if she did overreact passionately to everything about him, she didn't care; at least she knew she was alive and in love.

As she finished, he glanced at the balcony window. His full, soft hair, almost black in shadow, was sidelit by the fire to auburn and blood red. She knew he'd noticed blood spots on the carpet.

"You were seeing Mr Milner tonight to discover who he was. Not to feed on him."

"I didn't kill him!" she said. "I couldn't let him send the letter, or remember he'd met me. My family have to let me go, as I did them. Do you think I did the wrong thing?"

Karl paused. "It must have been hard for you, dearest. God knows, we are not made of stone."

"*But*," she said sharply. "I know what you're going to say."

"We agreed not to prey on guests. We should never feed in our own home. It's not necessary... and can be dangerous."

"Do you have to be so calm about this?" Charlotte flared. Since the day she became a vampire, there had been this conflict between them, never fully expressed. "Sometimes I wish you'd be angry with me, so I could argue back!"

"I've never noticed you have any difficulty arguing with me," Karl said drily.

"It's *your* rule, not to feed on people you know. What difference does it make if you know their name, or even feel affection for them?"

"Did you feel affection for this friend of David's?" Karl did not sound jealous. Sometimes she couldn't fathom his emotions at all, which frustrated her beyond reason.

"I liked him. Unlike you, I can't be impersonal!"

His reaction was measured, as always. "But why risk destroying people you like, or even love? We may not kill, but we cause untold damage that may be worse than death to some. And the more you feel for someone, the more dangerous. You know how close I came to destroying you. The more I loved and desired you, the greater the temptation of your blood. That's why I choose strangers: so that I don't betray someone who trusts me. And I know it solves nothing, makes me no less evil. But at least their faces do not follow me forever afterwards."

Charlotte couldn't answer.

Karl stroked her shoulders. "Yes, I agree you had to drink from Milner to cloud his mind; but is that why you did so? He was likeable, someone who would be a good friend to a mortal, such as David."

"Karl, stop this," Charlotte said, closing her eyes. "I can't help these feelings. I can't be perfect."

"I'm not asking that. I'm saying that if you drink from people you know, they will haunt you, in one way or another. You may never be free... neither physically, nor emotionally."

"Can't we even have human friends?"

"You know what happens!" said Karl. "You can never see them only as friends – and God knows, I have tried – without being aware of the blood under their skin, their cells changing with every moment they grow older."

Charlotte felt thirst clamp tight on her heart; an urge for more than blood. "But I want them. I need them."

"More than you want or need me?" Karl spoke lightly.

She broke away and sat on the edge of a chair. "Don't be infuriating. It's different, you know it is. Don't pretend not to understand!"

"Oh, I understand only too well." He spoke softly, but she heard many echoes in his voice: bitterness, empathy, regret, passion. "That's why I encourage you to think before these feelings overwhelm you."

"You imagine I don't *think*?" Charlotte retorted. "I wish I could stop!"

"But this is the point: the blood. It enables us to stop thinking. It's almost the only experience that obliterates our intellect for a few blissful minutes, isn't it so?"

Charlotte said nothing. She sat still, her gaze fixed on him.

Karl came to her, sat on the arm of the chair and put his hand over hers. "When you were human," he said quietly, "when I first knew you, all your attention and passion fastened on me. And I warned you it was for the wrong reasons."

"The glamour of vampires," she murmured. "No, always more than that."

"I know; but the magical veil drew us together so powerfully precisely because it threatened to keep us apart. Now the veil is gone, other forces are pulling you away from me. Inevitable, I know, but it still makes me sad."

She turned to him. His face was inches from hers, achingly beautiful, his hair a crimson halo. Ice-white danger to any human who came this close to him. His words unsettled her. She had to challenge them. "No, Karl, you're wrong." She touched her fingertips to his cheekbone. "You told me this wouldn't be easy. Every day I miss my family, and fight against what I've become, and hate myself for loving it so much. And you want me to be happy – yet you disapprove because I'm not tormented enough!"

Karl had the grace to look startled. Then he laughed. "Am I such a fiend?"

"Unbearable."

"But our debates are such a delicious pleasure," he said, "and such wonderful pain."

She wanted to be angry, but couldn't, because he was right. "My God," she said, "Karl, if I could for one moment make you understand what I feel for you – if I could find the words –"

They were moving towards each other, her hands sliding over his shoulders, his around her waist; each the predator, each the willing prey.

"There is something other than blood that saves us from thinking too much," said Karl, "and far sweeter than tormenting ourselves with words."

The bed under its shadowed canopy was never used for sleep.

On the cover their limbs shone with creamy luminescence in the darkness, moving, undulating. Their desire for each other felt human, sensual, compelling. Nothing to do with blood. Strange and wonderful that this pleasure hadn't been lost with their humanity – but then, it was a passion that could take dark, deceptive paths.

Charlotte had been a shy young woman of twenty when Karl met her: secretive, wary, sharply intelligent. He hadn't set out to seduce her, but neither had he tried very hard to refrain. A double sin, for while she worried about the potential disgrace, she was unaware that Karl, by his very nature, knowingly placed her in mortal danger. Unforgivable. Yet their attraction had been too thrilling to resist. Never would they forget their first time, in all its forbidden ecstasy... Karl so careful to ensure that she shared his exquisite pleasure. So cautious not to harm her, in any way. Resisting her innocent fervour had been impossible; delighting her, effortless. And at the end, protecting her from the peril of his blood thirst – sheer agony.

Now, though, they knew each other completely and held nothing back. Savage and divine was the fulfilment of this long dance. As Charlotte's head tipped back, her hair falling golden-bronze across the pillow, Karl felt her cling to him as he let go. The convulsive waves were delicious, human, deceptive... for they left him defenceless. Transported by bliss, Karl felt a surge of deeper lust, the vampire's true need.

When Charlotte was human, Karl had forced himself with every thread of willpower to turn his face from her neck. Excrutiating to resist: worse to have hurt her, or to admit that his suppressed urge for her blood had twisted into sexual desire and back into blood-lust again...

Ah, no longer. Now he let the feeling flood him. His face dropped to her throat and he bit, one swift savage action.

Then her blood was in his mouth, sharp and sweet like the juice of pomegranates. He could *taste* its colour: garnets, shining berries. *Ah, God*. Ecstasy. But a few sips only... to take more would weaken her. Just the very sabre-edge of rapture.

In the same moment, as Charlotte gasped her own pleasure – as her mouth opened with the cry – her lips and tongue latched hot onto his neck and her teeth stabbed into him. For minutes, blood passed between them; a circle of pleasure so extreme it verged on pain. Too powerful to be borne for long, while the exchange lasted it swept away everything else. This was the Crystal Ring in its deeper, hidden sense; a ruby-thorned rosary of paradise.

They broke the circle, lay gasping in each other's arms. Blood was scattered like jewels on their throats and breasts, while their wounds were already healing. Hair dishevelled, they lay gazing at each other. Every emotion shimmered between them. This was peace, chaos, contentment, yearning. An addiction that must be sated again and again, a lust that some would condemn as demonic; this was the nature of their mutual obsession.

And at the end of all, it was love.

In the deepest layer of the Crystal Ring, Andreas lay like a sea creature on the ocean bed, rolling with every surge of the tide. Half dormant, he could barely move or think. He could only endure the hideous crawl of eternity. Waiting... for what?

Somewhere in another time, he was talking rapidly, angry and distressed. The words and the setting eluded him. And then – Karl's face. Karl's hands on his shoulders, and the enchanting tranquillity of his eyes.

"Andrei, don't do this," said Karl.

He heard himself answer, "But Kristian took everything from me! He took my poetry, gave me this horrible darkness and his sick puritanism in its place! How can I bear it?"

"But what's to stop you writing poetry, as you did in life?" Karl was always so reasonable, curse him.

"You don't understand, do you?" Andreas said furiously. "I can't write, because there is simply no point! No point to anything, except blood! And Kristian calls this the way to God? Damn his God, damn them both to hell!"

Karl's arms went around him, lips against his cheek.

In the background, Katti's voice soothed, "There is still love, Andrei. And we love you. Kristian can't take that from us."

But he could. He could and he had.

A groan issued from Andreas's throat. The images dissolved and vanished, but the groan went on and on.

CHAPTER TWO

A DEADLY CALL

Benedict Grey did not consider himself evil. His activities might have generated lurid headlines had he attracted notoriety as other, more flamboyant, occultists did; but such attention was merely a measure of the public's ignorance. They could not comprehend that "occult" simply meant "hidden", that rejection of conventional religion did not equal devil-worship, nor that his quest was harmless and scholarly. Benedict would never dream of using his knowledge to hurt another living soul, hadn't even considered such danger.

Until today.

In an ashen sunrise, he stood looking out of a window, trying to clear his mind. The parlour was a cosy room with cream-washed walls, red rugs on dark floorboards, an inglenook fireplace. Outside, the winter-brown garden was sheened with buds. Daffodil shoots poked through the soil, and starlings squabbled over bread scraps on the lawn. After the previous night, it seemed miraculous that the everyday world was still here.

Outwardly, Benedict was conventional. A handsome ex-soldier who'd survived the War almost unscathed, he'd moved to Ashvale, a small market town in the middle of England, to be near his older brother Lancelyn. Ben and his wife, Holly, owned a thriving bookshop. That was all outsiders needed to know.

Their neighbours had no idea what took place in the privacy of the Greys' home. The brown brick cottage, with its slate roof and charming veils of creeper, looked as unremarkable as any other in the quiet old street. Only a chosen few knew of his arcane book collection, or the temple he'd constructed in the attic. Even Maud, his bookshop assistant, suspected nothing.

Ben and Holly alone knew what had happened in the temple last night.

Too stunned to talk, they'd retired to bed, but neither had slept. Holly was unsettled. Shortly before dawn, when she dropped off at last, Ben came downstairs to watch the sunrise while he tried to make sense of the impossible.

Lancelyn had taught Benedict that the astral plane was subjective; that every occultist's experience was unique, his perception of supernatural entities purely mystical. There were no horned demons waiting to be summoned bodily to Earth.

So what the hell was it that had manifested in his temple last night?

The ritual had been one of hundreds he'd performed, some with Holly and some alone. He recalled fragrant ribbons of smoke, the rhythm of incantation, lamplight gleaming on their robes – coloured lavender, for the border between night and day. Infinite corridors of reflection in the mirrors. The black Book in the centre of a ten-pointed star. And then, coalescing from air, a creature from the astral realm. Not a phantom but solid, maggot-white, *real*.

The difference, Ben reflected, was the presence of the Book.

He glanced at a small table, where the volume now lay like a slab of night on the lace cloth.

Holly was right, the creature had looked disgusting: a fossilised skeleton, horribly alive. Ben had needed no persuasion to banish it. Truth was, he'd been terrified. And now he was shocked rigid to realise he'd actually succeeded: summoned a being from the astral plane. Yes, he was appalled by its ghastly appearance, the aura of cold evil emanating from its pallid body, but...

By God – he thumped the wall in exuberance – *it was exciting!*

With the safety of distance, he regretted his haste in dispelling it.

Shouldn't have panicked, he thought. *Should have been more scientific, sent Holly out, tried to communicate. What if...*

Holly came in, interrupting his thoughts. Her normally pert face was stamped with circles of tiredness, her jaw-length dark hair a mess, but still she looked wonderful: a slim beauty in her white silk dressing gown. Their long-haired tabby cat, Sam, was in her arms.

"Still can't sleep, darling?" he said. She joined him at the window and stood looking out at her beloved garden. "Cigarette?"

She shook her head, so he lit one for himself and rolled it between his finger and thumb. Nervous habit.

"I've been thinking," he said. "The Book made the difference. We've proved there's power in it."

Her shoulders tensed under the white silk. She held Sam tighter until he struggled in protest and she had to let him down.

"Not still upset about it, are you?"

"I wasn't upset," she whispered. "I only wish I'd never seen the damned Book. I knew there was something evil about it."

"Oh, evil is subjective!" Ben exclaimed. "Just because something scares the life out of us, that doesn't make it *evil*. Simply unknown. Waiting to be investigated."

Holly turned to him, her eyes bright with fear. "You're not planning to try again, Ben." It was a statement, not a question. "You mustn't even think of it!"

Her emotional reaction began to annoy him. She wasn't saying what he wanted to hear. "But think, Holly; we succeeded! We summoned an entity from the astral realm. Even Lancelyn's never done that!"

"But it was horrible." She shivered. "Hideous."

"You couldn't see it properly."

"My eyesight may be poor, but I saw quite enough."

"It wasn't what I expected, that's true. But fascinating, you must admit."

"You have to draw the line at this, Ben. Fascinating, maybe, but dangerous."

Growing exasperated, he said, "Time of the month?"

She glared at him. "What has that to do with anything?"

"Well, you always get prickly–"

"Ben, I'm prickly because last night you materialised a *thing* in our attic that defied description! And you think it's *interesting*?"

He sighed, breathing out smoke. "I'm sorry, darling. I never meant to alarm you."

"Are you going to tell Lancelyn?" she asked sharply.

For some reason, the prospect was unwelcome. "Yes, yes, I'll tell him," he muttered. Holly walked towards the stairs, smoothing her hair. He didn't want her to go; he wanted to talk, if only she'd calm down. "Where are you going?"

"To have my bath," she replied, brisk now. "If Mrs Potter arrives before I'm dressed, would you give her the shopping list?"

"Yes," Ben said distractedly. Then, "Holly?"

She stopped in the doorway. Even angry and tired, she looked charming. "Yes?"

"You won't mention it to Lancelyn, will you? I intend to tell him in my own good time."

"Of course I won't," she said indignantly. "I never speak of such matters without your approval, not even to your brother."

Alone again, Ben drew on his cigarette and eyed the Book. Several hundred years old, perhaps a thousand, the volume was beautifully preserved. One of many books Lancelyn had lent him, this volume was exceptional, not least for the strange circumstances in which they'd found it.

Ben and Lancelyn were trying to translate the text. There were lists of names, apparently some kind of medieval register, pages of scribbled notes in Latinate code, virtually illegible. Hard going. During the experimental summoning, Ben had held certain passages in his mind like photographs, delving for power behind their unknown meaning. And a being from the otherworld had responded.

I must tell Lancelyn, of course.

Lancelyn was head of the Order. He should be told, but Ben felt reluctant. He said aloud, "That's just it. I tell him everything, because he's the magus and I'm still his apprentice. Eh, Sam?" The cat, sitting on the hearthrug, stared at him with large yellow eyes. "I never minded, but this is different. My first true breakthrough. My secret." He sighed. "But I'm being childish. Lancelyn and I share all knowledge. He didn't have to lend me the Book!"

Benedict had constructed his attic temple for his and Holly's use alone. The official group – the Neophytes of Meter Theon, as they styled themselves – met at Lancelyn's house every Friday night. Members came from all over the country, not gullible thrill-seekers, but intellectual men and women: writers, artists, even scientists. They sought higher spiritual advancement than convention could offer. The occult was one of many post-War crazes, but special because – Lancelyn asserted – a new spirituality was needed.

Of course, every little group thought their magus held the truth, but Benedict believed Lancelyn was different. He saw through foggy nonsense to the bright clear path of wisdom.

Once a month, Lancelyn spent the weekend fishing, leaving Benedict in charge of the meeting. Magus Adeptus for an evening. He loved those times. Always a wrench to hand the reins back to his brother. Imagine the Neophytes' reaction if he summoned such an entity in front of them!

I have to try again. Have to. But tell Lancelyn? Well... not yet.

Fear soared into excitement, and he forgave Holly her doubts. He sang as he shaved and got ready for work. Nothing more exhilarating than power. Mrs Potter the housekeeper arrived, made breakfast, fed the cat and went to the shops; Holly thawed and forgave him. They made small talk over the breakfast table. An ordinary couple.

Ben didn't hear the door-knocker. Entering the hallway, about to leave for work, he found Holly opening the door to a visitor: a plump woman enveloped in a full-length cloak of brown velvet with a matching floppy hat.

It was Deirdre, one of the Neophytes. She and her lover, James, were frequent visitors to the cottage. A strong-faced, attractive Dubliner of forty-odd, Deirdre favoured the unconventional look of an artist. Her face was white between wings of faded-red hair, and she clutched a carpetbag.

"I can't stay long," she was telling Holly. "I've a train to catch."

Ben greeted her, leading her into the parlour. "Come in, come in. We don't usually see you this early. Nothing wrong, I hope?"

Deirdre, usually full of life, was subdued. She said quietly, "You haven't heard, have you?"

"Heard what?"

"It's James," she said on a short breath. "He's killed himself."

Deirdre went grey. Ben caught her and helped her to the sofa before she fell to the floor. Holly unfastened the cloak, removed

Deirdre's hat and used it to fan her face, while Ben fetched a glass of brandy.

James had been a member of the Order, albeit an erratic one. And Deirdre, despite the fact that he was years younger and would never have married her, had loved him.

Holly said, "Oh, Deirdre, I'm so sorry. We had no idea." She glanced at Ben, her expression reflecting his shock. "What happened?"

Deirdre gulped brandy and composed herself. Sam jumped on her knee and she stroked him, oblivious to his claws catching her clothes. "I'm sorry. I refuse to cry, this is too important for tears."

"Take your time," said Ben. The news wouldn't sink in; unbelievable. Dreadful to see her upset when usually she was flamboyant and carefree.

"He hanged himself. It'll be in the papers tomorrow: a young barrister with everything to live for... You know the things they say."

"But why?" said Holly. She sat down by Deirdre, holding her hands, not far from tears herself. "He always seemed so happy and sure of himself."

"He didn't want to die," Deirdre said softly. "He was driven to it. A few days ago he told me he believed that someone had launched a magical attack against him."

Her words woke a degree of scepticism in Ben, but no surprise. He knew such attacks took place among rival occultists; whether they worked could never be proved. He asked, "Who would do that? Had he made an enemy?"

Deirdre looked at him with expressive brown eyes. He realised she was concerned for *him*. "It's difficult. The person he quarrelled with was Lancelyn."

Ben was incredulous. "Are you suggesting that Lancelyn would launch such an attack?"

He hadn't meant to speak harshly, but Deirdre flinched. "Please, Ben. I know you're close, but Lancelyn's no angel. He has a wicked temper on him."

"But what did they quarrel about? If there was a disagreement within the Order, I'd know."

Again a hesitation. "I – I don't know. But it was rancorous, and that's when James's troubles started. Nightmares, feelings of persecution. I could hardly believe what James told me, but I went and confronted Lancelyn and he –" She foundered, shaking.

"Take your time," said Holly. "Go on."

"Well, Lancelyn denied it, but his manner disturbed me. You know how he is. And now things are happening to me, too. That's why I'm leaving. So I came to say goodbye and –"

Ben cut across her. "What sort of things?"

They made a maudlin tableau in the half-light; a fading poetess with the younger woman sitting over her in concern.

Deirdre began softly, "I hear voices in my house when no one's there. My housekeeper seems to look at me with Lancelyn's eyes..."

"No," Holly whispered.

"Last night I had a nightmare. I was lying in bed when the room filled up with dank air, so thick I could hardly breathe. Usually I see a strip of light between my curtains but this time it was pitch dark. I sensed a *thing* coming towards me. Something heavy and massive. A current of absolute evil. The bedclothes held me down as if they weighed a ton.

"I heard a creature snuffling outside, like a huge pig. It got closer. Then the darkness split and I saw my curtains blown wide apart. A beast came surging in over the windowsill, breaking the glass and half the wall with it. It filled the room. And it was ugly, like an armoured rhinoceros, covered in tarnished brass plates, with a great head all dents and dimples. No eyes. A bluish-white steam came from under the armour plates, icy cold and stinking. I knew when the beast reached me, I'd be crushed to death. And it kept coming, pushing me up the bed until I was squeezed flat against the wall. I was suffocating. The weight on my chest was unbearable and I couldn't breathe –" She broke off, coughing.

Ben stroked her forehead. "Hush, you're safe. How did it end?"

"I woke up. I was dripping with sweat, but everything seemed normal otherwise. The window was intact and the curtains hadn't moved. I went to look out and all was quiet... but on the sill there were gouges in the wood like great claw marks. I looked again in daylight and the marks were gone, but the night before – I saw them."

Ben's reaction was absolute denial. He went to the window; birds fluttered and quarrelled outside. No one spoke. The clock cut the silence into hard sections.

At last he said, "I'm at a loss, Deirdre. I'm sure you're telling the truth, but Lancelyn can't be responsible. He's a scholar; he'd never hurt his friends."

Deirdre bowed her head, revealing grey strands in the copper. "I didn't come here to argue. I'm telling you what happened, that's all. If I don't leave, it will be me next." Her voice faded to a whisper. "It'll be me."

"No," Holly said firmly. "Lancelyn wouldn't harm a woman."

Ben stared indignantly at his wife. Was she implying that he might harm a man?

He said, "Have you considered that your mind is overactive because of James's death? That James and yourself might be the victims of suggestion, rather than actual magic?"

"Of course I have!" Deirdre snapped with a trace of her old spirit. "Don't you understand that control of someone's mind is the greatest power there is?"

Ben felt drained. This, on top of last night's work! "Look, if it will make you feel better, I'll visit Lancelyn, sort this out."

Terror flashed in her eyes. "No, don't! Don't tell him. I only came to say, be careful, both of you. Just be careful."

Disentangling herself from the cat, Deirdre stood up and squashed the floppy hat on her head.

Holly rose with her, concerned. "Where are you going?"

"Home to my family in Dublin. I'll be safe there."

"Don't go," Ben said helplessly. "You'll be such a loss to the Order."

"No I won't, because I don't care any more. I'm sick of the occult. The secrets were never meant to be used like this. Grown-ups dressing in silly costumes and playing power games; it's not worth dying for, is it?"

Ben smiled sadly. "That sentiment could apply equally to any great British institution. Why single us out?"

"Well, damn the whole lot of them, then," Deirdre said with feeling, trying to smile back. "God go with you."

They saw her off. Ben rocked on his heels, watching the autumnal gleam of her hair as her figure dwindled along the street. Then he and Holly went back inside, closed the door, and hugged each other.

"I don't believe it," he said. "Poor James, poor Deirdre. But how could she accuse Lancelyn?"

"It's true he has a temper, and the power to control people," said Holly. "But he wouldn't... He's like a father to me, more than my own father ever was. He wouldn't!"

"I don't think she told us everything."

"Probably not, but you didn't want to listen, did you?" she said. Ben glared at her, but couldn't reply. "Will you see Lancelyn? Will you tell him about last night?"

Ben looked into her bird-bright eyes, and read beneath the surface of the question: *Do you still trust Lancelyn? Tell me you do, so that we can both still trust him.*

"Yes, of course I'll see him."

"And promise me one thing. Never, ever try to repeat last night's summoning again!"

Deirdre's description of her nightmare had brought metallic revulsion to the back of his throat, a disgust that now extended to the previous night's visitation. He'd been too arrogant. Some things were not to be meddled with.

"I promise," he said easily. "I promise."

The theatre was in Milan, the performance the Ballet Janacek's *Giselle*.

In the foyer, the audience flowed to take their seats, a sea of voile and jewels, of dark suits, crisp shirts and groomed hair. Beautiful, ugly or mediocre; all were made elegant by fine clothes, by the glamour of theatre lighting and the heightened atmosphere. Glittering, the mortal crowd tantalised a vampire's senses on every level.

Karl and Charlotte moved with the throng. Their pretence of being human was a pleasure as satiny as seduction.

Karl usually wore black or charcoal. On him, a dark suit and white shirt, black overcoat, gloves, and a white cashmere scarf looked timeless and enticingly elegant.

Charlotte chose the muted colours she loved: shades of bronze and mushroom, dusty lilacs and sunset tints, sometimes a touch of gold, cream or silver. She liked soft fabrics, silk and lace and beads, ankle-length skirts with floating handkerchief-points. Everything soft, subtle, indefinable.

Often Charlotte would see someone glance at them, then blink and stare, as if in unconscious recognition. But no one guessed the truth. They did not see two monsters, only a tall, slim, charismatic man and a solemn-faced woman with crystalline eyes; and if anyone looked twice, they took preternatural glamour for surface beauty.

Karl drew the most stares, especially from women. Charlotte didn't mind. It suited her temperament to be in the background. She was simply glad to be with him, that he wanted her; because if he hadn't – if he'd left her or never loved her at all – she would have given up and died. Such was the extremity of her infatuation. Intoxicating and fragile.

Karl and Charlotte often travelled through the Crystal Ring to theatres all over Europe, to mingle with humanity and find victims in the dark backstreets afterwards, vanishing home by dawn. Although daylight held no danger for them, they both loved the velvet magic of night.

There was an added edge tonight, since David's friend had found them. Every time Charlotte heard an English voice among the flow of Italian, she shivered.

As they moved down the aisle, Karl was pensive. His gaze wandered over the baroque fancies of the ceiling, the gilded plaster and brass chandeliers. "I last came here with Andreas and Katerina. *Ach, du liebe Zeit...*"

"How long ago?" said Charlotte, startled. Karl rarely mentioned the friends whom his enemy, Kristian, had left to freeze in the highest circle of the Crystal Ring. Sometimes she wished he would say more.

"Forty years, at least. Yes, in the 1880s... It was almost the last time I saw them. This place has hardly changed, except for the electric lights in the chandeliers."

"What did you see?"

A faint smile touched his mouth. "It was a ballet then, too. We saw *La Sylphide*. A tale of a supernatural being falling in love with a mortal."

"Do you still miss them?"

"Less than I used to," he said, but she saw pain flicker in his eyes. "And it's no use to keep asking myself why I couldn't save them. They belong to the past, beloved."

"And so does Kristian," Charlotte murmured. "Thank God… or whatever gave us the power to destroy him."

In a cavern of crimson velvet, they waited for the overture to begin.

Charlotte's deepest pleasure lay in the pure joy of being at Karl's side. Horrible, the things she'd done to stay with him, not least the heartbreak she'd caused her family and her dearest friend, Anne. But given a second chance, she would do the same again because, if she'd remained human, Karl would either have left or destroyed her with his blood thirst. She'd commit any crime to keep him… And now she too was a crime against nature, a bearer of madness and death.

Incalculably expensive, their love.

Her personality hadn't changed, but continued to deepen in strange ways. As a mortal, she'd wanted to hide from the world. Now she was entirely detached from it, but the wounds of isolation she'd suffered as a girl lingered. In time she would rise above them; for the present, she had years of painful shyness to exorcise. Irresistible, to walk among people and think, *I'm not afraid of you any longer. Your judgment of me means nothing.* To know that with a look she could inspire fear or desire; or let them see she was not the demure young woman she appeared but something *other*. To turn their safe world upside down!

A sweet revenge; harmless, if self-indulgent. As a mortal, she'd craved affection, even while she hid from it. As a vampire, rather to her shock, she found the craving even more intense.

When strangers noticed them, she sensed their curiosity as strongly as she scented their blood-heat. Often she and Karl would strike up a conversation, forming superficial friendships that could never become intimate. That was how they'd met John Milner. Sometimes it happened that another couple would fasten onto them for the evening. The wife would flirt shamelessly with Karl – her poise torn to shreds by his allure – while Charlotte would brave her dagger-glances and charm the husband. This had led to many entertaining evenings. But here was a difference between them: Charlotte would sometimes feed on the husband, if she could get him alone. Karl, though, never touched the wife. Charlotte didn't fully understand why, yet – in a prosaically human way – she was glad.

Taking a victim was not infidelity. The notion was irrational, though it could seem perilously close, for blood was more than nourishment. Passion, conflict, excitement, pleasure and pain... everything. Never could blood be mere food. Never.

Charlotte remembered John Milner with mixed feelings.

Leaning close to Karl, she said, "I ought to feel guilty."

"Why?"

"It was that man, Milner, who suggested we see Ballet Janacek."

Karl's eyebrows lifted. "You are not still thinking about him, are you?"

"I'm only concerned that he might not forget. He could still return to David and tell him... something. Or if he doesn't go back, David may think the worst. Will he send someone else? Must we vanish from human eyes completely?"

"No," Karl answered firmly. "No one has the power to make us live as fugitives, not even the people we loved. The human world can't touch us."

He was right, and he was wrong, but it didn't matter. Calmness flowed into her from his amber eyes, and for the thousandth time his beauty struck her as if she'd never seen him before. Red and honey lights in his hair; rain beating against a window in another time, while the touch of his fingers soothed her into believing that her fall from grace would be divine.

"I know," she said. "But I don't want David to keep torturing himself."

"Then write to him yourself," said Karl.

"What's the point?" Charlotte said, resigned. "As you once told me, it's not fair to hope they'll forgive me. What we did can never be forgiven."

"No," he said. "It can't."

His fingers were twined with hers, and the murmur of the audience electrified her. At this moment she was so blissfully happy that she could forget what she was, forget the thirst. She was no longer outside the crystal world she'd first glimpsed in

Karl's eyes; she was inside, wrapped in velvet and golden light.

"What are you thinking?" he asked.

"That I'm perfectly happy."

He smiled. "And so am I, beloved," he said, kissing her hand. "These moments are worth any pain. They are what we live for."

He spoke her thoughts.

As the house lights dimmed, suspending them in crimson darkness, Karl looked at the programme. It was easy to forget that their ability to read in the dark looked strange to humans. "A small company, based in Salzburg," he said softly, "with dancers from all over Europe. Director and choreographer, Roman Janacek. The prima ballerina, Violette Lenoir, comes from Anna Pavlova's school in England. The critics are calling her the 'new Pavlova'."

"Well, they would," said Charlotte. "They always make such claims."

"And they're always wrong," said Karl.

As he spoke, Charlotte experienced a flash of anxiety. She was too new a vampire to have left her insecurity behind. *What if Karl is captivated by another mortal, as he once was by me? One of the dancers we're about to see. What would I do?*

Music was flowing around them, the curtains sweeping open onto a faked yet vividly real otherworld. Charlotte relaxed and let the story take her.

And found herself completely unprepared for her reaction.

She was spellbound. This *Giselle* was the most moving interpretation she'd ever seen. Janacek took liberties, imbuing the traditional choreography with breathtakingly fluid emotion. His risks paid off; the result was timeless, ethereal, raw.

Pain threaded through every joy; Giselle's fragile happiness, then her collapse into grief as her lover deceived and betrayed her. Every nuance seemed to have deeper significance that struck right to Charlotte's soul. And the heart of the enchantment was Giselle herself.

Violette Lenoir's dancing was transcendent. As she moved from innocence into passion, despair and death, Charlotte travelled with her. When Giselle died, Charlotte wept.

At the interval, it was all Charlotte could do force herself back to reality.

Karl smiled at her and said, "I wonder why it is so delicious to be made unhappy?"

In the second act, through darkness and moon-white mists, Giselle came back from the tomb.

Luminous in white and silver, she rose and whirled across the sweep of the stage, spinning, spinning. She seemed weightless, lost, as vulnerable as a dry leaf; an unbearable fusion of anguish and unearthly beauty. Charlotte watched with her hands tightening on the arms of her seat. The poignant story worked a sombre curse on her; death, resurrection, the undead haunting the living into their own graves... And Karl was right. There was terrible pleasure in the pain she felt.

Charlotte grew increasingly curious about the ballerina who inspired such powerful emotions. It was far more than technical skill or sheer beauty. She had that indefinable quality: *presence*.

With keen vampire sight, Charlotte watched every detail. Violette Lenoir's face was a pale oval, her eyes kohl-smudged and lips darkened to compensate for the bleaching effect of stage lights. Her black hair, flowing loose and lily-twined over her shoulders, had a blue sheen that enhanced the colour of her irises. Large, intensely violet-blue lakes – Lenoir's eyes were irresistible.

Humans are not meant to mesmerise vampires, Charlotte thought with irony. *It should be the other way round... but no, that's not true. Didn't Karl see something extraordinary in me, however well he hid his feelings? And don't I feel perpetually drawn to humans – if only for their blood?*

Oh God, I can't want to – no, she's an artist. Artists are perfect and untouchable, like us. But... I wonder if I could make her look at me?

Occasionally it happened that a performer would stare at Karl and Charlotte from the stage, as if, with heightened perceptions of their own, they sensed something amiss. But Violette Lenoir, although Charlotte willed her fiercely, would not look.

The ballerina was wrapped up in the story; nothing else existed. One of a band of souls betrayed, a victim whose only power was to haunt... and yet, in the end, what an insidious, lethal power that was.

The tragedy wound to its conclusion. The audience rose in wild applause and Charlotte rose with them, tears blurring her eyes. The stage was all light and colour again, the ghosts returning to vibrant life. Only a story.

As Violette Lenoir took her curtain calls and accepted bouquets, it seemed to Charlotte that her dramatic passion had switched off like a light. She smiled, but her eyes were glaciers. Her sudden aloofness only enhanced her aura; her darkness and paleness. The pain that had burned radiant while she danced was now locked away inside her.

And Charlotte went on staring, with a simple, burning wish to know what this mysterious creature was really like.

"Bravo!" shouted the man beside Karl. His accent was American. "Oh, marvellous!" He leaned towards Karl, raising his voice over the roar of applause. "Isn't she the most wonderful thing ever?"

"Perfect," Karl answered. "That was the most enchanting performance of *Giselle* I have ever seen."

The American was in his fifties, grey-haired, his neck webbed with lines like snakeskin. Charlotte tried not to notice the pulse jumping under his jaw.

He said, "Wonderful actress, too. Better than you think."

"In what way?" asked Karl

"They say she's an absolute bitch in real life."

A nervous thrill went through Charlotte. She asked, "Have you met her?"

The man glanced at her and huffed, embarrassed that she'd heard his off-colour remark. "Once or twice; I organised the publicity for their tour of the States last year. She makes the proverbial Snow Queen look as hot as Jean Harlow." He cleared his throat. "She's… chilly."

"Perhaps you got on the wrong side of her," said Charlotte. Karl's attention switched subtly to her. "I should like to make up my own mind."

"So would a lot of folk, but it's impossible to break through her entourage. She may love dancing but she sure hates people; so how does she pour out all that emotion?"

"She's a genius," said Karl. "Pavlova truly has a rival."

Charlotte was trying to gauge whether Karl found the ballerina equally fascinating. Unless he hid it well, she was sure he hadn't. His appreciation was sincere but detached.

"I'd like to see this again," she said.

"I got connections. I can get all the tickets you –" the American began, but Karl turned to Charlotte, cutting him off.

"If you wish," Karl said softly. "Now, shall we go?"

Charlotte and Karl walked slowly from the theatre, through the cool starry darkness outside; past posters announcing the ballet, away from the knot of hopeful worshippers waiting at the stage door.

The streets grew quiet and narrow. Charlotte couldn't banish the dancer's face from her thoughts.

Karl drew her hand through his arm and said, "When we saw the Ballets Russes, you were on air afterwards. We talked for hours, don't you remember?"

"I feel like being quiet now." She leaned her head on his shoulder.

"You needn't keep your thoughts from me. I have told you many times that there is nothing you can say that could shock me."

She looked sideways at him, startled. "Why would I be thinking anything that might shock you?"

"*Liebchen*, I saw the way you watched Violette Lenoir."

Charlotte stopped abruptly. She glared at him, defensive. "How can you always know –" Her lips softened and she looked away. "You always do this to me. I don't know why I fight you."

"You don't have to fight me."

She had to explain, not leave him with the wrong idea. "Anna Pavlova was magical but she seemed a universe away from us. She's part of a vibrant, energetic, real world that never touches the dusk we live in."

"And Violette?"

"Different. She projected anguish, pure shimmering pain. I'd like to ask her, 'What is it? Where does it come from, how do you turn agony into such magic?'"

"She may not have an answer."

Charlotte tried to sound off-hand. "You mean that what I *see* isn't who she really is. I know. I should like to ask her, that's all."

"If you want to meet Violette, do so," Karl said reasonably. "What's to stop you? In the Crystal Ring you can walk through walls, straight into her dressing room. Then what?"

"I wouldn't do that. It would be unfair and I'd hate to frighten her."

"Then, if the American gentleman is to be believed, you are unlikely to meet her." Charlotte was silent. He continued, "Any immortal might have the power to step into the room of Pavlova or Lenoir and destroy a great and shining talent, but none do; not even those who claim to have no conscience, like Ilona or Pierre. There's an unspoken law, an instinct. We still respect the human world. Why destroy the culture that gives us so much pleasure? Or ravage a world without which we could not exist?"

"I agree completely. I never said I wanted –"

"But understand, Charlotte! That is the very root of your fascination: your desire for her blood! So very like sexual attraction; the more enticing the human, the more you long to satisfy your thirst. Only for her it would be fatal. Do you wish to fulfil that need and stop her dancing?"

"Of course not!" Charlotte raised her chin in anger. "Was I merely a source of blood to you?"

"As I said, it is so like sex." Karl held her gaze. "You don't have to ask that, beloved. The more captivating the human, the more their blood means. That's the danger."

She looked away. "I couldn't bear to harm her. I'd simply like to reassure myself that she's real... to discover how a mortal can seem supernatural. But I never shall; it would destroy the magic. Karl, I wish I you couldn't see straight through me like glass!"

"I can't. I never could."

He bent to kiss her. She stretched her arms around his neck and pressed her mouth to his; eager, loving. A ruby-red flare of desire and thirst reminded Charlotte where she belonged now. Nothing mattered except being with Karl, and the taste of blood was a bitter-sweet ecstasy above all others. This was real; a distant figure on a painted stage was not.

"Come with me, dearest," he whispered, "into the Crystal Ring."

She went with him gladly. Like a doll in a music box, Violette pirouetted in a corner of her mind.

* * *

Deirdre stood at the post-box, the letter in her gloved hand.

How can I send it? she thought. *If Ben knows already, he'll realise I've broken a binding oath to write this. But if he doesn't, it'll break his heart.*

Ben, forgive me for not telling you face to face. I couldn't find the words. And if you think I'm a coward, don't judge me until you're as frightened as I am.

She loosed the letter, heard it fall into the darkness of the box.

A few minutes later, she was on the platform, waiting for the train that would take her to the ferry and safety. The occult had been her whole life, the Neophytes of Meter Theon her family... but all she wanted now was to escape. The wind blew fresh in her face and she tasted freedom. In her mind she saw the deep greens and the lovely, cloud-veiled mountains of Ireland.

Then – she heard the beast coming.

Again it began as a deep, rhythmic snuffling noise. A huge blind pig. She looked along the track in panic and saw the creature nosing towards her. The great eyeless head, the steam pouring from its joints, and the terrible stink of metal and oil...

She was dizzy. The day turned dark and the crowd on the platform vanished. Deirdre was alone in a land of demons.

It's only my imagination, she told herself. *Ben said it's only in my mind! If I stand and face the beast, it will go away.*

Her heart was racing hard as she moved to the platform edge. It was clear she must do this. *You don't exist*, she thought, jumping down onto the track. She flung up her hands, chanting a banishing spell, but the demon came on, huge, deafening, wreathed in steam. She yelled aloud, "You don't –"

Her cry was lost in the scream of brakes. The weight of the beast bore her down, crushed her, and passed blindly on.

CHAPTER THREE

INTO THIS SHADOW

As the atmosphere enfolded the Earth, so the Crystal Ring surrounded a warped aspect of it that only immortals could enter. Some vampires equated it with hell, others with heaven. Karl and Charlotte had their own theories. Like the universe itself, it could be explained a hundred different ways and no explanation could yet be proved.

Hand in hand, they let the world around them change. Trees became rustling black spires, walls snapped into impossible perspectives. Any witnesses would have seen Karl and Charlotte vanish.

At ground level the Ring was a dark, demonic hall of mirrors, but its sky flowed with fire and liquid light. Karl and Charlotte soared upwards. The air bore their weight like water. Ahead floated a great ridge, a cloud-hill in constant motion like a wave of gold-dappled glass. This realm was like an epic sky painted by a deranged visionary, suffused with the light of heaven and the glow of hell. Far above, canyons soared up towards thunderous mountains, stained blood-red and purple. Like clouds, these features condensed from air then frayed to nothingness in an endless ocean-blue void.

Radiant lines shimmered like an aurora, exerting a weird pull. This was the magnetic field of the Earth, made tangible and visible to immortals; the only constant by which they could navigate.

The structure of this realm, according to Charlotte, was created by mankind's collective subconscious, by the electrical outflow of minds. And its energy could warp humans into vampires, because vampires represented the most extreme of human emotions; the fear of death and of the dead returning to life; the desire for power and immortality.

There must be even more, Karl thought, but her theory was easier to accept than Kristian's doctrine: that this was the mind of a God who used vampires as pitiless envoys.

Karl also wondered if the Ring was simply a matter of altered perceptions. Their bodies were different here, as objects in water appear distorted. They became dark, thin demons, their earthly garments also changing beyond recognition into spangled webs. Clothes, small personal possessions; the Ring, following its own capricious laws, would rarely allow anything heavier to be brought here.

The Crystal Ring was empty, alien, hostile. Its sheer size was enough to provoke insanity. It could be lethally cold, even to vampires. Yet there was endless fascination in its wildness. The exhilaration of flying, climbing, floating in its strange atmosphere could be fatally addictive.

No vampire could avoid the Crystal Ring. It made them what they were. Only in its frigid arms could they find the rest denied them on Earth – but if they stayed too long, the Ring might keep them forever.

The distant moan of a gale rose and fell around them… then Karl sensed shapes around him, shadows printed on the clouds. He remembered the last time – when he'd been so shocked that he sprang out of the Ring in full view of a human.

He controlled the lash of fear, caught Charlotte's arm and held her. "*Liebling*, do you feel someone nearby, watching us?"

She turned slowly, blinking, her eyes like golden glass in her lovely darkened face. Her hair floated against a dark blue void. "No. Who was it?"

The feeling vanished. "No one," said Karl. "Imagination."

"Are you sure? It's not like you to imagine things." She looked drowsy. He too felt tiredness creeping over him.

"The Ring is enough, without conjuring anything worse."

"Perhaps it was Ilona."

"No," he said.

"She never hated you, Karl," Charlotte said sleepily. "Not in her heart." She stretched and turned over like a swimmer. "The Crystal Ring feels cold tonight. I am so tired."

"Then rest." Lying outstretched on the sapphire ether, as if floating face down in the sea, Karl put his arm over her waist, his head on her shoulder. He felt her sigh faintly as she sank into meditation; and he let go of his own thoughts, and touched infinity.

This was the nearest state to sleep that vampires could enjoy. All emotion suspended, Charlotte gazed in a trance at waves rising and falling, golden-bronze against indigo; the world shrouded in shadow far below. Her mind wandered, not into dreams, but through strange waking visions...

She imagined herself in an elegant garden; a terrace, wide lawns, trees and pools all silvered by moonlight. A huge plane tree cast a shadow on the grass. This was Parkland Hall, her aunt's house, where all her most vivid passions had flowered; where Karl had turned from friend to lover, in those sweetly innocent days before she knew what he was. The garden would haunt her forever, even if she never set foot there again. It had become a realm in its own right: the secret landscape of her mind, symbolising all fulfilment and all loss.

Her friend Anne was sitting with her on a marble balustrade that bounded the terrace. And Charlotte conjured a scene that she knew would never take place in real life...

Their friendship had ended in bitter words. Who could blame Anne for rejecting what Charlotte had become? Still, it hurt. The wound gaped open and stung with salt.

Yet here they were together. Anne was clearly nervous of her skin's pale glow and the brilliance of her eyes, but Charlotte said, "It's not so terrible. Please believe me. I've so wanted to come back and explain."

"I dreamed you would," said Anne. "I regretted the way we parted, dreadful things I said. Who am I to condemn you? The shell *seems* evil, but there's mystery and beauty inside."

"Beauty can be a warning of poison. I didn't know until it was too late; that was my downfall. But not yours, Anne; you have more sense."

"Have I? That's my trouble. I never understood what you were going through. I was only there to pick you up when you fell...."

"No. You remained yourself *because* it didn't touch you."

"Perhaps. But I couldn't help wondering... was almost envious, in a way. What an awful thing to admit."

Charlotte said softly, "Dearest... I had no idea." She rested a hand on Anne's neck and stroked her throat. Anne shivered, but her eyes were fearless, captivated.

"I'll never forget you, Charli. I'll never stop wondering what I missed."

Charlotte shook her head, helpless. Then she drew Anne towards her and they embraced. How she'd longed for this. Forgiveness, acceptance. How it had hurt, losing her dearest friend in such rancour. "If you really want to know, I won't deny you."

She bit into Anne's neck and swallowed. The blood tasted like champagne. Anne did not pull away, only made a faint noise in her throat. Charlotte stopped, and they held each other hard; friends, blood-sisters. This was a bond between them forever.

"But don't have bad dreams, dearest," Charlotte whispered. "It's also a gesture of love."

Anne smiled. With an arm around Charlotte's waist, she turned and said, "Look."

There on the dew-grey lawn danced a spirit in white satin and net; Violette Lenoir, the ghost of Giselle.

The scene vanished, like a bubble.

A vision beyond a daydream. Almost real – but false. They were not Anne's words, not her sentiments. Charlotte lived with the hard truth: that she would never see Anne again.

A dart of cold stung Karl to alertness. Something felt wrong. He looked around and saw black shadows undulating over the contours of the Crystal Ring, the hills changing shape like storm clouds on a strong wind. The watchers again?

No, nothing there. The moods of the Ring were changeable. A stream of coldness flowed heavily over him, and he knew it was time to return home. He tightened his arm around Charlotte's waist, trying to rouse her gently, but she woke with a start.

"Oh, is it time?" she said reluctantly. "I was so far away."

"We should go back. Are you cold?"

"I wasn't until I moved… but yes, it's freezing. And I'm thirsty."

The ether was a vast flow of ultramarine glass around them. Long strands of cloud traversed the blueness. The two vampires were fantastical sculptures of jet and coal-black lace, tiny against the rolling skyscape.

Below them, against a fleecy cloud, Karl saw a thin greyish shape. He touched Charlotte's arm. "There's someone down there, do you see?"

"Yes. But they look…"

She didn't utter the word "dead", but Karl had the same feeling. The vampire looked rigid, like a dark cross against the whiteness. As they drew closer, Karl saw no lustre on its skin, no cobweb wings to add grace. It looked starved, scoured, brittle. It was floating helpless in the Ring like driftwood.

Charlotte said anxiously, "Can you tell if it's someone you know?"

"Not yet." They were curving swiftly downwards. "Slow down. Be careful."

"This is what happens if we stay too long, isn't it?" she said faintly. "We grow too cold to escape, and starve."

They landed on the cloud, their feet sinking into its substance as it just bore their weight, like honey. Karl bent down to the creature. A stick figure, coated with ash; the face was blurred. Grief thrummed inside him. Charlotte uttered a moan of pity and horror.

"I think she's female, but I've no idea who she is," he said. "She must have been here a very long time. We're too late."

"What shall we do?"

"Leave her."

Karl touched the creature's thin arm. Searing cold bit him, so fierce it bonded his hand to the arm and he couldn't pull free.

"What is it?" Charlotte, alarmed, tried to help him.

"*Mein Gott*," he said. "Don't touch her! She's deadly cold. I think she's come down from the *Weisskalt*."

Charlotte glanced up, as if seeking a gap in the thunderous clouds far above. But the *Weisskalt*, the frigid outer skin, was too far above to be visible. Binding her tattered false-wings around her hands to protect them, she said, "I'll bite my wrist and squeeze blood on your hand to free you. You'll tear the skin otherwise."

Karl began to say, "No –" when the stick-creature thrashed into life and seized him. Its body was not fragile but heavy as stone, the thin limbs as strong as steel. Ice flared through him. He saw Charlotte over its shoulder, her eyes wide as she tried to drag the demon off him. Then he felt its fangs sink like sharp thick fossils into his neck.

There was nothing harder to fight than a starving vampire. Karl couldn't escape. He was paralysed, his ears full of the creature's convulsive swallowing. His blood leapt painfully through his veins, pulsing out of him in time to the numbing suction of the mouth.

He struggled, suppressing panic. It was vital his senses remained clear. "Charlotte, we must leave the Crystal Ring. Guide us down. Quickly, before she takes all my strength."

As he spoke, he sensed another vampire drawing close. No surprise, to see another dark form winging alongside Charlotte – red and violet glints on a swirl of blackness – nor to hear Ilona's light, abrupt voice.

"We'll take him together. One on each side."

"Hurry," said Charlotte. No time to be startled by Ilona's appearance, only to be glad of her help. "Don't touch the creature, she's freezing."

Ilona retorted, "She'll soon be warm as toast, if we don't prise her off my father."

The Crystal Ring spiralled as Karl fell in the vampire's grip. Ghastly, this helplessness. As his energy was stolen with his blood, he feared he would plunge through thin air to Earth – or be stranded in the Ring without hope of escape.

But he felt sure hands on his arms, drawing him down curving paths of ether towards the lake of shadows below. All the time Karl battled to keep his bearings, and to prise the ravening blood-drinker out of his flesh.

She was taking everything. Heat, strength, will. And as she surged frantically back to life, her *self* touched Karl and he realised who she was.

Instantly he stopped fighting, held her to him with both arms, even while his power bled away and his vision turned white.

Charlotte and Ilona pulled them both from the Crystal Ring and into the mortal world. He felt Charlotte's energy tingling into him through her hands, the only warm spots on his body. She'd lent her strength to bring him back. And so had Ilona; why had she helped?

As they tumbled to Earth, the creature's fangs came out of Karl's neck and she slumped in his arms. She was no longer stone-rigid but pliable flesh. In human guise again, all four collapsed exhausted on the ground. Karl blinked, and saw the faces of his lover and his daughter glowing ghostlike against darkness.

They were lying on grass, on a roadside. Dawn glimmered on steep alpine meadows.

"Karl?" Charlotte's arms went around him. Her clothes were torn, her hair tousled. "Are you all right?"

He hugged her, sat up, gently set her aside. "Yes, beloved. Thank you." He looked at Ilona's sharp oval face, pallid under her hair, the same near-black auburn as his own. Just a glance. She would only throw his thanks back at him.

Between them lay the naked, piteous form of the sick vampire. She tried to claw at Karl, who held her down easily. Her form had changed with the transition to Earth, but she scarcely looked human. Her body was dead white and skeletal. Skin and muscle were pasted on her bones like papyrus. Mummified. A thing that should have been dead; instead she was writhing, sounds of agony rattling from her throat.

Karl bowed his head. He was beyond weeping.

The three immortals knelt around her, silent – not with revulsion, but with the knowledge that they could each be looking at their own fate. To suffer like this, unable to die…

Karl pulled back his sleeve, and put his wrist to the vampire's mouth.

"What are you doing?" Charlotte cried.

The white creature, closing her eyes, sucked hungrily.

"Feeding her."

"Hasn't she already taken enough from you? Why?"

"It's Katerina," said Karl.

Charlotte and Ilona both gaped. Karl felt weakness weighing

him down. He knew he should stop while he could still move, but he was transfixed by Katerina's ruined face, by the way her pain lessened as his increased. Pinkness crept into her cheeks. Then Ilona swore in German, and began to laugh.

"Christ!" she said. "I might have known! She always led a charmed life, didn't she? I wonder how she pulled this trick?"

Charlotte closed her hand on Ilona's arm. "Don't," she said. Her voice was quiet, but her subduing effect on Ilona was – to Karl – unique and astonishing. "Karl, please stop feeding her. She'll kill you."

"How?" asked Karl. "If only it were that easy for us to die." He pulled his wrist from Katerina's lips and pressed his thumb to the wound until it began to heal. Then he took off his coat and covered Katerina's pathetic form. She uttered faint moans. There was no intelligence in her eyes.

"It is Katerina, without doubt," said Ilona, bending closer. "What happened? Where did she come from?"

"We found her drifting as if dead," said Karl. "I didn't know her at first. When I touched her, she attacked me. But, Ilona, why were you there?"

She glanced at him with her large dark eyes, looked away. "I am often near you, Father. I dislike entering the Ring, but every time I'm there I feel something... not right. I considered asking if you'd noticed the same, but I'd hate you to think I have such fancies."

"You should have told us," said Karl. "You know I would take you seriously. What was it you felt?"

Ilona's lips thinned; she loathed admitting to feelings that weren't flippant or callous. "Other vampires around me. Too many. And what was Katerina doing, floating like a dead fish in a tank, when we thought she was in the *Weisskalt*?"

"I don't know whether to be relieved or disturbed that my own visions were real," said Karl. "I wish I had an answer, Ilona."

"What are you going to do," said Charlotte, "about Katerina?"

"Cut off her head," said Ilona. "Put her out of her misery. She can't survive."

"Why not?" Karl said sharply. "I brought you out of the *Weisskalt*, and you survived."

"Yes, but I'd been there only a few days. She was there for forty years! Look at her!"

"I will not destroy her." Karl said evenly.

"God," Ilona muttered, raising her eyes at the sky.

"Are you going to help me or not?" said Karl.

Even Charlotte looked reluctant. Drawing back, she said, "What can we possibly do?"

"She needs human blood. She's drawn so much from me that I've no strength left to enter the Crystal Ring at present. Even if I could, Katerina's far too weak to go back in. So, first we must find out where we are."

"Somewhere in Austria or Switzerland," said Ilona. "Isn't that specific enough?"

Karl ignored her. "We'll arrange a place to meet. Charlotte, you can go through the Crystal Ring and bring a motor car; go home and bring ours, or hire one; whatever is quickest. Meanwhile Ilona and I will feed Katerina. Then we'll take her home."

"Can you enter the Crystal Ring for long enough to take her through a wall?" Ilona asked.

"I doubt it," said Karl. They stood in a valley with mountains rising around them, dawn lightening the shadows to steel-mauve. A spring thaw patched the snow with green. He held Katerina against him, wrapped in his coat; she was like a wax mannequin, her head drooping against his shoulder, her hair cobwebby like an old man's.

"We'll do it the easy way, then." Ilona pointed to a farmhouse sitting snugly in the valley. "I'll enter first and let you in. The inhabitants won't put up a fight. Can you sense them?"

Karl felt little discs of warmth touching him. He was drowsy, and didn't want to harm them. But for Katerina's sake...

They went down through the twilight, unobserved. At the house wall, Ilona vanished; moments later, a door of cracked wood swung open, and Karl took Katerina inside. He felt sickly cold, almost too weak to think. He scented blood in the gloom, deep under the stench of animals, of sour milk and cheese, washing, woodsmoke, human illness.

There was no one healthy in this house. The fit members of the family must be out in the meadows, for only two hot, quick-breathing entities pulled at him. Thirst ravaged him.

"Here," Ilona whispered, pushing open a door.

There were two beds in the little room. In one lay a thin boy, his breathing laboured in his sleep. On the other sat a grossly fat wreck of a man, with an adult's face and the eyes of a child. He watched the sick boy as if he'd sat there all night.

Seeing the vampires, the big man leapt up and screamed. Ilona sprang forward, felled him with a jab of her fingers. She tore into his throat, then recoiled and sat him upright, offering him to Karl.

"God!" she said disgustedly. "I don't think he's washed in his life! Let her take him, quickly."

Karl had only to help Katerina a little. Smelling the blood, she writhed like a baby seeking its mother's breast. She fell onto the child-man, began to lap from the wound Ilona had made as if demented. She absorbed his blood, his life-aura, everything.

The boy woke and sat up, staring with huge, feverish eyes at the apparitions in his room. His breathing was noisy, threaded with whimpers of fear.

Katerina will need him too, Karl thought. *God knows how much blood it will take*... but he, too, was starving.

He moved to the boy and sat down on his bed. The child stared at Karl in dumb terror. He was dying; tuberculosis, polio, some awful affliction. Karl pitied him; but sparing him was impossible. He could only clasp the narrow shoulders and look into his eyes.

Karl held back until the boy's expression changed from fear to tranquillity... even love. And then, sealing the deception, he bent and bit into the clammy throat.

He was famished and the blood was more delicious for being hot with fever. No human disease could affect him. His own unnatural body would destroy any trace, leaving only the rich crimson essence he needed. When the craving was strong enough to override conscience and compassion, he let it; accepting his nature without pride, without shame.

His thirst partly slaked, Karl forced himself to stop and leave the rest for Katerina – although, God knew, the child had little enough to give.

Two pitiful corpses, they left. Shells. Karl seemed to be looking at them from a great distance, unmoved. The river of life had caught them, carried them for a while, then washed them up like drowned dogs on the bank. So it did to everyone. But the gorgeous, glittering, crimson river flowed on forever.

Policemen came and asked questions.

Yes, said Benedict, Deirdre was grief-stricken over James's death. No, we've no idea why he killed himself. We didn't know him well. A suicide pact? I don't think so. She was on her way back to Ireland. Yes, they attended meetings of my brother's literary group, but this occult stuff has been greatly exaggerated. What we do wouldn't shock your maiden aunt. Come along sometime.

Holly sat listening to this, weeping.

She'd known about Deirdre's death long before the police called. One of her psychic flashes, like a punch to the stomach. That must have been the moment Deirdre went under the train.

Deirdre had been waiting to change trains at Leicester, the policeman told them, standing quietly on the platform with no sign of agitation. When the train came she jumped in front without warning. Witnesses said she held up her arms as if to stop it, but the driver couldn't brake in time...

She must have jumped on impulse, said Ben.

Eventually the police went away, satisfied there were no suspicious circumstances.

Ben and Holly comforted each other. Later, as she began to recover, Holly said, "I've had an awful notion, ever since Deirdre came to say goodbye. I thought, 'If anything happens to her, it will prove her right.'"

"About what?" Ben said thornily.

"Being persecuted by Lancelyn."

He shot to his feet. "Don't be ridiculous! She was upset, not in her right mind!"

"I don't want to believe it either," Holly said in a low voice. "But we have to consider the possibility, at least."

"I'm going to work," Ben growled.

Numb, Holly watched him walk out; tall, long-limbed, fair-haired. Always full of energy; a strange mixture of kindness and single-minded ambition. She worshipped him. That was why he could hurt her so easily.

When he'd gone, she went into the kitchen and made a cup of tea to calm herself. *Two of your friends die,* she thought. *You suspect that your own beloved father – father-figure, at least – as good as murdered them. What in the name of God are you supposed to do?*

Another image. A white envelope in a gloved hand. A letter on its way...

She pushed away the vision. Her psychic ability was a burden, not a gift. The random images were capricious, unreliable. They never presaged anything good.

Lancelyn and Benedict might possess higher powers to touch the astral world, but she had a simple clairvoyance that they lacked. As a medium, she was invaluable to them. The process made her uncomfortable, but she submitted out of a desperate need to be useful. Her own parents had regarded her weird gifts as unacceptable. So to be accepted and *needed* by the men she loved meant everything to her.

It was through her visions that they'd found the ancient Book. Why she'd had that particular vision, she'd no idea, unless Lancelyn had projected his complex desires onto her. "We need an earthly key to the astral realm, a link," he had said. Then he had hypnotised Holly, and she had seen the heavy volume on a table in a tiny cell that was thick with mildew, candlewax, soot and cobwebs. The cell was in a tunnel, deep underground, where no human had passed for centuries.

Further hypnotism and research helped them locate the tunnel. It was on a private estate in Hertfordshire, which meant, strictly speaking, they were trespassing. But, Lancelyn reasoned, if the owners were unaware of the tunnel's existence, how could taking the Book count as theft?

Holly hadn't gone with them, but on their return they described the place exactly as she'd pictured it. They'd broken into the cellar of a derelict house to find the entrance. A cold, subterranean place, full of death and ghosts. The lair of a mad hermit, long since dead.

She was profoundly shocked to hear that her vision was so

accurate. *Why do I see such things?* she asked herself. *Why can I never control or understand them?*

She hated the Book at first sight. Something deeply malevolent lingered within it.

No sooner had Ben brought the tome into the house than he'd summoned that ghastly, groaning corpse. Holly hadn't felt safe since. And now Deirdre. Impossible to be objective, when her deeper instincts screamed, *This is evil. You are right to be afraid.*

She went into the parlour and forced herself to open the Book. Cramped writing on yellowing pages. Paper, ink, leather. Nothing to be afraid of...

A terrible resonance flowed out and she slammed it shut, feeling ill. As she stood glaring at the slate-black cover, Sam snaked around her legs, mewing for attention. She gathered him in her arms, absorbing comfort from his warm, hairy weight. He seemed imperturbable.

"The Book doesn't trouble you, does it?" she said. "The evil's not directed at *you*, Sammy. But it's searching for... *someone*."

A knock at the door made her jump. Holly put Sam on the rug and forced herself to answer. The woman on the doorstep was Maud Walker, their bookshop assistant. Sighing inwardly, Holly asked her in.

"Mr Grey sent me to make sure you were well," Maud said with her characteristic nervous giggle. "He said you were upset earlier."

"He needn't have done," said Holly. "I'm perfectly all right."

"I'm so sorry about your friends," said Maud, as if James and Deirdre had merely encountered inclement weather at the seaside.

"Would you like tea?" said Holly, showing her into the parlour. "There's some in the pot."

Medium height and broad-hipped, Maud was beige from head to foot. Even her hair was the same beige as her cardigan, plain skirt and buttoned shoes. She was in her twenties, unmarried, almost pretty but for protruding blue eyes and overlarge teeth.

Holly wanted to like her. After all, it wasn't Maud's fault she lacked charm, a sense of humour or even natural tact. Everyone was different... Maud unfortunately came across as a flat-footed soul with a streak of cunning, someone who failed to rouse fondness in others and didn't care. At this moment, however, Holly was perversely glad of her company.

"Oh, is that a Bible?" Maud exclaimed, reaching for the Book. "I love the Bible, don't you? It's such a comfort."

Holly swept the Book out of her reach. It was a clammy lead weight against her stomach. "No, it's one of Ben's." She hurried out with the volume and locked it in the study. When she came back, Maud was crying.

"Are you all right?" said Holly in astonishment.

"I had a feeling about your friends," Maud said, sniffing loudly. "I knew something was wrong. I'm psychic, you know, terribly psychic."

Holly bit her lip to stem inappropriate laughter. She gave Maud a handkerchief and watched her drying her false tears. Maud often expressed such claims. Although she had only the vaguest knowledge of the Neophytes, she was always angling to join. "I'm psychic, terribly psychic," she would confide to the bookshop customers. And once she had turned to Holly and asked plaintively, "Why do people call me 'Miss PTP?'"

"Thank you, Maud," said Holly, "for helping to cheer me up."

Maud looked at her, her face suddenly frozen. "You are peculiar, Mrs Grey. I don't mean to offend, but you don't always behave..."

"Oh, how should I behave?"

"Well, you shouldn't laugh when people have died. And... if I had a husband like Mr Grey, I would *never* question his judgment."

Holly's mouth fell open. "Did Ben tell you to say that?"

"Of course not – but men know best, don't they? Life is happier if we obey them, as we obey God. You look a bit like a witch with your cat, Mrs Grey. It might give some people the impression you aren't altogether Christian, although I'm *sure* you are."

"Well, that's no one's business but mine." Holly spoke brusquely, too tired to be properly annoyed. "I assure you, there's nothing amiss between my husband and me."

Maud's stern look softened. Another giggle, a quick dip of her head between her shoulders. "Oh, I know. I spoke out of turn." Her tone became ingratiating. "I'm sorry."

"Go back to work," Holly said wearily. "Mr Grey needs you more than I do."

As she saw Maud out, a flood of unease hit her. She couldn't grasp the cause, and a moment later it was gone.

That evening, when Benedict came home, he went into his study and stood resting his hands on the Book's cover, deep in thought. Holly watched him from the doorway in the dim red-gold light. She said, "Thank you for sending Maud. She was the soul of tact, as always."

He winced. "Sorry. I felt bad about walking out when you were upset. Was she awful?"

"It's all right. She made me laugh. Miss PTP."

"I know she has her quirks, but she is a good worker. She's envious of you."

Holly was mildly shocked by this. "Why? Silly woman. Unless it's because I'm married to magnificent *you*, and she isn't."

"Does that mean I'm forgiven?" he said, smiling. "Come here."

"Move away from the Book first. I don't like it."

"It's just an old book, darling."

They hugged; she smelled the papery, leather scent of the shop on his waistcoat. Ordinary books, comforting. How warm and solid he felt.

Eventually he said, "I'm going to see Lancelyn tomorrow."

A twinge of anxiety. "What will you say?"

"That's what I'm working on. I'll give him a chance to clear himself – but I won't take anything less than the truth."

"And will you return the Book?"

A pause. His lips narrowed. "Not yet," he said grimly. "I haven't finished with it."

Katerina sat wrapped in blankets on a chaise longue, propped up by pillows. Her face, though still ghastly, was filling out into recognisable shapes, her hair acquiring a tawny sheen. Although she hadn't spoken, her gaze roved the room, taking in everything.

Charlotte tried to accept her presence with grace.

Katerina had been Karl's friend. For his sake, Charlotte should be happy to help, but unease gnawed at her. All she could think was that the sooner Katerina recovered, the sooner she could leave.

Over the past few days, Ilona had brought several victims to the house for Katerina. Rich drunks she'd picked up at theatres, innocent working men and women whom she had hypnotised or simply kidnapped. She delivered them with a kind of businesslike glee, watched Katerina drink each one dry, then casually helped Karl dispose of the corpses.

Karl supervised the process sombrely, showing neither regret nor pleasure. He never killed if he could help it; but if it could not be helped, he was capable of frightening ruthlessness. Katerina's recovery was his single-minded pursuit.

Charlotte would have assisted the bloody process if they'd asked, but was immensely glad when they did not. Her duties were to bathe Katerina, to wash blood from her lips, to keep her comfortable and sit with her when Karl was absent. She did them all, but with a sense of wrongness that bordered on resentment.

Hour after hour Karl sat with Katerina, stroking her forehead, holding her hand, talking or reading to her.

Katerina was a brooding presence in the house. Suddenly all Karl's attention was focused not on Charlotte but on her. *It won't be forever*, Charlotte told herself. She wanted to please Karl by helping him nurse his poor sick friend; she wanted to share his joy at Katerina's rebirth. But finding no joy in it herself, she felt guilty.

Often she went onto the balcony to escape the taut atmosphere of the house. She stood at the rail, poised above the dark-green cloak of forest, watching the great trio of mountains sparkling in the distance: the Jungfrau, Eiger and Monch. Once the spring thaw began it came quickly; the white meadows turned green, then to a riot of pink alpen roses, purple violets, blue gentians. Lake Thun and Lake Brienz unfroze and began to dance.

She thought, *Why is it one law for me, and another for Katerina? I am not allowed to take even a mouthful from a willing guest, yet he's dragging people here for Katerina to kill outright! Of course, I know there's no choice. She can't hunt for herself. I'm being unreasonable… but all the same I hate it and I want her gone.*

Why can't I be gracious about a wretched, sick friend of Karl's? Wouldn't I do anything for him? Yes, anything.

It's not forever.

With a soundless compression of the air, Ilona appeared beside her, stepping from the Crystal Ring. A slight, elegant figure with shingled mahogany hair: Karl's beauty feminised.

"You look miserable," Ilona said bluntly. "Have you quarrelled with Karl?"

"We don't quarrel," said Charlotte.

Ilona gave an acid smile. "That would be too human. But you can't stand having that sick woman lying about the place, can you?"

Ilona was brittle, venomous, unpredictably cruel. Karl had turned his daughter into a vampire because he'd been unable to bear the thought of her growing old. His motive had been love, but Ilona had hated him for it. She'd even killed Charlotte's sister Fleur, just to hurt him. Yet there was a complicated affinity between her and Charlotte that neither could explain. Charlotte was not vengeful by nature. Settling the score with Ilona would border on hypocrisy, since Charlotte had chosen to join their dark clan. So they maintained a fragile truce. In her heart, she would never forgive Ilona for Fleur, but she pushed her rage and grief to a corner of her mind where it lay dormant.

For now.

"I wish it hadn't happened," Charlotte sighed. "But now she's here I can't expect Karl to turn her out for my sake. I shouldn't even think it. I'm being selfish, but I can't shake off the feeling."

"Why should you? I'd feel the same, but I wouldn't be so noble. While he's out –" Ilona mimed an axe-blow.

"What are you talking about?"

"For heaven's sake, why are you agonising about this? You're jealous. It's perfectly normal."

"No!" Charlotte said, too vehemently. "I don't wish her harm. I just wish she wasn't here."

"But you've every reason to be jealous." Ilona spoke in a confiding tone. "Karl and Katerina were very close, you know."

"How close?" Charlotte asked before she could stop herself.

"Ask him." Ilona grinned. "No, don't ask. Just watch them together."

Charlotte knew what Ilona was doing, but fear rushed through her regardless. She suppressed it. "You're trying to cause trouble," she said calmly. "Don't. It won't work."

Ilona shook her head. "Oh, Charlotte. You're such a fool for love. God, you even have to fall in love with your victims before you can feed! It's terribly sweet, and terribly... bloodless, if you'll excuse the phrase. You're missing so much!"

"I don't think so."

"You try so hard not to frighten them, let alone kill them. I'm amazed you don't send a written apology afterwards! Karl is as bad. Seizing strangers so their faces don't haunt him."

Stung, Charlotte said, "Is your way so superior?"

"God, no. It's worse. It's horrible," Ilona said with relish. "Don't you know? I like to seduce mine. No, I mean really seduce them, make them fall in love and drag me to their beds. Haven't you discovered what fun that is?"

"I've no desire to. It would be repulsive."

Ilona nudged her. "I only do it with attractive ones, darling. God, they're such fools! If they please me, I'm kind; I keep them for a few months before I kill them."

"And if they don't please you?"

"I let them live."

"Is that unkind?"

"Mutilated, most men find it intolerable. I feed from the part that has most displeased me, you see."

Charlotte made a noise of revulsion in her throat.

"So squeamish?" Ilona laughed. "I despair of you. But don't change, Charlotte; you're so funny."

No point in arguing with Ilona; it only made her worse.

Charlotte said, "What I don't understand is why you are helping Karl. When I first knew him, he said you hadn't spoken for years. You still act as if you loathe him at times. Why help Katerina now?"

"Because I'm enjoying myself," Ilona replied. "He's always been too fastidious to kill on his own doorstep. What fun, to bring victims here and see their blood staining his carpet, while he has no choice but to condone it."

"Was Katerina your friend?"

"Never. I hated the bitch."

"You hate everyone."

"Not you, dear." Ilona put an arm around Charlotte's shoulders. "However, if Katerina comes between you and Karl, that will be even more amusing. They invented the word *schadenfreude* for me, didn't you know?"

"I don't believe a word you're saying," Charlotte murmured. She shrugged Ilona's hand from her shoulder. One glance seemed to dissolve Ilona's mockery. The humour bled from her face and voice.

"Aren't you curious," said Ilona, "to know how Katerina escaped from the *Weisskalt*? Something is happening. Did we imagine that we could kill Kristian without consequences?"

CHAPTER FOUR

THE EBONY GATE

The morning was fine, the cool air loud with birdsong. Benedict decided to walk rather than cycle to Lancelyn's; the extra time would help him to collect his thoughts.

The small town, Ashvale, lay between the rugged, bracken-covered hills of Leicestershire in the east, the mining villages of South Derbyshire in the west. Ben's cottage was off the main street, while Lancelyn lived downhill on the opposite side of town, in a large red-brick Victorian villa set in its own grounds.

There was little traffic about in Market Street; a few horse-drawn carts and delivery vans, cyclists, a crimson tram crossing the bottom of the road on its way to the station. Roofs shone under the ice-blue sky, trees were netted with faint veils of green. Ben enjoyed the stroll but his superficial confidence gave way to anxiety when he thought of confronting Lancelyn.

The truth was, Benedict didn't know his brother well. Lancelyn was eighteen years older, and had left home before Ben was three. All Ben recalled was a faceless youth who'd had constant shouting matches with their parents. He remembered hiding in his room during the fights.

Why Lancelyn left, he didn't find out for years. His parents refused to discuss their elder son. As far as his mother and father were concerned, Lancelyn was dead. It was only through tactless relatives that Ben knew he was still alive.

So to Ben, his older brother became a figure of mystery.

His parents, strict and religious, discouraged his friendships with "rough" boys in the village, so Ben created an invisible playmate: Lancelyn.

In those days, they lived amid wild hills near the Peak District in Derbyshire. Their huge, eccentric folly of a house never felt like home to Ben. It was more like living in a cathedral. The rooms were of bare stone, cavernous and echoic, with huge stained-glass windows in every room. On the dullest day there was colour, while sunlight threw floods of ruby and emerald light over his father's collected paraphernalia: brass candlesticks, incense burners, painted icons in starbursts of gold, crimson velvet cloths, paintings of the Madonna and saints. In later life, Benedict realised that his father had loved the trappings of religion as much as he loved God Himself.

This rare atmosphere of symbols and colours, of naked stone and lush rich cloths, permeated Ben in a strange way.

His father was a schoolmaster who always walked the two miles to school with his son. Ben lived for weekends, when he could venture out alone to explore. He loved the hills rising through the mist, their near-vertical flanks grazed by sure-footed sheep. Streams and waterfalls poured over rocks in the valley below the house. There were rumours of caves, too, although he never found them.

The imaginary "Lancelyn" was always with him. Ben pictured him as a shining, handsome hero from a *Boy's Own* adventure. Lancelyn led, Ben followed. The image stayed with him into adulthood.

Ben was nineteen when the Great War destroyed his dreams.

He served in the trenches in the worst of conditions, enduring cataclysmic battles. While he was there, the first letter came from Lancelyn.

Dearest baby brother,

Forgive me for never writing before. I wanted to. When I realised you were old enough to be dragged into this disaster, I couldn't bear to think I might lose you without even having said "Hello". Do you remember me at all? I still see you as a red-faced toddler covered in egg and jam. I can't believe they've sent you out there to be shot at.

I couldn't write to you at home. Mother would have destroyed the letters. Whatever she's made you think of me, I am not the Anti-Christ. Come home safely, so I can meet you and explain…

The letter began a correspondence that kept Ben from outright despair. Words from a distant golden hero, lifting him out of the filth and blood – for a brief time, at least.

Other soldiers broke down and went mad. Benedict's experience precipitated a revelation.

One night, sheltering behind mud-sodden sandbags under the hellish thunder of bombardment, Benedict saw an amorphous light on the lip of the trench. Crazed logic insisted that this was Lancelyn, come to guide him… where? Paradise? That meant death. He wept, but a voice in the cloud of light commanded him to stop and *look*. Disregarding bullets and shells, Ben saw that the mudscape of no-man's-land was actually a broad black river. He felt compelled to cross it… even knowing that to do so would be suicide.

The sky lit up with a shell-burst and stayed alight. The heavens shone like beaten gold. Clouds became mountains, castles, forests in the sky. Elongated figures moved up there, as dark as demons yet stately, like seraphim trailing wings of fire… neither angels nor demons, but something *other*…

Benedict knew that he was looking into the spirit-realm. *Leave Earth behind and enter,* Lancelyn seemed to say. *Cross the river, it's the only way!*

What could be worse than the hell he was enduring? Ben began to climb a ladder out of the trench. The vision ended as a bullet ripped into his chest and flung him back into the mud.

He was sent home, recovering from a wound that, the doctors said, should have killed him. A miracle; he was alive for a reason! While in hospital, he received another letter from Lancelyn.

My dearest Ben,
You're out of it! The moment the War ends, I am renting a villa in
Italy for the summer with some friends. Do join us.

Ben was thrilled. His heroic brother was real and they were going to meet at last! But then he thought, *What will Mother and Father say?*

He believed in honesty. When he broke the news to his mother, however, her reaction was extreme. If he went, she yelled, he need never bother coming back! He would be as dead to them as Lancelyn.

She forced the choice on him; Ben, knowing almost nothing about his brother, chose the new and unknown.

Thus he found himself on a tiered hill above the Mediterranean, sunlight glowing through cypress groves. As he reached a headland above the bay and breathed the warm fragrant air, he felt a glimmer of hope that life was worth living after all.

The sea was indigo, the sky deepest burning blue. Dust and heat and bare white rocks were softened by olive and orange groves spilling down the slopes. Ben saw the sugar-white walls of a villa with greenery spilling wildly over the boundaries. He climbed the hillside for a better view, until he could see over a wall and straight down into the grounds.

The sight made him gasp.

There were people in the garden, some stretched out on the grass, others playing tennis. Four women and seven men – all stark naked.

He'd heard of such goings-on among the "artistic" set; the puritanical father in him pounced, and his first reaction was disgust. Then he edged forward to take a longer look. He began to smile. *Good God, what a sight!*

A cough nearby made Benedict jump guiltily. Looking up, he saw a girl sitting on a rock above him, sketching. His first thought was that he must steer her away before she saw this decadent display.

She was pretty, with long dark hair flowing from beneath a huge sunhat, a loose white dress flattering her slim figure.

"Good morning!" he called out cheerfully. "Do you speak English?"

"I do my best," she said; her accent was educated British, with a trace of Norfolk. "Good morning. Isn't it a beautiful day?"

As he reached her, she smiled and put her sketchpad aside.

"May I see?" he said.

"If you like. It's not very good."

As he looked at the blur of brilliant colours on the page, he was aware of her gaze travelling over him. Although his parents had taught him that conceit was a sin, he'd often been called handsome; six feet four, with a strong face and a good head of blond hair.

"No, it's very good. Your use of colour is… bold."

"That's because I can only see the colours," she said. "Do you think the Impressionists were short-sighted?"

Benedict breathed a sigh of relief; no danger of her seeing the sunbathers!

"I wonder if you could help me," he said. "I'm looking for an Englishman, Lancelyn Grey. Is that his villa?"

"Oh, I'm staying with Lancelyn!" she exclaimed. She pointed at the sunbathers. "Yes, you found us."

"Good God," he said.

"What's wrong?" She laughed. "Oh, the sun-worshippers. Were you embarrassed? You shouldn't be; it's unhealthy to keep the body covered up, don't you think?"

All at once he saw this supposedly innocent creature in a different light.

"Well – yes I'm sure, but –"

"Come on, I'll take you down, Mr –"

"Grey. Benedict. I'm –"

"Oh, you're his brother!" she said, thrilled. "I'm Holly Marshall. Oh, he will be pleased you came."

She slid her hand through his arm and her scent flowed around him, like rain-soaked flowers. Ben was in love.

No ring on her finger; but what was she to his brother?

By the time they reached the villa, the sunbathers had vanished. He waited on a terrace in the deep green shadow of oleanders while she went inside, returning a few moments later to say, "That's a nuisance. Lancelyn and the others have gone into the town; we just missed them. He's left me some work. Do you mind waiting?"

"Of course not."

"Sit down, I'll bring some lemonade."

"You know I – I don't know Lancelyn at all. I haven't seen him for twenty years."

She blinked. "I know. He told me."

He sat in a fretwork chair and watched Holly, at a table on the terrace, copying a sheaf of notes into a book. Her sunhat made a big round shadow on the table. After a while she looked up, and he saw that her eyes were red.

"Anything wrong, Miss Marshall?"

She sighed, stuck her pen into an ink bottle, and rubbed her eyelids. "Eye strain," she said. "I have to copy these notes for Lancelyn, and I can't read his writing. It's giving me such a headache."

"Why don't you wear spectacles?"

"They don't help much. I was born with an eye condition that means I have to squint around the blind spots. I'm used to it."

"And Lancelyn makes you do this close work?"

"I don't mind!" she said fiercely. "I'd do anything for him. He's a wonderful man. You'll see."

Ben drew his chair beside hers. "Let me help," he said, but she pulled the papers away.

"They're private."

"I won't tell." His smile seemed to melt her resolve.

Warily she pushed the notes towards him. "You won't understand anyway. From here," she said, her fingernail indenting the paper.

Benedict read out, "'Initiate of the first level of I.T. makes r. as per Libris S. 1.1–5. Perambulate deosil. Examiner may determine if state of mind is open to receive secret Names of L.S. 2.1. Knowledge of secret N. direct from Raqia indicates imm. elevation to fifth.'" He stopped. She was right: gobbledegook. "Is that correct?"

"Yes, perfect." Her face was bright with relief. Huddling over the book, she began to write in a large, clear script. "Do go on. This makes it so much easier."

They worked with a delicious sense of collusion, their knees touching under the table, while their shadows moved with the circling sun.

When she finished, Ben said, "Excuse me asking, but is this a black-magic ritual of some kind?"

Her face dropped with indignation. "No, nothing of the sort! You really don't know Lancelyn, do you? The purpose of our Order is to train ourselves spiritually and learn secrets that are revealed only in a higher state of consciousness. It's absolutely nothing to do with…"

She stopped, staring at a figure in the arched doorway of the villa. He was dressed in loose Indian-style white clothes. The interior looked coldly blue behind him.

"Thank you, Holly," he said.

She looked like a schoolgirl who'd been caught at some mischief by a teacher. "I was only explaining –"

"It's all right, my dear." He stepped onto the terrace and held out his arms. "Benedict."

This couldn't be Lancelyn! He wasn't at all as Ben had imagined, a golden Greek statue come to life. He didn't even resemble Ben. Instead he was stocky, with big features and coarse skin roasted red by too much sun. He struck Benedict as not merely ugly but gnome-like. Under a mop of dark grey hair, his face was not so much lined as crumpled, the lower half coated with a sparse beard that resembled the hair on a coconut.

Then Ben was imprisoned in his embrace. He gasped, stunned and pleased. Lancelyn stood back and studied him.

"Benedict," he said again. "You are so much more handsome than your photographs."

"You never sent any," Ben said, laughing now. "You told me nothing."

"Well, now you know why mummy and daddy threw me out. They thought I was a Satanist."

"Are you?"

Lancelyn laughed. "They think anything outside their narrow brand of Christianity is Satanism."

Ben looked down. "Mother said if I came to you, I needn't bother going home again."

"Whatever do you mean?" When he smiled, his eyes became slits that gleamed with mischief. "You *are* home."

And Ben, despite his initial shock, felt excitement swell inside him. "Your letters saved my life."

"Me – not God?" said Lancelyn. "Well, Ben, what do you believe in?"

"Nothing. After the War, nothing."

"We'll see about that. Will you come to our Temple meeting tonight? You'll find us strange, but bear with us. We don't bite."

Benedict, although cautious, was ripe to become involved. With no sense of purpose, anyone who put a parental arm around him, especially if that person was *Lancelyn*, could ensnare his mind. More than that, his afternoon with Holly had induced a sense of otherness; he felt the world turning transparent, with shadow-figures moving in a dark landscape...

The first Temple meeting changed his life forever. It was alarming, ridiculous, inspiring, sinister. Embarrassing, at first, to see adults dressed up in robes, calling each other by made-up titles. In a cool windowless room, Lancelyn's temple had grey walls, white candles, enigmatic sigils drawn on the floor, a plain wooden altar; and clouds of incense in the air, richly intoxicating.

"The purpose of this meeting," said Lancelyn, "is to make our brother Benedict a probationer in the Order of the Neophytes of Meter Theon."

Benedict felt horribly self-conscious. Seven men, five women, all apparently well educated and bright, taking this so seriously. Lancelyn led them in a clockwise walk around the temple as they chanted set responses to his words. He called on obscure spirits to lend power. The chanting grew louder; the walk became a dervish dance.

Dizziness, incense, too little oxygen. Suddenly, Ben no longer found the ritual foolish, but hypnotic and liberating. They laughed as they whirled; the power they summoned became real, and it was the force of their own will. Ben felt it like heavy static, a cone of glowing light. Lancelyn's voice was deep and resonant; easy to believe he commanded demons and angels. He was a true priest, one who shouldered all burdens and gave all the answers.

At the peak of their euphoria, Lancelyn led Benedict to the centre of the circle and brought a figure before him, veiled from head to foot in black.

"She represents the Black Goddess," said Lancelyn. He drew back the veil. Underneath was a hideous mask that made Ben jump: a pallid, fanged crone. "Beware of the dangers before us! To unveil her brings wisdom – but only to the pure and strong. To the weak and corrupt she brings death!"

The veil fell to the deafening crash of a cymbal. Ben was made to lie face-down on the floor as he took a formidable oath of secrecy. Lancelyn's voice boomed, "We welcome this initiate to the path of Wisdom, she whom the ancients name Sophia."

Benedict opened his eyes, and saw the vision he'd had in the trenches; a glorious and terrifying skyscape. Ecstasy coursed through him. He knew, at last, that he belonged.

Afterwards, he told Lancelyn what he had seen. "Was it an hallucination?"

"My God, no." Lancelyn seemed delighted. "You saw the astral realm! You are like me. We share the same gifts! Father couldn't keep us apart. Conventional religion strangled me. Couldn't be doing with it. I studied other beliefs, joined various occult groups, but in the end the only way was to seek my *own* truth. Meanwhile, you've achieved a depth of vision that takes most initiates years of work. But understand: if you want to continue, the path will not be easy. There's a lot to learn."

"I'm willing to try," Ben said vehemently. "I'll do whatever it takes. But you must explain where this is leading."

"I would love to, if I could. However, I don't know – yet. The point is to search. *Meter Theon* means Mother of the Gods; the Greek title for Cybele, the Black Goddess. I see her as a rounded black stone, enclosed and secret as an egg. Her darkness does not represent evil but the quality of being *hidden*, obscure. Our task is to unveil her. When we do we will find Sophia, Wisdom herself. The path is not easy, because Meter Theon is a harsh and demanding deity – and how can we know what Wisdom will teach us until we find her? But when we do, she will rebirth us as gods.

"The vision you saw on the battlefield and again last night was the astral world, which I name Raqia, the firmament. That is Sophia's realm, where we must search. It is peopled by her servants, who may help or hinder us. You've seen Raqia, Benedict. The next step is to take courage and enter!"

The following day, Ben and Holly strolled through the white and emerald light of the trees, the sea breeze softening the sun's honeyed heat.

Holly said, "I knew you had psychic gifts as soon as we met. You have such a beautiful aura. Golden."

"You can see auras?" He felt that nothing could surprise him now.

"I see all sorts of strange things. I don't talk of it, because people think I'm peculiar. But Lancelyn doesn't."

"Neither do I," he said with feeling. Then, impulsively, "But why are you with him? You're so young. Don't your parents mind?"

He never forgot the awful vulnerability that flashed across her face, nor the shaky smile with which she tried to hide it.

"Oh well... you see, they were very young when they had me. My arrival was... inconvenient. I do love them, but they always saw me as a bit of a nuisance, I suppose. They couldn't wait for me to leave school and start work, but even then I couldn't do anything right. As for my psychic gifts, they thought I was making it up to show off, or even to be deliberately wicked. So I tried to hide my true self, but didn't always succeed, so all in all, the situation was making me rather unhappy."

"Poor Holly," Ben said quietly.

"I went to a medium for help, but she was a charlatan. Then I worked as a psychic myself for a time, but it was frightening. I saw too much. I was on the verge of a breakdown, when Lancelyn came to one of my seances. He was looking for genuine clairvoyants. He saved my sanity, made me see I was using the gift wrongly. I needed his guidance, Ben. That's why I went away with him."

"What did your parents say to that?"

"They made disapproving noises, but secretly they were relieved."

"They disowned you?" said Ben, thinking of his own family.

"Oh, nothing so dramatic. I still see them. They're nice enough in their way, but it's as if we're acquaintances, not family. The Neophytes are my family now."

Her loneliness made him feel intensely protective. They climbed down the rocks and stood at the sea's edge, gulls circling above them. Unable to hold back any longer, he took her in his arms and kissed her.

She opened to him, becoming warm, receptive, wanting him as he wanted her, but scared. He felt himself turning hot with embarrassment as much as desire, thinking, *How can I possibly admit that I'm a virgin?*

All the prudishness instilled by his parents reared up to torment him. He groaned and held Holly away from him.

"What's wrong?" She looked at him with dark, worried eyes. To his own shame, he was imagining her among the naked sunbathers.

He said, "I – I think you must be more experienced than me."

"Why?" She was angry. "I believe in free love, yes, but I'm not depraved. We hold the human body sacred."

"But you and Lancelyn…" he said helplessly.

"I'm his secretary. He's like a father to me!"

"I'm so sorry. I shouldn't have jumped to conclusions."

"This is my first time, Ben."

Her words sent a molten thrill through him, with the certainty that this was going to happen.

"Mine, too," he whispered. "But are you sure –"

"Ssh." She spoke sternly. "Don't say any more."

Wise advice. He'd almost spoiled the moment with talk, but she saved it, silencing him with her sweet mouth, drawing him down onto the hot firm sand. Awkward and laughing they undressed, and she pressed her golden body to his pale, war-scarred flesh. Not wanting to hurt or disappoint her, he let her guide him, responding to her needs, holding back his own delicious culmination with all his will until she had reached hers. And despite their inexperience, it was magical. Holly burned away his guilt, showing him that sex, even in all its animal, feverish urgency, was not a sin but an offering to heaven.

Afterwards, they lay folded together, melting like honey into the golden sand. Adoring each other in wonder. And Ben knew, they both knew.

"We must lie together like this forever. I never want us to be apart, Holly. Never."

The golden summer in Italy was the most glorious time of Benedict's life. However, it couldn't last. Returning to England, Holly insisted on a church wedding; she still had a childlike need to please her parents, and they *were* pleased that day, and quite charming. Lancelyn was benevolently thrilled that he'd brought Ben and Holly together.

When no children came, Ben and Holly were each secretly glad. They had no illusions about parenthood; how appalling, to inflict the same unintentional pain on their own offspring! Their families weren't around to drop irritating hints about babies, so they were left alone to pursue their rarefied lives.

Lancelyn helped Ben to establish his bookshop, but never interfered with its running. With no visible source of income, he spent his time studying the occult. He lived alone and – while he had relationships with some of the female Neophytes – seemed content to remain a bachelor. His only recreation, aside from fishing, was repairing mechanical toys.

He was a born leader, self-assured and inspiring. As a friend, too, he was delightful; warm, wise, endlessly helpful. Ben was certain he would never misuse his power.

Benedict was stunned to discover how much hard work the Order involved. He was required to study philosophy, religion, and physical and mental disciplines such as yoga. He mastered every challenge, and within a few years Lancelyn appointed him his second in command, Magister Templi.

The Order took itself very seriously. Lancelyn did not tolerate time-wasters. Some members were well known in their professions; judges, doctors, politicians, even aristocrats – but when they all dressed in robes with their faces covered, they shed their identities, relishing secret escape from their public roles.

For a few years, everything was perfect.

When things went wrong, the catalyst – Ben realised after the event – was their mother's death.

Holly sensed the death in one of her psychic flashes, soon confirmed by a letter from his parents' solicitors. Ben tried to attend the funeral, but his father, unrepentant, drove him away in a rage. That was Ben's last attempt to contact him. His father lived alone at Grey Crags now and could rot there for all he cared.

However, it was Lancelyn's utter indifference to their bereavement that crystallised Ben's frustration. As Ben grew into his own power, he began to resent Lancelyn's authority, his casual assumption that Ben and Holly were his protégés, eternal assistants. That was why Ben built his own temple. Working alone, he entered Raqia with increasing ease to soar through the ethereal mountains of the astral world. No esoteric words or symbols were needed; only the force of his own will. He saw wonders and sensed dark-winged creatures around him, beings who were frustratingly oblivious, untouchable.

If Lancelyn communicates with them, he thought, *he is either infinitely more adept than me – or he's hallucinating – or telling lies! Ha, heresy!*

The brothers were growing apart, though neither dared admit it. The process began even before they discovered the Book, long before the deaths of James and Deirdre. Ben finally acknowledged the schism as he walked along tree-lined streets to confront his brother.

Lancelyn, your meetings are fruitless and theatrical, he wanted to announce. *You have not unveiled Wisdom. You have done nothing new.*

I am younger and stronger than you. So why are you still in power?

Benedict stood on Lancelyn's doorstep, hands pushing his coat pockets out of shape. *I don't want to face this*, he thought. *I risk having all my dreams shattered. But I have to. I want everything, or nothing!*

A manservant showed him into the study. Lancelyn was sitting at his desk surrounded by his books and manuscripts. Another figure, a disembodied torso on the edge of the desk, made Ben start. Some sort of dummy, wearing a Mexican hat and striped shirt. One of Lancelyn's restored toys. Damned ugly thing, Ben thought.

"Come in," Lancelyn said gruffly. "Cigar?"

"Thank you," said Benedict.

Lancelyn leaned over to the dummy and pressed a lever. Whirring, it came to life, raising its hands to produce a box of cigars, then opening the lid to Benedict. The fixed grin on its badly painted face was unsettling.

"Nice toy, eh?" said Lancelyn. "I completely rebuilt the mechanism. Makes a pleasant change from brain-work."

Ben took a cigar. The automaton flicked a thumb, held out a light, then sank back to rest.

"Remarkable," said Ben, through clouds of smoke. He sat

in a leather armchair, putting on a show of relaxed confidence. "You've heard the unfortunate news about James and Deirdre?"

"Of course." Lancelyn sat down behind his desk. "Very sad. Most regrettable."

"Any possibility that it wasn't suicide? That they were victims of a magical attack?"

The magus's reaction was subtle. He became very still, face expressionless and eyes hard. "A strong possibility, I'd say."

"But who would do that to them?" Ben said. "Why?"

"They must have upset someone. No one with such powers uses them lightly, so it must have been very serious. Flouting the Laws, perhaps, or breaking their oath of secrecy."

Ben moistened his dry lips. Would Lancelyn speak so openly, if he were guilty? "D'you know who they quarrelled with? Does any member of the Order possess such power... apart from you?"

Cool amusement creased his brother's face. "What is this, Ben, a police investigation?"

"I need the truth. I understand that both Deirdre and James quarrelled with you."

"Indeed? What else did Deirdre tell you?"

"I never said she told me anything," said Ben, playing Lancelyn's game. "But she was afraid. She had a visitation. In the light of what subsequently happened, it sounded remarkably like a nightmare vision of a train."

"Perhaps she had a fear of trains; a self-fulfilling prophecy," Lancelyn said thinly. "Be careful, Ben. Be very careful."

The room seemed to darken. He blinked hard. "Why?"

"There is much you don't understand. Why d'you think I am head of the Order and you are not?"

Ben was stung. "Because I respect you!"

"Respect? Have you no ambition? Are you suggesting that your power is equal to mine, but you hold back out of brotherly love?"

"No. And I'm not here to argue, only for a straight answer. Did you have anything to do with the deaths of my friends?"

Again the room darkened. Lancelyn appeared tiny and distant, as if Ben were viewing him through the wrong end of a telescope. Ben began to shiver. Animal terror seized his mind. There was only one word for the current that surged into him: evil.

The feeling vanished. Too stunned to react, he heard Lancelyn's response to his question. "You disappoint me. First, there's no use you can make of the answer. Second, no magical attack is undertaken lightly; the reasons of the magus are deep and complex beyond society's shallow morality. One cannot be judged by the other. Third, you haven't so much asked a question as given an answer: that you do not trust me. Tell me, Ben, what use is a disciple if he lacks absolute faith in his master?"

Ben stood up, swayed, caught himself on the edge of the desk. He felt frightened, outmanoeuvred, and angry. "So, I am useless – for daring to question you?"

"Perhaps the fault is mine. I wonder why I promoted you to such high office when you clearly don't understand the rules."

"Since when has murder been in the rules?"

Lancelyn spoke with menace. "I am not a murderer, Ben, but I shall never forget your insinuation. Our search for Wisdom is a deadly serious business. If you don't understand how serious, you'd be better off out of it."

"Are you expelling me?"

"No, no." Lancelyn's hard tone softened. "I'm warning you. By the way, I hope you've brought back the Book."

"No, I haven't."

"How goes the translation?"

"Slow, but –" Ben stopped. He no longer had any intention of telling Lancelyn about the summoning. It was a matter of principle.

"Then if you can make no useful progress, I must work on it myself. Kindly bring it back immediately."

Ben straightened his jacket and said, "I'm afraid I can't."

"What?"

"I haven't finished my studies. I came here ready to give you the benefit of the doubt, but I won't be spoken to like an imbecile. I've as much right to the Book as you; I'll give it back when I'm ready. That's all. Now I'll bid you good morning."

"The message is clear," Ben told Holly. "Anyone who crosses Lancelyn will be punished. His warning is blatant: 'I have the power to kill with magic; no use rushing to the police because they can't prove a thing; but anyone who challenges me will meet the same fate.' Even me!"

Holly listened, her face pinched with misery. "I can't believe he'd hurt his own brother."

"Hang it, we aren't brothers any more!" he said. "We're rivals, and he knows it. But I won't take this. I'll find a way to defend myself – and you, Holly. Good grief, if he won't stop at me or Deirdre, why should he spare you?"

"Don't be ridiculous, he'd never hurt me!" She spoke more in fear than anger.

"I can't take the risk." He added sadly, "I don't know Lancelyn any more. Perhaps I never did. I was too busy worshipping him to see what he really is. But he's gone too far. I've got to take the Order away from him before he destroys it."

Benedict stood alone outside his attic temple, holding the Book. It was heavy as stone and icy to the touch, as if, instead of rotting, it had petrified.

Ben trusted Holly's intuition, but had been astonished when she'd envisioned the Book's location so accurately. When he and Lancelyn found the tunnel and saw the book in the tiny dank cell, exactly as she'd described –!

An unspeakably weird place, the lair of some medieval hermit. Eeriest of all, there had been five imprints on the cover, as if someone had recently touched the Book and snatched their hand away.

"I don't like it," Holly had said when they brought it home. "It has a horrible aura. I wish I'd never had the vision, and that you'd left it where it was."

But Ben had tasted its power. Now he was going to use it again – even though he was breaking his promise to Holly – in self-defence.

Wanting to avoid arguments, he'd persuaded her to visit a friend for a few days, insisting that she needed a rest. She'd gone reluctantly, saying goodbye with a sullen mouth and suspicious eyes. She must suspect… Still, now she was out of the way, he'd worry about the consequences later.

Lancelyn, you can send all the psychic currents and nightmares you like against me, he thought; *I am going to shape something real to send against you!*

He was ready to begin.

The attic was dismal, the outside panels of the temple as grey and dull as the surroundings. He'd constructed the shell within the roof space so he could walk all the way around it.

One of the panels was a door. Ben opened it and went inside.

Within, the ten-sided space was lined with mirrors, replicating each other to infinity. Ceiling and floor were black, each with a ten-pointed star painted in white lines. He lit an oil lamp and replaced the violet glass shade; he ignited galbanum and frankincense in a censer. Fragrant smoke filled the air.

Benedict was wearing his ritual clothes: pale mauve robe with the ten-pointed star on the breast, full-face mask and hood.

On the floor, in the centre of the star, he placed the Book. First, a meditation to settle his mind; then, breathing fast to make himself dizzy, he began to spin round and round the temple.

His mind was resistant to the trance. Trickles of doubt diverted his concentration. Although he dreaded failure, he was even more afraid of success.

Will it be the same being that answers, or a different one?

God, I wish Holly were here.

Lancelyn's fault... He began this... Does he think I'm weak, so easily intimidated? He needs to learn and he has to be stopped.

Breathe deep. Kill the doubts and concentrate.

As Ben trod the circle, he chanted a deep, piercing note until the bones of his skull vibrated. He found it easy these days to touch Raqia. He was an adept, in no need of the elaborate trappings and rituals of lesser initiates.

Reflections whirled past him, purple, black and silver. His vision darkened; green and red exploded across his eyes as he grew faint. Sweat poured from him, ice cold. His head ached from chanting, as if he were pounding his skull against a door... a vast ebony gate to hell itself.

The barrier burst open. He was out of his body and soaring through clouds. Dark gold, deepest blue. He leapt across a livid chasm and saw a vast white halo, scintillating far above.

He reached up to the halo and touched it! Shimmering coldness broke over his hand as he tried to grasp a piece of the higher realm and absorb its power...

Visualise... Power striking his enemy like lightning. A hellish wind blowing through the enemy's house. A cloud in the darkness of his bedroom, settling on his chest and sucking out his life...

Succubus. Lamia.

He cried, "Spirits of Raqia, you let me into your world; now come with me into mine! Hear the plea of your faithful servant. Aid me now and I'll repay you richly. Come to me... come now..."

Ripples flowed from his hand. He was plummeting backwards, losing his hold on the realm too fast. Yet the ripples flowed on. They shook the whole realm of Raqia; not a pebble but a boulder thrown into a lake...

Benedict burst out of the trance with a shout of pain. He ached and trembled as if he'd been crushed by a train. He struggled for control; now he needed all his strength to master the forces he'd called.

The temple swung into semi-focus. Something lay in the centre of the double pentacle, a white shape. Benedict stared. As before, it looked like a skeletal corpse, curled on its side like a crescent moon around the censer, lamp and Book. The lavender glow was as coldly mystical as moonlight.

"It worked!" he whispered. "By God Almighty and all the powers of Sophia, it worked!"

The first time had not been a fluke. He'd brought a solid, real being from another world into this. Again, his instinct was to recoil and banish it, but he controlled himself. *Be scientific...*

Had the transition killed it?

It looked dead, desiccated, ash-white. Cold vapour swirled from its skin and Benedict shivered. The entity brought winter with it, and snow lay on the floor as if blown there by the brief opening of an arctic door. Crystals glittered in the lamplight.

Benedict watched the creature. How to protect himself? He turned slowly, envisioning pentagrams in the north, south, east and west to guard the space... knowing that the true purpose of words and symbols was to concentrate his mind. That was where magic lay. In the mind.

Suddenly the apparition made a sound, a thin dry groan that went on and on. "*Ahhhh...*"

Fresh sweat burst out on Benedict's back. Not dead! He edged towards the mirror panel that concealed the door. This was too real.

"I am Benedict," he said, trying to sound authoritative. "I have summoned you from Raqia to Earth to do my bidding. You are here at my command. Can you understand me? Can you speak?"

It heard. The groan grew louder. It shifted a few inches with a scraping sound, and stretched out a hand with a terrible dry crackle, as if the effort might shatter its frame. It lifted its chin and Benedict saw the face. A mummified angel. He stared with overwhelming horror and pity at the papery skull and mindless, shrivelled eyes.

He tried again. "All respect to you, Spirit; you are safe here. I wish us to help each other. Tell me what it is you need."

The groan turned into a word: "*You.*"

The creature pushed itself up on bony forearms. Benedict wrenched open the temple door and was through in a second; he glimpsed a pale streak as it leapt at him, heard a leathery thud and the shattering of glass as he slammed and locked the door just in time.

He stood outside with the key in his hand, shaking, wondering how he would cope with the creature he'd unleashed.

Reduced at a stroke from adept to terrified probationer. This was the line between imagining he knew everything, and realising he did not; between belief and horrific reality. He'd imprisoned the thing, but there was only wood and glass between them.

Caught between terror and growing elation, he put his eye to a gap between panels.

In the glow he saw the bare wood of the damaged door, the creature lying at its base amid shards of glass. A corpse of ash. Tragic, it looked. Ravenous... for flesh, or blood? How on earth was he to control and nourish it?

The secrets were never meant to be used like this, he thought. *Worst possible abuse of privilege. God help me, I've done it now.*

Suddenly, as if the temple shell were transparent, the corpse stared straight at him, the wizened face feral and ghastly. He caught his breath. Then, in a white streak, it sprang.

Glass exploded like a shell-burst. Benedict screamed. The panel splintered and the creature came surging through and straight onto him, bearing him to the floor.

Its strength was impossible. Dead-white hands closed on his neck, forcing the screams back into his lungs... and as he strained, uselessly, to keep its fangs out of his throat, its wide-open mouth and staring eyes were a perfect mirror of his own.

CHAPTER FIVE

THE EYES OF A NIGHTBIRD

When Karl first mentioned Katerina, Charlotte had visualised her as small, gentle, and sisterly. The woman who bloomed from the husk was not at all what she had imagined.

Within two weeks, their care restored her to stunning physical condition. It was impossible to believe that the sleek beauty who reclined on the chaise longue was the same creature. She was stately, with glossy dark-brown hair that lay in skeins over her broad shoulders. Beautiful, but not ethereal; her features were strong, her mouth full, her brown eyes haughty.

Charlotte tried to dismiss Ilona's warnings, but all the same she couldn't stop herself watching Karl with Katerina. The more she tried to prove Ilona wrong, the more her worst fears came true.

Karl's attentiveness to Katerina ran deeper than kindness to a dear friend. She saw the way he looked at her, the tenderness with which he brushed her hair from her face. He would sit holding her hand for hours, talking softly, in both English and German. At first she did not respond, but soon she began to look at him, frowning a little, listening. Sometimes her lips would move, as if she were trying to speak.

At the same time, Karl became distant towards Charlotte, giving her minimum attention before returning to the patient.

He's preoccupied, he's concerned, it won't be for long, she told herself, but rationality failed to soothe her paranoia. She'd never seen him like this with anyone, even Ilona. The easy warmth he showed Katerina made her jealous.

When Karl went out to feed and to rest in the Crystal Ring, Charlotte no longer went with him. Instead she was expected to stay with Katerina.

Charlotte endured these times. She could barely bring herself to speak to the invalid. If she tried, Katerina's only response was a wary sideways stare.

Her unease deepened towards animosity.

The hostility, it seemed, was mutual. To please Karl, Charlotte would sit and read to her, but it was always with the creeping feeling that Katerina might attack her at any moment.

The difficulty of suppressing her true feelings made Charlotte withdrawn; but if Karl noticed, he said nothing. That alone was unlike him, and hurt her. He was too wrapped up with his "patient" even to notice.

I think Karl would have made a wonderful doctor, she thought drily. *In a different life, a different world. He has the hands and eyes of a healer... so people trust them, and find out too late that he has the fangs and appetites of a wolf...*

The room in which their guest was convalescing had yellow roses twining over the wallpaper, a peaked wooden ceiling, vases of alpine flowers: it was a room of warm spring sunlight in which vampires – deceptively – did not look out of place.

One morning, as Charlotte sat reading to Katerina, Karl came in and looked over her shoulder at the book of Goethe's poetry on her lap.

"Why don't you talk to Katti, instead of reading?" he said.

"Because I don't know her," said Charlotte. "And she doesn't know who I am."

"But she soon will. She sees you every day. I know from experience that it's possible to be *aware* for a long time before you regain the power of speech."

Charlotte nodded. For Karl's sake, she swallowed her resentment. She tried not to mind that he sat on the edge of the chaise and took Katerina's hand...

Katerina gave a start. She turned her head, blinked, and spoke in German. "Karl? Darling, has the world gone mad, or is it me?"

"Katti," he said warmly, smiling as Charlotte had rarely seen him smile. With his left hand he clasped her fingers; with the right he caressed her shoulder, his attention completely on her.

"I don't recognise this room." Her voice was deep and expressive; a voice to drown someone in love or kill them with hate. "Don't let go of my hand. I want to be sure you're real. I've had the most awful dreams."

"I am real," said Karl. "You're safe now. Do you know how long you've been here?"

Katerina looked around the room at the cheerful soft golds and yellows, the bright flowers. Her glance touched Charlotte briefly. "I have no idea. I feel as if I've been ill, and lost my memory, like a human. Give me a moment." She pressed a hand to her head. "It was like a dream... Were you and Ilona really bringing me victims? I couldn't get enough blood... I tried to speak but I couldn't move or make sense of anything. Before that there was blinding light and I was frozen and very afraid... Oh, my dear, hold me. I feel so strange."

"You have been ill, in a sense," said Karl. He hugged her to him; Charlotte stood and watched, feeling invisible. "As near to death as a vampire can be. Don't you remember how we found you?"

"Found me... where?"

"In the Crystal Ring. Don't worry, we'll explain later."

"Is Kristian here?"

"No," said Karl. "No, he is not."

"I knew you were with me, but on the other side of a glass wall. I couldn't reach you." Katerina stared at Charlotte over Karl's shoulder. "Who is she?"

Karl let Katerina back onto the pillows, and turned. "This is Charlotte." He switched to English, although Charlotte had understood their conversation perfectly well.

There was pure antagonism in the woman's eyes; a reflection of the emotion that leapt into Charlotte's heart. Hatred on sight.

"I didn't ask her name. I asked who she is."

"My companion," said Karl.

"Ah," said Katerina. "I see."

"She helped us to bring you back to life."

"Step forward, Charlotte. Let me see you properly."

Charlotte obeyed, but she felt she was being judged. Katerina's gaze trailed over her and found her sadly lacking. "What strange clothes you're wearing."

"My clothes are strange," Charlotte said coolly, "because you have been asleep in the *Weisskalt* for forty years."

Katerina looked stunned. Charlotte had used a cheap way to dent her composure, but for a moment it was worth it.

"Forty years?" She stared wildly at Karl. "What year is it?"

"Nineteen twenty-six. Spring." He gazed at Charlotte, his eyes saying, *Why could you not let me tell her more gently?* "Can you remember anything?"

"No. Let me think…" Her face went stiff with terror. "Oh God, where's Andreas? *Where's Andreas?*"

She was so distraught that Charlotte felt a pang of remorse. She wanted to comfort Katerina – even wanted to like her – but their situation made it impossible.

"We don't know." Karl held her arms to soothe her. "Kristian put you both in the *Weisskalt*."

"Why?"

"As punishment for deserting him for me."

"Of course. I remember… oh God, so he did it! The very thing we dreaded."

Karl said, "Forgive me, Katti. I would have stopped him if I could. I didn't know until it was too late. I should have tried to save you, but I didn't, through ignorance or cowardice."

"Don't, Karl. Don't blame yourself. The *Weisskalt* is too dangerous; but even if you had rescued us, Kristian would have devised some worse punishment." Katerina leaned her head back and looked out of the chalet window at the mountains. Remembering. "Oh, God. Andreas… It seems only yesterday we were all together. *Forty years?*"

"More."

"And I saw Ilona here? She's speaking to you now?"

"When it suits her."

"How things have changed." Katerina's eyes swivelled towards Charlotte, glittering. "How they've changed. Karl, would you bring me a mirror and comb? And something to wear, however dreadful. I should get up. I truly feel as if I haven't moved for half a century."

"Of course," said Karl.

Charlotte was poised to go instead, but Karl didn't ask; the request had been addressed to him. As he left, Katerina turned to Charlotte.

Her face was imperious, with a touch of softness that made it oddly painful to be disliked by her. She had all the confidence that Charlotte had never possessed.

"Well, how long have you known Karl?"

"Three years," said Charlotte. She spoke coldly, defensively.

"Such a little time. And were you human when you met him?"

"Yes." Charlotte gave an icy smile. "He brought me into the Crystal Ring."

Katerina paused, surprised and disapproving. "Well, I don't know what has befallen Karl in the time we were apart, but clearly he must have been *very* desperate, to have broken his vow..."

"What vow?"

"Never to make another vampire after Ilona."

"I know about Ilona. He kept no secrets from me."

"No?" A supercilious lift of her eyebrows. "I have to say, you are not what I would consider his usual taste."

"I don't understand," Charlotte said stiffly.

"You are a little cold shadow; he likes women with spirit; some blood, so to speak. He always insisted he'd rather be alone than drag others into Kristian's grasp, and that if ever we were separated there could be no one else... But then, he was always lying to himself."

Charlotte listened, feeling sick but trying to hide it. "If I hear you correctly, you're suggesting that I am a pale substitute for you?"

"Didn't Karl tell you what Andreas and I were to him?"

"Friends."

Katerina's eyes came alight with a knowing smile. "Friends only? I thought he had kept no secrets from you."

"What do you mean?"

"We were lovers, of course. I understand why he spared you the truth, but you ought to be aware, now I am here."

"You and Karl?" Charlotte spoke thinly, hardly able to form the words.

"Karl, and me... and Andreas. The three of us. You look

shocked. Have I upset you, dear? I didn't mean to."

"But it doesn't matter, does it?" Charlotte said fiercely. "That was in the past."

"It's in the present now." Katerina's certainty was absolute. Her will was an almost physical force that left Charlotte defenceless. "I'm here, awake, alive. And bear in mind that we were with Karl for longer than a human lifetime. Three years! How well do you think you know him?"

Karl was in the doorway. "Katti," he said quietly.

Charlotte knew that, with preternatural hearing, he must have overheard their exchange. Katerina had intended him to. Then Charlotte did what she'd always done as a girl when a confrontation became too much; she bit her tongue, made her face blank, and walked out. She left with dignity, but it felt like defeat.

Darkness fell; immortal eyes saw through it as humans could not, saw soft colours gleaming in the shadows, the glowing hidden beauty of the night. Charlotte buttoned her coat over her evening dress, settled the fur collar, pulled on her gloves and cloche hat. She did so briskly, staring through her reflection in the black window at the wind-blown world outside. A huge white owl sat in a tree top a few yards away, staring at her.

"Where are you going?"

Karl appeared at her elbow, as if from nowhere. She wanted his arms around her, his firm sensual mouth on hers; she wanted the perfection they had shared before Katerina came. But his past had become a solid barrier between them.

"To see *Giselle* again."

"Forgive me, I'd forgotten. I can't come; I must talk to Katerina tonight."

"So I assumed. That's why I'm going on my own."

"Charlotte..." He spoke calmly and rationally; his tranquil nature was one of the intriguing qualities that drew her to him. It also frustrated her at times. "I can't apologise on Katerina's behalf, because I don't know why she said what she did. But I am sorry you were hurt."

Both his gentleness and his distance scorched her. She could no longer keep her feelings secret; indeed, Katerina's hostility seemed to vindicate an outburst.

"Why don't you know? Because immortals aren't meant to feel petty emotions like jealousy?"

"Neither of you has any reason to be jealous."

"It's all I can do to share you with Ilona, and she's your daughter. Now this woman intrudes on us and tells me –" Charlotte stopped. She was almost too angry to speak, but still felt she had no right to her anger.

"There is no question of sharing. She hasn't come to replace you; how could you even think it? But we were close for so many years; you can't expect me to feel nothing for her. And I can't cast her out, any more than I could desert you, beloved."

"I know. I know. But you said you were friends, and she said lovers; who was lying, you or her?"

"I should have told you." His soft words pierced her like a white-hot dart; part dismay, part desire, inflamed by a brief image of Karl and Katerina lying naked together, kissing, biting...

Even though she'd thought could bear it, his admission flayed her.

"Why didn't you tell me?"

"I wasn't trying to deceive you. It was truly more friendship than anything."

"Strange friendship."

"Perhaps. But there seemed no need to complicate things unnecessarily. Call it an omission, not a lie."

"Well, now the owl has come home to roost." Charlotte wasn't sure why she said this, but from the corner of her eye she saw the white bird take off and flap away into the night. She went on, "Look at this from her point of view: she has woken in a world she doesn't know, and you are her only friend. She adores you; who wouldn't? Andreas isn't here to divide her attention, so she is bound to fasten onto you. I don't blame her, but that doesn't mean I have to tolerate it!"

Karl was shaking his head. "She's not like that. Give her time. I wish you would stay tonight and talk with us."

Torn, Charlotte longed to be healed, but Katerina was an implacable thorn in the wound.

"She wouldn't talk freely with me there, and I can't endure her condescension. I won't stay where I'm not wanted."

"Don't make this worse." Karl looked at her resignedly. "Perhaps it's best I talk to her alone, though. Come back soon."

He bent to kiss her but she evaded him and slipped into the Crystal Ring, unable to give him the briefest show of affection.

Katerina said she was tired of being inside, so Karl took her out and they walked slowly through the pine forest under a bright moon. The air was cold and fragrant, the forest floor as yielding as moss. And although Karl never forgot Charlotte, it was here that the wonder of Katerina's presence finally overwhelmed him. They embraced and held onto each other, weeping for the lost years, for the miracle.

At last Katerina stood back and said, laughing, "Well, how do you like the clothes?" She'd chosen a white shirt and trousers – Karl's clothes, not Charlotte's – which only emphasised her femininity. "Women wear men's clothes now, you said. I should bob my hair, too, to be in fashion, like Ilona."

"No, don't cut it. Fashions change so fast."

"And our hair grows fast, too. You always liked long hair. Is that why Charlotte's is down to her waist?"

Karl did not reply.

"Are you annoyed with me?" she said.

"How could I be?"

"I know." She laughed, showing strong pearly teeth. "Returning from the dead after forty years gives you licence to do and say anything, doesn't it?"

"For a while," Karl said, not responding to her self-mockery. "But I won't allow you to upset Charlotte."

Katerina stopped and leaned back against a tree, her arms folded. Her face was like marble in the moonlight, her lips silver-pale; she needed to feed.

"I behaved badly," she said. "I apologise. I wasn't myself; I wasn't expecting to see her, and I felt... possessive. What claim can she have on you, when I've known you so much longer?"

"That's irrelevant. I know I once said I'd rather live alone, but I didn't understand how much I needed her until I met her."

"The question was rhetorical, *mein Schatz*. You didn't have to answer; I understand." She sighed and brushed her deep-brown hair back over her shoulders. "Oh, what fools we are. We think we're above jealousy, but we're not. We are animals, defending our territory."

"I don't want you and Charlotte in conflict, Katti. There's no need."

"It wasn't only me, though. Why does she find me so threatening? I'm glad she went to the ballet alone. I can talk to you now."

Karl decided to steer her away from the subject of Charlotte. "Have you remembered anything?"

They walked on through the trees. Katerina said, "Certain things. I remember Kristian coming for us; God, such a bad dream. He accused us of leading you astray, daring to help you make Ilona a vampire without his permission. He said we'd disobeyed God's laws, and that made us like Lucifer because we had tried to put ourselves above God... Oh, you know how he is." Katerina gave a dismissive shrug, but Karl saw her submerged terror. She turned paler as she went on, "He brought accomplices, hooded like monks, but he didn't need them. Kristian seized both Andreas and me without help. Even together we could not resist him. He talked of betrayal and, God help us, I seem to remember him weeping. He took us into the Crystal Ring, higher and higher. Soon all I could see was blinding whiteness. The light and cold were unbearable. I knew what was happening because he'd done the same to many others... God, I was never so terrified in all my existence! I heard Andreas calling my name, and I was screaming for him." She paused, swallowing hard. "I couldn't see him. His cries faded and he was gone. I became too stiff and weak to move... and then Kristian abandoned us. I told myself he was trying to frighten us, that he must come back... but he didn't. He left me there. And my poor Andrei..."

"And were you aware of being in the *Weisskalt* for long?"

She threw back her head. "In a way. There was light and ice; no thoughts, no real pain. Certainly I didn't know so many years had passed. It seemed a single, long moment."

Karl hadn't realised how tense he was until she said this. He'd dreaded hearing that she had been aware of every second of those forty years. "But how did you escape the *Weisskalt*? Kristian used it as a death sentence. No vampire ever leaves without help. I wish I'd tried to find you, Katti, but…"

"No, dear, you'd only have been trapped with us," she said gently, touching his sleeve. "I've no idea how I escaped. Except that I heard Kristian's voice, and it woke me up."

"What?" Karl whispered.

"It's vague. I don't remember escaping. I found myself floating lower down in the Crystal Ring. The warm air hurt like fire. There were other vampires waking around me, but I couldn't reach them. The Crystal Ring is too vast; we drifted apart like leaves. I believe I floated for a long time, months if not years. I was aware enough to feel time passing… yet my mind was blank. Then something hot touched me and I leapt for the blood; I realise now that it was you, darling. I'm sorry if I hurt you, but you saved me."

"What makes you think it was Kristian who woke you?"

"I know his voice, although it was in my head, not my ears. Where is he?"

"It could not have been him," said Karl. "Kristian is dead."

Her lips parted, her eyes flew wide open. "It's not true!"

"I killed him, Katti. Others helped me – Ilona, Pierre, Stefan and Niklas, and Charlotte – but I was the one who lured him to a dark, cold place that sucked out all his strength so we could finish him."

Katerina stared, denying his words with a minimal shake of her head.

"It had to be done," Karl went on. "He held too much power over us. None of us wanted to slaughter him, but he wouldn't leave us alone."

Eventually she said stiffly, "You needn't justify your actions to me. I hated him, in the end. But I'm shocked. I never thought he could die."

"Believe me."

"But it was his voice! He said, 'Wake. Take revenge. Don't let them forget me… I commanded you to sleep and now I command you to wake!'"

"You must have imagined it."

Katerina turned in front of him and clasped his arms. "But if I imagined it, *what woke me?*" she exclaimed. "What?"

Karl had no answer. He'd told her with absolute certainty that Kristian was dead, but now he began to have doubts. What if Kristian had survived being drained of life, frozen, dismembered?

Revenge... Don't let them forget me...

Katerina's voice brought him back to himself. "Karl, talk to me. I haven't seen such a look in your eyes since..." She stopped short of mentioning the death of his long-dead mortal wife, Therese, Ilona's mother.

"I don't believe we are actually immortal," he said. "But we're so resistant to death as to seem so. A vampire is like some demonic insect that grows a new limb when it loses one, that can't be crushed or burnt... and if you cut it into six pieces, six whole insects come back."

Katerina, usually imperturbable, looked alarmed. "What's wrong with you? Beheading kills us!"

"Not always. Not if there is another vampire to save the head and feed it fresh blood. The body grows anew." He fell quiet, flooded by hellish memories.

She said quietly, "Do you know someone to whom that happened?"

"Stefan. A human beheaded him and Kristian saved him... And it also happened to me."

"My God. This is too much, Karl."

"It's the truth." He opened his hands. "Charlotte's brother cut off my head; Kristian wouldn't let me die that easily."

"Charming relatives she has! So, you killed Kristian, even though he saved your life?"

"I wasn't sure I wanted to live again. Now I'm glad to be alive and with Charlotte, but at the time... You cannot imagine the horror of what Kristian did."

"Tell me."

"Later. There's so much to explain. But knowing there was a possibility, however remote, that someone might revivify Kristian, we cut him into pieces. Severed his head, split the skull, cut up his torso and limbs."

Katerina was shuddering. Tears stood bright in her eyes.

"Are you weeping for him?" Karl asked.

"No."

"I did."

"It's the shock, Karl. Kristian was so strong! He was everywhere and everything. I can't imagine him brought so low. Did he cry out for help?"

"Yes. He said his only sin was to love us too much. And at the end, when I brought down the axe, he asked, 'This is how you love me?' And he said those words after we'd cut off his head. *After.* That was most hideous of all, though it did ensure that we destroyed his skull... But what if he came back, what if he simply *cannot* be destroyed?"

Katerina ran gentle fingers along his forearm. "What would you do if he had survived?"

"God knows."

"Well, we must find out if he has. And what of Andreas? If I'm alive, he might also be in the Crystal Ring, lost and starving. Help me find him! I need you, Karl; didn't we help you, all those years ago?"

Karl folded his arms around her and held her to him. She was taller than Charlotte, her face almost on a level with his. He'd never stopped loving Katerina, her calm strength and voluptuous warmth; he had only trained himself to survive the loss.

She kissed him on the mouth. He responded. So natural, so miraculous to feel her lips on his after all this time... but conscience stopped him. He drew back and turned his face aside.

"I see," she sighed, her arms slackening. "Forgive me. I forgot you were spoken for."

Karl thought, *Why didn't I foresee how difficult this might be? Dear God, but I did. I simply could not admit it.*

He kissed her forehead, determined to be brotherly. "Of course I'll help you. Anything."

Katerina smiled. "Then we'd better set about regaining our strength. I am so thirsty, aren't you?"

She strode off down the forest path and Karl matched her pace; vampires in their element, danger now to anyone they encountered. However, he didn't want to feed too near home.

"We keep a motor car in an old stable at the bottom of the hill."

"A what?"

"Horseless carriage," Karl said, smiling. "We brought you here in it, don't you remember? An elegant thing, really."

"I have some vague recollection of a dreadful noise, a stink of leather and oil." Katerina laughed. "Oh, let's walk, drive, fly; I don't care! How good it feels to move, to be alive again. I want a human in my hands, a sweet young boy, and his blood flowing over my tongue... Do you still insist on hunting alone?"

"I prefer to."

She stroked his shoulder, her voice honey-seductive. "Just for tonight, hunt with me."

After the ballet, Charlotte stood outside the stage door with Violette Lenoir's worshippers. She felt like an alabaster statue in the midst of their whispering excitement. There were young girls, aspiring dancers with their parents; folk of all ages, more women than men, each carrying a bouquet for Violette. To look inconspicuous, Charlotte also held an armful of flowers. A sweet fragrance swam up from the petals and she breathed deeply, trying to distract herself from the temptation of so much human blood.

Violette's performance had been as entrancing as the first. While watching her, Charlotte had not once thought of Karl or Katerina.

She had no intention of speaking to Violette; only wanted to see her close at hand. Why, she wasn't sure. Perhaps to draw out for as long as possible the magic that kept her from thinking.

After half an hour, a tall man with a mop of grey hair came out, and the girls greeted him with cries of delight. Charlotte realised he must be Roman Janacek, the director and choreographer; Lenoir's mentor, the newspapers called him, as if he'd created her like the puppet in *Coppélia*. He laughed and talked with the little crowd, but Charlotte stood apart, watching. His face was handsome in a ravaged way, his loose frame energetic, his movements extravagant.

As he signed their programmes, he kept glancing over the girls' heads, straight at Charlotte. She met his eyes without expression or invitation.

After a few minutes he went back inside. They waited again. Then a long black Mercedes glided to a halt in front of the stage door, ready to receive the star.

The crowd's excitement swelled. First came an assistant with armfuls of flowers that she arranged in the back of the car; then two women and a man emerged and took seats in the vehicle. Charlotte had no idea who they were, but one of the girls said, "Her friends, the ballet patrons, they're taking her to supper."

"I'd do anything to go with them!" another sighed.

Finally, Violette emerged. She was dressed in black, more petite than she appeared on stage, her face barely visible between a huge fur collar and her deep-crowned hat. The gleam of an eye, the tip of her nose, lips curved in an aloof smile. The flower-givers pressed forward, too shy actually to crowd her. Charlotte made no attempt to present her own bouquet. She simply observed.

Even in everyday clothing, Violette shone: an angel masquerading as human. Without stage make-up her features were softer, much prettier. She looked a little like Ilona; pale, with expressive eyes and dark lips. But her skin had a human radiance, and there were light freckles on her nose and cheeks. Her mouth smiled, but her eyes had the self-absorbed gloss Charlotte had seen in the eyes of film stars and royalty; cool, egotistical, gracious.

She accepted the tributes without a word, giving only a regal nod. An assistant spoke for her, "*Danke schön. Sie sind sehr freundlich. Vielen dank,*" then relieved her of the bouquets and held open the car door.

As she turned to step inside, Violette met Charlotte's gaze. For a fractured instant the dancer's regard held, then flicked away with apparent indifference.

I am just another stranger to her, Charlotte thought. And her detached yet fierce curiosity about the ballerina made her feel more alien, more like a vampire, than ever before.

With flowers filling the windows, the car slid away into the night; a perfumed, candlelit shrine. The fledgling dancers hugged each other, exclaimed and sighed and waved. Violette waved back with queenly grace until the Mercedes swept out of sight.

It would have been easy for Charlotte to follow, travelling invisibly through the Crystal Ring, but she did not. Somehow

Violette was as remote from her as from her human devotees. As they dispersed, Charlotte slipped in through the stage door.

Backstage activity was fading as the dancers called goodnights to each other, their faces shiny with cold cream. Charlotte passed unseen into the Crystal Ring, walked through the wall of Violette's dressing room, and re-entered the corporeal world.

The small room was a den of lace and tulle, satin and net. There were headdresses starred with gypsophila; a silk dressing gown hanging over the corner of a screen; hampers and racks of costumes half-filling the room. The floor had been swept, make-up neatly ordered on the dressing table. The ballerina was gone but her presence lingered; a fading warmth, the sweat of her exertion mingling enticingly with the scents of greasepaint and perfume.

Charlotte walked slowly around the confined space, looking, touching the costumes in which Violette enchanted her audience. *Why am I doing this, what do I want?* asked the voice inside her; but the only answer was a dull ache.

She placed her flowers on a couch. In the morning, someone would wonder how they had got there. On impulse, she took a lipstick and wrote, "From Charlotte" on the ribbon; a small, enigmatic tribute to Violette's genius.

She sensed someone approaching. A key turned in the lock, and as the door opened she quickly stepped into the Crystal Ring. The room became a warped, smoky jewel around her – but the human was visible by the glowing spines of his aura.

She wanted to see him properly. Moving behind the screen and back to solidity, she recognised the man who'd come out to commune with the masses; the choreographer, Janacek. He locked the door behind him, then – like Charlotte – moved pensively around the room, running his fingers over the chair-back. A lock of grey hair hung down over his lined face; he was in his fifties, she thought, with the easy charisma of the gifted.

Then, to her shock, he drew a costume from the rack – the one in which the spirit Giselle had danced back from the grave – and embraced it convulsively. Charlotte watched dumbstruck. The way he clutched the pearly satin bodice to his chest, rubbed his face into it as if to drink the scent, sent a shiver of distaste through her.

She had no wish to witness an act so intimate. Passing into the Ring again, she noted the colours of his aura; bright raspberry-red, mingled with spines of pewter that looked like bayonets. Oppressive, manipulative.

With that image in her mind she left the theatre, meaning to go home. Instead she walked for miles, lost in thought; hunted and fed; walked again under the clear black arch of night. And a long time passed before she went back to Karl and Katerina.

Violette sat in the car, a shrine of flowers, her mind wandering while she made polite responses to the small talk of her associates. They demanded nothing more of her; she was the goddess who'd given a great performance. She was not required to talk, only to *be*.

In truth, she would rather have dined alone. All she wanted now was the quiet of her hotel room, her maid Geli to ice her aching knees.

This darkness always fell on her after a performance. Ecstatic energy had burned out, the orgasm of applause was over; now there was only the flat silence of the night to face, and everything to do again tomorrow.

She knew her three tormentors would come to her tonight.

They never appeared in her dreams, only in the gap between waking and sleeping; tall shadows who said nothing but filled her with indefinable, ghastly yearnings. It was a childhood haunting that had never left her; the same primal neurosis that creates monsters from innocuous shadows. Violette had not grown out of her fear, but at least – so she believed – she'd learned to live with it.

Tonight, for no clear reason, the face of an unknown woman in the crowd had induced the dark feeling. Violette had no idea why. She could not even recapture the woman's face; only her unblinking, crystal-grey eyes.

CHAPTER SIX

INVITING DARKNESS

Benedict was dying. The monster clamped to him was like no living predator; a mantrap of rope and stone. Immoveable, mindless. His limbs tingled and his ears filled with a rushing sea. Pain, grinding pain from shoulder to head... the insatiable mouth like a giant leech on him...

Benedict refused to die.

He sucked lungfuls of air, opened his eyes wide, fought to stay conscious. Desperation lent him strength, brief and white-hot, born of the pure will to live.

His hands grappled the vampire's arms. Projecting the full power of his mind, he whispered, "I entered your realm, I summoned you. You cannot destroy me. You are subject to me, you must obey me. Let me go."

As he whispered, his hands tightened on the thin hard arms, trying to loosen their grip. Harder, harder. He shook with the effort. But slowly, inch by inch, he prised the creature's stone limbs from around him...

It wouldn't take its fangs out of his neck. He felt defeat rushing up to claim him. *No, God, don't let me faint, not yet –*

"There is a chain around your neck," he said. "If you don't release me, the chain will tighten until it strangles you. Feel it tightening. Now let me go!"

The vampire loosed him so suddenly that he fell. He landed on the floor in a heap of broken glass. Blood everywhere. Yet through

107

black dizziness he kept his wits, breathing deeply until his head cleared. The creature was lying against the shattered panel of the temple wall, white as a candle flame against the darkness. It was lapping at a pool of blood on the floor, its tongue rasping like a cat's. Was it less gaunt than before? Ben watched the faintest rosy tinge creep into its skin.

Benedict stood up, feet planted apart to keep his balance. He felt sick and ragged. But the whole aim of his occult training had been self-discipline, and now he called on all his reserves.

He must be calm, impartial, authoritative.

How shall I address it? As a god? No. I made it obey me, therefore it is vulnerable. I must establish my superiority while I have the advantage.

Ben's confidence returned. Something in his subconscious had snaked out and twined with the vampire's mind – the terrible power of a human who could touch the hidden realms.

He said, "Can you speak?"

The vampire ceased licking and stared up, mouth hanging open. "Ah," it groaned, like a baby imitating speech. Then, slurred, "*Ja.*"

"You will never attack me again, do you understand? You must not feed on me."

"*Ich verstehe.* I will not. I cannot." Then, agonised, "*Hilfe. Hilfe!*"

Benedict was speechless for a moment. He'd never expected a creature from the spirit world to speak German.

"Do you know where you are?" he said, slowly and clearly.

The vampire's eyes were dark gleams, deep in the sockets. "No. I was... I can't remember. Help me."

"I am Benedict, your master. I called you here to serve me."

The creature's face lengthened. "Who am I?" It curled up, one hand round its thin knees, the other clawing at its throat where Ben had made it imagine a chain. "*Mein Gott... Ich fürchte mich... Katti, wo bist du?*"

The vampire was frightened! Its weakness and confusion were pitiful. Not at all what Ben had expected or hoped for. With his hand pressed to the bite-wound in his neck, he stood over the pale being.

"Can you remember your name?"

Silence. The skull-like head fell sideways. Then it said, "*Ich heisse Andreas.*"

A human name! What could this thing be? Had he raised it from the dead?

"Where are you from, Andreas?"

Ben saw the almost-human lines of the face expressing misery and hunger. The thing raised its head and said with astonishing clarity, "Why do you stand there asking these puerile questions? I am starving. I don't know where I came from, or why you have this power over me. I never met a mortal who... I don't understand. I only know I'm starving, starving."

"What do you need? Human blood?"

"*Ja,*" said Andreas. A ghastly smile split his face. "Just that."

"Nothing else? Ordinary food? Animal blood?"

Andreas stretched out an arm with a rustling, dry-leaf sound. "Must be human. *Bitte*. I need it."

"How much?"

"*Ich weiss nicht.* A lot."

"Well, you can't have more of mine."

"I'd take it if I could. I'd kill you. I don't know why I can't. I've never felt such hunger. It hurts and I'm hot and cold." He clawed at Ben's foot. "If you won't give me blood, find someone who will!"

Ben stared at the monster, alarm singing inside him. He couldn't train a vampire to do his will, any more than he could keep a guard dog, without feeding it. So someone had to provide their blood. Their health and life, too, perhaps.

Ben had never meant to cause harm, only to protect himself and Holly. But no, that was a lie. He'd wanted to prove a point, to demonstrate that his power was superior to Lancelyn's. And this was the price.

"Let me out." The vampire's voice was guttural with pain.

Benedict shook his head. "Impossible."

"But you must. Don't you understand? I need blood! I am in torment; is this why you captured me, to torment me?"

Andreas rose suddenly to his feet, unfolding demonically. Ben stepped back, startled.

"You did it!" the vampire hissed. "You brought me here to starve. What are you? Torturer!"

Bleached arms outstretched, Andreas lunged towards the attic door. More glass shattered and fell.

Ben said softly, "The chain is tightening. It will take off your head!"

Andreas collapsed across the threshold, a gnarled silver branch. His fingers were frantic twigs plucking at his neck.

Benedict rubbed at the pain in his own throat. The creature's suffering woke his pity. Lancelyn had taught that any spirit he summoned would be an embodiment of his own qualities, focused to attain his goals . This was nothing of the sort. It was a separate entity, with its own inner life, a human name.

Ben made a decision. It meant following the Left-Hand Path and never turning back, but, grimly, he made it.

He bent over Andreas and said, "I'll make a bargain with you."

"Anything."

"Suppose I take you out and find you someone to feed on. Is that what you want?"

The reply was a groan of pure lust.

"In return, you will obey me in all respects. You will feed on no one without my permission. You will answer all my questions truthfully. And if ever I let you out alone, you will return to me. Do you agree?"

The vampire nodded. Ben picked up the Book and thrust it under his icy hand.

"Swear on the artefact that summoned you! That will bind the oath."

The vampire cringed and tried to pull away, but Ben held him in place.

"*Einverstanden. Ja*, I swear, I give you my word, I'll obey you!"

As Ben released him, Andreas snatched his fingers from the cover as if it were red-hot. Shuddering, he sat up and edged away.

"No need for that! Why shouldn't I come back? I've nowhere to go. Let me feed now and I'll do anything for you. Please. I can't think, can't move. I want my strength again." He saw himself in a piece of broken mirror and touched his own desiccated face. "God help me. Who did this to me? I can't bear to live like this. Either kill me or let me feed!"

Benedict watched with curiosity. Not true, then, that vampires cast no reflection. *He is truly in my power*, Ben thought – *or at least, he thinks he is, which is the same thing.*

He felt a spur of elation. Perhaps the path of darkness would be easier to follow than he'd thought.

"Calm yourself, Andreas. I shall look after you. It's the middle of the night, so we can go now, but you'll need clothes… You can wear my greatcoat, and a hat is essential."

"God in heaven," said Andreas, staring at Benedict with contempt. "Do you think I am some brainless savage, happy to go outside stark naked?"

The days and the nights folded down one on another; Katerina grew in strength, yet showed no inclination to leave. Charlotte was beginning to suspect that she never would.

Each afternoon they sat in the roseate glow of the drawing room; Karl, Charlotte, and Katerina. Three unnatural beings in the shape of humans – still with enough humanity to love and to hate one another.

Before Katerina came, Karl and Charlotte had spent nearly all their time together. They separated only to feed, each preferring, for different reasons, to hunt alone. In the morning they would enter the Crystal Ring to rest; evenings were often spent at the theatre. But the long golden afternoons and velvet nights were theirs. They would read to each other, talk, listen to the gramophone; or Karl might play the cello, which Charlotte loved. Often they took long walks through the night-blue woods, or climbed the white flank of a mountain that no human could survive; or simply rested together in contented silence, hands entwined, needing nothing else. These times were as delicious as the savage addiction of their love-making.

Everything they did together was absorbing, timeless, lined with gold and tinted with gorgeous colours. Not a human world. No dull moments; no division between pleasure and pain.

But since Katerina arrived, Karl and Charlotte had not made love. They were too often apart, to ensure their guest wasn't left alone. Karl even avoided sitting beside Charlotte as if he would not touch her in front of Katerina. Small consolation that he did not touch Katerina, either. This seemed diplomatic, to avoid either woman feeling rejected. But the distance he placed between himself and Charlotte made her feel she couldn't speak or act freely in her own house.

After her initial attack on Charlotte, Katerina had apparently called a truce. She became polite and gracious – enough to satisfy Karl, at least. If he perceived the barbs concealed by her gentle words, he didn't say so.

Charlotte found Katerina's sweetness intolerable. So false. At least open hostility could be fought. Instead, she too must play the courtesy game; to do otherwise would only place her in the wrong.

Katerina's disdain came through in subtle, sinister ways. She said nothing to cause offence; instead she was so kind and condescending that she left Charlotte feeling hopelessly inferior – precisely as if Katerina knew her dormant weakness, and deliberately set out to wake it. She behaved like the mistress of the house, Charlotte her maid. Their very temperaments made them slide into these roles. While Charlotte battled to keep her place, Katerina simply occupied hers, like a serene and smiling Madonna.

It's obvious, Charlotte thought, *that she means to claim Karl and usurp me. Why can't he see it? But she's a different person with him; warm, sincere, a dear friend. I could easily have loved her, in other circumstances... but that knowledge only twists the knife.*

Karl and Katerina's ease in each other's presence was instinctive, effortless; torture for Charlotte to witness. They spoke openly of old times, excluding her. No doubt there were a thousand more matters they discussed only behind her back

And there was the strain of keeping her dignity. She mustn't let Karl sense her jealousy, nor let Katerina think she cared.

For a time, Ilona came and went like a capricious breeze, all charm and cruel humour. She uttered venomous put-downs to Katerina that Charlotte longed to say but daren't; Katerina only responded with unruffled gaiety. Neither would let the other win. If anything, they thrived on their animosity. If Ilona made a show of affection to Charlotte, it was to irritate Katerina. Charlotte despaired at their bickering, the way they used her against each other.

Yet Ilona had a more serious agenda. Questions about Kristian's death, Katerina's rebirth, shadows haunting the Crystal Ring. When Katerina refused to supply straight answers, Ilona lost patience and ceased to visit them. Despite feeling used, Charlotte missed her. She felt she'd lost her only ally.

If Karl was aware of these undercurrents, he seemed to regard the situation with sad detachment. He believed that everyone was responsible for their own behaviour, as he was for his; a philosophy Charlotte found noble but infuriating.

When she was human, Karl had been unobtainable; beautiful, mystical, so far beyond her that she hadn't known how to reach him. Aching to touch him, yet terrified of what would happen if she did...

With cruel irony, the same feeling crept over her again. This time, though, the barrier between them was not Karl's vampirism, but his attachment to a past she could not comprehend.

She thought, *If Katerina really wants to get rid of me, she will. I should fight her, tooth and claw, but I don't know how!*

One night, to her relief, she came home and found Karl in the drawing room alone.

"Where's Katerina?" she asked.

"Gone out to hunt and explore on her own."

To her unspeakable delight, Karl came to her, kissed her, and drew her to the sofa. Just as if nothing had happened. She wasn't about to argue; they sat together in the fire's glow, hands entwined, her head resting on his shoulder, as they used to before the intruder came. Charlotte felt free to speak at last.

"It's wonderful to be alone," she said. "Able to talk."

Karl's eyes, reflecting tiny flames, became troubled. She'd seen that expression before she discovered he was a vampire; a look that said, *I am keeping a terrible secret from you.*

"You don't have to be quiet when Katerina's here," he said. "She is not an ogre. There's no reason for her presence to curb your freedom."

"You wish we'd get along like good sisters?" Charlotte said flatly.

Karl half-smiled. "Of course."

"You noticed, then, that we don't."

He didn't answer at once. His gaze drifted unfocused to the fire. "I am sorry that you are both finding this difficult."

"Have I said a word of complaint?" She kept her voice steady. "I did all I could to help, and I would have done more, if you'd asked. But you can't expect me to be overjoyed that she's here. There seems to be one law for her and another for me."

"You mean her victims? That was only while she was too weak to hunt for herself."

"Yes. I know. I understand. But she can look after herself now, so why is she is still living here?"

She hoped to find sympathy in Karl's eyes, and saw none. A touch of disappointment, perhaps, which hurt.

He said, "I don't want her presence to distress you. The last thing I want is to cause you any unhappiness."

Sudden anger boiled from nowhere. "That always was the last thing you wanted, yet you caused it regardless! First you took away my only defence against you, my fear – and then you took my heart, my virtue, my blood, my respectability, my family – and finally, my humanity."

His face did not change. She could have struck him.

"But you are still here." He stroked her cheek, turning her face towards him, his amber-crystal gaze intent on her. "Whole, beautiful, still completely yourself. What did I take?"

"Nothing. I gave everything freely. And I'd do so again." Shivers of desire ran through her, even while she was furious with him for beguiling her so easily. "Don't forget that!" she said fiercely. "Did Katerina ever give you so much?"

"It wasn't the same, *liebling*. She was one of the three who made me a vampire; she, Andreas and Kristian. And, as I've told you, you have nothing to fear from her."

"I think you're wrong."

The shadow fell across his eyes again. "She apologised for what she said when she first woke. She was not herself."

"She hasn't apologised to me. She is nice to me now only because you asked her. Isn't it true?"

Karl's only response was a slight lowering of his eyelids. His long, dark eyelashes concealed his irises.

"Don't you see?" Charlotte went on. "Katerina behaves as if she's your wife and I am her servant, and with such grace that I hardly realise what's happening until it's too late. She's too subtle, too clever for me; I don't know how to fight back."

"There's no need for you to fight her! It's simply her manner. There was never any guile in her, not even with Andreas, who would have tried the patience of a saint."

"Do you think I'm imagining things? That she's perfect and I'm making trouble for no reason?"

"Your words, not mine," he said. "But no, I don't think it."

"She's different with you, of course. She sees you as an equal, takes you seriously. She treats me as nothing, a child to be patronised. I suffered it from my aunt and sisters all my life and I won't tolerate it again!"

He touched her temple, brushing back strands of hair. How delicate his fingertips felt on her skin, warm silken ivory. "They had power over you, only because you let them. Don't you remember how you overcame it – long before I made you immortal?"

Charlotte said softly, "Katerina means to take you away from me. I know you don't want to believe any ill of her, but it's true."

"No. Dearest, try to forgive her. She has nowhere to go, no one except me."

"She's a vampire, not an orphan!"

"Kristian used to say, 'Our Father is God and our Mother is Lilith.' As they do not exist, clearly we are all orphans."

"Oh, well, that is a beautiful answer! The very thing that makes her dangerous is the fact that she has no one but you." Despair drained Charlotte of emotion and she thought, *God, why do I feel so helpless?* She turned to him, laid her hands on his chest. "Karl, I will be honest with you. I can't stand her being here. I want her to leave. Please."

He held her wrists, pressing her hands to him. She felt the warmth of stolen blood through his shirt, the lean contours of his ribs.

"I cannot ask her to leave, any more than I could you."

Her breath caught raw in her throat. "Do you love her so much?"

"Yes. If you want honesty. But it's not the same."

"Isn't it? How do I know you don't take her to our bed while I'm not here, and drink her blood? You must have done so in the past!"

"Charlotte," he said sadly. "I don't."

"But you've hardly touched me since she arrived. What am I

supposed to think? You haven't made it clear to her that you are with *me*. All I can see is that you refuse to choose between us."

Taking her hands between his, Karl bowed his head, touching his lips to her fingers. He was still closed away. She knew he wouldn't give a direct answer.

He said, "If I've done or said anything to make you doubt my feelings for you, I ask your forgiveness. But out of love, grant me this: don't ask me to discard a friend."

Charlotte could not answer. He kissed her, and as her lips opened to his, her anger dissolved into hopeless confusion. They were together, and talking. That in itself was such an exquisite pleasure, it hardly mattered what they said.

"Very well," she acceded. "For your sake, I won't ask. I understand your loyalty to her. But you know we can't go on like this. How long?"

"I don't know, beloved," he sighed. "She hasn't regained strength to go in and out of the Crystal Ring. She's more vulnerable than she seems."

"If I thought that was true, and she didn't hate me so violently, perhaps I could bear her," Charlotte whispered.

"Be patient." And Karl himself was so patient that she could refuse him nothing. "It's not a question of her vanishing from our lives the moment she recovers. It's more complicated. We don't know what changes Kristian's death may have caused. If his passing woke Katerina, what about the other vampires he imprisoned? We must find out."

"That could take years. If not forever."

"I promised to help her find Andreas."

Charlotte was silent, nurturing a small flame of hope.

"If she finds Andreas, will she be content with him? Or does she want you both to herself again?"

"Don't," said Karl. "Haven't I reassured you?"

"Katerina's the one I'm really afraid of. I can't help it, Karl. She makes me go cold. She would get rid of me if she could."

"No."

"Believe me." Charlotte stared languidly into the fire. "I never thought anyone could come between us, not even Kristian – until I met Katerina."

"Not your Giselle?"

She looked at Karl in surprise. "What?"

"The first time you saw her, I thought for a few moments I'd lost you. You've been to almost every performance since."

A cold feeling gripped her stomach, like the beginning of blood thirst. "And you were welcome to come with me, but you didn't! I needed to escape to another world where the most important person was not Katerina. Do you blame me? I remember all the dire warnings you gave against growing too close to humans, but I've never met Violette Lenoir, and I don't want to."

"Beloved, I can only say this: stay with us. Don't feel you're being driven away. You are not. Be patient with Katti, because this concerns all of us." Karl stroked her hair, and kissed her again. "Nothing can separate us."

"Then don't keep secrets. You used to tell me the truth, however harsh. Now I feel you're telling Katerina but not me, as if you imagine I need protecting from... what, I don't know."

Karl's pale, caressing hand paused on her cheek. "Very well. There is something else."

He went to put fresh logs on the fire. Charlotte sat forward. "What?"

"There is a faint possibility that Kristian might not be dead."

Charlotte gaped at him, horrified. "That's impossible! What makes you think that?"

"Because Katerina swears his voice woke her up."

She shivered, despite the fire. "No. He's dead. Do you think he would leave us alone if he'd survived? He died... and Katerina woke."

While she followed a black strand of thought along its unwelcome branches, she was conscious of a larger reality; that she and Karl were communicating soul to soul again, that she felt loved and whole within the crimson-golden sphere of firelight...

Logs popped and hissed, showering sparks. A draught sent gold motes whirling everywhere as the door opened and Katerina strode into the room. She brought a swirl of cold air with her, a surge of light and life.

Charlotte's mood fell like a dead bird.

"Still splendid, the world out there," said Katerina, unpinning her hat and throwing it on a chair. Her dark hair gleamed, and her face was flushed from feeding. "So wonderful to see and feel again, to walk among people and taste their blood. Warm, warm. But I don't like the fashions; how plain, how straight up and down they are. And those machines roaring about on wheels. How they stink! But it's so exciting."

She flung off her coat and sat down in an armchair, unbuttoning her shoes and rubbing her feet through her silk stockings. "I never knew such clothes for making a woman look as dowdy as a pauper, or as elegant as a Greek goddess. They look simple yet they're so difficult to wear. Whoever thought of these appalling button-strap shoes? And I tell you, I am not flattening my breasts for anyone. They'll be sorry, these women, when fashion changes and they've flattened themselves out of existence. Oh, but all in the name of freedom! What wonders that Great War has brought about."

"Be glad you missed it," Karl said drily, dusting ash from his hands as he turned to her.

Charlotte hated her for violating the mood. *Little cold shadow*, Katerina had called her, and at this moment that was how she felt. Here was Karl's "dear friend", radiating energy and *joie de vivre*; and all Charlotte had offered in competition was flat-voiced jealousy.

And all those unpleasant feelings, fused with the revelation Karl had just unleashed on her, made her ruthless. Ignoring Katerina, she pursued her unfinished conversation with Karl. "Why didn't you tell me before?"

Silence. Even Katerina looked startled, and asked lightly, "Why didn't you tell her what, Karl?"

"No point in worrying her, when we have no proof," he said.

Katerina blinked. "Proof of what?"

"That Kristian may have survived."

"Ah." Katerina flopped back in the chair and began to unpin her luxuriant hair. She looked majestic and seductive.

"I don't care," Charlotte said fiercely. "You should have told me."

Katerina stood and went to Karl's side in a single flowing movement. Both dark, she only half a head shorter than him, they seemed as close as twins.

"She's right, Karl," she said, looking down at Charlotte. "We should have told you, dear. But what can you do about it?" Again the honeyed condescension, calculated to make Charlotte feel an outsider. She was beyond tolerating it.

Staring hard at Katerina, she said, "I don't know. But I would like to help you find Andreas."

Unexpectedly, Katerina came and sat beside her. She put a hand on Charlotte's arm. "I appreciate it, but that's not a good idea."

"Why not?" Charlotte spoke thinly, glancing at Karl's half-shadowed face.

"I'm worried about how Andreas might be when we find him. He could be out of his mind; Lord knows how he might react, seeing a strange face." As Katerina spoke, her smooth tone frayed. She was speaking the truth, and couldn't hide the pain that gleamed through her facade. Charlotte felt brief but genuine sympathy. "You're a fledgling, Charlotte; how could you defend yourself, if Andreas attacked you?"

"I can look after myself," she retorted.

Katerina appealed to Karl. "You wouldn't put her in such danger, would you?"

"Of course not," he said.

"So you're saying you don't want or need my help, either of you?" said Charlotte.

"We're thinking of you," Katerina began, but Karl interrupted.

"I've told Charlotte that I want her help. Whatever the danger, I cannot tell her what to do. It's her choice."

"*Natürlich!*" said Katerina, as if astonished it should be otherwise. She stared hard at Charlotte, her face regal, full of dark strength. The contempt radiating from her chestnut eyes crushed Charlotte to ash. "Your decision; but ask yourself: suppose he was put in danger by having to protect you, do you *really* want to put Karl's safety at risk?" And the unspoken coda: "*When you know you aren't wanted, and you appreciate how miserable I can make your life?*"

Benedict walked through dark lanes with a vampire at his side, and more questions in his mind than he'd ever dreamed.

Lancelyn might create illusions or mind tricks to terrify people,

Ben thought, *but has he the power to call a supernatural creature in physical form? I doubt it. Surely, if he'd ever achieved such a feat, he'd never have been able to keep quiet!*

Andreas was silent, incredibly light and graceful under the voluminous greatcoat. A thin figure: just a glimpse of dead-white skin between hat-brim and scarf.

Ben took him to the canal a few miles away, where water lay turgidly brown under the shadow of warehouse walls. There the vampire took a victim, an old man lying asleep on a narrowboat.

Ben tried to watch – not to shy away – but it was dark. He heard more than he saw. The man starting awake, a muffled cry, the long thin form bending over him; the crunch of teeth through flesh and cartilage, a brief struggle, stillness. Then only a faint groan from Andreas. He lay down right along the old man's form, convulsing as if with sexual pleasure.

At that point, Ben could stand no more. He left the boat and waited on the towpath, feeling sick, shivery and depressed. *Christ, how often will he want to do this?*

He closed his eyes, opened them again to find Andreas beside him, silent and composed. His face looked polished, luminous. A great chilling wave of awe went over Benedict. He'd been so wrapped up in practicalities that the truth hurtled through and struck him like a spear. *This is a vampire. An evil spirit that should be dead and is not.*

Ben shook himself. He guided Andreas into the cover of trees, one hand hovering near the vampire's shoulder – not actually daring to touch him. They walked for a minute. Then Ben said, "Did you kill him?"

"Probably," said Andreas. His German accent was very pronounced yet musical; soft, dreamy. "Ah, but I feel better."

"Listen to me. You don't have to kill them, do you?"

The vampire didn't answer for a while. Eventually he said, "I don't have to, no."

"Then don't!"

"What does it matter?"

"This isn't London!" Ben said sourly. "We can't support a rash of unexplained deaths. People will talk, there'll be police and journalists everywhere…"

Another pause. "While I need the blood so desperately, I can't help draining them. I can't stop. But if I could, it still leaves them… unwell." Rough anger edged his voice. "What do you want of me? If you don't like this, Benedict, why in the name of hell did you bring me here?"

They did not speak again until they reached home.

Ben switched on a light, and watched Andreas remove his coat. The change made him gasp. Although the vampire was still pallid and skeletal, he was recognisably human; skin smooth, his limbs straight, his movements easy.

Ben said, "We have a lot to talk about."

"Have we?" Andreas said bitterly. His sunken face with its cobweb hair was unsightly – but what a change from his first appearance!

"I need to know what you remember of the astral world, and why you were trapped there. If you're a vampire, why weren't you free to roam the world? Were you dead? Were you ever human, or –"

"*Liebe Gott*, stop this!" the vampire said hoarsely. "I can't remember anything! Only flashes, which vanish when you ask these stupid questions. My head aches and I want to sleep, but I can't. Leave me alone!"

"I'm sorry," said Ben. "You need to rest. Is there anything… particular that you require?"

"A coffin?" said Andreas, mocking his tone. "No. I do not need to lie in a coffin, nor to avoid daylight or running water. None of the folklore nonsense. But protect me from bad musicians and bad poets, please. And the cold. I can't stand to be cold."

Sighing, Benedict took him to the guest bedroom. Andreas lay down and seemed to enter a state of catalepsy. Not breathing. Ben shut the door and left him.

He had a few hours fitful sleep, continually disturbed by the cottage cracking and murmuring around him. Bad dreams. Mice running about between the floorboards. The taste and smell of blood…

He woke to daylight, barely in time to dress before the housekeeper arrived. He checked Andreas, found him lying as before, staring at the ceiling. Ben locked him in.

When Mrs Potter came, he let her make his breakfast, then gave her the day off. She was surprised, but didn't argue. Ben would have to find excuses to keep her out of Andreas' way... *Hmm, awkward having a vampire guest, but I'll sort it out.*

He telephoned Holly and told her all was fine. She sounded unconvinced.

He meant to spend the day in his study, reading all he could find about vampires and their connection to the astral world. He'd just settled to the task when Maud arrived on the doorstep, indignant.

"Mr Grey, aren't you in the shop today?"

"No – I'm sorry, Maud, I should have telephoned. I've had a lot on my mind. Do you mind coping on your own for a couple of days? I'll pay you extra."

"It's no trouble," she said with a touch of petulance. "I don't mind if I *know*."

"Thank you."

She turned to leave, then pulled an envelope from her pocket. "This letter came to the shop yesterday, or the day before... I'd have brought it sooner, if I'd known you weren't coming in."

He took it from her. "My fault, but I wish you had."

She gave a martyred, ingratiating smile, as if to say, *I'm terribly put upon, but I suffer in silence.*

"Strange girl," Ben said to himself, closing the door. He sat down and stared at the envelope in shock. Deirdre's handwriting.

Dear Benedict,

I'll send this to the shop so you needn't explain to Holly if you'd rather not. I'm writing before I catch my train. There's more to tell that I couldn't say to your face. Too difficult. Call me a coward, but I couldn't have borne your questions and distress. I just wanted to leave.

I'm breaking an oath to tell you this. The story is that Lancelyn goes fishing once a month. He doesn't. He goes – went, rather – to James's country house and held meetings of a secret order he called the Hidden Temple. James and I were the only members from the NMT. The others were the usual: members of parliament, judges, aristocrats and the like – men seeking more extreme versions of the occult to stimulate their jaded appetites. Lancelyn supplied

the need. Opium, hashish, cocaine, women, boys, seances and sex
rituals – whatever they wanted.

I'm not coming over moral about this. I was all for free love
and free will. I enjoyed it to start with; there was some plausible
talk about communion with the Goddess through sexual union,
which Lancelyn may have half-believed. It was money that ruined
it. Once someone's initiated, he has them forever. He held enough
scandal, over every one of them, to have destroyed their careers
and lives – and he milked it. If you don't believe me, where do you
think all his money comes from?

Well, James got sick of it. I told him, "Refuse to let Lancelyn
use your house any more!" but when he tried, Lancelyn got
furious and tried to blackmail him. James said he had enough
evidence, of procuring, drug-dealing and the like, to do worse
back. Lancelyn was incandescent. That's why he killed James and
that's why I'm leaving.

You can go to James's house if you like, but you'll find nothing.
His relatives are in possession and Lancelyn will have removed
the evidence. What he'll do about the Hidden Temple now, I don't
know and I don't care.

Ben, I know you love your brother. If you knew about this all
along, I've made myself look a fool, which doesn't matter. But if
not – and knowing you, so decent and good, I'm sure you didn't
– I'm sorry.

Please burn this. Your friend, D.

Ben dropped the letter and put his head in his hands. "Oh,
God," he said.

That night, when Andreas needed to feed, Ben took him to a small
hospital and said, "Find someone who would die anyway."

Whether Andreas obeyed, Ben did not ask. The only way to
cope with the horror and hypocrisy was to shut his mind and
harden his heart.

"Good and decent," Deirdre had called him. *Christ.*

When they returned to the house, Benedict saw lights burning
that he hadn't left on.

He opened the front door, saw nothing unusual in the hall. The air felt taut and frosty, vibrating with the vestigial energy of his ritual. The place felt cold, heavy, frightening. He heard a faint scrabbling of mouse paws.

A strip of light under the drawing-room door filled him with unreasoning terror.

He glanced at Andreas, but the scoured face was devoid of fellow-feeling. Shuddering, he pushed open the door to the parlour.

Holly was sitting on the sofa, her feet tucked underneath her, her face deathly. Still in her coat, she held Deirdre's letter crumpled in one hand. For a heart-stopping moment he thought she was dead; murdered and posed there as some ghastly joke.

She looked up. Relief. But why was her face so white, why did this feel as alien as a nightmare? Holly could be volatile, courageous, bad-tempered, but he'd never seen her so pale and motionless, as if so terrified she could endure it only by sitting absolutely still.

Seeing Andreas, she stared.

Benedict said in dismay, "Darling, why are you home? I wasn't expecting you for at least a week." He glanced darkly at the vampire and added under his breath, "She is not to be touched."

Andreas only smiled and blinked. His eyes were long black crescents in his burnished skin.

"I had to come back; I knew you were in danger." Her voice was raw with tiredness. "How could you pretend everything is 'fine' when it obviously isn't? I'm not a fool!"

"Holly –"

She went on staring at the vampire. "What is that – thing with you?"

"A friend," said Ben.

"He has no aura," she whispered. "He's not human, is he?"

"Holly, this is rather difficult –"

"Not human." Her eyes were bird-bright in her ashen face. "Like the others."

"Others?"

She glanced at the ceiling. "In the attic and on the landing. White creatures like him. The house is full of them. In the name of God, Ben, what have you done?"

CHAPTER SEVEN

DANCER OF DREAMS

The search would begin when Katerina regained her power to enter the Crystal Ring. That could take days or weeks; Charlotte had breathing space. The minute she could escape without it seeming Katerina had frightened her away, she flew to her refuge, *Giselle*.

The truth was, Katerina disturbed her at the most primeval level. The gleam of her eyes, warm and wise and yet so sinister, as she softly crushed Charlotte's offer of help: *Ask yourself, do you really want to put Karl's safety at risk?*

No, Charlotte thought. *No, I don't. But I won't let you win!*

If not for Katerina, perhaps Charlotte would have forgotten Violette Lenoir. As it was, the ballerina remained the only creature who could soothe her. In the next few weeks she saw the Ballet Janacek in cities all over Europe.

Sometimes she lingered at the stage door until Violette emerged; at others, she left the theatre the moment the performance ended, found and took a victim with urgent fervour that left her shocked at herself.

Anger at Katerina? Frustrated desire for Violette's swan-pale throat? Charlotte's own feelings alarmed her. In the glorious freedom of being with Karl, she'd felt happy and in control. Then Katerina intruded, and a rope came untethered within her. She felt as if the first storm would carry her away.

The latest performance was in Vienna – Karl's home city, and he wasn't with her. A double sadness; the run of *Giselle* was almost over. *Tonight, and tomorrow; then*, Charlotte wondered, *where else will I find refuge?*

After the curtain calls, Charlotte left swiftly but didn't go home. She walked all night, feeding on three or four victims as she went. Easy for a pretty young woman to catch a man's attention; they were so pleased, so trusting, that she felt no guilt. The purple-red intoxicating juice of their veins swept away all pain; theirs, and hers. She took only a little blood from each but drank languorously, her mind as dark and dispassionate as the night itself.

Wind, rain, spring flowers nodding under a glaze of light. In the Vienna Woods she watched the sun rise like a pearl through a red ocean. Then she walked back into the city to lose herself in crowds whose rational, busy minds were oblivious to the supernatural. She floated on their oblivion like a feather.

Ugly, the workers' flats being built on the outskirts. Who could be so dull-minded as to defile this beautiful city with cold modern ideals? This was where Karl had lived, long before she knew him. As she walked past palaces and theatres, she imagined him everywhere; a ghost in nineteenth-century clothing, a musician in the time of Beethoven and Schubert. The sun came out and the wet cobblestones shone.

She entered an opulent hotel and sat in the lobby, stirring a cup of coffee that she would not drink. Gauze veils of sunlight gleamed on the dark panelled walls and brocade upholstery. All brown and faded gold, hushed as a library. She watched guests coming and going. Diamonds and fur. Lives untouched by the currents of change.

Last night had been given over to mindless sensation, but now she must think.

Karl has never given me cause to be suspicious of any human female, though God knows, he has enough temptation. Katerina's different. Immortal, powerful and confident. I can't challenge the link between them, their hold on each other; I don't know how.

Karl still loves me, I'm sure, but all his reassurances turn to dust in the face of one fact: he loves Katerina too.

Her brown eyes haunted Charlotte. Such withering contempt; *How*, she thought, *how can she make me feel so impotent? And her teeth…* a shiver of revelation. God, *she showed me the tips of her fangs!*

A clear threat; the ultimate way one vampire claimed power over another was to feed on them. Loss of blood meant weakness, while the dominant one's strength increased. That was how Kristian had made himself their leader, by being physically undefeatable. *And Katerina's older and stronger than me...*

Would she dare? Will Karl protect me?

I have to decide. Do I run away and let her win, or do I tag along and let her humiliate me? I'm so afraid, if I force Karl to choose between us, that he might not choose me. And he'd resent me for forcing him, I know he would.

Well, it's clear what I'm doing at this moment. Running away.

Sensing movement, Charlotte looked up and saw a couple coming in through the lobby doors. With tingling shock, she saw that the young woman was Violette, her companion the ballet's director.

While Janacek went to the desk, the dancer came and sat on a sofa opposite Charlotte. She was wearing a black fur-trimmed coat, a cloche hat half-shielding her face.

Violette took a newspaper from a coffee table, unfolded it and began to read. Charlotte covertly watched her. Was she really so interested in the news, or trying to avoid being recognised?

She willed the dancer to put down the paper, but she didn't. *Why do I want her to notice me?* Charlotte thought. *What can I possibly offer her, except danger?*

She leaned forward and said, "Excuse me, madame, would you like some coffee while you're waiting? There is plenty in this pot; I can ask the Fraülein to bring a fresh cup."

Violette lowered the newspaper. Her eyes were startling: dark sapphires. Her expression was supercilious. "No, thank you," she said, and returned to reading.

Her accent – despite her name – was upper-class English, clipped. She clearly didn't want to enter conversation with a stranger, and saw nothing in Charlotte to interest her. Charlotte felt disappointed but unsurprised; it was exactly the response she'd expected. Violette's mere proximity was weirdly electrifying. She tried to shut out her awareness of the dancer's blood-heat and the smooth skin beneath her clothes; tried not to see her as a desirable victim. Impossible. Violette was as self-contained as a vampire, which only made her more intriguing.

Struck with an awful image of seizing Violette, here in the lobby in front of everyone... Charlotte thought she had better leave before she was tempted to do just that.

Janacek strode over from the desk, his footsteps heavy on the thick carpet. He gave Charlotte the briefest glance as he sat by his ballerina and began to speak quietly to her. Their voices were hardly above a whisper, but Charlotte could hear them easily. They were discussing a private party to be held in this hotel, after tonight's final performance of *Giselle*.

Charlotte rose to leave, but couldn't go without saying something to Violette; just a word of appreciation. It might be her only chance. She looked straight at Violette as she spoke, not trying to conceal her vampire luminosity.

"Madame Lenoir, forgive me for interrupting, but I want to thank you for all the pleasure your dancing has given me. I've been to almost every performance of *Giselle*. Nothing else has helped me forget my troubles; only your dancing."

Violette had no chance to respond before Janacek leaned forward, shielding her. "Madam, don't you know it is extremely rude to interrupt a private conversation?" He spoke with a heavy Eastern European accent. "We appreciate the sentiment, but Madame Lenoir does not care for unsolicited approaches."

Charlotte's eyes flicked to him, widening, turning as frigid as Violette's. "Well, forgive me, Herr Janacek. I won't waste your time by praising your choreography. Good-day."

She walked away slowly, her head high, not looking back. Her only feeling was one of hollowness. *I said it would break the magic; feet of clay, all these great people.*

As she reached the glass-panelled oak door, she heard heavy footsteps behind her. She kept walking; Janacek caught her up as she stepped outside.

"*Gnädige Frau*, allow me to apologise. I show bad manners. Madame Lenoir has many, many people who wish to speak with her; it is a great strain, and always I must protect her. I am sorry."

Charlotte glanced behind him into the hotel, saw no sign of Violette. "It's quite all right," she said coolly. "I am very honoured to meet you, Herr Janacek."

"And I am honoured to be recognised. Most people only know the dancers," he said, nodding. His smile was warm and a lock of grey hair tumbled over his forehead. But she remembered the blood-and-metal spikes of his aura, and the way he had caressed Violette's costumes. "May I know your name?"

"Charlotte Alexander." That wasn't her last name; it was actually Karl's middle name, but it pleased her to use it.

"Charlotte?" He frowned suddenly. "You leave flowers once –?"

"I don't know what you mean." She turned away, but he came after her, as she knew he would.

"Wait, Frau Alexander. You spoke of troubles she helped you forget; your words touched me. I see in your eyes a tragedy…"

Hardly that, she thought, wondering if he assumed she had some fatal disease. In a way, she had. "I'd rather not talk about it."

"You are a great lover of ballet? It means much to you, to meet Madame Lenoir?"

"It would have done, had I actually met her," Charlotte said coolly. "I'm thinking of certain young girls to whom it would mean the world to meet their heroine; I hope she is kinder to them than she was to me, or who knows how many potential dancers she may disillusion for life."

The choreographer looked startled. "You are a teacher. I should have known."

Charlotte smiled. "What can I tell the children about the day I met the great Lenoir?"

He spoke with animation, words falling over each other. "You understand that there are many people who would make demands on Lenoir's time if she let them, but she is an extremely busy and hard-working dancer. She is shy, she does not trust strangers."

"I appreciate that."

"However, I might be able to arrange a proper introduction, if I can persuade Madame to see you. You would like this?" His eagerness, she noted with sad amusement, was not to be generous to a supposed ballet teacher, but to seduce her. On him, her beauty had worked effortlessly.

Although she tried to resist, the idea of meeting Violette again was enticing. She did not need this man to arrange an introduction, but she played the game.

"Perhaps I could come to the party tonight? I couldn't help overhearing…"

Sudden hardness in his eyes, charm switched off. "Ah no. Too soon. It is a private party." Then the warmth returned. "But if you would do me the honour of letting me take you to supper tomorrow night? I know. Come to the theatre this afternoon, while we rehearse. I make sure you have the best seat for tonight's performance, and we will arrange our rendezvous, yes?"

Charlotte put on an innocently awed expression, as if she couldn't believe the great man had asked her out. "That would be delightful." She turned, waving a gloved hand at him as she descended the steps. "*Auf Wiedersehen*, Herr Janacek."

A womaniser; very charming and brilliant, but a manipulator… That was the impression she gained of Violette's mentor.

That afternoon, she went to the theatre as suggested, but didn't announce her presence. Instead she moved in and out of the Crystal Ring, listening and watching. Janacek, an obsessive perfectionist, was drilling the *corps de ballet* through the fine details of their steps, shouting at everyone from musicians to stagehands about the minuscule imperfections of the previous night. Violette appeared late in the afternoon and marked her steps mechanically, conserving her energy for the performance. *She looks tired*, Charlotte thought, watching now from the wings; melting away into the shadows whenever she sensed danger of being seen.

When they took a break, Charlotte entered the Crystal Ring and followed Janacek and Violette to the ballerina's dressing room. Invisible, she saw the room as a mesh of silvery lozenges tilted at dizzy angles, while the humans were two auras; one harshly red like hot metal, the other a shimmer of lilac, indigo and silver.

She found an alcove and eased herself into the real world, hovering between two realms, in case she had to vanish again quickly. Wedged between a screen and a big square sink, she could see most of the room. No luxury here; cascades of fresh flowers did little to disguise the bare walls and noisy water pipes.

Violette was retying a *pointe* shoe, resting her foot on a wicker clothes-hamper. She was smaller than she looked on stage, her body breathtakingly slender and firm. Even in practice clothes, with her hair in a loose ebony coil on her neck, her presence filled the room like the white fragrance of lilies.

Janacek leaned on her dressing table and folded his arms, watching her. He said, "I went after that young woman who spoke to you."

"I know you did. I'm not really interested."

"Her name is Charlotte Alexander. Don't you remember, we found flowers in a locked dressing room, 'From Charlotte'?"

Violette paused, tensing like a bird poised to take flight. "So? I'd forgotten. There are hundreds of women called Charlotte. What was she, anyway, a journalist?"

"No." There was a sly, hungry look to his smile. "A ballet teacher. She wants to meet you."

"Oh, God." Violette tied and retied the white ribbons impatiently, as if taking out suppressed anger on them. "Why? What is wrong with these people? Does she think I can give her magic to dance or teach better? People and their questions. I get up, I work myself to exhaustion, I go to bed; why do they think a ballerina's life is so wonderful?"

"Come, my angel; the people you work with, the life you lead – so far from ordinary folk, of course they find you fascinating. The creation of beauty is magic to them. They want you to be the ice goddess who is also sweet and ordinary; irrational expectation, but it gives them hope that one day they may be like you." He sounded as if he were mocking her in some subtle way.

"I've nothing to give except my dancing. I can't waste time making small talk with strangers."

Janacek laughed. "You don't have to meet her. I only tell her I *might* persuade you."

Violette, repinning her hair, turned to him with narrowed eyes. "Ah. I see. You found her attractive, I suppose?"

He laughed. "Are you jealous? I could spin this out for weeks; drop her a crumb here and there, keep her dangling with promise that I *may* introduce you next time, if she is patient."

Violette turned away, cold disgust on her face. "I suppose you'll sleep with her."

"Of course. They do anything, these women, for a chance to get close to the famous genius."

"You make me sick," Violette whispered.

Janacek reached out to her, pulling her towards him and linking his hands around her tiny waist. "If we could, my darling, I would need no one else."

She stood rigid in his arms, pulling in her stomach so tight that her ribs showed. She said nothing, but the snake-glitter of her eyes made Charlotte shiver. How *dare* he fondle a woman who looked at him like that? How dare he touch her at all?

Janacek only chuckled and patted the dancer's taut abdomen. "Oh, I know. A little accident would ruin your career, not to mention your perfect figure. But while you keep saying no, you can't deny me amusement elsewhere."

Violette's face could have turned flesh to stone. "I don't care what you do. And I don't want to hear about it; not this woman, nor any other."

"You are ungrateful," he said, giving her a little shake. "At least they are women, not men."

"I don't care if you copulate with goats, as long as I don't find out!"

A lizard-like smile folded his features. "How tragic. A lovely woman, jealous of farmyard animals."

The instant he let her go, Violette rushed across the room to the sink. Charlotte slipped quickly into the other-realm. The dancer turned on the tap and splashed her face with cold water. Doing so, she stood half in Charlotte's space, so that her aura passed straight through Charlotte.

Unbelievably delicious. Tight-threaded with pain, yet silver-cool, jewel-like, intimate. It was all Charlotte could do not to drink the aura. When Violette moved away she was left stunned, aching from head to toe. She felt fiercely protective of Violette, outraged at Janacek's behaviour. How dare he treat her with such contemptuous familiarity?

"Can we please get on with this rehearsal?" Violette snapped. "I would like a rest before tonight. Torment me when it's over, if you must; until then, I don't want to discuss anything but *Giselle*."

She stalked out of the room, the choreographer following. As they left, Charlotte saw him slide his hand over her buttocks and between her thighs; a gesture not of affection, but of power.

A DANCE IN BLOOD VELVET

* * *

Karl found Katerina reclining on the sofa in the dying light of the fire. A book lay open on her lap, unread; her head was tipped back, hands lying loose at her sides. Her eyes, half-closed, formed two arcs of tear-soaked lashes.

"Katti?" he said, taking her hand. "What's wrong?"

She sighed and resettled herself against the sofa wing. "Nothing, really, my dear. I'm so tired. I wish I could sleep. I wish to God we could sleep; why must we go on and on, always awake?"

Karl thought, *If only Charlotte could see how vulnerable she is – if only Katti would let her see – there might be understanding between them.*

"Have you fed tonight?"

"Of course. It's not lack of blood; I've been feeding like a lion, not an invalid. It's tiredness of spirit, because I can't enter the Crystal Ring."

"I know," said Karl.

"I ache for it, more than for blood." She stretched out her arms, uncurling her broad, strong hands. "To dissolve... to feel that lovely glassy air around me and float on the clouds. The trance. The refreshing trance of infinity..." A tear left a silver trail on her cheek. Karl brushed it away with his thumb.

"Your strength will come back," he said.

"Why is it taking so long?"

"I couldn't enter the Ring for days after you bit me. Be patient. You have been very ill, and so weak."

"So dead, you mean."

"And that is why it takes longer."

"I know." She smiled, her brown eyes sleepily warm. "You always make me feel better. When I can travel again, we'll look for Andreas."

"And Kristian," Karl said heavily. "I must know what happened to him."

"You won't go without me, will you? We do this together."

"We agreed we'd wait until you are ready." He kissed her hand. All too easy to lose his detachment and forget how much time had passed... even to forget Charlotte, while she wasn't here. "But we

133

must find the truth. Haven't you wondered why it's so hard for us to die?"

"God's little messengers, aren't we?" she said, smiling. "That's what Kristian believed. God's revenge on mankind. The thoughts in His head cannot die."

"What if we aren't God's creations, but those of humanity itself? Imagine this: the Crystal Ring creates and sustains us. It is a replica of Earth and sky, recreated by a billion human minds. The energy of human thought made physical."

Katti's face turned stony. "And what does that make us?"

"The distillation of their greatest hopes and fears."

She reflected. "Well, their greatest hope must be eternal life... and their fear, death."

"Yes, we bring what they fear – but there's one thing worse than death, and that is the idea of the dead coming back. Death is merely tragic, but returning from the grave is both horrific and unnatural."

"God!" she exclaimed. "However much one misses dear Uncle Johann, the last thing one wants is him knocking on the back door all covered with grave-mud and worms." She started to laugh. "Is this what you believe now?"

"You know me, Katti. It's dangerous to be convinced you know the absolute truth; I've seen too many people, human and vampire, destroy themselves and others with dogma. I find it more interesting to remain an agnostic. But is this theory any more unlikely than believing that the Crystal Ring is the mind of God?"

"I liked that," she said. "It was one good thing that Kristian taught us. Comforting."

"In that it saved you having to feel guilty?"

She was amused. "I never feel guilty anyway. But yes. And don't ask me to change."

"I wouldn't dream of it."

"Where did you hear these strange ideas, anyway? From Charlotte?" Karl didn't reply, but she said, "I thought so. You should be careful of her. Humans have a word for people like her, who 'see things'. Fey. That's what she is."

Her words saddened him. She saw the cooling of his expression and said, "Don't look like that. You know I'm only teasing."

"And you know you're not, so don't pretend to be amazed that

I'm not laughing," he said softly. "Don't criticise her; you don't know her."

"And how well do you? Why does she keep going to the same ballet, Karl? I should watch her. If she's fastened on some human… It's all too easy. You used to resist, I know, but you were unnatural – and even you fell in the end. She's behaving like Kristian! Don't you recall? The way he went to your concerts and sat staring at you, night after night?"

"I could hardly forget." With effort, Karl spoke calmly. "I'm not unaware of what might be happening. I don't like it; I am selfish, I want Charlotte to myself, I can't bear the thought of her having divided loyalties. But then, I am inflicting the same on her."

"I know. And you can't convince her we are only friends… because we weren't."

Katerina was right; uncomfortably so. He said, "I wish you would be kinder to her."

"When have I been unkind? I am myself; not my fault she doesn't like that. Why does she keep leaving us alone together, unless a human is offering something better?"

She was trying to goad him. "Jealousy, as you keep pointing out, is a human reaction."

"A terrible strain, having to rise above such emotions," she said tartly. "Perhaps we are not as divine as we imagine."

"The point is this, Katti. If I forbade her to go, I'd be behaving just as her own father and brother did when they discovered our relationship. They tried desperately hard to protect her from me, but their efforts came to nothing. Trying to hold Charlotte is like trying to capture air in a net. But if I give her freedom, she will come back."

"You may only make her think you don't care."

"We know each other better than that."

"Do you really? Dear Karl, I know it's not in your nature to lay down the law, but it might be in your interests to find out where this caprice is leading."

He only shook his head. He didn't want to listen, but a cold pearl of dread had been growing since the first time Charlotte saw Violette.

"She will come back."

"Will she? She's already been away longer than usual. She doesn't understand you as I do! Oh, damn it." Katerina lost her voice. She turned her head away, pressed her lips together. Then she took Karl's hand. "I have nothing against Charlotte, truly. Only it seems the blink of an eye since we three were together. You and I and Andreas, I mean. But it's such a long time, and everything has changed. You're the only link, Karl. I'm doing my best, but it's very hard to share you."

Charlotte left the theatre without speaking to Janacek. He did not know she'd ever been there. But that night – still without having been home to Karl – she went to see the last performance of *Giselle*.

Perfection; no hint of disharmony behind the scenes. Violette's dancing was incandescent, as if she threw all her passion and energy into the closing performance. By the second act she'd half-exhausted herself – which gave Giselle's ghost a ragged, heartbreaking fragility. At the end, the applause was an uproar. Violette danced her curtain calls, each one a performance in itself.

Starving, her head swimming with the heat of so many mortals, Charlotte slipped away and hunted down a victim; a strong, handsome, well-dressed young man, who never saw who seized him in the shadows. *How it floods away all doubt and anguish,* she thought, *this gorgeous scarlet stream... How it sickens, that blood has such power over me, that I can't exist without it...*

She left the man fainting, as if drunk. Her attack would unhinge his mind – for a few days or forever – but that was something her conscience had to swallow. Too great a burden, to kill outright – although she would, if it were unavoidable. At her core, she could be harder than Karl.

Then she entered the Ring and went to the hotel where she'd met Violette earlier. The lobby was quiet, but her sharp hearing caught wisps of music and voices from a distant ballroom. In the cloakroom she rinsed a blood-speck from her cheek, hung up her coat, brushed and redressed her hair. Her evening dress was beige silk voile with handkerchief points, inset with panels of silver lace and sewn with silver bugle beads; soft colours that suited her, making her hair intensely golden. In the mirror, her face was pale but radiant, emphasising the dark lakes of her eyes. Her mouth was deep red from feeding, yet still she looked innocent. She smiled coldly at herself, at the deception.

Janacek had refused to invite her to the party, yet here she was.

She assumed there would be someone checking invitations on the door, so she entered the Ring and drifted through walls until she found herself in a great sweep of light. She tasted the thrilling heat of many auras mingling together in a glorious blaze of fire-colours. Voices buzzed like the rasp of loose violin strings.

She found a corner and slipped into reality behind a huge potted palm. If anyone noticed, they'd put the apparition down to too much champagne. A high ceiling, chandeliers, tall windows with blue velvet curtains; oil paintings of Hapsburg high society at play. A chamber orchestra played waltzes.

There were some three hundred people in the ballroom; members of Ballet Janacek with their rich friends and supporters. A gathering of the elite. The dancers were the stars, each one holding court in a circle. Charlotte couldn't see Violette. Instead, instantly, she sensed her presence among her admirers, an icy gleam amid the heat.

The ballerina was on the far side of the room, surrounded by a large group. As Charlotte threaded her way through, she was stopped several times and engaged in conversation, usually by men. She joined in graciously, enjoying the exchange of banal pleasantries. How she'd dreaded social occasions as a human; how deliciously easy it was, now she no longer cared whether folk accepted her or not.

Yet as she drew close to Violette, apprehension crept through her. She wanted the ballerina not only to acknowledge her but to *like* her; she wanted to humiliate Janacek. Why did this matter? It was more than pride, more than desire for blood. The need was so deep and sharp that she dared not disturb it for fear of what she would find.

First glimpse of the dancer through the crowd. In a long wide-sleeved dress of ivory satin, her black hair coiled under a bandeau, Violette was playing another role to perfection. The gracious goddess. She looked pellucid, crystalline; completely the exquisite spirit of Giselle. The faintest blue tracery of veins pulsed under her creamy skin. Her eyes were the only vivid colour about her. She would have caged any vampire's heart.

A corpulent German was vigorously shaking Janacek's hand, then kissing Violette's fingers with hardly more subtlety. One of Janacek's assistants diplomatically guided him away; no one was allowed to monopolise the stars. More well-wishers pressed forward to replace him. An endless stream of people waited to meet Violette, who, like a queen, could spare only a few minutes to each.

The dancer's face was a mannequin's; a white smile, beautiful but glassy eyes giving away nothing of her soul. Her sociable warmth was a shield. With a surge of sympathy, Charlotte saw that Violette hated this pantomime. She endured it because she didn't want to disappoint.

In a brief pause between greetings, Violette turned to Janacek and spoke very softly. Charlotte isolated their voices from all the noise around her. "What time is it?"

"We only just arrived," he said. "Give them an hour, at least."

"I'll stay as long as I must. Providing I can have some more champagne. Would you mind?"

Charlotte moved nearer, observing so intently that she forgot to worry how they would react when they saw her. Vampires drew people's attention with indefinable magnetism; a lure to their prey. And as a young woman alone she stood out; not part of a group, outside convention. Unnatural.

Several acquaintances descended heartily on Janacek, and while he greeted them, Violette's gaze found Charlotte. Her smile faded. Staring, she touched Janacek's sleeve.

"That woman's here!" she whispered. "Did you invite her?"

"Excuse me," said Janacek to his friends. He looked startled to see Charlotte. "No, of course not."

"Then what's she doing here? It was understood, no outsiders. I certainly don't want your affairs flaunted at me!"

"I tell you, I did not invite her."

"How did she even know?"

"She overheard in the hotel. But I tell her it is a private party..."

As they spoke, Charlotte moved out of their line of sight. Taking a glass of champagne from a waiter, she slid towards Violette and Janacek like a blade of starlight.

"Well, have her removed."

Janacek sighed. "Of course. Where is she? I can't see her now. You know, someone with such impudence has to be admired..."

"Don't be absurd," Violette said flatly. "It's the principle."

"Oh, does it really matter?"

"Yes it does! I keep seeing her, and she's beginning to infuriate me. There's something disingenuous about her that makes me go absolutely cold."

In the chilly wash of these words, Charlotte stopped. Two tall male friends of Janacek were all that blocked her way now. Recovering her composure, she brushed their arms with her fingertips. The lightest of touches, yet they leapt apart as if she'd delivered an electric shock.

Stepping between them, she smiled into the hostile faces of Violette and Janacek. She offered the glass. "More champagne, Madame Lenoir?"

The dancer's eyes opened wider. Her face was a composed mask, but Charlotte thought, *She's frightened of me! I don't want her to be afraid...*

Janacek found his voice. "This is a private party, madam."

"It was rather impulsive of you to invite me, then."

Violette said nothing.

"Frau Alexander, you made a mistake," Janacek said, flustered. "I said, not tonight. You cause embarrassment."

"Forgive me, Madame Lenoir," Charlotte said innocently. "I didn't mean to start an argument. Herr Janacek led me to believe he could introduce us, but I wasn't quite sure what he expected in return."

As she spoke, she let her true nature shine through, holding nothing back. They would not guess "vampire", only see a woman of uncanny beauty with hypnotic violet eyes. A vampire trick, to hold the gaze of potential victims a little too long; men and women alike would become fascinated, tongue-tied, over-eager to please. Then it was easy to control them; and if she wanted to touch them, to kiss their necks, they were only too happy to oblige. *Yes, anything!* their eyes would say, not understanding what they were permitting until it was too late.

She saw Janacek fall at once, as he had before, his brain interpreting the feeling as simple lust. Sweat broke out on his upper lip.

But Violette... How coldly polished the ballerina's eyes were; how could mortal eyes be so chilling? It was near-impossible to hold the look, as impertinent as staring at a princess – but Charlotte persisted.

Violette, however, did not react as she had hoped. Far from softening, her eyes grew more aloof, even contemptuous. It was she who severed the contact, not Charlotte.

"This is a simple misunderstanding –" Janacek began.

Violette turned to him and snapped, "I don't know what this woman is insinuating, but please ask her to leave."

The crowd around them fell quiet, watching.

Charlotte was devastated. How could Violette be so completely impervious? She'd wanted to prove something, to melt Violette's reserve into soul-deep empathy, and she'd failed. Not a word, not a smile, not even the barest semblance of courtesy could she wring from the dancer.

Is it possible, she thought, *that she sees right through the glamour and hates what I really am? No, no, it's something else. It's* him.

Janacek opened his hands, shaking his head a little. "I'm sorry, madam, but really you should not have –"

Violette gripped his arm. "For goodness' sake, don't apologise to her. Enough."

At that, his expression turned flint-black. Charlotte had lost him. Forced to choose between them, he sided with Violette; he might have power over her, but clearly she also had a hold on him stronger than any Charlotte could conjure. His feelings were transparent in his face; he was inwardly furious at having to send away a woman who – he supposed – would have been an easy conquest; and he turned that fury full on Charlotte. If she hadn't infiltrated the party and upset Violette, he could have played her like a kitten on a cotton reel for weeks.

So he imagined. Charlotte, intuiting his thoughts, gave a thin smile.

"I am sorry you have wasted your time." The malevolent weight of his glare would have terrified the human Charlotte. "Obviously I did not make clear that Madame Lenoir does not permit unsolicited contact. Now, if you would leave quietly, to avoid a scene...?"

As he spoke, she recalled his hands on Violette's waist, his taunts, her revulsion. It was *his* fault the dancer was isolated. Janacek was not her shield against the world, but her gaoler. All Charlotte's emotion condensed to a single point.

"Don't trouble yourself, I'm going. And I'm the one who should apologise." She stared at him as she spoke, her eyes widening, letting him see her pupils turn to ice, windows onto night. Again she snared him, not with lust this time, but fear. To see him draw back, unsettled, was gratifying.

Then, acting on a cold, swift impulse, Charlotte did something she had never done before. Without even touching Janacek, she sucked out his life energy. Radiant needles of heat left his skin and entered hers; the sensation was a brief, unpleasant prickling, then tingling fire. She turned hot as if she'd swallowed his blood – but without the luscious satiation. The peculiar austerity of the feeling made her feel ruthless.

Janacek didn't seem to notice. Like everyone else, he stood waiting for her to leave. Then his face turned grey, and he staggered as if about to faint. People flocked round him in concern, but he shook them off, insisting testily that he was perfectly all right. Violette simply watched, expressionless.

"You should take care of your health, Herr Janacek," Charlotte said icily. "You don't look at all well."

She turned and walked away, burned by dozens of stares following her; everyone affected by her presence, no one understanding why. She felt Janacek's gaze boring into her spine. He knew she'd done *something* to him, and was scared to death...

In the hotel lobby, Charlotte leaned against a column and closed her eyes. Shock washed over her. *God,* she thought, *what have I done? Unforgivable. God, him... I can't really have done this!*

Then coolness flowed back into her, as frigid as Violette's eyes. The one person she wanted to reach had been unmoved.

"It was for you, Violette," she whispered. "I did it to free you."

CHAPTER EIGHT

THE LEFT-HAND PATH

"They're in the attic," said Holly, "and out on the landing. White creatures like skeletons. I don't know how many."

"You've been up there?" Ben said anxiously.

She nodded. "I took one look and ran straight down again."

"Did any of the creatures hurt you?"

"No."

Holding her chin, he turned her head side to side, studying her throat. No marks, thank God. "You should have left the house, old girl."

"I had to wait for you," she said gravely.

Benedict flattened his hands on the air. "Stay here. Don't move. Andreas, come with me."

"Be careful," she said. "For heaven's sake be careful!"

He went into the hall and ran lightly up the stairs. Andreas, still muffled in his hat and scarf, followed unhurriedly. On the landing, at the foot of the narrow flight that led up to the attic, Benedict paused.

The atmosphere rippled. The house no longer felt familiar but many times its real size, a huge dark edifice sprawling into other dimensions. The walls reverberated with ponderous shudders and crashes, like a glacier shedding icebergs…

A pale body lay halfway down the bare wooden steps. It looked dried-up and dusty grey. Impossible that it had moved at all, let alone crawled so far!

Ben gave Andreas a grim glance and began to climb towards the attic.

His heart accelerated as he picked his way over the prostrate figure, expecting its hand to snake out and seize him. Was it possible to establish control over these entities, or was he too late?

He got past the thing. It didn't move, only lay like a spider-husk, cobweb-draped, devoid of life-signs.

Andreas whispered, "*Mein Gott*, was I like this?"

The top landing lay in sepia half-light under one dim electric bulb. The attic door was a lightless rectangle. Ben moved softly to the threshold, staring at a white wrist and hand that stretched out towards him. A skeleton hand.

"Don't go too close," Andreas whispered. "If it smells your blood…"

Not replying, Ben stared into the darkness.

The temple was ruined, four panels shattered so he could see into the shell. Luminous shapes hung on the blackness; he counted six. None were inside the temple itself; they were out in the attic, lying motionless as if the effort of crawling that far had exhausted them. With one at his feet and another on the stairs, that made eight… was that all? Might there be others he couldn't see?

The air shivered in a ghost-wind. Compelled to close his eyes, he found himself gazing up into a blizzard-racked firmament.

Ben understood. He was seeing into the astral world. The vast skyscape always turned him giddy with awe. There were mountains above him, split by gaping chasms, distant peaks towering into violet infinity. A dark, shifting world, lit by gleams of fire. An appalling coldness sifted down… a dull copper-red light suffused everything, unearthly and baleful…

This is my fault, he thought. *I tore a rift between the Earth and Raqia and I didn't seal it properly! What did I do wrong? I failed to end the summoning… or it went on after I'd stopped, like radio waves on the ether.*

"What are you doing?" Andreas said urgently, as anxious as any human.

"Hush!" said Ben. "Don't interrupt me."

He squeezed his eyes shut, held out his arms stiffly. He let his mind blend with Raqia, and then, with all his might, he willed the beings back into their own realm and the rift to heal.

Dangerous to do this cold, with no preparation. He felt himself falling, thrown into a chasm. *Freezing... ahhh...* And then he came back to himself and saw nothing behind his eyelids except dull red starbusts.

He reached for the door frame to steady himself, opened his eyes and stared into the attic. He saw roof-struts, shadows, the temple shell...

The pallid figures still gleamed in the darkness. He'd failed to banish them. There were too many and he lacked the strength. Shaking, he leaned against the wall, whispering, "Oh, God."

The next he knew, Andreas seized his arm and cried, "*Vorsicht!*"

Ben saw the corspe in the doorway rise up in a pale loop. Andreas hauled him out of the way just as it struck. He heard a soft thump as it landed headlong on the floorboards, felt its fingernails scratching at his ankle. Feeble yet hideously cold and grasping.

Ben snatched his foot out of its reach. "Christ!" he exclaimed, pressing back against Andreas; forgetting that he had the same hungers.

He saw Andreas's white face from the corner of his eye, felt the chill of his skin. Horrified, he pulled himself free. He was trembling uncontrollably. The attacker now lay rigid and blank-eyed, as if it had spent all its energy in that one leap.

Enough, he told himself. *I'm behaving like a slave to this situation and I must become its master. What would Lancelyn do?*

"You are in danger if you stay here," said Andreas.

"I am gratified that you care."

The vampire shrugged.

Ben said, "But how dangerous are they? Can you remember how it felt when you were – like that?"

The black eyes gleamed angrily. "*Ja, leider.*"

"Well?"

"It was extremely unpleasant. I don't know how to describe it. Have you ever woken in the night with a dead arm, having slept on it?"

"Yes."

"Imagine feeling that all over, but worse. Your body is dead but your mind is awake and confused. You have no memory, only fear.

And then excruciating pain, as feeling comes back to your limb?" Ben nodded. "That's how I felt when I smelled your blood. A stinging fire like pins all over me. Jumping at you was a reflex. But when I failed and fell back to the ground, the numbness returned."

"So, you believe these creatures are suffering?"

"Yes, that is a safe assumption," the vampire replied acidly.

"But unless they're provoked by the smell of blood, they are helpless? Well, I shall lock them in the attic."

"They will sense humans in the house. Despair may make them stronger. They'll break out; a locked door won't stop them."

"Well, what will?" Ben said through his teeth.

He stepped cautiously over his attacker towards the attic. Inside, the others sent up an eerie groan that went through him like a chorus of damned souls.

In the gloom, an oblong block caught his eye, lying in the centre of the ten-pointed white star. Of course! The Book! He'd been too occupied with Andreas to think of it. No vampires were near it. In fact, they were pressing towards the walls as if it repelled them.

Ben moved slowly towards the wrecked temple, shoes crunching on broken glass. The dormant vampires looked pitiful, like shrivelled pupal cases. One or two twitched as he passed, and he began to sweat. Hardly daring to breathe, he crossed the white lines of the star and reached down to the Book.

As he made his way back, a vampire reared like an albino cobra and lunged. Benedict flung up the Book like a shield. The vampire swerved away and collapsed to the floor, uttering faint, piercing wails.

Ben fled through the door.

Hugging the Book to his pounding chest, he pointed to the creature by his feet and its fellow on the stairs. "Help me get them back inside."

"What?" said Andreas, recoiling. "I'm in as much danger as you! What do you think I can do? I don't know who they are. You've no idea what you're doing!"

Ben lost his temper. "Just help me, damn it!"

Resentfully, Andreas obeyed. How cold the two bodies felt to Ben's touch, peculiarly weightless yet rigid, like pumice. The one on the stairs lashed out, but Ben pushed its hand away with the Book and it shrank back. Shutting his mind to revulsion, Ben helped Andreas to haul them inside the attic.

He shut and locked the door, wiped sweat from his face.

"You're insane," Andreas muttered.

"This Book," said Ben, holding the volume towards him. "Any idea what it is?"

"A Bible?" Andreas drew away, folding his arms. "Take it away, it stinks of damp."

"Please, look." Ben opened the thick cover and turned the yellowing pages. "Can you understand it?"

"No. It might as well be written in Chinese." He turned away. "What do you want me to say? Get rid of it!"

"Why are you frightened?"

"I don't know. For God's sake, let me go downstairs, I –"

"Stay where you are. Answer me. I made you swear an oath on this Book and you recoiled as if it were on fire. Why?"

"It makes me feel cold and sick. It's disgusting. It saps my strength."

Ben closed the Book and took it out of Andreas's reach. "It's all right, you've told me enough. This Book has power over your kind. Logically, then, if I place it against the door, the others won't be able to come past it. Agreed?"

"Why ask me?" Andreas said thinly. "Some vampires are superstitious, but I never was. I don't believe in the power of artefacts to repel or control us. So, if I think the Book is evil – or holy, or whatever – it merely indicates that I've lost my mind. You had better be careful, my friend."

Ben leaned the Book against the door. Inside, there was silence. Sighing, he straightened up and gingerly touched Andreas's shoulder. "Come downstairs. We must talk."

Holly was waiting anxiously in the hall. Seeing Ben, all her feelings gathered in her face. Questions, and a desperate relief that she was too angry to express. Wordlessly, Ben took her arm and led her into the parlour.

"Everything's under control," he said. "They're safely imprisoned in the attic."

"You mean you didn't banish them?" She turned away, tight-lipped, and fetched a decanter and glasses from the sideboard. "Brandy?"

"Yes, please. God, I need it."

"And your friend?"

Andreas sank down on the floor against a wall, knees drawn up to his chin. The hat hid his face. Ben didn't suggest he remove it; the pale gaunt skill was an ugly sight, and he didn't want to give Holly any more shocks.

Ben said, "I don't think he –"

Andreas looked up. "Forgive my bad manners, *Gnädige Frau*. We have not been properly introduced. I am Andreas."

"Holly Grey," she said, her eyes opening wide.

"I am delighted to meet you," Andreas said with hollow courtesy. He lowered his head, and withdrew into silence.

Holly glared at Ben. "Are you going to explain this to me?"

Ben coaxed the fading fire to a blaze, then, shivering with cold and delayed shock, he flopped gratefully onto the sofa and pulled Holly down beside him. They sat in silence for a few moments, sipping brandy from balloon glasses. How deceptively cosy and normal the parlour seemed; firelight glowing on creamy walls and on the dark polished furniture. A paper fortress.

"I didn't mean to put you in danger," said Ben. "You should have stayed away."

"How could I? I knew you were doing something wrong! Why?"

The tension of the night dissipated, and the brandy made him heavy-headed. He felt suddenly depressed. "You've read Deirdre's letter, haven't you? She posted it just before she –"

"Yes."

"Do you believe her?"

Holly lowered her head, pressed knuckles to her forehead. "No. Yes."

"Lancelyn and I are at war. It's been building for a long time, only we wouldn't admit it. I can't let him go on like this, but when I try to stop him I have to be prepared for a counter-attack. That's why I performed the summoning rite again."

"You promised you wouldn't," she said. "You promised!"

Unable to deny it, he continued evenly, "A creature materialised, as before. It was Andreas. I wasn't expecting the others; the summoning must have been more powerful than I realised. I sealed the rift, but I can't send them back."

"But what are they? They give out no aura. They're like corpses – yet they can move and cry out! Most horrible thing I've ever seen."

"I wish you'd stayed away. Gods, you might have been killed!"

"But what business had you, messing with something so dangerous?" she said furiously. "They're not good or protective spirits, are they? Were you trying to raise the dead? Because that's what you've done!"

Ben found it difficult to defend himself when he couldn't even answer her questions. No good dressing up excuses in esoteric language; Holly would never fall for it. He asked quietly, "Andreas, what would you call yourself?"

"A vampire, *natürlich*," Andreas said flatly, "unless you want to be poetic. We are Lamiae, Children of Lilith. Immortals."

Holly said, "And were you like the others, when you first came through?"

Andreas did not reply. Ben answered, "Yes."

"But he can walk and talk now. How?"

"I took him out to feed and he's a little stronger," Benedict said uncomfortably.

"And he fed on –" she whispered.

"Human blood."

"Ah," she said. "I just wanted to be sure." She poured more brandy with a shaking hand. Her face was grey. Silence fell, thick with tension.

Ben thought he heard Andreas murmur, "Christian."

He leaned forward. "Do you fear the symbols of Christianity?"

"What?" Andreas looked up irritably.

"We are not exactly what you'd call regular church-goers."

Sarcastic amazement glittered in the dark eyes. *Extraordinary eyes*, Ben thought.

"No? I would never have guessed. No, it's a man's name, Kristian, with a K. He was the Devil. I wonder where he is? What year is this?"

Ben told him. He saw Andreas's hands tremble, almost saw his mind recoil behind his eyes. "All those years!"

"Who was he?" Ben ventured.

"Enough! I can't tell humans these things! How can I remember, if you won't leave me in peace to think?" He pointed at the ceiling, his coat sleeve falling to reveal his thin white wrist. "You called the Crystal Ring up there! No human can touch it, they shouldn't even know it exists – yet you called it, and then you're surprised there are vampires everywhere! You don't even know what I'm talking about, do you?"

Muttering viciously in German, Andreas leapt up and marched towards the door.

"Please," said Ben, "tell me about the Crystal Ring. If you help me, I'll help you. You're alive because of me. You must do my bidding."

"Pompous idiot," Andreas snarled. He paused, added, "I have to obey, because you have this power I don't understand. I wish you'd leave me the hell alone to think."

"Very well. Sit down and I'll leave you in peace. But you'll tell me eventually."

The vampire sank into an armchair, uncannily motionless in his reverie. Ben was stunned by his apparent mental anguish. Who would think that an evil, undead creature could feel fear, confusion, or grief? Andreas puzzled him deeply. He'd expected an astral being, good or evil, to be a fount of higher wisdom. This man, though clearly supernatural, was strangely human in his weakness.

"So," said Holly, "we have an attic full of the undead, all starving for blood. What are your plans for these... vampires? To send them against Lancelyn?"

"They're for self-defence only."

"But what if Lancelyn attacks us? Would you actually let them kill him?"

"No! I don't want that!" Holly's questions exasperated Ben. Of course he must address them, but he wanted to do so in his own time. "I intend to render him powerless. Too scared to practise magic or threaten us, ever again."

"But this is dangerous. You can't guarantee he won't be hurt."

"If he is, he asked for it! What about James and Deirdre? What compassion did he show them? Holly, please!" He so rarely raised his voice to her... foreboding struck him. It had never occurred to him that this might damage their marriage, along with everything else. "I have to work this out for myself."

"No. You involve me when it suits you, but when difficulties arise, you shut me out. I've known Lancelyn longer than you, and I can't stand this ill-feeling. I don't believe he's guilty, but even if he is, I can't turn against him."

"Whose side are you on?" Ben demanded.

"Yours, of course, but it's unfair to make me choose!"

"Don't blame me, blame my brother. I haven't abused my position to exploit and murder people!"

She turned away, biting her lip. "Ben, I'm on your side. But how can you control these vampires, or feed them? Does the Book explain? Don't lose your temper, just because I ask a question you can't answer."

Ben looped his hand through her arm, but she remained wooden. "Come on, old girl," he said gently. "I'm sorry. I don't know, but I'd better find out fast."

"How?"

Ben lit a cigar, staring through blue haloes of smoke as he pondered. *What the hell shall I do?* He pictured the Book standing sentinel outside the narrow attic door. *Do you contain the secret of transforming a nest of adders into a demon army? Give me answers, damn you!*

He said, "Andreas?"

The vampire gave him a cold, bitter stare.

"If the vampires have blood, I assume they'll begin to recover. How are they likely to behave?"

Andreas laughed. Barely audible over the crackling fire, he replied, "I have no idea. We were all human once. Like humans, we are all different."

A chilling thought. "You aren't saying that you all died human, and I resurrected you as vampires?"

"No, Benedict. We were vampires before." How crisp was his accent, how beautifully precise his English. Delicately self-mocking, hypnotic. "You didn't create us, only woke us. When they taste blood they'll begin to recover – and they'll be savagely angry and hungry, as I was. But I should admit, my friend, that I am a coward as vampires go. I like being looked after and I'll do anything for a quiet life. You find me easy to control, yes? I am a kitten. What you have in your attic, quite possibly, are eight ravenous tigers."

Benedict poured more brandy and swallowed it, grimacing. *God, what a nightmare!* Bad enough, taking Andreas each night to hunt humans; doing the same for nine vampires was unthinkable. They were in pain, suffering, and useless to him... but how in all conscience could he let them feed? How the hell to control them, if he did?

Andreas had been too easy.

As if reading his thoughts, Holly said, "I can't see an answer. It's inhuman and dangerous. You'll have to swallow your pride and ask Lancelyn for help."

"Never!" Ben shouted.

"You can't cope alone!"

"Yes, I can!" He lowered his voice. "I've made a decision. I'll leave the creatures as they are for now, with the Book to control them. When Andreas is stronger, he can help me with them, one by one."

Her mouth began to form denial, but she only shook her head in despair.

"Support me, Holly, please. Lancelyn must not find out. It's essential! Promise me!"

Not meeting his eyes, Holly promised.

There was no telling what Lancelyn might do next.

Benedict could not face another visit. The less contact they had, the better.

He endured the following days in a state of tension. Leaving the house was unavoidable, but he dreaded leaving Holly alone, even with the protection of the Book. He tried to send her to her family in Norfolk, but she refused.

The best solution, in the end, was for Holly to work in the shop while he stayed at home. He gave Maud various excuses; that he had flu, or needed to work at home. Holly returned each evening, complaining that Maud had driven her mad all day, that Ben hadn't instructed Mrs Potter to do the right jobs. Their bickering was a symptom of darker anxieties; the intrusion of the otherworld, the constant pressure of presences behind the attic door.

Ben let Andreas hunt alone each evening, trusting him to

return. He always did, as if content to be at Ben's command. Soon there were rumours of a flu epidemic around Ashvale... even a few deaths.

Andreas should go further afield to hunt; I'll buy a car and teach him to drive, Ben thought. And then he put his head in his hands and groaned at the awful banality of evil.

At night, unable to sleep, he stared at the ceiling for hours, hearing faint scratches and moans above... *I can't bring victims here,* he thought. *But even if Andreas were to take them out one by one... filling the town with vampires is unthinkable!*

Amid his fears, he acknowledged a terrible fascination with these beings. Andreas's transformation was remarkable. Every time he returned from feeding, there was visible improvement. His shrunken skin filled out, becoming smooth and radiant. His hair, black, soft and wavy, grew so fast that Holly had to trim it every day. And his face had an extraordinary beauty that Ben had only seen in paintings; ethereal with long, delicate features, deep green eyes with a wary gleam, a sculpted mouth. He was tall but finely built, a rarefied creature, almost translucent.

He looked like a poet, and had the melodramatic temperament to fit. Ben was intrigued. Andreas couldn't be judged by petty human standards, after all.

He tried everything to deflect Ben's continual questioning, insisting he couldn't remember, still less confide in a human. If Ben persisted, Andreas would sulk. But, slowly, information emerged. Ben's ideas began to change.

The Crystal Ring was another realm, but whether it was the astral world – Lancelyn's Raqia – he was unsure. There seemed to be no spirits, angels or devils there; only vampires – which were, perhaps, all of those. Yet Andreas seemed to have no deeper insights than a human.

And Ben thought, *Lancelyn's been deluding himself. I know more than he does!*

One Sunday afternoon, Benedict heard the hiss of bicycle tyres, and looked out to see an unwelcome figure dismounting from his cycle at front door. Holly was in the back garden, Andreas in the study with Ben.

"God Almighty, it's Lancelyn!" Ben cried, jumping up. "He

mustn't see you. Go into the kitchen, shut the door and stay there."

"*Liebe Gott*, isn't it enough that I must hide when your housekeeper's here or the baker at the door? I'm bored with it." The vampire obeyed wearily, while Benedict opened the front door with a show of composure.

"Good afternoon. To what do I owe this – honour?"

"Oh, don't be sardonic, Ben." Lancelyn spoke gruffly, removing his bicycle clips. "It doesn't suit you. How are you? There was a rumour you'd had the flu."

How ordinary he looked, a flush-faced gnome with dishevelled hair; how harmless!

"No, I'm in fine fettle."

"Are you sure, old man? Pale and tired, I'd say. Hope you haven't been overdoing it. Can I come in?"

"Of course." Benedict showed him into the parlour, offering cigarettes and whisky. They sat down in apparent civility, Ben feeling as deadly calm as his enemy looked. Playing the British game.

"I regret our argument," said Lancelyn.

"So do I."

"So I've come to make peace – if you want it."

Ben was startled and suspicious. "Oh yes?"

"You haven't been to a meeting for two weeks," said Lancelyn.

"I thought you'd expelled me from the Order."

"Nonsense. I need you."

"Ah, yes. Your fishing trip next weekend, isn't it?"

Lancelyn clearly heard the edge in Ben's voice; he gave a long, cold stare. "Anyway, Ben, I've come for the Book. Give it back now, and no hard feelings, eh?"

"I told you, you can't have it"

"Don't be ridiculous," Lancelyn said crisply. "Where is it?"

"Never mind the damned Book!" Ben pulled Deirdre's letter out of his pocket and put it into Lancelyn's hands. "Read this. It can't do her any further harm, now she's dead."

Lancelyn read it swiftly, his only reaction a frown. Then he tore it in half and threw it on the fire.

"Not much point in burning it," said Ben. "I won't forget what she said. You can't tear my mind in half, can you? Is it true?"

Lancelyn said nothing. Ben shouted, "Is it true, damn you?"

"For God's sake. Yes, it's true."

Ben was devastated. For a white-hot moment, he felt like a child betrayed by his father. "So you provide drugs, sex and occult thrills to rich fools, and then you blackmail them? When James and Deirdre challenged you, you killed them! How could you? I looked up to you!"

"What upsets you, little brother?" Lancelyn said without emotion. "The nature of the Hidden Temple? Or the fact that I kept it secret? I didn't tell you because I wanted to protect you."

"What the hell from?"

"Oh, come on! You were always disgusted by sex. I've never known such a prude; you must get it from Father. For heaven's sake, you were a virgin at twenty-three! You'd still be one now if I hadn't set Holly to seduce you."

Ben was outraged. "Holly and I found each other without any help from you. I'm all for free will – but blackmail is the exact opposite! Your Hidden Temple is about nothing but corruption."

"The type of people who join are corrupt," Lancelyn said smoothly. "Don't they deserve what they get? The higher their status, they more they want to roll in filth. I tell you, I could bring down this government and the next with what I know. Now that is power."

Although Benedict was aghast, he felt an awful excitement. Firm ground to challenge Lancelyn at last. "Maybe so, but it's not what we set out to do. Where's Sophia in all this? What's happened to Wisdom?"

"Can't you work it out?" Lancelyn said archly.

"You're playing games. You can't wriggle off the hook by pretending there's some higher motive. James and Deirdre – what had their deaths to do with the path to Meter Theon?"

Lancelyn was immovable. "They knew what happens to Neophytes who break their oaths, but I didn't kill them. I only played on their fears. How they chose to face those fears was their affair."

"I can't believe I'm hearing this. How could I be so wrong about you? I thought you were noble, perfect!"

"Well, I'm not." Lancelyn leaned back his head and blew smoke rings. "What are you going to do about it?"

"I'm going to take the Order away from you and put it back on the right lines."

"Really?"

"Really."

"This sounds like a declaration of war."

"It is," Ben said passionately. "It's been undeclared for quite some time."

"My dear boy, I *am* the Order. Even if you seduced my neophytes away, which you can't, I'd start another. The Temple of Meter Theon is where *I* am."

"Not any more. By the time I've finished, you won't want to be magus of anything. You'll want nothing to do with the occult ever again!"

A long pause. Lancelyn seemed disturbed, at last. "These are bold threats, Ben. If there's nothing to them, you're going to look foolish – but if you mean what you say, I will win. And you'll lose Holly for certain; she'll come back to me."

"No," said Ben, controlling his rage on a wave of conviction. "You've already lost her. But I ask one thing: leave the other initiates out of this. If there's a war, let's keep it between the two of us. A little cowardly to throw others into the firing line, don't you agree?"

Lancelyn looked surprised. Then his mouth spread into an unpleasant smile. "You're quite right. Just the two of us; that's only fair."

"But try anything like the tricks you worked on Deirdre, and you'll be sorry."

"I wouldn't dream of it. Nothing so crude." Lancelyn drained his glass, flicked his cigarette end into the fire, and stood. "Well, I'll be going. So glad we had this little talk to sort out our differences. And now, the Book, if you please."

"No," said Ben. "It's not yours. I'm keeping it."

"Something in it, is there?" Lancelyn winked knowingly. "I'm sorry about this, Ben – but not as sorry as you will shortly be."

Ben showed him to the door and watched him leave.

Lancelyn mounted his bicycle and rode away whistling.

* * *

The garden was Holly's refuge. She'd been on her knees all afternoon, digging up weeds until her hands ached; now, pulling off soil-plastered gloves, she sat on her favourite bench and watched the evening sunshine slanting golden-red through the fresh young leaves.

Physical tiredness helped her relax. The house was full of unpleasant vibrations, and strong instinct warned her to stay outside.

Nothing but trouble since this argument with Lancelyn began, she thought. *I wish it were over, I wish I'd never been psychic or joined the Order.*

She loved both Ben and Lancelyn, but could not keep them from each other's throats.

The garden was lush and full of life, the only fragment of the world she could control.

"May I join you?" said a soft voice. She started. Andreas stood gilded by the sunset.

"Of course," she said guardedly, moving along to make room. "Sit down. You don't seem to mind the daylight."

"What do you expect me to do, catch fire?"

"I don't know. I've never met a vampire before. I'm curious about people, so why should I treat you any differently? Is there a special way I should address you?"

He half-smiled. "I hope not. Your husband makes me feel less a vampire than a zoo exhibit."

"Why don't you leave, then?"

"Nowhere to go," he said. "I'm content here. I like you and Benedict, however infuriating he can be. By the way, his brother was here."

"When?" That was the feeling of unease she'd had! She made to stand, but Andreas held her back.

"He's gone. Stay and talk to me. They had quite an argument. Benedict shut me in the kitchen, but of course he doesn't realise that vampires can hear through walls."

"What did they say?"

Andreas told her. Holly shut her eyes and said, "Oh dear God. What next?"

He went on, his voice soothing. "Lancelyn is like Benedict; he also has strange gifts, I could tell. I've never before met humans who recognise what I am, *and* hold power over me. Ben reminds me... There's a vampire called Kristian who rules us, but Ben is different; not yet sure of his powers, whereas Kristian is overconfident... I wonder where he is? The last I remember is Kristian's face gloating over me as he left me for dead in the *Weisskalt*." Andreas shivered. "Now I learn it happened forty years ago. I am in a foreign country... and I don't mean England."

"Were you always a vampire, or did you become one?" she asked softly.

"I was human once. I was born in the eighteenth century. I planned to be a great poet, but Kristian came along and said that because I was so beautiful, he wanted to make me immortal... so I took his offer greedily, and found that when you enter the Crystal Ring, human ambitions such as writing poetry don't matter any more. Then I knew which kind of immortality I would have preferred – too late."

Holly heard immense anger buried in his soft tone. "What is the Crystal Ring?"

"It's what your husband calls Raqia, although we never called it that. Kristian said it was heaven, the mind of God. It is our realm. That's why I don't understand Benedict's ability..."

"Do other creatures live there? Are there spirits, or angels?"

"Oh, you can't imagine the emptiness! I call it hell! Only vampires can enter... but then, Kristian claims we are angels of a kind, the bringers of God's vengeance. Thankfully I had friends who rescued me from his madness. I wonder where they are?"

"In our attic, perhaps," said Holly. Andreas turned, staring so hard that she recoiled. "Did you live in the Crystal Ring or on Earth?"

"Both. We enter the Ring to travel or rest. Otherwise it was France, Germany, Italy; we were always on the move. Hoping Kristian wouldn't find us. But he did, and imprisoned us there in the ice... the *Weisskalt*, the highest level of the Crystal Ring. I can't forget the cold and the light. Agony."

Holly had one of her unbidden visions. A sweeping plain of ice, scattered with figures like dark, bandaged mummies.

"What else can you remember?"

"I heard his voice, commanding me to wake and take revenge.

For what, I don't know. I floated in the Crystal Ring for months. I saw images and faces from the past, but I was helpless. Then it went dark, and I was lying in a circle of mirrors with Benedict leaning over me. You were there too. You screamed, 'Banish it!' and I was thrown back into the Ring. I lay there, starving, until your husband saw fit to summon me again." The glittering darkness of his stare had a strange effect on her. "I feel safe in your house. People, mortal or immortal, drive me mad, yet I need them. Here are two people who want me, although I don't know why."

"It was Ben who wanted you," she said.

"Don't you want me, Holly? I'm disappointed." He stretched out a hand above his knee, spreading the long fingers. "I feel transparent. My hands are like white glass. Can you see through me?"

"Almost," Holly half-whispered. "I never thought a vampire would be so beautiful. I could never mistake you for human; you have no aura – or only a faint one, like the moon."

"Very few humans see such things," Andreas said, echoing her soft tone. Sitting close to her, he pressed one hand along her cheek, turning her face to his. Cool, his fingers, and so gentle. She was leaning towards him… and he embraced her suddenly as if desperate for comfort. His arms were slender yet so strong, and he was hurting her now.

She could barely breathe, and yet she felt languid. So lovely, this embrace, and natural. His breath against her skin made her shiver all over. She felt his lips against her neck, the tips of his teeth…

At once she snapped back to herself, shocked awake by a fierce inner alarm.

"Don't!" she gasped, losing her voice. Then, more firmly, "Don't, Andreas, please."

He pulled away from her, his face lengthening. He gasped and scratched at his throat. "Damn it. *Verflucht!* I can't do it."

Her composure in tatters, she watched him, in shock at the danger she'd narrowly avoided… almost disappointed.

Andreas leaned back with a mocking, angry smile. "I can't touch you," he said.

"Why not?" She probed her neck where his fang-tips had left tiny imprints.

"Benedict forbade it, you see, and I can't defy him."

Her shivering grew worse. "Oh, because *Ben* told you? Otherwise you would have done it, wouldn't you, whatever I said? What you are is a lie; charming and gentle, but all you really care about is blood – and you would've left me sick or dead, and not cared."

"Or mad." Andreas gave her a chilling sideways look. "Don't forget mad. Forgive me, Holly. I can't help it."

"It's Ben I'm angry with," she murmured. "Once an occultist uses his knowledge for evil, he can't go back. He knows the law, that wicked acts rebound on the sender with three times the force, but he won't listen! I have to stand by while he and Lancelyn destroy each other, and there's nothing I can do. Nothing."

Andreas put light fingertips on the back of her neck, gently stroking her. She didn't object.

"Poor Holly," he said. "So we both are helpless. Shall we be friends in our helplessness?"

Footsteps behind them, and she heard Ben's voice, sharp and suspicious. "What are you doing?"

"Talking," said Andreas. But Holly turned, furious.

"Why didn't you tell me Lancelyn was here?"

"I didn't want to –"

"Don't lie, don't say anything! Andreas told me what was said. And then he tried – he tried to bite me."

She stood. Ben, horrified, looked from her to serene-faced Andreas. "He did what?"

"It's all right, he stopped," Holly said coolly. "But if you don't banish the others soon, what do you think might happen?"

Ben pushed a hand through his hair, angry and distraught. His handsome face was lined with strain, and his eyes had an unbalanced glint. "Try to be patient."

"Have you seen yourself in the mirror?" she exclaimed. "Gods, if there were *anything* I could do to stop this, I would!"

With that retort, Holly walked away before frustration made her scream.

That night, Ben took Andreas along the tree-shaded street past Lancelyn's big red-brick house. There were no lights, no sign of activity.

"That's where he lives."

"You'd like me to go inside and kill him?" asked the vampire.

His bluntness stunned Ben. The thought of Lancelyn actually dying horrified him. "No, no, that's not the idea at all! I want to prove I'm stronger. I want him to *acknowledge* it. I don't want him hurt, only humiliated."

"Ah, a game."

"It's not a game! The whole spiritual future of mankind is at stake!"

At this, Andreas laughed so uproariously that Benedict was afraid someone inside would hear him. He pulled the vampire further along the street, but Andreas went on laughing until tears ran down his face and he could hardly stand.

"For God's sake, will you stop it?" Ben exclaimed.

"But you people, you have such pretensions! Everything in the name of religion... You take yourselves so seriously!"

"You don't understand. I thought you would, but you are just –"

"What, human?" Andreas snapped. "Hardly. Don't be so touchy; I like to see people playing dangerous games that might destroy them. I approve. It's... poetic."

"Very well, it is a game," Benedict said grimly. "But it matters. Don't you see? Your existence is proof that it matters!"

Holly was trembling as a manservant showed her into Lancelyn's study. Her stomach felt small and knotted. Guilt prickled hotly over her.

Lancelyn stood up behind his desk as she entered, all smiles. "My dear, how delightful to see you. I thought you were avoiding me. Sit down. So, how is everything?"

"Not good, actually," she stammered. This was so difficult. The atmosphere of the house filled her lungs, familiar yet unpleasant; musty, damp, redolent of bare linoleum and dust-heavy cobwebs. She'd often sat here in the past, performing secretarial duties for the Order. Not for some time, however.

He resumed his seat with the aloof air of a doctor. He prompted gently, "Does Benedict know you're here?"

"No."

"Ah. Naughty girl." She looked away in discomfort. He added, "I'm only teasing. I've missed you, Holly; I haven't asked you to work lately in order to avoid embarrassment, but really, you don't need Ben's permission to see me, do you?"

She gasped, "I'm in an impossible situation."

"Impossible? How?" He spoke with an insouciant, mocking smile.

"I want to be loyal to you both, but I can't. He'd be horrified to know I'm here. But I want no part in your so-called war; I'm here to ask you to end it. Please."

She folded her hands in her lap to stop them shaking. He regarded her with something close to admiration.

"Ah, my little peace-maker. Perhaps you should address your appeal to your husband. I'm terribly sorry you're upset, but conflict seems unavoidable."

"Nothing is unavoidable," she said, quiet and fierce. "I'm worried for both of you."

"Am I in danger?" He raised his thick eyebrows.

He was too perceptive, reading into the slightest remark. She tried to repair the damage. "I mean I don't want you to hate each other. What are you trying to do to Ben?"

"Nothing. He listens to rumours and jumps to wrong conclusions, I fear."

"Then can you look me in the eye and tell me Deirdre's letter was a lie? That you had no involvement in her death?"

He leaned back, gazing at the high ceiling. "James and Deirdre lost their nerve. Fear killed them. These aren't gentle powers that we deal with; lose courage, and you're done for. Holly, I'm sorry you learned about the Hidden Temple. I never wanted you sullied by the darker side."

"Why not? If you hadn't concealed your extra activities, I might not be so convinced they're bad."

"The sin lies in the secrecy, eh? Come now; with your talent, what could I possibly keep hidden from you?"

"That's not fair." She steadied her voice. Confronting Lancelyn was infinitely harder than arguing with Ben. "You made me take an oath never to use my gifts against you."

"And knowing what happens to Neophytes who break their oaths, you've been a good girl. But supposing I released you from your vow. Look at me and describe what you see."

She gazed. Just a man, as beloved as a father despite his faults. Then, for a moment, there were great winged shapes flapping all around him, coal-black yet only half-seen. The shadows of his soul, towering above him, capering on the wall...

In her poor eyesight, Lancelyn was blurred but so were the shadows, which meant they were *real*. Horror thrashed inside her and she looked away quickly. When she dared to look again, the shadows had gone.

"Well?" he said. "What did you see?"

"Nothing."

"Indeed?" He stood and came to lean over her with his hands on the arms of her leather chair. She shrank away. She couldn't avoid his sparkling, mischievous eyes; felt herself slipping towards a trance out of habit. "I think you saw something. Let me hypnotise you, Holly. I want to know what you saw."

"No!" If she let him, he'd drag Ben's plan out of her, and Ben would never forgive her. In panic she tried to duck under Lancelyn's arms. He clutched her shoulder, holding her petrified with one hand.

Then he released her and moved away. "Why are you frightened of me?" he said sadly. "You know I'd never hurt you."

"I don't want you thinking I've turned against you," she said, her voice small, "but I have to stand by Ben."

"You were with me a long time before you met Ben."

In distress, she gazed at the stocky, solid figure who'd offered the kind acceptance denied by her parents. The risk of losing his approval filled her with terror. Defying him was agony.

"I'll make a deal," she said with all the control she could gather. "I'll tell Ben nothing about you, but I won't spy on him for you, either."

Lancelyn smiled, shaking his head, but the smile was cold. "You're treading on dangerous ground, Holly."

"It's all I have. I should go." She felt herself breaking. Enough. Swiftly she rose and marched towards the front door, chin held high. She collided with a hat-stand, thanks to her patchy eyesight, quickly regaining her dignity as she left. She was gone before Lancelyn had the chance to notice her eyes were full of tears.

* * *

Benedict spent hours on the landing outside the attic, studying the Book. Each time the text verged on making sense, he lost the thread again. The grimoire had a definite ambience: a feeling of grey misery, of immeasurably ancient times and secrets better not known... yet he couldn't leave it alone.

From behind the door came eerie vampire groans, the snake-rustle of their bodies across the floorboards; but when he peered through the keyhole, he never caught them moving. They'd gathered in the temple shell, away from the door. Dead white moths.

This is cruel, Ben thought. *But I have no choice.*

He brooded on Lancelyn's visit. He pondered the undead creatures beached in the driftwood of the temple, on the best way to unleash them on his enemy... *God, I must act soon!*

Andreas's near-attack on Holly had alarmed him. Even more disturbing was the fact that she hadn't seemed afraid.

He encouraged her to go out, to help Maud at the shop, visit friends or go shopping. But when she wasn't at home, he found himself wondering, *Where is she? Who is she seeing?*

Has she gone to Lancelyn?

Terrible, to mistrust his own wife when they'd been so close. Vampires had brought paranoia into the house. He trusted no one.

Benedict bought a second-hand motor car, a black Morris. In its dark interior, uncanny passengers would go unnoticed. One afternoon, while Holly was at the bookshop, he took Andreas for a drive.

"There are several large towns in driving distance," he said. "Birmingham, Derby, Nottingham; places where you can satisfy your thirst without attracting attention. When we revive the other vampires, it will be essential to travel further afield."

Andreas didn't reply. He was fascinated by the vehicle, entranced by its speed.

"Do you agree?" said Ben.

"You're very calculating," said Andreas.

"I have to be."

"And yet you're hot-headed. You are a strange man, Benedict. I think you would make a very good vampire."

Arriving home, Ben parked outside the cottage, unlocked the front door, removed his coat. Holly wasn't back yet. Andreas entered the study, as he often did, to read history books about the years he had missed, and newspapers, which he loved. Ben went upstairs to check on the vampire invalids. Outside the attic door he stopped in dismay.

The Book had gone.

He checked the door was still locked, looked through the keyhole and counted eight pale shapes. As usual, they lay as if dead – but they'd all moved closer to the door.

Ben ran downstairs and confronted Andreas.

"Have you touched the Book?"

"Of course not," said Andreas. "You know I can't stand the damned thing near me."

"Well, where is it?"

"How should I know?"

"Someone's moved it."

"Not me. How could I, when I've been with you all afternoon?"

Ben turned away, suddenly realising what had happened to the Book. He checked all windows and doors; nothing had been disturbed. That proved it. Burning with rage, he sat and waited for Holly. If she'd betrayed him, perhaps she wouldn't dare come home – but minutes later, he heard the front door open.

"Holly!" he shouted, striding into the hall. "You've taken it to him, haven't you?"

Hanging up her coat and hat, she turned, looking astonished to be greeted by this outburst. "Taken what to whom?"

"You know what I'm talking about! The Book's gone. You took it. Where the devil is it?"

"I've no idea!" she cried indignantly.

"Don't lie! You've taken it to Lancelyn! How could you?" He stepped towards her.

"Ben, don't!" she cried, leaping backwards. "Stop! You look demented."

He mastered himself, thinking, *Surely I wasn't going to hit her?* "Where is it?" he demanded. Andreas came into the hall and stood leaning in the doorway with a slight smile.

"I don't know." Her voice dropped. "Perhaps someone broke in."

"No," he said flatly. "I've checked the whole house. Whoever entered had a key. Who has a key, except you?"

"Mrs Potter."

"No. I took hers, so she can't come in when no one's here."

Holly went white. To Ben, she appeared a stranger, not his wife. She blinked, parted her lips and said quickly, "Wait, Ben. You keep a house key in your drawer at the shop, don't you?"

"Yes, but…"

"Maud went out this afternoon. She asked for an hour off. She may have gone into your office first…"

"That's preposterous! Why her? She knows nothing about the Order, still less that the Book even exists!"

"That's not true. She saw it once, when you'd left it in the parlour. And she's always angling to join –"

"Oh, so Lancelyn's got to Maud, has he? She's never even met him!"

"She must have done," Holly said patiently. "He's often in the shop, isn't he? How could she *not* have met him?"

"This is ridiculous." He grasped her shoulder and she winced. "Bad enough if you've betrayed me, without blaming an innocent girl. Maud couldn't…"

Dismayed, Holly retaliated, "Ben, are you losing your mind? I *know* it was Maud. How can you not believe me?"

"Because you were always Lancelyn's pet! Remember, you said you'd do *anything* to stop this battle. And the only thing was to give him back the blasted Book. Doubtless you told him about Andreas and the summoning. It's logical. You probably knew about this 'Hidden Temple' all along, and denied that as well."

"I never did! I knew nothing, I swear!"

"Perhaps you took part in the orgies, for all I know!"

"How *dare* you not trust me?" she cried, seething. "Damn it, I'll prove Maud took that Book!"

"Holly –" he began, but she marched to the front door, seizing her coat as she went. She slammed the door so hard that the whole cottage shook.

Still trembling with rage, Benedict heard the reverberation go on and on. The house cracked and shifted eerily. He looked up the stairs, then, his tongue thickening with dread, he began to climb.

"Don't go up there," said Andreas.

Ben paused, sudden fear dousing his anger. Andreas was at the foot of the stairs, gazing up at him. And as Ben stood there, shaking, he heard the sound of wood splintering above. The attic door.

"My God, they're breaking out. You must help me."

He glanced down at Andreas, but the vampire shook his head, backing away, eyes blank. He looked terrified. Ben discovered then that a vampire's fear was more infectious and horrifying than that of any human.

"I'm leaving."

"No!" Ben shouted. "I forbid you to leave!"

Andreas carried on towards the front door.

Ben said, "The chain is tightening."

Andreas stopped and doubled over, hands flying to his throat. After a moment he straightened up and turned to glare at Ben. His eyes were circular pits in his skull, and a necklace of red fingerprints marked his neck where he'd plucked at the invisible garrotte.

"Please help me," said Ben.

"You can keep me here, but there's nothing I can do," Andreas said hoarsely. "They're as eager for my blood as for yours! You're on your own, my friend."

CHAPTER NINE

POPPY WINE

For two weeks, Charlotte waited for news of Janacek. She could have spied on him in person, but the thought repelled her. She'd come too close to him and to Violette; now she needed to keep her distance in every sense.

Every day she would travel through the Crystal Ring to Berne or Interlaken to look at the newspapers. Late one morning, as she was about to leave the house, she found a newspaper already open on a table in the library. Her gaze went straight to the headline: renowned choreographer Roman Janacek had died after a short illness. His death was unexpected, a cold that turned to pneumonia. The funeral would take place near Salzburg in two days' time.

Charlotte had been expecting this moment, yet it was still a shock. As she stood reading the story for the third time, Karl entered the room and walked soundlessly to her.

She turned, but there was no need to speak. From his expression, he knew what she was reading.

"Did you put this paper here?" she said, her voice almost failing.

"I left it for you to see. I thought you should know." His voice was grave.

Charlotte couldn't speak. Karl voiced no accusation, but he was clearly waiting to hear what she would say. When a vampire spent time with humans, and one suddenly died – of course he was suspicious. And she was terrible at lying.

"It says he died of pneumonia," she said at last "I did not drink his blood."

Karl's gaze was unwavering. "There are other ways."

Her tense silence was as good as a confession. He might not stand in judgment, but his disapproval lay heavy on her. He added, "If you feed on their life energy instead, the damage is invisible. That's what Kristian would do, because he couldn't bear to touch humans. The victim never knows, until they die of the first minor infection they catch. It's often a cold, I've heard."

She dropped her head in shame.

"Why, Charlotte?" he asked.

She made herself meet his eyes. Their calm amber glow still had the power to squeeze her heart white. "He was a vile man. He had power over Violette, and used it to torment her. He treated her like a slave."

"Would a jury sentence him to death for that? He may have been vile, but he was also brilliant. What if you have not only destroyed him, but broken up his company and ended Violette's career?"

So quiet, Karl's voice, and impersonal. Charlotte felt ashamed and angry, burned by his words even though his tone was so carefully neutral. She said, "You're a vampire too, Karl. Don't tell me you've never killed anyone. I know you have."

"I've done many things to regret, even though they were necessary to my survival. But was his death necessary to yours?" Then, to her amazement, Karl's face changed. He frowned and drew away from her, at a loss; failing to keep his dismay hidden. "I can't believe you would do this. It's so unlike you. Or is it? Perhaps she was right."

He started to walk away. Then, only then, did she see how much pain she'd caused him, and knew with horrifying certainty that she couldn't put it right.

"She? You mean Katerina?" Charlotte said, following him. "She's labelled me a murderer, has she?"

Karl stopped, half-turned without looking directly at her. "No. She only suggested that perhaps I don't know you as well as I thought I did." And he resumed his walk into the drawing room, so distant that the few feet of air between them might have been an ocean.

Charlotte stayed in the library. She sat at the table, staring at the print that condemned her. Not for a moment had she worried that Karl would find out, nor considered his reaction if he did. His withdrawal left her impaled and helpless, thinking over and over, *He's going to Katerina. I've driven him to her.*

She felt deathly, yet she couldn't cry. Her only emotion was bitter numbness.

I meant to kill Janacek, and I'd do it again, she thought. *It can't be undone. How can Karl understand what compelled me, when I don't understand it myself?*

For two days, she hardly saw him. What was there to say? Katerina's presence made it all too easy for them to avoid each other. When the time came, Charlotte dressed in black and travelled alone through the Crystal Ring to Austria.

There was no colour in the graveyard, only tones of grey as rain sifted over the rough hillside outside the church. The trees sheltering Charlotte wove a black web, glistening with silver. Such a crowd outside, more people than could possibly fit into the church! Stunned, she watched horse-drawn carriages arriving; the hearse, the mourners following. Black horses, white flowers; Violette's colours. She sensed human radiance barely warming the chill interior of the church, while the hymns floated thinly into the damp air.

I caused this, she thought. *The death of a great man, a national hero. All these people are mourning him.*

She felt no sense of triumph. If this proved her power, it was not the kind of power she'd ever wanted. Neither did she feel sorrow, only a detached spiritual greyness.

I stand here like a ghost. Outside humanity. Undead.

When the mourners came out and assembled round the grave, Charlotte looked anxiously for Violette. There she was, black-veiled but unmistakable, dainty even in grief. Her head was bowed; her hands, encased in black silk gloves, clasped in front. A man and woman moved close beside her to comfort and guard her. Some of the mourners were sobbing. Charlotte could not hear Violette's voice among them.

The coffin was lowered, prayers said, flowers and clods of earth and ballet shoes thrown into the grave. The mourners began to drift away until only Violette remained. Charlotte watched as her companions tried to persuade her into the carriage, out of the rain; she shook them off. "Leave me alone for a few moments," she said.

The crowd lining the road from the churchyard was silent, indistinct behind a veil of rain; the minister sheltered with the gravediggers inside the porch; one carriage waited for the dancer. They might as well not exist. There was only Violette.

She stood on the lip of the grave, a slim figure as austere as a headstone in the misty half-light. But she no longer looked down at the coffin. She was staring straight at Charlotte.

Charlotte simply looked back, willing her to walk over, thinking, *If you want to speak to me, come; if not, you will never see me again.*

Then Violette walked around the grave and across the wet grass to where Charlotte stood under the dripping trees. No one came after her. For the first time, the two women met alone.

"I thought it was you," said Violette. "What are you doing here?" Her voice was calm and precise, giving nothing away.

Charlotte opened her umbrella and held it over them both; a subtle cage. "I came to pay my respects, Madame Lenoir."

Violette's face was a fleeting pearl behind the net veil. Her cheeks were dry; no tears. Sable, black feathers and jet beads suited her so exactly that she took Charlotte's breath away. What was it about this woman? Not sexual, Charlotte's feeling, more like a passionate response to a work of art. Indefinable, spiritual yet almost covetous. Infinitely more than a desire for blood.

"Why?"

"For your sake. I had to speak to you."

Violette stared at her, pupils expanding. "I thought I'd seen the last of you."

"Yes, you dismissed me like an empress sending away some peasant not fit to kiss your feet. Will you do the same this time?"

"I would, but you have me at a disadvantage," the dancer said thinly. "You force me to ask you who you are."

"You know my name."

"But *what* are you? A witch? You told Janacek to watch his health. Two days later he was dead. How did you know he might die? Did you put a curse on him?"

"I only observed that he looked unwell. Surely you're not superstitious?"

"There are no folk more superstitious than performers, and dancers are the worst." Her self-mocking tone was grim. "You come to every performance; you leave flowers in a locked room; you appear at a party that no one could enter without an invitation; then Roman upsets you and suddenly he is dying..."

"And I thought you were too wrapped up in your work to notice me at all," said Charlotte.

Violette blanched. She tried to remain aloof, but Charlotte saw tension and fear roiling under the mask. Remorse hit her; not that she'd killed Janacek, but that his loss had hurt Violette. She touched the dancer's shoulder at the base of her slender neck.

Violette froze; clearly, she didn't like to be touched. Charlotte held her gaze, wanting to calm and entrance her as Karl had once done to her; wanting to fill her with the same blissful tranquillity. The ballerina remained impervious.

"I'm sorry," said Charlotte, letting her hand drop. "I didn't mean to intrude on your grief. But Janacek was doing you no good. He had nothing left to teach you."

"I owe him everything. He saved me from spending my life in the *corps de ballet*; he gave me that chance!"

"He would have destroyed you! He was jealous, wasn't he?"

"He loved me."

"If he did, his idea of love was possession and control. Wasn't that his scheme, touching, taunting you, telling you what he planned to do with me?"

The dancer whispered, "How could you know that? *How the hell could you possibly know that?*"

"What I don't understand is why you let him do it. Did you feel in debt to him? So? That gave him no rights over you, none at all."

Violette closed her eyes. She was shaking. "No one could know these things unless they were a witch."

"I know it can be impossible to break away from someone, no matter how much you want to. If you loved him, I'm sorry."

For a moment, Charlotte thought the ballerina was going to faint. She'd imagined some magical communication and friendship between them; instead, all she had achieved was to make Violette miserable and frightened.

Charlotte said softly, "I had no right. How could I forget that it's possible to adore someone, no matter how wicked they are?"

Silence, except for rain dripping onto the grass.

Violette drew a shuddering breath. Sobbing, she said, "I hated him."

Not sobs, Charlotte realised, but humourless laughter. "Violette?"

"I hated him! You are exactly right about everything. My God, trying to pretend to be grief-stricken. I would like to dance on his grave!"

"Don't," Charlotte said quietly. "You're upsetting yourself."

Violette put a black-gloved hand to her lips. "I loathed him, but I don't know what I'll do without him. He was all I had."

"There must be something better."

"But what? How is my life any of your business? You still haven't explained who or what you are. A too-persistent devotee, I thought at first; I've met enough of those. You're not a ballet teacher, nor a journalist."

"I never said I was. And I'm no witch, I promise. You said I forced you to talk to me, but I cannot force you to do anything at all."

"Can't you?" Violette's eyes were netted sapphires. "When you know things about me that no one could? When you can kill a man, so you imply, without even touching him? I suppose you could kill me too. With those eyes, you could make me do anything. All I'm asking is that you tell me why. What do you want?"

"To be your friend, that's all. To watch you dance."

The ballerina's stare was cynical. She looked ill. "My *friend*? You scare me to death. Does that satisfy you? But I warn you, I'm no coward. I will not give in."

Violette's fearful defiance made Charlotte feel ashamed, hopeless. She dropped her gaze and said, "I admit, I frightened you because it was the only way to catch your attention. Despicable. I thought that once we met, you'd feel differently, but all I sense is... dislike."

"You are correct. I dislike you intensely."

"Then I'll leave."

She gave Violette the umbrella and turned to walk away. To

her surprise she felt the dancer's hand catch her elbow. The neat fingers in their black satin sheaths seemed to fire a chain of lights in her arm.

"Don't go."

It was a command. Charlotte stopped and turned back. "Why not?"

"Because you are a trial to be faced. It's no good trying to escape you."

Charlotte was stunned. She feared Violette was unbalanced; was it grief for Janacek, or a pain far older and deeper? "What do you mean? I'm not here to torment you."

"Perhaps you don't know it, but you are my punishment. I don't want you near me, but I can't send you away. You have a greater hold on me now than Janacek ever had. It's what you want, and what I deserve."

Aghast, Charlotte said, "What punishment? I can't imagine you have any cause to deserve that."

Violette smiled. "You mean there's something about me you don't know?" She pointed to the distant carriage. "Come with me. Come back to Salzburg."

Karl waited a long time for Charlotte, but she still did not come home. *Every time she goes out,* he thought, *she stays away longer.*

Katerina occupied his attention, so the hours passed swiftly and Charlotte would return before he knew it. This evening, however, he was alone. Too much time to dwell on Charlotte's absence.

He sat in the library, gazing out of the window at the forested hills and cloudy night sky. Firelight filled the room with flickering shadows, glowing orange on the book that lay open on his knee. He tried to read, but the words failed to engage him.

Where did the rift begin? he thought. *Was it when Katerina came... or did Charlotte's obsession with Violette begin before that? Have I driven her away – or simply given her an excuse to seek freedom?*

It's hard to forgive her for Janacek, but I miss her... desperately. How dare I condemn her for killing, when I made her what she is? The human Charlotte would not have harmed a fly.

I never rejected Ilona for her cynicism and brutality; not for long, anyway. But to think Charlotte killed a man, not from hunger but from malice, as Ilona might... Why is it so hard to accept?

Because, he thought, *I expected Charlotte to be perfect; no, not perfect. I only wanted her to remain herself. I dreaded her changing, as Ilona changed when I made her immortal. And I hoped, because her self survived the transformation, that all would be well. I assumed that the change would occur drastically or not at all; never that it would be slow and insidious.*

The person she is now seems so unlike the innocent, passionate girl I first knew... or has this been dormant in her all the time? That's what she used to say. "The fact that I am with you proves I am a bad person."

It doesn't matter what I tell myself. I don't know her. That is the sad truth. I do not know her.

I suspect she attacked the choreographer because he came between her and Violette... But I won't know the truth until I talk to her. I should have given her a chance to explain; but if she can't forgive me for Katerina, and thinks I cannot forgive her, will she ever come back?

Karl closed his eyes against a stab of fear. He had lost so many people he loved: Therese, Andreas, Katerina – Ilona, too, emotionally if not physically. Now it seemed his happiness with Charlotte was too bright-burning and fragile to last. Immortality and contentment were incompatible conditions; but still, to lose her, for whatever reason, would be unbearable.

His thoughts began to circle endlessly, self-destructive. He needed rest. Katerina had gone out to feed; she was physically strong now, but still mentally exhausted. If she didn't recover soon, Karl decided, he would begin the search for Andreas alone.

Now he found relief in blending into the Ring, arcing upwards through the roof of the chalet like a seal through water, leaving the human world behind. Karl fell through the firmament, found a pathway, and began to climb towards dappled cloud-hills.

The Ring was dark, all violet, blue and black. He climbed higher than usual, looking for light. Floating in a swirl of peacock radiance, half hypnotised by the slow-rolling motion of the peaks below him, he sank into a trance.

Visions came. Memories. He was back in the nineteenth century, a lost country of elegance and squalor, of bright satins and drab stinking shadows. The exquisite red fire of blood... and the black cold emptiness of undeath. A time dominated by Kristian's all-pervading power.

Kristian: a great dark figure of a vampire, who believed himself the chosen prophet of a vengeful God. His fanaticism and his irresistible strength had made Karl's existence a misery.

In the Vienna of 1820, Karl had been mortal, perfectly happy with his wife Therese and their baby daughter, Ilona. But Kristian, scouring Europe for beautiful disciples, abducted him and transformed him into a vampire. The next time Karl saw Therese, she was dead; butchered at Kristian's command, to sever him from earthly bonds. Incredible, after that atrocity and others, that Kristian had still expected Karl to love him!

The pain of losing Therese – of failing to save her – was intolerable. Karl bore it, but he could never forgive.

As often as possible, Karl would escape the drab castle on the Rhine where Kristian held court, and live alone until his master came to fetch him back. He hated what Kristian had done to him... and yet, he could not regret becoming immortal.

In many ways, Karl was an excellent predator. He fed without compunction, not merely to survive, but because the rapture lifted him beyond conscience. He would walk softly through the streets – in a huge city, or a remote village – looking for a person alone who dawdled with no sense of danger. It was a rare human who sensed him before he struck. And he did not discriminate; he didn't seek derelicts, criminals or prostitutes, thinking they had less right to life and health than others; nor the rich to punish their privilege. He wanted to know nothing about his victims. Whether a drunk lying in an alley was a loving father, or a woman walking demurely from church a sadist who beat her servants, he did not wish to know.

Strike like a bolt from God, Kristian had told him; but that was not the reason Karl took victims at random. He simply accepted he had no right to judge them.

Kristian, who loathed humans, believed that taking their blood was disgusting and sensual. Like an archbishop preaching that although sex existed, they must not indulge, he required his vampires to feed only on life energy. An austere commandment that Karl, like most vampires, found impossible to keep. (Kristian knew, of course; but what use was his band of sinners, if they failed to sin?) Taking blood need not kill, but stealing life energy nearly always did. And to have a human in his arms, to feel the soft warm weight against him and the red pulse of their heart... it was the only release.

Hardest for Karl to tolerate was his appalling loneliness. Great, passionless sweeps of existence were punctuated only by the hot red bliss of killing. For company, there was only Kristian, whom he despised, or Kristian's acolytes, who were worse. Although he would glimpse a spark of rebellion behind another vampire's eyes, it was a caged passion that dared not break free. Perhaps he should have stayed and nurtured potential rebels, but they were too set in Kristian's ways, dry creatures scratched in chalk.

The only vampires to whom he felt attachment were Andreas and Katerina, despite the fact they'd helped Kristian initiate him – or because of it. Transformation was a raw, overwhelming experience that forged complex bonds. Katerina's statuesque warmth and Andreas's dark neurotic beauty drew him, but he kept his distance because they seemed devoted to Kristian. Yet they often spent time away from Kristian in a small house in Paris. Sometimes Karl detected irony in their devotion that their egotistical master did not perceive.

Wishful thinking, perhaps. He dared not risk friendship with anyone.

Karl had to fill the emptiness between skirmishes with Kristian and the pleasure of hunting, or go mad. He didn't brood on Therese or the life he had lost. Being a vampire was to be an ice-hard creature, touched but not torn apart by mortal loss, set apart from mortals but still able to pass among them.

There was still the world: cities, with their theatres, taverns, art galleries, busy squares. With sensitive vampire perception, he gained more from aesthetic pleasure than he had as a human.

Once he went to Paris when he knew Katerina and Andreas were there, although he had no intention of visiting them. He went to *The Marriage of Figaro*, and minutes after the house lights went down, he noticed a woman watching him.

She was seated in a box opposite to his across the auditorium. Her eyes gleamed like diamonds in the darkness. She was half-visible in the shadows, in soft shades of crimson. Her hair was deep brown... Like a flood of fire, memories of his long-dead wife leapt into his mind. Not only Therese, but the loneliness he'd endured since... He'd thought the grief bearable; but in the light of a stranger's eyes, it became a torment.

The woman was alone. At the interval, Karl asked if he could join her. She assented, clearly delighted. Close at hand, she hardly resembled Therese at all; she was taller, much quieter in manner. They said little, but there was no need; understanding flashed between their eyes.

False understanding, Karl thought sadly. She saw a handsome man to whom she was deeply attracted, not knowing what he really was: a crystalline replica, animated by stolen blood.

He had no intention of harming her. Sitting beside her in the warm darkness, he shut down his vampire instinct. All he wanted was her company, to be close to a human for a while, as he hadn't been for what seemed eternity. To pretend he was still mortal. Then he would kiss her hand and leave.

When the music ended, she told him her name, Yvette. Her story followed; and although Karl did not want to hear it, by telling him she unwittingly protected herself. She was married, she confessed, but her husband was old and they'd never loved each other. Besides, he was away in the country and she hated staying in the town house alone...

The invitation was not blatant, but sad, poignant. She was genuinely lonely. And Karl, against his better judgment, accepted. *Why am I doing this,* he thought, *when I cannot give her what she wants?*

As they travelled through the dark wet streets in her carriage, Karl found himself becoming more aware of her, not as a potential victim, but as a woman. Her creamy shoulders, the crimson velvet sculpted to her body, the soft loops of her hair. Her natural scent was delicious. To his own amazement, he felt no need for her blood; only a longing to kiss her... to let velvet and satin fall to the floor, and to feel her flesh pressed against his.

Yvette was talkative now, showing no concern that he said

little. In fact, he could hardly speak. Since his transformation, he'd never felt natural passion for a woman; only a desire for blood, which was lust of a different kind. Kristian encouraged the belief that vampires had no needs other than to steal human life. What was the point? And yet...

Kristian the puritan would not have approved... but Kristian was the last thing on Karl's mind as Yvette led him into her house.

The rooms were huge and draughty, much of the furniture covered with dust sheets. A few candles barely made an impression on the cavernous darkness, and her two elderly servants seemed as lifeless as the house itself. But in her chamber, she and Karl gathered all the lamps and made a bower of honey light around the four-poster bed.

God, this desire was real, so strong. He couldn't say no; it was like falling. He felt euphoric, as if she'd broken the curse, and by some wondrous holy magic made him mortal again.

Yvette welcomed him into her arms with joy. She was no innocent, but an experienced, passionate lover who'd been alone for longer than she could bear. She made Karl feel purely, blessedly human. He sank into her warmth with complete abandon.

No thought but to please her; no fear of harming her. His only emotion was this river of joy and heat... and so natural, then, in the delicious bliss of release, to lower his face to her neck, to kiss her skin through the damp tangled strands of hair...

There was no warning of the treachery. With a soft motion as gentle as a breath, Karl's fangs were in her throat, her blood surging into his mouth, and he could not stop drinking. Could not stop.

At first she pulled him hard against her with a cry. Then she seemed to realise what was happening, started to struggle and push him away. But the compulsion was sovereign, a blind impulse he couldn't fight. This was the treachery, that it felt too beautiful to be wrong; as if they were inside each other, every cell united in rolling red fire that pulsed on and on... slower and slower... into stillness.

Karl came back to himself as if drenched in ice. His lover's mouth was open, her eyes staring upwards past his shoulder, her body limp and waxen...

He pulled away, dizzy and intoxicated. Yvette lay beneath him like a ravaged mannequin, her cheeks sunken. Her white skin was turning blue... and on her throat was a purple wound, across her shoulder a splash of crimson the colour of her discarded dress.

He staggered back, half-sliding off the bed, the floor a swaying deck beneath him. All his pleasure turned ash-cold with her death. *I never intended this*, he thought in blank self-loathing. *Dear God, this was the last thing, the last thing...*

But even as he stared at the result of his desire, he understood.

This was inevitable. The uncomplicated lust he felt for her had been a posturing liar. Pursuing it could have no other end. *If I'd known*, he thought, *if I'd only known, I would never, ever have let it begin.*

Now it was not Therese but another's wife who lay murdered; and this time, he, not Kristian, was the killer.

Karl hardly remembered gathering his scattered clothes, dressing, fleeing into the Crystal Ring; despair and a red haze of tears blinded him.

He spent a long time alone, but coming to terms with what he'd done was impossible. Eventually, in complete despair, he went to the house of Katerina and Andreas.

Katerina was there on her own; uncannily similar to Yvette in the candlelit parlour. Creamy skin, long brown hair. But she was no lonely innocent in danger from him.

"Karl, what a wonderful surprise," she said. "How lovely to see you."

Unable to utter the most basic pleasantry in response, Karl began to pour out the story. He held nothing back; she was the only one he could talk to, and he was beyond caring what she might think. He paced the room until the candles died, and starlight fell silver through the darkness.

When he finished, Katerina rose and lit fresh candles, shaking her head. She looked both astonished and sad. Karl's agitation had faded at last to leaden dullness.

"Even another vampire is disgusted," he said. "Or are you amazed that I'm such a poor disciple of Kristian's, not to delight in causing horror?"

"No, dear; it's only that I've never known you so upset, or

pacing about like a lunatic. This is the first time you've spoken to me so openly. I'm glad you felt you could tell me. Ah, *liebe Gott*; what you have been through…"

Katerina's strong face was receptive and warm, but he felt she was making light of the matter. "Me? What about *her*?"

"Well, at least she enjoyed herself. I trust you saw to that?" Katerina said acerbically.

"For God's sake."

"Of course you did; it's not in your nature to be selfish. The irony, Karl, is that you don't actually need to be an unselfish lover; with beauty like yours, one look would send any woman into raptures. There are worse ways to die."

He sat down, his white hands stiffening on the chair arms. "You're being ridiculous," he said in a low voice. "Can't you be serious about this?"

"But I am, dear." He felt her hand on his arm and jumped; she approached so softly. "There would have been a worse way. Alone in that ghastly house, of some horrible disease passed on by her husband. Of consumption. In childbirth. Of old age, waiting in vain for children who've long since abandoned her… oh, there are many worse ways than with an angel sucking gently at your throat."

Karl remembered Yvette's dead eyes, and shuddered. "There's no way you can soften this."

"No." Her whisper cut like diamond. "This is the hard truth; you cannot have contact with humans except to drink their blood. Don't you see? You told yourself, 'I won't harm her,' but your need for blood is cleverer; it took down your intellectual defences with sexual desire. That's why we still feel these desires, my dear; didn't you realise? Kristian never told you, but he wouldn't. He deplores sex, just as he despises anything passionate or physical."

"Why didn't you tell me?"

"You never asked," she said, "and you were so self-contained, it never occurred to me you didn't know. I'm only amazed it took you so long to find out. Some vampires take their prey like that every time. The pleasure is… beyond compare."

He suppressed a shudder. "Well, I never shall again."

"Won't you?"

Karl was silent for a long time. Katerina knelt by his chair and watched him, motionless as only a vampire can be. Then she asked, "But how did it feel, to make love again?"

"Wonderful. As sweet as taking blood."

"I know," she said. "Difficult to give up."

"Not at such a price."

"But it doesn't have to be like that. Do you think Andreas and I just read poetry to each other?"

"Hardly my business to think anything," said Karl, but emotions stirred amid his pain and guilt.

"Kristian would disapprove. His law is that we may love no one but him – and then only spiritually, of course. But I cannot give up my pleasures, whatever he says."

"But if we feel desire only with the object of taking human blood, why should one immortal feel passion for another?"

"You forget, we can drink each other's blood too. And you forget that we can love each other passionately. The secret is that with another vampire, it doesn't matter if you lose control –" she bit at the air, and smiled – "because for us, it's not fatal. Far from it, sharing blood is the most divine experience you can imagine. Think about it."

"What for?" He was listening from a grey level of consciousness.

Unexpectedly, Katerina sat on his knee, put her arms around his neck and kissed him, long and passionately. He responded, despite himself.

"Don't you feel anything for me?"

He shut his eyes, rested his head against hers. "Of course I do. But –"

"Because I love you, Karl."

"But what about Andreas?"

"I love him too," she said simply. "I have the most terrible weakness for beautiful men. So does he, I'm afraid. We both love you. Andreas won't be jealous; he's too in love with himself for that. We aren't human, so why should we be constrained by their morals?"

"What makes you think humans are any more moral than we are?" Karl said drily.

"That's better," Katerina laughed. "Oh, stay with us, Karl."

Too seductive, her arms, the promise of friendship, love, sex;

everything for which he was starving. He held her tight, kissing her cheeks and neck. "I want to," he sighed. "But what part does Kristian play in this arrangement?"

At that, she was sombre. "None. I think it's understood that we share the same feelings about him. As a very young vampire, I adored him; I was disillusioned soon enough. Not my vocation to be a little Sister of the Grim Reaper. Still, it's safer to play along than rebel openly, as you do. Don't we fake it beautifully? I don't know how you get away with being so disagreeable."

"If I come to you, he'll know that you've rejected him," said Karl.

He thought Katerina would hesitate, but she replied, "It's dangerous, but you, my darling, are worth the risk." Suddenly she bit his throat, taking a single swallow of blood. "Do the same, Karl. It's our bond."

"I cannot," said Karl, the image of Yvette haunting him. He stood up, planting her on her feet. "I cannot."

He left her then; but the next night he went back, took the sacramental mouthful from her throat, and from Andreas's; kissed their hands, embraced them. He was lost, but it was the most welcome surrender.

Some time passed before he and Katerina became lovers. He held back, feeling that in becoming a vampire he'd forfeited his right to companionship or pleasure. But it happened, inevitably; and while he took her blood in the last blissful convulsion, she also drank from his throat. Nothing was lost. "This is the Crystal Ring," she whispered. "This is what it really means." And she was right; once he fell, the rapture was impossible to give up.

Andreas didn't take as easily to the arrangement as Katerina had predicted, and was often moody. Perhaps he had reason; it wasn't sharing Katerina he minded, but knowing Karl favoured her. Karl had no homosexual inclinations, it was that simple. Or at least, he hadn't as a man; their angel-demon status blurred the boundaries. He felt affection for Andreas. To embrace and exchange blood was an affirmation of love as deep as any. If Andreas wanted more, he was disappointed. However, Karl soon learned that Andreas was happiest when he had a grievance, and an audience to play to.

"You are like Kristian," he would complain. "You're cold."

Katerina responded, "I assure you, Karl is anything but cold. You have as much of him as he wishes to give; and everything you want of me. Stop complaining!" And she would take Andreas away and console him. She was in her element with two lovers, yet Karl, strangely, never felt possessive. He loved them both; the arrangement felt warm and natural, free from mortal pain or jealousy... or true passion.

For a long time they were happy. There were dangerous periods spent hiding from Kristian or placating him, but they had many years before Kristian finally lost patience. He came while Karl wasn't there, and took Katti and Andrei away into the *Weisskalt*.

"If I didn't have you," Karl once told Katerina, "there would be no one."

And that remained true for forty ice-cold years. He kept himself apart from other vampires, allowed himself no desire for humans except for their blood.

Until he met Charlotte.

Sweet, shy, enigmatic; unpredictable, cynical and self-willed. Without trying, she slid through all his defences as no other mortal ever could. In different ways, they seduced each other. Insanity, after what happened with Yvette, knowingly to put Charlotte in the same danger... yet that was the point: the desire and the danger together were irresistible. Even though he loved her too much to hurt her. Even though he averted the danger, forcing himself in the last dizzying moments to turn his face away from her throat... hard to admit, but the risk, the knife-tip struggle, was in itself an unholy pleasure. He could not stop being a vampire, for love of a human.

When Charlotte joined him beyond the veil, the transformation only magnified everything she had been in life. Shining hair, shimmering eyes. Her waywardness. The unnerving sense that she was searching for something intangible and would pursue it to the edge of destruction... Still mysterious, irresistible to him.

Karl came out of the trance, one step behind the present. Katti gone... Charlotte beside him instead. The Crystal Ring's fantastical sky-scape tilted around him. The air was bitingly cold. Had he stayed too long and slipped into torpor?

As he began to glide down through the deep-blue air, his

mind snapped into full alertness. *God, Katerina alive again... but Charlotte?*

He heard voices murmuring on the wind. Shadows again, three presences rising up past him behind layers of cloud. Close yet distant. He felt ripples of cold magnetism tugging at him... heard monotonous chanting that filled him with irrational dread.

Karl dived through nothingness, rushing swiftly home. Weird terror filled him, expansive, fragile and crystalline as the Ring itself. This transcendent realm, perilous yet as constant as an ocean – how could it change?

With relief, he felt the house solidify around him. Grey dawn seeped into the room; the furniture, fireplace, paintings, familiar in cold shadow. He'd barely stepped out of the Ring when a figure rushed at him and threw her arms around his neck.

Katerina. He held her tight until she broke the embrace and looked at him, her eyes shining eerily bright in the gloom.

"Oh, Karl!" she said. "It's happened, I can enter the Crystal Ring at last! Isn't it wonderful?"

"I'm so glad," he replied quietly. "Did you spend long there?"

She put back her head, like a cat stretching. "Long enough to rest. Such a relief. I took a gentle walk through the past... remembered conversations with Andrei and you. It helped put my thoughts in order."

"Did you... hear anything?" he asked. "Voices?"

He expected her to dismiss the idea, but she frowned and said, "I think so... I felt odd vibrations, at least. A sort of pulling."

"Did you see shapes that might have been other vampires?"

She shook her head. He saw her through visions of the past that hadn't quite faded. Katti, friend and lover, always to be trusted.

"No, but what do you think they were?"

"I don't know, but I've seen them before, and so has Ilona." As he spoke, Karl loosed her and went towards the library. He paused in the archway, turned back. How empty the house felt. "Have you seen Charlotte?"

"No." Katerina's voice hardened. "Hasn't she come back? She's been away for days, Karl."

He was silent, gazing into the dead fire grate.

Katerina said, "Well? Darling, tell me what's in your mind."

Karl leaned on the mantelpiece, thinking, *I can't believe she still isn't home*. He kept the thought to himself and said, "If the manifestations in the Ring are anything to do with Kristian, we must discover whether he's alive or dead."

"How?"

"By going to the site where we killed him. I should warn you, it was a deadly subterranean place."

"Deadly to vampires?" she said, incredulous.

"Particularly to us. We'll have to take great care."

"Well, now I can travel again, we can go at once!"

Karl sighed. "Charlotte and I agreed that if ever we had cause to go back, we would do so together. I don't want to go without her."

Katerina sat down on the arm of a chair. "But Karl, we can't wait. We really should go immediately." He understood her excitement at her renewed powers. And he shared her urgency, but he wanted to give Charlotte a few more hours.

"Not until tonight. I want the cover of darkness."

"If you insist," she said impatiently. "But if Charlotte's not back by then, we must go without her. Promise me, Karl. Anyway, if it isn't safe, surely you wouldn't wish to put her at risk?"

He looked broodingly at Katti. She added, "She's had days to come back! Has it occurred to you that she is not interested?"

Karl dismissed the idea. Charlotte had a passionately enquiring mind. He couldn't bear to think that their last conversation meant she would never come back... indeed, he was sure she would – but when? And how would she feel, finding out he'd broken his word and revisited the manor house without her?

Disregarding Katerina's remarks, he said sharply, "We shall go tonight, whatever happens."

A smile touched her full rose-red mouth. "I shan't mind a little danger. Not if it is with you."

Holly ran along the main street, thinking only of Ben and the accusations he'd made. She saw a man walking towards her, but didn't see who he was until he stepped into her path. She ran straight into him.

Lancelyn. She looked up into his bearded, familiar face, saw his expression crease into lines of concern.

"Holly," he said. "My dear girl, are you all right?"

"Perfectly," she gasped, round-eyed.

She'd always been a little frightened of him, but had trusted him with her life. Now all her rocks had dissolved in waves of confusion. She loved him, but again she glimpsed three tall figures behind him, rippling on the air like watered ink.

She tried to fight free but he held her arms. "I want you to understand," he said, "whatever happens between Ben and me, I will never hurt you. I love you. You can always come to me."

"Yes," she said, distressed. "I must go."

"Don't let Ben use you against me," he said softly. "The oath you made to me still binds you. Remember."

He released her and she hurried past, away from him. Yet she could not resist looking back.

There was no one. Where Lancelyn had stood surrounded by his shadowy companions, the street was empty.

CHAPTER TEN

VIOLETTE

In the car that was taking them to Salzburg, Violette sat pressed in the corner, slender legs outstretched, her face an exhausted white oval amid her mourning black. Charlotte, sitting beside her, gave her only an occasional glance. The driver was closed away by glass. Rain sheeted onto the car roof; outside the streaked windows, the Austrian countryside rolled by in lush green beauty.

Violette had made her assistants travel separately, telling them that Charlotte was an old friend. Charlotte wasn't sure why she did this. Violette was determined to treat her as an unwanted spectre whose presence she must suffer. Charlotte wished it were not so... but Violette was exhausted. There would be time later to gain her trust.

Charlotte had hoped for friendship, a dark sisterhood. There was communication, at least, albeit reluctant and threaded with unease. Neither understood the eerie equation that was at work.

They sat in silence, Charlotte respecting her need for peace. After a while Violette said, "I don't know what will happen to Ballet Janacek now."

"What do you want to happen?" asked Charlotte.

"God knows. It was his company. It will have to be disbanded."

"Why? You could take over yourself, or start your own company with the same people."

Violette closed her eyes. "I'm too tired to think of this. I only want to dance, I don't want to be bothered with all this trouble."

"But you would be in charge." Charlotte sat forward, trying to inspire her. "You could choose the dancers and musicians, and perform whatever ballets you wished. You would have complete control."

Violette's eyes half-opened, slips of jet. "I don't know."

"You are as creative as Janacek was! He was holding you back. Without him you could... fly."

"What do you know about it, really?"

"It's true. Anyone could see it."

"It's so much to organise. I can't bear the business side, legal people, accountants... the thought depresses me."

"Then let me do that," Charlotte said softly.

"Why?" Violette raised her head, startled. "What can you do?"

"You'd be surprised. I'm good at organising, and I understand figures. Most of all, I am very good making people agree to things and sign the right documents..." She smiled, recalling the vampire glamour that she and Karl used on officials at times. Such subterfuge was necessary for creatures who never grew older, who used different names to protect their identities and travelled without passports. A compliant solicitor was essential; shaping such people was second nature to Karl, and he had tutored Charlotte well.

"Janacek's business manager can do all that." Violette gazed listlessly out of the window.

"Not as well or as fast I can. How do you know he's on your side?"

A flash of anger. "How do I know *you* are? Are you trying to save the ballet for me, or steal it? I can't decide whether you're my fairy godmother or a confidence trickster."

"Neither, I swear. I want to help you. Please trust me, Violette. We'll keep the company together and all you'll have to think about is dancing. Isn't that what you want?"

"All I want," said Violette, "is to sleep." She closed her eyes and was silent for the rest of the journey; but Charlotte knew she was not asleep.

They came down into Salzburg between the mountains and arrived at an elegant almond-green house, four storeys high with tall windows. The home of Ballet Janacek. The river Salzach flowed in front, swift and silver-green. On the far bank stood the old town, where the many church domes were dominated by the great forested ridge of Mönchsberg and the Hohensalzburg fortress. *Loveliest of towns*, Charlotte thought.

"Come in," said Violette as the chaffeur helped them from the car. "Let me show you round. I'd let you stay in Janacek's rooms, but I can't, until his family have taken his effects away."

"There's no need. I can find a hotel."

"Nonsense," Violette said thinly. Her words were polite but her tone was brittle. "You must stay here. We'll find a room for you upstairs, I'm sure."

The house was quiet; many dancers who'd been to the funeral had not yet returned. An elderly woman, a young man and two girls came out to welcome Violette. She greeted them with kisses. They obviously adored her. A tall, thin Austrian maid took their coats; Violette said, "Thank you, Geli. Go and make us some tea; we'll be up in a few minutes."

Her warm, confident manner was in sharp contrast to her wariness with Charlotte.

As they climbed the stairs, Violette paused to explain the function of each floor. There were rehearsal rooms for the musicians, offices, storerooms for costumes, and on the third floor a huge mirrored studio for the dancers.

Violette went in and leaned against the barre, looking up. "There are two apartments on the next floor; one is mine, one was Roman's. Then there are some attic rooms where the *corps de ballet* live. I think there's one vacant, though they are a little basic." Her voice was frosty. "I hope you don't mind."

"I told you, you don't have to do anything for me."

Violette turned to her, her eyes elongated; black and deepest blue, narrow with unease yet hauntingly beautiful against her milky skin. "Forget what I said in the graveyard – about punishment. I was upset, I wasn't myself."

"It's forgotten."

"Perhaps I'm wrong about you, Charlotte," she said. "If you can do what you said – do it. I want this ballet to go on – in Janacek's name, but under my direction."

Charlotte felt a rush of excitement. Violette was softening by degrees. "Whatever you want."

They went to Violette's apartment, and took tea – or rather, the dancer did, while Charlotte pretended. She didn't let herself dwell on what she really wanted. That would be an easy appetite to feed, after dark – *and*, she thought, *I don't want Violette's blood. I don't.*

I can't stay, Charlotte thought. *I must go back to Karl.*

She was alone in a spartan bedroom, leaning on the windowsill and gazing at the great forested shoulder of rock across the river, the fortress walls rising into the sky; and below, the sunny Rennaissance elegance of roofs and spires.

How weird this is. I never dreamed I'd come here. I never even meant to speak to her.

I said that meeting Violette would destroy her magic, but it hasn't. She is so strange. I can't leave her alone…

I should go back to Karl now. But what is there to go home for? His disappointment in me, and Katerina's contempt. If I leave him to her, will he miss me at all? A flash of memory, a deep twisting pain. *How can we ever restore the perfection we've lost? We can't… is that why I'm clinging to Violette?*

Surface matters had proceeded smoothly. Charlotte had met patrons, administrators and solicitors; legal and financial difficulties were raised, only to dissolve under the spell of her shining, persuasive presence. She'd taken a couple of the men aside, flattered and entranced and fed on them… so easy. And now the Ballet Janacek belonged to Violette.

The ballerina expressed not a word of gratitude.

Charlotte hadn't expected or even wanted thanks; as the days passed, it became clear that nothing was going to change. Violette did not want Charlotte there; she merely tolerated her, a strange, unwelcome benefactor.

As the dancers returned, Violette threw herself into work as if nothing else existed.

Karl was constantly in Charlotte's mind, a deep-red ache. They'd never before been apart for so long, and she grew restless to see him. Yet she hesitated. She couldn't forget the pain of their parting conversation. *If only he'd forsake Katerina,* she thought, *and if only I hadn't killed Janacek...* To go back was to risk rejection. But the longer she stayed away, the harder it was to return.

Besides, Violette had let her into the enchanted circle of her company, and held her there with an unseen force like gravity.

Charlotte watched her preparing for *Swan Lake*, mesmerised by her energy, the miracle of beauty unfolding. In rehearsal she was strict, an obsessive perfectionist, often short-tempered. Never unfair. Her dancers, male and female alike, feared, respected and worshipped her.

But she has no friends among them, Charlotte thought. *Even the ballet patrons who socialise with her are no more than acquaintances. She will let no one close – least of all me. Why?*

Violette had told the company that Charlotte was her "business assistant", which was loosely true. No one questioned this. They were simply glad that the ballet had survived.

In the evenings, when Violette finally rested, she would collapse on a chaise longue and eat a huge meal while Geli iced her knees and massaged her shoulders. She seemed to be in constant pain.

"This is what ballet is," she said dismissively, when Charlotte expressed concern. "It's not glamorous, it's hard work. If I don't complain, nor must anyone else. I always tell my dancers, if you can't endure the pain, find another career."

Once or twice Charlotte persuaded Violette to walk along the river with her. They talked, but Violette was not the kind to confide, and Charlotte, too, had secrets. So their conversations were only about ballet business, and they trod warily around each other, not really knowing why they were together at all. Still Charlotte's obsession was increasing.

She would watch the dancer's slender neck and the movement of her throat as they talked, the lovely soft inkiness of her hair and the darkness of her brows against the pearly cloud of her face... and as soon as darkness fell, Charlotte would rush through the Crystal Ring and feed on a victim as if possessed. But never did she lay a finger on Violette.

She'd been there almost two weeks – it seemed longer, so much had happened – when restlessness compelled her, one night, to enter the rehearsal studio. She took in the empty, mirrored sweep of the room, moonlight fanning through the uncurtained windows, and imagined Violette there, pirouetting fluidly across the studio as she practised Odile's steps.

How does she move like that? Charlotte wondered.

She took off her shoes and began to move experimentally. Raising her arms she spun in a *foutté*, then lifted one leg in a high *écarté*. Her soft full skirt swirled round her legs. It felt pleasant, exhilarating. She ran on the tips of her toes and leapt in a *grande jeté* – and then something made her stop dead. Violette was in the doorway, dressed in a grey satin robe, glaring at her.

"You didn't tell me you could dance." Her tone was one of grave accusation.

"I can't," said Charlotte. "It was the first time I've tried."

This was the wrong thing to say. Violette came towards her, eyes burning. Charlotte had never seen her so angry. "You liar! You were dancing *en pointe* in stockinged feet; that's almost impossible, not to mention stupid. You'll injure yourself. But no one can dance like that 'the first time'. You're mocking me. Why?"

"I'm not, I swear," Charlotte said quietly. "I copied what I've seen you doing, that's all."

"Excuse me, but you cannot 'copy' the years of work it takes to become a prima ballerina." Violette was furious, but Charlotte saw fear behind her eyes. She was telling Violette the truth; but how could she explain that immortal bodies were not like those of humans? They were strong and fluid, not bound by tight muscles, stiff joints or lack of coordination. Imitating humans was effortless. It was what vampires did to live.

"I'm flexible, and a good mimic... If I looked more than a clumsy beginner, that was only due to poor light, and luck."

"No." Violette turned away and held onto the barre. Charlotte saw her reflection, the stiff terror of her expression. "I would ask you to stop mocking me, but that's why you're here, isn't it?"

"I don't know what you mean."

"You aren't human, are you? I tried to convince myself otherwise, that the things I said over Janacek's grave were foolish fancies – and I almost succeeded, until I saw you dancing. I thought I could cope with you, but –"

"Don't feel you must 'cope' with me," Charlotte said softly. "I hoped you would grow fond of me."

She touched Violette's shoulder. The ballerina shrugged her off with revulsion. "I never knew," she said, her face turning white, "that Satan craved affection, as well as one's soul. How touching."

"I'm not from Satan," said Charlotte, thinking, *Yet you are so nearly right!* "What on earth do you think I am?"

"A creature sent to tempt me. I'm going to tell you something now that I've never told anyone. You may think I'm mad, but it hardly matters. Other people think they have guardian angels; I have demons. They lean over me as I'm falling asleep, three tall shadows. They don't speak but they imply... that I will face temptation, and my fall will affirm their belief that I am wicked to the core."

Charlotte was stunned, wondering if Violette was sane. "What are these demons?"

"My guilt, I imagine. I don't actually think they're real, obviously. Temptation was bound to come and I'm fated to succumb, and then I'll be damned, like my –" She stopped. After a second she breathed again, and went on, "I'm frightened to death of you, Charlotte. Your presence here is killing me. It's temptation and punishment together. I thought I could prove something by resisting you, but I can't."

"Oh, God," Charlotte breathed. "I don't know what to say. The last thing I wanted was to cause you pain. I'll go." She began to walk away. Violette, she sensed, did not turn round but watched her in the mirror as she went. "I'll go."

Once Charlotte decided to return to Karl, she realised in horror how long she'd been away.

Did he wonder where I was? she thought as she travelled through the Crystal Ring. *He must have guessed I was with Violette. If he's given up on me... I couldn't blame him, but it would kill me.*

How have I let this happen?

She felt abandoned and terrifyingly lonely. The rolling mountains of the Crystal Ring filled her with fear.

She arrived to find the chalet in darkness. No sense of Karl's presence; without him, the place was a shell. Weighed down by disappointment, Charlotte moved listlessly around the rooms, lighting lamps.

My fault, I should have come back sooner. Her throat was burning. *Karl, where have you gone? I should have stayed. Why did you give so much to Katerina; why did I let you both get away with it?*

Violette, from a distance, seemed a heartless Snow Queen who had enticed Charlotte away from her true place.

In the glow of a Tiffany lamp, filtering through stained-glass lilies and dragonflies, she saw a note lying on a sideboard. She read in Karl's elegant, slanting handwriting,

> *My dearest Charlotte,*
>
> *Katti can travel again, so we have gone to search for Andreas and the truth about Kristian, beginning in the place where we last saw him. We could wait for you no longer. How long it will take I have no idea, a few days perhaps. If you must depart again before we return, leave me a letter. Tell me where I can find you.*
>
> *K.*

The place where we last saw Kristian...

That meant they'd gone to Parkland Hall. Charlotte held the note against her chest, stunned. *My fault for not being here... but to think that Karl would go without me, that he's gone with Katerina instead!*

At least he'd let her know. She thought of following, but decided better of it. If she missed them, she didn't want to be there alone. If she found them, though, she had no wish to encounter Katerina in the garden that had been sacred to her and Karl. How foolish this jealousy was, yet how sharp, a knife in the heart.

She dropped the note where she'd found it, left no message in return. She couldn't bear to wait for them. *We agreed to go back there one day... But I should have been with you, Karl, not that woman.*

Turning away, Charlotte threw herself into the Crystal Ring. She was going back to Salzburg, to Violette.

* * *

What is the use of anything, Holly thought, *if Ben doesn't trust me?*

She hurried down Market Street, round a corner into the cobbled alley where the bookshop was. She'd meant to go to Maud's lodgings, but the encounter with Lancelyn had shaken her badly. She needed to gather her thoughts, and the shop was her only refuge.

Holly reached the doorway and fumbled for her key. The bow window was unlit, but the small panes glinted; she was glad of moonlight as night fell. As she put the key in the lock, she froze.

There was someone inside.

Pressing her face to the glass door, Holly saw Lancelyn and Maud. He was talking, bending towards Maud, touching her hand; Maud's eyes were huge with awe, her mouth open. Holly looked on in wild dismay. She saw them sharp and clear as if lit by a cocoon of light even though the shop was dark...

She shut her eyes tight, cursing. When she looked again, they'd gone.

She opened the door and entered. No one here. The interior was indistinct to her imperfect eyes. Only a vision... but of a genuine encounter? Her psychic intuition rarely misled her. She felt drained by the conflicts of the past few days. Locking herself in, she sank onto a stool behind the counter, and dropped her head on her arms.

Is Lancelyn trying to slither inside my mind, as he did with Deirdre? He promised not to hurt me, but how can I believe him?

And again, *What's the use if Ben doesn't trust me? If Lancelyn's somehow poisoned him against me... but why? What are they doing, fighting each other, tearing me apart like a rag between two dogs?*

Holly thought about Andreas. Despite what he was, there was such sadness about him, an endearing melancholy. He'd once spoken of his lost friends Karl and Katerina so longingly that she'd touched his hand – and in that touch, received an echo of memory from him. Two figures from the last century, drawn in black and white and faded reds, with lovely, pitiless faces. The image still hung in her amazed mind.

Are they still alive? Might Andreas's friends help him? she wondered. *Would they help Ben – or only bring more danger?*

Holly went into a narrow recess between ceiling-high bookshelves. This would be her temple. Raising her arms, she began to turn in circles, chanting.

She felt ridiculous, without incense and paraphernalia, without Benedict or Lancelyn to lend the weight of their conviction. She was a mere handmaiden to the Order, with no authority to conduct a ritual of her own.

Yet, with a kind of shuddering desperation, she went on. She uttered the secret titles of Meter Theon, summoned Andreas's friends by name, wove mental barriers to protect herself from evil... but she sensed no energy gathering. Hopeless. Her heart wasn't in it.

She was too afraid.

At last she sank down onto the worn carpet, drained. Nothing happened. The shadows remained motionless. *Must go*, she thought. *Must find Maud, then go to Ben...*

Deep torpor flowed over her, and she slept.

Karl looked up at the Georgian mansion standing square against the sky. Foliage flowed from its flanks, curtaining the steep gardens; tree bowers, ornamental lawns neatly enclosed by shrubs, an occasional monkey puzzle tree or sequoia standing in exotic silhouette. The moon swathed the landscape with silver gauze, catching jewel-points of colour that only vampires could perceive. How different England felt from any other country. Gentle, ancient, redolent of lost lives...

Karl had always felt fated to come here again... but not so soon, and not without Charlotte. He wasn't unduly worried about her; she was a vampire, not a vulnerable mortal. He knew she was staying away of her own will, and he understood her reasons. All the same, he ached with regret.

"Memories?" said Katerina.

Karl half-smiled. "Can you tell?"

"I always could, my dear. I don't know why people find you mysterious. Will you tell me, or shall I just be quiet?"

"I am so glad you're here," said Karl. "I still can't believe it, after all this time." He fell silent, listening to the air breathing softly through the leaves. There were no humans in the garden; he sensed a few motes of heat in the house, but didn't probe too closely. He had no desire to encounter any of Charlotte's family.

He and Katti were dressed in greatcoats, gloves and heavy shoes; tonight's work would be unpleasant.

Eventually Katerina said, "Well, won't you tell me about this place? Describe your life, while I lay frozen asleep..."

"I met Charlotte," Karl said quietly, "because I was looking for a way to kill Kristian. I thought a scientist might help me find answers; why vampires exist, what our fate might be when the universe itself isn't eternal... and how we might be destroyed."

Katerina said sharply, "And did you find your answers?"

"There are none. Only theories. Humans can't fully explain the natural world; how can we expect them to understand the supernatural? But Charlotte was the scientist's daughter. Dr Neville; a kind and trusting man whom I deceived utterly."

"Not deliberately, Karl? It's not in your nature."

"That hardly salves my conscience. We cause harm, whether we mean to or not. Simply seeking his help, pretending to be human, was a deception."

"And then you stole his daughter."

"Among other crimes."

"Poor Dr Neville," breathed Katerina. "But tell me about Charlotte. Why her? You swore you'd never make another vampire, after Ilona."

Karl smiled without humour. "Surely I don't need to explain what I see in Charlotte? Anyway, this is her aunt's house. This is where..."

"Enough," said Katerina. "I'll use my imagination."

"The irony is that through Charlotte, I *did* find a way to destroy Kristian. There's a medieval manor not far from here, with an underground tunnel leading into these gardens. Charlotte and I had to use it as an escape route... and it almost killed me."

Katerina blinked in disbelief. He'd told her very little, preferring to show her. "How?"

"Come with me." Karl tucked her hand through his arm.

The ice house was a small stone and brick chamber sunk into the side of a slope, hidden in a thick belt of trees where the gardeners seldom worked. Parts of the garden were left deliberately wild, enhancing its charm. To Karl's relief, the chamber had not been pulled down or bricked up; it looked exactly the same as when he'd escaped with Charlotte.

"This is where the tunnel emerges," he said. "The ice house extends under the hill…" He ducked under the low lintel, Katerina following. "The opening is at the very back."

"Where? All I see is mouldering stonework…"

"In the floor, where it joins the wall. It's clogged with leaves."

Karl bent down and scooped away damp decaying layers. Insects scurried over his gloved hands. He relied on vampire sight in the darkness, not risking torchlight until they were underground. Soon he found soil under his hands, and saw the small fissure yawning downwards, uninviting. No surprise that no one had ever explored it – except Charlotte.

Discarding the soil-crusted gloves, he paused, staring into blackness so absolute that even vampire sight could not penetrate. He waited for the keening of ghost voices… the touch of searing coldness.

"If you sense anything strange, tell me," he said

"What?" Katerina was kneeling close beside him, her face moon-pale, her eyes intent. "Don't tell me you believe in ghosts now?"

"Listen; if you feel cold and weak or hear strange sounds, turn round and come straight out. I mean it, Katti. There's a presence here that almost killed me. And it destroyed Kristian."

Her eyes showed white with shock, but she nodded.

Karl eased himself feet-first into the fissure, found the sloping floor, and edged down until it levelled out and he could stand. Then he helped Katerina down after him. She looked around her as he flicked on his torch. Rotting bricks, soil, tree-roots; air saturated with a musty stench.

She said, "There is something… an evil feeling. What's causing it? How did Kristian die?"

Karl was reluctant to answer. He wished they were not here at all, but suppressed his revulsion. "A vampire made this place his lair, centuries ago. He killed all his victims and hoarded their corpses here. Thousands."

She gave a soft *Ohhh*, then whispered, "He sounds as obsessive as Kristian, in a different way. But how can this affect us?"

"I don't know think it's correct to speak of ghosts. The stealing of victims' energy, over years and years, left an incredibly voracious vacuum. So when a vampire walks into it, the victims take revenge. Their wraiths suck back the stolen life. This place becomes as cold as the *Weisskalt* and far more terrible."

The tunnel extended deep under the hill, narrow and claustrophobic. Karl recalled ghastly hallucinations, the dead souls dragging him towards their own cavernous realm of death...

"How did you survive?" said Katti.

"Charlotte saved me. She gave me her blood."

"Of course. And then you brought Kristian here deliberately?"

"Yes," Karl said without emotion. "He was so easy to deceive, suspected nothing until it was too late. Once he became too weak to move, I drained his blood to save myself. And when he was paralysed, we cut him to pieces to make sure."

"God," she whispered. "I wouldn't have believed you, if I hadn't come here myself. This is a terrible place..."

The tunnel was chilly, dank, unpleasant, but the perilous atmosphere felt muted.

"Last time it was far worse. I wonder if the wraiths sated themselves on Kristian; took out their rage on a single vampire?"

A few hundred yards into the tunnel, they rounded a bend to a wider section where the earth floor was churned up.

"This was where we buried him," said Karl.

"Where?" Katti seemed calm, but a tremor in her voice betrayed her.

"Everywhere," said Karl. "I told you, we dismembered him."

As he spoke, he stared at a pile of crumpled blackness lying against the wall, half-buried. It reflected no light from the torch. He bent down to touch it.

Dark coarse material, saturated with damp and mould. Kristian's coat.

"Dear God," he whispered.

"You can't want to do this," Katerina said faintly.

Karl ignored her. He propped the torch in the soil and began to dig with his bare hands.

Worms, grit, sparkling bits of mica stuck to his flesh; his skin gleamed through the filth like alabaster. He burrowed into the ground, with an image of a vampire digging itself out of its grave; an old superstition that still retained horrible resonance. Katerina watched, wide-eyed, as if she wanted to help but could not move.

He found bones. Soil-caked, no flesh left on them. A skeletal hand with a plain gold ring that fell off as he lifted it; unmistakably Kristian's. Horror filled him. Kristian's clothes, wet and rotting... his naked bones... *But his skull, where is his skull?*

"Karl, stop!" Katerina's voice sliced through the freezing veil of mist before his eyes. "Please stop."

Karl sat back on his heels, hands black with earth. He was gasping for breath like a human; held himself still until the feeling subsided.

"I can't find his head."

"It must be here. Oh, leave it, come away."

"But Katti, don't you understand? If his skull isn't here – if some vampire came and took his head – they might have resurrected him!"

"No. No, Karl." She knelt beside him. "You cut the skull into pieces, didn't you? How would his acolytes know he was here, and how could they survive this poisonous place to find his remains?"

He let out a deep sigh. A nightmare. But he thought, *I will not give in. I shall be like ice, detached, as I have always been...*

Karl stood, lifting Katerina with him.

"Please, let's leave," she said.

"Not yet."

She frowned at him, disturbed.

He said, "Every trace of doubt or dread we feel is a victory for him, whether he is alive or not. We cannot give him that power. There's something else I want to find before we go."

He led her onwards, surrounded by hideously vivid memories. Past a chamber stacked floor to ceiling with human bones, brown with age... Katerina wanted to look, but Karl pulled her away. He was waiting for the deathly drop of temperature and the heart-stopping wails of the dead to begin...

Further on, another chamber. Torchlight revealed the bare walls and candle-blackened ceiling of a long-deserted monk's cell. Karl stared at an ancient table that squatted in the centre.

"It's gone."

"What's wrong?" said Katerina. "What are you looking for?"

"Someone has been here," Karl said at last. "There was a black book lying on that table. Charlotte and I had no time to look at it. That's why we planned to come back, to see what the vampire who once lived here had written. Who could have taken it? To my knowledge, only Kristian, Charlotte and I ever saw the Book."

Katerina walked into the cell and stared at the greyish oblong where the book had lain. "Humans," she said. "They always leave a trace of warmth behind."

Karl played the torch over the floor, then flicked it off. Easier to see without the dancing shadows. Footprints in the tunnel floor led in the direction of the manor. He, too, caught the scent of humans... too faint to be recent. "These tracks are months old. So they may have taken the Book at any time within the past year."

Katerina touched the cracked surface of the table. As she did so, the whole chamber seemed to vibrate with a scream barely inside the threshold of vampire hearing. She shivered.

"Come away," said Karl. "Don't touch anything. The presences have lost their potency, but they're still here."

The quickest way out was through the manor house. As they made their way towards the steps that led up to the cellar, she said, "Can't we enter the Crystal Ring?"

"I wouldn't try it here," said Karl. "This place seems to exist in both realms. Kristian tried to escape into the Ring, but when I followed, something held us like tar, and the wraiths were everywhere."

"Don't," she said, shuddering. "I believe you. This place is abhorrent."

They ascended steep narrow steps into the cellar; more memories. Karl noted that the chest he'd left concealing the trapdoor had been moved, the cellar door left ajar... and as they climbed more stairs into the kitchen, he saw that a leaded window had been forced.

"The house is derelict," he said. "Anyone might have broken in."

"Let's leave," said Katerina.

"Yes..." Karl hesitated, looking around the shadowy medieval kitchen... he recalled the ringing echo of Anne's and David's laughter; remembered Charlotte walking fearlessly into the cellar's depths as if she shared affinity with its secrets...

"You're finding it hard to be here, aren't you?" said Katerina. "At least... you wish she was here with you, instead of me."

Karl didn't reply. He took her hand, then turned and wrapped one arm around her, feeling her breath against his neck, her hair – not soft like Charlotte's, but strong and smooth – between his fingers. "Katti."

"If only she understood how much you love her," Katerina said against his neck.

"She does."

"Don't be so sure. Our minds tell us we can love more than one person, but our hearts won't believe it; and there's always one who is more precious than any other. You want to be with Charlotte, and I..." He felt her throat move, suppressing tears. "I want to find Andreas."

"We will," said Karl, drawing her into the Crystal Ring.

As the world dissolved to dark silver around them, she said, "Where now?"

"Schloss Holdenstein."

"Oh, not that place! Must we?"

"It's almost our last resort. I vowed I'd never set foot there again, but if there *are* any answers, we may find them at the castle. And I'll call the others to meet us there; Ilona, Pierre, Stefan and Niklas."

"Karl..."

"If Kristian survived, where would he go, except back to his old lair?"

That evening, when Charlotte returned to Violette, she went straight into the ballerina's rooms without knocking. Since becoming a vampire, human conventions often went out of her mind. She sensed two humans inside; the dancer and her maid, Geli.

Violette, in a long dressing gown of mauve silk, was lying on a huge sofa of almost the same shade. The maid sat on a stool beside her, pressing packs of ice onto the dancer's knees.

She looked exhausted. She pressed one hand to her colourless forehead as if to smooth the lines of tension. A bottle of

much as men. Famous actresses, some of them; you will know them from the theatre and the movies. They wear men's suits and look divine and make no attempt to keep their lifestyles secret. They send me violets – for my name, they say, even though I know perfectly well what violets signify. I never respond. I can't work out why you are different."

"I approached you as a friend, not a lover."

"I have no friends," Violette said. "Professional associates, with whom I perform a social charade." She slurred the words, laughed at herself. "But no friends."

"Why not?" Charlotte thought of Anne, and the particular closeness and comfort no male lover could give. She, too, was starved of female companionship. "You need a friend who will support you, not put you under pressure, as Janacek did."

"I can't. I trust no one." Violette leaned her head back; languid, but not as drunk as she wanted to be, Charlotte suspected. "I don't like men," she said with sudden passion. "Do you?"

"Some. I loved my father and brother... even Henry, my ex-husband, in a way, but they all..."

"Betrayed you?"

"No," said Charlotte. "I betrayed them, and they never understood why. They couldn't forgive me. We all hurt each other very badly."

Violette's eyes widened. "You are human, then. You have a family."

"Not any more."

"Nor me." Before Charlotte could ask her to explain, Violette said, "How did you betray them?"

"I ran away with a man they disapproved of."

The dancer laughed. "How banal! I'm disappointed. I thought you were a spirit of some kind, a sylph. Why aren't you with that man now?"

"I am, but... I'd rather not talk about it."

"Here we are, then, both preferring to keep our secrets." Her tone was nightshade-bitter. "What is there to do, if we can't talk? You're here only because you've fallen out with your lover, and I –"

"What, Violette? Tell me."

"What's the point? Confide in someone and you become vulnerable. They use your pain as a weapon against you. I have no friends because I have only one passion: to dance."

"No, you're only telling half the truth. You dance to blank out your pain, don't you? It stops you thinking of anything else."

Violette's silence was icy. Charlotte had touched a nerve of truth. She went on, "But all the passion in your dancing comes from that pain, doesn't it? Why be ashamed, when it makes you great?"

The dancer drew a breath, exhaled. Then she undid the sash of her gown. "Would you massage my back? It aches abominably."

"If you like."

Violette placed her glass inaccurately on the table, slid her arms free of the sleeves and turned onto her stomach. Her back was bare under the robe. It was the first time she had willingly let Charlotte touch her.

Charlotte sat beside her hip and began to knead the creamy-pink flesh.

"Your hands are cold," said Violette. She turned her head to the side, one eye glittering up at her. "Do you know why I hate you, Charlotte? Because I desire you. You see straight through me and... I might almost start to love you."

Electric stillness; such a shock to hear her admission.

Violette went on, "Now I'm going to say foolish things and blame it on the champagne. I prefer women to men, only it's not the sort of thing one is meant to admit in polite company. You don't look shocked."

"I had guessed."

"Would you be surprised if I told you I've never done anything about it?"

"Yes, a little."

"I can't stand men touching me." Violette shuddered under her hands.

"What about your male partners?"

"That's separate, it's work. If ever one touched me in anything but a professional manner he'd be dismissed on the spot; we all know the rules. But I've never had a lover. That's why Janacek controlled me, because it was so easy for him to make me suffer. Always hints, threats... he truly despised me for refusing to sleep with him. But with women... well, with your own sex it's wrong, isn't it? It's a sin."

"Is it?" said Charlotte. She was so amazed at Violette's confession, she hardly knew how to react.

"The ballet is my lover. I don't want strangers intruding, tantalising me with the sins I must avoid. You call yourself a friend, yet you torment me as Janacek did, in a different way. Why? What is it about me?"

"You made me weep when you danced *Giselle*," Charlotte said helplessly.

"Don't stop massaging. Your hands are warm now. Higher."

"It's not your fault, that people love you. You see it as a curse, but it's a gift."

"And vice versa," said Violette. "You frighten me. I don't want you here, but it's beyond my power to send you away. Have you any idea what you're doing to me?"

She sounded near despair. Charlotte had never seen her so defenceless.

"I'm sorry. I didn't mean to..." She slid her hands to Violette's shoulders and pushed the heavy soft raven hair aside. "If you really want me to leave, I will. I almost did, yesterday."

"No, Charlotte. I don't want you to go. But if I let people near me, they take parts of me away!" She twisted onto her back. "Don't you see how helpless that makes me feel? I hate you and I want you... and I don't understand why."

Charlotte was unfurling her vampire bewitchment on Violette without trying, unable to keep it from shining palely in her eyes, in her touch and voice. "I'm afraid of what I feel for you, because I don't understand it either," she whispered. "And you only pretend to be cold because you are frightened too. But there's no need."

With one forefinger, softly bent, she traced the curve of Violette's small breasts. She didn't mean to. It was like being in a trance.

With a sound that was half-sigh, half-gasp, Violette put her arms around Charlotte's neck. Her grip was tight, strong, filled more with tension than affection. Her soft perfume, mingled with her natural fresh scent, filled Charlotte's head. The way her hair pooled in black whorls on her collarbones was breathtakingly seductive. Charlotte hugged her with pure tenderness.

As if she had not learned how deceptive the feeling was.

She found herself kissing Violette's neck. Silken lips on silk.

Violette pulled Charlotte down until she lay on top of the dancer with one knee between her thighs. And she went on kissing the smooth throat, only kissing, touching with her tongue... and, without conscious will, she felt her fangs slide down and into the flesh; without effort, like biting into a peach.

Violette made no sound; only the tautening of her body betrayed any feeling. Charlotte drew her blood slowly, passionately... a succulent juice laced with fire.

This divine pleasure... she remembered how it bonded her to Karl, how deep it could reach when it happened not from appetite or violence, but in pure love...

Violette's ribs began to heave. She held her breath between gasps, moving, convulsing. Charlotte held her tighter, trying to soothe her as she drank, and suddenly it seemed that the dancer was all around her and inside her; midnight hair writhing, white limbs and red blood snaking out to enmesh her... eyes flying wide open, her pupils expanding sightlessly. She clutched at Charlotte, rocked against her, and fell back, drained, expelling all her breath in one long sigh.

It was easy then for Charlotte to stop and let her sharp teeth slip back into their sockets. She had not taken much and yet she felt sated, glowing from head to foot, deliciously happy. With butterfly touches of her tongue she licked the fang-wounds clean and watched them fading to silver-mauve crescents. Violette lay languid in her arms. And to realise that the dancer had experienced rapture, not pain – that Charlotte had given her pleasure equal to her own – filled her with relief and inexpressible joy.

"Dearest," Charlotte whispered, bending to kiss the hollow of her throat. Violette jumped and began to shudder. After a moment Charlotte realised that she was sobbing.

She propped herself on one elbow and looked down at the dancer's closed eyelids and the trails of tears on her cheeks. "Why are you crying? Don't. There's no need to be afraid."

Violette's eyes half-opened and slid to stare at the vampire under a shimmer of tears. There was no surrender, no warmth in them. To Charlotte's shock, her eyes spat fury and revulsion.

"What have you done to me?" Violette hissed.

Her voice and her eyes slammed into Charlotte, breaking

the spell into shards. She drew back, speechless, as Violette struggled from under her, exclaiming, "What are you? Get out of here, get out!"

Violette was on her feet and staggering to the door, dizzy with alcohol and blood-loss. She snatched her robe, holding it close around herself with one arm. Reaching the door, she faced Charlotte, her free hand on the brass handle.

"Wait," said Charlotte. This wasn't what she'd envisioned at all. "Violette, please. Let me explain. Come back and sit down..."

"I do not want to hear an explanation." The dancer's voice was low, stiff with cold spines of rage. "I never want to see you again."

"You don't mean it."

"I do!" Her hand flew to the fading marks on her throat. "What in hell are you? You used me! God, I was right, why didn't I listen to myself?"

"No!" Charlotte, now on her feet, went towards her. To her dismay Violette drew back, flattening herself against the door.

"You betrayed me! I thought – I thought a woman could be a friend as no man could, that she might heal when men only try to possess. That's what you told me yourself. Liar! You're just as bad as them. I hope my blood poisons you, I hope you go to hell!"

Nothing Charlotte said could placate her. No words, no hypnotic looks would win her over. Violette's disgust and sense of betrayal went right through to her soul.

Misery flattened Charlotte like a hammer. In a last desperate gesture she held out her hand, but Violette's reaction was to wrench open the door, holding it against herself like a shield.

"Don't touch me!" she snapped. "Get out, *get out*!"

Charlotte wanted to say sorry, but could not. She picked up her coat and hat and walked through the doorway, her face blank.

"If it's what you want," she said quietly, "I won't trouble you again."

Afterwards, walking for hours with little awareness of the city around her, Charlotte came to understand that the dancer was right. She *had* betrayed her. The treacherous thirst that masqueraded as love had betrayed them both.

That's all it was, Charlotte thought. *I fell in love with her because I wanted her blood.*

Violette never wanted to know me. I forced my company on her, I killed to get closer to her, I cajoled, I played on her vulnerability and, God help me, I even got her drunk like some second-rate libertine. She never wanted me; not as a simple human friend, not even with all the supernatural allure. How could she be immune? She asked what I was, but God, what is she?

All she wanted was for me to leave her alone but I couldn't. I seduced her.

I violated her.

That horrific thought hung in Charlotte's mind, painfully bright. She couldn't see beyond it. It was like the sword of God hanging over her, the terrible vengeful God she thought had died with Kristian. And she wished the blade would fall. Cleanse the Earth of the obscenity of a vampire's presence.

CHAPTER ELEVEN

THE TWISTED BLACKTHORN

Benedict stood on the stairs, frozen there by the piercing sounds from above; the echo of wood splintering, dry flesh slithering across broken glass on floorboards, the open-mouthed, mindless groans of famished vampires.

His head ached with terror. He wanted to flee, slam the door, and run. *Save my skin or I'm going to die...*

Andreas was down in the hallway, flattened against the front door, still here only because Ben forbade him to go. He said in a hollow voice, "I wouldn't desert you, Ben. But come away with me, please."

Ben didn't move. He heard the dull thuds of something sliding down the attic stairs.

Not breathing, he climbed slowly to meet it.

"Don't go up!" Andreas called. "Leave them, let's get out!"

Andreas's panic was contagious. A head and torso appeared at the top of the stairs; a skeleton clad in rags and ash. It reached down to him with a taut, bony arm.

Andreas ran up the stairs and grabbed Ben's elbow. "What the hell are you doing? They'll kill you!"

"You tried, but I stopped you," Ben said grimly.

"I was alone and weak, but it was still a near-death struggle between us." Andreas held him back. "How can you fight so many? They'll be stronger, more desperate –"

Ben shook Andreas off. His throat stung with fear and rage.

"Don't you see, I must prove I control them by will alone, without help from the Book or Lancelyn. If I can't, I may as well die anyway!"

Andreas stepped back, amazement in his pale marble face. "You're crazy. Why am I trying to protect you?"

"If you are so keen to leave and you want to help – go to Lancelyn's and get the Book. Don't hurt him, just bring it back as fast as you can. Go!"

Andreas glowered. He began to retreat, moving backwards, turning as he went. Then he was gone so fast, it was as if he vanished in a rush of blackness, the slam of a door.

Now Benedict was completely alone. A demon that consisted entirely of appetite stared at him from round, black sockets.

With the self-discipline of training, Ben pushed all emotion from his mind. *If I die*, he thought, *it doesn't matter. Not to me, at least; but it will matter to others. If they feed on me, it will give them the strength to escape and feed on innocent people. Maybe Holly, dear God, Holly...*

I must win.

Normally he needed careful preparation to connect with Raqia. Now he had no choice but to do it cold. He flung himself into a higher state of mind, seeing two worlds at once; one with his eyes, the other with his mind.

The skeleton above him showed no sign of life. Holding his breath, Ben took one step – and it rose and surged at him like the impossibly long tongue of a frog.

Its hands closed on his upper arms like rings of freezing metal. Shocks ran along his nerves. His limbs went numb. He stared into huge, hollow eyes in an ivory face; a beast fighting frantically for survival, moved by dumb instinct.

"I summoned you," Ben gasped. "By the power of Raqia, you are subject to me. There is a chain around your neck. If you touch me, it will strangle you until it severs your head."

The creature took no notice. Open-mouthed, it strained towards his neck. His arms were pinioned but he flung up an elbow against its chest and held it off.

Ben was beyond fear now. There was only the incandescent fight for life. A battle of wills wouldn't work this time. He needed a real weapon.

He opened his mind to the astral world, caught and moulded it, set the firmament shimmering like a harmonic to his thoughts. With all his will he shaped the idea and projected it into the vampire's skull. "I control the Crystal Ring and therefore I control you."

The fanged mouth snapped shut. Still it leaned into him, but Ben began to force it back upstairs. He was winning! But in that breath of victory he slackened his guard and was pulled around, twisting, falling.

The attic stairs caught him painfully across his spine. Another skull-face arced down from above and he turned ice-cold, convulsing.

"No!" Ben screamed, flinging up his arms. He drew down the Crystal Ring like a curtain, caught the creatures in its folds, bundled them away. "I am the master of your realm and I control you, all of you. Go back where I command you. Go back!"

The effort turned his body into a sheet of pain. He crawled upwards, driving the two demons before him. The battle raged on every level. He tried to banish them into the astral world, but they wouldn't go. He could only use his power like a whip to subdue them. His head sang with hideous pressure.

There were three more on the attic landing. They writhed like white beetles, pitiful yet repulsive. With sheer force of will he drove them back into the ruined temple, the effort leaving him sick and drained.

Finally all the vampires were inside, and Ben sat cross-legged in the doorway. He was their master, by the merest paper-edge. He trembled with exhaustion.

Appalling knowledge seeped through him. The heat of his blood maddened them. They clawed the air and shrieked, their hunger a force that plucked at his control, threatening to unravel him.

He thought, *I cannot ever leave this spot. If I relax my guard for one second they'll break loose and destroy me. If Andreas can't find the Book, I shall have to stay here until...*

Sweat poured from him. *I can't do this. But I must.*

Come back, Andreas. For God's sake, come back.

* * *

213

When Karl returned home, he knew Charlotte had been there. The note had been picked up, slightly crumpled, dropped; but she'd left no message in return. Smoothing the paper under his fingers, he sighed. This set a seal on the empty horror of looking for Kristian and the lost Book.

"Don't be sad, dearest," Katerina said behind him. "If she's been home, she hasn't come to any harm. She must still be with Violette; you know how enticing humans can be, how hard it is to leave them alone."

Saying nothing, Karl took a fresh sheet of paper and wrote the date.

"Why leave messages, if she can't be bothered to answer? It's a waste of time, she won't come. She doesn't seem to realise the importance of our search." Katerina's voice was gentle, consoling. "She's making things so difficult for you. I'm sorry."

Karl, however, did not want sympathy. Grimly, he went on writing. An impersonal note; no affection, no recriminations.

> Charlotte,
>   I have called our friends to meet me at Schloss Holdenstein tonight. If you read this in time, join us there. It is vitally important; please don't fail me.
>
>   K.

Age softened the outlines of Kristian's Schloss, making it seem organically fused to the ridge on which it stood. A mass of dark walls, turrets and chaotically angled roofs, it resembled a dozen such castles on the Rhine; a dreamlike place to inspire fairy tales. To Karl, though, its silhouette against the lavender sunset looked inexpressibly malevolent. Such grim memories. He and Katerina stepped from the Crystal Ring at the base of the ridge, and climbed the steep wooded hillside towards the castle. On their left the river lay dark as iron.

Spring flowed towards summer; grapes were swelling on the vines all around, trees danced in rags of green taffeta. The castle remained chill and barren.

Katerina said, "It seems a century since I was last here. How desolate the Schloss looks. Does anyone still live here?"

"I've no idea," said Karl. "I haven't set foot here since Kristian's death."

"Did anyone tell Kristian's followers of his demise?"

"Not to my knowledge. I certainly had no intention of admitting my guilt."

"So it's possible they don't know?"

"They must have found out by now," Karl said indifferently. "I had no reason to care what his acolytes thought. Some would have been glad."

"And the others?"

"Would want to avenge him, I imagine."

He began to climb faster, moving sure-footedly over outcrops of rock and near-vertical paths. Katerina hurried to keep up. "And if anyone's there," she persisted, "what shall we tell them now?"

Karl did not reply.

It hadn't been difficult to contact the vampires who'd helped him to kill Kristian. Ilona had readily offered to help. Pierre liked Vienna and Paris; Stefan and his twin Niklas were usually in London. While it was unlike Ilona to be so helpful, Karl knew she was more concerned about the consequences of Kristian's death than she would admit.

Karl made sure, though, that he and Katti arrived well before the others. He wanted to know what danger waited at the Schloss before anyone else walked into it.

Reaching the walls, they entered the Crystal Ring to pass inside. Even in the ghost-world, the stonework felt dense and coarse, holding them like molasses. As they pushed through, Karl sensed the presence of several vampires, like jewel splinters in his mind. Walls of bare stone hardened around them, becoming a corridor with a low roof and sloping floor. No luxury here; Kristian had kept the castle as plain as a monastery. The flagstones were spotless, freshly swept.

Karl and Katerina looked at each other. "Well, let us see who is here," he said.

As they walked towards the heart of the castle, the atmosphere was that a crypt; an echo of the manor house tunnel. The lingering agony of victims had soaked into the ancient walls like blood.

This can happen anywhere, he thought. *Wherever vampires dwell for too long... the curse will rebound on us.*

They descended a curving flight of steps. At the bottom, in the doorway to a chapel, a female vampire stood looking at them. She was slender, almost childlike, with straight dark-gold hair. In her dark hooded robe, with a broom in her hands, she seemed part nun, part fairy-tale witch. Karl remembered her. She'd rarely spoken, never smiled, and had obeyed Kristian with fanatical devotion.

"*Grüss Gott*, Maria," he said.

She gave a minimal nod of respect. She didn't appear surprised to see him, he'd stayed away far longer in the past. But then her gaze moved to Katerina, and the broom fell from her hands.

"Katerina," Maria whispered.

"Yes, dear," said Katti. "Back from the dead."

Maria had been trained never to question Kristian, with the result that she never questioned anything. She only blinked solemnly.

Karl said, "Kristian is not here, is he?"

"No."

"When did you last see him?"

Maria's eyes hardened. "He has not been here for a long time."

"Almost two years?"

"Calendars are props for mortal insecurity. We are timeless."

A phrase straight from Kristian's mouth. Karl sighed inwardly. Maria had been a true believer, forbidden to think for herself. Now, with no inner resources, she was worn thin by her master's absence. Karl wondered, *Is it too late for her to change?*

"Surely you notice the seasons passing. In your estimation, how long? Many months?"

"Yes, many," she conceded. Her hard mouth turned down at the corners. "We thought our lord Kristian was with you."

"Well, he is not," Karl said softly, thinking, *I cannot tell her, and break her heart... not until I'm certain that he's truly dead.* Sensing other vampires converging from different parts of the castle, he tried to count them; three, four...

"Where is he, Karl?" said a voice behind him. Karl turned and saw a young man with a cherubic face, fair hair, clear grey eyes; the look of a keen young priest about him. Cesare. He, too, was a passionate follower of Kristian's creed; unlike Maria, fiercely evangelical.

"Have you not seen him?" Karl said lightly.

"Not since he left here – with you," said Cesare. "And you're right, it is almost two years. Where is he?"

"I don't know," Karl said truthfully.

Other vampires appeared, drawn by Karl's arrival. He counted seventeen. Like Cesare and Maria they all wore black monastic robes. Although their faces were half-hidden by hoods, Karl recognised them all. His gaze moved over them.

"Are you all that's left of the faithful?"

"We wait for our leader," said Cesare in strange tone. "Some drifted away, claiming that Kristian had deserted us – for you, Karl. But we never give up hope that the Father will return."

"So no one here has seen him?"

The hooded ones murmured denials. Karl touched Katerina's fingers, a secret communication of relief as he dared to believe that no one had resurrected Kristian. That they were truly free of him forever.

"I have something important to tell you," said Karl. "I've called other immortals here; when they arrive, I want everyone to meet in Kristian's chamber. Will you come and listen?"

The acolytes nodded. Their eyes, lit from within like the eyes of cats, rested hungrily on Karl as if he held all the answers.

The Schloss felt austere and frigid. Karl had always loathed it. Even in the master's absence, he noticed, the atmosphere hadn't changed. No laughter, no affection, no humanity was allowed to dwell here. Only celibate adoration of Kristian, and worship of his singular savage God.

No wonder so many of us risked hideous punishment for the sake of freedom, he thought.

Ilona arrived first with Pierre, an immortal who was sometimes an enemy and occasionally a friend to Karl. He had curly brown hair and cold blue eyes, a handsome, sardonic face. Pierre and Ilona were allies in their flippant attitude to life, yet here they were subdued. For once they made no sarcastic remarks, no cruel jokes.

Next came the blond twins, Niklas and Stefan, like porcelain angels. They were physically identical but for their eyes; Stefan's were blue and mischievous, Niklas's topaz-yellow and blank. Stefan was full of life, while his brother followed in mute, emotionless compliance. A law unto themselves, these two, though Karl trusted Stefan.

The newcomers in modern dress made a striking contrast to the hooded disciples, who greeted them with searchlight stares, deep suspicion on both sides. No love lost here. The atmosphere was thick with shadows.

No sign of Charlotte.

Karl couldn't wait for her. He was sure, now, that she would not come. Presently he called everyone into the deep windowless chamber where Kristian used to hold court. As he watched them filing in, he thought, *I should have gone to find Charlotte myself... Perhaps she takes my failure to do so as rejection, but surely she knows me better than that? I will not be heavy-handed. That was Kristian's way, not mine.*

Katerina whispered in his ear, too softly for anyone to overhear, "Don't worry. Kristian is gone for good, I'm certain."

"I knew of no more than sixty vampires," said Karl, "and Kristian claimed to control them all. Nearly half are here. It's possible that someone unknown could have healed him... but I knew him. If he could, he *would* have come back by now."

"Well, everyone's here," said Katerina. "Will you begin?"

Everyone except Charlotte, Karl thought. Her absence deepened his sense of foreboding.

The chamber was bare, but for a carved black chair that stood on a stone dais like a throne. Torches flamed on the walls. There was no sign here that the world had moved beyond the Middle Ages. As Karl went to the dais, the vampires waited in silence, Katerina and his friends standing apart from the hooded ones.

Cesare, with his hands folded inside his wide sleeves, headed the faithful. Looking into their solemn, guarded eyes, Karl felt no regret for what he was about to say. He had no pity for them.

"Nothing stays the same forever," he began. "Not even for immortals. I fear you've wasted two years waiting for your master to return, because Kristian is dead."

A moment of stillness, like a held breath. A female voice, Maria's, cried, "No!"

Someone else shouted, "Liar!" and then a wave of angry denial began. The only one who did not react was Cesare.

Karl's voice cut through the uproar. "It is the truth."

Dull silence rolled in, broken by whispers and moans.

"And how would you know?" Cesare said hoarsely. "What proof do you have?"

"That he hasn't returned."

"But he went away with *you*. You are the one he placed so far above us! What happened to him?"

Karl closed his eyes briefly, sickened by the pain in the priest-vampire's voice. "I killed him."

If they decided to take revenge, he was ready. For long seconds no one moved.

"Impossible," Maria moaned. She started forward, but another vampire held her back. She doubled up, her hands clasped over her heart.

Cesare said bitterly, "We know he's dead. We know!"

The uproar began again, this time directed at Cesare. He faced them and shouted in anguish, "It's no good! We all felt the vibration of his death; the whole Crystal Ring shuddered and wept with outrage. And we have wasted all this time pretending it never happened. Admit it!"

His passion shocked Karl. Cesare forced acknowledgement from the others like blood. Their grief was a tangible web. Karl almost felt sympathy... almost. As Cesare confronted him, he was unafraid.

The fair vampire said, "Why in the name of God have you come to tell us what we already know?"

Karl rested a hand on the high-backed chair, fixing them with baleful eyes. All at once he realised they were afraid of him, as they had been of Kristian. "If you knew, you plainly did not want to face it, but you must. Your master is dead. You should consider how you are going to exist without him, for there's no need for you to live like slaves a moment longer."

Cesare's boyish face twisted with loathing. "Kristian trusted you, Karl. He loved you more than he loved all of us together. He *chose* you!"

"Well, perhaps he chose me as his executioner," Karl said acidly.

"Listen to me. He was a tyrant. He had to die so that we could think for ourselves, and it has never been more important that we *think*. Someone such as Kristian cannot die without affecting everything. When he died, Katerina woke from the *Weisskalt*. Other vampires may also have woken. Have any of you seen unknown immortals in the Crystal Ring, or sensed unexplained presences?"

A hesitant murmur of assent. A woman wept on her neighbour's shoulder; Maria was down on the flags, arms outstretched in grief. Karl took any reaction as a sign that there was still hope for them.

Cesare said, "How did he die?"

"You don't need to know."

"But we do. We won't believe it until we do!"

So Karl began to tell them. Why spare them anything? They were vampires, not children. He would not implicate his accomplices, unless they chose to stand with him, but he had no reason to deny his own guilt.

As he spoke there was movement in the corridor outside. Smoke and flame flared in a draught; a figure appeared in the doorway, hair shining bronze and gold under the torchlight, her gleaming eyes fixed on him. Karl's hand tightened on the black chair, but he contained his reaction to the briefest pause between words. Then he went on describing Kristian's death in passionless, clinical detail.

When Charlotte left Violette, she fled straight home – but Karl, again, was not there.

Her attack on Violette, the whole of their disastrous relationship, had shattered her. It was all she could do to think of anything else. She found the note, stared distractedly at the words. Schloss Holdenstein? *Why, what does this mean?*

She had to go, for Karl's sake, if nothing else. She obeyed the request mechanically, feeling only a wisp of anxious curiosity as she travelled through the Crystal Ring. Her mind was elsewhere, bound up in barbed wire.

She was horrified at herself for betraying Violette's trust. Worse was her own hypocrisy; the betrayal only mattered, she knew, because it caused Violette to reject her. *Never mind the harm I've caused*, she thought wretchedly. *If she hadn't minded me drinking her blood, that would have made it all right. But she was disgusted and I can't bear it. That's all. I wanted her to love me, despite what I am...*

Why? Because Anne couldn't? Yes... but I've only done to Violette what I desired from the moment I saw her. How dare I pretend to be so amazed at my behaviour, or so aggrieved by her reaction?

But I never wanted to hurt her... Oh God, this is what Karl used to tell me. "I want you, Charlotte, but I cannot have you without destroying you..." But we went on anyway, because it was too delicious to stop.

The ballerina's blood danced through her in thrilling lines of garnet light. *Too delicious, too gorgeous to stop... and I felt such passion for her that I couldn't believe she didn't share it. I thought, I thought... I don't understand any of this. How can I face Karl, feeling like this? Ashamed. A violater. I can't.*

Charlotte stepped through the thick stone walls of the castle and sensed vampires gathered in a deep chamber. The meeting had begun. This place held unpleasant memories... Kristian had imprisoned her here and forced Karl to discard her, the worst moment of her life... and then he'd starved her of blood, unspeakable torment to a new vampire. But now the pain was distant. She saw the world through a frost of numb shock.

She walked the corridors until she saw torchlight spilling through an open doorway. The vampires – silent monk-like figures whom she hardly knew – were gathered in Kristian's audience chamber. Karl stood on the dais, one hand resting on the ebony throne, addressing the group.

He was explaining how Kristian had died.

Charlotte entered softly, but everyone looked at her. Karl barely paused, but as he went on speaking he gazed at her, his eyes intense – with relief, passion, anger? All of those. His gaze scalded her like liquid fire in the eerie light. And as he described how he'd lured Kristian to the manor house and hacked him to pieces, he went on staring at her.

Charlotte knew all this; she had been there and she'd helped. But to hear him describe it, in cold blood, to disciples who had revered Kristian as their prophet... Even Pierre, Ilona and Stefan seemed stunned. She pressed against the stone archway, shivering.

Karl. She saw him as if for the first time. Graceful, lean and imposing, his red-tinged dark hair massed softly around a sculpted face. So finely carved, his features, a seraphim's face darkened by suffering that had pooled into deadly tranquillity in his eyes. A heart-stopping combination of beauty and strength. His presence never ceased to invade her, thrusting into every cell like the thrill of blood itself, igniting her with scarlet flame. And his power enveloped the stone chamber like a blood-red velvet cloak, as Kristian's once had.

He finished, having shaped the narrative to sound as if he'd acted alone. *He protected us, his accomplices*, she thought with surprise.

Why weren't Kristian's devotees demanding Karl's execution in revenge? Instead she sensed grief, confusion, directionless outrage. A fair-haired male vampire at the front said, "You cannot take away our leader and give us nothing in return."

"I'm not asking for understanding, Cesare, still less forgiveness," said Karl. "I came to tell you the plain truth. Also to suggest that we could help each other."

"If you want to help us, become our leader," said Cesare. "Take Kristian's place!"

Karl was visibly shocked. "No."

"You must. We need someone. You cannot slay the king and not replace him!"

"My intention was never to usurp him." His voice was subdued, full of anger. "I did it to free us all."

"We didn't ask to be free!" Cesare exclaimed. Cries of assent. "We needed him!"

"You are intelligent beings with powers that humans would envy. So why are you behaving like sheep without a shepherd?"

Cesare's eyes widened with rage. "Even the strongest need a spiritual guide. What would the Church be without the Pope – and what are we without Kristian?"

The darkening of Karl's face held Charlotte mesmerised. Easy to forget how forceful he could be when the need arose. The very strength he used to reject the suggestion only drew them towards him. All the more startling because he showed this side of himself so rarely. His strength was as magnetic as his beauty.

"Be whatever you wish," he answered. "Learn to think for yourselves – unless you don't want to. You were willing slaves; for that you deserved Kristian, and you deserve this limbo you are now in. I will not take his place."

Cesare was shaking. Tears ran down his face. "You can't imagine the agony of being without him! You've no soul! How dare you call us slaves, when we loved him; how dare you take him from us and give nothing in return? You killed him to free *yourself*, not us. Never say you did it for us!"

Bronze fire glinted under Karl's dark brows. "Is freedom 'nothing'?" He spoke with stony contempt. "I don't know whether to pity or despise you. This meeting is over."

With a roar of anguish, Cesare drew his hands from his sleeves and rushed at Karl. A glint of steel; Charlotte saw with horror that he had a cleaver, and was swinging it two-handed at Karl's neck. No one was close or fast enough to protect Karl.

Rather than backing off, Karl met the attack. As Cesare lunged, Karl's hands shot out and seized his left wrist. In the same movement he turned, using the attacker's momentum to heave him over his shoulder and onto the floor.

He lay helpless, Karl leaning over him. The cleaver was still in his left hand, but Karl forced his wrist back and down until the blade cut deep into Cesare's own throat.

Blood sprayed from crescent wound. A scream became a bubbling rasp as his body arched in pain. His hand sprang open, releasing the handle. The blade remained stuck in the wound, then slid sideways under its own weight and clattered onto the flagstones.

Karl let him go and straightened up, his expression coldly furious. "Does anyone else wish to vent their feelings on me?"

Horrified silence, thick with unease. Charlotte could only press against the wall in relief and shock.

Cesare lay convulsing on the dais, slow blood oozing from his throat. Karl could have beheaded him, Charlotte knew, but had spared him. Cesare's wound would heal. And although Karl could have drunk the acolyte dry to prove his superiority, the fact that he disdained the blood only made him seem stronger.

The immortals knew, and dared not challenge him. Only Ilona smiled, whispering to Pierre.

Maria spoke. "But you have proved your power. That makes you our leader, whether you want it or not."

"Take responsibility for yourselves," Karl said in a low voice. "No one rules over me – and I refuse to rule over others."

He strode off the dais and towards the doorway. Charlotte saw Ilona, Pierre and Stefan glancing at each other as they turned to follow him. Niklas and Katerina were behind them. As Charlotte waited for them to reach her, she saw Cesare rise up on the dais, hanging unsteadily onto the throne with one hand, the other pressed to his gashed neck. His face was a ghastly bluish-grey.

"You have made bad enemies here, Karl." His voice was a thick, fluid rasp.

"Enemies, for telling the truth?" Karl said coldly. "The worst foes you have are yourselves."

"We'll wait for a new leader to come – and one surely will. Leave and never come back!"

With a look of disgust Karl turned away, not bothering to reply. Reaching Charlotte he stopped, letting his companions go through the archway before him. Ilona and Stefan acknowledged Charlotte with brief smiles as they entered the corridor and vanished into the Crystal Ring. Then she found herself facing Karl, alone.

His eyes moved over her. She had no idea what to say. Karl held out his hand to her, but she saw no warmth in his face.

He said, "Are you coming home?"

"Why didn't you finish off that idiot Cesare?" said Katerina.

The seven immortals had gathered in the drawing room of the chalet. Charlotte watched, contributing little to the conversation. Pierre, whom she'd never trusted even though he had helped transform her, leaned on the mantelpiece. Niklas sat like a golden-haired doll in a chair, with Stefan – deceptively sweet-natured – perched on the arm. Ilona was as striking as ever; fashionable in a black, beaded dress, her hair cropped and wavy. She stood by the gramophone, looking through their record collection; an exact replica of a bored debutante.

Katerina was stretched out on the sofa, Karl standing near

Pierre by the fire. Charlotte sat in an armchair, separated from them by her own black guilt.

"I think they're all mad," Karl said, "but if I can't change their minds, I won't kill them just for disagreeing with me. As long as they leave us alone, I have no desire to trouble them."

"But Karl, what did you expect?" said Pierre. "All those with any sense have already left. The ones who remained were bound to act like idiots, because they're idiots to have stayed!"

"Some will have listened to you," said Katerina, "but they wouldn't dare admit it in front of poisonous fanatics like Cesare."

How extraordinary they looked, thought Charlotte, glowing with the enticing radiance that only vampires possessed. She could barely believe she was one of them; she felt like an outsider, filled with human wonder.

"It doesn't matter," Karl said wearily. "The point was to make sure that Kristian is dead."

"And are you?" snapped Ilona.

"As sure as I can be."

Stefan said with good humour, "To be honest, Karl, I think you made a mistake. Why not agree to lead them?"

"Because I refuse to behave like Kristian."

"Your pride will kill you, one of these days."

"It's nothing to do with pride," said Karl. "If they want to live on, worshipping Kristian's memory, they're free to do so. The point is that Kristian gave us no choice. That was why he had to die."

"But they won't forgive you," said Stefan. "They see a light in you, Karl. I would have followed you happily."

He spoke lightly, but his smile faded at Karl's answer. "As you followed Kristian? With dog-like devotion until the moment was right to turn and savage him? You were all the same, even Ilona. Even you, Katti. All of you except Charlotte."

Their silence writhed on the needle tip of truth.

"For pity's sake," Katerina said, low and angry. "That is unfair, Karl."

"Nothing about our existence is fair."

Stefan said calmly, "If you won't lead them, they'll find someone else."

"That is up to them."

Ilona added, "Someone worse than Kristian! At least Kristian loved us!"

"Exactly," said Stefan. "I would rather have Karl, wouldn't you?"

Charlotte listened to them arguing as if watching a play. This had nothing to do with her. She felt dead inside; all she could see was Violette's blanched face and the revulsion in her eyes.

"Enough," said Karl. "I'm as certain as I can be that Kristian is dead. But if his death woke Katerina, what of the other vampires Kristian left in the *Weisskalt*?"

Pierre said, "Leave them alone! The world is a big place. I agree with you, my friend; we are all loners."

"But are we?" Karl said. "Kristian united us, even while we defied him. He was the tyrant who made it unnecessary to think for ourselves; by which I mean that we didn't think beyond escaping him. But now he's gone, we have no focus. You saw how they were in the castle! And as for the vampires he may have woken – we know nothing about them. What might they do?"

"*Mon Dieu*, who cares?" Pierre exclaimed.

"Some of us!" Katerina said heatedly. "What about Andrei? Have you forgotten him?"

"Hardly, the self-centred brat."

Katerina glared at Pierre. "That, as mortals say, is the pot calling the kettle black."

"Kristian's death has caused changes we don't understand," Karl persisted. "I'm not the only one to sense unnatural shadows in the Ring, am I?"

"No, I've seen them," said Ilona.

"Well, I haven't," said Pierre, folding his arms. "We're flocking together like frightened birds! What's the matter with us? We're vampires, nothing can hurt us!"

"No?" said Katerina. "Tell Kristian that. Tell Cesare, who was a spine's width from death. Or tell *me*. You haven't the slightest idea of the agonies I suffered when I woke from the *Weisskalt*!"

Pierre rolled his over-large blue eyes.

"I simply want answers," said Karl. "I don't seek power, only knowledge. Do you understand?"

"Of course." Stefan put his hand on Niklas's arm, as if to communicate with his mute double. "And we'll help you, as we always have. What do you want us to do?"

Karl's eyes softened, and his lids curved down. "Anything you see fit. Travel through the Crystal Ring, observe anything strange, search for other vampires. Katerina and I will look for Andreas... and for a lost Book."

"Well, you can count me out," said Pierre. "You're wasting your time."

"*Something* is happening, and you won't make it go away by pretending otherwise," Ilona said crisply.

"I am surprised at you, *chérie*. Since when are you filled with philanthropic concern for your fellow vampires? You're only afraid of an interruption to your pursuit of pleasure." Ilona opened her mouth, but he added, "I know, because you're just like me."

Pierre walked to Charlotte, lifted her hand and kissed it. She jumped; she'd been in a reverie, half-listening.

"You are the only one with sense, Ophelia," he said. "You have nothing at all to say to this nonsense." Pierre bowed, and vanished.

With that, the meeting was over. Ilona began talking with Stefan and Katerina. Charlotte stood and went towards Karl, forcing herself to face him at last.

Before she reached him, Katerina stepped between them and caught his attention. She appeared to do so without malice; not trying to exclude Charlotte, but barely even aware of her.

"Karl, I was thinking..."

"What is it, Katti?"

A frown creased her smooth alabaster forehead. "The disturbances in the Crystal Ring – perhaps we should seek them deliberately, try to understand their cause, regardless of any danger."

"Yes, I agree," he said. "It's time to explore, not bury our heads like Pierre." They were intent on each other, ignoring Charlotte. Swallowing anger, she subtly changed direction towards another room as if their bond was of no consequence to her.

Karl found Charlotte alone in the darkened library. Normally she loved light, music and company. Something was very wrong; her silence throughout the meeting had emphasised her unspoken distress. She'd lost her spirit, all her bright passion.

Charlotte stood looking out of the rain-dashed window. She didn't respond as he approached. Her hand was dead to his touch.

"*Liebling*, what's wrong? Why did you leave us?"

"It took you long enough to notice I'd gone. Can Katerina spare you?"

Her words saddened him, but he reacted gently. "I'm here now. I am so glad you came back at last. You sent me no word…"

"You went back to the manor house without me," she said. "We agreed we would go together."

Karl was so relieved to see her that he would forgive her anything, but her toneless voice and blank expression woke a sense of dread. "I'd rather you'd come with me. You know that. I'm sorry; we should have waited. What assurance can I give, that Katerina does not come before you and never will?"

"It's not Katerina!" Charlotte snapped. She bit her lower lip. Blood rushed rose-red into the flesh, making him long to kiss her.

"What, then?"

"I can't tell you."

"Why not?"

"Because… you would despise me, and I couldn't bear it." Her head dropped forward. He pushed her tawny hair aside and saw that her face was blank with absolute misery. Her skin was white, her eyes deep in shadow. She began to shiver.

"You need to feed," he said gently. "Come, I'll go with you…"

She resisted the light tug of his hand. "No. I can't feed."

"You must. You will feel better."

"I know! But what right have I to feel better?"

"Why do you say this?"

No answer. Quietly he said, "Charlotte, I've often seen vampires reach a crisis when they are forced to confront their nature, and cannot accept it. Some conquer it, others never do. You seem so instinctive an immortal, I hoped this would never happen to you… but if it has, it's my fault. You have no reason for shame, but please tell me what's happened."

A single shake of her head.

"Is it Violette?" He felt her hands turn colder. Her temperature actually dropped at the question.

Eventually she whispered, "I drank her blood, Karl. Everything

I swore I wouldn't do, had no desire to do..."

"Ah." He felt no surprise, only sadness. The dragging sorrow grew heavier as she went on.

"What if she can't dance again, if I've made that light go out... because I thought I loved her? I don't understand. Why should I feel such attraction to her, when I had you? It was terrible. I tried to tell myself it was friendship when in truth it was an obsession. I lied to her."

She stopped, anxious for his reaction. Karl could not be warm, in the face of what she was telling him. He could only be impartial. "Go on," he said.

She frowned. "Do you know how cold you sound? But I'm glad. I'm not asking you to forgive me."

"Forgive you for what?"

"For being unfaithful."

"Is that what you feel you have been?"

Another silence. Then she said, "I killed the choreographer, because I thought he was keeping me from her. That was insanity, wasn't it? The truth is, it was *she* who didn't want me. She didn't want anyone, but I was hell-bent on breaking down her barriers – and when she surrendered, when she let me in at last, I betrayed her. I took her blood. If you'd seen the horror in her face afterwards... I thought I loved her. Instead I've wrecked her life. I can't run away laughing like Ilona, I can't make myself not care."

Karl breathed out slowly. His hands travelled over her arms and shoulders, but she remained like a statue under his touch. "Only strangers, Charlotte. Never look at their faces or ask their names, or they will tear you apart. But it's no use to say this now. You understand what you've done. I can't condemn you, when I've done worse, nor judge you more harshly than you judge yourself. I cannot tell you it doesn't matter, because it does. But how did you expect your... liaison with her to end?"

"Not like this."

"Did you hope she would love you after you fed on her? What then?"

"No. I don't know."

"One of our most blissful dreams is that the abyss between human and vampire does not exist. How I longed to drink from your throat again and again, without you ever growing sick or terrified... Impossible."

"But now you can!" Charlotte exclaimed. Her voice was a bayonet; he thought, *Yes, I made her like me so I could keep her, and now here she is in ice-cold anguish because of it...*

"And this is the price," he said. "The pain you are in."

"But I was willing to pay. I'd have let you take my blood anyway, because I loved you so hopelessly. I *did* let you. But Violette isn't like me. She isn't so sick and twisted that she finds what we are... desirable. She thinks I am a punishment, not a prize. She thinks I'm her damnation."

Violette thinks she is damned? Karl was mystified, but let it pass. "You saw Violette onstage as a goddess you could never touch or control – so you set out to prove otherwise. It was always her blood you wanted. That's what the blood is; power."

Her head drooped. And yes, he felt dismayed with her, whether or not he had any right. He added softly, "You let the dream get the better of you. We all do in the end."

"I don't –" she shook her head. "I wish I knew what to do."

"Do nothing. Let her be."

"Why are you so understanding?" she said bitterly.

"How else would you like me to be? Violently jealous? Completely unconcerned?"

"That would be what I deserve."

"Ah, I see. If I punish you, that will alleviate your guilt?"

"Bastard," she said under her breath.

Karl drew the curtains, lit a lamp. "Well, I have been called worse." He took her hands and said, "Beloved, I must ask you to make a decision."

Her tension worsened visibly. "What?"

"We are going to search for Andreas. We may be away for a long time."

"You and Katerina," she said woodenly.

"I'd like you to come with us."

For the first time there was a flash of life in her violet eyes. "It comes to something when you feel you must *invite* me, as if I'm a stranger. Once we would have taken it for granted that wherever you go, I come with you. No longer."

The truth of her words grieved him. "I'm telling you that I want you with us."

"Katerina won't."

"Does that really matter to you?" Karl was nearly exasperated with Charlotte, but her obdurate manner held him back. He'd seen her distressed or angry many times, but never so impervious. Almost as if she couldn't see him any more.

"No. I don't care what she thinks. But I can't come with you, Karl."

"Why not?"

"I can't bear to be with anyone. I can't love you while I hate myself."

Karl gripped her hands. "I will not leave you in distress. The search can wait, or Katti can begin on her own. Dearest, don't let this guilt consume you."

Charlotte's shoulders jerked – a single sob, firmly suppressed. "No, you must go. All we'll do is argue ourselves in circles, and I'll feel more guilty for keeping you here." She turned her cool amethyst gaze onto him. "When I was human, and we first grew close, you were terribly kind to me. And secretly I almost hated your kindness, because in my heart I didn't want you to be 'nice' to me; I wanted you to love me savagely. Now you're doing it again. Don't you realise it can be the subtlest, most horrible form of rejection? Don't stay because you feel sorry for me; only stay if you desire me! I wish things hadn't changed... but they have. Katerina came, and I turned away to Violette. That can't be undone."

"While I was being 'kind' to you," Karl murmured, "it was all I could do not to..." He trailed off, knowing, helplessly, that she was right. "Even immortals cannot stop the world intruding on them. I would still rather not go without you."

"I insist. You have a purpose, and I need to be on my own."

"On your own?"

She paused. "To watch Violette. Not to trespass on her life again; only to see how she is, if I did her any lasting harm..."

"Ah," said Karl, releasing her hand. "The truth."

"Karl, my dearest Karl. I'm sorry."

"And so am I," he breathed. Hopelessness settled through him. How had this happened? Like a creeping weed, fate had put out tendrils to drag them apart, unnoticed until it was too late. Neither of them wanted this, but there was no answer.

Tears shone in Charlotte's beautiful, expressive eyes, but he had no comfort to offer her.

"Go," she said without expression. "Please go."

Andreas looked across the darkened room at the man in bed. Middle-aged, plain; his face was florid against the white pillow, his hair a peppery mix of greys, a sparse beard like lichen adding to the horror. Grim, but his looks didn't matter. The blood was all that mattered. A fat, juicy heart pumping red elixir through the moist web of his lungs and on through the swollen vessels...

Andreas felt a tugging pain around his neck. He stopped. *Not allowed to touch him,* he thought sourly. *I'm only meant to look for the damned Book.*

Nevertheless he took a step towards the bed. He saw his own hand, slender and pale against the black sleeve of his coat, resting on the bedside table.

Stupid, Benedict. I could finish this for you now...

They came out of nowhere; from the floorboards, from the air. Lightless shapes, elongated, hooded. Silver fire blinded him. Andreas fell back, not understanding; swept from quiet reality into a nightmare. The shapes had black wings outlined by pale flame...

Shadows without substance... Yet Andreas heard voices whispering, felt their cold hands all over his body... cried out as their hard teeth drove into his neck and stole the red fire of his life.

"You're such a fool, my dear." Ilona's voice. Charlotte looked up from her chair and saw her slim silhouette. Firelight from the other room shone plum and scarlet through the edges of her hair. "Such a fool."

"I know," said Charlotte. She felt nothing now. Ilona sat on the carpet at her feet and draped her arm over Charlotte's knees. Musky perfume and a hint of human blood rose from her.

"You cannot be a vampire and live like this. You aren't mortal, you must stop behaving as if you are!"

"What do you suggest?"

"Don't agonise over your victims. Laugh at them." She gripped Charlotte's leg so hard that it hurt. "Go back to Violette and finish what you started! Don't flinch and run away from her horror; relish it! Relish your power. Have her completely and leave her behind like a broken lily. Then you can cry. You will sink so deep into your own evil that you will really have something to grieve about."

"You're hurting me," Charlotte said acidly. She plucked Ilona's hand off her leg, holding her bony, bracelet-adorned wrist tight between her fingers. "I'm not you, I can't behave like you!"

"You'd better try," Ilona said, smiling. "If you go on like this, you are going to destroy yourself."

PART TWO

The rose and poppy are her flowers; for where
    Is he not found, O Lilith, whom shed scent
And soft-shed kisses and soft sleep shall snare?
    Lo! as that youth's eyes burned at thine, so went
    Thy spell through him, and left his straight neck bent
And round his heart one strangling golden hair.

DANTE GABRIEL ROSSETTI, "BODY'S BEAUTY"

CHAPTER TWELVE

SHADOW LIGHT

Violette had what she wanted; Charlotte had gone. So why couldn't she keep the demon-woman out of her thoughts?

When the day's rehearsal was over and her dancers had gone to their beds or lodgings, Violette would spend an age in the empty studio. Not dancing, not even thinking. Just staring at moonlight fanning across the floorboards, and the subtle light-patterns made by river reflections on the ceiling. She saw Charlotte everywhere. A motionless shape against the blue glow of the windows; the silver-gold crescent of her hair catching the light; her grey-violet eyes, tranquil as lakes, shining straight through her...

A shift of Violette's head and the apparition would vanish – only to coalesce in another place, a different play of shadows. A ghost, a fetch... some dead thing masquerading as human. Thin disguise. Charlotte was no human, but a seductive lamia sent to tempt her and gloat at her fall.

Then Violette would rub the ache in her throat where Charlotte had bitten her... and loathe herself for the feelings that ran through her loins, proving her father's assertion that she was evil.

The day after Charlotte left, Violette had tried to go to confession. Her first time for years. She'd rejected her family's religion, but Salzburg's churches were Catholic, and their passionate vision of God spoke straight to her pain. The tiniest chapel held incredible riches. Towering altars of red marble, sunbursts of gold, robed saints yearning towards heaven...

But outside the confessional, a sudden wave of nausea choked her and she had passed out. She'd been unable to go through with it.

Rest, the doctor said. You have worked too hard and you are anaemic.

Violette could not rest. The permanent soreness of her back meant she slept badly at the best of times. Now, when she dozed, she had nightmares; but if she stayed awake, the fearful visions came anyway. Her three shadow-companions were growing taller, more solid and oppressive as they leaned over her, soundlessly whispering...

In this fatal slippage of reality, she became obsessed with the colour black. Such a beautiful non-colour. So rich, so uncompromisingly stark. Black, black. Jet and flowing feathers glossed by the light... naked skin gleaming through lace... net dewed with beads... a figure veiled from head to foot in a black shroud... and a huge ebony serpent with glittering scales, hiding in every scrap of shadow, rearing over her bed in the dead of night...

These images haunted Violette without mercy. *Charlotte has done this to me*, she thought. *When she bit my neck, she opened a door in my mind that should have stayed closed. She sucked from me the strength I needed to keep the door locked.*

It didn't occur to Violette that she was no longer sane. No one around her noticed, either. She'd never allowed her colleagues to see her inner self; no one dared try to penetrate her aloof shield. They still saw her as she'd always been: brilliant, self-sufficient, an obsessive perfectionist.

Violette could keep the demons at bay only by working. She danced until the ache of her muscles counterbalanced the pain in her joints, until exhilaration carried her beyond pain. Yet rehearsals grew harder each day. Not that she didn't want to perform... only that *Swan Lake* had begun to seem hollow. White swans, magic... she began to consider putting another ballerina in the role of Odette. Violette found she was interested only in dancing Odile, the evil sorcerer's daughter.

Traditionally, the same ballerina danced both characters, good and bad. It would be unconventional to split the roles, but...

Violette stood in the costume store, in the drear glimmer of a single light bulb. Three o'clock in the morning, and the building was deathly quiet. Her spine was a solid column of fire, each disc of cartilage swollen, red-hot. She'd been almost in tears, but now she rose above the pain as if it belonged to someone else. She stood stroking Odile's costume; stiff tulle, satin and beads... as black as night, gorgeous ebony, with sequins flashing red and purple, like snake scales, to indicate her sorcerous, serpentine nature... Hidden, forbidden, wicked.

The three were here, lurking behind costume racks and wardrobes; silhouettes with round blind heads, like monks, like phalluses. She imagined their accusing words, *You fell, Violette. You let her touch and invade you, and you wanted her. No good protesting afterwards, after your lust was sated. No good being horrified that she took your blood; you were the one who invited the lamia onto your couch. You unleashed your own depravity. Now you must play out the rest of your story. All of it.*

Violette felt no fear, only cool acceptance. The demons weren't real; her mind was playing tricks with tailor's dummies in the darkness. She went on stroking the rich raven gloss of the costume and a thought came to her.

A ballet just for Odile...

The idea germinated and began to branch, transmuting fluidly as images flowed one after another through her mind. *A new ballet!* Her heart was pounding as darkness folded over her like thorns on bare skin. She had no defences. She became the idea's avatar.

She saw the work as a whole; every scene, every dance. Now this... now that. Yes. A ballet of the greatest tragedy ever to befall mankind... told from the other side. The Serpent's side.

Unblinking, Violette left the storeroom and walked upstairs, dazzled by her personal vision. In a few hours her dancers would wake, her set designers and musicians present themselves to her... and for those few hours she would not sleep. She needed all the ideas at her fingertips, ready to break the news: "*Swan Lake* is cancelled. Today we start work on a brand new ballet."

Benedict had been alone for hours. The cottage was silent; he heard nothing outside, no birds singing, not even the friendly rattle of the milk cart. He felt as if a blanket lay over the house, compressing his whole world to the murky gloom of the attic. Inside, the vampires lay like heaps of dust and cobwebs. Sometimes one would twitch frantically and groan, then fall back into dormancy; but their thirst, anguish and malevolence struck him in constant waves.

Ben, too, was thirsty and hungry. He was desperate to relieve his bladder, and his legs were numb. But he dared not relax his attention for a second.

A knock at the front door hit him like a shell-burst. *Who the hell–?* Must be Mrs Potter. He imagined her waiting, tutting, walking away.

But where were Andreas and Holly? What the hell was keeping them? Although he didn't want Holly to walk into this, he wished with all his heart she was there.

But she betrayed me. She's probably gone back to Lancelyn. And Andreas… impotent rage dragged talons through him. *No, Lancelyn can't have taken everything from me!* And yet the idea held weight, and grew. The whole ghastly situation began to seem like a plot, manipulated by Lancelyn all along…

No, this is paranoia.

The day passed. Ben was forced to urinate where he sat. His mouth was dry and sticky, his head ached. Tormentingly, the telephone rang for an age. When it stopped, the silence shrieked in his ears.

Darkness fell again. Discipline sustained him and would do so for perhaps another night and day… but what then?

The hollow eyes in the darkness seemed to speak. *Come to us, nourish us with your life-blood. It will happen eventually, so why not give in now?*

"No!" said Ben, forcing himself to draw his fraying strands of power together. *Get thee behind me…*

Then he heard a sound downstairs. A soft tap that might have been the cottage creaking.

"Andreas?" he called.

The faint sound came again. Someone was moving in the hall… and then he heard the rhythmic whisper of feet climbing the stairs.

"Holly, is that you?"

No reply. Soft and insistent, the footsteps came on.

* * *

Karl and Katerina travelled the Crystal Ring together, two dark scraps working their way across the vast, steel-blue flank of a mountain. The skyscape was wild, cloud-hills billowing like sails. Karl detached himself from sad thoughts of Charlotte and turned his energy to the present... but the sense of loss remained.

"You know what you should have done, of course," said the creature of lacy darkness that was Katerina. "You were too soft with Charlotte. You should have ignored her words, seized and kissed her, bitten her, dragged her into bed. She would have forgotten Violette soon enough."

"I expect you are right," Karl said wearily. He'd wanted to do exactly that, and now wished he had – too late.

"I'm always right. It's what she wanted; did you need her to spell it out? Sometimes words are a waste of time."

"Should I have made things easier for her? I try to warn her against mistakes, but I can't prevent her from making them. Protecting her from the consequences will not help her."

Katti looked at him with dark, unhuman eyes; an aurora drifted in fiery veils behind her filigree false-wings. "I take it back, *mein Schatz*: perhaps you weren't too kind, but too hard on her."

Karl had no more to say.

They climbed to the peak and paused there. The mountain's substance, no denser than blood, only just bore their rarefied bodies. Golden clouds crashed around them like waves, sifting down the pleated sides... down into the night-violet abyss below. Karl took Katerina's hand. They launched themselves into thin air, and fell.

The descent was exhilarating. Karl closed his eyes, almost in a trance... then Katerina suddenly released his hand and said, "Karl, the pull is there again! Can you feel it?"

She was drifting away from him, silhouetted against the deep blue chasm. Karl swooped down to reach her. Not safe to lose contact. As he caught her, he felt the entire Crystal Ring shiver. Alarming sensation, as if they were goldfish in a bowl, and a cat had struck their world with a paw...

She clung to him. "It's dragging me downwards. I can't fight it. Karl, help me."

For some reason Katti was more strongly affected, the current trying to snatch her from his grip.

"But this is what we came for," he said. "Let us go with it. Don't be afraid, Katti, I won't let you go."

"It's coming up from Earth. I've felt it before, but never so powerful..."

"Don't fight now," Karl said softly. "We must follow the current to its source. Close your eyes and float."

Her eyes flickered, betraying anxiety, then fell shut. Her darkly angelic form went limp; Karl curled his fingers lightly around her arm, letting her guide him. She drifted northwards, reeled in by an invisible line.

Now Karl heard eerie sounds... a faint echo of voices chanting. He thought, *If this dimension is the massed psyche of mankind, could they deliberately change or influence it with their thoughts?*

The pull was strong now. Frightening sensation, like being drawn into a vacuum left by turbulent air. Rainbow lines of magnetism, more stable than the cloudlike terrain, helped him to keep his bearings. Katti was being drawn towards England, descending in a vast, inexorable curve.

But this is fascinating, Karl thought. *What is this power? Is Katti more affected than me because she woke so recently from the* Weisskalt?

They were moving across England now, or at least the Ring's distorted version of the land. Descending fast, Karl saw the lowest level of the Ring as a cloudy forest, deep in purple twilight.

Katerina gasped. "Don't let me go, I can't stop!"

She was almost torn from his hands, but he stayed with her. Light faded from violet to near-blackness. Now they were accelerating out of control through blurred shadows, sucked fiercely into a dark funnel towards the ground. A hard sloping surface like a roof rushed to meet them –

A new sense of peril hit Karl, almost too late. He held Katti's arms, resisted the pull with all his strength and swerved aside. All was confusion; he couldn't tell which realm they were in. They tumbled over and over and came to rest in darkness.

Karl became aware of grass beneath him, a mass of foliage above, the cool clean scents of early summer. The real world felt comfortingly solid, enfolding them in the sweet balm of night.

He grasped Katerina's arms and helped her to her feet. They

were in human shape again, ethereal wings changed back to plain dark coats.

"Katti, are you all right?" he said.

"Yes," she said. "Only shaken. What happened?"

"We were torn out of the Crystal Ring and thrown down here. We're in England, although I'm not sure where."

Katerina looked up, smoothing her hair. "Someone's garden, evidently. Did we nearly crash through their roof? That was a neatly avoided disaster."

"By a miracle," said Karl. He saw shrubs and trees, lavender bushes, drifts of late spring flowers, lawns and rose beds surrounding a slate-roofed cottage. "Did the call emanate from here?"

"I'm not sure," said Katerina. "It happened so swiftly at the end. Dreadful sensation – if I discover who did this to me –"

"If the summons came from a human…" He spoke softly. "How is that possible?"

Katti put her arms around him and they stood holding each other. Listening. Clematis and roses stirred in a breeze; a mouse scuffled in the undergrowth. Beyond the cottage, a motor car sputtered along a street. Then silence. Karl extended his senses to the interior of the dwelling, trying to gauge who was inside. He discerned a little cloud of warmth amid shards of ice…

"There is a human inside," he said. "And several vampires."

She gripped his arm and said quickly, "I know, I feel them, but hush… There's another one, further away."

Karl raised his head. He felt a splinter of quartz touch his mind… familiar, but too distant to identify. "Katti, wait."

"No." She drew him across the garden, brushing past damp shrubs. "We find that other vampire first, then we come back here. Don't argue with me."

Karl acquiesced, trusting her instinct. They passed along the side of the cottage, along a narrow street to the centre of a small, ancient market town. As Katti drew him across the road to a lane on the far side, he felt the other vampire's presence growing sharper. Georgian houses, a handsome church and tall shadowy trees in the churchyard gleamed with detailed richness in Karl's eyes.

"Hurry, Karl, while he's still there!" Katti breathed, clutching his arm. Her eyes were bright with excitement.

"We don't know who it is. It could be anyone," he said steadily, not wanting her to be disappointed. She didn't answer, only rushed through the churchyard as if towards a beacon.

Beyond, a footpath brought them to a ruined castle. They climbed a low wall and stepped onto an undulating bowl of grass, emerald blades sparkling with tiny diamonds. High castle walls, a shell, stood dark against the glowing night. A sharp crescent moon cast light onto the black hair and white face of a vampire.

The vampire, however, was lying flat on the ground as if injured. Katti ran to him, reaching him before Karl. She lifted the thin dark form in her arms and turned his face to the moonlight.

"Oh, Karl, it's him!"

Karl fell to his knees. He'd felt nothing but suddenly he was weeping as he touched the white hands, stroked the deathly pale cheeks and curly hair. The long, green eyes half-opened and Andreas said drowsily in German, "Where the hell have you been?" Then the revelation hit him and he struggled to sit up, clawing at Karl's coat. "Or are we all in hell? Karl, is it really you? Speak to me. Katti?"

"It's us, Andrei." Katerina was laughing and crying. "Darling, you're safe, we're with you. But what are you doing here? What happened to you?"

Together, they helped Andreas sit up. He was cold, weak and disorientated, as if he'd been attacked. Karl thought, *But he's alive!* They gathered him in their arms and there was a long, poised moment in which they held each other in pure rapture.

Andreas wept. A hundred questions, a thousand answers. They spoke in a rapid stream, giving only half-explanations, understanding each other without words. All the years they had lost were swept away, while the horned moon rose gradually above the castle ruins.

"I was attacked," Andreas said. "Some devilish vampires leapt on me and drained me... I don't know how I came here. I remember crawling from the house, starving, in torment. I fed on some boy in the street but it wasn't enough. I fell and I couldn't move."

"Hush," said Katti. She pressed her wrist to Andrei's mouth and he drank, eyes closed, an expression of relief on his pallid, delicate face.

Karl simply stared at him. He thought he'd seen everything, that there was nothing left that could shock him, but this was a miracle he could not grasp. He hadn't seen Andreas for forty years, yet here he was, perfect. More stunning than Katti's rebirth because he hadn't witnessed the stages... And vaguely horrific. He felt as a human might on discovering a long-dead relative alive again, unaged. Then Karl thought of his own human family, how aghast they would have been if they'd ever discovered he was a vampire. *Thank God they never knew. Only Ilona knew, and look what has happened to her...*

He came back to the present and watched Katti, cradling Andrei as he fed. Karl touched her pinioned arm. "Don't give him too much."

Katerina freed her wrist. Andreas fought for a moment, lunging with fangs extended. Then his head fell back and he sighed as blood coloured his cheeks.

"If you need more, we'll find you someone else," Katerina said softly.

"No. I must go back." Lifting his head, he tried to stand; Karl and Katti helped him. They stood in a circle, embracing each other; together again, outside time. Lips on each others' skin. Exchanging the miracle without speech.

"These vampires that attacked you," Karl said at last, "where are they now?"

"I don't know. They were not like us... don't ask me this now."

"But where are you going?"

"I have much to tell you." Andreas's lips thinned in a smile. "Come and meet my friend Benedict."

The footsteps seemed to approach from a vast distance. Ben's control was loosening. His shirt clung to him with sweat, an unvoiced scream clawed up his throat, but he must hold himself together.

The intruder was reaching the first landing... crossing it... now mounting towards the attic.

I mustn't take my eyes off the vampires, he told himself. He called aloud, "Andreas, for heaven's sake, say something!"

Mustn't look, but I can't help myself...

Ben turned, and almost leapt out of his skin. A stranger gazed down at him. A tall man, dark overcoat unfastened and swathing his lean form like a cloak. A mass of glossy hair shadowing a face of incredible beauty, expressive eyes under dark eyebrows... Astonishing eyes like auburn jewels; tranquil, questioning, contemptuous, all at once. Obviously a vampire.

Benedict was riveted. While his attention was on the stranger, one of the attic creatures leapt for the doorway.

Ben saw it from the corner of his eye, felt a sword-thrust of despair. Nothing he could do. He flung up his arms – but the pale form went straight over him and hurled itself onto the stranger.

Benedict stared, petrified. The succubus was tearing at the stranger's collar, straining to attach itself to his throat with open jaws; but the stranger seized its arms, forcing it away. His calm face was suddenly feral.

Now he gripped the creature's head, wrenching it to one side. There was a horrible grinding noise, then the snap of its neck breaking as he exposed its throat... lowering his own mouth and biting savagely... but the creature was ashen grey. No blood left. The stranger flung the bony husk with such force that it went clean over Ben's head, crashed through one of the remaining temple panels and collided with the rafters on the far side.

The beings in the attic retreated, groaning.

The look the unknown vampire gave Benedict was both horribly calm and furious. He had an aura of power that Andreas had never possessed...

Of course! Obvious who this was!

Benedict stood up. His numb legs almost gave way, but he clung to the doorway and said, "Good evening. You must be Kristian."

His voice shook, but his words stopped the vampire in his tracks. He looked astounded. Then he smiled, and the smile was not pleasant.

"What gave you that idea?" Beautiful deep voice, a slight Germanic accent. Ben shivered involuntarily. Such a presence about him. "Who do you think Kristian is?"

"An immortal of great power."

"And you are –?"

"Benedict Grey." Ben drew himself up and folded his arms;

he matched the vampire's height, which made him feel less intimidated. However, he was aware of being dishevelled and exhausted, and that he stank.

"Well, Mr Grey, count yourself lucky that I am not Kristian. If I were, you wouldn't be talking to me now; you would be dead. My name is Karl."

"Andreas's friend?" he said in sudden excitement. "Karl – I can't recall your second name –"

"It doesn't matter. Just Karl."

"But have you seen Andreas? Where it he?"

"On his way," said the vampire, gazing into the attic. "We found him at the castle. He can tell you what happened, if he wishes. He told me how he came here, and how you summoned these others..." His tone was deceptively conversational, so when Ben looked round, he was stunned by the hostility in Karl's face. "Have you the faintest idea of what you've done? How long do you think you can control starving vampires? You are a damned fool to meddle with this."

Ben responded thinly, "I don't answer to you."

The too-perceptive gaze raked over him. "Andreas says you have a hold on him that he doesn't understand. Perhaps you do have power, but it isn't enough. You should look at yourself, Mr Grey. You're on the verge of a breakdown."

As Karl spoke, Ben heard the front door open. The noise jolted his raw nerves. After a few seconds, a woman mounted the attic stairs, followed by Andreas. Another of them, Ben realised in dismay. Her radiance was unmistakable. She had one arm around Andreas's back, the other hand stroking his shoulder... suddenly Ben knew that this must be Katerina!

Andreas looked ill, disorientated. Ben found himself both angry and relieved to see him. "Where the hell have you been?" he said. "The Book, have you got it?"

"No," Andreas said flatly.

"What? Why the devil not? What happened?"

"Don't ask!" There was a crazed look in his narrow green eyes. "I'll tell you later. Not now!"

"Let him be," the woman said protectively. She was as extraordinary and unnerving as Karl, and Ben felt like an outsider in his own home; acutely aware of being in the presence of unholy angels.

Trying to regain command, he said, "Excuse me, madam, I'm delighted to meet friends of Andreas, but would you please explain how you found him?"

Her eyebrows rose. "You called us, I believe."

"Didn't your invitation extend to all vampires?" said Karl. He stepped past Ben and entered the attic, looking around unhurriedly.

"Be careful!" Katerina said, but the creatures played dead and made no move to attack him; perhaps they didn't dare.

A flame of resentment lit in Benedict's brain. *I called these beings to serve me, not to act as if they own my bloody house...*

Karl's face was impassive as he moved among the vampires, but his eyes were dark – with pity? Presently he came out and said, "This is disgusting."

Benedict was startled. Could a vampire feel disgust? He didn't understand these beings at all. He tried to stare Karl down, to prove himself equal, but Karl – to his annoyance – wouldn't play the game. When Ben asked, "How so?" Karl addressed his answer to Katerina.

"This is cruel, keeping them in a state of starvation."

"Yes," she said. "I know how it feels. It is horrible."

"But we cannot bring them back to life."

She gazed at Karl, dark eyes expanding. "Why not?"

"It would be irresponsible. Restoring these old vampires would be as bad as creating new ones. How do we know what we might unleash?"

"What are you saying? There's no alternative."

"Yes, there is. Behead them."

"Would that end their misery?" she said passionately. "Are you absolutely sure?"

"No, not absolutely," Karl replied, "but I believe it would."

Ben watched impotently as she seized Karl's arms. "How can you even contemplate this? They aren't animals, to be put down! They're immortals; some may have been my friends, and others may have knowledge of the old times, before Kristian! How can you throw that away?"

"Because the price is too high!"

"Would you have struck off my head, Andreas's too, never realizing whom you'd slaughtered? You can't want to do this, Karl!"

He shook his head, not answering, clearly troubled.

Benedict listened grimly, gathering his strength. "Excuse me," he said sharply, "The decision is not yours to make. I summoned them here and their fate rests in my hands, not in yours."

"Does it, really?" Karl said. "What in heaven's name do you plan to do with them?"

Katerina gazed at the undead husks with revulsion. "I was like that when Karl found me," she whispered. "It seems unbelievable now."

"So was I," said Andreas, moving to her side. "It took me a few days to recover, although I can't enter yet the Crystal Ring."

"Days? My healing took weeks!" she said. "We must help them."

"Why?" said Andreas. "Kristian put them in the *Weisskalt* because they were trouble. If we bring them back, they'll be nothing but trouble to us."

"Not to mention their victims," Karl murmured.

"So behead them," said Andreas. "Put them out of their misery."

"What if you or I or Karl had been among them?" Katerina exclaimed.

"Help them, then," Andreas said, off-hand. "It's all the same to me."

Karl sighed. "Very well, Katti. We'll revive them. I've no right to pronounce death upon them; even Kristian didn't do that."

"I am glad you realise it," Ben said, trying to re-assert his authority. "Their right to survive was never in question."

Karl fixed him with impassive jewelled eyes. "Then would you like us to go, and leave you to it? How will you cope? You'll have to take them out one by one to feed – assuming their first victim is not you. The process could take months. Perhaps you have the strength, Mr Grey, but looking at you, I doubt it. And if these creatures don't kill you, we might. You *may* have the means to control us as you control Andrei – but do you really want to put it to the test?"

Benedict hated Karl, because every word he said was true. He glared at him in frustration. Then he leaned on the wall and pushed a hand through his unwashed hair, sighing deeply. "You are correct, sir, and I don't want to make an enemy of you. I have one powerful enemy, and that's enough. I need help. I'd be grateful for your assistance."

"Our pleasure," Katerina said archly.

The three were close together in the doorway, excluding Ben. Seeing only each other. The change in Karl's expression was striking; no longer hostile, he looked as tender as a lover. Ben watched in fascination and resentment as they whispered, caressing each other with an abandon no human displayed in public. An unholy trinity.

He burned to break them apart, to re-establish his leadership. He persisted, "It must be understood that we work as a team."

"Benedict," Andreas said mildly, "go to bed."

Ben felt chains of fatigue on him and decided to take this advice before he collapsed. In a softer tone he said, "Do me one favour, Andreas. Go and find Holly."

Holly woke with a jolt of shock, wondering what on earth she was doing in the shop, in darkness... Her neck ached and her right arm was numb from sleeping on the floor.

Her heart sank as she remembered. At that moment, she became aware of someone standing over her. A thin black figure with a long, pallid face...

With a gasp of terror, she sat up.

"It's me," said Andreas's voice. "Whatever are you doing here?"

She crouched miserably over her knees, trying to rub life back into her arm. When she didn't answer, he leaned down to help her to her feet. His face was close to hers, and in the dim glow of pre-dawn she saw he was smiling.

"Oh, God, have I been here all night?" she said, her mouth thick. "Has anything happened?"

"Ben is all right. You look so worried, Holly, but there's no need."

"And you look happy," she said suspiciously. Being close to him was like being drugged by an exotic poppy. She fought the feeling.

"Because my friends arrived last night."

"Friends?"

"Katerina and Karl."

At that, her legs almost gave way. He helped her to a chair and she sat, fingers pressed to her face, unable to speak or breathe. He left her, and she heard him in the little kitchen at the back of the shop. Returning, he placed a glass of water in her hands.

"What's wrong?" he said. He was being so kind.

"I – I tried to reach Raqia last night, and summon them. Your friends, I mean. But nothing happened – I thought – I can't believe –"

Andreas crouched beside her and stroked her knee, looking at her in wonder. "*You* brought them?"

"I don't know. I don't think so."

"But you must have done! Why else would they appear now? They're helping Benedict with his guests, so the poor man can sleep. Did you know they would help?"

"I hoped – but I was afraid I might make things worse."

"No, you did the right thing! Dearest Holly, how can I express my feelings? I'm in awe of you."

His gratitude embarrassed her. "Please don't be. They may have heard Ben's summoning, not mine. But if you think it was me – please don't tell Ben!"

"Why not? Might it dent his ego?"

She smiled wanly. "That's one reason. Besides, I'm in enough trouble already." In her distress, she forgot what Andreas was; he became a simple, human friend. "Ben and I used to be close. I don't know what went wrong. Now he's fixated on higher beings, and he doesn't see me any more. Lancelyn's the same. Yet I still can't believe Lancelyn is evil... I suppose it's true, but I can't accept it."

"The death of illusion," he said, his cold breath brushing her cheek. Suddenly he hugged her, kissing her cheek and then her mouth, holding her tight in a paroxysm of emotion. Holly received the embrace with a shivering mixture of alarm and excitement. Then he drew back and looked at her. "Men are wicked, human and vampire alike; don't let them make you so sad."

"I'm not sad, really," she said, struggling to retrieve her composure. Andreas was so strange; as pernicious and falsely consoling as opium, and just as seductive. She needed to escape his influence. "Once I've combed my hair and had a cup of tea, I'll be ready to face anything."

"Shall we go home?"

"You go. There's someone I must see."

* * *

Benedict slept with the dreamless abandon of a child. When he woke, he found sunlight shining through the curtains, and Holly standing over him.

"Ben!" she said. "Ben, are you ever going to wake up?"

Gods, what a lovely sight. Her face was flushed, brown eyes shining, bobbed hair pushed untidily behind her ears. Not a statue animated by stolen energy, but pink and soft and alive.

"Mm, m'awake." He reached for her, but she stepped away.

"Get up!"

He pushed himself onto his elbows – then the memories came back. Her betrayal, and their house full of dangerous guests.

"Maud's downstairs. Please come and talk to her!"

He dressed hurriedly, fully alert now, and ravenously hungry. "Where have you been?" he said. "You just walk out and disappear –"

"Do you blame me, after the things you said? You didn't come looking for me!"

"How could I, when –" He stopped, and clasped her shoulder. "Look, Holly, no more angry words. Whatever our differences, let's be calm about them. What do you say?"

She lifted her chin. "Very well. But I didn't take the Book! I – I spent the night at the shop, then I went to Maud's lodgings first thing this morning."

"The shop? Where, on the floor? Good grief. Are you all right?"

She nodded. "Perfectly. Let's go downstairs and have breakfast in a civilised fashion."

They went onto the landing; the cottage was quiet. Ben noticed that the doors to the three guest bedrooms were shut; he glanced at the attic stairs, but saw nothing. "Did Andreas find you?"

"Yes," she said briskly. "Do you seriously think it's a good idea to send vampires looking for your wife?"

He drew a heavy breath of guilt, and made no reply.

Maud was at the kitchen table, pouring cups of tea. "Hello, Mr Grey. There's yours, two sugars. I thought I'd make myself useful."

"You always do. Thanks," he said, draining the cup in a few swallows. Ah, the restorative power of tea. He studied Maud –

fawn skirt and jumper, fawn hair brushed back from her almost-pretty face. The big spheres of her eyes and her prominent teeth gave her a look of breathless innocence; he couldn't perceive any hint of guilt in her.

Holly leaned towards Maud, resting the heels of her palms on the table edge. "Tell my husband what you told me. About the key."

The innocent eyes grew larger. "The older Mr Grey came into the shop one day and asked if you kept a house key in the office, and could he borrow it one afternoon. So we arranged a time and I took it to him."

"Did he give a reason?"

"No. I thought it was all right because he is your brother."

Ben sank down on a chair and groaned. "Oh, God. So he came in and took the bloody Book himself."

Maud blinked. "Did I do something wrong, sir?"

"Yes! No. You weren't to know. He... borrowed something I didn't want to lend him."

"I'm sorry, sir."

Holly went on glaring at Maud, not satisfied. "Didn't it strike you as odd that he asked you instead of me? Did he offer you a reward?"

"Holly, for heaven's sake –"

"How well do you know Lancelyn Grey?"

"Look, drop it, will you?" Ben said. "Maud, did you know Lancelyn had a sinister motive?"

She shuffled, adopting a wounded voice. "Of course not, Mr Grey."

"Right, that's an end to it." He stood up. "Go and open the shop, would you, Maud? Just carry on as normal. But if my brother approaches you again, you must let me know at once."

They saw Maud out. Closing the door behind her, Ben put his arms around Holly and they stood in the hallway, holding each other. "Holly, I'm so sorry. How could I doubt you?"

Holly was unresponsive in his arms. "She's not telling the truth."

"Well, what is the truth?"

"I don't know! I can't be psychic to order! But how can you tell her to 'carry on as normal', after she helped Lancelyn break into our home?"

"She didn't mean to. I know she's a little odd, but not sly.

Darling, she's just a simple girl who'd help anyone and never suspect any harm."

Holly seemed about to argue. Instead she relaxed and hugged him, her head on his shoulder. "You were a beast."

"I know, I behaved unforgivably," he said. "I'm sorry."

"You weren't yourself. This is the effect the vampires are having, if you could only see it! I'm frightened of what's happening to us."

"Don't be." He kissed her glossy brown hair. "Come and talk. There's a lot to tell you."

He led her into the parlour, pausing in shock as he saw Karl and Andreas sitting on opposite sides of the dead fire grate. They were silent, as if they weren't there at all.

Seeing Karl, Holly stared, pressing a hand to her chest. She uttered a faint, "*Oh*."

Her shock is understandable, Ben thought. He closed the door, and made introductions.

"I am charmed to meet you, Mrs Grey," said Karl. He took her hand but she froze and pulled away. Still glaring at him.

"I'm sorry," she said. "I'm finding it rather hard to be polite, when I know what you are. I find all of this… impossible."

"Sit down," said Ben. "Where's Katerina?"

Karl answered, "We took the first one out after you'd gone to bed. He is doing well. Katerina's sitting with him."

Ben saw the blood drain from Holly's face. He took her hands and told her what had happened, as briefly as he could.

"It won't work, Ben." she replied. "I've told you all along, this can't work!"

He felt such sympathy, affection and remorse that he would have done anything to reassure her; unfortunately, he feared she was right. "Love, I'd like you to go away for a while. It's too dangerous for you here. Do you mind? You can go to your parents."

She looked less than thrilled at this suggestion.

"For how long?"

"Until it's over."

Ben expected Holly to protest vehemently, but she didn't react. Her eyes were gravid with unexpressed thoughts. Before he could press her, Andreas spoke. "Is no one interested in my adventures? I saw Lancelyn when you sent me to his house last night. I had no chance to take the Book, didn't even see it. He was asleep, but three shadow figures set on me and almost killed me. All I saw of them were black shapes and silver fire, but their fangs and appetites were real enough. I don't remember escaping, or how I ended up near the castle. If Karl and Katti hadn't found me..."

"Three shadows," Benedict said grimly, "that drank your blood?"

"Yes. I'm sorry to tell you this, my friend, but however terrible your vampires are, Lancelyn has something worse."

In a small voice, as if forced to confess a secret, Holly said, "I've seen them too, Ben. I met Lancelyn in the street and they were with him. Three shadows."

Ben only believed the tale when Holly confirmed it. Then a huge shudder of emotion went through him from head to foot; pure, searing rage against a foe who could never be outwitted. He hadn't realised how deep his animosity ran until that terrible moment.

Lancelyn stole the Book and now he has weapons to outdo mine...

"No," Ben whispered. "Can I *never* be one step ahead of him? Damn him to hell, the bastard!"

Karl and Andreas merely looked at him, then at each other; figures carved of milky jade, too lovely and too cold to share any human empathy.

"Well?" said Katerina. "What do you think of our friend Benedict?"

She sat on the edge of a bed, tending to the first vampire they'd taken out to feed. He'd fought them all the way, taken three victims, killing two outright. The transformation wrought by the blood was astonishing.

A tall well-muscled male was already discernible, fleshing out the framework of bones. He lay motionless as she gently sponged his naked body; Karl had a fleeting impression of a nurse preparing a corpse. Katerina was intent on her task, her strong hands moving over the pale-gold flesh as if to explore every nuance of its texture. The vampire's eyes were closed; his hair, already growing, a flaxen mane on the pillow. His face was strong and strangely timeless; his race, impossible to pinpoint. Karl suspected that he was very old.

"Benedict is a driven man," said Karl. "He's misguided, but he has power that he clearly doesn't understand. Have you ever met a mortal with knowledge of the Crystal Ring – let alone any power to control it? That is dangerous, like a child with a bayonet. He's bound to injure himself or someone else, eventually. And it's his wife I fear for the most."

"We may be here a long time," Katerina said, smiling. "You're hating this, aren't you, my dear?"

She was right. "I still feel it's wrong to bring these vampires back to life – but equally wrong to destroy them. I'm appalled, actually, to find a human interfering in vampire affairs."

She shrugged. "Interesting, though."

"You don't look unhappy about it," said Karl.

"Oh, it's an adventure. And I have you and Andrei again! That is all I could ask for. Anything else is... what do you say? Icing."

The vampire on the bed opened his eyes. The irises were topaz yellow, like a cat's. Katerina paused, startled. The golden one smiled faintly at her, and closed his lids again.

"He's going to be beautiful, isn't he?" she said.

"Divine," said Karl. "Have you ever seen an ugly vampire?"

Katerina only laughed.

"Do you know him?"

"No, never seen him before," she said, "but he spoke earlier. Only a few words. He said his name is Simon."

As she spoke, Benedict appeared in the doorway. He looked quietly furious and not rational. *Difficult*, Karl thought, *for humans to have close contact with vampires and retain their sanity.*

"So, I'm misguided, am I? A child playing with dangerous weapons? I will not be patronised, not even by you."

Simon moved; his limbs twitched, his head tilted up. Katerina went towards Benedict, her hands raised to push him out of the room.

"Mr Grey, for your own safety, you should not –"

The pale-gold vampire surged past her, leaping for the heat of Ben's blood. Karl felt no impulse to protect him; he simply watched. A certain detachment – exercised with cool judgment on occasion – allowed him to be scientific rather than heroic.

Benedict's hands hit Simon's chest with a slap; he struggled against the predator with more than bodily strength. His eyes were wild. Unintelligible words rumbled from his throat. The vampire backed him into the door frame but Benedict kept him at arm's length, his face crimson with effort.

Suddenly Karl felt the fabric of the Crystal Ring in the air, like ice particles on a thin breeze. The room darkened and trembled. Simon's grip broke and he backed away, falling to his knees, tearing at his throat as if he were being choked.

"And I can do this to all of you!" Ben shouted, shaking a fist in Katerina's shocked face. "I keep you all like dogs on invisible chains. If you threaten me, the chain will tighten until it takes your head off."

Katerina gripped her own throat and backed away from him, looking bewildered, completely human for a moment. The threat didn't seem to touch Karl. He felt no pain, no constriction.

"Stop this," he said quietly. "Leave Katerina alone!"

He lifted Simon and helped him back onto the bed, then went to Benedict and seized his arm. Shocked by his speed, Ben tried uselessly to break Karl's grip.

Katerina gasped with relief. "That hurt, Mr Grey," she said furiously. "How dare you!"

Karl's grasp seemed to sober Ben. His face blanched patchily from red to white. Shock and unspent energy swam in his eyes.

"Not me," said Karl, his mouth close to Ben's ear. "I don't know what this hold is that you have over the others – but you cannot wield it over me."

CHAPTER THIRTEEN

IN THE GARDEN

The plush gloom of the theatre felt as familiar as home to Charlotte; the atmosphere sank into her pores like prickles of velvet, thrilling and disturbing. The collective warmth of the audience tempted her; resisting temptation was a physical ache.

Charlotte waited for the curtain to open in a state of unbearable tension, praying for the ballet to work some healing miracle on her.

The past few weeks had been the strangest and most wretched Charlotte had ever known. After Karl and Katerina left, she'd existed in a haze; shell shock, it might be called in a mortal. A void. Although her emotions were harsh, she found the strength to bear them, as if watching her own pain from the outside.

At the beginning she hadn't fed for days, becoming nearly as white and spare as Katerina. Unable to forget Violette's horror, she punished herself for it. Starving, Charlotte lost touch with reality. She saw visions of black and silver figures that terrified her; she understood how mystics – such as Kristian – thought they'd seen the face of God. At the end of all, though, they were only hallucinations, dust.

Everything seemed worthless.

Difficult for a starving vampire to be rational. Eventually, blind appetite drove her to seize a victim without conscience and – above all – without illusions of love. Only then did she enter a calmer state.

Karl sent letters that revealed only vague information; they'd found Andreas in England. He gave the address. Charlotte felt nothing; her only thought was, *Thank God it's not Cambridge.* And she wrote back, but there was little to say; Karl wouldn't want to hear about Violette, or how concerned about her Charlotte still was. The only thing she truly wanted to say could not be said, because of the way they had parted.

I miss you.

Ilona and Stefan visited her, but Charlotte found reasons to send them away. Ilona was too unsympathetic, mocking; Stefan too kind. She couldn't bear company, nor could she bear being in the house alone.

For a long time, she dared not seek news of Violette. To hear that Violette had stopped dancing, that she'd gone mad or even died – because Charlotte had indulged in one moment of sensual pleasure – would be unbearable.

At last, unable to tolerate the lonely chalet any longer, Charlotte moved to a hotel in Salzburg. Built high on the Mönchsberg ridge, the lovely building was swathed in ivy, and gave a breathtaking view across the town and river valley to the mountains opposite. From her window she could see the almond-green house of the Ballet Janacek. Still she kept away. Numb, she simply waited, read newspapers, listened to gossip in coffee houses.

The Ballet Janacek was still in business. Occasionally she saw a dancer or musician in the town, but never Violette. The temptation to seek her out grew stronger, but Charlotte resisted. To relive it all, to be rejected again – no, it would finish her.

One morning, as she sat in a dark café in the Getreidegasse – coffee steaming untouched in front of her – she saw a newspaper announcement that shook her to the soul.

Ballet Janacek announced the debut of a brand new ballet, *Dans le Jardin,* in Vienna. *Prima ballerina assoluta* – Violette Lenoir.

Relief consumed Charlotte like a flash of fire. She dropped the paper and walked out, giving the startled waiter a lavish tip.

And now she was in Vienna on opening night. She sat at the front of the balcony, no longer aware of the miasma of perfume and body heat around her. All her attention was on the stage, her breath held.

The curtains unfurled on darkness. A curved blue line

glimmered... shafts of light shone from clouds... music rolled like thunder. And in one of the most glorious solos Charlotte had ever seen, a muscular male dancer portrayed God's creation of the world.

Green light shimmered through a scrim, creating the illusion of a garden. The Tree of Knowledge was rooted in the earth and stretched its branches up to heaven; under its foliage, God brought the beasts to life. Delightful, the *corps de ballet* dressed as rabbits and birds and deer; but a sinister undertow was developing. There was menace in the modern angularity of the music, the eerie use of lighting. A story everyone knew – but why had Violette chosen it?

Then God beckoned Adam and Eve to life. Two pale sinuous figures in flesh-coloured body-stockings – shocking to see them apparently naked beneath trails of ivy. Charlotte stared at the female dancer's yellow hair. Why wasn't Violette dancing the main role?

Most shocking of all – God was portrayed as a leaping, clowning trickster. A dream figure from a William Blake watercolour, with the malicious intelligence of Puck. The dancer was magnificently believable. He took not so much pride as glee in his creation, placing the Tree in the Garden of Eden as a deliberately cruel temptation.

Then came the Serpent.

Even before the creature slid onstage to weave magic around the sweet blonde Eve, Charlotte was dizzy with anticipation. Violette appeared all in black, sinuous, glittering, full of energy. A world away from the innocence of Giselle. Incredibly evil and seductive, she courted Eve with the allure of a vampire. At the same time, she achieved the incredible feat of making the Serpent sympathetic, God the malevolent one.

Take the apple. Eat. Make a fool of God.

Violette in this role was completely in her element.

Charlotte actually shut her eyes at times, thinking, *This is impossibly daring. I dread to think how it will be received.*

The sin was committed and the Fall began. In a spectacular change of lighting, the softness of the Garden turned to harsh spiky angles, as angry and modern as the music. God's pleasure in his creation became implacable rage... *But you put the Tree there*, Violette told him with expressive hands and eyes. *You made me, too.*

God crushed her underfoot. The audience gasped.

With a pointing finger he'd created Adam and Eve; with a pointing finger he drove them from the Garden. Now the *corps de ballet* became fiery angels set to guard the gates of Eden, and Man began his eternal exile.

No happy ending to this tragedy. The end was the beginning; the whole history of mankind unfurled from this moment like an infinite tapestry on the red darkness... down through the ages... to the present, to the sinners sitting in this theatre.

Utter silence greeted the curtain. Charlotte guessed how the audience would react; their disapproval had been tangible throughout. When she was proved right, though, she was furious. The polite applause that finally broke out failed to mask the babble of people surging rudely towards the exits.

Technically the ballet was breathtaking. Emotionally, too. But it was wrong. There was a taint of insanity on it. It was too serious, too full of pain. Blasphemous.

Charlotte made her way into the foyer, feeling stunned. *Dans le Jardin* was glorious... but it was the creation of a deranged mind, too far ahead of its time. She sensed disaster.

She pushed impatiently towards the outer doors, famished. Anger made her thirsty... as did love, paradoxically. *Must hurry or I'll take one of these sneering idiots where they stand...*

"*Entschuldigen Sie bitte, gnädige Frau,*" said a voice behind her, "are you not Charlotte Neville?"

Charlotte turned as if jerked by a chain, and looked into a face she'd never seen before. A man in his mid-fifties gazed at her over black-rimmed spectacles. He had a beautiful, sharp-boned face, a shock of soft grey hair, bushy iron-grey eyebrows.

"I think you've made a mistake," she said thinly.

"Forgive me, but you look so very like the daughter of an old friend. Or rather, I should say, like his wife."

His words swept Charlotte abruptly into a different world. The notion that this man had met her mother transfixed her.

"George and Annette Neville," he said, then shook his head. "I'm sorry, I'm being foolish. If you say I've made a mistake..."

"Did you know my – Mrs Neville well?"

He smiled, more confident now she'd given herself away. It was a very warm smile. "Hardly at all, I regret to say. My name is Josef Stern. I'm delighted to meet you, for the second time. I don't expect you to remember me. I met your father at a scientific conference before the War, you see, and a few months later while I was in England he kindly invited me and my sister Lisl to visit his house. We spent a delightful afternoon. You were barely two years old at the time, but I remember you distinctly. An enchanting child, so shy."

Charlotte was suddenly her human self again. Her mouth softened. "That would explain why I don't know you, Herr Stern. I'm astonished you recognise me."

"You're so like your mother. I recall that Mrs Neville was expecting her third child at the time…"

"That was Madeleine," Charlotte said quietly. "Mother died soon after her birth."

"I know, I heard. I was so very sorry."

"But what was she like, my mother? I was so small when she died, I barely remember her."

The man held her gaze. His eyes were almost black, very kind. "Shall we escape this crowd and stroll together? You will call me Josef, please. I hate formality."

"So do I," she said.

Outside, in the cool air of the street, they walked through avenues of trees and into a public garden. Charlotte forgot her thirst.

"She was very like you," Josef went on. "She had a glow about her. Hospitable, but rather aloof and fragile; the sort of person of whom they say, 'She was not meant for this world.' And I fell hopelessly in love with her, of course."

Charlotte was shocked, but his smile made her laugh. "Well, if you only met her once, I still envy you."

"I understand," he said. "So sad, hardly to have known her; such a lovely woman. But many years have passed since then. Your father, is he well?"

"I – I'm afraid I haven't seen him for two years." Odd that she was compelled to be honest, but the stranger felt like an old friend. "I heard his health is not good… but there are certain reasons why I can't go home."

Josef raised a hand. "Please," he said. "I don't mean to intrude. Shall we talk of something else?"

"If you don't mind."

"Very well. How did you like the ballet?"

"I thought it was wonderful. It's a shame the audience were too stuffy to realise it."

Josef chuckled. "I am inclined to agree. Also a shame Madame Lenoir took the theme so literally, however."

"I don't think it was at all literal!"

"No, no, but she lifted the story we all know straight off the page. She didn't look behind it, to other versions, the derivations. For example, did you know that the myth of Eve's creation from Adam's rib may have been a misinterpretation of an ancient relief?"

"No," Charlotte said, fascinated.

"The relief shows the goddess Anath, watching her lover Mot murder his twin Aliyan. The goddess is mistaken for Eve and Mot for Yahweh, who is actually driving his dagger beneath Aliyan's fifth rib, not removing the sixth."

"Indeed? Why are we never told these things?"

"It wouldn't do to disbelieve the official version, would it? Still – of course she had to use the familiar creation story, or no one would have understood."

"Are you a scholar of Hebrew mythology, Herr – Josef?"

"Oh, it is only an interest; I moved from science to psychology, which seems to have helped me understand nothing at all about life…" For a moment he stared at the ground, lost in thought. Then he glanced sideways at her and smiled. "Still, let us be glad we have people like Lenoir to make great art out of sorrow."

They walked on through the park, at ease with each other. Charlotte found Josef's company soothing; he was courteous yet outspoken, reminding her of Karl. In fact his face captivated her, because Josef was so very much as Karl might have looked – had he stayed mortal, and grown older. *And then I would never have met him,* she thought with a stab of pain.

"My dear, you looked unwell for a moment," he said. "Or unhappy?"

"No, it's nothing. Memories."

"You know, I neglected to ask if you are married."

Without thinking, she said, "I don't know," and was astonished when he burst out laughing.

"Of all the things to be unsure of! 'Do you believe in God?', 'Will it rain next Thursday?', 'Are you married?' – 'Oh, I'm not quite sure.' Forgive me, I've no right to make a joke of it. Perhaps you are separated from your husband and don't want to be."

"Something like that."

"And it's none of my business, anyway."

She half-smiled, to show she wasn't offended. "And you?"

"I never married. The only girl I loved turned me down, which was very sensible of her; I could never have been faithful, and would have made her terribly unhappy."

They stopped under a tree. Streetlights made the foliage a web of radiance. "At least you are honest," said Charlotte, looking up at him.

He paused, as if tempted to kiss her; and the awful thing was that she didn't mind, that she liked him very much. So easy to let this go further. It would be wonderful and comforting; he would make her feel safe, cherished. But that treacherous moment would come when she could no longer resist the thirst... she saw Violette's stare of betrayal and horror, heard Karl's sad voice, "*Never look at their faces or ask their names...*"

Oh God, but she was thirsty and he was so close and there was no one near...

With a great wrench she turned her face aside and pulled away.

"Forgive me," he said sadly. "I was too forward. Such a fool, I forget I am no longer twenty-five. It is not to be, is it?"

"No," she said. "Not because I don't like you..."

"My dear, no need to explain." He looked wistfully at her. "You are so young and I am so old..."

"Nonsense," Charlotte said softly. "You're not old, and I'm not as young as I look. But I can't, because... I'm afraid I might hurt you."

A quick, indulgent smile. "How could you possibly –" Josef stopped. She was looking straight at him, letting him *see*. The glassy light of her skin, the tips of her canines.

He went deathly pale and took a step backwards, swaying. She thought he was about to faint or run away, and she didn't want that. Taking his arm, she guided him to a bench and sat beside him. A statue of Mozart gazed benignly down at them.

"Don't be afraid of me," she said, clasping his hands. "Please. I let you see what I am because I trust you. I didn't want to deceive you – and I think you are the exceptional kind of man who can accept it. Can you?"

The stiff revulsion in his eyes began to soften. Warmth returned to his clammy hands. "Oh my God," he said, taking a deep breath. "*Mein Gott.*"

"Forgive me, Josef. I didn't mean to shock you. I simply couldn't lie."

"Such creatures exist, then. Ones who are not quite alive, but prey on the living. And if we'd grown close, would you have killed me – like a black widow spider eating her mate?"

"I might have done."

"There cannot be a pleasanter way to die," he murmured.

"That's what they all think," she said drily, "until it's too late."

He blanched. "How strange. My friend's little daughter." He looked intently at her, frowning in curiosity. "But how did this happen to you?"

"It would take forever to explain."

"Does your family know?"

"Yes. That's why I can't go home." Suddenly she no longer felt that this mattered. She stood and began to walk away, but he followed.

"This is terrible," he said. "Don't go. I'm not afraid. Let us talk."

Her thirst was growing too strong. "Please, you're in danger if you don't let me go."

"Charlotte," he said with sudden intensity, "come home with me."

"I told you, I can't."

"Not for that reason." The sadness in his face was something far deeper than horror or infatuation. And she knew her instinct had been right; Josef did possess the calm intellect to accept her. "I believe you won't hurt me; we will just be friends, yes? But please. There is a reason."

Without knowing why, Charlotte gave in and went with him. Fatalistic curiosity took over.

They reached a dark cobbled courtyard, a stone staircase leading up to a flat. Inside, the low-ceilinged rooms were crammed with furniture and books. A miasma of sickness lay on the place.

Josef asked Charlotte to wait in a parlour and closed the door;

she heard voices, Josef asking someone to leave, the front door closing. Then he came back and said, "I've sent the nurse away."

He took her into a stuffy bedroom. In the bed lay a woman with greying hair coiled about a lined face, eyes open, mouth gaping at the ceiling.

"Who is she?" Charlotte whispered.

"My sister, Lisl," said Josef. She glanced at him but he looked away, trying to hide his tears.

"What's wrong with her?"

"A deterioration of the brain," he said. "Premature senility. Lisl is only a year older than me. First there were little lapses in memory, changes in her personality. Eventually she could not feed or dress herself and would cry when I left her alone. Now she does not even recognise me. She has no life. She simply exists, and her lungs are failing too. She's not my Lisl any more."

"Can nothing be done?"

"Nothing," he said. Tears ran down his face. "And I think it would be better if she were dead. I only wish I had the courage to do it myself."

Charlotte stared at him, horrified. "You cannot be asking me..."

"Yes, if it will be painless," he said. "And peaceful. Will it?"

Her instinctive horror vanished almost as it appeared, only a remnant of human emotion. "Yes. But how can you trust me like this?"

He didn't reply. Charlotte moved to the bed. She did not want to do this, but knew she was going to regardless; her fangs slid out of their own accord and the thirst was like a weight falling through her. No going back. *Why not*, she thought, *when they are both in such misery?*

She bent down and took the woman's thin wrist. The skin was loose and dry but the pulse thudded fast against her thumb.

Charlotte hesitated, gazing down at the face concealing a fragmented mind. Lisl's expression was tragic in its vacancy, a pearl of saliva poised on her slack lip, a stale smell rising from her even though she was kept clean and her hair was neat. The little violets embroidered around the neck of her white nightdress... every detail shimmered through a haze of tears.

And Charlotte thought, *What if I could make her a vampire*

now? Would her mind and youth return? Or would she be frozen like this forever?

She lifted the hand to her lips, then changed her mind and folded it gently across the woman's chest. *Not the wrist*, she thought. *There is no need to be impersonal; I am not afraid of your sickness, Lisl.*

At the last sharp moment, Lisl was as desirable as any mortal, her blood as rich and luscious. Charlotte was almost delirious with hunger, yet she leaned down as gently as she could. *Did I meet you once, when I was a child? I don't remember.*

For a second the woman's cloudy eyes caught hers. The slack mouth moved. Charlotte seized the last spark of awareness, saying with all her soul, *Don't be afraid...*

"Is there anything you wish to say to her?" Charlotte said.

"Why?" Josef said thickly.

"Because someone killed my sister Fleur, who wasn't ill but young and strong. I never had the chance to tell her all the things I'd failed to say..."

"My God," he whispered. "No. It is all said..." But he clasped his sister's other hand and bent his head against her fingers, murmuring unintelligible words.

Then she slid her hands into the neck of the nightdress, and bit gently into the woman's throat.

Memories rushed through her in a stream of vermilion light; Lisl, young and laughing, and Charlotte, hardly out of babyhood, being bounced on her round firm knees, while her father and a brown-haired young Josef smiled at them –

Gone. Salt-richness filled her mouth, divine liquid surging through her throat and stomach and veins... all sorrows quenched in a violent spasm of ecstasy.

It was over in a sigh. Lisl's heart gave up without argument, then Charlotte let her fangs retract and lifted her head, licking blood from her lips, letting the last sip slide down her throat; tidying away the evidence. All she felt was relief.

When she looked up, she found Josef staring at her with the same sick look Violette had given her; the sudden shock of understanding, the horror that she herself had experienced when she'd first realised the truth about Karl.

Now Josef saw, under the soft feminine layers of her clothes and skin and hair, a hard, luminous core that craved blood and fed without conscience. More than evil; simply untouchable, impossible to grasp.

Charlotte rose, eager to be away from her victim – and from Josef. "I must go," she said, glancing back to see him pulling the sheet over his sister's face. She walked on through the front door and down the stairs, but he caught her up in the courtyard.

"She's at peace," he said. His cheeks were tear-streaked, but she was taken aback to see that the stiff horror in his face had softened. "I've no idea what to say, but I must say something. I've done a terrible thing, yet I don't feel it to be terrible. Lisl is at peace. Thank you."

"Don't thank me. You may regret it later, and hate me."

He shook his head. "Never. Tonight has changed everything for me. Whatever you are, Charlotte, I hope you'll visit me again."

"Why?" She looked at him, aware of an affinity between them that lay beyond logic or analysis.

"How can I be content to bury myself in dead mythology, after living mythology has revealed itself to me? How can I feel anything for Lamia, succubus, incubus, Lilith and her demon children or all the angels of heaven, when I have met a real being who is richer and stranger than anything on the dry page of a book?"

"Do you want to write me into a book, a thesis?"

"It's tempting, but no, no more than I'd put a bird of prey in a glass case," he said with a wry look. He took her right hand, and kissed it twice; first the back, then the palm, as Karl had often done… The gesture made her shiver. "If ever I can help you in return –"

"Even though you know what I am?"

His lips thinned in a sad smile. One more minute and she could have fallen in love with him; even after Karl, even after Violette. It seemed she fell all too easily.

"You have been so kind to us," he said. "Even kinder than I could have dreamed, no?"

"One thing," she said. "If ever you see my father again, don't tell him you've seen me. Goodbye, Josef."

"Never say goodbye to an Austrian. The phrase is *Auf wiedersehen*."

* * *

Violette was alive, healthy, hard at work; Charlotte was desperately relieved that her attack had caused no apparent harm. Soon, though, her initial relief turned sour.

Dans le Jardin had nothing but bad reviews. The ballet disturbed and confused its audience; critics universally loathed it. Churches called for it to be banned.

The work was accused of being too modern, too simplistic, obscene, grotesque, a waste of Violette Lenoir's huge talent. It proved the folly of a woman trying to replace the great Janacek. Yet the worst accusation was that it was too serious. The mood of these times was one of frivolity; Violette had tackled a theme too dark and disturbing.

"Lenoir was pupil of Pavlova's but will never be as great as her teacher because she lacks warmth," one critic wrote pompously. "She is a superb actress but it is an *act*; her emotions do not come from the heart."

You blind idiots, Charlotte thought in fury. *Her dancing is completely from her heart. Her coldness stems from her pain. It's self-protection!*

One day, in more enlightened times, *Dans le Jardin* might be revered; but now it was a disaster. At every performance, Charlotte was disheartened by shrinking audiences. Once the public decided to hate the ballet, nothing would move them to love it.

Now Violette was newsworthy again; the Ballet Janacek faced ruin.

The tour was cancelled halfway through, and the company returned to Salzburg. Charlotte retreated to her hotel, thinking of Violette alone in her flat across the river; imagining the disappointment and worry she was enduring. And she longed to go to her...

The following day, as she sat reading in her hotel room, Charlotte felt a wave of heat scamper over her. A human approaching. She threw aside her book, knowing who it was even before she heard light footsteps in the corridor. Opening the door with undignified haste, she found Violette standing there with her gloved fist raised, about to knock.

Charlotte didn't know whether to laugh or cry. She did one sensible thing: refrained from throwing her arms around the dancer. They stood and looked at each other; Violette unsmiling, unreadable as always.

"It's so lovely to see you," Charlotte said at last. "Come in. How are you?"

Violette walked in, not replying. Her coat was deep blue, trimmed with black fur. She looked around the room, went to the window and stared out.

"I didn't think I'd ever see you again," Charlotte said, subdued. "Won't you take off your coat?"

Violette turned and gave her a long, hostile look.

"I won't touch you," said Charlotte. "I swear. Please. You're in no danger." Then Violette hesitantly took off her coat and hat and laid them on the bed. Underneath she wore a lavender dress with silk roses on the shoulder. No jewellery.

Charlotte said, "How did you know I was here?"

"I know you've been in Salzburg for weeks, and at every performance."

"Why have you come to me now?"

"I wish I knew," Violette said abruptly. "I tried to stay away but I couldn't help myself."

And nothing's changed, Charlotte thought helplessly. "I loved *Dans le Jardin*."

"I'm so glad." Violette gave an ironic smile. "It's a shame no one else did. It came about because of you, you know."

"How?"

"After you..." The ballerina unconsciously rubbed her collarbone. "After what you did to me, I went out of my mind for a time. A sort of creative frenzy. It was very strange... not pleasant. *In the Garden* was the result."

Charlotte found herself laughing. All at once it was hard to be polite. "Shall I drink your blood again, to repeat the effect? Is that why you're here? I should have asked for royalties."

"For all the good it would do," said Violette, eyes narrowing. "Ballet Janacek's finished. I put everything we had into that ballet, and lost it all. Doubtless I can find another position, and so can my dancers, but what about the rest of my people? I care about them, even if I seem not to. They are everything to me."

"I'm sorry. If I'm meant to feel guilty, I do."

"No, I didn't come here to blame you!" Violette exclaimed. "I blame only myself. *Jardin* was an insane project. I was insane; unfortunately, no one dared tell me."

"But the ballet was wonderful!" said Charlotte. "It was too progressive, that's all. You know that."

"I don't know what my life has come to," said Violette, "when the only person to whom I can admit that my heart is broken – is you." She sat on the arm of a chair, turning her back. Charlotte left her to cry for a few minutes. She found a handkerchief in Violette's coat pocket and offered it, careful not to touch her.

"Would you like a drink?"

"No. I've been drinking too much."

Charlotte fetched a glass of water. "This is what I meant." She gave her the glass, leaned on the chair back. "Your company isn't finished. There's a simple way to save it."

"What?"

"Put on *Swan Lake*."

"With what? I told you, we're bankrupt!"

"I'll give you the money."

"I couldn't possibly take it."

"Pay me back later, then. It doesn't matter. And I'm not offering out of guilt; I can't bear to see you fail because of the public's stupidity! For God's sake, will you stop being so stubborn? You'll drive me mad!"

She grasped Violette's wrist. The dancer glared. Charlotte loosed her, but as her hand slid away, Violette caught and held it, digging her nails in. "I want to thank you, but I can't. This is like selling my soul to the Devil... Where does your money come from?"

"It's mostly Karl's, actually," Charlotte breathed. "It's very easy for us..."

"To steal?"

"We don't need to. He has property, investments... and it's hard to stop people giving us gifts of their own free will."

"After falling in love with your beguiling demon eyes? It sounds like fraud to me."

"You don't really think I'm from the Devil, do you?"

"I don't know, Charlotte. All I know is that when you left me, I went mad. I give in. I'll do anything to save my ballet, but what's the price? My soul, my blood? Take it. I belong to the Devil, anyway."

Charlotte longed to embrace the slender woman and console her... but even as she denied her nature, she couldn't trust herself. With the memory of Violette's disgust fresh in her mind, she would still give anything to taste the burning jewels of her blood...

Again, with effort, she held back.

"I promise," she said, "I will never prey on you again. We'll be friends, that's all. I'll prove you can trust me."

"I wanted us to be more than friends. That was my downfall." Violette stood and went to a mirror, trying to compose her face. "Friends, yes. Let's draw a line between us, like a business agreement. This Karl; he's your lover, I take it?"

A pang went through Charlotte from head to foot. "At the moment, I'm not sure."

"Is that why you're so unhappy? He drew you into the kingdom of the undead with his fatal kiss, then deserted you?"

"Not exactly. We have terribly complicated lives, just like humans. And you won't turn into a vampire, Violette; it's not that easy."

"But I already am one," said the ballerina, staring at herself in the mirror.

Charlotte started, wondering what she had missed. "No, you're not."

"All women are bloodsuckers. That's what my father told me."

"You didn't believe him, did you?"

"Part of me always has. It's a form of obsession, isn't it? You know something is ridiculous, yet you cannot stop thinking it."

"But why would he say such a thing? That's cruel."

"I don't think my poor father was in any state to realise he was being cruel."

"Tell me what happened," said Charlotte.

"I don't want to. It's sickening." Violette roved the room like a cat unable to settle. She was fragmenting before Charlotte's eyes, her outer shell falling to reveal a raw, defenceless creature who'd never breathed the air before.

"I may not be human, but I can still understand..."

"If I tell you, it's only because you *aren't* human." Violette sank onto a corner of the bed. How like Giselle she looked; exhausted, almost destroyed, yet heart-breakingly beautiful. "The awful thing is that, because of you, I now know my father wasn't mad after all…" She trailed off, then began, her voice light and rapid as if to skim over the pain. "From the outside, I had an ordinary middle-class life in Surrey. I was born Violet Birch – a ballerina needs a more exotic name, of course. My mother had no more children. My birth was difficult; I tore her, and she was never really well again… Nothing was spelled out, you see. There were only hints and mysteries. So that's what I remember of childhood; not understanding, and feeling frightened.

"My father wasn't the easiest of men. He behaved in extremes. Sometimes smothering us with affection, at other times cold and sarcastic. He scared me out of feeling any fondness for him. My mother refused to share his bed, and sometimes at night I heard them quarrelling, my father trying to persuade her into some awful act she didn't want. All I knew was that it sounded dark and terrifying. She would say, 'What if I had another child? It would kill me. We agreed!' He'd say, 'I know, but I'm your husband, I'm only human!' And she'd shout back, 'Do you want me to die?'"

Charlotte put in, "That must have been horrifying. Especially to a child."

"Well, I became convinced that my mother's poor health and unhappiness was *my* fault. I don't believe my father ever forced her, but some mornings they'd be in a foul mood, snapping at each other and at me. Then my father would feel guilty and apologise to her – almost wheedling, while she sat as cold as a nun. And this, I thought, was 'love'.

"We presented a conventional front, and did all the usual things like church-going. My parents appeared an ordinary, quiet couple. But… I'm sure mine was not the only home full of hidden tension, resentment, unspoken dangers.

"My mother accused my father of going with other women. I was old enough by then to suspect what their quarrels were about. He would deny it, but then blame her – admitting his guilt, in effect. They tore each other to pieces with this toxic mixture of possessiveness and rejection. And all I learned of sex was that it was dangerous and wicked, something men used to torment women.

"I was eleven, I think, when it happened. Father came home late one night in a terrible state, blood all over him. First we thought he was drunk and had got into a fight. A neighbour brought the doctor. But Father was so distraught he confessed everything, and no one could silence him. Mother pushed me out of the room, too late. I'd heard most of it and I heard the rest through the door.

"A woman had picked him up in the street, he said, and taken him to a hotel. She seduced him and he couldn't resist, even though he was disgusted with himself. She was a demon, he kept saying. 'A demon, a demon.' She insisted on climbing on top." Violette shuddered. "And when it was over she wasn't pleased with him, so she leaned down and bit him – God, it's so hard to say. She bit right through his male organs."

As she spoke, Charlotte thought, *Ilona*...

"I was spared any more details, thank goodness, but I gather the mutilation was permanent. But all these ravings in front of our stunned neighbour and the doctor! My mother was devastated. She rushed out of the room, saw me and knew I'd heard everything. I think in sheer rage, and grief that she'd failed to protect my innocence, she took it out on me; slapped me, shook me violently, shouting, 'This is what lust does! It's sent from Satan to destroy us!'

"So those were my first lessons in physical love. Blood, pain, terror and rejection.

"Mother died a few weeks later. Shame killed her; she went into a decline, stopped eating, succumbed to pneumonia. My father was ill, too. Partly from his injury, but mainly in his mind. The attack unhinged him.

"He decided he and I were both evil. 'This black hair,' he would say, pointing from his head to mine, 'it's the mark of Satan. We're from the Devil; we drove your mother into her grave. How can we save your soul, Vi?'

"I can't express how terrified I was. He talked endlessly about evil and demons; often he locked me in my room for days. He got so deep into my head, I thought I was damned, that I'd wilfully destroyed my mother. And he..." Her voice gave out. She twisted her fingers together and went on, in a whisper of revulsion.

"There's worse. Sometimes he came into my room at night, sleepwalking, and exposed himself. He'd stand by my bed, saying nothing. How was I meant to react? I'd shut my eyes tight until he left, but I couldn't avoid glimpses of... the injury. There was almost nothing left. A stump of flesh, scars..."

She put a hand to her lips, her eyes blank. Then, her voice level, she went on, "By the time the doctors took him to an asylum, I was nearly as mad as he was.

"I was sent to live with an older cousin who had her own children and didn't really want me. Fortunately they were well off, and she was happy to send me away to ballet school. I was so lucky. I poured all my energy into dancing and shut the past away. Oh, I was tough on myself... but even so, I couldn't erase the nightmares completely.

"Father died in the asylum. I was fifteen when I last saw him, and he was still talking about the demon who'd mutilated him. 'She was a lamia,' he said. 'A temptress, an instrument of Satan. All woman are the same inside!'

"His words made me ill. I said, 'Not my mother.'

"'No, she was saint,' he said, as if he'd forgotten the bitterness of their marriage. 'The Devil made me defile her, and she gave birth to a demon.' He pointed at me. 'That's what killed her, Violet. *You*!' Then he lunged and tried to strangle me. The attendants restrained him before he did any real harm. I never saw him again."

Charlotte, reeling, struggled to find words. "Gods, I'm so sorry. But he was ill; surely you know that nothing he said was true."

Violette's eyes flashed open, accusing. "It wasn't you in some disguise, was it? My father swore she had teeth like a wolf and sucked his blood. It would make sense; you destroyed him, and now you've come for me." The dancer's face paled to greenish-white.

"It was not me, I swear," said Charlotte. "Did he give a description of her?"

"Her hair was the colour of blood. She called herself Ilona. That's all."

Charlotte closed her eyes in utter dismay. *Ilona, would you feel remorse if you heard this – or would you just laugh?* "Does it help to know that it wasn't your father's fault, either? He was the victim of a vampire. Knowing that, could you forgive him?"

Violette rushed into the bathroom and slammed the door. There was silence, then the sound of water running. Charlotte waited a minute, and went after her.

She found Violette leaning over the sink, splashing water on her face. "Are you all right?"

"I felt faint. I thought I was going to be sick, but I can't. I've eaten nothing today."

"You must eat. There's no sense in punishing yourself. Let me take you out for lunch; you'll feel better." She led Violette back into the bedroom; the dancer was passive, exhausted. "Don't you understand? None of it was your fault."

"Of course I understand! That makes it no less painful. However many times my rational mind tells me it wasn't my fault and I did nothing wrong – my inner self refuses to listen. My father's word was law. My voice is nothing."

Then, at last, Charlotte took Violette in her arms and held her. The dancer did not resist. She wrapped her slender arms around the vampire's back, dropped her head onto her shoulder, as if giving herself up to death. Her cheek felt deliciously cool against Charlotte's... and although the vampire in Charlotte longed to bite down and feel sweet hot blood pouring into her mouth, tenderness won.

"I can't love anyone, because I don't know how," said Violette. "My father warned that my true nature would come out one day. Desiring women instead of men doesn't make me feel safer, because he convinced me that women are devils. You came along to prove it."

"A sort of guardian demon?" Charlotte said.

"Yes," Violette laughed drily. "Isn't that what you are?"

"I suppose so."

"Do you know why I made you leave, that time in my flat? It wasn't because you bit me, or the shock of realising what you are; I think I already knew. It was because I let myself lose control, and I was frightened of what I felt. Disgusted."

"But you're not driving me out now? Nor running away?"

Violette shook her head. "You win," she whispered.

The dancer shed a few tears, but Charlotte remained dry-eyed, feeling hollow as they held each other. Knowing that Violette accepted her, not as a friend, but as the embodiment of her surrender to the evil side of her nature.

She gave in to Charlotte hating herself.

CHAPTER FOURTEEN

MIDNIGHT ANGELS

A Sunday evening; it seemed to Holly that she and Benedict had spent the whole day quarrelling. He wanted to send her away, but she refused to go.

"For goodness' sake, Holly, you're not safe here! You've been in danger several times. I can't risk it happening again."

"It's not safe for you, either!" Her face was hot with anger. "That's why I'm staying."

"I can't allow it. You must go to your parents'."

"Why should I be any safer there? The supernatural takes no account of distance. Besides," she added bitterly, "how would you know I wasn't consorting with Lancelyn?"

"I trust you," he growled. "How can I concentrate on the situation while I'm worrying about you?"

"What am I supposed to do with myself, a hundred miles away? Doesn't *my* worrying matter?"

Neither would back down. The parlour door was open; she noticed Andreas in the doorway, witnessing their quarrel with no hint of embarrassment. As Ben paused for breath, Andreas walked in and said lightly, "You're too hard on her, Benedict. She is only trying to protect you."

Ben glared at him. "Yes, but she can't."

"Really? Where do you think we'd be without Karl and Katerina?"

"What has that to do with Holly?" Ben said, exasperated.

Drenched by foreboding, Holly awaited the inevitable reply.

"She called them, of course."

Dismayed, she said, "Andreas! You swore you wouldn't tell him!"

He shrugged. "I am not very good at keeping promises, I'm afraid."

Ben turned almost yellow with anger, then went icily quiet. The change unsettled her. He couldn't tolerate the idea of anyone surpassing his occult skills – least of all his own wife. Knowing that, she'd resolved to keep her efforts secret.

At last he said thinly, "How could you possibly have called them?"

"I don't know," she said, flustered. "I'm not sure I did. I imitated the ritual, but nothing happened. It could be the echo of your original summoning that brought them, not me." She finished lamely, "I only wanted to help…"

"How dare you even try?" he hissed, colourless. "How dare you interfere with this?"

She had no defence against his fury. Seething, she retreated to the kitchen, only to find Katerina there with the cat in her arms. One of the new vampires stood beside her; a thin, pale woman with red hair.

Dear God, Holly thought, *is there nowhere I can escape?*

Katerina turned and looked sympathetically at her over Sam's tabby head. She said, "Your husband doesn't deserve you, my dear."

Holly stopped, keeping the table between them. "Have you been listening?"

"It's difficult not to overhear, in such a small house. He doesn't deserve your loyalty."

Holly looked stonily at her, thinking, *I want my cat back and I want you gone, all of you!* The flame-red of the new vampire's hair reminded her of Deirdre, and a horrible flashback hit her; Deirdre falling under the train… the image subsided and she let her breath go.

"Are you all right?" Katerina, with apparent concern, walked around the table and unloaded the indiscriminate Sam into Holly's arms. "If you like, I'll reassure Ben myself that I will let no one harm you. But ask yourself: is he trying to protect you, or merely to exclude you? Hard not to notice a touch of jealousy in his voice."

"Did I summon you?" Holly asked, suddenly fierce. "Or was it Benedict?"

"I'm sorry, my dear. I have absolutely no idea."

Holly glanced down at Sam, now rubbing his face against her chin in an ecstasy of affection. *This*, she thought, *after you were all over Katerina*! "Well, I don't care what my husband says or thinks. I am not leaving."

Karl found Benedict in his study; still raw from the argument, to judge by his sour demeanour.

"Must you be so uncivil your wife?" Karl said pleasantly. "She has everyone's best interests at heart. I don't know who summoned us, but it's clear she was trying to help."

Ben glowered at him. "I don't need a lecture, even from you."

"Very well, no lecture. You are right to be concerned for her; after all, why should these vampires obey you?"

Benedict stared, his expression guarded. Karl sat facing him across the study desk. A candle spilled a pool of light between them.

"Why should I justify my actions to you?" Benedict said stiffly. "Presumably you could kill me at any time, yet you haven't."

"There is a great deal you do not understand."

"I think there's a great deal that neither of us understands."

"True," said Karl. "We're both reluctant to give away secrets, but this is arrogance, which achieves nothing. I suggest we forsake our pride and talk openly."

"Well..."

"Are you afraid of me?" said Karl.

"No."

The candle burned to a stump and began sputtering in liquid wax. Karl snuffed out the flame with his fingertips. Smoke ribboned upwards, side-lit by the dull red glow of a lamp. With the eerie lamplight outlining his pale face, Karl stared at Ben from unblinking amber eyes...

After a moment Ben looked away, his posture softening. "Yes," he breathed. "Yes, of course I'm afraid. I'm not an idiot. And I know I'm out of my depth, but I'm damned if I'll let it defeat me! Why are you the only vampire I can't control?"

Karl leaned back, folding his hands on his knee. "Possibly because the others were dormant, while I was not. My question is, what gives you power over *any* vampire?"

"I thought it was the Book, but Lancelyn's got it now and I was able to subdue Simon without it. I'd like to think the power's within me. Natural aptitude honed by mental discipline." Benedict began to tell his story. He spoke flatly at first, then feeling crept into his voice and he spoke fervently of the Neophytes of Meter Theon, his dispute with his brother, his astral journeys into the realm he called Raqia.

When Benedict mentioned Holly's vision of a black grimoire in an underground passage, and their quest to find it, Karl's amazement grew.

"Why should she have that particular vision?"

"Lancelyn had a way of directing her to the result he wanted," said Ben. "How, I don't know. She can't give any rational explanation."

"I know where those tunnels are," said Karl. "I've been there, too often."

Ben's eyes grew wide as Karl told him a little about Kristian, the *Weisskalt*, and the ancient passageways beneath Parkland estate.

"I saw the Book in the cell," said Karl. "And I went back, only to find it gone. At least I know now what became of it. But I had no chance to look inside, and I'm curious."

Ben was restless with excitement now, his resentment of Karl forgotten. "There were lists of names, and scribblings in a sort of coded Latin. Lancelyn and I were working on the translation together, until the trouble started. It was only after I brought the Book here that I was able to summon Andreas. Only an experiment, the first time..."

"If Kristian's death woke vampires in the *Weisskalt*, they must have been drifting in the Ring for months. They answered your call because they were weak; other immortals were strong enough to resist. I'm not denying you have extraordinary talent..."

"Thing is, the Book itself seems to have an intrinsic hold over vampires. As if they fear it."

"I see." Karl was carefully not telling Benedict too much. "But when you speak of entering the astral world – surely you don't do so bodily?"

As far as Karl knew, only vampires could enter the Crystal Ring. A mortal taken there, on the point of death, became a vampire.

"No," said Benedict. "Only in dream form, as it were. Lancelyn describes the spirit world as subjective, a journey into the self. That's not to denigrate its importance. The microcosm contains the macrocosm; each man contains the universe within himself. But the point is that when I found Raqia – the Crystal Ring, as you call it – I knew it was *real*. Then I began to doubt that Lancelyn's spirit realm and mine were the same. I decided that mine was real, his wasn't – egotism, perhaps, but that's where the rot set in. My desire for superior knowledge clashed with his refusal to see me as equal."

Karl said, "But if the Crystal Ring is the human psyche, his ideas weren't inaccurate. I've never heard of a mortal discovering our realm. It's impossible..." He went on, half to himself, "But why should it be? If the Ring, or Raqia, is a realm of the subconscious, surely all humans have the potential to enter. Why shouldn't a highly trained mind do so consciously?"

"You mean I may not be unique?" said Ben.

Karl half-smiled. "Does that matter?"

"Yes, it does." Ben grimaced, self-mocking. "Naturally I want power that no one else possesses. Why deny it?"

"Well, you're certainly not alone in the desire."

"No. Lancelyn and I are very alike."

"Is he so terrible, your brother?"

"He was everything to me. I couldn't believe it when I learned how he was abusing his powers. He's utterly depraved, immoral; he effectively killed two of our friends! I have to seize the Order from him. He says he won't hurt Holly, but I don't trust him any more. I love her; I'd rather die than let her come to any harm. Can't you understand why I must defend myself?"

Karl regarded the earnest face under the blond hair, and felt sympathy for Ben. He was not a bad man... misguided, perhaps, but Karl was in no position to judge him.

"Assuming you wrest the Order from him, what then?"

"I'll guide us back to our proper course: the search for Wisdom. Lancelyn – before he took the wrong path – personified wisdom as a hidden goddess whom we must unveil."

"Do you believe in God?"

"I believe in higher powers that are concealed from most mortals. If that is God, yes. That's what we're looking for: complete knowledge. Enlightenment. And by the way, our quest is nothing to do with Satanism. Only the ignorant paint occultists with that brush! We are Gnostics of a sort. That's why I can't stand what Lancelyn's done with his bloody 'Hidden Temple', because it panders to all society's misconceptions."

"Very pure, your motives sound," said Karl. "But aren't you fighting evil with evil? You condemn him for murdering your friends, and yet you're happy to unleash vampires in pursuit of your goal."

Ben's eyes narrowed. *Pointless to ask*, Karl thought. *His ideals and his actions operate on different moral levels, as with most men.*

"I have no choice! Who are you to condemn me?"

"I don't condemn you," said Karl, smiling. "I was only asking."

Ben stared down at his hands. "Well, I don't know what my quest is now. Everything's changed. Raqia is real, and inhabited by..." He looked up, his eyes alight. "How did this happen to you?"

Karl didn't answer.

"Could you make me like you?" No inflexion in Ben's voice. His gaze was candid and steady.

"No. And I wouldn't if I could."

Surprisingly, Ben said, "Well, I don't want it. I might change too much. I need to understand this from a human perspective before I move on to anything... higher."

"You seem sanguine about the idea of becoming unhuman."

"Lancelyn convinced me that if we follow the path to Wisdom, we can and will become gods."

"Do you believe him?" Karl, to his own surprise, found himself enjoying Ben's company.

"Not quite. But that doesn't mean it can't happen."

"What do you think Lancelyn is trying to do, if he's abandoned Wisdom?"

"God knows. He's shut me out. Offering drugs, sex, occult thrills and blackmail to the rich – well, there's only one crude goal, power and wealth," Ben said with contempt. "But I don't underestimate him. I don't believe he's found vampires of his own; I think it's another mind trick. However, if he *has* got something real, some entity that attacked Andreas – I take the danger seriously."

"And you want us to protect you."

"More than that; to help me defeat him. I can't sit and wait for his next move. I'm seizing the initiative. First, we retrieve the Book. I can't let him use it against us."

Karl stood and placed his cold hand over Benedict's. Ben gave a start.

"Very well, let us find the Book," he said. "And we'll help you, for the time being – but it can't go on forever. You cannot keep a coven of vampires, Benedict."

"I'm sorry," Ben whispered in the darkness of their bed. "So sorry, Holly. Can you forgive me?"

As he gathered her in his arms and held her warm and safe, in absolute, unconditional tenderness, Holly forgave him. They made love with intensity, a crucible to melt every angry word. Afterwards they lay at peace together, healed.

"I'm staying," she said firmly. "You need me."

"I know."

"I only want to help."

"I know."

"I'm being practical. You can't leave Maud to run the shop, not after she gave Lancelyn our house key. You need me to keep an eye on her."

"Yes. You're absolutely right..." He was quiet, then added, "And, of course, I need you to keep an eye on Lancelyn."

She stiffened. "No, don't ask that! I took an oath not to use my psychic gift against him. If I tried, he'd know. I can't, any more than I could spy on you for him."

She felt a jolt go through Ben's body, as if she'd speared a nerve. "Ben, I told you I would never contemplate it. Trust me."

"I do," he said. "We can trust each other."

"Maud, I'll watch happily. Not Lancelyn."

He kissed her, conciliatory. "Not Lancelyn," he agreed. "You're right, it would be unfair."

She relaxed, relieved of a horrible burden. "Thank you."

"No." His mouth was by her ear, yet his voice sounded distant and hard in the darkness. "Lancelyn is mine to deal with."

* * *

The next day, Holly went to the bookshop with a sense of purpose; to purge Maud's muddy swirl of lies. There would be a new start.

Holly wasn't looking forward to the task. Maud was difficult; not stupid, exactly, but somehow on a different plane, naïve yet cunning, like a shell inhabited by different personalities that she presented to suit the occasion. With customers she was efficient, over-friendly and gossipy, but normal. With those she envied, such as Ben and Holly, she was a compulsive actress. A breathless admirer, or a wheedling child, but never natural. Holly also had to suffer her bouts of holier-than-thou superiority. Today, though, Maud's fakery would end.

As Maud arrived and hung up her coat, Holly marched her into the small, dark office.

"Tell me the truth," said Holly. "You entered our cottage and stole the Book yourself, didn't you? You didn't innocently lend Lancelyn a key; you knew what you were doing!"

The girl's face dropped; she looked indignant, then frightened. Hugging herself defensively, she tilted her head, her protuberant eyes glazed with wronged innocence. Then her manner changed, lips pouting. "Yes," she said defiantly. "Yes, I did it."

"Why? What did Lancelyn say to you?"

Behind the wide orbs, Holly saw a prickly ego that distinguished between right and wrong only as they affected Maud herself.

"He told me my psychic abilities were the most remarkable he'd ever seen, and that if I helped him, I could join the Order."

Holly bit back the obvious retort: *You idiot, can't you see Lancelyn was using you?* She kept her tone neutral. "My husband seems to think you barely know him."

"Oh, I've known him a long time," Maud said smugly. "He often comes into the shop when Mr Grey isn't here. He says you want to keep me out of the Order because you are jealous of my spiritual talents."

Holly gasped, almost laughing. "He said that?"

"Lancelyn said Mr Grey had stolen a certain Book, and that if I returned it to him, he'd reward me. I've been in Lancelyn's house. He told me about a secret Temple that you and Mr Grey know nothing about. He said he'd make me a special disciple."

"Good God, Maud, you believed him?" Holly shook her head. "Don't you know what they do at the Hidden Temple?"

"It's secret until you join," the girl said archly.

"It isn't like the real Order, it's –" Awful images surged up of naïve Maud being abused. "When you met Lancelyn, did he ever try to – touch you?"

She dreaded the answer. Holly had thought Lancelyn so pure and honest when he preached unrestrained sexuality to his followers. His teachings had seemed natural, not sinful. But after Deirdre's ugly revelations about the Hidden Temple, Holly no longer knew what to think. His noble philosophy was no more than a lace cloth over a swirling, sordid pit.

Maud responded with a doll-blank stare, as if she had no idea what Holly meant. "He said it's your fault people make fun of me for saying I'm psychic. Why is it all right for you, and not for me? Why do you hate me, Mrs Grey?"

"I don't hate you," Holly said, dismayed. "Lancelyn can be very persuasive. I should know. I don't blame you for being taken in; I'm angry because you were disloyal on purpose, and now you stand here telling me how clever you are!"

Maud stubbornly refused to acknowledge Holly's words. "You're jealous of me, Mrs Grey."

"No," Holly said, infuriated. "You couldn't join the Order because you were unsuitable."

"Unsuitable, how? Because I happen to be a good Christian? Lancelyn said my gifts bring me closer to God. There's no conflict between the Church and the Order."

"No. It's because you're too empty-headed and devious to see the Order as anything but a status symbol to boast about!" Holly knew insulting Maud was not going to help, but she was too angry to stop. "You flaunt your piety in the same way, because you'll simply do anything to be noticed. I feel a little sorry for you, but the fact remains you broke into our house, and lied. Ben should have dismissed you."

"Oh, he wouldn't do that." Chilling nastiness entered Maud's tone. "He needs me. He says he needs a real woman. No, if anyone desired to *touch* me, it wasn't Lancelyn but the younger Mr Grey.

He always said nice things when he brought me into the office and locked the door..."

"Stop it!" Holly cried. She felt blood rush from her head in a wave of sickness. It couldn't be true – but the insinuation was a stab of doubt, like poison. "How dare you insult Ben with such an accusation?"

"It's easy to call someone a liar, Mrs Grey, but it doesn't prove I am one," Maud said blandly. She was right – and that gave her undeserved, terrible power. Suddenly she looked utterly malevolent.

"My husband would never touch a creature like you," Holly said with icy disdain.

"Why don't you telephone and ask him, Mrs Grey?"

Yes, prove her wrong now – but Holly stared at the black mouthpiece sitting on its stalk on the desk, and knew she couldn't. She had a brief vision of slapping Maud, hard, and sacking her on the spot – but wasn't that what Maud wanted, to be centre stage in a melodrama?

Holly would not give her the satisfaction.

"Don't be ridiculous." Her heart was lurching, but she spoke sternly to put Maud back in her place. "Do you like your job?"

"Yes, Mrs Grey."

"Well, then, I suggest you get on with it. And if you're thinking of crying to Lancelyn – remember that I know him far better than you. You might actually be in danger from him. Don't you realise that?"

Maud had the grace to look scared then, and spent the rest of the day in sulky silence. Superficially, Holly had won.

The next day, Maud was bright and over-eager to please, as if nothing had happened.

But... she'd forced the toxic needle of doubt under Holly's skin. Ludicrous, obscene, the idea that Ben would ever touch Maud. Holly trusted him. The trouble was that she could never be *entirely* certain... there would always be a tiny seed of suspicion, whispering *What if...?*

And Maud knew it. Hence her breezy good cheer.

All I have to do is ask Ben for the truth, Holly told herself. *But I can't. I will not dignify Maud's spiteful allegations by asking!*

And he'd deny everything, of course. That was the point.

Whatever he said, doubt would remain. So she kept silent, and if Ben noticed any change in her, he made no comment. But the secret spectre of infidelity fed on her. She remembered their love-making after the argument as the last time she'd felt absolutely sure of his integrity and love.

The loss felt like death.

Without hope of ever knowing the actual *truth*, she passed her days in slow-burning agony, dangling by a wire over a cold silver sea.

And Maud, after all, had won.

Lancelyn's house was a double-fronted red-brick villa set behind a wall in a mature but neglected garden. Tall sycamores, ashes and Scots pines loomed around the dwelling. Karl went in first, entering the Crystal Ring to melt through a wall, then letting Benedict in by the back door. The darkness felt cold, stark, deserted.

Ben entered stealthily, the whites of his eyes gleaming.

"There's no need to creep about," Karl said at normal volume. "There's no one here."

Ben started. "Are you sure? He isn't one for lots of staff, but he has a couple of servants."

"I know when there are humans nearby," said Karl. "If anyone challenges us, I'll deal with them."

Ben swallowed, as if suddenly aware he was alone with a vampire. "Well, we can't risk putting lights on," he said. "I'll use the torch."

"As you wish. I don't need it."

Ben glared, his lips thinning. "Of course you don't."

"Where do you wish to begin?"

"The study's the obvious place, I suppose." Ben directed a thin light-beam into the front hall.

Karl took a dislike to the house. It felt hollow and musty, unclean. The ceilings were too high, the floors bare. A faint leathery stink of damp hung about the place, which seemed not to have been decorated in fifty years. Dead animals stood frozen in glass cases.

A tunnel of bookshelves led into the study. As they emerged,

Karl saw a grotesque face staring at him. He froze, thinking, *Why didn't I sense this?* Then he saw that it was a torso resting on the desk. A dummy, he realised. God, what an ugly thing!

He glanced at Ben, who looked back with a grim expression – as if the dummy reminded him that Karl, too, was inhuman, and far more dangerous.

"Only a toy," said Ben. "An automaton. Damned thing produces a cigar and lights it for you; sort of rubbish Lancelyn collects. Now, if he's using the Book, it could be around here – or hidden anywhere."

As Ben searched piles of books and papers on the desk, Karl looked along the shelves. All these ancient volumes; he wished he had time to study them. There were gaps where books leaned at angles, as if many had been removed. He said softly, "Ben, I don't think the Book is here."

"What?"

"I have no sense of its presence."

Ben glared at him, dismayed. "Well, let's have a damned good look, anyway. I'm not giving up! You know a lot about this Book, don't you? Things you haven't told me."

"Not as much as I'd like." Karl wondered why he felt compelled to answer this mortal's questions. Perhaps he possessed more power than Karl would acknowledge. "The fabric of the tunnel where you found the Book was once a vampire's lair which had absorbed the echo of a thousand deaths. The victims were long gone, but left their pain and emptiness behind. Eventually they turned on their killer and destroyed him. They still wait to take revenge on any vampire who sets foot there."

"Revenge?"

"Too strong a word, perhaps. They steal back what was taken from them, as coldness steals warmth. It was as mechanical as that."

"Were you afraid?"

"Terrified." Karl gave a ghostly smile. "It was enough to bring down Kristian, the strongest vampire I've ever known. That's why the Book repels us."

"Could it kill you?" Ben asked quickly.

"Do you wish to brandish it against me like a gun?"

"No, no. I'm simply curious. Is the effect actual or psychological?"

"I wish I knew," said Karl. "When we returned to the tunnel and found the Book missing, I felt the wellspring had been torn out. So perhaps the Book was the source. I would dearly love to know."

Ben went on searching as they talked, eventually crying in exasperation. "The bloody thing's not here!"

"I did tell you."

Ben insisted on searching the whole house, and Karl helped with infinite patience. Interesting place, despite its hostile atmosphere: an academic's lair, frozen in the last century. They explored the temple where, Ben explained, the Neophytes of Meter Theon had met: a grey room, with the windows blacked out, symbols painted on the floor and artefacts strewn on a wooden altar. It seemed paltry and unimpressive to Karl. There was no sense of power here – and no sign of the Book.

Finally they returned to the hall, where Ben sank onto the stairs with his head in his hands. "I've this horrible feeling he's gone, and taken it with him."

"Where would he go?"

"I've no ruddy idea!"

"How much does he know about your vampire guests?"

"For Christ's sake, why all these questions?" Ben said furiously.

"I am trying to help you," Karl said patiently.

Benedict sighed and stared at his hands, making fists, flexing his fingers. "Sorry. The extent of his skill is impossible to measure. Sometimes our workings are effective, sometimes they aren't. Lancelyn and I are not psychic on an earthly level as Holly is; that's why we'd hypnotise her to find things out. Didn't always work, of course; sometimes worked too well. He was deadly jealous when I married her. He thought he could keep control of both of us, and he damned well couldn't. Anyway, if he poked around my house when he took the Book, he may know everything."

"The deaths you say he caused," said Karl, "are you sure they were due to a supernatural attack, and not coincidence – or Lancelyn planting suggestions in vulnerable minds?"

"It's the result that counts," Ben said irritably. "Causing change in accordance with will. That *is* the magic." He started to laugh.

"What do you find so funny?" Karl asked.

"That you can be cynical about the supernatural! For heaven's sake, you can walk through walls! What sort of proof do you want?"

Karl smiled. Ben looked startled, disarmed. "Gods, you look human when you smile," he muttered.

"Perhaps it is ridiculous for me to be cynical," said Karl. "However, I can't tell where the boundary lies between the tricks of clever men and the genuine occult – which is, by its nature, hidden from most mortals."

"Like the existence of vampires and the Crystal Ring."

"Quite."

Ben stood, shaking creases out of his trousers. "Let's try the study, just once more."

They looked again, half-heartedly this time. Ben muttered expletives as he searched.

Eventually Karl said, "Benedict, enough. I'm certain the Book is not in this house."

"Right. We'll have to think again."

As Ben spoke, Karl felt a thread of fiery coldness, like a sword-cut down his arm. Mortal heat, and something else. A door opening soundlessly.

He gripped Ben's arm but it was too late to hide. Pointless, anyway. A stocky, bearded man emerged from the tunnel of books and stood regarding them shrewdly. The shadows behind him seemed to thicken.

"You can think until you're purple in the face, dear boy," said the man. You can't outwit me with your –" he waved a hand at Karl "– friends."

"If you took the Book from me, I can take it back," Benedict said, remarkably composed.

"I was wondering when you'd try."

"Where is it?"

"You don't need it," Lancelyn said softly.

He had an aura of strength, Karl observed; like a tree, rooted in the earth. Lines of thirst rose in his throat and burned in the tips of his fangs. Taking the blood of a strong man was a rare pleasure and all at once he craved it...

Faster than they could see him move, he grasped Lancelyn and was leaning over him. He heard Benedict gasp, "Karl, don't hurt him!" For a moment he had the satisfaction of seeing terror on the magus's face.

"Are you going to help your brother?" Karl whispered.

The shadows around Lancelyn solidified and lunged. Something seized Karl and flung him away so violently that he collided with the desk and almost fell. He saw three figures, solid and human-shaped, yet near impossible to see directly; black from head to foot, but surrounded by a corona of sizzling platinum light.

He'd seen them before in the Crystal Ring. They'd alarmed him then, and now they terrified him, sapping his will...

"What have you done?" Ben cried. "What are these things? Did the Book bring them?"

Lancelyn chuckled, folding his arms. "No, Ben, I brought them. I don't need tools to enhance my powers. They've always been with me; but they've become more substantial of late. What the hell were you doing, summoning undead things against me? You fool. They're useless against my three."

"What are they?" Ben's voice was hoarse with fear.

"Not demons but *daemons*; guardian spirits."

"My vampires are stronger!"

"Really? Stand aside, I don't want you hurt."

A figure detached itself and rushed at Karl. Karl tried to escape into the Crystal Ring, couldn't move. The room was spinning. He glimpsed an oval face, long nose, narrow shining eyes like two sabres. Slender hands clutched his wrists as he tried to fight it off.

It was so strong! Karl felt his own limbs turning to rope as it clung to him. What was this entity? Stronger than Kristian, it seemed... It might drink his blood, or worse... but *what was it*?

A human shout, sudden movement in the corner of his eye. Karl saw Ben moving to seize the Mexican dummy from the desk. Then he swung it hard at the daemon's back.

Blue flame flowered in the darkness.

Karl heard Lancelyn curse. The shadow loosed him and vanished in a sudden flare of light.

The automaton was on the floor leaning drunkenly against the desk leg, its torso licked by flames. It still grinned as its painted face began to melt. Ben was backing away, staring at the light as if hypnotised.

"Christ," Lancelyn shouted. "The bloody cigar lighter must've sparked off the fuel reservoir. Help me put it out!"

As he floundered, searching for something to smother the flames, the desk caught light. Papers spilled onto the floor and flared up with daylight brilliance. The dummy collapsed sideways and flames chased lines of spilled fuel all over the carpet. Fire roared towards the curtains, towards the priceless books. Bitter smoke billowed.

Lancelyn was beating at the blaze with his hands and feet, his face wild and lit from below by red fire. "Help me, damn you!"

Karl only stared at him through a veil of flame. "Where are your guardians now, Mr Grey?" he said softly.

Then Karl lifted Ben bodily, rushed towards the window and leapt through in an explosion of glass. He ran into the cool of the night, flung Ben down under the cover of bushes, turned to stare back at the furious orange light blazing in the windows. Black smoke surged out against the light.

A figure danced like a maddened demon. Lancelyn's voice drifted after them. "Damn you, Ben, you'll pay for this!"

"Christ. Christ," Ben gibbered in disbelief. "We can't leave him, we've got to get help."

He scrabbled to get up. Karl held him down with the pressure of one finger and watched the fire, thinking in a remote vampiric way how beautiful it was... and then he said, "I don't think so. It's his own fault, *nicht wahr*? Let us go home, before the whole street wakes."

After the fire, Lancelyn vanished.

There was half a column in the newspaper: fire had damaged the house of Mr Lancelyn Grey, renowned scholar, but the fire brigade had arrived in time and confined the blaze to the study. Many rare books had been lost but there were no casualties; his servants were on holiday and Mr Grey only just home from a trip. The fire was accidental, caused by a faulty cigar lighter...

"He didn't implicate me," Ben said, stunned. He sat in the parlour in the depths of gloom, couldn't shake himself out of it.

"You wanted to help him. And he didn't blame you for the

fire," said Karl. "Are you sure that you hate each other?"

"Habit," Ben said bitterly.

Several days had passed since the fire. Lancelyn's house was locked and silent, the brickwork smoke-darkened above the boarded-up study window. Lancelyn's expected revenge never came; Ben heard not a word from him.

Ben contacted every member of the Order, convinced that someone must know of Lancelyn's whereabouts – and intending to enlist their support. Now was the time to seize control over the Neophytes of Meter Theon.

To his dismay, everyone refused to speak to him. Most lived too far away to visit easily. There was one man only a few miles away, towards Nottingham, so Ben went to his house and put his foot in the door. Through the gap, the nervous acolyte told him that Lancelyn had suspended the Order until further notice and expelled Benedict. No one was to communicate with him... or they would suffer, as James and Deirdre had.

Benedict returned home in despair and fury.

"He'd destroy the Order, rather than let me have it," he told Karl, Andreas and Katerina. "And I'm the last to know! He understands the Book in a way I never could, and he's summoned creatures even Karl can't defeat... God, is there nothing, *nothing* I can do to get the better of him?"

The three vampires seemed to sympathise. Karl said gently, "This is no longer a rivalry between overgrown boys, but something infinitely more sinister. Andreas and I have both encountered the creatures Lancelyn called daemons. We do not take the threat lightly."

"Were they afraid of the fire?" asked Katerina.

Karl shook his head. "It merely distracted them. But any danger they pose to us is beside the point; I want to know what they are."

"So what shall we do?" said Katerina.

So warm, so lovely she is, thought Ben. *It would be easy to get too close to her... and she's a vampire, you fool. No, must keep my distance, keep control.*

Karl opened his hands. "Continue as we are. Simon has recovered fast and he's intelligent and amenable; he will cause no trouble. We'll go on restoring each one in turn. Until then, Benedict,

I suggest you forget Lancelyn. While he leaves you in peace, let him. I'm sure he will return to torment you soon enough."

Under Karl and Katerina's care, the vampires came slowly back to life. Ben watched their recovery with growing excitement, fascinated by the gleaming beauty that swelled from the husks. *But what are these creatures*, he thought, *who don't follow any traditional folklore? They walk about in daylight, even if they prefer the night; they show no fear of holy symbols, garlic, running water, any of that nonsense. They rest in the spirit-realm, not in graves... Surely they are closer to angels than demons!*

Ben relied on Karl and Katerina to control the vampires still in a semi-dormant state. Once they regained a measure of intelligence, he could dominate them with the technique he used on Andreas, Katerina and Simon: an unseen chain around the throat. He was subtle, though, not wanting to alienate them. He would only use the power if any rebelled; meanwhile, he left them to Karl and his friends, while he went back to the bookshop. It was either that or close the business.

He'd decided, at last, that Maud had to go.

Still no word from Lancelyn; no taunts, no threats. Only silence. Ben should have felt relieved, but he did not. He'd lost his brother, friend, and enemy all in one, and he felt bereaved.

He tried not to dwell on Karl's grisly task – taking each vampire out at dead of night to spill the blood of unsuspecting men and women into its ravenous mouth... Ben was hardening himself to the horror.

We ought to leave, Ben thought. *The cottage is too small, too near the neighbours; someone will wonder why we have so many guests coming and going at night! I'll vanish, as Lancelyn has. But where to go?*

My father's house in Derbyshire would have been ideal. Shame the old fright's still alive. Never mind, I'll come up with something... So I can't keep a coven of vampires, eh, Karl? We'll see.

* * *

The attic was empty now. The vampires were recovering on beds and couches in the guest bedrooms. They were all – except one – taking on their true forms and personalities.

"Do you know any of them?" Karl asked, watching Katerina as she tended one of the patients in the small bedroom. There was a low, beamed ceiling, a rug on dark floorboards, fresh flowers in the tiny window.

"Some of them. The two quiet ones, John and Matthew, were on speaking terms with me, though we had nothing in common. They had strong religious beliefs that didn't accord with Kristian's. They thought he was a false prophet from Satan, and tried to kill him. They hurt him quite badly, I believe, but he was too strong for them. I remember others whom Kristian put in the *Weisskalt*, but they aren't here."

"For that, we should be grateful," Karl sighed. "At least Benedict hasn't summoned every single vampire in the world here."

"But where are they?"

He went to her and stroked her shoulder. "Wherever they are, they can take care of themselves. I think we should concern ourselves with these, don't you? Do you know this one?"

The woman on the bed had dark brown skin, so deeply black it was almost blue. She looked Indian; she had that carved, silken beauty.

"No, I've never seen her before," said Katerina. "She looks at me but won't speak. Nor will the African man in the next room, but I've seen him before. He was often in the castle, but I don't know how he upset Kristian. I never heard him speak, come to think of it. We called him Malik. I don't know the pretty silver-haired male, but Rachel was a friend of mine."

In the corner sat an attenuated woman with white skin and a flame of red hair. Karl had heard her talking to Katti, but now she gazed out of the window as if in a trance. A waxwork princess.

Katerina went to her and stroked her fiery hair. "You knew Rachel, didn't you?"

"No," he said.

Katti looked pensive. "Of course not. Kristian disposed of her just before he found you, now I think of it... She was like you in many ways, *mein Schatz*."

"Another thorn in Kristian's side?" Karl said drily. "Shall we see if the last one has made any progress?"

"The runt of the litter," said Katerina. She kissed Rachel's cheek and followed him into another bedroom.

On the bed lay a brittle ashen figure who'd shown no improvement, the only one who hadn't fought them or raged for blood. They'd taken him to victims without success; he had no interest in feeding. As they looked down, the papery mouth cracked open and he mewed feebly.

"I wonder who he is?" Katerina said. "What does he want?"

Karl felt a stunning pang of pity. He answered quietly, "He is telling us that he wants to die."

Katerina stared at him.

"It's hopeless," Karl went on. "He won't feed because he doesn't want to live. He must be another whom Kristian took by force, who never wanted to be a vampire. We're only torturing him."

"You can't want to –"

"Yes. We must make an end of him."

The decision was made. Karl fetched an axe from the garden shed and they laid the thin figure on the floor. Then he struck off its head, as easily as splitting rotten wood. No blood fell, and the skull crumbled to dust.

As they buried the remains in the garden, Ben appeared through the twilight, anxious to know what they were doing. Karl explained without emotion, but inside he felt a dreadful chill winding through him; part hope, part terror.

He put his arm around Katti's shoulder and they hugged each other. Wind blew rain-clouds across the sky and tore healthy leaves from the trees. Benedict seemed far away, a paper figure of no importance.

"Can you imagine the strength of will it takes to refuse blood?" Karl whispered in awe. "Even in the utmost misery, blood rules us and saves us. To possess such strength, in the depths of despair…"

"We don't even know who he was," said Katerina.

"Only that he wanted to die."

"And we can die, Karl," she said, her voice trembling. "We can."

* * *

Summer deepened towards autumn. Karl had not seen Charlotte for months. They wrote to each other, but cold sea and ice-capped mountains lay between them. They transmitted plain news to each other, not emotion.

Often Karl longed to write the truth: "Charlotte, can we not admit what we are doing? We may live from day to day without feeling pain, and be deluded into thinking that no harm is being inflicted. But we are wrong. We must stop this; we must talk."

The words were in his mind, but never flowed from the nib of his pen.

After the burial of the vampire that had wished to die, Katerina was depressed.

"Take me to London, Karl," she said. "Simon can cope here for a day or two. I need to escape this prison and see life."

Benedict was surprised. A trip to London? He seemed to find it incredible that supernatural beings could want to indulge an ordinary, human pleasure.

The pleasure, Karl thought, *is really not ordinary at all. We might live half in another realm, but we are tied to Earth. We were all mortal once, and even a creature of extremes – such as Kristian – could not completely sever himself from the world.*

Kristian, naturally, had had minions to perform such mundane tasks as buying clothes, but Karl preferred to act for himself. It was an excuse to move fully in the mortal world. There was the poignant delight of innocent encounters with tailors or shop assistants; engaging them with cool courtesy, while secretly tantalised by the scent of their blood. Knowing how easy it would be to bite into an unsuspecting mortal neck... but knowing, also, that he would not.

So he found great satisfaction in taking Andreas and Katerina to the London stores, observing their fascination with new fashions and electric gadgets. Andreas deplored the modern styles, but Katerina was won round by the geometric boldness of everything from buildings to tea-cups to stark, colourful posters. She loved the mix of motor cars and horse-drawn vehicles in the streets, the trams and charabancs, the noise, the electricity. She gazed at film stars flickering in black and white on silver screens, so like vampires with their smoky eyes and porcelain faces.

"Does it seem strange to you, Karl?" she asked. They stood in Trafalgar Square, watching pigeons wheel against the grey sky, basking in the warmth of people around them. "All the fashions that passed us by while we slept, all the inventions! Were you aware of changes, or did they creep in day-by-day so that you barely noticed?"

"I noticed," Karl said, smiling. "Some transformations were quite sudden. I don't think it is unique to vampires, these days, to feel that you've stepped into a foreign world."

"You've always had too much empathy with mortals," she said. "The wonderful thing is that we're together again, we three, as we were before. And there's no reason for us ever to part again."

They walked arm-in-arm with Katti in the middle. Even Andreas was happy. When darkness fell they moved through the theatre crowds, intoxicated by heat and gaiety. Andreas's eyes misted with thirst, and he left them. Karl watched him moving down an alley beside the theatre, and knew that some victim would find himself staring into an ethereal white face with long green eyes; soon to be struggling in panic and awe as the fangs stabbed and hot blood flowed out of his heart...

They waited for Andrei, standing by a pillar in front of the theatre. And Karl saw a poster announcing a future production. The Ballet Janacek's *Swan Lake*, starring Violette Lenoir.

"I am so happy tonight," said Katerina. She embraced him with a passion to which Karl could not respond. She pulled back, her hands stiffening on his arms. "Why is it that every time I kiss you on the mouth, you turn away and kiss my cheek like a brother?"

She was distressed, but Karl felt only vague sadness. "I'm sorry."

"You were never like this before! What is it; that you needed me then, and don't need me now?"

"You were always telling me how dangerous it is to need anyone, Katti," he said gently. "Times change, even for us."

She shook her head, lips pinched. "I can't stand this any more. I only want you to make love to me, Karl, not to throw yourself off the Eiffel Tower. It's only pleasure, and nothing we haven't done before!"

Passers-by were looking at them. Karl held her arms. "Katti, please."

"This is the first time I've complained. I've been patient for months, waiting for you to get over Charlotte. What will you achieve, saving yourself for a lover who has deserted you? It's so human, so banal! Pointless! I know you still want her, my dear, but what if she never comes back? Life, our immortal life, must go on."

He knew she was right, but it made no difference. He could easily have given in to desire, taken her, tasted her blood... it would be wonderful but, in the end, it would be empty. He tried to shut away the winter landscape in his soul. "I never meant to upset you," he said. "Katti, I love you and what you suggest would be very easy, but I can't. After Charlotte – whether I see her again or not – I cannot feel passionate about anything. I'd be betraying her and lying to you. This is nothing to do with moral sensibilities. It is simply the way I feel."

"Oh, God." Katti turned away, briskly wiping her cheek. A blood-tinged tear soaked into the finger of her cream glove. "Forgive my outburst, and forget it ever happened. My dear, I hate to see you unhappy, but it won't last forever. When your sorrow has passed, I'll still be here."

Holly lay in bed, dozing restlessly. The dark mood that preceded menstruation was on her, distorting simple unhappiness into grey webs of nightmare.

Ben's strong smooth body was beside her, but she might as well have lain alone. He slept soundly, divorcing himself from worry as men could. The soft rise and fall of his ribs was like the Earth itself breathing in and out.

Holly wished she could escape as easily. Every time she looked at him, Maud's sick lie hung between them, a demon of self-destruction.

We swallowed Lancelyn's notions of sex being natural and sinless, she thought. *I was the one who seduced Ben, down on the shore of that lovely blue ocean in Italy... I wanted it to be true, it should be true, but it isn't. To think of him with Maud makes me ill! What did she offer that I couldn't give?* the demon whispered. *What did I do wrong?*

She was sure Maud was lying and yet... no amount of reassurance would ever expunge the doubt. It was like a sickness, her desperate need to trust and love her parents, Lancelyn, Benedict, someone – yet never being fully able to do so. Sometimes she felt like a child.

She kept seeing Lancelyn's face, but the image was tainted. The idea of his "Hidden Temple", where he used his followers as whores to exploit those with more money than sense, lay in her stomach like wet sand. Perhaps they deserved it, the thrill-seekers he blackmailed, but that didn't make it right. She'd loved him as a father... heartbreaking to be told he was a villain. *How can I possibly accept that I adored a murderer?*

And Benedict... what has he become?

Sleep smothered her thoughts in heavy, roiling blackness.

A muffled storm raged, filling the sky with lightning and the streets with torrents of water. Holly floated, disembodied yet stifled by thunderous heat. Maud's face solidified in front of her, her orbs brimming with disingenuous excitement.

"I must see you, Mrs Grey," she said. "I've a message from Lancelyn. Meet me in the Temple at his house."

Holly found herself in the street, frantically struggling through the storm. She was floundering towards Lancelyn's house, wading through waist-deep floodwater. Debris surged past on the grey foam as the water invaded shops and dwellings, bringing down walls in its wake. The sky roared and flashed. There was not a soul about, no one to help her. Hot rain whipped her hair into her eyes and mouth. She stumbled and gasped as the water nearly carried her off her feet, but she kept going. *Must know...*

She saw figures on an altar. A woman, robe pushed up to her waist, a man's hairy buttocks bouncing between her legs. Maud and Lancelyn. She almost retched.

Now she was free of the flood and running along the tree-lined street to Lancelyn's house. She dreaded reaching it. But there it stood, red and shadowy under the swaying branches, the windows dead and empty; the boarded study window like a sewn-up eye.

Her perception shifted again and she was inside the plain grey room that was the temple. She was dry, the storm forgotten, but panic and exertion drained her. She felt heavy, powerless. The temple was dark, lit by a single mauve candle on the altar; the only furniture, three empty chairs. Maud was there alone, dressed in a ceremonial robe the same mousey-fawn as her hair. Her prominent eyes and teeth gleamed.

"Actually," Maud said airily, "I was in the Hidden Temple all the time, so I know all Lancelyn's secrets. Now I'm going to tell you the secret, Mrs Grey."

In a flash of clarity, Holly knew that her dream was trying to reveal some fundamental truth.

"What is it?" she whispered.

"There's going to be a Dark Bride. And guess what, Mrs Grey? The Dark Bride is you."

"And the bridegroom?"

Maud sniggered, dipping her head. "Your bridegroom is Lancelyn."

Holly gasped. "Do you expect me to believe this?"

She felt herself drifting upwards...

"Lancelyn will marry you," Maud insisted, "and then I can have Benedict."

...upwards and outwards, until she was looking down on herself: a woman under a black bridal veil, carrying a violet candle. Horror raced through her like floodwater. The bride moved slowly forward as if at a funeral, watched by three figures who now occupied the three chairs. They were silhouettes of angels; one black, one white, one red. They inclined their heads and applauded as she passed, their palms making the sound of rushing rain.

There was hideous logic in the vision. She thought, *So Lancelyn always really wanted me after all?*

"Where's Lancelyn?" Holly asked. No answer. "Why isn't he here?"

"It's all a trick, really," said Maud. Her face was inches from Holly's and she was giggling, her eyes white and mindless. "Lancelyn told me to lure you here. Because the groom who really marries the Dark Bride, you see, is Death." Maud put her hand to her mouth as if shocked at her own audacity. Laughter spilled between her fingers. "Ben and Lancelyn despise you, Holly. They want you dead so they can raise me in your place."

Some force took Holly and threw her backwards onto the altar. The angels rose around her, now all inky dark, and she felt this had happened before, to someone else, and that other person had also drowned in despair. She tried to scream. Fear leapt like a cavorting devil inside her, and she could produce only whimpers of desolation.

"Oh, dear, dear," said a voice from somewhere deep in the room. Lancelyn.

"Oh dear, Maud," he said with chilling joviality. "I wanted to see if you'd go to such extremes, and you have."

Holly saw Lancelyn standing there, smiling, as real and ordinary as life. Maud turned, her hand falling from her slack mouth, her face suffused with terror.

"Someone has been tricked here, and it is not Holly," he said.

The altar beneath Holly became a bed. She was in her room again, yet it was subtly wrong; Ben wasn't there, and another bed appeared where the wall should have been.

In that altar-bed lay Maud.

Lancelyn stood over Maud, his gnome-like face radiant. Holly was an unwilling witness.

"You foolish girl, Maud," he said. "You have the psychic ability and spiritual potential of a cockroach. Yet you would betray my brother and hurt my Holly, in return for a little flattery? Betray me to them in turn, just to boast of your exploits? And then you'd lure Holly to her death, like the cutthroat whore you are. Go back to your church pew, your Bible. Pray for your soul."

Silence. In a faint radiance that fell through the curtains Holly saw a dark shape near the door; a tall shadow, nothingness.

Holly watched the shape drift into the gap between the two beds. Fear floated like an unattached entity inside her.

The figure was like an eclipse: black yet dazzling. She watched it move to Maud's bed. Translucent, it obscured Maud's shape under her eiderdown like an inky waterfall. It bent lower until it seemed to lie across her. The girl did not stir.

Then Holly became Maud.

She stared up into fierce silver eyes, felt its weight like a cold sheet folding over her. The coldness began to suck out her warmth, pitiless...

The vampire drank. Not blood but something more essential. *The will to live.*

Holly surged up and out of the nightmare, drenched in sweat, noiseless screams tearing her throat. Ben slept as if dead beside her. Where Maud's bed had stood there was only a wall.

CHAPTER FIFTEEN

A DANCE IN BLACK VELVET

The Ballet Janacek's *Swan Lake* was magnificent, as Charlotte had known it would be.

The critics greeted it with relief as "a glorious return to her true vocation by Violette Lenoir after the unfortunate diversion of *Dans le Jardin*". At last, they said, she was realising her potential and lifting her company to the heights of the Ballets Russes.

Patronising fools, thought Charlotte. Who were they to pass judgment on Violette's art, when she was so far above them? The company's tour took them to the major cities of Europe. Charlotte watched every single performance, yet Violette's spell never palled.

There in the darkness, Charlotte would sink into the green, silver and blue world of the swans as if drugged. Bliss, to have nothing in her mind but the beauty of this floating world; no thoughts of Karl or her family, no memory of Josef weeping over his dying sister; no reminder that after this she must walk through the darkness and drive hard fangs into some victim's neck... No, here and now there was only Odette in white, and Odile, enthralling in gorgeous black. How like the Serpent from *Dans le Jardin* the dancer seemed then; sinuous, cruel, yet with a strange integrity that wrung sympathy for evil. As the virtuous Odette, Violette was acting; as Odile, she was so completely herself that it was frightening.

Charlotte always sat alone in a private box. She kept her distance from other members of the ballet, aware that they thought her

304

strange. She saw little of Violette either. From a distance, it was easier for them both to be friends and business partners; easier not to torment each other. Violette seemed happy to know that Charlotte was nearby – but not too close.

Sometimes Charlotte would watch rehearsals. She became increasingly suspicious that the pain Violette suffered for her dancing was not normal.

She was taking longer to warm up, and sometimes her movements lacked their usual fluidity. At first Charlotte thought she was conserving energy for the performance, until she fell twice while executing simple pirouettes. Violette never fell.

Her performances remained flawless; but in Amsterdam, in rehearsal for their last night on the continent, Violette actually cried out with pain as her partner Mikhail lifted her. To his solicitous concern she insisted she was fine; but her face was colourless and she left the practice session early. Unprecedented.

Charlotte followed her to her hotel room. They were due to sail for England in the morning... Karl was there, but Charlotte tried not to think about that.

Violette had her back to the door and was executing slow *pliés*. How cautious her movements seemed. Her shoulders were rigid, her neck tendons standing out. Once or twice she gasped through her teeth.

"Violette," said Charlotte.

The dancer started and turned round, raising a hand to rub her shoulders. Her skin, always pale, was more drained than radiant. "I wish you wouldn't creep up on me like that. I should be used to it."

"I'm worried about you. You're obviously not well."

A small dry smile. "No? What is your diagnosis, doctor?" Violette put on a robe and sat on the arm of a chair.

"I think you're working too hard," said Charlotte. "You will injure yourself."

Violette hugged herself and stared down at her bare right foot, which she pointed, flexed, pointed, flexed. "Oh, you are a long way behind," she murmured.

"What do you mean?" Charlotte moved towards her then stopped, her anxiety growing.

"I thought you would have guessed. Don't you know everything?"

"Of course I don't. What's wrong?"

"I've told no one yet. I can't bring myself to."

"But you can tell me."

"Yes." Violette went on staring at the movement of her flexuous foot as if mesmerised. And Charlotte realised that she was trying with all her strength not to cry.

The spasm over, Violette spoke, her voice low and hoarse. "I found out before we left Salzburg that I have a degenerative condition of my joints and spine. If I don't stop dancing I'll put myself in a wheelchair within five years."

Charlotte swallowed the words like poison. God, how to react to such news! Whatever she said would upset Violette; sympathy worst of all. "The doctor might be wrong."

"I've seen four doctors and they all say the same! I'm crippling myself."

"What if you do stop?"

"Then I'll have ten years of hobbling around, if I'm lucky.

"Can't they do anything?"

"No." Again the hard smile. "I wouldn't trust doctors to touch my body, even if they claimed they could cure me. But there is no cure. If I rest, lie about in hot spas like an invalid, I will preserve my health a few years longer, that's all." She sighed, then looked straight at Charlotte. Unbearable, to see that hard pain in her face. "You see choreographers teaching and directing from wheelchairs, don't you?"

"Yes," Charlotte said fervently. "Yes."

"But not me. You will never see me like that."

Violette rose and came to Charlotte with all her dancer's grace; silk robe floating, her hair loose on her shoulders. "I want people to remember me dancing." She stopped inches from Charlotte, gazing at her. Dazzling, those indigo eyes.

She said, "Charlotte, kill me, please."

Charlotte turned away, dizzy with shock. "No!"

"If you won't, I'll do it myself!"

"Don't talk about death! Your doctors must be wrong. If you rest, you'll get better. Cancel the remainder of the tour!"

"Never."

"Then rest as soon as it's over! You're bound to feel better if you'd simply recuperate for a while."

"Stop this, please." Violette held out her white, expressive hands, curling the fingers. "Look. I can feel the disease, like sand in my joints, wearing them away. The pain when I get up in the morning... It's not that bad, I suppose, no worse than any poor old woman has to suffer, but to me it's death. I may have brought it on myself, by dancing too hard as a child, or at least made it worse. Now you look as if you're going to weep. Please don't. I can't stand sympathy, that's why I won't tell anyone." Violette's voice was surprisingly gentle, but her face was china, containing no self-pity. "I shall dance until I drop, of course, but I won't let them see me deteriorating; I won't have them shaking their heads and muttering in pity. The moment I am no longer 'the great Lenoir' – I want you to do it." Charlotte half-turned away, but Violette stepped around to face her. "Do what you did to me before, only don't stop."

As she spoke, she laid her hands on Charlotte's shoulders.

The sensation was poignantly thrilling, bird-delicate. Violette rarely touched her voluntarily. Now she moved closer, and her body pressing lightly against Charlotte's felt warm; so fragile and yet real, vibrant with blood. The blackness of her hair against the pearl of her skin...

Charlotte seized the dancer's hands, thrust her away, and stumbled to the far end of the room. Thirst rushed crimson and silver through her. Almost impossible to think clearly, let alone to resist but she must, she must.

From the darkening of Violette's eyes, she was clearly aware of Charlotte's struggle; a stark reminder that she wasn't human, that the blood thirst was not to be played with. She looked suddenly terrified, but did not react or try to escape.

"Don't," said Charlotte, moving behind an armchair and gripping its brocade back for support. "Never tempt me like that or I won't be able to stop myself. You don't understand how strong the thirst can be!"

"But I want you to." Violette's voice trembled.

"Not this minute, though, surely! And that's not the point! I don't want to kill you, Violette. I couldn't bear it! You don't know what you're asking!"

"Don't I? Were you just playing with my life, Charlotte – wanting to be near a dancer for the glamour, like some star-struck girl? Or did you come to be with me through life and death?"

Charlotte turned away. Violette made her feel powerless, as if she were the vampire and Charlotte the mortal.

"I could kill myself, of course," Violette added with chilling flippancy. "I thought it would hurt less if you did it."

The thirst receded. Charlotte was in control again, or as near as she could manage.

And now that she saw clearly again, the solution hung bright and inevitable as the sun before her.

She remembered how Karl had resisted the decision to transform her for as long as he could. *It is so lonely*, he'd said. *Your conscience could not bear it. You might change, as Ilona did. You could grow to hate me. You might die.* God, a hundred reasons... and in the end, it was only love that had taken the choice out of their hands.

Amazing, then, that with Violette she could make the decision in a split second, with no doubts. Fear, yes – but no doubts at all.

However, Charlotte could not make the transformation on her own. She would need help.

"Listen to me." She went to Violette and touched her cheek. No hunger in the gesture, only tenderness. "There may be something I can do to help you. I can't promise, but as soon as we arrive in London I shall find out."

"Whatever are you talking about?"

Violette closed her fingers over Charlotte's wrist. Close enough to kiss, they looked at each other solemnly.

"Do you trust me?" said Charlotte.

"Yes," said the dancer. "God help me. Why shouldn't I? You've saved my ballet twice. Whatever you are... that hardly seems to matter. It all feels part of the plan."

"There was never any plan, believe me." *If I'd made a plan,* Charlotte thought, *it would have been for Karl and me to stay together... And how on Earth can I expect him to help me now? But he must!*

"No cure, either," said Violette.

"No guarantee; only trust me, and don't worry."

"You ask the impossible."

Charlotte let her power shine from her eyes to Violette's soul, simply to tranquillise her and numb her pain. And Violette – perhaps because she guessed what Charlotte meant and dared not consider the implications – was receptive for once.

"Concentrate on the ballet, nothing else. My dearest, beautiful Violette. Forget the future. Dance."

"As if there's no tomorrow," Violette said softly.

As soon as they arrived in London, Charlotte went to see Stefan.

The house in Mayfair looked just the same; a touch dilapidated, plaster flaking from the columns at the front door. The hall, with its black and white tiles and a staircase winding around the walls, was as impersonal as ever. How eerie it felt to be here. For this was where Karl had brought her to be transformed into a vampire.

They'd visited Stefan and Niklas since, but the place never failed to awake echoes of thrilling fear. On the dreary landing of the top floor, she knocked at Flat 5. The door opened at once to reveal a glittering eighteenth-century palace.

Framed against the splendour stood the blue-eyed Scandinavian angel Stefan, his arms open to welcome her. Charlotte walked into his embrace. How good it felt to hold him, how comforting. Over his shoulder she saw his twin, Niklas, watching impassively. She should be used to Niklas by now but he still disturbed her. He was Stefan's perpetual, silent reflection.

"Charlotte, how lovely to see you," Stefan said warmly.

"You always seem to know I'm coming," she said.

"Have you forgotten that I'm a vampire?" Stefan's smile was warmly innocent. And Niklas echoed the smile, though his pale-gold eyes were empty. "I sensed you climbing the stairs. And before that, believe it or not, I looked out of the window and saw you walking along the street." Then, unexpectedly, he kissed her on the lips like a lover.

The gesture was so natural that Charlotte didn't think of resisting. She opened her lips to the warmth of his mouth, and put her hand in his hair; and when the kiss ended, she didn't feel remotely embarrassed.

She thought of Josef, how easy it would have been... Such moments reminded her of how far she'd come from being human, when she would barely let anyone touch her.

"Come in, come in," he said. "Sad, isn't it, that we poor creatures have to do without life's basic courtesies. I can't offer you a drink."

"Not from a glass, anyway," she said. Stefan appreciated the joke.

She took Niklas's hand and kissed him on the cheek. Even if he had no true awareness of the world around him, she knew it pleased Stefan for his companion to be acknowledged. Then Stefan led her into the parlour, an array of shining Italian furniture, chandeliers and lush Persian carpets. She walked to the window. Stefan didn't offer her a seat; he knew she felt at home, and would stand or sit as she wished.

"What brings you here?" he asked.

"The Ballet Janacek is in London."

"Ah. *Swan Lake*, of course."

She asked the question, the whole reason for her visit. "Have you seen Karl?"

"Naturally. I saw him last week." Stefan's off-hand reply gave her a pang of envy. Karl only had to be absent for a few hours to be transformed in her mind into a creature of myth, infinitely desirable yet unobtainable... And this time they'd been apart for months.

"How is he?" she said, too quickly. "Still with Katerina?"

"It depends what you mean by 'with'." Stefan shook his head, gave her a chiding look. "They found Andreas; did you know?"

"Yes. He wrote to me."

"And they found some crazed occultist who has summoned several of Kristian's discarded vampires to him. He hasn't told me much."

"I'm sure you know more than me," said Charlotte.

"Well, it's very strange. Kristian dies, and the sleeping ones wake? Yet... we are all still alive and going about our business. What could be wrong?"

"I wish I knew."

"You look cold, Charlotte, like a human in a snowstorm, all huddled and shivering. What is it?"

Charlotte made herself relax. "I must see Karl."

"You know where he is, surely?"

"Yes, but... Stefan, this is so hard to explain. The way we parted was awful. I can't bring myself to approach him. I was the one who told him to go, in the end."

"Ah. So now you can't say, 'Come back.'"

She smiled ruefully. Stefan always made difficult situations easier, which made her feel guiltily grateful.

"Don't worry," he said. "I will arrange something. Meanwhile, why don't you forget all this, come and enjoy yourself? There's a party in a few days' time. It will be a lovely affair, fancy dress, a grand house."

"Where?"

"Oh, not far. Kensington, I think. We were invited through friends of friends, you know." He winked. "Niklas and I are still popular at the most fashionable parties, jazz clubs... everywhere."

Charlotte held herself steady against the sleet of memories. Long ago, when she'd first known Karl, Kristian had sent Stefan and Niklas to infiltrate her sister Fleur's clique of friends. They had welcomed twin vampires like a new drug, cultured them as rare narcotic flowers that brought bliss and madness – without understanding the serpents they embraced. A kind of sickness. And it had ended in Fleur's death at Ilona's hands.

Not so long ago, Charlotte thought. It seemed a century but was barely three years. Sometimes it shook her rigid to realise that she was part of this world now; that these deathly creatures who wreaked such havoc were her friends...

"I don't feel much like enjoying myself."

"That's obvious; that's precisely why you need to try. It will be delightful. Besides, you'll be in costume; I'll arrange that too. I can see you in a certain painting... oh, lovely."

"You're too good to me."

"Why not? I'd do anything for you, Charlotte." He spoke with a wry smile. This was the trouble with Stefan; she could never be sure he was serious. She paused, wondering whether to take up the challenge.

"Anything? Would you help me... to make a vampire?"

He blinked. So captivating, his sapphire eyes, hopelessly seductive to his victims, whom he would leave obsessively in love, mad – but rarely dead.

"Perhaps."

"Stefan, if a mortal was seriously ill, and they were brought into the Crystal Ring, would they be cured – made perfect, as we are?"

"That would depend on their strength. If they had the spirit, they'd be healed and become a flawless immortal. If they were very old or sick, the transformation would kill them. There are no half-measures."

She remembered Josef's sister, and bowed her head. *But Violette is fit and her will is like steel.* She said, "The person is young and strong, but their joints are degenerating."

"They would have a very good chance," said Stefan. "But who is it?"

"Does it matter?" said Charlotte. "Don't you trust me enough to know that I wouldn't ask this lightly? It's someone who will suffer unbearably if they stay human. I'm deadly serious, and I need your help."

"And you have it," he said warmly. "But we need a third. You know Niklas can't help; he lacks the power and understanding."

"Yes. That's why I need to see Karl."

For a rare moment, Stefan looked serious. "Charlotte, ask someone else. Pierre, perhaps…"

"No, not Pierre! We've never been friends, you know that. I won't ask him for anything."

"Someone, else, then. Karl will never agree."

"It must be Karl."

Stefan gave her a look of affectionate resignation. "Well, you are the only one who could persuade him, after all."

"And you'll ask him to meet me?"

"Of course, as soon as possible. But never mind him. This party; all you need do is come here in the afternoon; I'll dress you and we'll go together. Think of the entrance we'll make! You in the middle, with Niklas on your right hand and me on your left: three golden angels."

When *Swan Lake* came to London, Karl went to the opening night.

He went alone, without telling Katerina or anyone. He wanted to remind himself of Violette's magic; to understand how she'd seduced Charlotte away from him. A deeper lure than beauty, he knew.

More than anything, he wanted to see Charlotte.

Karl entered the theatre only after the doors were shut, the house lights down. Then he slid through the Crystal Ring and took his aisle seat in the back row. He didn't want Charlotte to see or sense him.

As the orchestra played the overture, he thought briefly of Benedict and Lancelyn. At times Karl was sorely tempted to kill them both – that was how dangerous they seemed – to scatter the vampires, and bury the whole affair. Yet he couldn't let go until he learned what lay behind it all.

But forget this now, he told himself. *Tonight, it does not matter.*

He could feel Charlotte somewhere in the theatre, a cool soft diamond touching his forehead.

Although vampires could sense each other from a distance, some could make themselves all but invisible. His daughter Ilona was hard to perceive; she touched the mind as a sliver of clear glass rather than a reflective jewel. Perhaps she inherited that trait from Karl, for other vampires complained that they didn't always know he was nearby. And now he hoped Charlotte would not notice him. What could be said, after their parting conversation? Their letters had conveyed nothing beyond fragments of information. They had both held back, giving nothing from the heart or soul.

In the magnificent gloom, Karl suddenly saw Charlotte. She was in a box above the left side of the stage, alone. He saw her as the curtains opened, and stage lights brushed her profile with delicate silver. As the ballet began she leaned forward and the light slid over her bare shoulders and her hair, glittering on her bandeau and diamond choker. Her attention was completely on the stage. Whoever would guess she was not human?

Swan Lake, as he expected, was wonderful; a lavish, romantic feast for the worshippers, everything it should be. And Violette, of course, was sublime. As Odette in white feathers she captured the audience's heart; but to Karl's preternatural eyes, it was only as Odile, the sorcerer's daughter, that she truly came alive. Showing her true colour. The sleek black costume, throwing flashes of purple and crimson, was the vivid symbol of her soul; dark, pitiless, strangely desperate.

Yet Karl watched without emotion. Violette Lenoir puzzled him, but failed to move him. He could not afford to let her touch his soul.

When he looked at Charlotte... *God, how far away she seems,* he thought. *Not even aware that I am watching her... once, she would have been aware of nothing else. Was this inevitable? Mein Gott, so easy to seduce humans; look at them a moment too long and they fall. So easy – so cruel – to let myself become the centre of Charlotte's life, because I fooled myself that it could last. But to hold another vampire... to compete with the lure of a human like Violette... ah, that is something else entirely.*

The magnetism between human and vampire is sovereign because it is the ultimate relationship. Unthinkable, forbidden, therefore infinitely alluring. So, was I always to lose her, whatever happened? If she'd stayed human I would have lost her to death. Would that have been worse than this slow drifting away?

No. Even if I am right, these ideas are not law... and there is no law that says I cannot fight them.

Karl made to grip the velvet arm of the seat, and instead gripped the forearm of the woman sitting next to him. She started and gasped, indignant.

"Forgive me, madam," he whispered, releasing her. She was looking at him now, her frown becoming a wide-eyed stare as she took in his fine-boned face, dark hair, consuming eyes. Her lips parted and her eyes moistened.

She was a bonny, handsome woman in her thirties, radiating good health. Plump with blood. The warmth of her filled his senses.

One glance, and she was ready to do anything for him. Karl was usually slow to anger, but for some reason the ease of potential seduction made him furious.

"That's quite all right," she said.

"But it isn't," he said under his breath. He should have left then... but he did not. Violette wove her enchantment onstage and Charlotte watched raptly, but they were far away, a shining, blurred backdrop to this tiny drama in the darkness. Coolly he took the woman's hand as if to kiss it, turning it over at the last second and pressing his lips to the inside of her wrist. Then, softly, he let his fangs slide out and stab through the skin.

Her eyes bulged, but she didn't make a sound or try to stop him. He held her gaze over the plump heel of her thumb. Then came the gorgeous rush of blood, and it was all he could do not to seize her bodily. *Oh, God, the cruel wonder of it...* They sat motionless, victim and vampire, her wrist at his lips. No one around them noticed a thing.

Eventually the woman passed out, her head lolling as if in sleep. Karl folded her hand into her lap and quietly left. The ballet was almost over. Despite the blood filling him, he felt empty.

He didn't look back at the woman, nor wonder whether she would live or die. He'd wanted to punish the lie of vampire glamour, but in the end had only punished another innocent victim.

Karl walked away from the theatre, his long legs carrying him swiftly through the crowded streets. The blood had sharpened his appetite, and although he didn't want to hunt, he knew he must. He had no thoughts of Katerina or Benedict... The only image in his mind was Charlotte, glowing above him like the moon, oblivious to him, her amethyst eyes locked on a stranger.

No, Karl thought. *I will not let Violette Lenoir win.*

The party had already begun as a taxi-cab brought Charlotte, Stefan and Niklas into the square. The house dominated a grand Georgian row, its windows sparkling white against pearl-grey walls. Music and laughter struck Charlotte's sensitive ears like the chime of glass bells. A red carpet beneath a canopy led from kerb to front door, where two footmen stood ready to greet guests.

As soon as she saw the house, Charlotte knew with dismay that she could not enter. She stopped, looking up at the long, shining windows.

"What's wrong?" said Stefan. His hand was through her left arm, while Niklas, mute, walked on her right. He'd dressed Charlotte as the "Lady of Shalott" from the painting by John William Waterhouse; she wore a simple medieval dress, close-fitting at the waist and elbows, flaring into a full skirt and long sleeves that touched the ground. Stefan and Niklas were twin knights in chainmail and white surcoats. The party's theme, he'd told her, was simply "black and white".

"I've been here before. The hostess, who is she?"

"Lady... oh, some ridiculous name." Stefan took an invitation card from his pocket. "Lady Emerald Tremayne."

"Well, I can't go in," she whispered. Such painful memories...

"Why not?" Stefan asked patiently.

"Because I've met Lady Tremayne. She's a society hostess, she knows my aunt. I came to one of those dreadful debutante parties here. God, how I hated them! She's an awful snob who couldn't stand me."

"Charlotte, my dear friend." Stefan put his hands on her shoulders. "What are you saying? This is the human part of you speaking, but she's dead and gone. You don't have to be frightened of some harridan who terrified you in the past."

"But what if she recognises me? Or if other people here know me? There might even be members of my family..."

He only smiled. "If they recognise you, what does it matter? Tell them they've made a mistake. You can convince them of anything you like. Remember what you are!"

Still Charlotte hung back. Then she made herself release the fear, shocked at how tense she was. "You're right," she said, exhaling. "What am I thinking?"

"All you have to do is have fun," he said. Then the three of them strode up the steps beneath the canopy and into the hard shine of light.

Charlotte's overwhelming impression was of silver and white. A grand entrance hall, a stairwell with a massive chandelier shedding rainbow glints. Some guests at the foot of the stairs were all in ivory and pearl, the only colour about them the flash of gems and the golden-pink of their flesh. Through double doors that gave onto a vast ballroom, Charlotte glimpsed Greeks, Egyptians and Romans in white silk and jewels. They resembled extras from an epic film more than genuine characters; not that it mattered. This was fun, a fashion show. The rich inside their little fortress were shielded against poverty and the endless rows of slums outside in the spinning darkness...

"Charlotte!" said Stefan.

She blinked. She'd turned dizzy; how unreal this felt, as fragile as spun sugar. "I'm sorry, I was miles away."

"You almost vanished into the Crystal Ring! Don't do that in public, it's very embarrassing."

She tightened her hold on his arm. "I don't want to be here."

"Obviously, but you are. Come and be introduced like a good girl."

As Stefan had predicted, they made a wonderful entrance. Her magnolia-white dress was adorned with a long golden necklace, bands of gold embroidery around her upper arms. Her hair, autumn-coloured, flowed loose to her waist.

"In the painting," Stefan had said, "the tragic Lady drifting away in the boat is utterly unconscious of her own beauty. That's why you are perfect to portray her, Charlotte."

He was right; even now, Charlotte had no idea that she looked breathtaking. She was aware of heads turning, but it seemed they were staring at Stefan and Niklas; her knights.

A small, nervous young man in Greek costume came hurrying towards them; Stefan's human friend, who had invited them. *Victim, more than friend*, Charlotte thought, seeing his pallor and the way his feverish eyes hung on Stefan and Niklas. Breathlessly he introduced them to Lady Tremayne as "Jan and Johann Kessler and their sister Eva."

The hostess, an attractive woman in her forties, shrouded in layers of cream lace and camellias, stared hard at Charlotte. "But my dear, I swear – you look exactly like the niece of a friend of mine... Charlotte –"

"What a coincidence," Charlotte said sweetly, affecting a vaguely Germanic accent.

The woman's scarlet lips hardened into a smile. "But – well, forgive me, of course you couldn't be Miss Neville."

As Stefan spun a confection of lies about his "family", loving every moment, Emerald Tremayne went on staring suspiciously at Charlotte. But "Eva" found she couldn't care less what she thought. *Yes, wonder about me. Tie yourself in knots, because you'll never know the truth.*

And then they were moving into the ballroom, swimmers in a foaming tide. More chandeliers, a polished hardwood floor, curtains of creamy damask. A dance band played jaunty popular tunes and the dance floor was full, the air thick with laughter and smoke. Among the film extras she saw other costumes; the inevitable harlequin, some comical, ungainly chess pieces, even a couple dressed as a snowflake and a piece of coal. On the far side of the room, rows of windows reflected the scene in bright squares.

Thank heavens, she could see no one she knew. Perhaps it wouldn't have mattered if she'd met her Aunt Elizabeth, since she was the only one who'd even partially understood Charlotte's decision. But to see her sister Maddy again... she couldn't conceive of it. There were a few half-familiar faces, but shyness and anxiety had stopped her making friends. She doubted anyone would remember her.

Charlotte felt light-headed. The scene was too sharp, like glass; she felt as if she'd been thrown back in time, into her girlhood, when such maelstroms terrified her. And yet she wasn't afraid, just vibrantly aware of the crowd's blood-heat. She felt like two people at once – both outsiders.

I shouldn't have agreed to this, she thought. *I wish I'd gone straight to Karl instead.* She pressed her tongue to the tips of her fangs. *God, why am I so thirsty?*

Already Stefan had infiltrated a group of young men and women who were braying with laughter at each other's jokes. Charlotte stood silently apart, observing the guests like zoo exhibits. There was something pleasing in the way people would turn and stare at her. But how empty, that tiny sense of triumph...

The black chess piece was shouting drunkenly into her ear, "Miss Neville! How perfectly wonderful to see you! Care for a dance?"

She turned and looked coldly at a square puffy face inside a frame of chicken wire and paper. He was some friend of her sister's she barely knew.

"You've made a mistake. My name is not..."

"Oh no, I haven't. You're Charlotte. Not got any friendlier, have you?"

She turned to him and smiled. She felt like tearing the wire from his sweating neck. "Would you like to come into the garden and see how friendly I can be?"

The young man looked astonished. And she would have done it, taken him outside and sucked his blood, if Stefan had not touched her arm. He must be clairvoyant, the way he always guessed what was in her mind.

"Eva, dear," he said, pulling her away.

Then Charlotte felt the black-diamond presence of vampires, out in the entrance hall. She froze, staring at Stefan, everything else forgotten.

"Who is it?" she said.

He only smiled. "Come along." They moved through the crowd, Niklas following serenely.

Through the wide doorway, she saw Karl and Katerina, with an unknown dark-haired male vampire, being greeted by Emerald Tremayne. Her heart leapt violently and she turned on Stefan, accusing. "You knew he was coming!"

"Of course," the angel replied serenely. "I invited him."

In luscious contrast to the white chosen by most guests, the three were in black velvet costumes of the eighteenth century. How gorgeous, how striking they looked! So artlessly true to their nature, there seemed no point in trying to disguise what they were. Her Ladyship, clearly taken with them, was chatting animatedly.

"Did Karl know I'd be here?" Charlotte whispered.

"Yes. That's why he came. Andreas is with them."

He knew, she thought, *and yet he brought Katerina with him...*

Charlotte, her arm linked through Stefan's, could not take her eyes off Karl. He wore breeches and a waistcoat, a tailored frock coat flaring elegantly from the waist; white stockings, black buckled shoes, white lace at his throat and cuffs. Almost exactly as he'd appeared at Madeleine's birthday party, the first time she had truly *seen* him.

She recalled the cat-grey gloom of a garden, Chinese lanterns in the trees; seeing her brother, earthly and familiar, talking to a stranger who was plainly not of this world; infinitely beautiful, infinitely terrifying. Promising to take her world apart... and proceeding to do exactly that.

And the effect Karl had on Charlotte now was just the same. No, more intense, because now she knew everything. All the terrors and wonders promised by the first glimpse had come true, and far more... and the thought that she might have lost him was agony.

My God, is he doing this to me on purpose?

Stefan was drawing her and Niklas forward, mischief in his eyes. Lady Tremayne turned and waved imperiously at them. "Ah, do come and let me introduce you. I never knew they bred such a handsome race on the continent. These are the Kessler brothers, Jan and Johann; forgive me, I can't remember which is which."

"Neither can we," said Stefan, winking at Katerina.

"And their sister Eva. Miss Kessler, may I introduce Karl von Aschbach..."

Karl, his face betraying nothing, kissed Charlotte's hand as if they had never met before. His fingers felt glacial, and he barely touched her before he let go.

"I am charmed," he said. "And these are my friends..." he reeled off more false names.

"I'm pleased to meet you," she said, barely glancing at Katerina or Andreas. Karl looked into her eyes for the briefest moment; he gave nothing away, but neither did she.

"How charming you look, Miss Kessler," said Katerina, shaking her hand. Her expression was warm, but condescending. As always. How confident and regal she was, firmly in possession of both Karl and Andreas.

"More than charming," said Andreas, sombre and sincere. Charlotte smiled guardedly. So this was Andreas! A long face with a rose-pearl translucency to his skin, dark curly hair, sensuous lips. She sensed a self-absorbed moodiness about him, but thought she might like him regardless. How frustrating that they couldn't initiate a truthful, open conversation.

"Do come and join the party," said Lady Tremayne. "It's almost time for supper; only a buffet, but we can gain a head-start on the vultures."

"Thank you, I'm afraid we've already eaten," said Katerina.

If only she knew, Charlotte thought, *what manner of vulture she is actually entertaining.*

Karl turned away as Lady Tremayne led her favoured guests – like a flock of glossy ravens – into the ballroom. Charlotte followed, looking at Karl's straight, ebony-clad back, the mahogany sheen of his hair. Oh, so painful, having to hold back and play this human charade! Was he cool to her because they were in company – or because he'd regarded their last parting as final? She could hardly blame him – but not knowing was anguish.

"Enjoy the evening," Stefan whispered very softly. "One of you will have to swallow your pride, eventually. And you do look heavenly, though I say so myself."

"It's all right for you. You love this! Teasing humans, telling lies, seducing them."

"Of course," he said. "Don't you?"

Lady Tremayne organised them into a circle, and the vampires stood with champagne glasses in their hands, pretending to sip. Other men and women joined them, but Emerald and Katerina flanked Karl. The conversation was the social trivia Charlotte had always detested, although she could mimic it with ease. Stefan was right; in other circumstances this would have been amusing. She resented bitterly the way Katerina stood at Karl's side as if she belonged there – Karl making no move to dispel the impression.

Through everything, there was the tormenting thrill of being so close to Karl, unable to reach him. This feeling never died. She thought, *How could he bring Katerina? It's a cruel way to tell me, if that's what it is. I never dreamed it would be so difficult to see them together; I thought I could bear it but I can't. But I won't let him see I care; I won't even look at them.*

Instead she watched Andreas. He had the seductive glow of their kind even though he looked bored, as if was too much effort to smile. That sullen beauty was enough to draw people to him. Emerald was clearly fascinated. Charlotte distracted herself by guessing what was in her mind. She was very like Charlotte's Aunt Elizabeth: supreme in her confidence to conquer any man she wanted. And although Andreas and Stefan (Niklas too – imagine the novelty of seducing blond twins!) were equally enticing, the prize would have to be Karl – simply to prove she could steal him from Katerina.

You poor fool, Charlotte thought. *All you'll get from him is a sweet smile and a graceful refusal.* Then, with a shiver, she wondered if Stefan, Andreas or Katerina might feed on Lady Tremayne before the evening was out.

While she ignored Karl, she felt him watching her. The temptation to glance at him was overwhelming. She resisted, but still his eyes scorched darkly into her. Turning hot, she edged away to the satellite group forming around Stefan and Niklas.

Shielded by others, she glanced back and saw a Roman emperor leading Emerald Tremayne onto the dance floor. The band was beginning a slow waltz. She could just see Karl; he was excusing himself from the group, moving away. Where was he going?

To Charlotte's surprise, he was coming towards her. The group parted to let him through. She saw the dismissive coolness of Katerina's expression as he said, "Miss Kessler, may I have this dance?"

Charlotte felt like refusing, but could not. He led her onto the floor, slid one hand around her waist and twined his fingers with hers. They looked at each other; no word was spoken. They were both holding back. His eyes and face were a distracting veil over his thoughts; she dared not let their beauty slide through her guard. She was thinking, *Has he dismissed me forever, because of Violette and Katerina? Is this a polite goodbye? Or is he saying nothing because he's not sure of me, either?*

After a time, he said, "Can we stop pretending now, Charlotte?"

"Meeting at this party was not a good idea," she said flatly.

"No, it wasn't."

"Stefan didn't tell me you were coming."

"He meant well." His tone was off-hand. Her fears welled up and she felt dangerously close to crying. More than ever she tried to make her eyes blank and cold.

Yet as they danced, something happened. She avoided his gaze, looking over his shoulder at other couples. But how lovely Karl's hands felt. Nothing more deliciously sensual. And he was holding her closer with every step.

"Charlotte, look at me," he said. "You really are not aware of it, are you?"

"Aware of what?"

"The effect you have, all in white, with your hair loose." Now Karl was gazing at her as he always had, his irises deep amber lamps. His intensity left her defenceless... because he was bewitched by her, too. Useless, pretending to be reserved or cold to each other.

Then she understood, if she hadn't known all along. Their

passion for each other could never be divided among others.

"I think I have some idea," she said, and he smiled.

Artifice fell away. Charlotte found herself smiling back at him. Ah, the contour of his shoulders under the black velvet; the touch of his fingers on hers. The soft near-black chestnut of his hair, light sheening the strands with blood-red... His eyelids swept down, his long lashes dark against his cheeks as he looked at her throat. Desire. She turned hot and cold like the human she'd once been; a girl too nervous even to dance with him.

Charlotte sensed people watching them; Stefan with approval, Katerina and Lady Tremayne with mild disgust. She didn't care. *Let their jealousy eat them; they can never know how we really feel!*

As the music ended, Karl kissed her on the mouth, long and passionately, as if they were alone. Charlotte heard Emerald – a few feet away – gasp with shock. For all she knew, they'd only met an hour before!

Karl and Charlotte looked at each other, sharing the joke. "And your conduct in public is usually impeccable," she said.

"We should go somewhere more private, don't you agree?"

They moved through the crowd and slipped discreetly through some French doors. Outside, they found a lovely, intimate garden, divided by hedges and trellis into separate arbours. It was a town garden, not large, but curtains of foliage made it seem dense and endless. Karl and Charlotte walked slowly through the maze, hand in hand, letting the clear air and the subtle colours of night wrap round them. Each arbour had its own ambience; some were spacious, with a statue or fountain as a focus; others were tiny, swathed in clematis, climbing roses, wisteria. Plenty of places for lovers to hide. *Guests must love this garden*, Charlotte thought, although the air was too cold for more than a few courting couples to be outside. None turned to look as Karl and Charlotte passed.

In the furthest corner, they found a small bower, hidden by ivy and climbing roses. There was a wall-fountain, a stone bench, a bank of moss sloping into a tiny pocket of wild garden. They sat on the bench, but it seemed the cool breeze blew distance between them, and Charlotte became nervous.

"I sometimes wondered if we'd ever see each other again," she said.

"I knew we would. I only wondered if you wanted to."

"Well, now you know," she said. "I always did."

Karl stroked her cheek, gazing seriously at her; she was trembling, couldn't stop herself.

He said, "I went to *Swan Lake*."

She was startled. "You didn't tell me! Why didn't you come and sit with me?"

"I didn't say which performance I saw."

"But I've been at every one! I never knew you were there."

Slight sadness touched his mouth. "And that's why I didn't come to you."

"But I wish you had! Karl..." And Charlotte knew that she could not mention Violette. If he thought she only wanted to see him to discuss Violette –!

"I still can't entirely forgive you for not coming with Katti and me." He spoke with a touch of humour, but meant it, she knew.

"Have you anything to tell me?" she asked softly.

"A great deal." Karl began to tell her about Benedict, vampires rescued from the *Weisskalt*, the fire at Lancelyn's house and the confrontation... And although Charlotte listened with interest, and it was bliss simply to be with him, none of it answered her question.

"But," she said, hardly able to force out the name, "Katerina..."

"What about her?"

"Karl, for heaven's sake! Must I share you with her? Or are you about to tell me that you've abandoned me for her?"

Karl's reaction, as usual, was infuriatingly minimal. "If that were the case, I would not be here now."

"Well, why ever did you bring her? If a man comes to a rendezvous arm-in-arm with another woman, he can only be saying one thing. And pardon me, I'm not yet old or wise enough to rise above jealousy. I can't bear to think of you making love to her while I wasn't there..." Feeling tears in her eyes, she turned her head away.

Karl let out a soft breath. All the time he spoke, he stroked the long skeins of her hair. "We were playing games, you and I, when we met this evening. Both pretending not to mind what the other did. But it's pointless, and only hurts us, because neither of us are game-players at heart. I have not made love to Katti.

She's offended that I refused, even though she has Andreas now. I brought her tonight, not to parade her as my lover, but to convince her that I still love *you*. No one else, ever. And I agree, these things shouldn't matter to us, who are immortal and supernatural; but they do. They still do."

"Oh, God." Charlotte sighed. Her tears became those of relief. She could say nothing articulate; *I love you to distraction and I hate myself and I've missed you, forgive me, forgive me, please...* Only, "God."

"Beloved, when will we know each other well enough to have absolute trust?" Karl sank his fingers through her hair and kissed her; and they both knew. Katerina didn't matter, Violette was forgotten. There was only this.

Charlotte tipped back her head as Karl rested his lips on her neck; the gentlest, most loving of gestures, because he could have bitten her, and chose not to. She put one hand in his hair and held him lightly, feeling the moment whip through her, like a breath held too long.

Then, without another word, Karl took her hand and led her down into the wild garden. Under the foliage of birches and weeping cherries, she took off her dress and spread it on the moss-cushions, and they lay down together on its soft white folds. The night-chill, too cold for humans, was no more than a prickle on their flesh.

"How have we let so much time pass?" Charlotte whispered. Karl was removing his velvet coat, but she pulled him to her, still half-dressed. "Never mind that."

Smiling, he did not protest.

An imperative fever took possession of them, humanly urgent, weirdly heightened by the dark sweetness of the garden. Like falling, like flying. Karl's heat swept Charlotte into a pleasure so searing and convulsive that afterwards she was left shaking and almost too weak to move. Too drained to slide her canines into Karl's neck, as she would usually have done... And she realised that Karl had not bitten her throat, either. For some hazy reason, she was glad.

They had no wish to go back into the house. They dressed, not speaking but kissing often; began to tidy each others' dishevelled clothes and hair, then stopped and clutched each other – her head on his shoulder, his head resting on hers – under the dappled trees.

Leaving the garden through a side gate, Charlotte took Karl back to the hotel where she was staying with the Ballet Janacek.

There, on her bed in the big shadowy room, they made love again. More gentleness and passion this time, no sense of the hours passing. With snowflake delicacy they stroked each other's gleaming bodies, feeding on beauty without ever taking a drop of blood. *This is almost too exquisite to bear,* Charlotte thought; *why does there have to be anything to life but this?*

Again, at the end, orgasm did not plunge her into the deeper lust for blood. She wanted to... but let the feeling go. And although Karl pressed his lips to her neck, he did not break the skin.

He lay across her, teeth just grazing her shoulder. When he lifted his head and gazed down at her, dark red hair falling into his eyes, he looked as shaken as she felt. He was no longer smiling. Neither was she.

"This is the danger, is it not, *liebchen*?" he said softly. "That desire can take us completely out of ourselves."

"Completely into someone else," she said. "Yes. Like feeding ..."

"No, even more than that, because in taking blood you gain control; in sex you lose it. And to surrender our power like this is frightening..."

"To a vampire?" she said. But she knew exactly what he meant. "Still?"

"But I haven't seen you for such a long time, Charlotte. The memories fade a little, so when we experience this again, the intensity is devastating. It can never lose its hold."

"I remember the first time," she said. "I was a girl, ridiculously innocent until you seduced me. I had no idea such feelings existed; not outside guilty dreams, at least. Then you showed me and, God, I didn't know what had hit me. I have never been so terrified, discovering how it could take me over, mind, body and soul. Just that tiny word that could never be mentioned. Sex. Infatuation, passion, love..."

A faint smile lengthened Karl's mouth. "I know. But let us be honest, neither of us was sorry, were we? And I tell you, it's worse for a vampire, because we are not used to giving up our power in such an abandoned way."

"I had a foolish thought, just now. I wished we were both human. I wish we didn't have to hunt for blood to live. That we had no worse cause for guilt than the fact that we aren't married. But these thoughts are an irrational weakness, aren't they?"

"No, but they cause you pain," said Karl. "And such pain can be dangerous. Sometimes I understand why Kristian forbade us from loving anyone but him and his God."

Charlotte turned on her side, propped her head on one hand. "Well, which do you prefer, love or self-control? Would you leave me, rather than be a slave to passion?"

She asked idly, but regretted the question at once. *If you can't bear the answer*, she thought, *never, ever ask*. She closed her eyes, felt Karl's hand on her hip. Warm and divine his fingers felt, like silk.

"Now, I never said that, beloved. But I might be forgiven for wondering if you distanced yourself from me for the same reason?"

Charlotte thought of Violette and her heart sank. She shook her head. "It's a lie," she said, "this talk of self-sufficiency. We're always in thrall to something. Someone."

"The dancer?" said Karl.

"Don't," said Charlotte. She lay back, pulling him down. "Shh."

His long, leanly muscular body pressed the length of hers, and she felt the two sharp points of his fangs puncture her veins... Her back arched with the stinging pleasure. No human terror, but still there was an acute thrust of disbelief that he was not human... delicious amazement that she was unhuman, too.

After a time, Karl curled his arm under her hair and drew her down to his throat. "Share the milk of Paradise," he whispered.

Hours later, Charlotte saw dawn glimmering through the windows. Time to enter the Crystal Ring to rest. Lying here with Karl, she should have felt supremely happy, but could not. She hadn't asked the question. She'd put it off all night in favour of pleasure, but it hung in the twilight, a great iron bell that must toll eventually.

While they bathed and dressed – Karl still in his black velvet – she was trying to summon courage to speak. *Now, before it's too late!*

"After the Crystal Ring," he said, "I'm going back to Benedict. Will you come with me?"

"Karl..."

"It's not an ultimatum, beloved. Stay here for now, if you wish. I only ask that we don't spend months apart again." He looked closely at her, concerned. "But be honest with me, and tell me what is troubling you."

Ask him! "I need your help."

"Yes?" He looked wary, but resigned, as if he already knew.

"You're going to say no, but please don't, not at once. I want you to help me make Violette into a vampire."

"*Liebe Gott*." He turned away from her. "I knew you were going to ask this."

"How?" she cried.

"Instinct. Why else did you want to see me, after all these months?"

"Karl, don't! I'm asking for your help. I could have asked someone else, and never told you at all. But I don't want secrets. I want you to be part of it."

"Charlotte, you cannot just –"

"No, listen to my reasons! Don't turn away. You can't think I'd do this on a whim. Even Stefan has more faith in my judgment than you! Violette is ill. If we don't transform her she won't be able to dance much longer. She will be crippled."

Karl reacted calmly, but she felt him withdrawing with every word. This was precisely as awful as she'd dreaded.

"Is her disease likely to be fatal?"

"I don't think so, but she will die if she can't dance. She asked me to kill her; she said if I don't, she'll kill herself."

"A dramatic threat."

"But she means it."

He half-turned and said gently, "Then I am sorry she caused you pain. But the transformation cannot be used as a panacea for mortal ills. And whatever the reason, it would be wrong."

"Was it wrong to transform me?" she said. "Do you regret it?"

"Yes, it was wrong, and no, I don't regret it, but all the arguments still stand. Bringing you through the veil did not negate them. Don't do it, Charlotte. Let her be."

"Let her die, you mean! Don't you think it would be selfish, to keep this from her?"

"Unselfishness is not the most notable attribute of vampires."

"Why do you hate Violette?"

"Why do you hate Katerina?"

She shook her head. "I don't. Not now."

"Because I told you the truth; you have told me nothing. I don't hate Violette, I feel nothing for her. But why do you care so passionately about her fate?"

"She's my friend, but she is something special; almost more than human already. I can't explain," Charlotte said fervently. "I don't ask lightly; I never asked this for Anne, or Maddy, or..."

"Exactly. What makes her so compelling?"

"Her talent."

"There are many talented ballerinas. Don't you realise that, as a vampire, she may have no desire to go on dancing? Do you care about your father's atomic research? Do I play the cello, except for idle amusement? Does Andreas write great poetry? No, because when we enter undeath, mortal achievement becomes meaningless."

His intractable, quiet anger floored her. "Not Violette."

"Her art and her talent will outlive her. Isn't that immortality enough?"

"Not for her! Karl, please."

"No. I will not make another of our kind. You never know what you're unleashing on the world. I took the risk with you because I couldn't bear to lose you; but she is nothing to me."

"But something to *me*; doesn't that count?"

Karl ignored the question. "The transformation may kill her."

"Not her. She's too strong." Charlotte despaired of changing his mind. Hopeless, this argument; neither of them could or would give way.

"How many of us can the world support before we are discovered, exposed, openly feared?"

"How would they destroy us?" Charlotte said scornfully. "You carried out experiments in my father's laboratory and found nothing... almost nothing."

"That is irrelevant. My fear isn't of being destroyed, but of too many vampires being made. Perhaps Kristian had the right idea, to put certain vampires in the *Weisskalt*. He may have been justified in guarding his flock so zealously."

"You can't be saying you'd kill other vampires, so a precious few could survive?"

"Why not?" Karl's tone was detached, inscrutable. "Are you and I and our friends not precious? Only so many wolves can prey on the sheep."

"Don't." Charlotte shuddered. "I never think of them as sheep, or as prey!"

"I know, dearest. You find it so distasteful to touch a stranger that you have to believe you love them before you can feed." A sound of denial escaped her throat but he continued, "And I am the opposite; with me it must be strangers, because I can't bear to hurt those I know. But it doesn't matter. These are delusions. We are predators, they are our prey. And they cannot support huge numbers of us."

Charlotte moved around him as he spoke, studying him from every angle. He changed with the light, like the sea. How icily ruthless he looked one moment; and then how troubled.

"Just one more vampire, Karl. Not a legion. Why do you fear her?"

Karl was hard to read, but from the merest lift of his eyebrows, Charlotte knew she'd hit the truth. He seemed startled that she noticed.

She asked again, "What are you afraid of?"

"You, sometimes," he said, taking her hand. "I don't know, Charlotte. I am not afraid; I simply feel that with Violette it would be dangerous, very wrong. You know it too, don't you? I could stop you. If not with words, with force." His hand tightened on hers and she stared at him. "But you know I'd never use force against you. I am not Kristian. The decision is yours."

"But what if you don't agree with my choice?"

"Leave her alone," he said. "Come away with me."

"Dear God, do you think I don't want to? If only! But I can't."

They were both silent for a time. Karl's eyes were contemplative, baleful. Eventually he said, "Well, in truth, the decision should be Violette's. Dare you give her a choice?"

"No," Charlotte admitted. "I don't think she'd understand. You said it yourself; no one can understand, until they pass through the veil."

Karl dropped her hand. "So I'm wasting my breath."

To her shock, he made for the door.

"Karl!" When he didn't stop, she said in distress, "If I transform her, will you ever forgive me?"

His only reply was a brief backward glance, but the look said, *I don't think so.*

CHAPTER SIXTEEN

"GAZING WHERE THE LILIES BLOW"

Karl returned to Benedict's house in the morning. Looking at the brown-brick cottage in the quiet leafy street, no one would dream that anything extraordinary was happening inside. Ruffles of Virginia creeper on the walls glowed vividly crimson.

Karl stood outside for a few minutes, a familiar despondency spreading within him. *Violette already has too much power over Charlotte*, he thought. *She's the last person I'd wish to see made immortal. But if nothing I say will make Charlotte stop, it is going to happen.*

A horse-drawn cart clopped past; an old man in a cap cycled laboriously towards the town centre, trousers flapping. Ah, the sweet song of robins, even as autumn gathered...

Perhaps I should be angry with Charlotte, Karl thought, *but that would only drive her further away.* Anger was not what he felt, anyway. He was calm, but dull pain made him long to feed; to recapture the pleasure of being with her, to release sorrow in a rush of blood-red ecstasy.

That, however, would have to wait until dark.

Entering the house, he heard voices in the parlour. Ben and Holly were talking in hushed, stricken tones as if they had received a monstrous shock.

Karl found Holly huddled on the sofa, Ben leaning on the sofa-back with clasped hands, Katerina and Andreas listening. The fire burned strongly, painting their faces with orange light. Katerina, perched on the arm of Andreas's chair, looked up at Karl with her strong eyebrows raised. Cool surprise, as if she hadn't expected him to come back.

Karl asked, "What's wrong?"

Holly had been crying; she was pale, her head bowed. Benedict straightened up and answered hoarsely, "We've had some bad news. My assistant at the bookshop, Maud, passed away this morning. Thing is, Holly woke me at dawn, frantic because she had a nightmare that Lancelyn had killed Maud. I told her to go back to sleep, but she couldn't. So, to put her mind at rest, we went to Maud's house to make sure she was all right." He swallowed, turning greyish. "Her landlady was on the doorstep, seeing the doctor off. They told us that Maud had died about an hour earlier."

"From what cause?"

"The doctor was cautious. Said it was probably a lung infection that worsened, or a severe asthma attack..."

"Had she been ill before?"

"Never, as far as I know. But Holly's dream..."

"Mrs Grey?" Karl said softly. "You've had these premonitions before."

She looked up, her eyes starkly bright against the ash-rose pallor of her cheeks. Although he felt intense sympathy, he knew that the attention of a vampire would not comfort her.

"It wasn't a premonition," she murmured. "I actually saw it happening. It was like a weird, horrific dream, but somehow *true*. I saw Lancelyn telling Maud that he'd used her, and she'd let him down. Then a thin black figure appeared and leaned over her. I became her; as the creature leaned down, I felt all my heat being sucked out, a crushing coldness and languor falling on me – but I knew it was happening to *her*, not to me. It was horrible, I can't tell you how horrible."

Karl thought for a moment. "It sounds consistent with the way a vampire might steal vitality rather than blood. The effect is to make the slightest illness fatal. It's not usually so swift, but certainly possible."

Holly shivered at his stark confirmation. Karl said, "Well, Benedict, do you believe that Lancelyn was responsible?"

"I'd rather not believe some of Holly's visions, but... it's so similar to what happened to James and Deirdre. The black figure sounds like the shades we saw at his house. If Lancelyn's 'daemons' are some kind of vampire..." Benedict moved to the mantelpiece and lit a cigarette, hands shaking. Karl found the smoke unpleasant. "The victim could have been Holly! It doesn't bear thinking about!"

"No, I still don't believe Lancelyn would hurt me," she said. "Not fatally, anyway." She raised her chin and gave Ben a painfully complex look. "I haven't finished. In the vision, Maud lured me to Lancelyn's house with a message that he... wanted to marry me in some kind of occult ceremony."

"*What?*" Ben gasped.

Holly went on with obvious difficulty. "Then she claimed that she'd tricked me to my death, because – because you and Lancelyn wanted to get rid of me. But Lancelyn appeared to tell her, no, *she* was the one who'd been tricked. He'd set this vile trap for her, knowing she'd walk into it. So perhaps part of her message was real; that Lancelyn intends to steal me from you, Ben. What is the 'Dark Bride'?" She spoke accusingly, through fierce tears. "How much of the vision is true? I'm damned if I know!"

Ben looked blank, but rage glimmered in his eyes. "I don't know, love. Perhaps he invaded your mind as he did with Deirdre. If so, if he imagines he can take you away from me and – God, he doesn't deserve to live!"

His vehemence made Holly wince. Remorseful, he went to her and touched her shoulder, his voice soft and pleading. "Look, darling, I know you're reluctant to think ill of Lancelyn, and furious about my summoning rituals – but can't you accept now that I'm justified?"

Karl saw her freeze under his touch. Anger flushed her cheeks, but her voice was small and diamond-edged. "Yes, Ben, I know. I had little sympathy for Maud, but the way Lancelyn dealt with her was brutal, completely unforgivable. Everything I felt for him died with Maud. I'm on your side, Ben. I support you absolutely, unconditionally, in everything."

His face shone as she spoke. He opened his mouth to express delight, only for Holly to push his hand off her shoulder, almost slapping it away, as she leapt up and marched to the door. Ben stared after her in dismay. "Holly!"

The door slammed and she was gone. Ben turned and thumped the mantelpiece so hard that a vase fell over and smashed on the grate. "Damn it to hell!"

"I'll go after her," Andreas said, standing up.

"I shouldn't," Karl said sharply.

Andreas gave a twisted smile. "She trusts me."

"All the more reason for you to stay away from her, then."

Andreas blinked, cat-like, as if to say, *What are you going to do about it?* but he remained in the room.

"Why are you angry?" Karl asked, turning to Ben. "This isn't your wife's fault."

"I'm not angry with her. It's bloody Lancelyn. I thought I'd got the edge on him. But he's mocking me, showing he still has the most power and can do what the devil he likes – and I can't retaliate because I don't know where in hell he is! Can I never bloody well win?"

"But why should you win?" Karl said coldly. "Have you a God-given right to win, or to use unnatural forces as a weapon?"

"No more and no less than he has," Benedict said through his teeth. "We've got to find him. Finish him before he finishes us."

Katerina said, "He's right, Karl. This may have begun as a foolish human affair but it affects us all now. Lancelyn is dangerous."

"I know," said Karl. "Benedict, if I were you, I would make sure Holly is safe. Are you sure you have full control over the other vampires?"

"Yes," Ben said, "but I'll go after her anyway. Damn, I wish she'd gone to her mother's!"

"She's probably safer here," said Katerina. She rose and went to Ben; effortlessly maternal yet seductive, as she always was with men she liked. "We should call everyone together and explain. Some are asking questions. I've told them a little but I should warn you, they aren't happy. They are not all sweet reasonable creatures who will do anything you ask."

"Thank you for the warning," Ben said grimly, and left.

Katerina walked to Karl but stopped an arm's length from him, when normally she would have kissed him. She looked well-rested and rosy with stolen blood. Perhaps Karl's paleness betrayed him; she seemed to know that all was not well between him and Charlotte.

"My dear, what a surprise to see you," she said in German. "After you vanished last night, I didn't expect you back so soon. Didn't you bring the errant waif with you?"

"If you mean Charlotte, you can see she is not here,"

"And I was so sure you were reconciled."

Andreas strode towards the door, his face a map of disgust. "Excuse me," he said viciously. "I cannot listen to this."

He left the door open; Karl heard him running upstairs after Ben. "So, you've been giving Andreas a hard time?"

Katerina faced him, quietly hostile. "About what? It's nothing to us that you disappeared with her."

"Katti, there is no point in our quarrelling about this," he said gently.

"No point in even discussing it, I suppose."

"Not really."

She glared at him. Then her coldness dissolved into concern. "Karl, you look so worried. I'm sorry. I didn't mean to spit poison at you the moment I saw you."

He enfolded her in his arms; her body felt different to Charlotte's, taller and firmer, not as slender or deliciously rounded – but just as familiar and warm. He was thirsty and could easily have bitten the sweet flesh of her neck – but he resisted. "Forgive me. I wouldn't hurt you for the world. You haven't lost me. You never will, but Charlotte…"

"Is your soulmate?" Katti said with a sour smile. "I understand."

"We had a difference of opinion, but it changes nothing. There is no force that could weaken our love for each other. I wish you would accept that."

He felt her breathe in and out against his shoulder.

"Of course I accept it. I've been foolish; I was frightened. That's what the *Weisskalt* does. We'll always be close, Karl, whether we make love or not; what is sex anyway? Such a human weakness, when there's so much else. I have nothing against Charlotte; I'm sure I'll grow to love her, as I love Rachel. After all, I am a graceful loser. So, won't you tell me what happened?"

Karl shook his head. "There is no point," he said wearily. "Katti, would you do something for me, please?"

"If I can." She detached herself from him, self-contained now.

"What you said to Ben is true. If he tries to keep a nest of full-grown fledglings they will start killing each other. Once they're able to enter the Crystal Ring again, he cannot hold them. So we must reach an agreement before any blood is shed. When we call them together, I'd like Stefan and Ilona to be here. Would you go and fetch them?"

"Of course. What about Pierre?"

"If you see him, but I don't think he's interested."

"And Charlotte?"

He did not reply.

"Karl," she said chidingly. "She's clearly hurt you and you don't want me to say, 'I told you so'. But it's not for me to pass judgment on her." She caressed his hair. "In the past you always told me everything. That hasn't changed... has it?"

He looked at her lovely face, and knew there was no point in keeping secrets. "Charlotte wants to bring Violette Lenoir into the Crystal Ring. I can't stop her, but I won't help her."

"Ah. But you can't destroy Charlotte's obsession by refusing. You might make it worse. Would it be easier to share her with another man than with a woman?"

Karl smiled thinly. "You don't realise, I share her with her victims all the time. Whether their relationship is friendly, or sexual, or one of vampire and enthralled victim, it doesn't matter. In a way, it's all one; for us, the boundaries hardly exist. I don't mind her having friends, even other lovers, as long as they do not supplant me. But there's something about Violette..."

"What? I am intrigued, dear."

"Nothing I can put into words. I feel that Charlotte and Violette... will destroy each other."

Katerina looked thoughtful. "You could put a stop to their association."

"But I won't."

"Nothing that would tar you with Kristian's brush?"

"No freedom without responsibility, Katti. She must do what she thinks is right, and bear the consequences."

"I'll never understand you!" she said. "For one of the kindest, most passionate people I've ever met, Karl, you can also be the most ruthless, cold-hearted –"

"Close the door on your way out," said Karl.

Violette danced a glorious final performance of *Swan Lake*, unaware that this would be her last night as a mortal.

Charlotte had to make a decision, but could not tell Violette. *Asking* her, discussing it at all, was out of the question; she knew the ballerina would refuse, and she dared not take the risk.

"It must be that night," she had told Stefan. "The company travels back to Salzburg the following day. I have to bring her to you while we're still in London. If it's going to happen, let it be as soon as possible."

"If you are sure you're doing the right thing," said Stefan.

As the time came closer, Charlotte was racked by apprehension – but not indecision. "No, I'm not sure," she said. "All I know is that I am going to do it."

"Well, you'll be pleased to hear that Ilona is happy to help us."

"Good," said Charlotte, then stopped to think. *My God, it was Ilona who attacked Violette's father! We can't possibly – but no, there's no reason for Violette to guess who she is. It will be all right.*

Stefan saw her expression. "Oh, not another objection, surely? I'm running out of immortals to ask!"

"No," she said quickly. "Ilona is ideal."

"I'll make certain she is there on the night. All you have to worry about is Violette."

That, thought Charlotte, was worry enough.

Superb as the last performance was, Charlotte could not enjoy it. Seeing Violette dance like a feather, despite her pain; to witness the audience's adoration, the ocean of bouquets, the endless curtain calls, moved Charlotte to tears. Violette laughed and wept and looked genuinely happy. And Charlotte thought, *What right have I to take her away from this? To change the course of her life, to decide that I know better than nature? Yes, I might make her immortal... but I may cause her death, or turn her away from dancing forever...*

What is this voice inside me that insists I must do this?

Violette made a token appearance at the after-show party, seeming overwhelmed and embarrassed by the adulation showered on her. She drank too much champagne and left early – not with her usual poise, but hurriedly and in tears.

Charlotte followed her back to the hotel – walking, while Violette went by car – and waited until she dismissed Geli. Then Charlotte entered softly, without knocking.

She was trembling from head to foot, as nervous as any human. Only vampiric strength of will pushed her on. *It is going to happen tonight,* she told herself. *Tonight.*

The suite was decked with white flowers and porcelain swans, gifts from well-wishers. The gorgeous scent of chrysanthemums filled the air. There was even a flower sculpture in the shape of a swan, a work of art, beside the chaise longue where Violette lay.

The dancer, in the lavender georgette dress she'd worn to the party, was embowered by lilies, her lapis-lazuli eyes reflecting petals and leaves in perfect miniature. Seeing Charlotte, she smiled and raised a languid hand to greet her.

"Are you in any pain?" Charlotte asked.

"No, none. I feel wonderful."

A sudden rush of hope. "Is there any chance the doctors were wrong, that you're getting better?"

Foolish question; Violette didn't know her fate hung on the answer. "Do you have to? I was happy until you mentioned it."

"I'm sorry. You were crying when you left the party."

Violette pursed her lips and gave a quick shake of her head. "It's a dreadful responsibility, to be almost... worshipped. I try to tell them it isn't just me, but my dancers and musicians, my set designers, everyone... but they won't listen. I want to say, will you still love me when my joints are like footballs and I walk with a stick? I can't accept it gracefully, being feted. Not like Pavlova." She gazed down, brooding. "Their love made me cry. The audience, and the company. So wonderful. This evening has been perfect. One minute I'm crying and the next laughing; that's why I'm here. I can't cope with it."

Charlotte moved to a sideboard and uncorked a bottle of wine. "This is the price of genius, my dear friend."

Violette laughed. "I don't deserve perfection, but who cares? I have it, apparently. Why not enjoy it? Bring me a glass of that wine, darling."

Charlotte had already poured a glass and added drops from a small bottle. She took it to Violette, but paused, twisting the stalk between her fingers.

"Are you going to give me the glass or just stand there waving it over me?" said the dancer.

Charlotte was finding it hard to behave like anything but a vampire. She forgot human niceties and spoke her thoughts. "Even if you weren't ill, you would die anyway. It's only a matter of time. You can't dance forever."

Violette blinked, as if alarmed by her tone. "What's the matter with you?" She sat up, putting a protective hand on her throat.

Charlotte gave her the glass. "I'm sorry, I don't mean to upset you."

"You haven't." Violette swallowed half the wine and made a face. "Ugh, this tastes coarse after champagne. Never mind, it has the same effect. Didn't you tell me to forget the future? Today, tomorrow, I can still dance. As soon as we reach Salzburg we'll start something new. They want us to tour America again; there's talk of South America, too, and even Australia. I wonder if I'll ever go there?"

She went on sipping. Charlotte sat beside her, watching. After a few minutes she said. "Of course you will. Everywhere. A new ballet – of your own?"

"After *Dans le Jardin*? I don't think so."

"But if you chose a less sensitive subject..."

"Something frivolous, to suit the mood? Perhaps. Why should anyone be interested in my dark side –" Violette stopped, took a quick, deep breath.

"What's wrong?" Charlotte said softly, knowing.

"I – I'm not sure. My chest feels heavy. The room's going round."

"You drank the wine too fast. A walk in the fresh air will help." She went to the wardrobe, found the drab coat and hat Violette wore when she did not want to be recognised.

"Oh, I'm too tired, I can't..."

She didn't resist as Charlotte raised her to her feet and dressed her. She staggered and blinked, confused. As they descended in the lift she leaned on Charlotte, giggling. Charlotte prayed she would not pass out in the lobby.

She hurried Violette outside and into a taxi-cab. Only as the vehicle pulled away into the street did Violette seem to realise that something was amiss.

"S'sn't a walk. My head... feels like a lead weight on a rope, whirling," she slurred. "Something in the wine."

"I told you, you drank it too fast."

"No. Not wine. Opium... you drugged me?"

"Yes," said Charlotte.

As the cab took a corner, Violette fell heavily against her, unable to right herself.

"Why?"

Charlotte put an arm round her. Oh, the lovely pliancy of her limbs, the slow thunder of her heart as it fought the drug to keep the blood flowing around her young body... "I said I'd help you, dearest. But you mustn't fight me."

Violette, heavy-lidded, looked hazily into her guardian demon's face. And even through the fog, Charlotte felt her stiffen with fear, saw the awful realisation dawn in her clouded eyes.

Violette knew. *She knew*.

By the time they reached Stefan's flat, Violette had almost no control over her muscles, but was fighting oblivion with all her might. Charlotte had only wanted to spare her any terror. As Stefan greeted them, though, she physically felt a rigor of fear travel up the dancer's throat.

"I think you've overdone it a little," Stefan said drily.

"No, I didn't give her enough. She's still frightened."

They sat Violette in Stefan's glamorous drawing room and she lolled like a rag doll, eyes rolling under the lids. Then she roused again, stared at Niklas – a silent pale-eyed ghost of Stefan – and shrank back with fear that was pitiful to witness.

Horrible, to see Violette stripped of her supreme poise and self-control. Charlotte thought, *How can I do this to her?* And yet Violette still retained her grace, and that more than anything made Charlotte wretched with guilt. For the hundredth time, she pushed her foreboding away.

"Oh, God, let's do this as fast as possible. Where's Ilona?"

"On her way, I hope," said Stefan. "Does Madame know what's going to happen?"

"I haven't told her, but I think she's guessed. I knew she'd fight me. That's why I gave her laudanum. I'd never have got her here otherwise."

Stefan gave her a quizzical look, eyes wide. "Persuasion?"

"You don't know her!" Charlotte snapped. "Will it matter, if the laudanum's in her blood when we transform her?"

"No. Drugs have so little effect on us. It may make us light-headed, which won't matter as long as we don't lose concentration. Will you be the one to take her life?"

Horrifying thought, yet she felt a swell of desire. To hold Violette in her arms, to feel that perfect skin against her lips; the hot burst of blood in her mouth... and this time, no need to stop, just to draw out her life, on and on...

"Yes, I'll do it." Charlotte turned away quickly, so he wouldn't see her trembling.

Violette cried, "No!" Far from calming her, intoxication was making her panic.

Stefan said kindly, "Shouldn't you explain what to expect, calm her down that way?"

Charlotte knelt by Violette's chair. "Don't be afraid. We're going to make you like us. The process takes three of us; we're waiting for the third. Believe me, it's nothing to be afraid of. And afterwards you'll never be ill. You will be able to dance for eternity."

"But the Devil..."

"The Devil is not involved, I promise."

Violette went on shaking her head. Tears flowed down her face. She could barely speak, but her posture was expressive of profound grief, like Giselle in the ballet. "Don't, Charlotte," she whispered. "If you love me, please don't do this."

The plea was a powerful wave that hit Charlotte full in the chest. *How can I go on with this? It's the last thing in the world she wants, the cruellest thing...* But she said harshly, "It will be all right." She pulled away, paced across the room. "It will!" She had to make her heart fossil-hard – frightening that she could do it so easily.

Violette closed her eyes and shuddered from head to foot.

"Where's Ilona?" Charlotte said again.

"Relax." Stefan stroked her neck. "She's coming. Are you absolutely sure this is what you want?"

No. Yes. I don't know but I cannot stop it! She nodded mutely.

A short time later, a rift opened the air like the tearing of tissue-paper and Ilona stepped into the room, a neat figure in a maroon cloche hat, coat and leather gloves of the exact same shade. As she removed the hat, smoothing her shingled plum-red hair around the perfect heart of her face, Violette gave a hoarse cry.

"Good God!" Ilona said indignantly. "What's wrong with her? Is my hairstyle out of fashion already?"

Charlotte went to Violette and tried desperately to console her. "Hush. Don't be afraid, she's here to help us."

At last Violette forced out the words, "You called her Ilona!"

"Yes."

Hard to hear the words, but Charlotte made out, "My father, my father..."

Ilona said, "Charlotte, dear, whatever is she saying? Can't you quiet her?"

"I'm trying!" she said, but Violette was writhing under her hands, repeating, *"Father, father..."*

In dismay, Charlotte understood. "Oh, God," she breathed. "She once told me that a vampire attacked her father and caused his madness and death. She thinks it was you, Ilona. She recognised your name."

"I've never met her wretched father! She's demented!"

"How do you know?" Charlotte said angrily. "The way she described the attack, it couldn't have been anyone else!"

"Well, what if you are right?" Ilona glared at Violette. "I can't be expected to remember individuals. If I killed your father, dear, he must have deserved it."

Violette lunged drunkenly forward, almost falling off the chair. Charlotte held her back.

"She doesn't want this, does she?" Ilona leaned down, her face near the dancer's. "I didn't want it either, dear, but I got it. I didn't even know what was happening; at least you seem to have some idea. Am I right, Charlotte? She doesn't want it – but you do, therefore it must happen? Just like Karl. In the name of love, his will must be done. And the irony is that now he refuses help you in exactly the same violation – so here I am instead."

"Why did you agree, if you're so bitter?"

"Anything to upset Karl," Ilona said. "Why should I care what Violette wants anyway? Let's get on with it."

But Violette shrank from Ilona, clutching at Charlotte; even grasping Stefan, who was on the other side of her chair. "Not her! Anyone but her! If I can't stop you, please, I beg of you, don't force me with her. Not her, not her."

Ilona stood glowering at Charlotte. "Charming. If that's the way she feels, she can go to hell."

"Wait –" Charlotte began helplessly, but in the face of Violette's revulsion and Ilona's rage, she knew there was no point in arguing.

Ilona leaned down and touched Violette's hand. "And if they transform you into a vampire, you *will* go to hell, of course."

"Stop it!" Charlotte cried. "Get out!"

Karl's daughter picked up her hat, smiled sweetly, and vanished.

The moment she went, Violette seemed to lose all her strength and slumped over, clinging to Charlotte's hands. Stefan, giving Charlotte a resigned look, carried Violette into the bedroom – the room where Charlotte had talked to Karl, just before he, Stefan and Pierre had transformed her; their last conversation and last embrace as human and vampire.

Charlotte sat at the polished Italian dining table with her head in her hands, thinking, *What are we going to do? I wanted this to take place gently, with love.*

Stefan came back, pulling the door to behind him.

"How is she?" Charlotte asked.

"Asleep. Passed out," said Stefan. "Lord, she is beautiful. Just like Snow White. I would love to wake her, a prince with a difference."

"Make her spit out the poisoned apple and come back to life," Charlotte murmured. "What can we do now? Could just the two of us –?"

He sat beside her and placed his hand over hers. Through everything, Niklas sat like a mannequin, a faint frown shadowing his crystal-gold eyes. That was all the emotion he ever showed, an indistinct echo of Stefan's.

"I won't risk it. Without enough energy to take her into the Crystal Ring, she'd die. We'll find someone else – if you still want to go through with it."

Pain settled around her throat. "I can't go back."

"There is Pierre, if you could stand him, or one or two others I could ask, though it may take time to find them."

"I wonder if Andreas would agree?"

"He wouldn't want to displease Karl." They were silent for a minute, then Stefan said, "Why are you crying?"

"I don't know," Charlotte said. "It's ridiculous."

"Tell me."

She took a quick, sobbing breath. "Karl never had this burning desire to make me a vampire, as I have for Violette. It didn't possess him so strongly that it nearly killed him. He didn't take me away and simply do it. It wasn't a burning light!"

"Charlotte..."

"And I'm crying because he's not here now. Because he wouldn't help me, wouldn't see..."

"Charlotte, try to understand him. What you're doing to Violette is what he did to Ilona! And he thinks you'll live to regret it, as he did. Then, next time the desire comes to transform someone, you'll fight it and it will be agony, whatever your decision. How can you say he didn't burn? You were there. You know everything he felt and the anguish he endured. You know."

"Yes. I know." She let her head drop. The tears eased their hold. "Why are you so good to me?"

"Why not? It's easy to be kind. It's especially easy with you, because you respond so sweetly. Besides, it gives me pleasure." Stefan leaned over, lifted her chin, and kissed her lips; the kiss of a lover and friend, such a rare combination, electrifying and soothing all at once.

"I could fall in love with you, Stefan," she said.

"I am in love with you, Charlotte."

"No, you're not. You only love yourself."

"And Niklas!" he said indignantly.

"As I said; yourself. But then, I seem to fall in love with almost anyone."

"Oh, now I am insulted," Stefan said lightly.

"I'm sorry, I didn't mean..."

"Oh, don't apologise. I know you think the world of me."

Charlotte laughed. "Well, I do." They kissed again, and the kiss was delicious, lingering, poignant because they both knew it would never go any further. Stefan's lips slid down to her neck and she thought he would bite her... but he only planted a kiss on her collarbone, and pulled back.

"It's easy for us to love each other, because we will never cause each other pain," he said. For once he was serious, even sad. "You'll never make demands on me, because there is nothing you really want of me. And I will never tear your heart to pieces, because only Karl has that power. Hasn't he?"

"Only Karl," she agreed.

Stefan went to his twin, stood behind him and stroked his blond hair. Niklas looked ahead with a slight smile: a porcelain doll. "It's Niklas I feel sorry for. He can never share the pleasures of helping friends or kissing lovers."

"But he never feels pain, either, does he?"

"Is that good? It only means he can never understand." Stefan seemed far away, and for a moment sorrow burned from him like a white sword. Then he was himself again. "Why don't you go and look at Snow White?"

Charlotte went into the bedroom and sat on the bed. Violette lay with her head on one side, her bare left arm an ivory curve against the covers. She was awake. Her eyes glistened darkly under not-quite-closed lids.

"I'm sorry, Violette," Charlotte whispered. "I've made such a mess of this. I never meant to frighten or force you, but I couldn't see any other way. I don't know how to explain!"

Violette half-turned her head to look at her. Her voice was languid and hoarse, as if she barely had strength to speak. "It's all right, Charlotte. I know. I always knew this was going to happen. I was born with this curse... What use is it to fight?"

"You make it sound so negative, so evil."

"But that's what I am. I can't resist my own nature."

"You are not evil!"

"According to the Church, the tiniest unrepented sin may condemn us to hell. What does it mean then, to lie willingly in the arms of a vampire while I wait to be taken into your ranks?"

Charlotte gripped her arm in frustration. "But if there's no God – if mortals can be as bad as we are – oh, I don't know what to say, because you're right! There are no excuses. We have nothing to commend us. What I intend to do to you is wrong. But tell me you don't want it, that you'd rather sit crippled in a wheelchair, or give up and die, and I'll let you go."

Violette only sighed. "It doesn't work that way," she said tiredly. "My intellect rejects you, but my instinct says I have no choice. It's nothing to do with dancing or cheating illness. It's something quite separate... I don't understand. Perhaps it's the wine and opium. I won't fight you... but I'm still frightened, Charlotte."

"Don't be." She kissed Violette's limp hand. She preferred it when Violette fought; this bleak acceptance of the inevitable was ghastly.

"But I'm terrified." Violette took a short, dry breath. "I'm so damned terrified I could die."

Voices from the outer room. Charlotte sensed another vampire and thought *Karl!* – even as she knew it was not him. Giving Violette's hand a squeeze, she went into the drawing room and was astonished to see Katerina there, majestic in white fur.

Seeing Charlotte, she gave a start. "My dear, I didn't expect to find you here. But of course, I should have realised."

"Should you?"

"Karl told me of your intention to bring Violette into our circle." Katerina looked at the bedroom door. "She's in there, is she? Still human."

Charlotte was incensed by her arrival, her patronising omniscience. Stefan was unperturbed. "We had a little trouble with Ilona," he said ruefully.

"How astonishing." Katerina let her fur coat slide into his hands. "If ever you did *not*, that would be news."

"What do you want?" said Charlotte. "Did Karl send you?"

Katerina gave her a cool look that became suddenly conciliatory. "I don't blame you for snapping at me, but must we stay on bad terms? He sent me, but not about Violette."

"Why, then?"

"He wants to see Stefan. It's not urgent." Her voice was quiet and Charlotte noted a difference in her demeanour. She was less regal and condescending, more vulnerable. She sat down, folding her arms on the table and looking up at Charlotte. "All the same, hasn't it occurred to you that Karl might be right? It's a terrible, momentous thing to end a human's life like this."

"Do you think I don't know that?" Typical that she'd take Karl's side! "I've been through it all. Did you and Andreas plead for Karl's life when Kristian decided to make him a vampire? He didn't ask for it, either. Well, did you?"

"No," said Katerina.

Charlotte was struck by the openness of her admission. Why had she changed? "No, you helped. Why?"

Katerina's full deep-pink lips parted. She seemed taken off-guard. "Kristian was a hard master to disobey."

"And the rest! Don't tell me Karl's beauty played no part, that you didn't want to see such beauty live forever. You couldn't care less for his human life!

"It's true. I loved him. We all did. Kristian fed us the idea that vampires were meant to be solitary creatures with only one attachment: Kristian himself. Easy to believe, when you first pass through the veil. Suddenly humans seem a world apart, and it's difficult to feel for anyone when your strongest emotion is a craving for blood. You feel cold, isolated, afraid, and Kristian is the only one you can turn to."

Charlotte thought, *This is the first time she's actually talked to me!* Disarmed, she said more gently. "Was that how it felt for you?"

"At the beginning. I had been very religious. I was sincere in my faith, so I was sincere and passionate in my devotion to Kristian. But, with being the devout acolyte Kristian demanded, there came terrible pain. The truth is, we need companionship. We are not austere creatures like monks. We are profligate with our passions, we crave affection just like the humans we once were, if not more so. In other words, to comply with Kristian's image of a vampire is a lie. That's why Andreas and I turned away from him. He demanded the impossible. That's why he lost almost everyone in the end. How could he expect me to look on the beauty of Andreas and Karl, and not want to touch them and love them?"

"Why did he choose people who were bound to let him down?"

"He was the world's worst judge of character. Don't you agree, Stefan?"

"Thank heaven," Stefan said with a grin.

"He saw what he thought he could make us, not who we really were." Katerina's gaze drifted into the distance. "Karl was a soft silent creature; a cat, keeping to the edges of the room, observing without being observed. You catch a glimpse of him in the shadows; his dark brows indented over his lovely eyes, a shine of red fire on his hair, the faintest smile on his lips. All the rest is darkness; but his face, you would die for. Kristian was fooled; he imagined that because Karl stays in the shadows and says little that he is not strong, not dangerous."

"You don't have to tell me this," said Charlotte. "I know him."

"I'm simply describing him; isn't this the man, the vampire, we both know? But your reaction proves my point! You can't bear the thought of sharing him. I don't condemn you, because I'm guilty too. He makes us both possessive, because neither of us *can* possess him."

A strange calmness washed over Charlotte. At last she felt able to talk to Katerina. The war between them was over, although neither had won. Charlotte said, "I lost almost everything I had for him, and my soul is damned – by the laws of common decency, if not by God Himself. Yet I still think I'm the luckiest creature in the world. But I never stop paying. Every moment we're apart is... agony."

Katerina looked candidly at her. "I had no idea you felt such pain. I've never suffered to that degree over anyone. It sounds nightmarish."

"It can be. But it's worth anything to be with Karl. Or was, if he will ever speak to me again."

"How can you have anything left for Violette?"

"Precisely because she's the only being with the power to stop me thinking about him."

Katerina gave a disapproving huff. "Dangerous to give others such a hold on you. Love them, by all means, but don't let love kill you. The way to survive is to need no one; then no one can hurt you."

"Oh, that's a fine principle, that goes all to pieces when a

certain person intrudes on your life. I tried to convince myself I
could exist without Karl, and I can. Exist – not live."

"Then why risk it, for the sake of this woman?" Katerina
asked softly.

"I have no idea," said Charlotte, bowing her head.

Katerina came to her and stroked her arms. "I'll help you
transform her."

Charlotte was astonished. "Why?"

"Because she's important to you. Sometimes the only way to
release an obsession is by pursuing it to the ultimate degree."

"But Karl..."

"What made you think I'm bound by his ideas of right and
wrong?" Katerina smiled with real warmth. Sadness, too. "I'm
sorry I've been such a harpy, Charlotte; can I begin to make it up
to you? Go in to her."

The bedroom was dark, but Charlotte saw subtle shades of gold,
crimson and brown in the shadows. In contrast, Violette was a
creature of moonlight, stark black and white. Diffuse light from
the main room lay across her creamy arms and ice-maiden face.

Charlotte leaned over her, gently tracing the contours of her
body. Knowing the time was here at last, her thirst was so powerful
that she shook with the effort of holding back. She pushed her
hands under the dancer's hair, felt the silken weight across her
hands. Violette stirred, frowning.

"Shh." Charlotte bent down, breathing the fragrance of her hair
and skin. Faint remains of dusty theatre smells, smoke from the
party; lily-of-the valley perfume, the clean sweetness of her skin.

Violette opened her eyes, saw the vampire bending over her.

Charlotte thought she would be afraid, and was ready for a
struggle – but the dancer's eyelids were heavy with laudanum, and
she only sighed and whispered, "Charlotte..."

She tipped back her head, revealing her long throat. Charlotte
stared, hypnotised, anticipation throbbing and expanding all
through her. Then Violette stretched out her arms and put
them around Charlotte's neck. How strong she was! She pulled
Charlotte down until they lay face to face, the vampire half over

her, vibrating with this moment. She kissed Violette's cheek, moved downwards to suck the tender flesh of her neck between her teeth; stayed there a moment, telling herself, *Don't do this, don't... but I must, I can't wait...*

Her fangs lengthened of their own accord, pierced the vein.

The rapturous flood burst into her mouth, a red wave rushing through her. All the time – as if she saw herself from outside – Charlotte was aware that this was horrible, to be drinking blood... and yet too compelling to resist, a dazzling, unholy ecstasy. *Violette... ah, God help me, Violette.* And she felt the rich fluid running into her own veins, branching through her body until she tingled with bliss. She tasted the sacred magic of all Violette's creations; Giselle, Odette, Odile, Serpent.

Never had she felt such overwhelming love for Violette, nor such ghastly awareness that its fulfilment was killing her.

Through the crimson dream, someone began pulling at her. Charlotte tried to shrug off the irritation. It became more insistent.

"Gently, Charlotte," came Stefan's voice. "She mustn't die yet."

Miraculously, Charlotte managed to stop. She let the killing teeth retract, licked clean the wounds she'd made, kissed Violette on the neck and lips. Drowsy now. It was not opium but the blood itself, the satiation of desire.

They carried Violette into the candlelit bower of the main room, where Katerina waited.

"A little more," said Stefan. He took a mouthful from Violette's neck, passed her to Katerina, who did the same with surprising tenderness.

"Drain her now, Charlotte," said Stefan. "Take her to the edge of death, but no further until we form the circle. Then, just as we enter the Ring, take her life energy."

Charlotte wrapped the fainting dancer in her arms. Her violent thirst had abated, but still it was luscious to bite down again, to drink more tenderly now.

As she did so, Violette burst into life and began to struggle with incredible strength. Charlotte could barely hold her, as if this were not a dying human but a thrashing white demon, with serpents for limbs, snakes for hair.

Now they were all fighting to hold Violette. And never would

Charlotte forget the look on her face; blanched to silver-grey, skin drawn taut against the bones, and horror glaring from her huge blue-black eyes.

"Finish it!" Stefan cried.

God help me, I've done this to her –

She went on sucking, felt Violette's pulse slowing, her heart rolling to a stop. Yet still she fought! And when Charlotte released her in order to seize her hand and form the circle, Violette nearly slipped from her grasp like soap... but the circle held. Stefan gripped Violette's other hand, with Katerina between him and Charlotte.

Then, as they hung between the world and the Crystal Ring, Charlotte saw Violette's aura. Spindles of silver and violet and jet... Impossibly lovely.

The aura was Violette's essence, cool, tantalising, mysterious... and Charlotte must destroy it. She drew the spines of light into herself. The pleasure was heartbreaking... for with the fulfilment of her last need, Violette ceased to exist.

Fear rushed through Charlotte like a storm.

But Katerina was tugging her hand, the room dissolving. By instinct Charlotte released the stolen energies to flow around the circle and back into Violette as they drew her slender body physically into the other-realm.

And there they began to replace her warm, quick, vulnerable life with a hard cold fire that would endure forever.

Violette found herself lying in a wild garden. A drift of fallen leaves cushioned her. Beneath, she felt wet soil, mould, crawling creatures.

She had no memory of how she'd come here.

A man lay beside her, his head propped on one hand. A perfect, muscular man with a mane of red-gold hair. A god. He looked like Mikhail, her principal male dancer in the role of Adam in *Dans le Jardin*, yet Violette knew it wasn't him. His beauty failed to move her. The look in his eyes only made her loathe him.

"God made me from the pure dust of Earth," the man said reasonably, "but he formed you from filth and sediment. That is why you must always lie beneath me."

Violette felt that this argument had lasted for eternity. She sat up, dead leaves and mud falling from her. Her hair was full of leaves and cobwebs. Although the man's words made no sense, they dripped oppression like honey. The pull of nature held her, soil and gravity dragging her down into the Earth's embrace.

"No, I won't lie beneath you," she said. "I will not lie with you at all."

"But you are my wife," said the man.

"I am no one's wife!"

"God gave you to me. He made you for *me*."

This was ancient theological myth, the story of *Dans le Jardin*, and yet it was real. Violette felt she'd sunk into a deeper layer of reality. This struggle was fundamental and absolute. It was the substratum of existence, and must be acted out. Again.

"Who are you to call me filth?" she demanded. "Or lay claim to me?"

"Your husband, sweet Lilith."

"Why should I lie underneath? Dust, sediment: earth is earth. I am your equal!"

Trees clustered thickly above her and she saw the sky only as pin-points of light. Dense, fecund, obscene with life was this garden. A set from a ballet, more vivid than reality. Reptile eyes gleamed among the branches. Spiders and tiny snakes fell on her like rain.

"God ordained that you be my helpmate and subordinate," said the red-gold man. "If you will not obey, fair Lilith, I must force you. It is my right."

And he reached for her, this great and terrible bronze statue of a man. As he loomed over her, Violette saw that his face was that of her father.

She tried to scream, uttering not a cry but a word. It flew out like a stream of fire, incandescent, unknown and instantly forgotten. The ineffable name of God.

The forest canopy burst apart. Lilith tore herself out of the Earth's embrace and Adam's grasping hands, soared upwards. The sky was a lake of flame, her element, welcoming her back. She flew in awe and exultation.

Adam's voice followed her, thin and plaintive. "You can't leave me!"

"I wasn't made for you!" she cried. "I was created for myself!"

She glanced back to see the man gazing after her, as baffled as an ox.

Now Lilith-Violette knew she had done something terrible. She had broken God's Law. She had become the Enemy.

Her flight became a fall into sleep. All she could see was roiling fire. The only sound was a heartbeat rolling slower and slower... fingers touching her, voices whispering in another dimension... slower until it stopped...

Violette stood in a desert. The arid beauty made her want to weep for joy. Here was purity. No grasping, moist vegetation, no crawling things, no sweating male to weigh her down. Only a sweep of dry red sand, studded with rocks like giant rubies. A clean glassy sea washed the shore, reflecting a pure, pale lilac sky.

But she was being pursued.

God would not let her alone. He had sent envoys after her. She sensed them hunting her down on heavy, slow wings.

Terror. Yet she would not run away. Now she had found her dwelling place, not even God would drive her out. She would fight to the death for her freedom.

She saw them coming for her: three silhouettes swooping down against the curving void.

"No!" she shouted. "You can't take me back to the Garden, I won't go!"

They only smiled as they surrounded her; barely touching the shore with the tips of their toes, like dancers, like angels. She shielded herself, but they were all over her, kissing, stroking her hair. "Come with us. Come now," they cooed. "You'll die if you leave us. You've gone too far to turn back."

And Violette saw that the three were Stefan, Charlotte and Katerina. They were dark and divinely beautiful – and she hated them. "No. I won't. You can't make me –"

She fought ferociously, but they were stronger. They lifted her between them. Her feet left the lovely sterile desert. She was flying again, this time helpless in their grasp.

They carried her in a great arc over the ocean, and dropped her. She plummeted through thin air, hit the shining surface. Waves swallowed her, and light filled her like water; flooding her mouth, lungs, heart, her whole body. She *was* the light. Yet there was nothing holy in its brilliance. It was hard and glassy, too bright, unforgiving.

Yes. It was her light, completely.

Violette came out of the transformation screaming.

CHAPTER SEVENTEEN

NIGHTSHADE

Holly was in the garden, attacking the ravages of autumn with shears and a rake, when the vampires came to her through the dusk.

Andreas was sitting cross-legged on the grass, watching her with a sleepy half-smile. She still found his presence disturbing, though not unwelcome. As the others approached, he rose to his feet.

Holly strained her eyes to identify their vague, grainy forms; their faces were pearly ovals, wreathed by tendrils. One was Katerina's friend Rachel; she could tell by the red hair, like feathery flames around her thin shoulders. The two small men who moved like monks were John and Matthew. And behind them came Malik; almost seven feet tall, his face long and serene like a sculpture, his skin midnight black. Holly hadn't yet heard him speak a word, but his eyes contained frightening intelligence.

She was glad Andreas was with her. "What do they want?" she whispered, but he only shrugged. Facing them, she leaned on the upright handle of the rake as if it were a spear.

Rachel seemed to be their spokeswoman. Her voice was clear and sweet, like a glass bell. "We must speak to you, Mrs Grey."

"Of course. What is it?"

"Mrs Grey, can you contact the dead?"

Holly was stunned. She gathered her wits and answered honestly, "No. I won't use my psychic abilities like that. It's too easy to fool yourself. That's why I don't trust the gift. I let others interpret what I see."

"So, you think mediums fool themselves?" Rachel's voice, eyes, face, her blade-thin body, everything about her was piercing.

"Some do. And they fool gullible folk, which is cruel. And some may be genuine, but I don't claim... Why do you ask?"

"Karl and Katti and I wondered if vampires live after death, as mortals are supposed to; if we have anything resembling a soul. Do we go to hell, or float in limbo, or is there nothingness? We wondered if you could contact a dead vampire... such as Kristian."

Holly was aghast, but felt herself sliding under Rachel's influence... then Andreas spoke, shaking her out of it. "Why in hell would you want to do that?"

"Perhaps he'd explain what is happening."

"Are you out of your mind? Make contact with his ghost? He was insane enough in life! I tell you, it's better not to know."

"Have you finished?" said the crystalline voice. "Mrs Grey?"

"Andreas is right," she said. "I'm not sure there is life after death for anyone. I think vibrations remain, but not consciousness... as in the Book."

"Yes, what did you glean from the Book?"

Gooseflesh made a shivering path down her back. "Annihilation."

"Of what?"

"I mean that I sensed nothing from it but loss and obsession. Negation of life. But what I picked up was only the effect of the Book on vampires. Isn't that so, Andreas?"

"Exactly," he said.

"And when you look at us with your occult vision," said Rachel, "what do you see?"

Holly's reply seemed to startle her. She startled herself. "That you are like humans, looking in only one direction. You don't see the danger behind you. Three huge winged spirits rising over your shoulders..."

"What are they? Lancelyn's so-called daemons?"

"I think so, but I don't know *what* they are. You'd have to ask Lancelyn." Grief stabbed her throat. She swallowed.

"Are you really so afraid to have theories of your own?" Rachel spoke with sudden contempt. "You give the impression of waiting passively – to become Lancelyn's 'Dark Bride', or a sacrifice, or whatever fate holds. As if you're only here to play a role."

Her words cut savagely into Holly's fragile confidence. "You asked what I saw, so I told you," she said tautly.

"So should we help Benedict against these great shadows?"

"I think you should listen to him, yes," Holly riposted.

"Thank you," said Rachel. "We shall." She turned and swept away, the others following. Holly almost collapsed into Andreas's arms.

"But you did beautifully," Andreas said, steadying her. "What's wrong?"

"I'm furious that I'm still afraid of them," she sighed.

"Well, that is common sense." Again she felt the chilling fascination of being too close to him. He only stroked her shoulders and withdrew rather fastidiously from her. "Don't tell Benedict they asked your advice," he said, amused. "What would it do to his pride?"

Violette became a vampire in anguish and fire. Charlotte was the reluctant witness to every birth-pang; the fire lashed her, too, for she had engendered it.

Even as the Crystal Ring's fierce energy filled Violette, she shrieked with agony and denial. As her initiators drew her back to the real world – her human life extinguished, a new light blazing in its place – she went on writhing against them, clawing at her own hair and arms.

Her screams pierced Charlotte to the core.

They tried to soothe her, but Violette was beyond consolation. White as quartz, as strong as a snake, she threw off their hands and broke loose. Charlotte thought she would fling herself through a window, but once free of them, her agitation died. In the centre of a Persian rug she crouched in sudden, deathly silence, a changeling under a wreath of wild black hair.

Stefan, Charlotte and Katerina watched her.

Eventually Stefan said, "I've never seen anyone react so violently. Usually they are too stunned even to speak."

"Well, it is done," said Katerina, her voice dry.

Stefan said, "She needs to feed. We're all insane until the first taste of blood."

Charlotte sensed human heat in another room. Stefan was never unprepared. Memories flared of her own initiation; the cadaverous artist who'd offered himself eagerly to her, and the uncontrollable compulsion with which she'd leapt and gorged on his blood. The horror of it...

"You'd better bring him in," said Charlotte. Her own thirst rose. Violette's blood was in her, but the transformation had exhausted her. It had been exhilarating, but now she felt scoured.

Stefan and Niklas went to another room and brought out a young man between them. He looked dreamy, as if drugged. He was the one who'd invited Stefan to the party; Charlotte recognised his eager face and feverish, rapt eyes. He adored Stefan and Niklas. He did not realise – or care – that he was about to die for love.

Stefan led the man to the edge of the rug. Violette looked up, her face wild; Charlotte thought, *She scents his blood. Even his sweat is a lure. I remember. It's so alien and repellent, yet you can't resist...*

"Take him," said Stefan.

Violette's eyes opened wider. Her eyes were unchanged, still bright and preternatural. Expressive, tormented, as if she were forever balancing *en pointe* on the lip of a pit.

One emphatic word burst from her throat. "No!"

"He won't mind. He's willing. See, it is easy..." Stefan bent and pressed his lips to his friend's throat, took a swallow. A string of red pearls oozed out. "I've made the wound for you. Taste it."

She flowed to her feet. Her eyelids flickered; clearly the blood-aroma was tormenting her. "No," she repeated. The hard edge to her voice was impossible to disobey. A tone Charlotte had often heard her use when schooling her dancers.

"It is horrible the first time, but it will soon be over," he said. "Delaying the moment will only increase your distress."

He pushed the human towards Violette. Her eyes grew round, her eyebrows crimped with rage. "NO!" she cried, and fled to the door.

Stefan and Niklas followed, caught her before she touched

the handle. She struggled, but Stefan held onto her and looked at Charlotte. "We should leave her alone with the victim," he said matter-of-factly. "She'll take him eventually."

"What if she escapes into the Crystal Ring?" said Charlotte.

"She won't. No one can enter straight away, it's too overwhelming."

"Violette is capable of anything," said Charlotte. "I'm not leaving her like this."

"Don't talk about me as if I weren't here!" Violette said fiercely. She broke free of Niklas and stood rubbing her hands together as if trying to scrape off the skin. She looked from Niklas's blank face to the feverish human, seemingly horrified by everything. "I don't care how long you leave him there, I won't do it!"

"This is regrettable," Katerina said, "but I must leave."

"Where are you going?" said Stefan.

"Back to Karl. He wants you to come too, but I fear your hands are full here. I wish you luck with her; you'll need it." With that, Katerina vanished into the Crystal Ring.

Charlotte and Stefan were alone, staring at the apparition that was Violette. Charlotte felt no resentment at Katerina's departure; after all, she had not asked for Katerina's help, and had no reason to demand it now. Violette was her responsibility alone.

The prima ballerina who made audiences weep, who shone in the spotlight as she gracefully gathered more bouquets than she could hold, now crouched like a lunatic and began to rip out strands of her lovely black hair.

"What do vampires fear?"

Simon moved towards Karl across the darkened study as he spoke. One lamp burned under a red shade, dimming Simon's blond radiance to copper and earth tones. For a vampire, he had an attractive openness that reminded Karl of Charlotte's brother David; decent, trustworthy. Unnerving qualities in a predator, Karl thought. He must seem godlike to mortals.

"What have vampires to fear, really?" Simon asked again.

"Everything," said Karl. "Pain, death, not dying. Discovery by humans, if only for the anguish it causes. Hating what we are, fearing ourselves damned. The loneliness of the Crystal Ring; imprisonment in the *Weisskalt*. And discovering humans who have power over us."

Simon started to laugh. "Yes, you are right! But you're the first vampire I've heard admit it."

"I'm merely being realistic," Karl said with a smile.

"And the entities that Lancelyn has supposedly summoned against us; should we fear them too?"

"I believe so," said Karl. "They appear to be far older than us. But you have lived for centuries too, haven't you? Surely you must be aware of such creatures?"

"Yes, I am old. I remember Greece in its glory." Simon ran his fingernail along the edge of the desk, extruding a line of dust. "And I've heard of vampires more ancient still, possessed of unknown qualities. Alas, I know nothing of them."

"Kristian was rumoured to have been tranformed by three ancients," said Karl. "Perhaps that was what gave him such power."

"Perhaps."

"It's said he destroyed his own creators," said Karl. "I assume that means he put them in the *Weisskalt*."

"He must have been inconceivably strong to have done so." The fair vampire gazed candidly at him. "So, Karl, to have destroyed Kristian – you must be even stronger."

Karl sat back in his chair, eyebrows raised. Then a savage memory took hold and he said, "No. Love brought him down. There, something else to fear. Love, the subtlest weapon of all."

"Why so melancholy?" said Simon. "I'm simply glad to be alive again!"

"Then I'm pleased for you," Karl said drily. "But what if Kristian's creators woke when you did? Are they the ones attacking us?"

"Possibly." Simon paused in thought. "But these self-styled occultists, Benedict and Lancelyn – how would Kristian have dealt with them?"

"Killed them outright," said Karl. "He wouldn't have cared about the loss of potential knowledge."

"Ah, prudence was never among his virtues. Benedict seems to control us all…" A pointed stare. "Except *you*, Karl."

"Are you suggesting I kill him? I could, but I won't. This isn't finished yet. Surely you don't agree with Kristian's attitude that slaughter is the answer to everything?"

"No, my friend." Simon looked amused. "I was simply trying to judge whether you and I are in agreement. We are, to some degree."

"How do we differ?"

Simon half-sat on the edge of the desk, arms folded. "Whatever we tell ourselves, vampires need a leader," he said. "We need guidance."

"Not you, too," Karl said, dismayed.

"What?"

"There are still vampires at Kristian's castle who can't accept his death. They seem unable to exist without a master telling them what to think and how to live."

"Don't despise them. Not everyone is perfect."

"I wasn't implying that I think I'm perfect," Karl said thinly, "but there will never be another Kristian."

"Do I detect sadness?"

"I loathed him, yet I understand why some needed him to say, 'It is acceptable to be a vampire, because you are the Chosen of God.' But he lied. His whole existence was a lie! He filled himself with his ideas of 'God' because he was empty... I don't want to pursue this. He's gone, and they cannot make me, nor anyone else, into him."

"So, it's time to seek new strategies."

"But I have no desire to meddle in anyone's affairs. I wish others, human or vampire, felt as I do."

"How marvellous that would be!" Simon struck the desk. "No wars, no commerce, no art, no marriage; the human race would be dead in a generation. Impossible. Every time you feed, you affect someone's life!"

"Of course," Karl said wearily. "Since that is the case, we can only exploit this situation to gain knowledge."

"You feel as I do," Simon murmured. "Wisdom, that's the goal."

"Aren't you wise already?"

"I've seen generations rise and pass away, and I have learned that true wisdom is to set yourself apart and simply *watch*. Isn't that what we're doing? And it's a great deal more interesting than lying undead and mindless in the *Weisskalt*."

Karl heard light footsteps in the hall, and knew it was Katerina. The study door opened; her face appeared in the gap, her brows drawn together in worry. Seeing Simon, her expression brightened. She came in and kissed him before she kissed Karl.

"Where's Stefan?" said Karl, ignoring her blatant transfer of affection.

"He can't come yet," she said. "He will, as soon as possible, but Charlotte needs him."

"Why?" Karl tried not to betray his concern. "Is anything wrong?"

Katerina unpinned her hat and smoothed her hair. Then she sighed. "I'd better tell you. You will find out soon enough, and I'd rather you heard it from me. Charlotte has brought Violette into the Crystal Ring."

Karl had guessed she was going to say this. For a few moments he felt nothing, not even surprise. Then sorrow rolled in, like heavy black sand on a slow tide.

Then she added, "I helped her."

"Helped? Katti, why?"

She turned to him, passionately defensive. "Because Charlotte would have done it anyway! I thought that if she was so determined, perhaps there's a deeper reason and it should happen. Fate, if you like." Reading the dismay in his face, she said, "I'm sorry, Karl."

"Why be sorry?" he asked. "I didn't forbid you to help her. You're free to act as you wish."

Katerina sat on the desk beside Simon, her thigh pressed against his. She looked drained, and humanly distressed. "I am, but I believe you were right after all. Too late, I know. Violette came out of the transformation insane. She won't feed. I walked out; I feel rather ashamed of deserting them, but I had to. I couldn't watch; I've never seen anyone react so badly. They can do nothing with her. You knew this would happen, didn't you, darling? Charlotte wouldn't listen, but, my dear, how I wish I had."

Karl was silent. There was nothing to be said.

"What will you do?" said Katti. "Will you go to her?"

"No." Aware that he sounded cold, Karl saw shock in her face. Strange, when Katti had disdained Charlotte for so long, that she now cared about her. "If I seem callous, perhaps I am, but I won't help her. She wouldn't want it, let alone expect it. Charlotte's responsibility lies with Violette, and mine lies here."

"I wonder about you, Karl," Katerina whispered. Simon touched her arm. "I wonder if you still have a heart at all."

The last vampire to recover was Fyodor, a Russian with snow-blond hair and silver eyes. He'd switched from catatonia to glass-sharp reason in a moment, and had not stopped asking questions since.

Karl had gathered them all into the parlour, which seemed too small to contain so much unnatural beauty. Even he felt uneasy among them. *No wonder*, he thought, *we can so easily unhinge human sanity*. Andreas and Katerina – by virtue of familiarity – seemed pliantly warm and unthreatening by comparison.

Neither Ilona nor Pierre appeared, but Karl had expected nothing of them.

In the glow of electric lamps and firelight, the vampires were luminous. Their shining beauty was magnificent and monstrous, lethal like that of venomous snakes or birds of prey. Karl studied each one in turn. Rasmila fascinated him; she said little but seemed so sweet-natured and cheerful, he could barely imagine her drinking blood. So lovely, the sheen of her fine dark face, the indigo-black hair falling to her waist... *Her victims must love her*, he thought.

John and Matthew had been monks in medieval times. Now they believed they served the horned Devil that had afflicted their mortal lives. Their existence was a struggle to pacify their dark master, paying continual penance for their sins, terrified of the God who'd abandoned them. Thin, rarefied creatures, they seemed too frail to survive the modern world. Their crime against Kristian, as far as Karl could tell, was refusal to accept his belief that God and Lucifer were the same being.

Fyodor, by contrast, believed in nothing but the glory of what he was. He was exuberant, heartless, mocking. His colouring, in contrast to his personality, was ethereal; ivory skin, white-blond hair, irises of bleached silver. Andreas had taken an immediate dislike to him, and Karl understood. *I don't think Fyodor is very different from the man he was in life*, he thought. *Cruel, even obnoxious.*

Fyodor was talking to Rasmila, but she only listened, smiling.

Katerina's friend Rachel sat apart in a corner; a siren, combing her hair. Slender and translucent, with her fiery hair she would not find it easy to pass as human. *Like me*, Karl thought, *she wishes to be left in peace; that, too, was her only crime against Kristian.*

The tall African, Malik, still hadn't spoken, although he seemed fully aware. Now he sat playing chess with Simon. *His mind is sharp*, Karl thought, *so perhaps he simply feels no need for human chatter.* His face was long and sedate, like an ebony sculpture. A wonderfully striking figure – but how he must terrify his prey.

Karl trusted none of them.

Even Simon, who seemed reasonable and helpful, might have hidden motives. A red-gold creature with the tawny eyes of a lion, Simon could have been taken for a war hero. An unfortunate weapon of seduction, Karl noted.

Extraordinary, he observed, how swiftly most of them were adopting the speech patterns and behaviour of the present day. This was vampire camouflage at work, of course. Yet, like Karl, they all retained an old-fashioned quality that fascinated humans, playing disastrously on their love of mystery and nostalgia.

As they waited for Benedict, Karl murmured to Andreas, "I wonder why we felt the need to heal them? They feel no loyalty to anyone. No mortal would thank us for this. They – *we* are a plague on mankind."

"But mankind created us," said Andreas. "So you've been saying. We were transmuted by the touchstone of their dreams and desires. So why feel guilty about anything we do to them?"

"It's too easy an excuse to say, 'Humans want us.'"

"Do you want to save the little darlings from themselves?" Andreas sneered. "Whether mortals asked for us or not – they've got what they deserve!"

Benedict entered at last; he was clearly on edge, but alight with energy. He brought Holly with him, keeping her close with his arm around her shoulders. The aroma of her fear and the rapid pulse of her blood caused a tangible stir among the vampires. Even Karl responded. They all rose to their feet, facing Benedict – their saviour and captor.

Ben cleared his throat. "Well… I would like to begin."

"We've been waiting," said a hostile voice; one of the monks, John.

"They won't give you an easy time," Karl said, moving to Ben's side. Then he addressed the others. "Benedict is an adept who can see and control the Crystal Ring. I suggest that we all treat him with respect."

"Thank you," said Benedict, standing taller. "You are powerful beings, but so am I. Don't let us underestimate each other. I summoned you and I can control you."

"We know," said Rachel, "but will you treat us with equal respect?"

"I have the utmost respect for you! Haven't I saved you from starvation and exile?"

"Kristian's death released you," said Karl. He'd told each vampire individually; some had reacted with joy, others as if they couldn't take the news in. "If not for Ben, however, you might still have been stranded."

"Wonderful to be alive again!" exclaimed Fyodor. "And to hear that Kristian is gone – but now you tell us we have a human in his place? This is a lamb trying to rule wolves!"

"I am not appointing myself as your master," said Ben. "I summoned you to help me against a dangerous enemy. I'd rather ask for your help than demand it."

"Vampires do not *help* their prey," Rachel said crisply.

Murmurs of agreement. Karl, Simon and Katerina looked at each other.

"We must be allowed to go our separate ways," Rachel went on. "Let us go."

Colour rose in Ben's face. "I cannot."

"At least hear Benedict out," Karl said reasonably.

"Yes, listen to him," said Simon. "We must reach an agreement. In Kristian's absence there will be anarchy unless we find a new leader."

John's companion, Matthew, said, "Are you suggesting that we make this whey-faced man a vampire and let him rule us?"

"No, of course not," said Karl, giving Simon a dark glance. "If anyone wants another Kristian – in my opinion they are insane, but I won't deny them the right to their belief. If any of you want that, return to Schloss Holdenstein; Cesare and others are still there, waiting for a new leader because they lack the imagination to decide their own destiny. Does anyone wish to go back?"

A brooding silence. No one wanted that. Karl added, "However, I believe we face a genuine threat. We should co-operate."

Rachel said, "Vampires aren't meant to help each other. We're predators, not Samaritans."

"I won't accept this." Matthew stepped forward, his small hard face full of hatred. "This Benedict is from the Devil, like Kristian, sent to test us."

And he rushed at Benedict, hands outstretched. Holly gasped and pulled away, Karl and Simon moved to intercept him – but as the monk reached Ben, he vanished.

Ben's eyes were closed, one hand raised and so taut that the tendons bulged. In front of him a column of air turned cloudy with frost feathers, and Karl saw the faint form of Matthew, suspended between Earth and the Crystal Ring. He was plucking at his throat, choking, his eyes round and swollen. His fingernails broke the skin as if trying to reach inside his own flesh to break the invisible chain...

Stunned silence held the other vampires. Seconds passed, then Matthew solidified and collapsed at Ben's feet. A rash of blood-beads encircled his neck. Karl had a ghastly vision of the unseen chain tightening like a garrotte until it severed his head.

"Stop!" Karl cried. He seized Ben's shoulders, felt a jolt like an electric shock. "Stop."

Benedict's unholy strength dissipated. He slumped suddenly, and left Matthew writhing on the carpet. The others were motionless, tangibly shocked.

Fyodor turned on Karl, face distorted with fury. "How can he have this power?"

"Apparently he can project his mind into the Crystal Ring," said Karl. "If he controls its fabric, he controls us."

"This is nonsense!" said John, on his knees at Matthew's side.

"Then furnish us with a better explanation, if you can."

John said, "He is from the Devil!"

Andreas laughed out loud. Benedict said, "Lucifer gave me power over his own minions, is that it? No. Karl is correct. I've achieved this through mastery of my own will; that's what magic is. *Will*. I know it's hard for you to accept, but try to understand. I need your help. I insist on it."

"But this is wonderful!" Fyodor exclaimed. "You are dangerous *and* mad! How can we say no?"

Karl raised his hands to quiet them. "Ben, you had better let them go."

Ben stared at Karl. "What are you saying?"

"Rachel is right, we are solitary creatures. Yes, you have power over them, but how far does it extend and how long will it last? If you force them to stay against their will, you will make enemies for all time. You'll never sleep again."

"I need them."

"And perhaps they need you – but give them a choice."

Ben bowed his head. Holly's eyes were fixed on Karl, shining with gratitude. Then John said, "I would rather die than do a mortal's will."

"Go and die, then!" Andreas exclaimed. "God Almighty, I'm sick of this bickering! I wish you'd all stayed in the *Weisskalt*, you miserable ungrateful bastards!"

He marched out of the room, followed by baleful stares. Ben said aridly, "Nice to know someone is on my side."

Fyodor said, "What case can you present for us helping you?"

"My enemy, Lancelyn, has summoned three supernatural spirits – or more, for all I know – which are dangerous to vampires and humans alike. It's in your interest to help me find out what they are, and defeat them."

"It's true," said Karl. "Andreas and I have both been attacked by them. If you think Benedict is your enemy, you are wrong. Lancelyn is more dangerous. But what are these shadow-vampires? Does anyone know?"

Silence. Then Matthew whispered. "They are from Satan and cannot be fought."

Rachel said, "We don't belong here, caged. That was Kristian's mistake, trying to make us a flock as if we're all the same. I want solitude."

She spoke Karl's own thoughts.

"All right," Benedict said finally. "Go. I relinquish my power over you. Stay only if you want." He exhaled heavily and closed his eyes.

He's acted bravely, Karl thought. If any vampire tried to attack Ben now, Karl was ready to defend him – but no one moved.

A collective sigh rippled through them, a release of tension. Karl heard John murmuring to his companion, "No, Matthew. Satan sent Benedict, so we must aid him and appease our master."

Matthew's eyes were closed in pain, his voice thick. "Yes. Yes."

Ignoring them, Rachel smiled at Benedict. "However," she said, "now you have so graciously granted our freedom, I am prepared to help – on the condition that once the threat is removed, you let us go."

Hope flashed in Ben's eyes, but his tone was cautious. "You are already free. So, you will stay, after all? What about the rest of you?"

Karl's gaze moved over them; Malik nodded sombrely, John and Matthew had already made their decision, however spurious their reasoning.

"I can't resist," said Fyodor, laughing.

"Rasmila?"

"I want to help, yes," Rasmila said, inclining her head with a charming smile, light sliding on her blue-black hair.

"We all want to learn about Lancelyn and his friends," said Simon.

"We wanted to be given a choice, that is all," said Rachel.

Katerina smiled approvingly at her and added, "It certainly took enough effort."

Ben gave Holly a reassuring hug, but she did not look reassured.

"You were right, Karl," he said. "I'm grateful. I would rather have you all here of your own free will than under coercion."

"You took a risk, Benedict. That was brave," said Karl.

"Thanks," Ben replied grimly.

Fyodor tilted his head, his mouth a papery silver line. "Tell me where your enemy is and I'll suck his heart dry. All your problems will be over, no?"

"No," Benedict said emphatically. "It's not that easy. First we must find him. Then I want to disempower him, not take his life."

Fyodor shook his head in disgust. "You don't know where he is?"

"No, but I will find out. If you'll excuse us?" Ben took Holly's hand, but Karl touched his arm.

"The last thing you want is Lancelyn's death, isn't it?" Karl said quietly. "You won't admit it, but what you truly want is to prove a point. But if this escalates beyond your control and Lancelyn dies... how will you face the consequences? Or if *you* die – what about your wife?"

Ben's face froze. He said tightly, "If we sit around asking such questions, we'll get nowhere." He walked to the door, but as he made to pull Holly with him, she staggered and swayed.

"They're here," she said. Her face was blanched and she gasped for breath.

"Take her upstairs," said Karl.

"No," she rasped. "Lancelyn's shadows are already here."

Karl and Katerina looked at each other, then at Ben's stunned face.

"There's nothing here," Katerina said soothingly. "If there was, we'd know."

When Andreas left the meeting, he went into Ben's study and slammed the door. He was sick of the other vampires; sick of everything. He wanted to be alone in the leather-scented darkness; he also hoped Katerina would follow, so he could vent his feelings to an audience. She did not.

As he closed the door, he realised he was not alone. A lamp shone, and in the far corner, reaching up to take a book from its shelf, was a slim figure in red crushed velvet: Ilona.

She turned, replaced the book, smiled. "What's wrong with you?" she said. "Got out of your coffin on the wrong side?"

"Everything's wrong. All of them in there, with their stupid arguments, mysteries, ridiculous attitudes." He leaned on Ben's desk with braced arms.

"I know, I was listening. Why do you think I didn't come in? But I've seen those shadow-creatures myself. I'm not closing my mind, unlike Pierre. We may not need the help of these fools, but we must find out –"

"I don't need a lecture from you, of all people. I hate this existence." He turned his back on her, but she came up behind him and placed a long, fine hand on his shoulder.

"I'm not lecturing. Hate it, h'm? Would you rather be back in the *Weisskalt* than standing here moaning? I don't think so."

"Why not?" Andreas said, sweetly acidic. "The *Weisskalt*'s cold, Katerina is cold; what's the difference?"

"Ah." Ilona moved in front of him. Lamplight gave her hair a red halo. "Tell me."

"Katti is offended because Karl refuses to resume their relationship. So she punishes *me*."

"But it isn't your fault. It's his – not to mention Charlotte's."

"Did I say that logic features in this? She is oh-such-good-friends with Karl and Charlotte; I'm the easiest target. Besides, I made the mistake of saying, 'Why the hell should I sympathise with your unrequited desires, when Karl never gave himself to me?' She's been impossible since. It's true. We were always a triangle that was open at one end, but Katti never cared, as long as she had her own way. And now we are nothing."

"Poor Andrei," said Ilona, smiling. "They're both impossible; you are caught in the middle, as usual."

"It's all so pointless." He spoke bleakly. His rage faded, but the feelings of loss and betrayal were real. "What's the use of being immortal, outside life, when we're still in thrall to these pathetic emotions?"

"Write a poem about it," she said blithely.

Andreas turned, one hand raised, almost tempted to strike her for her blindness to the age-old depth of his pain – or at least to punch the wall. She caught his wrist and said, "No. If you want to take it out on me, don't do it like that. Stop complaining, Andrei, and stop being a victim!"

She raised her other hand to touch his hair. "All dishevelled," she said. "Such beautiful green eyes. You are so lovely, Andrei."

"So are you," he said, surrendering. He seized her shoulders and pressed his mouth to hers. Then he was pushing her down, and she was pulling him, they were tearing at each other's clothing, kissing as if to suck out each other's breath. Half-naked, they grappled savagely on the carpet beside the desk, regardless of the unlocked door.

Ilona had fed recently, and was warm under his hands. The red-rose flush of blood in her veins maddened Andreas and he bit her throat as he thrust into her. She gasped and laughed, encouraging him. But Andreas was not naturally savage and she outdid him, ripping his back with her nails, stabbing her fangs into his neck, chest, arms, anywhere she could reach; leaving a dozen wounds. Not neat pairs of holes, but blood-filled gouges and pits. She tore out chunks of his flesh, convulsing so violently with her climax that she almost broke his back.

Andreas's pleasure was sharp, exquisite, over too soon; and after, Ilona still clung to him, drawing hard on a vessel she'd opened in his chest. His strength was gone. He knew, too late, that she'd stolen too much of his blood.

Now he was fighting to escape, hair falling into his eyes as he struggled against the pale steel of her limbs. "Stop, for pity's sake! You – fiend from hell – you'll kill me!"

He felt her fangs retract, stinging pain rushing into the holes she'd left. He hurt all over. Ilona smiled lazily at him, her face beautifully flushed. "Did that give you something else to think about?"

"You're insane," he said.

"That's not very romantic."

"No one's ever tried to half-kill me before."

"You should go out more." She turned on her side and leaned on her elbow. "Don't tell me you didn't enjoy that. My God, you needed no enouragement! Oh, get up and rearrange your clothing before someone walks in."

"I can't move."

"Nonsense." She straightened her rumpled dress, refastened Andreas's buttons. Then she dug her fingers into his collarbone and pointed at the window. "Go out there, find some luscious young man, and take back the blood I drew from you. Take more. Maybe then you'll remember the point of this pointless existence."

"You're right," Andreas said languidly. "Wounds heal." And he grabbed her relaxed arm and bit hard into her wrist before she could stop him.

Ben took Holly to their bedroom and sat her in an armchair by the small fireplace.

"I'm all right. Don't fuss," she said.

Clasping her limp hand, he asked gently, "Did you really feel Lancelyn's daemons in the house?"

"Perhaps not inside... but somewhere near. Everything's black and cold... I'm so tired." Her face was horribly pale. "Karl's right," she said. "What if you or Lancelyn should die?"

"Holly, don't." He embraced her and they hugged each other fiercely.

"I couldn't bear it."

"No one's going to die," he said into her hair. He felt like crying; he saw now that all Holly's spirit and happiness had faded, and he hadn't even noticed. "Hush. Karl and the others are our friends."

"How can they be? They're savage creatures, elementals. They don't care about us; they'll use you and... It's suicidal, Ben. You've known it from the beginning but you wouldn't stop. You never would listen to me – neither you nor Lancelyn."

"I know, love, but it's too late now." Ben pressed her down with his hands, soothing, restraining. "There's no choice. We need to be strong. Finding Lancelyn is a matter of urgency. Have you any idea where he is?"

"None." She went stiff under his hands, defiant.

"But you've had visions of him. Was there no clue?"

"No, nothing at all."

"Well, we're going to find him anyway. Relax."

There was fear in her eyes. "I can't, Ben."

He felt refusal in every line of her, and knew in his heart she was too exhausted to endure hypnosis. His heart, however, was not ruling him. Lancelyn's face filled his inner vision, grinning and mocking, with three inky figures looming over his shoulder. Holly's reluctance became a vexing obstacle between him and his opponent.

"Look, I know you're breaking an oath, but he's hardly kept faith with you, has he?"

Her silence was ominous, sullen. Then she sat up, and the look in her eyes flayed him. They burned with betrayal, as if he'd done her some monstrous wrong. "Have *you*?"

"What on earth are you talking about?" he exclaimed.

She went still, her face mask-like. Eventually she forced out the words. "Tell me the truth about Maud."

"What the devil's she got to do with this?"

"She claimed that you used to take her in the office and…"

"What?"

"For goodness' sake, you know what I'm asking! She claimed you wanted to leave me for her." Holly spoke rapidly, one hand on her forehead as if overcome by shame.

Ben was sincerely astonished. "Maud and I – lovers? That's preposterous. I've never laid a finger on her, never wanted to, thank you very much."

She groaned. "I knew you'd say that!"

"What am I supposed to say?" He was irritated now. The last thing he needed was this complication. "One shouldn't speak ill of the dead, but you said yourself she was a cunning, manipulative liar."

"I know, but you don't see," she persisted. "However much you deny it, I can never be completely *sure* you're telling the truth. And I've given her victory by asking the question, which I swore I never would."

Although he desperately wanted to reassure her, the difficulty of doing so angered him. He wanted the matter settled so they could get on with finding Lancelyn. At that moment, Sam, who'd been flat out on the bed, stalked over and leapt onto Holly's lap. She plunged her hands into his fur as if he were her last hold on sanity.

Ben took her pale cheeks between his palms, beginning the hypnotism without permission. "Darling, please believe me. I've only ever wanted you. You know it in your heart, don't you? Maud was jealous; she wanted to hurt you. This is what Lancelyn has done to you, through her."

"Oh, I want to believe you…"

"Hush. It's time to find him. The sooner we sort this out, the sooner it will be over, and then I'll make it up to you, Holly, I promise. You do trust me, don't you?"

Her face was a portrait of resignation. "I believe you, Ben. I want it to be over, too."

"Come on, then. You're not too tired, are you, love? Sit quietly. We've done this a hundred times."

He felt her relax at last. She never could resist him. "I'm sorry, Ben. Sorry…"

Long years of conditioning let her slip under Ben's influence almost too easily. Her face was colourless, etched with anxiety, but he told himself she would be all right.

Ben, kneeling beside the chair, talked her swiftly into a trance. Her head tipped back, her hands curled limply on the tabby cat's flanks.

"Let your astral body fly free," Ben whispered. "Look for Lancelyn. He's drawing you to him. Feel the pull. You are bound so close that he can't hide from you. Search!"

"I'm flying," Holly whispered.

"Where are you?"

"Don't know."

"Are you in Italy, Holly? Has he gone to the villa?"

Her face furrowed with tension. "Don't know. Can't see…"

"Try!"

"Can't, I'm dizzy." She gasped and her body jerked. "Help, I'm falling!"

"It's all right, Holly, you're safe," Ben said quickly. "Tell me what you see."

"Hills. Not Italy. Steep hills… too tired to climb them, I can't…"

"No need to climb. You can fly."

"Bracken and stones. It's cold. Grey granite. There's a house in the mist."

"Describe it."

"On its own… on a hillside. Great walls and towers, a chapel with tall windows…"

Ben was trembling. "Are there –" He nearly said "stone lions", but did not want to plant ideas in her head. "Are there statues at the front door?"

"I can't see." She groaned. "It hurts. Being pushed away."

"Try! Go on, Holly, closer." Ben's voice grew more urgent. "You must! Are there – I mean, what shape are the windows, is there water nearby, what?"

He heard the door open, glanced round in irritation. Katerina came in and said, "What are you doing?"

He waved at her to be quiet.

"She's too tired for this, Benedict. You'll make her ill."

Taking no notice, Ben persisted, "Can you see statues?"

"Two stone lions."

"Yes!" he whispered, triumphant. "And?"

"Pointed windows with stained glass. A stream below." Her back arched with pain. Sam stood up and began to knead her lap with his paws; Ben impatiently shoved him onto the floor.

"Yes, and do you see the name of the house?"

"Grey Crags."

"Oh my God," Ben clutched her hands, breathing fast. "All right, old girl, steady. Can you get inside? Is Lancelyn there?"

"Think so. Can't get in. Barriers…"

"Push through! He's placed them to stop you but you can break through. Come on, Holly!"

She writhed and grunted, as if in childbirth. "Can't…"

Katerina knelt on other side of the chair, watching Holly intently. "You must!"

She gave a short scream. Her eyes opened wide, bloodshot and straining. "Coloured light everywhere. There's green and blue… And so much red, splashed over the room like blood. He's coming…" Her breathing grew quick and shallow. Her face drained to a deadly blue-white.

Katerina said softly, "Wake her, Ben."

Benedict ignored her. "Holly! Is it Lancelyn?"

Holly was fighting for every breath. "Yes – And three figures, burning so bright I can't look – they've seen me!"

Katerina reached across Holly and gripped Ben's arm. "Bring her out!"

He pulled free, annoyed by the pain. "Hold your ground. Steady now. They can't hurt you. What are they?"

Between high-pitched shallow breaths, she gasped, "They – they're bringing the Dark Bride. They are metamorphosis. Lancelyn's here, he's laughing at me… reaching for me… Help!"

"You're all right! Hang on."

A searing pain struck Ben in the scalp, making him yelp. The bloody cat! It had launched itself at his head, claws unsheathed, as if to protect its mistress. Cursing, he struck it away, feeling scraps of his skin torn out as it leapt to the floor.

In that moment, he lost Holly.

"For heaven's sake, bring her out!" Katerina snapped.

"All right, keep calm. Lancelyn can't hurt you, Holly. You're leaving now; gently drifting away and coming back to me."

"I can't –"

"You're calm. You're safe."

"No, can't escape!"

Ben was scared now. "Yes, you can! Come on, break free!"

Holly struggled, fluttering on the edge of life. Then, with a scream that seemed to tear her apart, she jerked upwards, convulsed, and lay still.

"All right, I'm going to wake you now." He could hardly keep his voice level. "You're home and safe. Wake up, Holly."

Nothing happened.

In panic he seized her wrist, found a mouse-rapid pulse. He repeated the words, trying to ease her home. At last her eyes half-opened. Her eyelids flickered heavily over slits that gleamed red with blood, with the lingering nightmare-trance. She heaved in a long, laboured breath.

"Relax now," he said. "How do you feel?"

No answer. She only stared at him from a web of helpless pain. Ben had a sudden, terrible fear that she would never speak again, that he'd pushed her so deep into the abyss that she'd never claw her way out. Then he thought, *But this is Lancelyn's doing. By God, I'll find him and make him pay!*

He touched her cheek, suddenly aware he was bathed in sweat. "You saw Lancelyn," he said in a low voice. "He's at Grey Crags, our parents' home. Now tell me exactly what you saw."

Still no reply. Katerina said, "For pity's sake, leave her alone. Anyone could see she was in no state for this. What have you done?"

"She's tired, that's all." But Holly began to tremble, her gaze swivelling over the ceiling. Filled with alarm, Ben looked up.

And there was a thunderous shuddering of the air, like wings beating in the attic, huge birds breaking through from another dimension. Even Katerina looked petrified. The room dissolved in a harlequin whirl of black and grey. Three shining apparitions rushed past like ribbons of light, gone as fast as they appeared. Reality fell back into place.

In the stillness that followed, Katerina said, "Lancelyn knows you've found him. That was a warning."

Ben, overwrought and unable to accept that he'd harmed Holly, spoke into her face. "Describe the nature of the enemy! What is the 'Dark Bride'? Don't be afraid; I won't let him near you, but you must explain what you saw!"

Holly fixed him again with a deathly stare as if gazing from the pits of hell. At last she spoke. Her tone, to his amazement, was conversational; but the voice and the words were not her own.

"Why not come and find out for yourself, little brother? I've been waiting patiently for weeks for you to guess where I am. Took long enough – but I'm ready when you are."

Karl had talked to Katerina and Simon for a while, but now he wanted time alone to think.

He went to the study, too preoccupied to sense anyone inside. Opening the door, he was startled to see two figures on the floor. One was Ilona; the other, with his back to Karl, his black hair a mess, was Andreas. He lay beside Ilona with her wrist at his mouth. Feeding on her.

With anyone else, Karl would simply have closed the door and walked away. But his daughter's presence in the scene clawed away his usual detachment.

"What the hell are you doing?" said Karl.

Ilona saw him first. She shook Andreas, wrenched her wrist out of his grasp. "What does it look like?" she said coolly.

She rose to her feet like a cat, utterly unembarrassed, taking time to smooth her crumpled dress. Andreas stood slowly and leaned on the edge of the desk. His shirt was ripped and blood-stained, hanging off his shoulders. His chest and neck were ploughed with wounds, scratches, bruises. He stared unsteadily at Karl under half-closed lids.

Karl felt like striking him. "How could you, Andrei?" he said quietly.

A look of defiance came to his face. "It's nothing she hasn't done with a thousand other men, human or vampire."

"But she's still my daughter." His voice was very low, but Andreas seemed to perceive something terrible in Karl's face, a frozen blood-lake of ancient wounds and sorrows. He blinked and drew away.

"Karl, for God's sake – I didn't do her any harm. I'm the one who got torn to pieces."

Karl strode to him, grasped his arms. Andreas, alarmed, tried to pull free. "You're a fool, letting her do this to you. You realise you'll be too weak to enter the Crystal Ring, perhaps for weeks? You should have had more sense."

Ilona touched Karl's elbow, as if worried that he was actually going to attack Andreas. "You are really upset about this, aren't you?" she said. "Why?"

Karl turned to her. Her twisted expression was an alloy of bitterness and triumph. "I don't care what you do, as long as I'm not forced to witness it," he said tonelessly. "Particularly not with my friends. You could at least have chosen somewhere private."

She shrugged. "It was rather too... spontaneous. Andreas jumped on me. Has it occurred to you that his sudden desire for me might have something to do with you and Katerina?"

"Ah, so I'm to blame?"

"For the love of God, I've had enough of this," Andreas said, folding his arms. "Ilona, shut up."

Ilona moved closer to Karl, pressing against him. "I can't believe you're reacting like this. If we were human, and I was fifteen years old and you caught me in bed with your best friend, then I'd understand your anger. But we're not father and daughter now, are we? That stopped the day you brought me into the Crystal Ring. We were almost the same age in human years, and a century has passed since then. We cannot be parent and child any more. We are not human."

She put one arm around Karl's waist, slid her hand under his shirt and caressed his lower back, flesh to flesh. "So what is wrong with you?" she said. "It's not fatherly love, is it? It's jealousy. Because you want me for yourself, don't you?" She stood on tiptoe and kissed him full on the mouth, lips parted.

Karl did not respond. All he felt was sorrow. There was no truth in Ilona's words, but her need to play this game made him despair.

When he stood like marble under her hands, she pulled back, angry. "You must have turned to ice when you were made a vampire!"

"But how can I win with you, Ilona?" said Karl. "If I'd kissed you back, you would have been completely disgusted. And rightly so."

"You're lying to yourself." She walked away from him.

"And you're playing games. What is this? You want to prove that my remaining scraps of morality are a lie, and destroy my friendships at the same time? That would be two victories in one, would it not?"

"Oh, damn you to hell," said Ilona. "I thought we could work together, for once. I was wrong."

She vanished so suddenly that Karl barely heard the soft crackle of the Crystal Ring receiving her. He exhaled, weighed down by regret.

Andreas's hand touched his forearm. "I am sorry, Karl."

"There's no need. She's only behaving as she has always behaved, to punish me for changing her. I don't know why I still hope for anything different."

"Katti and I miss you."

"What are you talking about? I'm with you."

"In theory only."

Karl turned Andreas to face him. The wounds Ilona had made were already healing, but he was still horribly white. Karl said, "Come here," and they embraced, everything forgiven, nothing resolved. Andreas's lean body felt ice-cold. "Are you so unhappy?"

"I've been thinking of leaving you both," Andreas said miserably.

"Andrei, don't."

"I wish you meant it."

"Go and feed. You're freezing."

He kissed Andreas on the cheek; they looked at each other, not quite smiling, resigned. A scream arrowed into the silence; Holly's voice, torn with agony. Then Karl felt the flutter of demonic wings all through the house.

Andreas gasped. "My God, what was that?"

Not answering. Karl ran into the hall and upstairs to Benedict's room. There he found Holly in an armchair, Katerina and Benedict leaning anxiously over her.

"I'm ready when you are," she said, her light tone incompatible with her ghastly expression.

Ben ground the heels of his palms into his forehead and moaned.

"What has happened?" said Karl.

"Oh, God. Holly, where are you?"

"Leave her alone," Katerina said briskly. "Give her a chance to recover, at least."

Ben straightened up, grimacing. "We've located Lancelyn," he said grimly. "He's at our parents' house, Grey Crags. Good God, I can't believe he'd go there! But no, it's perfect… the bastard! There's only my father left now. Neither Lancelyn nor I have spoken to him for years. It's the last place I'd expect my brother to go – which is precisely why he chose it. A twisted joke. Karl, we have to assemble the others and travel there immediately."

Holly said, "Whenever you're ready, little brother. I'm waiting." She laughed. Her eyes were mindless.

Karl looked closely at her. She was in a deep state of shock, possibly beyond recovery. Repulsed by Ben and his methods, he said, "What about your wife? You can't leave her. She's ill."

Ben turned on him, eyes ferocious. "D'you think I want to leave her like this? If she's in Lancelyn's power, the only way to help her is to stop *him*. I'll get the housekeeper to stay with her, invent some story to cover myself, and tell Mrs Potter to call the doctor if need be." He gazed helplessly at his wife. "I know it's not good enough but it's the best I can do."

"And if Lancelyn attacks her while you're not here?"

Ben drew himself up to yell at Karl, then his fury dissolved. "I can't cover everything. Too dangerous to take her with us. I have to make a decision – and we're going to Grey Crags."

Katti looked at Karl. "Well?" she said.

"I suppose we have to go with Ben."

"If Lancelyn's still there to be found."

"I've a feeling he will be," said Karl.

He touched Holly's wrist, wishing he could soothe her. Yet as he felt the hammer of her pulse, desire for her blood surged through him. God, that rich dark pull… Karl dropped her wrist quickly and moved away.

Vampires cannot help humans, he thought. *How often do I have to be reminded? We can only destroy them. This is the one immutable law of the Devil's maze.*

* * *

"Well, why not leave immediately?" said Simon.

Karl and Katerina had explained to the others, who received the news with pleasure, glad there was to be action at last. Fyodor and Rasmila flanked Simon, seeming too serene, too eager. Karl thought suddenly, *They are all still an unknown quantity. I trust no one to guard Holly. This cannot end well.*

"There is no real hurry," Karl said wearily. "Benedict says the house is near a small village north of Bakewell, by the Peak District. About sixty miles from here. He's told Katti and me how to find it. We can travel swiftly through the Crystal Ring, but he cannot – and neither can Andreas. They'll have to go by car, which will take a couple of hours at least."

"Well, we have time to rest and hunt, then," said Simon. "I think we should, don't you?"

"Yes," said Karl. "Benedict is getting ready to leave. We'll meet outside Grey Crags as soon possible. It's best if the vampire contingent arrives first, to estimate any danger."

Katerina said, "Stefan hasn't appeared. If he comes now, he'll find no one here, except Holly and the housekeeper. I trust he has the sense not to frighten them to death."

"We'll leave him a message," said Karl. "Ilona was here, but decided not to stay."

"Another quarrel?"

Her words induced a sting of pain. *Always*, he thought, *when I think I've resigned myself to Ilona's nature, something happens to reawaken the futile anguish of hoping she will change.* He only said, "It was nothing."

"Then why do you look as if you want to kill someone?" Katerina said, smiling. Her remark did not require an answer. Andreas, Karl noticed, was carefully looking in the opposite direction.

"If we're slightly reduced in number, it doesn't matter," said Simon. "We are still ten against three; surely that will be enough?"

"If it is not," said Fyodor with fierce amusement, "we deserve to die anyway!"

"Speak for yourself," said Andreas.

Karl felt apprehensive. He thought, *I've seen the daemons, I know they're more powerful than us... if there is no resolution to this, if they only want to fight and destroy us...* He felt a sudden violent thirst, and a need for the silence of the Ring. Oh, for the sweetness of Charlotte's embrace...

"Shall we begin, then?" Simon said cheerfully. "Don't be afraid, Karl. We are immortal!"

Rachel, Malik and the two monks stood at the fringes of the parlour, with Karl at the centre. Simon, Rasmila and Fyodor formed a triangle around him. They were smiling for no reason, he noticed; strange smiles, without warmth. Katerina stood nearby but seemed excluded. Karl found himself blending into the other-realm without trying, as if they carried him with them. The room vanished, but the vampires were all around him, changing colour and form. Only Andreas was left behind.

The sky exploded into life above them. The nine were gossamer moths against the cloudscape. They rose fast. Karl flew without conscious effort, as if the others were lifting him; it felt pleasant, exciting.

The realm became dark and tempestuous. Thunderous purple clouds congealed from nowhere. The ribbons of magnetic force, usually a reliable guide, rippled as if caught in turbulent water.

Simon set the pace, Rasmila and Fyodor flowing effortlessly with him. Karl looked down and saw Katerina, Rachel and the others struggling to keep up. As he watched, they dropped further back.

"Slow down," he said, but no one answered. He felt invisibly linked to them, unable to pause and wait.

Katti drew ahead of the others below. She had one hand outstretched, a cloak of torn lace and snakeskin swirling around her in the wind.

This felt wrong. Karl looked into the too-benevolent faces of Rasmila, Fyodor, and Simon; they grinned, teasing him.

"Of course, you have realised who we are," said Simon.

"Who are you?" said Karl.

"We are the immortals who created Kristian."

A dark and terrifying excitement rushed through him, too electric to be pure fear. He was horrified yet bewitched.

"Why did you do it?" he whispered.

Fyodor answered. "It seemed an excellent joke. In life Kristian was devoutly religious, a preacher of hellfire and damnation. What better way to plunge him into sin than to make him a vampire?"

"It didn't work, though."

"Oh, it worked all too well," said Simon. "The change made his beliefs even more gloriously extreme."

"And he turned on you and put you in the *Weisskalt*."

"But now we're alive again," said Rasmila. "Alive!"

Air-currents rushed loudly in Karl's ears. The skyscape raced by so fast that he no longer saw detail, only billowing cream and golden surfaces. Sketched on this blankness were three dark figures... not attenuated beings like him, but huge transparent shapes, like shadows thrown from the feet of Simon, Fyodor and Rasmila...

Lancelyn's daemons.

He tried to shout a warning. Everything was streaming out of control. He looked down for Katti, saw her climbing frantically to gain height. Her mouth moved but he couldn't hear her.

"Simon, look out!" Karl cried.

The three daemons swooped. Oblivious to Karl and Katti, they threw themselves at Simon, Rasmila and Fyodor, who spun, arms raised to defend themselves...

As if in an underwater dream, Karl watched them engage soundlessly.

He wasn't sure what happened next. There was no attack, no fighting. Rather, there was *assimilation*. Shadows and vampires dissolved into each other; in their place appeared three gleaming shapes.

One was fire-red, one white, one blue-black. Not bright, yet hard to look at directly, elusive like after-images of the sun. At first he felt no fear. He simply watched, certain he was hallucinating, that the Ring was playing eerie tricks.

He saw Katerina flailing upwards, and heard her voice calling faintly, "Karl! Karl!" Behind her, very small now, came Rachel, Malik, John and Matthew.

What was the danger? Karl looked at the three fiery figures. Insubstantial, as if seen through water. Serene and deadly. *Angels*, he thought, *who can crush vampires as we crush mortals...*

In a fluid movement that he did not see coming, they seized him. Arctic cold enveloped him and he thought, *They're taking me to the* Weisskalt! Fangs unsheathed, he began to struggle.

Below his attackers he saw Katerina arrowing closer. He must warn her away...

Karl felt wolf-teeth freeze into his throat. The white one – Fyodor still, or something else? – was biting him. Hideously strong... rousing memories of his battles with Kristian... but this was worse. This being had no weight, nothing to fight, yet it was sucking out all his strength.

Katerina reached him and began to claw the indigo daemon that was clinging to his back. "Let him go!" she shouted, but her voice was tiny and distant. "Let go, let go!"

Suddenly Fyodor released him, lunged, and grabbed Katerina. She struggled and screamed, a fox in a steel trap. "Karl!"

The darkest one peeled away and plunged at Malik, John and Matthew, scattering them like leaves.

Now the copper-red angel bore Karl away. His limbs were useless, as if chained. Twin needles pierced his veins. His strength faded with his blood... he was dissolving like an ice-crust, yet in clear focus he saw the white daemon tear Katerina's flesh, drink, then fling her aside like a broken doll. He saw the vermilion wound in her throat as she arced away against the vast canvas of the Ring; dwindling, gone.

Katti...

They were all lost to sight now. Karl was alone. The dark angel and the light one flew back towards their red companion, the purge complete.

In a fluid motion, the red-gold angel whirled to face him and Karl found himself looking into Simon's face. His eyes were spoked golden wheels filling Karl's vision.

"We made Kristian," Simon whispered, "and you killed him."

The three held him between them, taking turns to sip from his throat until he lost the power of movement, speech, even reason. Still they sucked at his veins. Dogs licking a dry marrow-bone. And yet they held him gently, as if he were made of eggshell, and their hands felt delicious, and their unintelligible voices were like birdsong.

CHAPTER EIGHTEEN

THE KINDNESS OF DEMONS

"Her refusal to feed isn't unusual," said Stefan. "Her reaction is the most extreme I've ever seen, but thirst will overcome her eventually."

"I'm not sure," Charlotte said, distressed. Violette was pacing restlessly like a panther maddened by the scent of meat, yet she ignored the passive young man who offered himself as her victim. "I know her. She means it. Send your friend away and leave me alone with her."

Stefan shook his head doubtfully. "If you are sure. Niklas?"

He made a small sign, and his mute *doppelgänger* lifted the young man and bit his throat. Charlotte felt a spurt of surprise, and thirst; she hadn't expected this. Niklas fed quietly and neatly, his serene expression unchanging, until the man slumped in his arms. Then Stefan guided the victim out of the flat as if discretely ejecting a drunk.

"I've called a taxi-cab for him," Stefan said as he returned. "He will feel faint, and won't remember anything clearly."

He's been spared, Charlotte thought. *Violette would have killed him. Does he even realise?*

"Call if you need us." Stefan took Niklas's arm and led him to another room, closing the door. Charlotte knew he would hear everything, but she was glad he was there.

Violette circled the room, sat, then jumped up and resumed her demented pacing. *Has the transformation destroyed her mind?*

Charlotte wondered. *Why am I treating her like a wild animal?*

She caught Violette's arm, halting her. "Violette, do you know what's happened to you?"

"No." The dancer shook off her hand, glaring at her.

"Do you know where you are, who I am?"

"Don't treat me like an idiot! I don't *understand,* but I haven't lost my mind. You've made me like you, a beast that drinks blood. But I won't, I can't!" Arms crossed, she clawed at her own shoulders.

"You can't scrape off the power like a skin," said Charlotte. "It's part of you. It's a tiny fire inside every single cell. I know drinking blood seems unthinkable, but that's only the remnant of your human nature. You are one of us now. It's natural to us. Wonderful."

"I know all this!" Violette spun away, pulling at her hair. "You don't understand! If I swallow blood, something terrible will happen. It's already happening."

"Do you mean something other than becoming a vampire?" Charlotte asked carefully. "Your mind will play games with you while you're starving."

Violette faced her. Her fierceness vanished and she looked defenceless, confused. "Was I supposed to... Did it happen to you, did you...?"

Charlotte held her wrists, trying to calm her. "Everyone sees strange things during their transformation. Is that what's frightened you? Tell me what you saw."

Violette chewed her lower lip with the tip of one sharp canine. She said, "Who is Lilith?"

Charlotte frowned. "Why?"

"Tell me!"

"A character from mythology," said Charlotte. "Wasn't she Adam's first wife, in some Jewish writings?"

"Yes, and she was evil. She's the embodiment of wickedness; proud, arrogant, malicious, vengeful. She encourages sin, she feeds on men and murders children. She's the bride of the Devil, mother of demons, the Serpent itself."

Violette trembled as she spoke. Her expression was ghastly. Charlotte asked gently, "And did you see her?"

"I am her," said Violette.

Charlotte, speechless, could only think, *God, she has lost her mind! Careful, I must help her through this.* "What do you mean?"

"After you drained my blood and I passed out, or died, I found myself in a garden. It was disgusting, wet and crawling with insects... so much life, it was obscene. There was a man..." She seemed physically to shrivel, losing her ballerina grace. "He tried to force himself on me, and when I wouldn't submit he kept arguing, tormenting me. Like Janacek, but worse, because I couldn't stop him. He said I wasn't allowed to refuse him because he was my superior. This made me so angry I thought I'd go up in flames... and I did. I flew up into a sky of fire... and I spoke God's secret name to escape, and that was wrong too. I broke God's law and sided with the Devil. I only wanted to be left alone, but that seemed such a great crime! I came to a beautiful red desert but God wouldn't allow me to stay there. He wanted me to return to the man, so he sent three angels to fetch me. I saw them coming, I felt them seize me and throw me into an ocean of light..."

"And then?"

"There was only the light, and fear and pain. Feathers cutting me like steel. I was in this room again but the pain and the light came with me."

"It must have been me, Katerina and Stefan you saw," Charlotte said gently. "We would have looked different to you. I should have explained more."

Violette seemed impatient. "Yes, obviously I saw you, but you were something else as well. I knew it had happened before; my escape, the envoys coming for me. I was an outsider. I hated Adam, I hated Eve who replaced me, I wanted revenge on all their children. So I became the serpent who destroyed their innocence and got them cast into the wilderness. It was me. Lilith."

"You were dreaming," said Charlotte. "You got this from *Dans le Jardin*. You can't believe the story was literally true."

"But I wasn't dreaming. I was *remembering*. The story is eternal, always happening. Explain how I know so much that I never knew before!"

Charlotte was at a loss, wishing Stefan were there. "The transformation plays tricks on the mind," she said weakly.

"Well, this is quite some trick! Tricks, dreams – I thought you'd explain what all this means. But you don't know, do you? You've done this to me without even understanding it! You don't even know what I'm talking about."

"You're still Violette! These feelings will pass if you'll only come out with me and feed."

Violette sat down, stretched out her left arm and stared at it. Without warning she bit savagely into her forearm, jerked back her head and stared at the wound she'd made. Two pits filled with purplish gel. "No blood," Violette said hoarsely.

"Don't!" Charlotte cried, catching her wrist before she tried again. "No blood, because I took it. All that's animating you is the energy of the Crystal Ring."

"Will I die if I don't feed?"

"No, but you'll experience terrible pain. I won't let you suffer that."

"Why do you care? These hands will strangle children. I'll tear infants from their mothers, I'll straddle and torment sleeping men. Steal their seed and give birth to all the demons in the world. All the vampires."

"Violette, for God's sake!" Charlotte spoke in despair. She remembered something Karl had told her; that after his own transformation, he had asked Kristian, "What are we?" and Kristian had replied, "Children of Lilith."

"For *God's* sake?" said Violette, with a thin smile. Anguish made her hideous.

"This is a delusion. Trust me. It will pass if you –"

Violette jumped up with a strangled cry. Charlotte leapt out of her way, suddenly mortally afraid of her. Stefan came running in, Niklas close behind, but Violette stopped short of attacking Charlotte. She stood scarecrow-rigid, clawing at her own arms.

"I can't feed! For this miserable, unforgiving God's sake, will you listen to me?" Violette cried. "Yes, I'm Violette, I'm still myself, just. But if I once taste blood, I will become Lilith completely and I'll never be able to go back. That's why I can't do it!"

She tore her own flesh in self-hatred, but tears gleamed in her eyes. Regret, compassion and sorrow overcame Charlotte as she moved towards the dancer and embraced her.

With terrible strength, Violette threw her off and backed

away. A feral glitter entered her eyes, something beyond reason. Charlotte gazed helplessly at her.

"Leave me alone!" Violette screeched. She ran at the mantelpiece and swept several valuable ornaments to the floor. In the explosion of bright sound, she turned and ran at Charlotte. Stefan and Niklas caught her in mid-flight and she writhed in their hands, snatching at the air.

"Perhaps she'll calm down if you leave, Charlotte."

"I can't possibly –"

"Let's try!" said Stefan. "You're the one she's trying to kill. Go, before she wrecks the entire flat!"

As he spoke, Violette slumped in his arms. He sat her down on a chair and she stared into space, unspeaking, catatonic.

Eventually Charlotte said, "Stefan, what are we going to do?"

"I have absolutely no idea." She'd rarely seen him so serious. "If we can't persuade her to feed, in the end…"

"What?"

"We would have to decapitate her, or put her to sleep in the *Weisskalt*. It would be the merciful thing to do."

Charlotte almost broke down with horror. Concerned, Stefan said, "Go and hunt. You need it; you're exhausted. We will look after her, don't worry."

She nodded wearily, glad of his kindness. She let herself melt into the Crystal Ring and rose slowly, leaving behind the warped shapes of the lower ether. Gilded hills drew her upwards with all the majesty of clouds. How she'd longed to fly among the clouds as a little girl; and now she could, now she could.

Ah, but the price…

I have to find help, she thought. *Karl is the last person I can ask… but can any vampire help me? Has this ever happened before? And what if there's no cure for Violette because she really is Lilith? No, no. Think straight. She could not become Lilith any more than I could become the Virgin Mary.*

Then she thought of someone. A kind, sad face; an older, gentler Karl. Josef. Suddenly he seemed the only person in the world to whom she could go.

It was a long journey through the Crystal Ring. The skyscape shone like a dying fire; dark coals backlit by a crimson glow. So vast and lonely. She was a snippet of black thread in the void. She felt cold, but distanced herself from physical discomfort and let the wind blow fiercely through her, cleansing her.

Stop being a fool, she told herself. *Don't weep for Violette. Just help her.*

It was a journey of hours; still far swifter than boat and train. She knew the ways well now, fitting the magnetic patterns and flowing currents of the Ring over the contours of Earth without effort.

Here were the streets of Vienna... the square white building, the little courtyard and drab unwelcoming stairs she remembered... Josef was at home. She felt the mote of warmth within the apartment, like a rushlight inside her.

She moved through the walls and saw him – or rather, saw his outline drawn on the Crystal Ring by his aura. Mushroom, dusty brown, a hint of silver; austere, gentle. An strong aura containing no malice.

Charlotte blended into the room and stood motionless, watching Josef. He sat bent over his desk, working by the lamplight. The glow outlined his curved back and put sparks of gold in his grey hair; threw lozenges of shadow across the desk and the dark furniture. She watched him with the still, feline concentration that only vampires possessed.

The flat felt different, now his sister Lisl had passed away. It was less cluttered, fresher, more studious. Yet empty, almost sterile. No one here but Josef and his books.

A photograph of a young woman rested in a silver frame on the desk. Someone important in his life. Charlotte felt strangely peaceful yet full of curiosity, seeing the human world as something alien and fascinating.

A cuckoo clock chirped the hour. Josef looked up and saw Charlotte's reflection in the uncurtained window in front of him; an apparition with a diadem of shining hair. He clutched the arms of his chair and his face dropped.

"Don't be alarmed," she said softly, in German. "It's me, don't you remember?"

He turned round in his chair, removing his spectacles and rubbing his brow. "Of course I remember you, Charlotte. How could I ever forget?"

"I didn't mean to frighten you."

He stood and kissed her hand, keeping a cautious distance. "How long were you standing there? You can't disguise what you are, my dear; you never looked anything but unearthly to me."

"Not pleasant, to find a vampire looking over your shoulder," she said, half-smiling.

"Isn't there some rule about you being unable to cross a threshold unless you are invited?"

"Ah, but you did invite me, once."

"But I'm not on my deathbed. I hope you haven't come to take my life, because I'm not ready to go."

"I'm glad," she said. "I'm not the Grim Reaper, Josef. Your time hasn't come, I promise."

He began to relax and his expression eased. "Then why are you here? I thought I'd never see you again."

"Nonsense. You knew you would," she said, smiling. "I have an ulterior motive, I'm afraid. I need your help. Information."

His eyebrows rose; he looked amused, fascinated. "Yes? Anything I can do, I will, but…"

"You said you study Hebrew mythology. What can you tell me about Lilith?"

"Lilith, oh my goodness." He was on his feet, looking along bookshelves. "She's barely mentioned in the Bible, you know, but she was at large in Babylonian and Sumerian myth long before the Talmud and the Zohar got hold of her. Won't you sit down? We can study the books together."

Charlotte sat down at the desk and picked up the photograph. A pretty woman in a crushed velvet dress; a society portrait. "Who is she?"

"My niece Roberta."

She heard regret in his voice. "Lisl's daughter?"

"No, I have another sister; she's her child. But they live in America so I rarely see my Roberta. I miss her. Even an old bachelor needs someone to look on as a daughter… Anyway, about Lilith."

He placed a pile of books in front of her and leaned on the desk by her right shoulder, opening the first volume.

"Different stories of her origin, as with everything," he said.

"In Sumer she was Lil, a destructive storm; in Mesopotamia she became a night demon who preys on sleeping men and women, causing erotic dreams."

He opened another book, quickly finding relevant sections. "Lilith is described as a hot, fiery female spirit in the abyss... Always a wild and destructive force. The Zohar calls her the ruin of the world. God formed Lilith as he formed Adam, but he used sediment instead of pure dust. Adam and Lilith never found peace together... She refused to lie beneath him, claiming equality, but when she saw that Adam would overpower her, she fled to the desert on the shores of the Red Sea. She is still by the sea, trying to snare mankind...

"God sent three angels to bring her back to Adam. Strange names, the meanings of which are unclear: Senoy, Sansenoy, Semangelof. Lilith refused to go with them, preferring to consort with demons.

"When Lilith saw Adam with Eve, she was reminded of God's glory and flew up to join the cherubim, but God cast her down." Josef paused, his finger on the text. "This is connected, according to the Zohar, to the moon's argument with the sun; the moon demanded equality and was punished by God by being diminished and set to rule over the night. But after the Fall, Lilith is connected in sin to Eve. God brought Lilith out of the depths and gave her power over all children who are liable to punishment for the sins of their fathers... Whenever men sin, Lilith is charged to rule over them. She is the woman of severe judgment; the flashing revolving sword of God."

A chilling thought thudded like a spear into Charlotte: *That sounds so like Kristian! He thought he was God's vengeance... Oh, don't let Violette be like him!*

"Is anything wrong?" Josef said.

"No, go on."

"She also becomes the bride of Samael, the Devil. The Kabbalists call her Harlot, Tortuous Serpent, Alien and Impure Female. She is seductive and nightmarish, murdering the men she has seduced. She is equated with the Greek Lamia, who sucks the blood of sleeping men. Sometimes she is the Serpent who tempted Eve, thus sharing Eve's guilt for the Fall."

Charlotte put in, "Do you have nothing good to say for her?"

Josef smiled softly. "The men who wrote these books did not."

"God diminished her, because she refused to obey Adam?"

"So it says. But she disobeyed because she is unruly, jealous, angry, ungovernable, destructive, murderous. The female counterbalance to God's goodness and maleness."

"You don't believe all this?"

"I am a Jew, my dear. That does not mean I literally believe every word, but I have respect for these writings." He went on turning pages. "She is the owl in the night, whose screeching drowns out the prayers of the righteous... Might I know why you are so interested in this?"

Seconds passed before Charlotte could answer. "Someone I know has got the idea into her head that she is Lilith."

"Oh?" Josef looked at her over the top of his spectacles. "Then you want a psychoanalyst, not books."

"That might be a little awkward. She's a vampire."

"Ah." He paused, frowning. Then he exhaled and said softly, "Oh, dear Lord in heaven. They also call Lilith the Mother of Vampires, of course... I don't know what to say, because I understand so little of what you are. Has she held this belief for long?"

Charlotte shook her head. *So easy to tell Josef,* she thought; *Why can't I be having this conversation with Karl?* "She's only just become... one of our kind. It happened during her transformation. She knew little about Lilith before, yet afterwards she suddenly knew many of the things you've told me, facts only a scholar would know."

"Is she dangerous?"

"She might be. She's in great distress."

Josef put his fingertips together. He thought for a minute, then said quietly, "Perhaps you should destroy her. Would it not be a merciful release?"

Charlotte sat motionless, but a chill crept over her. "Are you telling me she's unredeemable?"

His lips narrowed, and he shook his head. "I am telling you nothing, Charlotte. Is she Lilith, or does she only *think* she is? The latter is more likely, is it not? I try to answer your questions, that's all. I can't tell you what to do. A human could be helped, but a vampire – I don't know where one would start."

"I love her," said Charlotte. "It's my fault she's suffering like this. If killing her was the only way – but no, I won't consider it! The more I understand about the creature she thinks she is, the better I can help her, do you see?"

"Of course." He took her hand, light and cautious. "What we learn is that Lilith is many things, all of them destructive. You are a companion and daughter of Lilith, and yet you are compassionate... Is it compassion, when vampires care for each other?"

"Don't torture me with philosophy. I'm too tired. I must go."

He stood up as she did, still holding her hand. "Come to me again," he said. "I wish to see you again before I die."

"You're not an old man."

"No, but not young. No one knows how long they have left. I'm not being morbid; only realistic. There may come a time when I need you, as did my sister... Or will I look at you and wonder how it is to live forever?"

The image held her rigid. Yes, Josef would die; but she had the power to change that; to restore his vigour, bestow immortality... then she saw Violette's anguish, and she knew she couldn't take the risk.

Everything Stefan had said was coming true. *"What you're doing to Violette is what Karl did to Ilona, and he thinks you'll live to regret it. Then next time the desire comes to transform someone, you'll fight it and it will be agony, one way or another, whatever you decide.*

"I couldn't," she whispered, looking into his kind face.

"Is it so terrible?"

"You'll never know." She lifted her face to his and Josef wrapped his arms around her and kissed her gently, with a longing that wrung her heart. And she dissolved into the Crystal Ring even as he held her, leaving him alone with the image of a ghost; to meditate forever on the kindness of demons.

On her way back, Charlotte had a premonition that Violette would have vanished by the time she reached London; or worse, found a way to kill herself. So she was relieved to find her still there, Stefan looking after her. She sat curled in a chair, hands around her knees, her slim form half-hidden under a shower of sable hair.

Charlotte realised with astonishment that she was asking Stefan a question.

"But who is Niklas? Why doesn't he speak?"

"He can't." Stefan glanced at Charlotte, greeting her with a nod. "He's an example of the extraordinary things that can happen to us. The only way we can reliably be killed is by beheading. Even that need not be final. Feed the head with blood, and a new body will grow, as perfect as the old. But there's another trick. Feed the old body and it will grow a new head. A *doppelgänger* of the first, you see? A near-perfect replica, but with barely the intelligence of a cat." He waved a hand at Niklas, who sat impassively at the dining table. "He echoes what I do, but has no motivation of his own. Who knows what goes on in his mind?"

Violette looked up, momentarily shocked out of her misery. "How did this happen?"

"We were an experiment by Kristian. A sword-happy soldier decapitated me. Kristian kindly brought me back to life in duplicate."

"Why didn't you destroy the other one?"

"Because he's my brother," said Stefan, with an odd smile. "Because he's *me*."

"You're all mad," said Violette. She glanced at Charlotte then disregarded her.

"How are you?" asked Charlotte. No reply.

Stefan sighed. "She hasn't fed. But she's been asking questions; I've been telling her a little about the bad crowd she's fallen in with."

Questions. That was a hopeful sign. Charlotte knelt down by the chair and touched Violette's arm; at least she didn't pull away. How gaunt she was with lack of blood! A vampire's blood was better than nothing. A start; if she got the taste, she would want more.

"Drink mine. It won't hurt me."

Violette only stared at her with dead eyes.

Charlotte bit into her own wrist, held the oozing wound to Violette's chin. "Taste it." The dancer shut her eyes, wincing with revulsion. "Darling, you'll starve! You won't die but you'll wish you could! But if you feed you'll feel better in every way, I promise. Please."

"Stop it," Violette said in a low voice. "Don't try to force me. I won't do it. Don't look at me with those hopeful eyes. Nothing's changed!"

Charlotte let her go in despair. "I love you. I thought you loved me. Does that mean nothing?"

"I don't know what you mean by love! It's blasphemy, it's the excuse for everything, it's the cheapest threat there is! *Leave me alone!*"

Charlotte backed off. Devastated as she was by Violette's state of mind, she knew that to help her, she must detach herself from human emotion, as other vampires could. She looked sideways at Stefan.

"We may have to force her," he said.

"No," said Charlotte. "It would be disastrous. Stefan, why don't you go to Karl? I'll stay with her."

"Are you sure? I should perhaps go and see what he wants with me."

He took his twin's hand, and they vanished. Charlotte sat on a dining chair, watching Violette. She resembled a Lalique glass figure, knees drawn up, ankles crossed, head bowed. Dumb as stone, closed in on herself. Misery and physical pain flowed from her.

"I asked a scholar about Lilith," Charlotte began. "He told me the myths and they correspond with everything you say. He couldn't explain why this has happened to you, Violette, but I'm sure of one thing: this is important. Lilith wasn't a simple being; she had many aspects. If you'd stop fighting, we could face this together. You are more than human. You don't have to be ruled by pain!"

"If I drink blood, she will rule me."

"No."

"How do you know?"

"If I tell you that the Crystal Ring is a creation of mankind's subconscious, that vampires come into being through those subconscious fears and desires, and that Lilith too is a product of human imagination... then perhaps it's possible that you truly believe you are her. You've taken on her persona, and now she's real to you, subjectively real –"

"Oh, you are so clever! Perhaps you're right and I'm crazy –"

"I didn't say that."

"– but if I am crazy, it changes nothing. This *is* real. And I think I always knew it would happen, but that doesn't mean I want it. I'd rather die. I'm so frightened of the angels."

"Angels?"

"God's envoys, they call themselves. Sent by God to hunt me down. I don't know why I'm afraid of them but I am. I'm so cold, Charlotte. I hurt all over."

"Tell me their names," Charlotte said softly.

"I can't remember. Sibilant names all beginning with S. One was Senoy, yes..."

That was close to one of the names Josef had told her. Charlotte thought, *If my theory's correct and she has absorbed some myth from the Ring, does that make it any less true, less terrible? I would give my life to help her, but what if there is nothing I can do?*

She felt the atmosphere tearing, a vampire stepping from the unseen realm. She looked up, expecting to see Stefan and Niklas. Instead, three strange figures appeared that reminded her bizarrely of the chess pieces at Lady Tremayne's party. One was black, one white, one scarlet. They were as beautiful as saints and they gazed at her with the same beatific sadness that Kristian had once shown her.

Violette screamed.

Charlotte sprang to her feet, dazzled by terror.

"Who are you?"

The next thing Charlotte knew, the pale one was at her throat. She felt the stinging pain almost before she saw it move; bony hands held hers in a vice, milk-white hair brushed her face as its fangs tore her flesh... and her strength was draining away at horrifying speed with her blood...

A blur of darkness in the background, a brief struggle, voices that echoed and made no sense –

Then Charlotte was lying on the floor, too weak to move. The room tipped in duplicate around her. The eerie attackers had gone... and Violette had vanished with them.

"I'm so frightened of the angels..."

* * *

"Charlotte!"

The room tilted and Charlotte went dizzy. Hours must have passed. It was daylight. Someone was pulling her upright; she blinked hard and found herself looking into Katerina's distraught face.

"Katti... what are you..."

Katerina shook her. "What happened to you?" she demanded.

Charlotte hurt all over, and burning hunger pinned her stomach to her spine. She needed blood, as a drowning man needed air. "They took Violette," she said in a raw whisper.

"Who took her?" Katerina's face was white, her eyes too big. Her obvious terror inflamed Charlotte's fear.

"Don't know. Three of them. Vampires, I think, but like none I've seen before..." The effort of speech exhausted her. She rubbed her throat. The wound was healing but sore. "Fed on me... I'm making no sense, sorry..."

"No, you've made perfect sense." Katerina dragged Charlotte to her feet and they stood unsteadily. "I've seen them too. Come with me."

She pulled Charlotte towards the door.

"Where are you taking me? Can't move..."

"You must! You need to feed. Where's Stefan?"

"He went to Karl."

"Well, we haven't seen him, but he'll find the message we left."

"But why are you here?"

"Because those monsters have taken Karl as well."

Alarm seized her. She stumbled as Katerina hustled her through the front door, onto the landing. The stairs heaved under her feet. "Taken him –?"

"They attacked him in the Crystal Ring. I went after them and fought with all my strength." Katerina's lips drew back to show her fangs. "I'm strong. Almost no one gets the better of me; in the past I feared no one but Kristian. But these creatures are so powerful! They fed on me and threw me away like a child skimming a stone. I sailed through the Ring with no control. When I fell back to Earth, I hit trees and landed heavily on grass.

It hurt, but I was more furious than in pain; some human saw me, but it didn't matter. I fed on him. Then I walked until my head cleared and found I was in a park in London. I'm too weak to re-enter the Ring, so I came here. Thank goodness I did."

"Why would they want Violette and Karl?"

"I've no idea," said Katerina, "but Karl needs us. We must help each other."

"Oh God, where is he?"

"They may have taken him to some house of Lancelyn's in Derbyshire."

"But that's miles away! And neither of us can enter the Ring."

"Then we'll steal a car, take a train, anything!"

As they emerged into the street, Charlotte perceived the city as an iron blur in which every human glowed like a magnetic red fire. Katerina steered her between them. They passed through a little garden square enclosed by railings... and Charlotte saw a girl coming towards them, no older than herself, with a cheerful open face, an expensive coat, a terrier on a lead. In that moment, though, she was not a person. She had no purpose but to slake Charlotte's wrenching thirst.

The girl stopped, staring at Charlotte; first confused, then captivated. "Excuse me, but do I know you?" she said.

They appeared as sisters, embracing. Charlotte pressed her face into the girl's fur collar, seeking a vein. And then came the gorgeous spurt of blood and convulsive, excruciating relief...

And guilt. The beauty of it, and the horror.

Charlotte managed to leave the girl alive; but with what nightmares, she would never know.

Violette was in a desolate, storm-torn landscape that was in perpetual motion. She sat cross-legged on a mountain that bore her weight with the buoyancy of liquid, not rock. The peaks around were the colour of slate; the sky – if it could be called a sky – the most glorious deep blue she'd ever seen.

She knew this was the Crystal Ring. An ocean of wild, hallucinatory colour where clouds became mountains and the earth below was mist. A kind of hell, formed of pure energy. Lethal energy that could flood human cells and veins with demonic immortality and vile appetites.

Her captors stood around her. She now knew their names; the golden one, who glowed with red fire, was Senoy. The pale one with milky hair and silver eyes was Sansenoy. And the dark one, crowned with long blue-black hair, was Semangelof.

"Lilith," said Senoy. "Beautiful Lilith."

God's envoys had come for her, just as she dreaded. She was cold, achingly cold to her bones, and so hungry that every fibre of her body screamed for blood. But her discomfort was only a backdrop to her burning fear and rage.

"You will not refuse us again," said Sansenoy. He was icy and domineering; the leonine Senoy exuberant and warm. Semangelof seemed quiet, even empathic, but Violette knew their personalities were deceptive. Masks on sticks that angels held up to shield their true nature.

"I won't come back," Violette whispered. "I won't be Lilith any more."

"You can't *not* be Lilith, dear," said the dark female. "You always have been and always will be her."

"My name is Vi–" She couldn't utter the word. It seemed so far away, and a lie. She was Lilith.

"We offer you redemption," said Senoy. "You disobeyed God, yet God in His mercy gave you a role; to become his His retribution against those who stray. The greatest evil is disobedience. If sheep stray, they become fodder for the wolf. You are the wolf of God!"

How lovely, their singsong voices. Violette closed her eyes, lulled.

Sansenoy said, "To be God's sword on Earth, you must submit to His will. You are Mother of all Vampires, Lilith, the scourge of mankind. God cast you down and He raised you up to be his lash! Take your responsibility!"

Her eyes flew open. "God has done nothing for me," she said. "I won't repent, I won't do His will! I was punished for the crime of wanting freedom. I won't repent. I will not be used to punish mortal sinners."

"Then you will remain the outcast of outcasts," said the scarlet-gold angel. "The screech-owl in the night. You cannot disobey God without paying."

"Have I not paid?"

"Come with us now, and all debts will be settled."

She couldn't think straight, with these dazzling creatures staring through her. She was drunk on hunger and madness. *Who was the ballerina who danced so ecstatically? Was it me? No, someone else. I don't even remember her name.*

She said, "Come with you, where?"

"There cannot be a queen without a king," said Semangelof. "You are incomplete. You rejected Adam. All your sorrow stems from this original sin. So come and be joined."

"To whom?" Violette spoke scornfully. "To the Devil? To my father? To Janacek? It's all the same. God wants me joined to some man who will absorb me completely into himself."

A faint sigh from Semangelof. "Ah, she understands."

"I understand that I'm not allowed the freedom I desire."

"Perfect freedom resides in perfect obedience," said the white angel. "Your last chance, Lilith: come with us to your new consort. Apart, you are both incomplete. Together, you will empower each other."

Violette said, "I am no one's consort." Her voice was faint, and reason was bleeding out of her.

"All your bitter loneliness," said the dark one. "Swallow your pride, and all shall be healed. You'll be complete."

"Aren't you a woman?" Violette whispered. "Why aren't you on my side?"

"A true woman knows that her place is at her husband's side."

Someone plucked a thread, and Violette's mind unravelled.

Sick, cold and lost, she surrendered to their convictions like a dead leaf to the wind. "Take me," she said. "Do whatever you must."

She felt their hands on her, scorching her fragile flesh as they lifted her up through the otherworld ocean of storm and fire. "You won't redeem me, you'll kill me." They weren't listening. Still the words fell faintly from her dry lips. "And it's not Lilith you're taking back to Adam. Only what's left of me."

CHAPTER NINETEEN

THE BLACK GODDESS

Karl's abductors flew so low through the Ring that he saw the strangely warped and compressed contours of Earth. Deprived of strength, Karl felt like a disembodied eye floating across the darkness. Farmland, villages, and a smoky city passed below. Then came deep-cut hills, valleys flooded with fog.

The three swooped down, holding him. Reality exploded around them; the hills became massive walls louring against the sky. Steep-shouldered peaks rose from a fast-running wide stream. The rush of water and the occasional bleats of sheep were muffled in the mist. Even to vampire eyes, the light was dim and eerie; grass and bracken, rocks and water were colourless.

Karl glimpsed a village far away. The inhabitants slumbered, unaware of preternatural creatures diving over the hills. He saw a mass of trees, and a railway line snaking away into the fog. Then the landscape tipped, and he saw a massive stone house poised on a hillside. The angels accelerated towards it.

Karl knew the house was Lancelyn's. He sensed power, too much like Kristian's. The dead stone hand of a despot… and this hill was a black slope in Hades where demons fought futile wars forever.

Karl saw the fortress wall looming fast. He thought, *We're only half in the Crystal Ring, we won't pass through!*

He felt the impact as a dense, grainy substance swallowed him. For a wild second he thought his abductors would leave him entombed in the wall. He floundered through the stone, slower and slower... until he pushed out a hand into clear air. With the last of his strength he dragged himself forward and broke through to the real world.

He was inside the house, leaning back against the now-solid wall. Dazed with blood-loss, Karl still felt the abrading, suffocating embrace of stone tingling on his skin. Without doubt, he was too weak to re-enter the Crystal Ring. He sensed granite all around him, thick-walled chambers stretching above and below.

Suddenly there was a grizzled human face staring into his. His captors had vanished. Gathering what remained of his wits, Karl found himself in a long, windowless gallery with a curved ceiling. Light came from a row of braziers poised on bronze tripods. Firelight flickered on the walls, throwing shadows from a collection of strange human-size figures... mechanisms made of metal, cloth and fur.

The man in front of Karl was the only living being. The only source of blood.

Yet Karl, although starving, couldn't take him as prey. He was powerless to do anything except stare at the crumpled face, narrow mischievous eyes, the coarse hair and beard. Could this be the arrogant magus he'd confronted before? The man was dressed in shapeless brown overalls. With a screwdriver and an oil-gun in his left hand, he could have been a workman. But his sheer, solid confidence could belong to no one else.

"Welcome to Grey Crags," said Lancelyn. He quickly wiped his free hand on his overalls, extended it; Karl disdained the gesture, only glared coldly at him. The man was unperturbed. "I'm delighted to meet you; sorry we weren't properly introduced last time. I'm Lancelyn Grey. You are the legendary Karl. I apologise for my over-familiarity, sir, but I understand that vampires change their names so often there's little point in calling you 'Mister' or 'Herr'."

Karl laughed, surprising himself. He should have been furious, but there was something oddly endearing about Lancelyn's manner. He said, "I almost did not recognise you as the infamous Lancelyn."

"Infamous. I like that." Lancelyn grinned. "Ah, well, can't play the great magus all the time. I've work to do. Have to give my brother a proper welcome. Will you excuse me?"

Lancelyn turned away and went down on all fours to worry

at the mechanism of a life-size fur-and-metal tiger that held a human figure between its paws. Karl thought, *Does he have no sense of danger?* He pressed his tongue to the tip of one fang, half-extended from its sheath with the pressure of hunger. And yet, he could not bring himself to strike.

Karl went a few steps closer. "Would you care to tell me why I'm here?"

"I wanted to meet you properly. I've heard so much about you. The only vampire Ben can't control, correct? Yet you've been working with him – not least in trying to burn my bloody house down, but I'll let that rest. And you are also, I understand, the one who killed the Lord of Immortals, Kristian. My daemons are not at all happy about that."

His casual tone barely masked an implied threat. Karl absently made to rest a hand on the tiger's head.

"Don't touch it!" Lancelyn exclaimed, straightening up. "Bloody dangerous, this thing. I've just got it working. Wonderful curiosities, aren't they? Damned sorry I lost that Mexican."

Karl realised he meant the ugly cigar-lighter that had sat on the desk in his other house. "Also a fire-hazard, if you are not careful."

Lancelyn gave him a dry, knowing look. "No hard feelings. I didn't keep the really important books there anyway. Nothing has happened that was not meant to happen."

Karl had an uncomfortable feeling that this was true. "Your 'daemons' – who are they?"

Lancelyn flicked a switch, and the tiger came to life. It turned its head from side to side, flicked its tail, roared. The puppet beneath its paws struggled, its painted face a caricature of mortal fear. Then the tiger opened its jaws, lunged, and bit off its head.

As the automaton came to rest, Lancelyn touch a hidden switch, made it disgorge the head, and reset the mechanism. "Excellent," he said.

"You haven't answered my question," said Karl.

"Well, it isn't for me to discuss the business of angels. They wish to have words with you, but I have no quarrel with you."

"Angels?" Karl felt a rush of shock and scepticism.

"Well, what should we call them? 'Vampires' hardly does them justice, 'daemons' or guardian spirits implies that they're here to serve me, whereas in fact they have their own reasons. I don't command them; we work together, which is the best way. Messengers of God, if you like. Incidentally, I trust they didn't hurt you?"

"I'll live," Karl said acidly. "But what are they, really? I was with three vampires who had agreed to help Benedict. We were attacked – so I thought – by three dark figures, yet suddenly there were not six vampires with me but three again. As if your daemons had taken over their bodies. Have I misunderstood?"

"Probably."

"Are you going to explain?"

"No. I'm not being difficult, old chap; I'm not actually sure that I can. Come with me."

Wiping his hands on a rag, Lancelyn walked the length of the gallery. Karl followed, thinking, *I've never met such a mortal before. Even Ben had respect for the beings he'd summoned, a healthy trace of awe. Yet Lancelyn isn't stupid; it isn't mere bravado. He has absolute confidence. Shrewder than Kristian, less heavy-handed; perhaps more dangerous for that.*

Karl, despite the discomfort of suppressed thirst and anger, was fascinated.

The gallery was a museum of automata. Some stood on tables – a silver, articulated swan swimming on a stream of glass rods, a rose-cheeked ballerina pirouetting on a spindle – but most were floor-mounted. Larger than life, grotesque. A gipsy with a moth-raddled dancing bear; a man repeatedly catching the same fish; a guillotine about to sever the head of a revolutionary, while a waxen-faced woman endlessly knitted the same square of wool. A hooded executioner bearing a huge axe...

At the far end, a spiral staircase led up into the body of the house. Water rushed somewhere deep below. The house was old, but the staircase and plaster-work around the stairwell, Karl noticed, were new.

Lancelyn led him into a huge cathedral-like room. Bare granite walls were softened by luxurious furnishings. Roman Catholic opulence, the organic richness of Art Nouveau, heavy fringed silks like altar cloths, candles in brass sconces, lamps glowing under Tiffany shades. Five arched windows of stained-glass dominated a semi-hexagonal apse that – as Karl recalled from his outside view of the house – jutted magnificently over the hillside below. The night sky did not do the windows justice, but he still saw gorgeous jewel-colours, Bible scenes as works of art, holy figures set in sweeping landscapes.

Yet there was a lump of coldness at the room's heart. Something that called to Karl and repelled him, clawing at his mind...

The Ledger of Death.

"Come in," said Lancelyn, exchanging his overalls for a dressing gown of maroon quilted silk. "Make yourself at home. Mind if I smoke?"

Karl saw the Book lying in the centre of a massive rosewood desk. The sight of it made him feel faintly ill. This was the concentrated essence of the horror that had brought down Kristian...

"Ah, you've noticed," said Lancelyn. "Benedict was rather upset at losing the Book, wasn't he? My dear sir, you look terribly pale."

Karl forced himself towards the desk. "You seem to know a lot about your brother's activities."

"Naturally." The magus smirked. "I know everything Ben's been up to. I have my spies."

"Who? Holly? The unfortunate Maud? Simon?" Karl reached towards the thick, pitted cover of the Ledger. No good, he couldn't touch it.

No reply. "Do you know what the Book is?" Lancelyn spoke from the side of his mouth as he lit a pipe.

"I have theories, but it was stolen before I had a chance to test them."

"You think it has power? You think it enabled Benedict and myself to summon vampires from their hidden realm?"

"I don't know." Karl leaned on the edge of the desk, staring at him. "Did it?"

"Look." Lancelyn opened the Book. On the age-stained paper, Karl saw for the first time the scrawl of ink in a barely legible, medieval hand. Names. *Iohn the Fisher. Iohn atte Ford. Mary Whelespinner. Aelfric Parsonservant...* And on the right-hand page opposite were notes in cramped, indecipherable Latin. The names vibrated inside his skull until he felt he would pass out – if vampires could lose consciousness. Unfortunately they rarely enjoyed the luxury of such an escape.

Karl asked, "Have you translated it?"

"Yes, though it wasn't easy," said Lancelyn. "The author used a code, not helped by the fact that he was barely literate. His grammar and spelling are abysmal. However, that's not to say he was stupid. He possessed uncanny intelligence within a deeply warped mind; a vampire more at the mercy of his victims than they were at his."

"And the names are those of his victims?"

"Is it usual for a vampire to log their names and store their corpses?"

"Quite the opposite," Karl said emphatically. "Our instinct is to distance ourselves, with good reason."

"This fellow was quite the exception, then. He not only recorded the names of his victims but also wrote detailed observations of how they died, documenting their mental and emotional response to the process of death. In doing so, he inadvertently stored their anguish, the emanation of those untimely deaths, until it reached critical point and claimed his life. Is it not so?"

"You are a very wise man," said Karl. He forced himself to touch the Book. Sour coldness bled into his hands, numbing them. This greedy vacuum had seized Kristian, bringing down an immortal that no vampire could touch... "Yes, they took back what he stole. Obviously the hermit-vampire didn't realise what he was doing."

"On the contrary, I believe he did. He was a scientist of a primitive sort. One who experimented to the ultimate limit: his own destruction."

Karl was struck by the twisted irony of this. He, too, had once sought a scientific way to destroy vampires, without such devastating success. Unable to endure the Book's malice any longer, he went over to the fireplace, craving heat. "How did you find it?"

"By hypnotising Holly, in search of a physical link to Raqia. She guided us to the tunnel, the vampire's cell, and there lay the Book."

"And did it give you what you wanted?"

"I believe it was a focus. The aptitude resides in here –" he touched his forehead – "not in any artefact. My three daemons have always been around me in shadow form. The Book enabled me to focus, to communicate with them. Ben absorbed some of the Book's aura, even Holly took in a little – and once absorbed, it remains. That's why Ben didn't need the Book to control his vampires, nor did Holly when she made her appeal to you and Katerina."

"You seem to know everything."

"If only." Lancelyn pulled a face. He picked up a sheaf of paper; the translation, Karl realised. "Listen to this. 'The lowest circle of heaven is dark and thickly strewn with human spirits and the ghosts of their dwellings. The second circle of heaven is the lake of fire-clouds from which pathless ways lead upwards. The third circle is the ocean of bronze hills that flow with the ineffable light of the firmament...' On it goes until we reach, 'The highest circle of heaven, the uttermost extremity of ice, beyond which lies the blinding glory of God.' What is that, but a description of Raqia? The subtle power of the Book is to leech strength from vampires while feeding their secrets to humans. Subtle, but dangerous, don't you agree?"

"I am impressed," said Karl, "but I need to feed. If you don't let me go, the victim may well be you."

"No, it won't," Lancelyn said with confidence. "I'm sorry, you'll have to bear with us a while. Won't you sit down?"

"Sitting would not help," Karl said thinly. It would be so delicious, so satisfying, to reach out and squeeze Lancelyn's throat, like bursting a plum... and yet he couldn't. He pushed the thirst away. "So, what do you intend to do with your powers?"

Lancelyn smiled crookedly, drawing on his pipe then speaking through billows of blue smoke. "Contrary to what Ben has probably told you, I am not a megalomaniac. I don't plan world domination, nor even to bring down the government – though I have enough on certain politicians to turn the country on its complacent head. I don't even care about the Order. No. A marriage is what I plan, sir. A marriage."

"To your sister-in-law?" said Karl.

Lancelyn looked blankly at him. "Holly? Good God, are you mad? That would be like marrying my own daughter! Whatever you think of me, I draw the line at incest!"

"But Holly was convinced you wanted her as your 'Dark Bride'."

"Ah." Lancelyn grinned. "Oh, I see. No, she perceived my intention without understanding, and mistakenly applied it to herself. Not her fault; she's intuitive but poor at interpretation. No, I'm talking about the marriage of Earth with Heaven, God with Sophia, Man with Wisdom."

"A symbolic marriage?" Karl spoke quietly, floating on the edge of his hunger. "With what purpose?"

"To bring completeness, to discover ultimate Wisdom. Rather a perilous undertaking; to unveil such a bride would bring madness or death to ordinary men."

"And does it involve your daemons initiating you into the Crystal Ring?"

Lancelyn laughed, his face turning red under the coarse beard. "Is the thought of my becoming immortal really so horrific?"

Karl didn't reply, but he thought, *Yes, actually; you would make the most dangerous vampire since Kristian.*

"No," Lancelyn went on. "I am going to enter Raqia through the strength of my own will."

"That isn't possible."

"How d'you know? Not possible for ordinary men, obviously. But I am going to enter through the Goddess, my bride."

"Forgive me for being obtuse," said Karl, "but is she real or symbolic?"

"She is Sophia, Wisdom – but yes, she's embodied in a real woman. My angels are bringing her to me now. I wish I could explain better, but the thing is this: no one, not even I, can understand fully until they draw back the veil and discover Wisdom."

There was something terrifying in Lancelyn's self-importance and conviction. Yet he was uncannily likeable. Repulsive, yet attractive. *A human who controls vampires*, Karl thought. *Where does that leave us? And, God forbid, what kind of vampire could he become? We can't allow it to happen.*

"You know, you are the most beautiful young man I've ever seen," Lancelyn said thoughtfully. "Women must die for you. Ha, literally, I suppose. I hope my daemons aren't *too* angry with you about Kristian. I'd rather we could be friends, truly."

"I suppose anything is possible," said Karl.

This remark appeared to galvanise Lancelyn. "Oh, for heaven's sake! Don't you ever say what you really feel? You're bloody furious with me, but you think I'm rather interesting – no? Admit it!"

"Benedict loved you," said Karl. "He thinks you have degraded yourself. And I think it a shame that a decent young man like Ben has overturned every principle of decency in pursuit of revenge."

Lancelyn's jovial expression turned rancid. "Degraded myself – he thinks that, does he?" His merriment returned. "Ha! Of course he does! And doesn't he realise that I could have killed him ten times over, if I'd wanted?"

"But there's more fun in playing cat and mouse."

"That's not the point. He's my flesh and blood, but pig-headed young men will sometimes respond only to the lash."

As Lancelyn spoke, Karl sensed a dark bustling of the air. Out of the Crystal Ring stepped Lancelyn's allies, the vampire-angels, holding between them a female with wild black hair. Her lavender silk dress looked more suited to a cocktail party than a lofty stone mansion. Her aura was that of a captive leopard, frightened, ferocious.

She lifted her head, and Karl found himself looking into the eyes of Violette Lenoir. It took a moment to recognise her. He'd never been so close to her before, and she was no longer human...

Lancelyn turned and stared. Never taking his eyes off her, he carefully balanced his pipe on an ashtray. Then he went to her, fell to his knees at her feet, and began to weep. Over his bowed head, Violette stared blankly at Karl.

The three ancients also regarded him, but they were hard to see clearly, at once too bright and too ghostly. Silver, scarlet, raven's-wing blue.

"Most revered Sophia, highest of the high," Lancelyn said. "Be welcome here, Goddess and Bride." Words of ritualistic courtesy that Karl only half-heard as he studied Violette.

Katti spoke the truth, he thought grimly. *Charlotte can't have wanted this.* How different she was from the sublime dancer he remembered! Her hair was tangled, her skin stretched like silvery birch-bark over the lovely bones of her face; a starved caricature of beauty, yet still radiant.

Clearly she hadn't fed, and was in the full agony of thirst. But an ethereal vampire shimmer enhanced her natural allure, and her eyes were magnificent in their depth and pain; endlessly blue-violet as night. The colour of the Crystal Ring itself.

She unnerved Karl in every fibre. If she'd been a threat when human, as a vampire she was deadly. Everything he'd dreaded had come to pass...

And this is Charlotte's doing.

Lancelyn rose from his knees and turned eagerly to Karl, laughing and crying with joy. His naked emotion was embarrassing. "Dear God, she's beautiful!" he said hoarsely. "So beautiful. I knew she would be. Karl, you are privileged indeed to meet my bride-to-be."

"Madame Lenoir, I am charmed," Karl said without expression, inclining his head. "I am Karl von Wultendorf."

Violette stared at him through a wild mesh of hair. She looked demented. He wondered if she could speak, but after a pause she said, "So you are Karl. Charlotte speaks of you. But you've made a mistake; Violette Lenoir is dead. I am Lilith."

Karl's unease grew. What had the transformation done to her? "Why isn't Charlotte with you?" he asked, seeing a vision of her trying to defend Violette, the daemons savaging her and flinging her aside. "Where is she?"

"I've no idea."

"Did your captors hurt her?"

Her lips drew back. "I don't know, I don't care! You're her lover, are you? I despise the lie of love. All it brings is disaster, as vampires do!"

Her fervour shook him, but it sprang from the maelstrom of despair in which she was quietly drowning. Despite everything, Karl's strongest feeling towards her was sympathy.

"And you," he said kindly. "Are you hurt?"

She drew away from him, her eyes aflame with hostility. "What is it to you?"

Karl looked from her to Lancelyn, who was watching them intently. *Doesn't he wonder how we know each other? He can't possibly be unaware that she is – or was – a famous dancer.*

He looked at the serene faces of her captors and said, "Why have you brought her here?"

The scarlet angel spoke, in Simon's voice. "Don't interfere. You've done enough."

"Envoys of God," Violette said quietly. "I'd tear your wretched eyes out, if I could. Why can't God leave me alone? There is nothing in this world of any worth, nothing."

The envoys seemed sadly amused.

"Something of worth, surely," said Lancelyn. He went to Violette and touched her cheek.

Princess and toad, Karl thought, gazing at them in the honey sheen of firelight. *Lancelyn's taking a risk; the state of mind she is in, she may kill him.*

Strangely, his touch seemed to quieten her. "I am so glad you came to me at last, beloved Sophia."

"Why do you call me that?" she said. "I am Lilith. God made me from filth and drove me away to consort with demons. I am no one's 'beloved'."

"But you are more than Lilith," Lancelyn said with feeling. "You're in distress and you don't fully know yourself. You are the Veiled Goddess, soon to be my wife."

"A chance to be redeemed," said the dark one who had been Rasmila.

Karl said, "Is this what you want, Madame Lenoir?"

Out of natural chivalry, he wanted to help her. *I don't hate her*, he thought. *I even understand how she came between Charlotte and me. Even wrapped in hostility, she is magnetic.*

Violette's reaction was to turn her head away in sour amusement. "What do you care?" The whites of her eyes became shining circles. "No one cares about anything at all in this world. I care least of all!"

In the scorching desert of thirst, everything around him – shining chalices, red velvet and rich brocade, the windows set like jewelled dragonfly-wings in the stonework – seemed to throb with the pressure of unanswered questions. He wanted to help, but her savage indifference warned him to harden his heart.

"Am I to take it," he said, "that I need not waste my strength trying to rescue you?"

"You can go to hell!" said Violette. "Rescue me? Who in this godless Earth do you think you are?"

Lancelyn added, "Don't try anything noble, my dear friend. There's no point. This conversation is unseemly and I will not have my lady Sophia upset." He turned to Rasmila. "Kindly take the Goddess away and prepare her for our wedding. Most revered lady, until we meet again…" Lancelyn bowed deeply.

Violette did not spare her husband-to-be a glance. With the passivity of a slave, she let Rasmila lead her towards a door on the far side of the room.

Sorrow descended on Karl. He remembered her radiant genius, and mourned her lost humanity. And although he tried not to blame Charlotte, it was hard. *Why couldn't she listen to my warning? But she did what she believed best, as I did when I transformed Ilona…*

He went after them, moving in front of Rasmila to make her stop. "What has happened to you?" he said, staring into the glow of Rasmila's face.

"Let them pass," said Fyodor, moving behind them. "I could tear out your throat. Nothing would please me more."

Ignoring him, Karl said, "Answer me! Who are you, what do you want with Violette?" Rasmila looked solemnly at him with no hostility in her face, only the unreadable compliance he'd seen there before.

Simon spoke. "Without a consort, Kristian was incomplete. That's why you were able to destroy him. We will not make that mistake again."

"I thought you'd be glad of Kristian's death." Karl said calmly, ignoring his fiery thirst. "Do you mean to make Lancelyn into another Kristian?" Simon – who'd once seemed to be a friend – only smiled and shook his head. "Why won't you answer my questions?"

"Why should we?" said Fyodor.

"Enough," said Lancelyn, stepping between them to usher Karl aside. Karl stared at him, goaded by his audacity. Scenting the blood-heat that flowed from him…

It was clear to Karl that he must kill Lancelyn. Confounded by weakness and thirst, he couldn't unravel the situation. But to destroy Lancelyn, rather than see him exalted as a worse tyrant than Kristian… that was essential.

Karl moved towards Lancelyn. He no longer saw him as human, full of enthusiasm and learning; he saw him only as prey. A sweet sac of nectar. Karl closed in…

Lancelyn began to chant.

The words made no sense, yet they stopped Karl dead. Ice-waves broke over him, nauseating weakness pulled him down.

The words were only names. *Thomas New-come. Tom Thomas's son. Mary the Spinster...*

Names from the Ledger of Death. Even the names of the dead had power.

Karl half-fell against a chair. His thirst became grinding pain. Lancelyn's jovial face peered down and Karl saw that his lips were not moving; the names vibrated inside his head. Although the scent of blood was agonising, Karl could not touch him.

"I know it's hard to admit defeat, sir, but sometimes one must," said the magus. "Benedict may be unable to control you, but I can. I'm sorry, but I'm giving you over to my friends now. We have a use for you. Best of luck, old man."

Two faces, one silver and one golden, rose over him, moon and sun. Karl felt their cool hands take hold of him, felt fangs tearing and sucking at his throat. Paralysed, he could not fight. Simon and Fyodor bore him out of the room, down twisting corridors into a cave.

They threw him into darkness, and he landed painfully on dank earth. A circle of brown gloom above... and Karl found himself at the bottom of a deep black pit, too weak to climb the sides or even to move.

Then came waves of fear, terror he hadn't felt since being human. *I will never die,* he thought. *I'll lie here with the agony growing ever worse... and I'll never know why.*

If this is punishment for killing you, Kristian, I hope you are happy now in hell.

Benedict drove as fast as the old Morris and the cart-rutted lanes would allow. He had to stop twice to let the famished Andreas hunt, which further delayed them. They had just reached the valley mouth near Grey Crags when the engine finally overheated and died.

In the dreamy blueness of pre-dawn, Ben and Andreas left the car where it was and began to climb the valley on foot. A ragged path ran beside a stream, hills reared into heavy cloud; he remembered this wilderness so vividly from his childhood that it brought a cargo of mixed emotions.

Ben saw the mansion poised on the hill: part cathedral, part fortress. "Well, there's the house," said Benedict. "We couldn't have motored much closer, anyway. There's only a footpath."

They crossed a wooden bridge over the stream and climbed a steep path, winding between boulders, to the front door. The house loomed over them; light glimmered from stained-glass windows, high above. Two stone lions, weather-worn yet menacing, guarded the iron-studded doors.

"Where is everyone?" said Ben. "I thought they'd be here by now. Perhaps they're hiding behind the house?"

"No," Andreas murmured. "They aren't here."

Too soon to start panicking, Ben decided. "I can't believe Lancelyn's here," he breathed. "I can't believe his cheek! What the devil has he said to Father?"

"Perhaps he cut short the argument by murdering the old man," said Andreas.

Ben looked at his handsome, blood-flushed face, and shivered. "Don't. Come on, let's go closer to the walls before we're spotted."

Andreas went with him reluctantly, staring up at the pointed windows. "I don't want to go inside."

"What are you talking about?" Benedict looked at his watch. "Where the hell are the others? I thought they'd be here hours ago."

"They should have been. Something's wrong."

"Always the optimist, aren't you?" Ben leaned on a lion-statue. He looked at the heavy door knocker, a lion's head with a ring in its mouth. Andreas went to the door and pressed his ear to the oak panelling.

"Well?" Ben whispered.

"Some of them *are* here," Andreas said quietly, startled and worried. "Inside."

"What?"

"Karl's presence is very faint. There are four others, but I can't identify their auras. And one human. Katerina... I can't sense her, I don't know who is there."

"Only four? Where are the others?" Ben's confidence sank into frustration. The plan had gone wrong already. "Can you hear anything?"

"Only voices, too far away to distinguish... I don't want to go in, Benedict."

"What do you mean?"

"There's an evil energy inside that's stronger than us. Can't you feel it? I'm not such an idiot as to walk into a trap. What if our friends are in Lancelyn's power?"

"In that case," Ben said, "we should save them, shouldn't we?" He tried the door, found it locked. "Too much to hope we could just walk in."

"We could break a window," said Andreas.

"You're joking! Those windows are priceless!"

"Oh, the windows are more important than Karl's life, are they?"

"This is wasting time," said Ben. "Let's do the obvious."

He strode to the top doorstep, grasped the lion's-head knocker, and pounded three times.

A slow minute passed before the door split and one half creaked ponderously open. Two weird, shining faces peered out, making Ben start violently. Shaking himself, he realised they were costume heads on the shoulders of two tall, robed figures.

One was that of a lion; a mask wrought in polished gold with a mane of rustling foil, like a sunburst. The other was a silver bull with curved horns like crescent moons. The lion was robed in yellow, the bull in white.

The lion spoke, its voice muffled behind the mask. "Welcome, Benedict."

"Will you take me to Lancelyn?"

"That is our intention."

As Ben moved forward, Andreas seized his arm and pulled him back, wild with fear. "Come away! Don't go in!"

"I must. You can stay here." He crossed the threshold, seeing a flight of stone stairs curving up in the gloomy interior. Home, after all these years!

Andreas followed, frantic. Ben turned to see the silver bull thrusting Andreas back with gloved hands. "Your presence is not required."

Andreas staggered backwards, his face aghast in the narrowing gap. Then the door slammed shut, and Ben was alone with his bizarre welcoming party.

The darkness made him near-blind at first. He felt them removing his coat and jacket, then pulling a heavy cotton garment over his head. It felt like a ritual robe of the Order; he smelled incense in its folds.

"What are you doing?"

"Lancelyn wants you suitably attired," said the lion. Ben knew that neutral, ageless voice...

"Just take me to him, will you?"

The bull laughed softly. He recognised the laugh, the heavy accent. "It is not so easy."

"Fyodor?" Ben said accusingly. "Simon? What the hell's going on? You're meant to be on my side!"

Without responding, the lion-mask spoke. "Your right to see Lancelyn must be earned. He has sent us to test you."

"Get out of my way. Where is he?" Seeing a faint grey glow from the first-floor landing, where the living rooms were, Ben strode towards the stairs. Lion and bull seized him. He struggled violently, to no effect. Their fingers were delicate, yet hard and strong as handcuffs.

Recollecting himself, he began to exert his will over them. "You forget, I am your master. There is a chain around your necks –"

"No longer," said Simon. "You forget that you set us free."

"Let me go!" he cried. "This is bloody ridiculous!"

"No, Benedict," said Fyodor, a cruel smile in his voice. "This is bloody serious."

They led him between them, not upstairs, but through the doorway that led to the kitchens and storerooms.

"You traitors. How did he get his hands on you? Or were you with him from the start? Answer me, damn it!"

They were mute. A door shut, enclosing them in blackness. He felt Simon leave him, heard a heavy creak. Another door opening, a sudden chill breeze... Then they led him forward again.

"Mind your footing," Simon said helpfully. "There are steps down."

The warning came too late. He trod on thin air, pitched forward, found strong hands bearing him up until his groping feet found the tread. Then, in the after-shock, a wave of fear wrenched his guts.

"I know what your costumes symbolise," he breathed, counting steps as they descended. "The lion represents the sun, the bull is the moon; symbolising the study of nature as the path to high wisdom. This is aninitiation, isn't it?"

"Yes. An initiation for the adept," the lion replied.

Forty-three steps, then an uneven, rocky surface tilted downhill under his feet. He heard water running, smelled the subterranean clamminess of a cave. A tremor of excitement broke through his fear. *These must be the caves I could never find! Mother told me they were blocked off. Has Lancelyn re-opened them? How, why?* As they moved through darkness, Ben's mind worked furiously to comprehend what Lancelyn was after.

A scream of metal and a blaze of light made Ben's nerves explode, unravelling his hard-won calm into a tangle of terror. A hooded silhouette rushed out of the blaze, swinging a scythe at his head.

A scream leapt from his throat before he could stop it. He couldn't move. The scythe swept over him with a *swoosh*, the blade's draught ruffling his hair. Then the hooded figure shot backwards and jerked to a halt. As Ben's eyes adjusted he saw what it was: one of Lancelyn's damned automata, poised on a rail in a small, natural chamber. He swallowed, trying to slow his shallow breathing.

"The scythe-bearer welcomes the postulant to his initiation," came Simon's voice. The lion-mask was suddenly burnished bright by lamplight.

"Very impressive," Ben said harshly. "I suppose there's someone behind a curtain pulling wires?" No reply, but he sensed their amusement. Probably Fyodor himself had pulled some hidden lever. "So, Lancelyn insists I prove I'm worthy to speak to him? Incredible. All right, but tell me – is this a grotesque pantomime, or does he mean it?"

"His motives are his own affair," said Simon, "but you'd be well advised to take him seriously. As a postulant, you have certain choices. Make the wrong one, and you die."

The weight of the warning sobered him. *Lancelyn would*, he thought. *He would actually kill me. And the vampires I nurtured to protect me have turned against me.*

"What if I refuse to go along with this?"

"You have already begun," said Fyodor, "but you can choose to stop."

"But that choice will result in my death?" Ben said, his throat dry. "Very well, let's get on with it."

"Well chosen," Fyodor jeered.

"Your way lies through there." The lion pointed to an aperture in the far wall. An Alice-in-Wonderland rabbit hole, barely two feet high. "It symbolises the tomb through which the postulant must pass before reaching enlightenment."

Ben recognised the words from an ancient ritual. "Go and triumph over the terrors of the tomb," he murmured to himself. The smallness of the opening made his stomach recoil. Setting his jaw, he dropped down on all fours and entered.

It seemed a natural fissure, rough-walled, very narrow. Earthy, damp air filled his throat as he felt his way into the blackness, the robe catching annoyingly under his knees. *Lancelyn may be several steps ahead of me, but he hasn't won yet. Not while I'm still alive.*

Two minutes into the fissure, claustrophobia hit. Sweat drenched him. He was on fire and shivering, his heart drumming madly. His tiny world rotated and he thought, *God, my heart's giving out! I shall be buried alive.*

He crawled faster, scraping his hands and his knees. The roof touched his head; his whole body tingled with sick fear. *Dear Lord, if I'm going to die here, let it be fast...*

Now he was squirming on his stomach, breath chattering in and out. An inflow of fresh air reached him. His fear, having reached its peak, began to recede; then it dawned that the tunnel roof had risen, and there was space around him.

Ben's panic subsided, leaving him shaken and humiliated. He stopped and sat on a rock, drawing deep breaths, chastising himself for allowing intellect to be submerged by primeval reflex. *That won't happen again,* he told himself. *To die, without scoring a single point against my brother, to die a fool? Not a chance. Death itself does not matter and I refuse to fear it.*

Eyes straining against darkness, he felt his way across a rock-bed, edging between slabs and boulders. His fear had subsided to a background tremor, unpleasant but bearable.

Lancelyn, you're out of your mind, he thought. *A true initiation should be a test of the mind, not of someone's ruddy pot-holing abilities... If it's test of courage, though, I've hardly passed with flying colours.*

His feet found a lip of rock and he dipped his hand into empty space beyond. A chasm, barring his path? On hands and knees, he worked his way along the edge, discovering that it was roughly circular, some twelve feet across. As he completed the circumference, he was startled by an alien substance pricking his knuckles. Something snake-like, tough and bristly yet warmish...

Rope! A rope ladder, in fact, lashed to a rock and hanging down into the pit.

Ben wiped sweat from his forehead and neck. A choice, obviously. *Do I find another way out – and there must be one, since whoever put the ladder here is unlikely to have crawled through the wormhole – or do I climb down? Taking the easy way seems cowardly but might be wise; the difficult way, possibly courageous, probably stupid. Which of those am I, in Lancelyn's opinion?*

Well, we'll see.

Gripping the ropes, he swung himself over the drop. The ladder creaked alarmingly. His descent was slow as he tested each rung before trusting his weight to it. He counted them as he went; twenty-nine, thirty – then his foot pawed at nothingness.

He stopped, hanging like a spider on a thread. His nerves threatened a second betrayal, but he shut down the turmoil. The utmost in bravery or misjudgment was required now. *A gamble,* he thought; *if I let go, perhaps I land on my feet and find a tunnel to safety – or perhaps I fall to my death.*

His hands were in a spasm on the cold, damp rung and he thought, *I can't let go. I'll have to climb up again... No. wait. If I remove my robe and tie it to the bottom rung –*

A voice below him almost dealt a fatal blow to his heart. "Benedict!"

Ben stared down and saw, gleaming like the moon floating on midnight water, Karl's face. His heart jolted, blood galloped through his aching head. The visage shone with its own light, like some deep-sea creature with blood-red eyes.

"Benedict." Karl's voice was strangely hollow. "Help me."

"What are you doing here?"

"Lancelyn's creatures captured me. They drank me dry and I can't escape."

"There's no way out below?"

"Nothing. Only stone and water." Two pale hands floated up, disembodied. "If you'd come further down the ladder, I could reach your ankle and haul myself out."

Karl's eerie, coaxing tone was far from normal. Ben didn't move. "What do you mean, Lancelyn's creatures?"

"Simon, Rasmila and Fyodor. I can't explain what I saw, but they joined with Lancelyn's daemons and *became* them, like souls rejoining bodies. They attacked Katerina and the others. None of us had a chance."

"Are the other vampires dead?"

"I don't know."

Ben groaned in bitter dismay. Not merely defeated, but betrayed. "And you, Karl," he said, "whose side are you on?"

"Yours, Benedict," came the reply, "but I can't help you until you help me escape. Reach down to me. It's not far."

Ben was uneasy, but couldn't leave Karl. "Wait," he said. The ladder shuddered as, with difficulty, he pulled his robe off over his head. With one end wrapped tight around his hand, he leaned out, dangling the garment into the lightless well.

Ben was rigid, breath held. He felt Karl grasp the cloth, his weight less than he'd expected. And then, in a rush like the killing leap of a panther, the vampire surged up towards him, his face pallid as tomb-marble, his eyes red pits of famine.

Ben gave a hoarse scream and loosed the robe. White fingernails scratched his hand, fell away into blackness.

Frozen, Ben clung to the ropes and stared downwards. Horrified, he knew Karl was famished beyond caring who became his prey. He had almost died to find it out.

"Benedict, come down to me," said the voice, softly compelling. "I need you. Come…"

"No," said Ben. Tears squeezed from his eyes with the sheer effort of resisting, with the harsh blow of treachery. "I should have known that a vampire's blood-lust is stronger than loyalty, even yours."

"I am in agony. You can't leave me."

"I'm sorry, Karl. Lancelyn's used you against me. If I try to help you, I'll die."

Silence. Then Karl spoke, his voice parched but controlled. "You're right, Ben. You've seen that I can't stop myself. Leave me, quickly! If you linger… I will persuade you. I think there's a way out above. Go, before –"

That was the last Ben heard. He was already climbing out.

As he climbed over the lip of the pit, he saw a patch of pewter light a few yards away. A tunnel, high enough to admit a man! He made his way across the rocks and entered, feeling calmer but very grim. The glow, filtering along the twisting passageway, sculpted sooty masses of shadow more threatening than simple darkness.

Ben shivered in his shirt-sleeves, aware he might be walking into another trap. The tunnel led into a cavern of columns and rounded stumps of dripstone. He sensed watchers in the shadows, waiting, like Karl, to leap out and seize him.

He chanted softly to himself, channelling his mind towards Raqia. Hardly breathing, he waited for the silhouettes to pounce… He could hear a stream or spring, and over its soft bubbling music, an eerier sound like the silvery chime of bells.

A hundred shadows leapt and froze. Ben stopped in alarm. Yellow light spilled suddenly from above, sending fingers of flat darkness towards him. Squinting, he saw a doorway cut high in the cave wall, with light glaring through iron bars. Steps cut in the wall led to the aperture. He spun round to see what lay behind him; no watchers in the darkness after all. But seeing the cavern through which he'd walked, he gasped.

The whole cave glittered. It was a grotto embellished by human hands; every surface encrusted with crystal, amethyst, amber and seashells in swirling patterns. The shallow stream threw back reflections to dance on the ceiling. Cherubs stood on boulders, gazing into the water. Ben was amazed. To think this folly had been under the house, undiscovered, all through his boyhood!

He ran to the carved steps and ascended towards the light. Through the iron bars he saw a long, cream-washed gallery bathed in golden light. The unlocked gate swung inwards at his touch, and he entered.

The walls were painted with arcane symbols. Eleven bronze tripods stood along the length of the gallery, a bright-burning path to an altar at the far end. The peppery smoke of incense wafted to him.

The chime of bells grew louder. Life-sized automata acted out the tiny loops of their existence as he passed; a swan turned its head from side to side, a ballerina pirouetted, an angler played for a metal salmon, a revolutionary lost his head, and a black-clad executioner waited for a struggling wax queen to place her head on the block... and each one had its own music box, producing a weirdly celestial dissonance.

Benedict was transfixed, until the last model – a magus pouring chalices of wine at the altar – threw back its hood and revealed itself. Not an automaton, but Lancelyn.

Ben was so shocked that he could not react. He walked to his brother, speechless.

"Welcome, Benedict," said Lancelyn. "You look cold and you appear to have mislaid your robe – but never mind, you survived."

Lancelyn wore a black robe under a white cloak, a ten-pointed star on his chest. Otherwise, he looked as plainly familiar as ever. Ben's heart twisted in rage and regret.

"You bastard, what the bloody hell is the meaning of all this?"

"Such language." Lancelyn tutted, and smiled broadly. "I'm sure postulants in ancient times never swore at their examiners."

Ben leaned on the altar before he fell. The surface was inlaid with white, black and red marble in a pattern of stars within circles. An inch from his fingertips lay the Book, like a block of slate. Ben groaned. *After all this, he flaunts the Book at me.*

"I'm sure they were never so sorely tried," he said. "I'm disgusted that you would defile a sacred ritual for the sole purpose of mocking me. On second thoughts, I'm not surprised at all. It's just about on your level."

Lancelyn blinked, raising his unruly eyebrows. "No, Ben, you don't understand. I am not mocking you. This is a genuine initiation."

"Into what?"

"You'll find out. But you've endured a lot; won't you have a drink?"

Lancelyn indicated two glass goblets, one silver and one gold.

Both brimmed with red wine. Ben looked at them with suspicion. "Is this part of the initiation?"

"The final part. And I do mean final. One of these goblets contains wine, the other a lethal poison. Choose one and drink it."

"All right," Ben said, holding the omniscient gaze. "I will, if you'll drink the other."

"What?"

"Well, it's not much of a choice, is it, if I'm to be killed for refusing?"

Lancelyn paled a little, but he said, "Very well. It's fair. You choose."

When Ben took the silver goblet, Lancelyn expelled a little breath of approval. Ben's apprehension surged and his stomach churned. "Cheers," he said flatly. Eyeing each other, they raised the goblets and drank.

The wine tasted bitter. Ben waited for pain or some ghastly symptom to start; all he felt was warmth. He glared at Lancelyn, hating him, but his brother only looked back with an arch, sly expression.

Suddenly he grinned and clapped Ben on the shoulder. "Neither was poisoned. Just as well; you got the one with a drop of myrrh in it."

"I know." Ben adopted the same steel-edged, cheerful tone. "After all, you'd never set up a situation that put your own life at such obvious risk, would you?"

Lancelyn laughed. "A nice guess; still, I'm proud of the way you passed the tests of endurance. I know it was unfair, but that was part of the trial."

"But Karl would have killed me. I could have died!"

"Of course. It would not have been a true test otherwise. Still, you came through. I trained you well."

"Oh, you did," Ben spat. "No doubt of that."

He flung the goblet away, heard it smash as he swung a hard, accurate punch at Lancelyn's jaw.

The magus went down, landing with his legs splayed naked, his robes settling like a heap of unwashed laundry. Eyes brimming with water, he stared up at Ben in stunned indignation. It was a sharp reminder that, however bright Lancelyn might be, Ben had the advantage of youth and strength.

"What was that for?" Lancelyn exclaimed, his voice muffled, fingers pressed to his swelling chin.

"For Holly!" Ben shouted. A pathetic retaliation, he knew – but it had felt wonderful. "Can your daemons get here before I kill you?"

Lancelyn looked scared, his smugness gratifyingly knocked out of him. He clung to the edge of the altar and dragged himself to his feet, keeping his distance from Ben. "What about Holly?"

"I know you've got your claws into her mind, you pervert! Whatever designs you have on her, you can just –"

"Ben. Ben." He raised his palms in contrition. "Come with me. I need to sit down, if you don't."

Ben had released a lot of anger in the blow. Smouldering quietly, he let his brother lead him up a spiral staircase into the main body of the house. Ben looked back at the doorway, which in his childhood had been a plastered alcove with a bookshelf... *Ah, but this room*, Ben thought, staring around him. Everywhere was light and colour; magnificent windows casting gorgeous hues over the furniture. Ruby-red and green, azure and gold. *God, how I've missed this place*, he thought, taken aback.

"Sit down," said Lancelyn. "You can have a nice hot bath and breakfast, but first let's talk. Whisky?"

"No, thanks."

"Oh, come on." Lancelyn pressed the glass on him anyway, and they sat in armchairs on either side of the fireplace. "We should celebrate our reunion."

"What the hell have we to celebrate? Holly is ill and out of her mind because of you! You will let her go, because you're not having her!"

Lancelyn gave him an indulgent look. "My dear chap, I don't want her. Not in the way you think, at least. Who's the one with the filthy mind, h'mm? On the contrary, her illness concerns me greatly, but it happened because you forced her to break her oath not to spy on me. So, if you want to help her, look at yourself – not me."

The words filled Ben with horror and impotent rage. He knew by instinct that Lancelyn was right, but it galled him to accept it.

"If I'm to blame, we both are! And what about Father? What the hell have you done with him?"

"Don't jump to conclusions. The old man is getting on, you know. He couldn't cope with this place on his own, so I packed him off to a cottage in the village, with a couple of servants. He's perfectly happy, which is more than he deserves."

Ben felt relief, even though he'd had little affection left for their father. "But why?"

"Why do I want Grey Crags, you mean? To do it justice. To open up the old passageways, to appreciate the full glory of a nineteenth-century folly. It'll pass to both of us when the old fellow goes."

"No," Ben said impatiently, "why go to all this trouble with me?"

"Haven't you realised? It was a test."

"So you said."

"No, I mean it was all a test. Everything, for a very long time."

Aghast, Ben sieved his memory. "Since the time James died, followed by Deirdre?"

"No, long before that. The moment I met you in Italy, I knew you'd grow away from me and rebel. So I made preparations to bring you back."

Ben uttered a humourless laugh. "By running a brothel and drugs den under the guise of the Hidden Temple?"

Lancelyn tutted. "The Hidden Temple, my dear boy, was a shell concealing the Inner Sanctum of the Veiled Goddess. I was exploring the magical energy of sexual union, spiritually through the Neophytes, physically through the Temple – which by its nature attracted the morally dubious. I had to make them pay for their shallow disrespect."

"Financially?"

"Financially, and in sleepless nights worrying about their jobs, reputations and marriages. But this is irrelevant now. In reality it was another path to the Goddess."

Benedict didn't believe him, but strangely, he wanted to. The loss of Lancelyn-as-hero had hit him hard. "Are you suggesting that Deirdre lied?"

"She told you what she believed to be true. I wanted to see what you'd do if you thought me a murderer, a procurer and blackmailer;

to see what extremities you'd go to, what inner resources you'd find. And I was richly rewarded. You made instinctive use of the Book, allowing it to amplify your natural power. You summoned dangerous beings and handled them with skill."

"So you set me up for all this? I did nothing of my own volition?" Ben said sarcastically.

"On the contrary. Your actions provoked me to bring my own daemons into their full power. Don't you see? We are not enemies, Ben, and never were. I started this because I love you and I want you at my side. War was necessary to bring out the deepest courage in us both!"

Benedict stared. He couldn't believe Lancelyn was sincere. "All this trouble and pain... just a test?"

"A crucible. You cannot refine base metal without fire."

Ben was still raw with anger, yet he thought, *What if I assume Lancelyn is telling the truth?* He tried, and was astonished by the perspective that unfolded... "Are you telling me you haven't abandoned the search for truth in favour of money after all? But how can you excuse the wicked things you've done?"

"Imagine a higher plane where morality is subservient to the greater good."

"Complete amorality, you mean."

Lancelyn sat forward, his bruised face shining. "In the search for the Veiled Goddess, any means may be employed. And I've found her, Ben. I've found the Meter Theon, the Black Goddess."

Ben gaped at him. Lancelyn meant it. "And this is not Holly."

"Nothing to do with Holly. There is to be a marriage."

"What are you telling me?" Ben was shaking his head, incredulous.

"A story, dear boy, in which you've played a noble part. My daemons are intermediaries between the astral world and me. They are Senoy, Sansenoy and Semangelof, the angels who always accompany Lilith. They came back to Earth to find her, and she came into existence for them. And they came to help me because they saw my unique qualities, and they've awoken the Black Goddess in all her guises – Sophia Nigrans, Cybele, the Black Virgin, Lilith – to be my bride. This is a circle of causality at work, without beginning or end. Our marriage will be the union of Earth with Heaven, the Goddess with the Dying and Rising King, God with the Shekinah, Lilith with Samael. I shall do what no mortal has achieved: uncover the darkness of ultimate wisdom."

"Are you saying that the Goddess is a real person?" Ben's anger dissolved in confusion, but his suspicions lingered.

Lancelyn's narrow eyes sparkled. "Yes, and she's the most beautiful creature you'll ever set eyes on. Come and meet her."

"What?"

Lancelyn rose and beckoned, his face full of joy. Bemused, Ben followed him down a short corridor towards the family chapel.

"Three of your vampires were with me all the time, Ben."

"How? They couldn't be in two places at once."

"Let's say they were halves that have been reunited; Senoy with Simon, Sansenoy with Fyodor, Semangelof with Rasmila."

"So I never stood a chance?" Ben said acidly.

"You have great talents; all you lack is the confidence to use them." Pausing with his hand on the chapel door, Lancelyn turned to him, his expression sincere. "Benedict, you still see this as a battle. It isn't. Your vampires didn't betray you; as they became whole, they drew us back together. We're all on the same side, and this is a new beginning. I need you as my right-hand man."

"Nothing's changed, then. You're still the leader."

"Someone has to lead; to be first through the gateway and take the risks. You will follow. In our new state, hierarchy will be irrelevant."

Benedict saw Lancelyn in conflicting lights; one as hero-brother, the other as cynical manipulator. He could hardly voice the question. "Do you mean we shall become vampires?"

"Immortals, please. Yes, but by entering Raqia through the ecstasy of union with Meter Theon, we shall be immeasurably greater than any other immortal, even my angels."

He opened the chapel door. Ben's scepticism lingered until that moment – then vanished in a downpour of brilliance.

Light flowed around the crucifix above the altar, bounced off brasswork, pooled on the marble floor and the polished oak pews. The source of radiance was a magnificent trinity of seraphim that seemed to fill the whole chapel. Rasmila's beauty was a dark, shimmering veil; Fyodor, a white magnesium fire; and Simon, the lion, was a rippling fall of gold between them. Where their auras blended, arcs of glorious colour sprang out. The air shimmered with eldritch music.

Ben cried out in awe, all doubts annihilated.

Lancelyn said, "Bring Lady Sophia into view. I want my brother to see her."

Rasmila obeyed, somehow human-sized yet infinite at the same time. Ben blinked, his vision confounded as she guided a slight, black-clad figure into the aisle. The veiled woman moved in a dream. She was like a frail, graceful widow, tiny in comparison to her guardians. Yet she captured his attention like a single star in the vault of heaven.

Then she lifted her veil.

Down the length of the aisle, Ben glimpsed beauty that felled him like a shaft of sacred light. Her face was a creamy cloud, with huge dark eyes, her black hair a wreath of thorns. The veil fell. Ben couldn't speak.

He forgot Holly entirely.

"She is the future," Lancelyn said reverently. "Wouldn't you forsake your earthly wife for such a bride?"

As Lancelyn's letters used to lift him out of the misery of the Somme, so the words lifted him now. Truth blazed in glory. Lancelyn-as-hero regained his mystique. "Oh God, yes," said Ben. "Yes, I'd do anything."

"Today your role is to act as guardian, an utterly vital role to prevent any interruption to my wedding – but believe me, Ben, your time will come." Lancelyn turned Ben to face him, his smile one of blissful contentment. They clasped each other in a heartfelt embrace, and Ben felt a wonderful surge of faith and optimism. Holly, Karl, everyone else was forgotten.

"Welcome to the Inner Sanctum, brother," Lancelyn said with tears in his eyes. "Welcome home."

CHAPTER TWENTY

PRIEST OF NOTHING

Charlotte and Katerina found the village in a chill grey dawn.
In London, a spellbound gentleman had offered them a lift
in his Bentley. He had driven them much further, and given them
far more, than he'd ever intended.

They abandoned him when his motor ran out of fuel and he
passed out from blood loss, and walked the last few miles. There
were cottages along a curving street, houses built high on tree-
covered hills. Autumn fog clouded the landscape, dripping from
red and bronze leaves. Charlotte asked a startled milkman for
directions. He sent them past the railway station, up a narrow
lane alongside a stream.

Beyond the village, the trees thinned and houses were few.
There were barren sweeping hills crowned by rock. Where the
lane petered out, a high-roofed black Morris stood crookedly as
if left there in a hurry.

"That is Benedict's car," said Katerina.

"It's cold," said Charlotte, touching the bonnet as they passed.

In the neck of the valley, there was no human habitation, only
high, bare hills steeped in fog. A stream cascaded towards the
village, sheep bleated on the peaks.

Charlotte saw the house rearing out of the greyness. She reached
out with her mind for the presence of vampires, felt nothing. Too
far away. The scents of earth, rock and wet grass invaded her,
muffling her senses.

Despite the blood she'd taken, she was still weak from the attack of Violette's "angels", and not fully herself. "I can't find anyone…"

"They must be here. Come on," Katerina said firmly. Arm-in-arm, they climbed a footpath that was little more than a sheep track.

As they climbed, three figures came rushing towards them. The angels again? Charlotte clutched Katerina's arm in warning – then the forms resolved themselves into friendlier shapes. Andreas, Stefan and Niklas!

"Oh, Charlotte, thank heaven," Stefan exclaimed, hugging her tightly. Startled, relieved, she clung to him, her calm centre of safety. Katerina took Andreas in her arms and they held each other, hard. "We found the message at Benedict's house," said Stefan. "We came as fast as we could and found Andreas; he's told us all he knows, which isn't much. Violette's inside, I can sense her."

Charlotte received the news more with dread than relief. "I thought she might be. And Karl – is he here?"

"Yes." Stefan looked gravely at her, as if to break bad news. "But his presence is very weak. He may be in danger. Does anyone know what happened?"

Charlotte and Katerina each told their stories of the vampire-angels who'd abducted Karl and Violette; Andreas added his account of Benedict entering the house.

Charlotte said, "So, you haven't been inside?"

"Not yet," Stefan replied. "We've only been here a short time, talking."

"I've warned Stefan it would be suicidal to go in," said Andreas, "but I suppose we must."

"Of course we must!" said Charlotte. "That, or stand here agonising until it's too late!"

"Well, we have a choice," said Katerina. "We can all go in together, or enter separately to cause confusion."

"Then what?" Andreas broke in. "This is madness. We've all seen those three daemons and we know we can't defeat them! We have no weapons against them, nothing."

Charlotte turned on him. "But what choice have we? To leave Karl and Violette here and save our own skins, not even knowing what the three want with them? How long before they come after us?" She began to climb briskly the path towards the forbidding edifice. "I'm not running away."

Without hesitation, the others followed. Stefan caught up and took her arm. "Charlotte," he said firmly, "we'll all go in together."

Violette had overcome the thirst. She placed it outside herself, like a huge pane of glass between her and the world, or a gauzy shroud, clinging to her, webbing her down. She distanced herself, but couldn't escape entirely.

She was alone in the chapel. The angels had left. She had no thoughts of running away: the self she wanted to flee would only come with her. The slightest movement made her feel ill, as if fever waited to flash up and consume her. She must simply hold still against fear, the pain of memory, the constant dry burning of her veins. Sit very still.

"Lady Sophia," said a voice behind her. The self-styled magus.

She heard his footsteps in the aisle as he approached and sat beside her on the pew. No ostentatious reverence or tears this time, and she was glad. His first display had repelled her.

"My dear lady," he said, "are you afraid?"

With an effort, she turned to look at him. She could not focus properly – or rather, she focused too well. His face was too large, too full of colour and detail; she saw every pore in the florid skin, every whisker. Even the sight of him invaded her, like a violation. Light poured onto him from the tall windows above the altar. Her vision pulsed like a heart, expanding, contracting. Nothing made sense.

"The angels said I must obey you in all things," said Violette. Her voice was small, without emotion.

"Will you?"

"Yes."

"Why?"

His question penetrated the glass wall and shook her. He rested his fingers lightly on her hand. His touch disgusted her. He was Janacek, and the too-handsome Adam who'd tried to subjugate her in Eden, and her own father. He was every male who'd ever asserted dominance over wives, sisters, daughters...

"Why do you need to ask *why*?"

"Lilith does no one's will except her own," said Lancelyn. He spoke as gently as a priest. "Who tells the Black Goddess what to do? I am asking you not to obey me, but to join me. To let me in."

Violette could not speak for a time. There was nothing to say. At last she said, "I have nothing to offer you."

The words felt hollow. She'd thought the same about Janacek, and all the men and women who approached her with feverish eyes and bouquets in their clammy hands. She'd even thought the same of Charlotte. "What do they want? I give them my whole self on stage, there's nothing else – yet they seem to want more, something I don't understand. Embraces, kisses, sex? Why? It means so little."

She didn't realise she had spoken aloud, until Lancelyn said, "But it moves the stars."

"That's sentiment," she said. "No, it's about possession. They want to control me and I don't know why."

"When you dance, you control them." Again the intrusive fingers touched hers. Sickening pain gripped her heart. "Yes, I know who you were," he said. "But through each other we'll both become different. It's alchemy, transformation." \

"But I'm afraid. I don't want to change." She added, her voice knife-edged, "I resent the intrusion."

Lancelyn leaned back, unconsciously giving her more space. His voice was like velvet, or the plush fur on an old toy, comforting. "When I was young, I kept seeing three dark angels. Others would have been scared to death. But I knew, even as a child, that their darkness was to protect my eyes from their brilliance. You are like that, Sophia."

Another shiver that made her whole body hurt. "You saw them too? I dreaded them!"

"Why?"

"Because I knew they'd come from God to punish me."

"A different interpretation, that's all! Don't you see that we are linked? God's envoys have guarded us both, waiting for the right time to unite us. Me, a seeker of wisdom, and you, Wisdom herself."

Violette felt something break through the glass shroud; a tendril of hope. "You really saw them? I thought I was alone, and mad."

"No," he said. How tender he sounded. "Of course you were frightened; only a fool would feel no awe. But they are our guides, not our foes."

Violette swallowed, her throat thick and bitter. "My pain won't end until they have their way."

"Think of it as a change, not defeat."

"No, it must be defeat, a surrender to the forces I loathe. It's the only way to atone for all my sins..." *Tearing my mother apart,* she thought, *which drove Father away and made him prey to a lamia who destroyed us all; my original sin, my black hair, my depravity... the prophecy fulfilled when I gave in to Charlotte.*

"Then we both capitulate," he said. "We give up our egos and throw ourselves into the Abyss. No magus reaches enlightenment unless he surrenders himself. You are prey to darkness, by which I mean superstitious ignorance; that's why you are confused. You don't know yourself. We'll find the light together!"

She saw Lancelyn as her father – her father as he should have been. *And Janacek loved me,* she thought, as if she'd never realised before. *He was cruel because he couldn't have me. If I'd given in, he would have been happy – but would I?*

Stop fighting. Let it happen.

But Janacek was afraid of me! That's why he never dared force me... My dancers jump when I shout, my assistants are deferential, strangers so nervous. All scared of me. Even Charlotte!

"Do I frighten you?" she asked.

"Of course." Lancelyn half-smiled. "All men fear you, because you represent sexuality and knowledge. To us wretched men, that is a truly terrible combination in a female. Who would not fear Lilith or Kali? She is not a gentle goddess but harsh, unforgiving and truthful. That is why the man who dares to enter her risks so much – but will gain everything if he survives."

"I don't wish to frighten anyone."

"You can't avoid it," he said, with rueful affection. "Don't be kind to me. Be yourself."

"Do you love me?"

"With all my soul."

She lifted her hand a fraction of an inch, a small gesture, letting him fold his fingers around hers. His grasp roused no feelings, only held her steady, and she badly needed that. She needed to be confined, made safe.

She said, "You're the only person I have ever spoken to who seems to understand me."

"I wouldn't claim that, but believe me, you are among friends here. Only let me through to the hidden sanctum, beloved Sophia; then I'll truly understand."

"I'll do it," she said softly. "I'll do the thing I dread. There's nothing else left."

The well, Karl's prison, became a physical manifestation of his thirst. Lightless, relentless, inescapable. A sucking pit.

His mind was disembodied yet lucid. He thought, *How did I let this happen? Even Kristian never reduced me to this. Even he allowed me some free will and dignity. I thought that once he was gone, there'd be nothing to fear...*

Words he'd once spoken to Charlotte's brother now echoed with cruel vengeance. "We are very hard to kill, David. Rather like trying to cut the heads from the Hydra; strike us down and more of us come back." *I slew Kristian and now I have three enemies in his place.*

Karl hallucinated that Kristian was with him in the darkness. The space around them was no longer a pit but a castle balcony overlooking the Rhine. Schloss Holdenstein; another prison. And Kristian, unseen yet tangible, was a wall across the sky.

"I was the shield between you and God," said Kristian. "You shattered me and now there's no veil to protect you from the dazzling scythes of His wings. This is what you wanted, Karl. Don't complain that you didn't guess how terrible this would be. I warned you, but still you would have your way."

Karl tried to answer. Something about redemption... "If I asked forgiveness... if I told you I loved you, Father..."

"No, you trod that path before," Kristian replied. "It was all deceit. You told me you loved me; I believed you, and you used the lie to lead me into danger and death."

"Even lies contain a seed of truth," Karl murmured. "It took an axe to end your tyranny. If only a kiss of friendship had been enough..."

"Judas," said Kristian. "You killed me with a kiss, as you kill your victims. How can I save you now, when you destroyed your saviour – me? There is no second chance."

Karl was holding onto Kristian's hands, only to keep himself from plunging into the chasm. Strangely the hands were no longer huge but small, feminine...

The hallucination slid towards reality. There was someone in the pit with him; not Kristian, but a woman. First he saw a black shape outlined by a crackling aura... then he made out her features, as if through inky glass. Nut-brown skin, big kohl-ringed eyes, midnight hair sliding over her shoulders. An angel, with a vampire's face. Now she was in his arms. So slender, she felt, so warm, hardly supernatural at all...

God, how he needed her blood. But he must be careful...

"Rasmila," he said.

"Or Semangelof." Her voice was soothing, with a lovely, precise Indian accent. "I am both now, and neither."

"Were you ever human?"

"Once, very long ago. It was hard for me because my people are not allowed to kill any living thing. But in my transcendent form I become God's messenger and shed all my earthly ideas..."

"How did this happen?"

She only gave a chiding smile. "This does not matter now."

"Of course it matters. Am I to believe there is a God after all?"

"Am I not proof?"

No, Karl thought, *nothing is proof*. But she was right. She was in his arms, so close... And vampire blood, although less luscious than that of humans, was every bit as desirable when the thirst was intense. Karl felt desire sear through him, an intolerable pull that settled in his chest and hurt like a blade.

Yet he knew how strong she was. If he tried, she might destroy him. A mercy, perhaps.

"Do you know why you are here?" she said.

"Wasn't there something about punishment?"

"That is to come. You were put here to test Benedict."

"Ah, yes." Karl looked softly at her, knowing his eyes were

jewels that could seduce any mortal... No heavenly creature would be taken in, but his thirst demanded that he try. "I might have killed him. That was cruel to us both."

"Not cruel," she said. "What use is a test that doesn't try the postulant to the utmost? Cruelty does not exist on this level. He saw the danger and evaded it. You must be famished now. Are you not? Isn't the hunger agony?"

Karl turned his face away. "I can bear it."

"I've come to take you out of here."

"I'd go with you gladly, if I could move, but I can't. You and your friends took my strength."

"And I am here to give it back," said Semangelof.

He looked into her black eyes. His thirst surged like a cobra. "I can't drink the blood of an angel – can I?"

"Just a little," she said.

"Just a little," Karl agreed, electrified. He tightened one arm around her; with the other hand he stroked her cheek. Rather than strike immediately, as thirst commanded, he paused to kiss her lips, cheeks, chin. From the way she pressed against him, he knew that he had seduced her after all.

Gently he let his lips travel down her neck. He nipped the skin, let his fangs slide into her; holding back with all his will. And even when the lovely ruby beads oozed into his mouth he pushed aside the surge of relief and drank slowly, holding her with tenderness, as he would have held Charlotte.

When the time came to stop – the balance point, when he had sufficient strength, and she could spare no more without losing her own – she said nothing. He went on drinking, and she let him. He expected her to struggle out of his embrace, to cry, "Enough!" Yet she did not. Seemingly lulled into delicious languor, she let him drink and drink...

Eventually Karl could draw no more blood from her. Her veins were dry. Reluctantly he ceased, kissing the wound he'd made; feeling the edges heal under his tongue. God, how lovely to have fed from an angel. Paradise.

Then she pulled back, a crease between her thick dark eyebrows. "You've taken a lot," she said.

"Only what you and your friends took from me."

"You've taken too much."

"You could have stopped me," he said, half-smiling. "You did not, *mein schönes Engelein*." He stood, lifting her to her feet. "Is it my fault?"

"No," she said. "I mean you have drunk too much for your own good."

Karl paused, distrustful. "What's this, another ploy to disarm me?"

"No, I speak the truth. My blood has put you in our power."

He felt disbelief and dull apprehension. "How?"

"I'm sorry, Karl. This has to be. You are guilty. For as long as my blood sustains you, you are part of us."

Karl realised that their communion had been illusory. Her face faded behind an inky veil. She became taller and colder, her corona dazzling. He let her go.

"Guilty?" he said. "How can you defend Kristian, who tried to destroy you? Was that his secret, that people still loved him no matter what he did?"

"Come with me now," she said.

Karl, warm with the sparkle of her blood, began to climb the rough damp walls of the pit. He found the bottom rung of the ladder, and was out in seconds. So easy now.

She led him down a tunnel and into a startling cave like the interior of a jewelled egg. They must have dragged him through here on their way to the pit; he couldn't remember. Now he took in the riot of semi-precious stones, charming statues contemplating a spring that flowed on its glassy way to other, unknown caverns.

A rough-hewn stairway rose to a bright doorway some twenty feet above. At its base stood Simon and Fyodor. Their radiance was dim and they looked near-human.

Karl felt the fire of Rasmila's blood and the Crystal Ring's touch. Could they stop him if he tried to escape? Undoubtedly – but the awful thing was that he had no desire to try. All motivation gone, he was slipping into a thick garnet-red pool of lethargy. He thought of Charlotte and felt nothing.

It's true, he thought numbly. *The blood's put me in thrall to them.*

"Welcome, Karl," said Simon. "I am sorry our friendship has to end in this manner."

"Indeed?" Simon had a compelling air of authority, but Karl wouldn't admit defeat. "I thought you were glad that Kristian's death restored you to life. What am I missing? Have you forgotten our conversations, Simon?"

"You won't understand how we can be vampires, once human, and envoys of God at the same time. It is a mystery among many."

"We all have different aspects," said Karl. "Are you the only ones?"

"There may be others, but they're not known to us. Our purpose was to choose and create Kristian."

"For what reason? You claimed you made him a vampire in order to mock his piety. A joke that went wrong. A strange lie, was it not?"

"It was true, on the surface," Simon said benignly. "I know it's hard to comprehend."

"I'll try," Karl said aridly.

Fyodor interrupted, "We waste our time talking to him," but Simon held up a hand to quiet him and went on.

"We are dual beings. We retain our once-human forms, but the centuries drew us closer to God until we became the mercurial link between Earth and heaven. We exist on both levels. At the divine level is the true reason for Kristian's creation: we sent him as a priest to rule God's flock."

"He claimed he'd destroyed you," Karl said quietly.

"Because we let him believe it," said Fyodor. "We rested in the *Weisskalt*, beneath the Eye of God, because we were no longer needed."

"But we remained vigilant," said Simon. "As dual beings, we can divide and become, as it were, *doppelgängers* of ourselves. Our human forms slept while our divine halves watched."

"And served Lancelyn?"

"He drew our attention, as did Violette. In shadow form, we could do no more than observe. But when you slew Kristian, our sleeping halves woke. Gradually our purpose became clear, until body and spirit rejoined. The physical vessel refilled with divine fire and became whole."

"So, if you come from God," Karl said sceptically, "have you seen Him?"

Rasmila said, "The face of the Almighty is too bright even for angels to look upon."

"Or he doesn't exist!" said Karl. "Does he speak to you, issue instructions? 'Create a vampire priest', 'Capture a disobedient goddess'?"

"He speaks through our mercurial nature," said Simon, as if this made obvious sense. His eyes had the impenetrable glint of brass. Karl knew he'd never wrench the truth from them. The cloudy void between reality and imagination held no logic, only possibilities, beliefs and mysteries. There was no absolute truth.

"And your instructions now?"

"To raise another immortal to rule over vampires in Kristian's place."

Karl felt his grip on reason slipping. While Kristian's twisted evangelism had made the concept of God repellent, Karl had accepted Charlotte's theory that the Crystal Ring was created by mankind's subconscious. Now he felt a sudden fearful vertigo, logic sliding away on a slick of angel's blood.

What if Kristian was right? How can I doubt beings who speak with such authority?

"How can a loving God support the existence of vampires?" he said, cursing the futility of the question. *God allows all manner of horrors.*

"Who told you that God was loving?" Fyodor said mockingly. "Surely not Kristian. Vampires are the lash of God."

"And this immortal is to be Lancelyn?"

"He is a good choice," said Simon. "More intelligent than Kristian, less extreme. He will woo his followers, not drive them away. And we won't repeat the mistake of letting him minister alone. Kristian was vulnerable because he was incomplete. So we have found Lancelyn a wife, the only possible consort, the Mother of Vampires. Lilith, like us, is a dual being. She woke in Violette for this purpose. She symbolises the first woman, who strayed and must return to her husband. Thus Lancelyn represents Adam, the first male. In their union, both are redeemed and empowered."

Karl sensed his response to this would not be welcome.

Fyodor said, "Well, friend? Nothing to say?"

"If you want the truth," Karl said wearily, "whether you come from God or not, I don't care. I resent others interfering in my existence. I rejected it from Kristian, I reject it from Lancelyn, from you or anyone. You're making a mistake. Another mistake."

"You are unrepentent, then," said Simon.

"I never wished to kill him. I loathed the act and hated myself for it; but I don't repent. I would do it again."

There was silence. Karl felt a wrenching shiver pass over him.

"To Lancelyn also?" asked Rasmila.

"Why set up leaders, when you are so powerful?"

"We don't seek status. We do God's will," Simon answered sharply. "But you've set yourself against God. Such arrogance must be punished."

Karl laughed. "So, I'm the Devil now? This is ridiculous! You are under some delusion, this compulsion to control and manipulate."

"That's blasphemy." The quiet sadness of Simon's words filled Karl with dread. Nothing he said would change their minds. If they were intent on avenging Kristian and anointing Lancelyn, nothing would not stop them.

"What happened to Katerina, Rachel and the others you attacked? And Charlotte?"

"Nothing," Simon replied. "We only acted to keep them out of our way. They will recover... eventually."

"But their blood was delicious," Fyodor added. Karl could cheerfully have torn out his throat. "Keep your concern for yourself, friend. Your punishment will be appropriate."

Karl's lips thinned in a smile. "What will it be? The *Weisskalt*? Beheading? Perhaps you will torture me first. You could torture a vampire for years."

Simon's eyes were gold ice. "All we want," he said, "is for you to help ensure the smooth running of Lancelyn's wedding and consummation. Come with us."

Karl felt Rasmila's hand on his arm. He followed Simon and Fyodor up the steps.

"We are fair, not cruel," Rasmila whispered. "Do you think I would let them torture you?"

Karl did not reply. They'd been as close as lovers for a few moments; now they were nothing.

The doorway led into the gallery where Karl had first met Lancelyn. He was absent, but the braziers were alight and the automata all in motion. The air was filled with the whirrs and clicks of their sinister mechanical life, the silver cacophony of their music. Karl was surprised to see Benedict at the far end, leaning on the marble altar. He'd shaved, washed and trimmed his hair, and wore fresh clothes; grey flannels and a Fair Isle sweater. A ritual robe of bluish-lilac lay across the altar. Karl sensed the numbing presence of the Book, but the Book no longer seemed important.

Ben came to meet Karl, his expression serious. Rasmila, Fyodor and Simon watched their encounter in silence.

"I trust you found Lancelyn," Karl said. "What happened?"

Ben's eyes had a detached gaze. He looked at Karl without friendship or trust; it was not long since Karl had almost killed him in the pit. Their tentative allegiance was gone forever.

"It seems I misjudged Lancelyn," Ben said. "It was all a kind of... trial he'd set for me. I was judging his behaviour by ordinary standards, when I should have considered it on a far higher level."

"You don't sound convinced," Karl observed.

"It's been rather a shock, that's all. But we've sorted things out. I've seen the Dark Bride and..."

"Ah." Karl's tone was cool. "A glimpse of her was enough to make you forget all Lancelyn's misdeeds and cast your principles aside? I see."

Ben's eyes hardened. "No, you don't. Look, Karl, I don't know the whole truth, but Lancelyn has made promises to me. I know him and I believe in him."

"It's time for the wedding, Benedict," said Simon. "Explain Karl's role to him." The angel-daemons, a bright blur of copper, silver and ebony, vanished into the Ring. Ben and Karl were alone.

"Shouldn't you go with them?" said Karl, indicating the robe. "You will not want to be late."

"That depends," Ben said gravely. "Our task is to ensure that the ceremony isn't interrupted. If no one tries, all well and good. But Lancelyn fears that someone may want to halt the ritual."

Someone... Arrested by the thought, Karl let his senses reach out in a widening circle, through the walls to the dew-drenched slopes beyond. Five tips of diamond coldness pricked his mind... and a horrifying sensation ambushed him, like a blood-crimson curtain rippling down. His own thoughts were fogged, while the power he unleashed so easily was not his own. It was the ravening fire of Rasmila's blood. He'd become her spy.

Five... and he knew their auras intimately. Stefan and Niklas, identical. Katerina, Andreas, Charlotte. His heart sank in despair and he thought, *Why did you come? Stay away, then you won't be harmed!*

But his friends still approached. He sensed two of them slipping into the Ring, reappearing much closer. Stefan and his twin...

"What is it?" Ben said anxiously.

"They are already here," Karl said, unable to keep the knowledge secret. "Two of them are in the house. They're opening a door and letting in the others."

Ben's face flushed with determination. "All right, we're going to work together. Let's keep calm and draw them to us. Are you ready?"

Karl was not, but he felt Ben's mind thrusting into his on an alien red tide. The room tipped partway into the Crystal Ring. He was aghast but couldn't resist; his will was adrift in a body that belonged to his enemies.

"They are in the main living room," said Karl. He heard their voices; they knew the daemons were in another part of the house with Violette. "*It would be madness to confront them,*" Andreas was saying, "*Madness!*"

Then Charlotte's voice. "*Karl is here! Come with me!*"

"Call them!" said Ben.

"They're already on their way," Karl said leadenly.

Seconds later, he heard their footsteps on the spiral stairs, and saw them emerge one by one from the alcove near the altar. Charlotte was in front; she rushed towards Karl then stopped, inches from him, as if she'd seen the awful light in his face.

"Karl? What's happened to you, what's wrong?"

There was a moment of gathering tension. Katti, Andreas, Stefan and Niklas surrounded Charlotte, sharing her anxiety. The relief he felt at seeing their beloved faces was locked away inside the pitiless other-self, which simply did not care.

Charlotte's gaze darted to Ben and back to Karl. Her lips parted. "Where's Violette? What do those creatures want with her?"

Karl was able to answer calmly, "She isn't hurt, though she was in great distress when I saw her. They've brought her here so Lancelyn can marry her."

"Marry?" Charlotte laughed with disbelief. "She would never agree to that!"

"I asked her if it was what she wanted; she didn't seem to care. Lancelyn claims it is an occult marriage that will bring him some form of enlightenment. The angels say he is to be Kristian's replacement."

They were all looking at him in perfect amazement.

"But what does he think Violette is?" said Charlotte.

"A dark goddess. He had all manner of names for her." Not of his own will, Karl moved between her and the stairwell as he spoke.

"Lilith?"

"Yes, among others."

"God," Charlotte said, putting her hands to her face. Then she became electrified. "But we've got to stop them!"

"Don't even try," Benedict said sharply. She ignored him, starting back towards the spiral stair.

Karl didn't intend to touch her, but he was caught by the force of Ben's will, the dark mesh of Rasmila's blood. As she tried to run past him, he lashed out with forearm and fist to deflect her.

The blow caught her like a whip of lightning, flinging her off her feet and through the air as if a giant hand had thrown her. She hit the floor and skimmed across the tiles, straight into the base of the altar. Karl heard the crunch of her skull fracturing as it smashed into the marble. The noise squeezed his stomach like nausea.

Karl was aware of his friends' faces, white ovals of sheer incredulity stamped on his vision. Andreas and Katerina were clinging to each other. Stefan cried out, almost screamed in protest and fury, "No! Karl, what the hell have you done?"

"We must keep them here," Ben said, his eyes glittering. "It's a test of my strength, to protect Lancelyn without the angels' help!"

Karl barely heard him. All he could focus on was Charlotte, lying crumpled and deathly still against the altar, blood matting her hair. Her eyes were half-closed and unblinking, like a doll's. Above her, on the altar, the Book lay as if in humourless mockery.

Grief and despair drove him almost out of his mind. *I did this*, he thought. *Whatever forced me to do it, Ben or the daemons, I am the one who hurt her...*

Even as his powerless self wept, he felt the dreadful black pressure gathering again in his fingertips and he knew he couldn't hold back. The air throbbed darkly; all around them stood instruments – tiger, guillotine, executioner – that had been re-engineered to behead vampires. He would be made to torture and destroy the ones he loved...

Karl knew his friends, and knew they'd fight. He couldn't even speak to warn them. With a shout of anguish, Stefan launched himself at Karl, Niklas attacking Ben in mirror-image.

Pooling energy, Karl and Ben became a unit that could not have worked alone. Together they manipulated the fabric of the Crystal Ring, making it surge into the real world; a wave of storm-black, barbed force. Against it, Stefan and Niklas stood no chance.

Somewhere in the back of his mind, Karl heard Fyodor laughing.

Your punishment will be appropriate.

Violette was calm throughout the ceremony. She looked at the chapel through her veil, and felt nothing.

The angels had undressed her, bathed her, anointed her with fragrant oils and draped her from head to foot in black chiffon-silk. She held a bouquet of white lilies. Lancelyn, beside her, wore a long mauve robe beneath a gold cloak. What this signified, she neither knew nor cared. Scents of incense and flowers rose up through the soft light.

The scalding thirst grew worse, but stayed outside her so it didn't matter. She was a column of basalt.

The three angels acted as witnesses, attendants and clergy. Semangelof was her bridesmaid; the slender silver-haired Sansenoy gave her away. And the scarlet-golden one, Senoy, acted as priest.

The words were in Latin, the wedding like none she'd ever seen. Senoy blessed the unholy objects that lay on the altar. A knife, a knotted cord, a violet candle, a talisman in the shape of a ten-pointed star; he uttered exotic chants, made strange passes that turned her cold. Above the altar, amid a starburst of gold, the figure on the cross seemed to writhe in anguish against the un-Christian union that was being wrought below.

There were no hymns or prayers. At one stage Lancelyn launched into a long, unintelligible chant that made the bones of her skull buzz unpleasantly. Was he trying to hypnotise her, or himself?

The ceremony was incomprehensible, like a dream.

Senoy linked their wrists together with the knotted cord, and declared them man and wife. Lancelyn's face was radiant, like that of a saint enraptured by a vision of the Madonna.

Violette felt numb. *What am I doing here?* she thought.

"This was only a preparation," Lancelyn said softly, clasping her fingers. How hot he felt. "The real marriage is to come. When Jesus Christ died and was placed in the tomb, that was his sacred marriage to the Earth. He embraced the outcast black hag of death, and was resurrected."

Charlotte felt the impact of marble against her skull, felt the bones crack, the blood haemorrhaging into the lining of her brain. Everything turned crimson and purple... still she went on staring through the explosion of colour, conscious of pain yet not really concerned by it.

She thought she was dying. Although she knew that Karl had struck her, her main feeling was frustration at being paralysed. She couldn't even gather her thoughts to ask "Why?" It was obvious that he wasn't acting of his own free will...

Figures flickered in the coloured clouds. One moment Stefan was fighting Karl, the next he was falling... Niklas was already sprawled on the floor. Katerina was on her feet, arguing with the fair-haired man, Benedict. But she was backing away, while Benedict's eyes were swollen with a terrible bluish light.

Charlotte lost all sense of time. The fight diminished; Katerina and Andreas huddled by Stefan, enraged and helpless; Karl and Ben kept them netted in the Crystal Ring's chill substance. It was like a slow dream. She knew something terrible was happening to Violette – had already happened to Karl – and all at once her calmness vaporised. Rods of white-hot pain began to drive through her skull, striking again and again.

We are easy to hurt, Karl had told her once, *but difficult to destroy*. She realised that the terrible pain was caused by the bones and tissues beginning to heal.

But she was healing too slowly. There was an ice-rimmed slab of slate above her, draining her frail energy... the Book that had claimed Kristian.

Sudden movement; crisp coldness swirled in with three dark-bright figures. Laughter? A face stared down at her, pale as pearl, with milky hair and silver eyes. It was the one who'd drunk her blood when Violette was taken. He terrified her.

She heard him whisper, or speak mind-to-mind. *"These are the vampires who slew Kristian. Let Karl help us carry out the punishment."*

She saw as if through rippling water. Flickering, fervid light. A whirr of strange sounds as the pale one drifted down the gallery, resetting the automata... mechanical figures, meaningless and sinister... At the far end she saw a garish tiger biting off the head of a dummy that lay between its paws.

Another voice spoke, female, with an Eastern lilt. "No, let us talk to them first."

The three figures came into the centre of the gallery. Their brilliance hurt her eyes. Everyone was still, listening to the golden-red seraph's melodic voice.

"The ceremony is over and the consummation is taking place. You've done well, Benedict and Karl. As for the rest of you, can you not see that we do this for the good of all immortals? If you fight us, you only hurt yourselves. If we are to stand above mortals, we cannot grovel in their dirt; and we cannot exist in isolation. We must be a choir of angels, united in the firmament..."

Stefan interrupted, dragging himself to his feet. Charlotte had never seen him so angry. "Do you think we rid ourselves of Kristian so we could listen to this drivel instead?" he snarled.

Katerina caught Stefan's shoulders, as if to hold him back. She said, "He's right. How dare you violate Karl, and call yourselves 'angels'? Even Kristian never acted so despicably!"

Charlotte longed to join them. She fought a desperate private battle against her injuries, struggling to move.

"I told you this was a waste of time," said the pale one.

Then there was a flurry of movement, rippling laughter. Her

friends tried to escape, but the angels caught them effortlessly. She saw the golden one feeding on Katerina; saw Andreas attempt to flee, the heartless white daemon catching him. Benedict simply watched, but Karl...

The dark female and Karl had Stefan between them, drinking his blood, dragging him down the gallery... now they removed the dummy from under the tiger and strapped Stefan in its place, his head lodged in the tiger's mouth so that its metal jaws would close on his neck. Niklas followed, watching passively like another automaton. The female angel was smiling, but Karl had no expression at all.

Charlotte saw the tiger's tail swishing, heard the creak of its cogs and joints, its metallic growl. Its jaws began to close, engulfing Stefan's head completely. She saw the huge steel teeth, saw points of blood appear on Stefan's white throat. She cried out, "No!"

But she couldn't reach him. The Crystal Ring was coming through the walls in glass waves, purple as thunder. Karl looked up and for a moment she caught his gaze, a fatal blow. *They did this to you!* she screamed in soundless anguish. His eyes were bruised pits, passionless, as if he'd become a *doppelgänger* of himself.

She had to stop him.

She flung out a hand, found cloth under her fingertips and gripped it in the hope of pulling herself to her feet. But it was attached to nothing and slid off the altar to land in a lilac cloud beside her. It dragged something with it as it fell. A heavy, oblong block landed with a thump, emanating cold misery...

The Book. She would use it as a weapon to disempower Karl and Lancelyn's daemons.

Charlotte clutched the leathery weight to her chest, tried to stand, and collapsed. All that happened was that the Book weakened her instead. Unable to release it, she hugged it to herself, her tears turning to ice as the bitter truth of what she'd done to Violette stabbed her.

And the Book was telling her, *whatever you do will come back to haunt you.* It was the Ledger of Truth, pouring comfortless wisdom into her mind. The ancient hermit-vampire, its author, had lived his role to the full. He'd immersed himself in his victims' suffering and death, knowing they'd come back to claim him, perhaps inviting his fate. He was an experimenter on a grotesque scale. A primitive scientist, of a kind...

He'd known the Crystal Ring was the outpouring of mankind's dreams, that every human death caused a change in the Ring, however small. He knew that aware mortals could cause deliberate fluctuations that would enable them to control vampires...

Charlotte was fading, sliding away into darkness.

...that vampires were at the mercy of humans, at the end of all.

Lancelyn led his bride to the bridal-chamber.

The room seemed to Violette as precise and significant as the set of a ballet. It was all black marble, a dark glossiness reflecting specks of light and colour. Candles, censers on bronze tripods; the gorgeous smoke of frankincense, galbanum and sandalwood. In the centre was a huge bed with a sky-blue counterpane, embroidered with arcane silver symbols.

The angels had left them. She and Lancelyn were alone.

Fear gnawed at the edge of her composure.

"Sit down, beloved lady," he said.

"I'm afraid," she said. But she obeyed, sitting on the edge of the bed, her back straight and her knees pressed together.

Lancelyn stared at her. Then he came to her in a rush, went down on his knees, and put his arms around her waist.

"So am I," he said, laying his heavy, bristly head on her lap. "We're both afraid, my Sophia. But we'll guide each other."

Then, horribly, she caught the acrid scent of his sweat. He was hot and excited. And his excitement was sexual.

Sanctification had taken place in the chapel. This was to be the consummation.

She felt unreal, as if this was a nightmare of being on stage, with no idea which ballet they were performing or what her role was. But it was no dream. She took a breath. How raw and foreign the air felt, now that she no longer needed it. It stirred the thorn in her chest; the beast-like thirst that was slowly destroying her.

Lancelyn sat beside her and reverently lifted her veil. His crumpled face shone with love. Alarm went through her, like a match spurting and dying. His hands on her arms were clammy, shaking a little. She thought, *Don't touch me!* but held back her protest.

"In the consummation of our marriage," he said quietly, "all truth will be revealed. Lie down with me, Sophia Nigrans, bride of God."

Violette glared at him. The air burned her eyes, but she didn't blink. She discovered her voice. "It's dangerous," she said, not knowing where the words came from.

"I know the danger." His hands tightened; she could smell his body. He smelled exactly like Janacek, when he used to paw her revoltingly in the dressing room; the stink of a goat to her sensitive nostrils. "Only the weak and unprepared die. The brave survive."

"No one has ever survived me," she said.

"Let me be the first, then. All my life has been a preparation for this moment. Let me come inside you, right through the veil of darkness, to the light on the other side."

As he spoke, he stood up and began to undress. And there was power in the room, if only generated by his rapt excitement.

I've got to do this, she told herself. *I am going to do it. He says, "Trust me." It's revolting but that's only unfamiliarity, I must get used to it. I don't want to but that's the point, I'm meant to hate it because it's my punishment...*

He stood naked before her, hairy and stocky, his grotesque member already erect. It looked absurd and comical. He came to her, took her face between his hands and kissed her lips; if she'd been human, if she'd had anything in her stomach, she would have vomited.

Then he picked her up in his arms and placed her in the centre of the bed. He lay beside her, pulled her down. He did not command her to remove the layers of black silk, so she did not. She made no attempt to resist; she simply went with him, a straw carried on the wind.

He began to stroke her through the garments. She felt his damp heat through the delicate material. His hands were all over her; not rough, but hesitant in the most disgusting way, like a gloating schoolboy picking the icing off a cake. He touched her reverentially, but she found his awe vile. *He doesn't see me*, she thought. *He only sees an image. He's nothing to do with me...*

Why am I here, why am I letting this happen?

He kissed her again. She was so stiff under him that he drew back. "Don't be nervous," he said.

She remembered how kind he'd been in the chapel. He was the only one who understood her. *I'm being selfish,* she thought; *there's something wrong with me. If I can bear this I'll be healed. I must trust him...*

Lancelyn shifted to lie half over her, one leg between hers, his weight crushing her pelvis. He was fumbling with her robes, pushing them up over her legs. The angels had left her naked under the black chiffon. She felt the hot scratchiness of his legs against hers.

Violette turned her head away. Nothing connected her emotions to her will.

"Don't turn away," he said. "Kiss me. You are my wife, Lilith-Sophia."

"I don't want to be evil," she whispered.

"You're not. You are dangerous only to those who approach you without understanding."

"I'm not yours to judge."

"I do not judge you. You are the judge, Sophia. Let me pass into you and through you into Raqia. We'll taste each other's blood and it will be holy transformative wine."

His breath condensed with sour warmth on her neck. He slid his hand between her bare thighs. She whispered, "No, I don't want your blood."

He didn't seem to hear. He went on probing with sightless, rough insistence.

His fingers hurt her. The intrusion was insufferable, and she couldn't stand it. Her revulsion became drowning panic and she twisted under him, trying to escape. He stopped, face folding in puzzlement.

"What's wrong?"

The first tenuous connection between her mind and reality became a torrent. "I can't go through with this."

"What are you saying?" His fingers went on moving.

"I thought I could but I can't. Please stop. Please!"

Lancelyn's expression darkened, as if he finally realised she was serious. His face expressed more than words; he couldn't believe she wasn't compliant, that she was about to sabotage his perfect plan.

He held her down easily because she had no strength to fight him. "You must!" His hard organ pushed at her leg. His sweat grew more pungent.

"No. I mean it. Get off me."

"Don't be silly. It will soon be over."

"This is rape!" she cried. "You've no right, no one asked you –"

"Are you mad?" Lancelyn barked. How cold was his voice; how impersonal, his rutting heat. White-hot anger coursed through her and suddenly she felt centred within her own self again; deranged, perhaps, but no longer indifferent to her fate.

"No one's ever done this to me and you won't either. Get off me, *get off*!"

In fury, he forced her down and thrust his full weight onto her pelvis, splaying her legs. His head fell into the hollow of her shoulder; she felt his hot breath, stared at the sweat-slicked hairs bristling on his neck. How rough and disgusting the skin looked, in its endless variety of texture and tint, the tiny capillaries throbbing...

And then the tide burst over the sea wall. Some force sucked her mouth like a magnet onto his skin. She tasted acid salt. Her fangs slid from their sheaths, unstoppable, plunging through the skin into the fat artery until her mouth was filled with boiling fluid...

That moment changed everything.

How vile it tasted, yet how gorgeous. Like caviar, the compelling burst of salt on the tongue. Convulsively she sucked and swallowed... and as she did so she shivered with pure excitement, with the warmth that flowed through every cell... with the memory of Charlotte doing this to her, oh, the lovely tender warmth of it and the sweet-sharp fulfilment that went on and on...

Lancelyn went rigid. His hands gripped her shoulders, not to stop her but to control her. His seed spilled over her thigh but she didn't care about that. He cried out, with pleasure at first, then with discomfort, escalating fast to outright pain and fear. He moaned and struggled uselessly. But all this was very distant from Violette, because the blood on her tongue was the universe.

Electricity, a flood of rose-red sunlight, the most poignant coda ever heard... The room was far away, all sounds echoing faintly, beautifully around her. The stream of red fluid was the centre of everything. Fulfilment... *Ah. Images... Charlotte's hair, Charlotte's lips... a red desert, clean as rubies. The ecstasy of dancing, but nothing, nothing as complete as this, nothing so dark and so incandescent...*

And now Lancelyn was quivering in her arms, shrivelling like a salted slug. And the bliss had been all hers, not his.

Violette dropped him and pushed him away. She didn't want him near her. She was off the bed and in the doorway before she even realised she'd moved.

She stood and watched Lancelyn twitching on the azure cover, trying feebly to lift his head, staring at her with pleading eyes. She felt no pity, only a sickening fascination. Horrible, the colour of his face; dead white with blotches of red and bruise-purple. She saw the streaks of blood on his throat, and she shuddered as realisation broke slowly, cruelly over her.

He made me give in to the thirst.

"Damn you for what you've done to me!" she shouted.

Lancelyn shook his head helplessly, reaching out to her. "Did nothing," he slurred. "You wouldn't let me."

"You made me drink blood! You let me become Lilith and now I can't go back!"

In the quiet after she spoke, another layer of confusion peeled away and she perceived that some of the madness had left her. The agonising emptiness and hallucinations had gone. The blood made her feel solid and real. She was not Lilith. She was herself again... but that was worse. While she'd been crazed with thirst, she had placed all the horrors outside herself, but now, with the tang of stolen blood in her mouth, she had to absorb and confront them.

Lilith is a madness that will come upon me every time I need to feed and it won't leave me until I satisfy this evil lust... Again, and again...

"Damn you, Charlotte," she whispered.

"No, I see it now," said Lancelyn. He uttered a sound that was part giggle and part hiss. Violette watched in vague horror, caring nothing for him, only disgusted by the state of him. Then a tendril of regret came through. He'd been kind. He'd tried in some way to help her, to offer a future, which in the end she had refused. She'd never meant him any harm, but she seemed to poison them all: Janacek, her father, now this wretched man...

"Damn you for making me hurt him." She clutched the thin silk of her dress between her hands. "If I kill Charlotte and the others who did this to me, will that cure me? I have to purge this blood-lust. I cannot be Lilith!"

Lancelyn rose up on the bed.

"I couldn't do what the angels told me," she cried in despair, tearing at the garment. "They lied! I won't obey him, now or ever! Damn their God; they lied to me in His name!"

Lancelyn seemed not to hear her. He swayed, lost his balance and rolled onto the floor. She thought he'd fainted, but he reappeared around the corner of the bed, wriggling on his stomach across the marble flags, hands outstretched towards her.

"I found the light through you," he said. "I am become the Serpent of Wisdom."

And he came writhing towards her, undulating from side to side like some bloated, mottled worm. His eyes rolled back in his head and his tongue flickered between his wet lips.

Then Violette knew that he had met, at last, one of the threatened fates of those who dared to unveil the Black Goddess.

CHAPTER TWENTY-ONE

"DOES ANYONE KNOW HER NAME?"

Karl watched the steel-fanged mouth of the tiger closing on Stefan's neck as if in a nightmare, unable to prevent this horror.

As revenge this is perfect, Karl thought. *Kristian himself would have approved. Forcing me to destroy my own friends...*

"We are not cruel," Rasmila had claimed. In the three daemons' eyes this was justice, that Karl should be watching Stefan die in the jaws of a metal beast, that Charlotte and Katerina were struggling painfully for life only to face the same doom when their turn came. Meanwhile the angels merely watched and smiled.

All the time, Karl was aware of the blood-bond linking him to the daemons and to Ben; an open channel to their will. Like a blood-red cord it was tightening. Vibrations travelled through it, becoming images: a veiled woman rising up like a serpent, expressing denial in a voice like thunder. Surrender, pain, grief, release. The cord began to fray. And then the denial again, slashing like a knife-blade.

"*I cannot be Lilith. They lied. Senoy, Sansenoy, Semangelof, I defy you. I will not obey you, now or ever!*"

The cord snapped.

Karl felt the break deep inside his mind. It was like a sudden violent haemorrhage, then stillness, freedom.

The angels' power over him had gone. And, dear God, he knew why.

He leapt forward, slammed his hand onto the switch that stopped the tiger. It froze, teeth half in Stefan's neck.

"Keep still," said Karl.

Stefan whispered, very weak, "I am going nowhere, believe me."

Karl slid his hands into the hinged mouth and wrenched the lower jaw clean off, leaving broken wires and twisted metal. Stefan collapsed to the ground, a necklace of deep wounds oozing crimson blood – but they'd heal, Karl knew, and Stefan would live. He turned and, with slight shock, saw Niklas on his knees, holding his own throat, sharing Stefan's pain.

The intrusion of the Crystal Ring was fading. Ben could not sustain it on his own. He was leaning heavily on the silver swan's casing, white with exhaustion. Katti was with Andreas, shaking him, hugging him.

Karl's gaze swept to Charlotte, and his soul failed. She was face down on the floor, her hair a bronze cloud tangled with dried blood. He saw the corner of the Book beneath her shoulder.

He started towards her, but Simon, Rasmila and Fyodor gathered to block his path. Their radiance dimmed until they seemed more human than angelic. Clearly aware their power had gone; they looked at each other in consternation.

"It has failed," said Rasmila, plucking at Simon's arm. He seemed dumbstruck, and even Fyodor's arrogance had vaporised. Karl felt no sympathy at all.

There was distant scream. Benedict raised his head, exclaimed, "Lancelyn!" and fled the gallery, taking the spiral stairs three at a time. The three envoys started after him, moving, in Karl's perception, in slow motion. He went to the nearest tripod and seized the brass censer; a bowl two feet across, heavy, with red-hot embers still smoking within. Barely feeling its heat, Karl flung it at Simon. Scattering ash as it spun through the air, it caught Simon's skull hard and pitched him onto the floor. Karl was already running towards him, seizing the axe from the hooded executioner as he went.

The weapon was heavy and sharp. *God knows for which of us it was intended.* He put his foot on Simon's back, pressing him down; then he swung the axe at the golden-fair neck.

The blade struck bare tiles. Karl stumbled in the space where

Simon had been. An image lingered, a glowing body-shape fading into the Crystal Ring. Glancing up, he saw Rasmila and Fyodor vanishing, black and a white ghosts, frozen in attitudes of flight; now there, now gone.

He dropped the axe, and ran down the last stretch of the gallery to Charlotte. Lifting her up, he found her hands crabbed around the Book – but she was alive. Her eyelids fluttered heavily and she tried to speak. He began to prise the Book from her.

"Let it go, Charlotte. Let go!"

At last he wrenched the tome from her and hurled it away, straight into the smouldering embers from the brazier. Then he fell to his knees, holding her, his face hidden in her hair.

He stroked her head, felt her skull smooth and whole under his fingers. The injury had healed. *Thank God, or whatever powers rule us.* Relief flooded him.

"Forgive me," he said. "*Liebe Gott*, I never meant to –"

"Karl," she whispered, "Karl, hush. I know it wasn't your fault. There's no need to say anything."

"I want to kill those who made me hurt you! But what were you doing with the Book?"

He felt warmth returning to her hands. Her mouth curved with irony. "Trying to stop you."

He shook his head. "Oh, love, I doubt it would have worked; I'm sure the angelic envoys were immune, and I was under their control. But it might have killed *you*."

"I don't think so. I am not guilty enough." She sighed. "Yet."

As he helped her to her feet, she carefully probed the back of her head. Her eyes misted with disbelief. "Oh lord, it's healed. How wonderful... how horrible." She raised her face to his; still lovely, even after she'd come close to death and sprung back to life, as vampires could. "But what happened? Why did the angels leave?"

"I have some idea," he said gravely. "Lilith linked their circle of power, and she could choose to break it – which she did. But let us find out."

Stefan came to them, one arm around Niklas's waist. His wounds were healing – more swiftly than Charlotte's, but he looked deathly. "You believe in leaving things to the very last second, don't you, Karl? My God, what in hell were you trying to do?"

"It wasn't me, Stefan," Karl said, gripping his shoulder. "Believe me, I'm so sorry; you know I would not hurt you for the world."

Stefan nodded, kissed Charlotte's cheek and leaned his head against hers. There was no need to speak.

From the far end of the gallery, Katerina called, "Karl? We should go after Benedict."

"Yes, we're coming," he said, but Stefan shook his head.

"Not me. I'm not taking Niklas into more danger. What would he do without me? And if I lost him, I should die. I'm sorry if you think me a coward, but I will not take any more risks with his life."

"It's all right, we understand," said Charlotte. "Can you enter the Ring?"

"I think so, now those creatures and Benedict have stopped interfering with it. We'll see you in London. Be careful."

Stefan and his twin vanished. Karl sighed, feeling no resentment at their departure. "I doubt there's any more he can do here anyway," he said. "Come on."

When they reached the main room with its cathedral windows, Lancelyn's distress streamed to meet them, a tangible miasma. Exchanging a glance, Karl and Charlotte ran to the door on the far side, following Katti and Andrei, all drawn by the pungency of human sweat and terror. Sensory impressions streamed over Karl. The melting reds, greens and blues of the windows; the weight of stone walls, the grim cold atmosphere. He sensed water rushing through hidden caves far below, stillness outside... Two centres of heat that were Ben and Lancelyn. And a silver-purple storm waiting for them...

Human warmth drew them along a passage to a large bedchamber. Karl heard Ben's voice raised, almost screaming. The door was open, Violette standing just inside, Ben gripping her shoulders. Lancelyn was lying naked on his stomach a few feet away. Pushing past Katti and Andrei, Karl entered the room.

Benedict was shaking Violette, shouting, "What have you done to him? What have you done?"

He might as well be shaking an automaton. She stared through him and ignored his grip as if rooted in stone. Her mouth dripped blood.

Since Ben had forced Karl to act against his own friends – whether he'd known what he was doing or not – Karl had no sympathy left for him. He broke Ben's grip and shoved him back against the wall, so hard that he grunted with pain. "Leave her alone. Have you not done enough harm?"

Ben writhed, trying to escape, hardly seeing Karl. "She attacked my brother, she tried to kill him! Look at him!"

Karl looked down at Lancelyn. The magus who'd once seemed so poised, intelligent, humorous, now writhed in madness on the floor, all dignity gone. Karl saw two purple marks on his neck and his pallor, a sure sign of Violette's feast. His face was contorted, unhuman sounds hissing from his throat, a hideous grin twisting his mouth. All the light had gone from his eyes. Karl turned away in disgust and pity.

Looking at Violette, he asked, "What happened?"

She wiped her hand across her lips. "He forced me..." She trailed off. Karl sensed she was not ready to be reasoned with or consoled. She seemed primal, isolated.

Ben was leaning down to Lancelyn, weeping openly now. "Someone help me with him, please."

As he reached down, Lancelyn rose in a serpentine contortion and attacked him. His hands went round Ben's neck and the two men collapsed on the floor. Ben fought, choking soundlessly.

By reflex, Karl seized Lancelyn and tried to separate them.

Incredible, his strength, almost vampiric. Karl held the thick wrists and prised them slowly away, conscious of Rasmila-Semangelof's energy burning fierce but short-lived within him. The brothers' sweat-stench was now strong enough to mask the aroma of blood. Karl did not think of feeding. Ben's mouth was open, his face a purple mask of agony. Then Karl jerked Lancelyn loose. Ben scrambled up and ran, coughing and retching.

Karl held Lancelyn's wrists hard, trying to calm him. Lancelyn went on writhing beneath him, his tongue flicking from side to side in the red slot of his mouth. His eyes were white crescents. The revelation drove Karl almost to tears. Lancelyn was not hysterical, but completely unhinged. The brain behind the eagle-keen eyes dashed on the rocks of ambition. And although he'd hardly known the magus, the tragedy burned him.

"Get out, all of you," Karl said.

Karl flung Lancelyn aside and ran. As soon as he was through the door, Ben slammed it shut and locked it behind him. Katti and Andrei were in the passage, but there was no sign of Violette and Charlotte.

The door shook in its frame as Lancelyn threw himself against the other side. Ben jumped, wild-eyed.

"You must leave him locked in, for your own safety," said Karl.

"I can't leave him there forever!" Ben's voice was cracked and raw, and he rubbed at his larynx, coughing between words.

"I suggest you summon medical help. However, it will take strong men to restrain him."

"My God – are you suggesting... an asylum?"

They looked at each other as Lancelyn's hellish groans mapped his agitated, random movement around the chamber.

"What do you think?" Karl said coldly.

Ben raised both hands to rub at his face and neck. "I was meant to protect him! I was so busy thinking the threats were all outside – I never thought the danger was in bed with him! God forgive me!"

Karl took his arm, impersonal but firm. "Come away," he said. "We should find Violette, before she does any more harm."

He led Ben back to the main room. He'd expected Violette to flee, but she was standing below the central window like a supplicant before an altar. Slim as a lily-stem, trembling faintly, she was untouchable. The window, showing the Serpent in the Garden of Eden, spilled ruby and emerald light over her.

Charlotte was with Katerina and Andreas, watching from a distance.

"Was that her first taste of blood?" asked Karl, resting his hands on her shoulders.

"Yes, it was," Charlotte murmured, softening and leaning into his touch. "She gave in at last."

"Nothing more devastating. We never forget that first taste. Poor Lancelyn, to have been her prey... though perhaps he deserved it."

Ben rasped, "You witch! You might as well have murdered him!"

Violette spun to face him. "What have I done?" Her voice was flint-hard with fury. "He began this. What about the evil he's done to me?"

"How dare you –"

"He forced me to take his blood! Forced me. If he hadn't, I would never –"

She stopped, bowing her head, hands cupping her elbows.

Karl said, "That isn't true. The thirst would have overcome you eventually, whatever the circumstances."

"No."

"This is monstrous!" said Ben. "Lancelyn didn't deserve this! He acted from the highest motives."

"He was deluding himself," said Karl. "His motives were as selfish as could be. He sought immortality and power by taking an incredible risk. The vampire's bite can bring madness; he must have known this. He was a fool to imagine that enlightenment would come from it. But he thought he was different, superior to everyone else."

"What I did to Lancelyn was horrible," Violette said suddenly. "But he thinks he's found what he wanted. He believes he's become the Serpent of the Tree of Knowledge. Yet he's merely mad. Is that not horrifying?"

"You're mocking me," Ben said hoarsely. "God, Karl, can't you get her out of here? I want her away from Lancelyn!"

"Where were his precious envoys?" Andreas put in sardonically. "Why didn't they save him?"

Violette said, "They've gone."

"We know," said Karl, "but how?"

"I tried to do what they asked but I couldn't. I'm fated to disobey them. That was why they left. I wanted to obey – I thought if I surrendered, I might be saved – but I cannot stop being this – this *thing* for trying."

Charlotte left Karl and approached the dancer. Her deep-lidded smoky eyes were full of questions, compassion. She was pure warmth in Karl's eyes; golden-bronze and russet, aglow like autumn, while Violette was stark black and white. And Charlotte's obvious love for her still twisted his heart. Karl felt Katerina move close to him, her hand sliding through his arm.

"Are you any closer to understanding what you are?" Charlotte asked gently. She extended a hand, but Violette jerked away, stared sullenly from Karl to the others, her arms folded defensively. Unpredictable passions coiled in her eyes.

"I was reborn yesterday, but I feel ancient. My birth was painful, but when it was over I was five thousand years old. I remember being Lilith, the Mother of Vampires. I *am* Lilith."

No one spoke or drew a breath. They all saw that she was different, a black sun shining on them. She went on, "I know what I am, and yet I don't. I can't explain. All I know is that I am damned forever because I disobeyed God. His messengers came and gave me a new chance of redemption by lying underneath a disgusting man with too high an opinion of himself. *I could not give them what they wanted.* Neither Lancelyn nor I were what others thought. He was pride and I was the fall. A sacred marriage of Heaven and Earth, Benedict?" She spoke with contempt. "It was just a nasty, degrading fumbling – but he didn't succeed. I won't be possessed by anyone. I obey no one, not even God." She laughed. "I can't even obey myself! If I am a monster, Charlotte, you made me so."

"I hate to suggest this," said Andreas, "but is it possible that *she* is the leader who is going to replace Kristian? Even he used to call Lilith our mother, our creatrix."

Violette's arms tightened around herself. "I wasn't sent to lead you! I was sent to bring chaos! My business isn't to guide you, but make your lives hell. And I hope I do, because mine is hell."

Her gaze was on Charlotte, blue flames of passionate hatred.

"That is unfair," Charlotte retorted. At last, a spark of anger.

"I can't live with this evil, I can't bear the thirst!"

"Yes, you can." Charlotte seized her arms and wouldn't let her go. "You tell me this was your fate, then you blame me for it; you can't have it both ways. Take responsibility for yourself. Accept the thirst. It's part of you now!"

"Give me your blood, then." Violette's lips drew back and Karl saw her white fangs extending. Charlotte pulled back, startled, but the dancer's hands flew out and held her. "What's wrong? You were so eager to give it before. You took my life – give me something back!"

Karl and Katerina were moving towards them, too late. With a lithe twist, Violette bore Charlotte down and pressed her onto the hard floor. "Why didn't you end my life, as I asked? I'll end yours, for what you've done to me!"

Karl clamped his hands on Violette's shoulders, but her strength was immense, her limbs pliable yet immoveable. Her mouth was open, her long hard fangs a breath away from Charlotte's throat. Karl held her there but could not shift her; it was like trying to prise a limpet from a rock. Then Andreas came to help and at last, inch by inch, they hauled Violette away.

Katerina helped Charlotte to her feet, and drew her away protectively. Still Violette went on straining towards her in Karl's grip, eerily quiet in her rage, a lethal black sea-serpent. Charlotte's face was alight with hurt and anger.

"I think I'd better take her away from here," said Katerina, holding Charlotte's arm.

"Yes, go, both of you," said Karl.

"No!" Charlotte cried. "Let me talk to her."

"She's not listening to reason," Karl said tightly. It took all his and Andrei's combined strength to hold her. "Go with Katti. I'll find you later, don't worry. Go, before she breaks free!"

"Don't bother with Ben's car, it's broken down," said Andreas.

Finally seeing that Karl was right, that the danger from Violette was real, Charlotte let Katerina take her to the central doors that led towards the entrance hall. She looked back over her shoulder, distressed. "Karl, don't hurt her!"

Karl felt empty amusement. There was far more chance of Violette injuring him – and still Charlotte was concerned for her.

When the two women had gone, he felt Violette relax, but did not ease his grip. He didn't trust her. Ben, who'd been listening in silence, said bitterly, "I've had enough. Get her out, Karl, I mean it. I never want to see any of you, ever again."

"That sentiment is mutual."

Ben gave a grunt of disgust. "I'm going to see how my brother is."

As he strode out, Andreas said, "Well, what the hell are we going to do?"

"Keep her here for as long as necessary."

"Don't talk about me as if I'm not here!" the dancer said coldly.

"I was answering my friend's question," said Karl. "Whatever your grievance against Charlotte, I can't allow you to harm her."

"Who are you to 'allow' me anything?" Her voice fell, losing its clarity. "She did this to me. I said yes, but she'd cajoled me, she never told me how it would be! Don't tell me what to do. You don't know how I feel."

Andreas said in exasperation, "Do you think you're the only one who's ever suffered? It's hard for us all. The blood is the consolation, not the penance!"

"You don't know what the blood is to me!"

Karl shook his head to silence Andreas. He said more gently, "Violette, please calm down so we can talk."

"Why in hell's name would you want to talk to me? You hate me! Leave me alone so I can think."

"I'm not leaving you," Karl said wearily. "I don't trust you."

"You're under an illusion if you think there's anything you can say to make me feel better, or calm me down, or make me into a sweet-natured beauty like your Stefan. I am in agony! I don't need anyone to tell me how I *should* feel. I need no one to care, because I don't care a damn for any of you." Violette seemed relaxed in Karl's hands now, light and poised. "Lancelyn degraded me, but what I did was worse."

She caught her breath on the last words, sobbed. And before Karl felt her move, she slipped from his hands and was racing out of the door after Katti and Charlotte.

Karl and Andreas gave chase. Outside was a landing, a magnificent flight of stairs curving down to the hall and an iron-clad oak door standing open to the hillside. But no sign of Violette.

"God, she's fled into the Crystal Ring," said Karl.

"But Charlotte and Katti can't; they were too weak," said Andreas. "And I can't. You?"

Karl stretched his senses towards the astral realm, felt nothing. Rasmila's strength had deserted him. He shook his head, started downstairs. "Simon and his friends have handicapped us, but we still have our feet. Our only hope is that Violette doesn't know the Ring. She'll be disorientated and lose her way."

* * *

"I don't want to leave her," Charlotte said as they ran down the valley. "If I could only talk to her…"

"She wasn't listening," said Katerina. "You can't see how dangerous she is!"

"Of course I can! That doesn't mean I can desert her."

"Do stop arguing. Give her a chance to calm down, at least."

The hills were ghostly in the lingering mist. Although vampire sight could cut through the haze, Charlotte felt drenched and chilled. She was light-headed with hunger. Since the angels fed on her, it would take time for her full strength to return. Until then, weakness bound her to Earth and muffled her senses.

Through a mass of coppery mist-veiled trees she saw houses up on the hillsides, cottages along the winding valley.

As they passed Ben's broken-down car, Katerina said, "We'll soon find another motor." Then she stopped, her hand on Charlotte's arm.

They heard the deep slow chuff of an engine, a shrill whistle, saw clouds of white steam rising beyond the trees.

"The train!" said Katerina. "Nothing could be easier."

Charlotte laughed. So bizarre, to be fleeing on foot and rushing through the barrier of the tiny station like fugitives. *What must we look like*? Neither was wearing a coat. She was so dizzy with hunger she feared she must look drunk to onlookers.

Katerina guided her onto the platform; Charlotte hadn't seen her buy tickets, but it was easy to seduce officials with a certain look. A cold breeze blew along the line. Charlotte was only half-aware of climbing into the train through the steam billowing from the engine, of following Katerina down the narrow corridor to a compartment. Only two empty seats out of six. The train moved off as they sat down side by side. The other passengers were looking while pretending not to look.

The aroma of human blood all around was a virulent itch that Charlotte could not relieve. How strange this all appeared through her blood-delirium. *Years since I was on a train*, she thought, taking in the polished wood and neat brass fittings, the gas-lamps, the worn upholstery ingrained with the smell of tobacco. How drab the other passengers were in their dark blues and browns. There were two middle-aged women talking, a round-faced schoolgirl pressing her nose to the window while her well-dressed mother read a book and smoked. The blue skeins from her cigarette rose towards the ceiling, mingling with the sulphurous stink of the engine.

The noise and stench wrapped around Charlotte like armour, protecting her from the piercing tug of blood. *I can't feed on these people*, she thought. *How ordinary they are. I've spent all my time with Karl and Katerina, with Stefan and Violette... It's as if I'd forgotten these people existed! I used to live among them. I used to be like them. How dull, how prosaic, and yet...*

They spoke to her of safety. Of homeliness, kindness, humour. The wondrous, ordinary world that she had lost.

Charlotte bit her lip against sudden tears, closed her eyes. Katerina touched her hand and said, "What's wrong?"

"Nothing. Just the hunger," Charlotte murmured.

One of the women, rosy-cheeked under the wide brim of her hat, leaned across and said, "Hungry, are you, me duck? Here you are, I've got some sandwiches. Brought 'em fer' t' journey, but you look us if you need 'em more than us."

Charlotte stared aghast at the greasy white package that the woman was waving under her nose. "No – no thank you, I couldn't. Really."

The woman sat back, tutting good-naturedly. "You young people don't eat properly. They don't, do they, Mabel? Well, they're here if you change yer mind, love."

"Thank you," said Katerina. "My friend is a little unwell."

"Eeh, ah'm not surprised, running about wi'out y'coats on, you'll catch your death. What are you thinking of? You young people."

Her friend, Mabel, nodded sagely. They meant no offence, Charlotte knew; they were a pair of mother hens, generous-hearted, not a bad thought in their heads. And she wanted to take them, and –

"My friend needs peace and quiet. Excuse us," said Katerina. She turned in towards Charlotte, pointedly cutting off their eager expressions of concern.

"I'm all right," Charlotte whispered. "Just light-headed." Outside the window, hills and deep autumnal valleys rushed by. "And you?"

"I'll survive. I think we have to change trains for London. I'll ask when the guard comes."

"Ooh, no, me duck!" said the woman. "This train's fer London, from Manchester, straight through. Long way t'go wi'out food." She made to thrust the repellent package at them again, but Katerina stared at her, and she fell silent. Charlotte knew how easy, how very easy it would be to bewitch them all, the kind women and the immaculate mother and her child, to bite into their lovely red flesh...

She stood, hauled open the glass door, and escaped into the dark brown corridor. Katerina followed, sliding the door shut; cutting off the lure. "What is it?"

"I can't feed on them, I simply can't."

"Well, it's not a good idea, in broad daylight, with witnesses." Charlotte didn't bother to explain her real reasons. "Come along, let's go to the end, out of sight," Katerina added. "We could get off at the next station, feed, and then continue."

"I'm glad I'm not alone," Charlotte said, clasping Katerina's hand. "I'm glad we made peace at last."

The corridor swayed and rattled under their feet as they walked past a row of crowded compartments. Sudden darkness fell over the windows, and the train's noise was sucked to a different pitch as they passed through a tunnel. Daylight returned, but Katerina seemed arrested by shock. The moment passed and she shook herself. "Foolish ever to have argued. Karl can cope with Violette; she'll calm down soon, I'm sure. There's nothing to worry about now. You will see."

Charlotte smiled half-heartedly. She needed reassurance, needed Katerina's authority and warmth. Torture to recall the anguish in Violette's face. And what if she hurt Karl? *No, don't think of it. But God, this need for blood...*

At the end of the carriage, where the corridor opened into a space for the outside doors, Charlotte leaned against a wooden partition wall and sighed.

"This was a mistake," she said.

"No, it was an ideal opportunity." Katerina slid down the window in the right-hand door, leaned out for a moment. Cold air blew in. Then she turned to Charlotte and rested a hand on her shoulder. "It won't be long now."

"I can bear it."

"Were you feeling sorry for yourself, among those mortal passengers? You don't want to live their drab lives, do you? See how poor they are, how they struggle to maintain their petty respectability. They get ill, their noses run, they eat and excrete and squabble and die. How could you envy them, when you had Karl? And yet you gave him up for Violette. You don't deserve him." Katerina's tone was gentle, more chiding than critical.

Charlotte said softly, "That isn't fair. I never gave him up."

"Never mind. Everything will be as it should." Katerina's rose-red mouth widened, and Charlotte saw her pupils expanding in the velvet irises. Suddenly they were black drops of blood; demon eyes. Bitter poison oozed at last though her sweetness. "Just the three of us. Karl, and me... and Andrei."

Katerina lunged, and her fangs stabbed into Charlotte's neck.

Charlotte went rigid under the deadly grip. She was lightning-struck by betrayal, by her own blindness. *Why didn't I guess?* she cried silently. But she'd been lulled by thirst and complacency, so wanting to believe their rivalry was over...

"I thought..." she trailed off. *I thought we were friends.* Pointless to say it. The weight of Katerina's body pressed her against the woodwork and the train's chugging roared in her ears. She was drifting out of her body. Hallucinating. Weirdly, it was almost pleasant. Sensual. Katerina's victims must fall willingly...

But don't panic, Charlotte thought, holding herself still. *She can't kill me. There's only so much blood she can take and it will hurt, but I won't die. Be strong. It will soon be over.*

The spikes slid out of her flesh, leaving two fire-lined holes. Charlotte slumped in Katerina's arms, confused by the jolting and swaying of the train. She could hear human chatter all along the carriage, each voice distinct yet meaningless. She couldn't see properly.

"No more pain," Katerina whispered. Her voice was soothing but her face was blankly malevolent. "You cannot have Karl. You never could have him."

She turned Charlotte round, gripped her hands behind her back, and began to push her towards the open window.

She saw trees rushing past on the sides of the cutting, telegraph poles, a signal post, all a grey blur in the mist. Her head was spinning. Katerina leaned around Charlotte's shoulder to look out, then drew back.

"Yes, perfect."

"What are you doing?"

"You aren't well," said Katerina. "Some air."

Charlotte thought she was trying to throw her off the train. Instead Katti forced her against the door so that her hips were braced painfully against the frame, her head and torso out of the window. She was held in position by the vice of Katerina's hands. She tried to fight, but the older vampire was too strong.

She saw the tunnel hurtling towards them. There was barely any clearance between the train and the tunnel's unforgiving stone edge. Her head would be severed in the savage blow of contact.

She hung in a roaring furnace of terror, waiting for impact and darkness. It was like falling. Terror screamed through her like the onward rush into death –

Something happened that was beyond Charlotte's conscious will. Her head and neck were bending back in an impossible contortion.

The train slammed into the tube of darkness. In the rush of compressed sound, the flicker of gas-lights, she hung with her neck bent back, sooty brickwork racing past the tip of her chin. All that saved her was the survival instinct of vampires. Katerina's fury was transmitted to her through the spasm of her hands. The train's noise changed with a rush of air as they emerged into daylight.

Charlotte still could not move. What was Katerina doing now? Sliding an arm around her, fumbling at the outside of the door...

The cutting flattened into an embankment. Charlotte stared down at gravel streaking past. Then the door burst open, and she and Katerina tumbled out onto the ground.

They rolled down a steep slope, carried by their momentum, but Katerina never loosed her hold. Above them, the train went thundering by in a haze of heated metal and steam.

Charlotte's searing hunger was overlaid by the throb of bruises and jarred bones. Pain on pain. With vengeful black eyes and Medusa hair, Katerina rose over her and began to drag her racked body up the bank, towards the track again.

They were in a thick patch of fog. Charlotte's sight was dim with blood loss. All she saw was grass, a few straggling bushes, and the railway line. Otherwise, whiteness. She tried to speak, could not even produce a gasp. No strength to breathe. She was a wax taper, broken and hanging limp on its string.

Katerina went on dragging her, relentlessly mechanical. She felt stones abrading her hands and legs. She felt the hard metal rail scraping down her spine, the roughness of sleepers, then another rail. Katerina was hauling her to the adjacent line.

She managed to whisper, "What are you doing?"

"I told you we'd have to wait for another train, dear." Katerina's face hovered over hers, hideous and terrifying. "And wait we shall, for as long as it takes."

She pulled Charlotte to the outside of the other track and shifted her so that her neck was on the rail. She felt cold wet steel on the back of her neck, felt the ground shaking. Not their train racing away, but another coming towards them.

A film unwound in her mind, a frantic melodrama of a heroine tied to the rail by a moustachioed villain. But this was nothing like that. This was a heavy grey nightmare, awash with treachery and loss.

Katerina held her down, mouth curved with a rictus of determination.

"The driver will see us and stop," Charlotte said faintly.

"No, he won't, Charlotte. Not in this fog. Humans don't see as we do. He won't stop, dear, he won't."

The fog thickened around them. Evening was closing in early. The vibration became a rumble, then a dense thunder of wheels and pistons. Charlotte tried to cry out; terror paralysed her throat. She stared up at Katerina, pleading with wide, frozen eyes.

The face that stared back held no compassion. It drank and relished her terror. And suddenly there was a second face alongside it, someone appearing out of the gloom to look over Katerina's shoulder.

Violette.

For a second Charlotte thought she was imagining it. But no, Violette was real. And the two of them were leaning over her, luminously clear and large in her vision.

Oh God, their faces! Demented with hatred, eyes black with

lust for her death. The horror tore Charlotte's mind and soul to rags; that these people who'd appeared so beautiful and civilised, with whom she'd shared understanding deeper than any between mortals – that they could turn on her with such violent loathing when her only sin had been to love...

To love evil.

She wanted to die. With a bitter groan she turned her face aside and waited for the iron wheels...

Amid the earthquake of the train, she became aware of something happening. A struggle was taking place above her. Violette was pulling at Katerina. Then, with a gasp of effort, Violette dragged both Katerina and Charlotte up at the same time.

Charlotte was flung sideways like a doll. Grass and earth spun across her vision. The fight went on in the corner of her eye, but she couldn't move, could hear nothing but the train thundering past...

For long moments, the ear-splitting reverberation went on. Then it was gone, sucking air and swirls of leaves behind it. And Charlotte saw Katerina lying by the track, Violette crouching over her. Blood made a crimson smear along the rail. And in the train's wake, Katerina's head rolled to rest between the sleepers like a ghastly, misshapen football.

Strengthless, Charlotte lay where she was and watched. In disbelief, she saw Violette seize both head and body and drop them over the embankment. And then she came back, seized Charlotte and flung her over the same drop – a near-vertical valley.

Charlotte rolled through close-growing trees, over tree-roots and rocks, and came to rest amid thick undergrowth.

If the train driver stopped the locomotive and came back to look, he would find nothing. But the train did not stop. Silence fell, and Charlotte lay under a blanket of dead leaves in dense woodland.

She had a flashback of the two faces looming over her. To be so despised...

Then Charlotte understood what it meant to be damned. God had not merely forsaken her; God had never existed. There was no Lucifer, no fallen angels, no one to whom she could appeal. Nothing. *Why am I still alive? Is Katerina dead, did I dream it? Perhaps I am as near to death as I can be, and I'll never move again, only lie here forever in this pain...*

She thought of the kindly, ordinary people on the train and wept. *To be like them, to live blamelessly and then die at the proper time... how could I have ever thought this was better? I was never like them. But I should have tried.*

Time passed, an hour at most. Then she saw headlights on a road far below. *If a human came by I'd leap for the blood,* she thought – *but if no one comes, it doesn't matter.*

The car stopped. Figures climbed up through the trees, but she felt no human auras. These were vampires.

Two tall dark shapes. One came to her, caught her up in his arms, kissed her and held her so hard her body ached. It was Karl. The pain was blissful. She tried to speak but she could only laugh and cry.

Then he put his wrist to her mouth. For a moment she didn't understand what he was doing; she was weak almost beyond feeding. Then she drew his hand to her lips, kissed the palm and the soft inside of his wrist with overwhelming tenderness. And she remembered a time when she had done this for him... saved his life by giving him her blood, even though it might have killed her.

Gently she bit through the flesh. She tried to drink sparingly, to keep the pleasure at bay – but the feeling surged like a sexual flame. She couldn't hold back. She shuddered and cried as she drank, until he forced her to stop.

He cradled her head and kissed her. At last she could speak.

"How did you find me?"

"Violette came and told us where you were."

"Did she? She saved me," Charlotte said, more to herself than to him. She felt Karl's blood filling her limbs and moved experimentally. As if a scrim had been drawn back, the murky wood now glowed in colour and detail. Haltingly she told him what had happened. "Violette stopped Katerina killing me..."

"I know," he said gravely. "That's what she told us."

"And did you believe her?"

"I do now. I never dreamed Katti would do such a thing. I thought you were safe with her. If Violette hadn't found you, one more second..."

"I thought Violette had come to help *her*," said Charlotte. "The real horror wasn't in thinking I was going to die; it was their hatred pouring down on me. To be loathed like that, when I'd thought them friends…"

In response, Karl held her tighter. His arms around her felt wonderful. He rested his head on hers, so she could feel his soft hair, his warm breath. A trickle of liquid ran through her hair, down her forehead and cheek, to the corner of her mouth. It tasted of salt and blood. A red-tinged tear.

Karl, weeping? This astonished her as if she had half-forgotten or never fully believed the depth of his love for her… As if she'd known, yet not known.

"I thought I saw Katerina go under the train… did I dream it?"

Karl's silence was grim. Then he said, "Do you think you could stand up?"

"I'll try."

At last, some feeling in her limbs. Her body was slow to heal; her life hung by a spider-thread of energy. Karl helped, and as she rose to her feet she saw, some yards above them through the trees, Andreas sitting by Katerina's body.

He sat with his knees drawn up, arms folded round them, head bowed. Every contour of him was taut with misery. They were both half-concealed by undergrowth. Ivy, drifts of dead leaves, rotting branches. Charlotte could only see Katerina's feet, not the mutilated neck.

"Where is Violette now?" she said quietly.

"I don't know," said Karl.

"But why did she save me?" Tears again. "Why?"

"I have no answer, beloved."

Together they climbed up to Andreas. Charlotte was wary of approaching him, certain he'd reject their concern and blame her. But when she placed her hand on his shoulder, he accepted her touch. He looked up with no rancour in his eyes, only grief. Then she saw he was cradling Katerina's head in his lap.

Karl saw too. He broke down, quietly and without display. He crouched down by Andrei, leaned his head on his friend's shoulder, and wept.

She couldn't bear to watch. She turned away, and to her astonishment found Violette standing a few feet away between two tree-trunks. No longer the Dark Goddess, but troubled, pale with tiredness.

"I thought you wanted to murder me, Violette," said Charlotte.

"So did I." A brief, humourless smile. "But I was wrong. I was angry with you, that's all. I should have been angry with myself."

"Why did you save me?"

"I wanted to kill you; I had some twisted idea that if I did, it would cure me. But when that woman reached you first, and I saw her trying – I felt different. I wanted you to live. I realised I actually couldn't bear the thought of life without you... You don't know what I feel for you, Charlotte. You'll never know."

Charlotte longed to embrace her, but as she moved, Violette stepped away.

"Don't," said the dancer. "You mustn't make more of this than it is. And don't thank me for saving you. I won't hear another word about it. We're even now, are we not? Go to your friends."

"Please don't leave. Wait a moment."

Charlotte quickly went back to Karl and found him gazing at the head, eyes calm but brooding. She hadn't forgotten that if the head was intact, the vampire might be brought back to life.

Softly, she asked, "Karl, will you bring her back?"

Katerina's face was dead grey-white, the purple lips ringed with blue. Congealed blood clustered like garnets on the neck stump. He touched the left temple, tidying strands of Katti's hair; and even in that awful moment, Charlotte felt a pang of jealousy. She still resented Katerina, even in death.

"Andrei?" Karl said.

Andreas seemed to withdraw further into himself, looking sick. "I wouldn't know how. I couldn't. It's your decision, Karl. Your decision."

Karl rested his hand along the grey cheek. Charlotte's heart bled for him. Impossible decision. His face was frozen, his eyes dark.

After a long time, he spoke. "No. Let her rest."

Andreas's head dropped in despair. Intolerable enough, Charlotte thought, that this had happened; but when there was a chance she could live again, how much harder to face the loss... A thousand emotions rushed through her. Relief, guilt, infinite sympathy for Karl and Andrei, fear...

Choked, she said, "What if it had been me?"

The merest flicker on Karl's face. "If it had been you," he said gently, "I would have done anything to bring you back to life. *Anything*."

"But you loved her too."

"Which is more cruel: to leave her dead, or place your life in danger from her again? Yes, I loved her, but never as I love you. You know this, don't you? Why do you even ask?"

Charlotte nodded, lowering her eyes. Her bitterness faded and vanished. She understood. Karl would never hold Katerina's death against her, however much grief he felt, because it wasn't in his nature – and because she had let him make the decision freely.

"Let's go home," she said.

"We'll bury Katerina... not in hallowed ground, but in this wood where she can at least return to the earth. Then we'll go home."

Charlotte turned to Violette. "You'll come with us, won't you? And then return to Salzburg and the ballet."

"What is there for me, Charlotte?" Violette said dully. "I'm possessed. Whenever the thirst is on me, I become Lilith. Come back with you, for what? To hunt children?"

"To dance," Charlotte said softly.

Violette tugged at her long hair, smoothing out the tangles. She said, "I fed on Lancelyn because of the way he approached me; without thought for *me*, without seeing an individual soul in my eyes. Thinking only of himself. His own lust, his own gain, his own fulfilment. If I could have found one man, one woman who came to me in love, thinking of me and not themselves – but there's no one. I'll always be alone."

"But you have that, Violette!" said Charlotte. "Thousands worship you for your art, adore you with never an impure thought; men and women, young and old. You had that unconditional love! What did you do but scorn it?"

Violette looked away. "Love for my art, not for me."

"What's the difference?"

"There *is* a difference. You're right, I should be glad they love my art, at least. Anything more personal, I don't need." Charlotte watched her, wordless. Violette added briskly, "But this is self-pity." She smiled, her face diamond-hard. "Lilith is the killer of pity! I don't feel it for others and I'll kill it in myself."

To Charlotte's horror she began to bite herself, making swift savage gashes in hands, forearms, shoulders. The blood oozed slowly, unlike human blood. And the wounds were healing even as she made them, leaving only silvery marks under gore drying on her skin.

"Stop it!" Charlotte cried. She seized Violette's wrists and shook her. "Don't!"

Violette let her arms drop. The tension went out of her.

"But the pain doesn't go away," she whispered. "It never goes away."

She was fading as Charlotte watched, becoming a figure of smoky quartz with the dark woodland gleaming clear through her body. "Wait! You can't just leave!"

But Violette went on fading until the Crystal Ring swallowed her. Empty air blew through the space where she had stood.

And Karl said, "Let her go."

CHAPTER TWENTY-TWO

ROSARY OF THORNS

Benedict sat exhausted on the doorstep between the stone lions. He hung his head, arms resting loosely on his knees. He was waiting for the police and the doctor to come and take Lancelyn away.

The last thing he'd wanted was to involve the authorities, but there was no choice. Lancelyn was violent and would let no one near him; he no longer even recognised Ben. Left alone in a locked room for much longer, he might injure or even kill himself.

Ben knew they'd have to take him to an asylum. *Better if Lilith – whatever she was – had killed him*, he thought. *Even if they'd had me up for the murder, that would have been better than this.*

The mist thinned, revealing the beautiful wild valley, but it was one of those dull days that never really got light. Inside the house, Lancelyn still writhed and muttered. Ben couldn't hear him through layers of stone, yet he would never get those ghastly sights and sounds out of his mind. Lancelyn's madness hung in the air all around him, driving him to tears.

We've lost everything, Ben thought. *All our dreams folded into a cocoon that will never metamorphose into the glory we envisioned… I think I'm losing my own mind, if I haven't already. I'll never sleep at night, after this. I'll always be looking over my shoulder for Lilith.*

Suicidal craziness, trying to deal with vampires. Who the hell were we, to think we could meddle with the astral realm –

and worse, to control it? It was bound to recoil on us like this.
Bound to.

"That's it," he said under his breath. "I don't wish to see another supernatural creature again in my life. I want nothing to do with the occult. Oh, let me live in the sunlight, the mundane surface world where nothing's ever questioned and nothing leaps out at you from the dark. I never want to see a vampire again."

A shadow slid soundlessly in front of him. Ben glanced up, caught his breath, sighed; Andreas was standing over him, pale with thirst, his eyes like gleaming bloodstones. Yet he also looked oddly fragile, distressed. He flopped down next to Ben, mimicking his despondent posture.

"So, the Devil answers my prayers with the opposite of what I prayed for," he said. Although he was startled to see Andreas, he felt strangely glad.

"Better stop praying to the Devil," Andreas said flatly. "How is your brother?"

"No better," Ben said bleakly. "All I can think about is how he used to be. A kind, shrewd soul who could be expansive, generous, deceitful, challenging, aggravating... simply human. And this is what he's been brought to. I can't stand it."

Andreas looked sideways from under his dishevelled black hair. "Isn't it what you wanted? You've won. Lancelyn's finished. You intended to frighten him off the occult for life, no?"

"Stop!" said Ben. "If he's finished, so am I. I never wanted it to end like this!"

"But it was certain to!" Andreas spat the words. "Wisdom, madness or death, he said; well, he's got one of those. At least he's still alive. Luckier than Katerina."

Ben was too absorbed in his own misery to take in Andreas's words. Then the meaning sank in. "What did you say? What about Katerina?"

Andreas told him. His expression was bitter, his eyes too bright.

"I'm sorry," Ben said awkwardly. "I know you loved her."

"I don't know how to live without her."

"Can vampires truly die?"

"I hope so," Andreas whispered. "Yes, we can really love, and really die... the difference is, sometimes we are brought back to life."

A wave of mixed horror and hope. "Could she be –"

Andreas gave a savage shake of his head. "No. Karl decided to leave her in peace."

"*Karl* decided?" Ben didn't know why he cared, but Andreas's suffering woke a spark of emotion. "Don't you have a say? Couldn't you do it yourself?"

"It isn't easy." There was searing self-hatred in his voice. "And I don't want to make the effort. I would rather sit and feel sorry for myself."

Ben didn't know what to say. "Good God, you're strange. I don't understand you at all."

"Would you like to try?" said Andreas.

In the distance, Ben saw vehicles nosing their way up the valley; an ambulance, police car and the doctor's car, he guessed. *Christ, what am I going to say? Oh, anything. What does it matter? Just that I came to visit my brother and found him like this, I've no idea what's wrong. Bloody lies. Damn all this to hell!*

The vehicles stopped, unable to negotiate the rough ground. Men climbed out, tiny in the distance, and began to toil up the path. Ben felt he should go down and meet them, but could not bring himself to move.

He asked Andreas quietly, "What do you mean, would I like to try?"

"Has either of us anything better to do? No, Karl's right. Katti's at rest. It's time we let her go." Andreas put his hand on Ben's collarbone, leaned across him, kissed his neck – and bit him. Ben almost leapt out of his skin. Never had he thought Andreas could or would do this to him... yet the aching pain was seductive, the china-cold hands on his shoulders consoling... and the sucking kiss of heat at once unpleasant and peculiarly exciting.

The world lurched and he thought he would faint. Andreas drew back, smiling, red berries of blood on his lips.

"We must stay together, Ben."

"I don't control you any more," Ben said. He gasped for breath, as if he'd run up a hill. Shock, fear. "I've lost control; no, I've relinquished it, and I'm glad. You're free."

"Free to stay with you," said Andreas.

"I have to go back to Holly," Ben said, standing up. His hands and feet felt like ice. Weird panic spiralled inside him. His words were an incantation against it. "Once we've got Lancelyn into hospital, I'm going back to Holly."

Holly sat in the parlour by the telephone, raw and exhausted, the mouthpiece still in her hand. Ben had called to tell her what had happened.

His words remained vivid in her mind after he'd rung off, yet she could not grasp their enormity. Lancelyn, insane. They'd had to incarcerate him for his own safety. Ben would talk to the asylum doctors about moving him to a private home.

The image of Lancelyn locked in a cell, writhing in a strait-jacket, recognising nothing and no one, appalled her. But the tone of Ben's voice had almost been worse. He'd sounded wretched, hollow, as if life had ceased to matter. Holly was lost in confusion.

He turns against Lancelyn, she thought – *and even I finally saw why – and then goes back to him, as if they had some secret pact I knew nothing about! What am I supposed to believe?*

Numbly she replaced the mouthpiece, and wiped her eyes for the twentieth time. She gathered Sam on her lap and caressed his long, silken flanks. Her one friend.

The nightmare of the hypnotism still haunted her. She'd been possessed for a time, Lancelyn punishing her for breaking faith. He could have killed her, but finally he'd let her go, and she had slid through a long, dark tunnel into dreamless sleep.

When she had woken up, it was to find Mrs Potter beside her, and Benedict missing. She'd allowed Mrs Potter to fuss, make tea and toast, and to repeat the fatuous excuses Ben had left to explain his absence. Then she'd sent the housekeeper away, insisting in the face of her protests that she was fully recovered.

Even before Ben telephoned, her sixth sense warned her that something monstrous had happened. She raged against him inwardly. *He hypnotised me when I wasn't ready, forced me into it until I almost died to give him the information – and then I wake to find he's deserted me!*

She rested her head between the cat's sleek ears, talking half to him and half to herself. "It isn't only that he deserted me, Sam.

It's that he *excluded* me. I should have gone to Lancelyn with him, helped him in any way possible. Instead he leaves me behind! But when he comes home, I know he'll explain and he knows I'll forgive him." Tears burned her throat. "He loved me once... or has he always treated me like this, and I didn't see it? I don't know why I feel so angry, so helpless. I don't know why I'm sitting here waiting for him to come home!"

Sam tensed and gave a questioning, *mrreow*? He was not attending to Holly, but to the window.

The curtains were half-drawn, winter light gleaming in the gap. Holly sensed something wrong, an unpredictable yet familiar psychic shiver. Her head jerked up and she saw a figure against the light. Velvet darkness, no aura.

Holly scrambled to her feet in terror. *Enough*, cried a voice in her mind. *I've had enough of being frightened!*

The figure came towards her: a woman, birch-slim and as graceful as a dancer. She wore a black robe, not drab but as rich as raven feathers. Her hair, too, was a flowing black wing. Holly, despite her poor sight, saw every detail. A face like milky pearl, her eyes the violet of dusk lit by tiny stars.

And she looked curiously familiar... like a film actress. A veiled woman at the centre of a storm...

"Are you Holly Grey, Benedict's wife?" said the woman.

"Who are you?" Holly backed away.

"Lilith, though I have other names. I was with your husband and his brother a few hours ago."

"Oh God," said Holly. "No. You're the one who –"

"Who what?" Her voice was a razor cut.

"Who drove Lancelyn mad," Holly whispered. "The Dark Bride, the Black Goddess."

"Evil news travels fast, doesn't it?"

"He telephoned me." Holly wasn't obliged to explain anything to this apparition, but she couldn't help herself.

"I can only tell you that Lancelyn got what he deserved, because he drove *me* mad. Are you afraid of me?"

"Of course I am!" said Holly. "What do you want?" She backed up to the sofa, while Lilith moved around the room, looking at paintings, photographs, ornaments. She frightened Holly more than all other vampires together. She seemed a truly alien creature, the Devil's own. Sam merely watched, flicking the tip of his tail.

At the window she paused, looking outside. "What a lovely garden," she said. "It must be a picture in the summer, all those vigorous lush flowers and herbs climbing all over each other, all those insects and worms... I suppose you expend a great deal of loving care on your garden, don't you?"

"Yes," Holly said faintly, not understanding.

"But it's dead now, Holly. Look at the stalks, all dry and brown. Frost on the bare twigs. Your garden is cold and dead. I like it better that way."

Lilith turned, and the absolute certainty of death filled Holly. *I don't want to die!* Tears rose, but she gulped them down and said shakily, "I don't know how Ben and Lancelyn have upset you but I had nothing to do with it."

"Didn't you?" A meaningful pause. Then she said, "Your menfolk failed to impress me. I don't know why they imagined they could use me in their schemes. They've used you, too, haven't they?"

Holly was so taken aback by the question that she sat down before she collapsed. "What do you mean?"

"Think back." Lilith came towards her, her eyes huge like talismanic wheels. She seemed to know everything about Holly. "Didn't they exploit your talent to their own ends? They used you as secretary, housekeeper and medium, and you complied to keep a roof over your head. First Lancelyn, then Ben. Time and again they bled your mind of knowledge, then pushed you into the background. They excluded you from every affair that mattered! Didn't they?"

"Yes!" Holly cried. "How do you know?"

"You were no more than an appendage to them. You saw them as heroes but they were not. You still can't bear to accept it."

Lilith was unfurling, with painful clarity, all the truths Holly dared not admit. She held her breath until it hurt. At last she let go and said wretchedly, "What use is my being 'psychic'? I never foresaw this! I thought my visions were sharper than my eyesight, but they're not. I might as well be blind."

Lilith hissed, "Then why do you sit here crying for them?"

"Ben still loves me. So does Lancelyn!"

"Men like that only love themselves," Lilith said dismissively. "Shall I tell you how much Benedict loves you? Just before Lancelyn tried to rape me – to consummate a so-called 'marriage' to which I couldn't consent because I wasn't in my right mind – he promised Ben a bride of his own. Whether he meant to share me out like a temple whore, or find some other mystical creature, I dread to think, but Ben leapt at the idea. He didn't spare you a thought."

Her heart threw itself onto barbed wire. She cried, "You're lying!"

"No. He was seduced by Lancelyn's promises. Lancelyn said, 'Wouldn't you forsake your earthly wife for a bride like her?' and your husband answered, 'Oh God, yes, I'd do anything.' He was eager to discard you – and still you wail for him!"

"You're insane!" Holly cried, unable to stop her tears now.

"Perhaps – but I'm right. I can't stand to see your weakness! Hasn't he broken your heart? Hasn't he ruined your life with his ambition?"

"I need him, I have no one else."

"You have yourself!" Lilith said furiously. "That is all anyone has. Of all people, I should know!"

"It isn't enough for me!" Holly retorted.

"God, you make me angry." Lilith turned in a swirl of shadow. Her white hands came lashing out and seized Holly. Two ivory prongs rammed deep and vicious into her neck. In agony, Holly tried to fight free, but the woman squeezed her in snake coils. The cat leapt clear, making no attempt to protect her this time. They fell together onto the sofa-cushions. She felt the pressure of Lilith's body covering hers, rigid with unholy pleasure. A sensation of sick whiteness rolled through her and she began to choke.

Suddenly Lilith let her go and flung herself to the opposite end of the sofa. Holly, heaving frantically for breath, could only stare.

The vampire did not look sated or relaxed. Instead she sat stiffly, arms braced, eyes stretched wide as if in horror. And as Holly watched, a bead of blood appeared between her lips and travelled down her chin.

Lilith's lips closed on the reflux and she swallowed hard, eyes closing briefly. As the crimson bubble broke free, it did not so much fall as drift downwards, swelling as it went, its livid colour paling to vermilion. The bubble rolled over Lilith's knees and fell to the carpet, where it went on expanding, now the size of a kitten, a baby, a small child. Smoky shapes writhed inside the translucent sphere. It undulated, trying to put out limbs and a head. And at last it resolved into a human shape; a little girl, arms reaching out to Lilith, craving love and approval –

Holly recognised the child of blood and mist, but she had no breath to scream. The phantom child was *herself*.

The apparition went wobbling towards Lilith, at once nightmarish and pathetic. The vampire reached out and received it – not gently, but with clawed hands, her face death-white and ghastly. She slashed its throat, and as her fingernails penetrated its surface, the blood-child disintegrated without a sound. Nothing remained but a few blood-drops glistening on the carpet.

As the child vanished, Holly felt pain tearing her whole body – more grief than pain – then, in a flame of release, it was gone.

She looked up and saw the expression on Lilith's face. No cool, mocking beauty now. Lips parted, eyes stretched wide, she looked stricken. Holly thought, *She's as terrified as me! Why?*

A few seconds passed. Then the vampire reached out and grabbed Holly's hand as if for support. The hard grip made Holly wince.

"What was it?" Holly said, her voice failing. "What have you done to me?"

A gradual change came over the vampire. Her grip softened, and a faint pink blush coloured her face. She no longer seemed so demonic. And her face was lovely. A ballerina's face, perfectly shaped with infinitely expressive eyes. *I'd kill to be that beautiful*, Holly thought abstractedly...

And in that moment she noticed that she felt different. Calm, rising weightlessly above all her distress.

"Did you see a – a vision of a child?" Lilith asked softly. She touched the tip of her tongue to her lips, licking away red drops.

Holly nodded, and choked out a reply. "It was me."

Lilith looked closely at her, seemingly preoccupied with her own thoughts. "When I took your blood, I drew out the infant that you used to be... and I killed it."

"I don't understand."

"Neither do I. It didn't happen with Lancelyn, and you're only the second."

"You killed a frightened little girl!"

"Yes," Lilith said with intensity. "I killed her, Holly, but she had to die!" In a quieter voice she asked, "Has it driven you insane?"

"I don't think so. I feel different, that's all."

"This was different. Everything is new, I never know what to expect next…" Lilith was drawing away, mentally and physically. Lost in thought she stood up, becoming the dark goddess again. Holly knew she was leaving, and suddenly could not bear it.

"Don't go!" she exclaimed, jumping up.

"Why not? A few minutes ago, you were petrified of me."

"I'm not now. I – I want to know who you are."

Lilith's deep eyelids fell, making her eyes two black, feathery curves. She'd become distant in every sense. It seemed to Holly that although she was immortal, she was newborn; not yet in communion with her own nature.

"If you don't know, who does?" said Lilith. "You bemoan the limitations of your second sight, but you can't see because you won't let yourself. You've been hiding behind Ben and Lancelyn, as if you need their approval to exist, but you can't do so any longer. I won't let you. Don't you realise you helped to create me? Should I thank you or destroy you?"

Holly couldn't reply. She could only think of the Book, and her visions of the Dark Bride, of poor Maud, of Andreas pressing his cold lips to her face as he thanked her for the gift of Karl and Katerina. And of vampires coming to her through the dusk as if approaching an oracle…

It was true. Everything Ben and Lancelyn had done, her visions had been the catalyst. Good or evil? Both – but it didn't matter. The point was to take responsibility for her own visions from now on.

Lilith said more gently, "If I find out what I am, I'll come back and tell you." She took Holly's elbow. "Sit down. Rest. You won't die, and I don't think you'll go mad. But have I given you wisdom?"

Then she leaned forward and kissed Holly on the mouth. Startlingly warm and human, sending a flame of sensation through Holly – but as their lips touched, Lilith dissipated into the air. Holly was alone, staring at a strip of ashen light between the curtains.

Yet all her fear and anguish had gone.

A wonderful drowsiness overcame her, and she curled up on the sofa. The cat jumped up beside her. With one arm over him, his little rough tongue rasping her chin, she slept.

When she woke, it was to dazzling light and loud, excited voices. Sam had fled.

"Holly! Oh my God, look at the blood! Christ, is she alive?"

She shook herself awake, heart pounding. The electric lights were on and Ben was leaning over her, alarmed. Her shock passed and she sat up, easing her stiff limbs. Andreas was beside him but she only felt surprised to see him, not afraid. The drowsy calmness was still inside her and it felt delicious.

"Darling, thank goodness you're all right! I thought –"

"Your Black Goddess paid me a visit," Holly said languidly.

Benedict was aghast. "What?"

"She told me all about you, Ben. How eager you were to forsake me for a more thrilling companion?"

He looked stunned. He pushed his hair back from his creased brow, glanced at Andreas and back to her. "That's a lie!"

"Is it? I think she was telling the truth."

"Is this still about Maud?"

"No," Holly said, exasperated. "Maud was nothing. All she did was make me see I had good reason to doubt you! It's nothing to do with her, it's the way you've always treated me. You and Lancelyn both used me to get the knowledge you wanted, then pushed me aside, patronising me. You never took my warnings seriously – but it was all right to hypnotise me when I was distressed, to leave me half-mad with fear while you dealt with more important business. You only love me when it suits you. You and Lancelyn have used me for years, and I suffered it like the child I was. But I'm not a child any more."

From his expression, she knew that she'd hit the truth. He would never accept it; how many men dared view themselves in such a light? Ben was not deliberately wicked, but something demeaning that lacked all glamour: negligent and selfish.

"God Almighty," said Ben. "Don't go crazy on me, Holly. I've had all I can take."

"I am not crazy. I've never felt more reasonable. Lilith didn't hurt me. Quite the opposite."

"But the blood! And the marks on your neck! The state she left Lancelyn in – She could have killed you, anything!"

Holly retorted, "But you left me here at her mercy."

He gaped; she rose and pushed past him. In the mirror over the fireplace she looked at her sallow face, untidy hair, the faint crescent-bruises on her neck; she looked awful, but she'd never felt more clear-headed.

"I'm sorry," said Ben with genuine contrition. "I wasn't thinking straight. I had to go to Lancelyn, I had to…"

"There seem to be many things you've had to do at my expense."

Andreas looked over her shoulder; she met his lovely jade-green eyes in the mirror. "But we're back, Holly. Don't be angry, *mein Schatz*."

"What do you mean, 'we'?"

"Don't you want me to stay?" There was of note of surprise in the soft, seductive voice. "I have nowhere else to go… and I love you both."

Turning cold, she laughed in amazement. She saw Andreas exactly as he was: an alluring pearlescent shell whose charm masked a self-obsessed ego. A vampire in every sense, who would feed not only on their blood but on their minds, their relationship, their very selves.

"You can't possibly stay. Your kind of love would kill us."

She felt cool-headed as she spoke, untouched by Andreas's dismay. And for Ben, for the first time, she felt nothing. It was the most exhilarating sense of freedom she'd ever had. No, more than that. Her *first* sense of freedom!

His approval, Lancelyn's and even her parents' approval, no longer mattered.

"So," she said, turning to Ben, "after everything, you go meekly back to Lancelyn as if it were all a mistake? What did he offer, to make you cave in so easily? Some vague promise of bedding Lilith, and you were ready to abandon me?"

"It wasn't like that!"

"But you'd already deserted me, hadn't you, for something more important. You only came back because it went wrong! Well, you needn't go to the trouble of leaving me, dear. I'm leaving you."

His face dropped. Suddenly he was the child, and that woke her sympathy. "Don't say that. Holly, I'm sorry. I've been a total fool. I love you."

"We loved each other once," she said. "We almost had perfection. Until you staked it through the heart."

When Ben came to her and hugged her, she broke down. They both wept, because they knew there was no going back, and no reason to argue any more. Eventually Holly pulled away from him and walked blindly out of the room.

His voice followed her, distraught. "When will you come back?"

She paused. "Not before we're ready to stop acting like children," she said softly, "and live as grown-ups."

Later, she closed the front door behind her and stood on the step with her suitcase in one hand and Sam in a cat basket in the other. How sweet the air smelt, how vividly the frosted leaves and rooftiles glistened along the street. She had no idea where she was going. All she knew was that she was free.

Benedict stood disconsolate in the centre of the parlour as if rooted there. He couldn't believe she'd gone. Not Holly, who'd always been there for him.

That's the point, though, isn't it, he told himself grimly. *Because she was always there, I thought there was no limit to how badly I could behave. And she was right, our love has died... and I was too busy chasing Lancelyn even to notice.*

Holly, sketching in the Mediterranean sunlight... lying naked on the crystalline honey sand... "*I never want us to be apart, Holly. Never.*"

He would have changed everything to have her back.

He wanted to scream, to lash out at the cruel powers who'd taken his brother and his wife away. All he did was lean on the mantelpiece, put his head on his hands, and sob until his heart broke.

Andreas stood watching, saying nothing. How broodingly pale he looked... There seemed nothing angelic or inspiring about vampires now, only a shadowy-silver, thirsty darkness.

"That's it, then," Ben said eventually. "I really am alone. One minute I have everyone around me, everything happening. The next, deserted. Hard not to feel sorry for oneself."

Andreas unstoppered a decanter and poured a glass of whisky. "Sit down and drink this," he said. "I remember how comforting human remedies can be."

"I don't want a drink. It won't help."

But he let Andreas push him down and give him the glass. "You're not alone," Andreas said, sitting beside Ben, crowding him. "You need me now. We need each other. A sip... and a sip."

He pushed his fingers under Ben's collar, leaned in and nipped his flesh, taking only a sultry swallow or two of blood. *How horrible this is,* Ben thought, unable to stop him. *How lovely and how horrible.*

"Oh, God," Ben groaned, and closed his eyes.

There was a hard frost on top of the snow, and the world glittered.

Charlotte stood leaning on the balcony rail, aware of the cold as a pleasant needling as frost dissolved under her bare forearms, melted by the heat of stolen blood in her veins. It was so sweet to be home again... or should have been, but all pleasure was tempered by loss. Relief that Katerina was gone; then guilt, because of Karl's sorrow. And jealousy, regret, and relief again...

This was not an end. It was only a change.

The Alps stood white against the sapphire sky, and the forest was a cobwebbed fairyland. A huge moon floated above the Jungfrau. She imagined how Salzburg must look with the river frozen, the church spires and domes crisply sugared, ice crusted on the roof and windowsills of Ballet Janacek's almond-green house; the mountains flowing upwards in white veils all around.

Almost a month had passed since she and Karl had come home. Stefan had seen Rachel, Malik, John and Matthew, and reported that they'd gone their separate ways, dispersing into the ocean of humanity. But no one had seen Violette since the time by the railway line. Charlotte was haunted by premonitions that she would never see her again. A newspaper report brought her worst fears into being: "Mysterious disappearance of world-renowned ballerina." Madame Lenoir was believed to be suffering from exhaustion; no one knew her whereabouts.

Charlotte was doing her best to let Violette go, as a mother must let go of her child... but it was impossible not to think about her.

Where are you, what are you doing and feeling? I wish I could speak to you, Charlotte thought. *I wish you would tell me.*

Movement inside the house, a flitting shadow. Not Karl; Charlotte thought it was Ilona, arriving so subtly. Then the glass doors opened, and Violette stood in the doorway, outlined by light. She wore a long, heavily beaded black dress, a white coat trimmed with black fur, white silk lilies in her hair. A creature of crystal and velvet.

Charlotte laughed in pure amazement. "You must have read my thoughts," she said.

"I can read some people's. Not yours."

"I'm so glad to see you. I was afraid I never would." Charlotte gazed at her, not knowing whether to laugh or cry; simply overwhelmed by pleasure. "You look wonderful."

"You will be pleased to know I've gone back to the ballet. I told them I'd been away for a 'rest cure'." Violette's mouth curved in irony. "They were worried; God, if they only knew! Anyway, I came to give you back your money."

"What money?"

"The loan after *Dans le Jardin*. You can't have forgotten."

"I don't want it back."

"But I can pay it now. With profits." The flex of her mouth was almost a smile.

"Keep it," said Charlotte firmly. "Unless you no longer wish to consider me a business partner."

"What has business to do with anything?" Violette said, her voice low. "We will always be partners in something far darker, whether we like it or not."

Violette came forward, and Charlotte caught her hands, and they embraced. Violette bowed her head on Charlotte's shoulder; Charlotte softly folded her hand on the nape of her neck, relishing the glossy richness of her hair. And she longed to kiss the slender throat and taste the intoxicating liquor of Violette's blood... but the desire was sweeter for being held back.

"I'll continue to dance," said Violette. "It's still all I care about. And you were right, I can dance and dance and never grow tired."

"I'm so glad. But do your dancers realise that something has happened to you?"

"Of course not. I hide it, as vampires can."

"Aren't your doctors astounded at your recovery from an incurable condition?"

"What is my condition now, if not incurable?" Violette gave a soft laugh. "I shall not be seeing any more doctors, believe me."

"I'm so happy that you're staying with the ballet."

Violette drew back and looked at her with serious eyes. "Why? Does it ease your conscience, to know that you haven't wrecked my life and turned me into a perpetually murderous demon?"

"That isn't fair."

"Fair or not... The fact remains that I've changed. Yes, I can pretend to be the great Lenoir, and pretend very effectively, even to myself. But when the thirst comes, I am Lilith, and I don't stop being her until the thist is sated. And I hate it, Charlotte. I hate it."

Charlotte was silent, still holding her. Then she said, "But is it better than fading away into mortal sickness? Is it a price worth paying, so that you can still dance?"

"You want me to say yes, so you can stop feeling guilty."

"Don't play games with me!" Charlotte's hands tightened. "It doesn't matter a damn whether I feel guilty or not, to you or to me. You can't have it both ways. You consented, remember?"

A gleam of vulnerability in her face. "I had no idea it would be like this."

"Neither did I, nor Karl! No one ever knows, any more than we know what we are when we're born."

Violette fell quiet. "I don't blame you, Charlotte. You did your best for me. It's God I blame."

"There is no God!" Charlotte said, exasperated.

"How can you be so sure? Where did the three angels come from, if not from God? Why do I remember events that are meant to be myths?"

"Because the Crystal Ring gave birth to them! Man wasn't born from God's mind; God was born from ours. Raqia is swimming with myths and ideas that any vampire can absorb, especially if there's a resonance with our deepest fears or desires."

"How can you prove it? Does that make God real or not? The Crystal Ring, you say, is only a sea of dreams, yet it's real. And so am I, and so were the angels!"

"Are you still afraid of them?"

"No. They have no power over me. And I don't hate God, or whatever aspect of God seemed real to me, but I can't love a being that insisted on oppressing me. Yet I can't escape, can I? Whatever I do I am playing out a role. Lilith, Mother of Vampires," Violette said contemptuously. "Outcast forever, because there must always be a scapegoat."

"There is no God," Charlotte said helplessly. "You're doing this to yourself, for some reason. If together we try to work out why –"

"What, we'll all live happily ever after? I don't think so. But at least the Devil loved me."

"I don't think you have ever called me that before."

"I mean Lancelyn. I regret harming him. He asked for it, with his arrogance... but still, I'm sorry."

"Why?"

"Because he's the only one who ever saw me as more than I am... saw me as I *could* have been. He didn't dimiss me as a fearful demon, which is how Lilith is seen. He called me Dark Goddess, Cybele, Sophia of hidden wisdom... as if to say that darkness isn't simply evil, but a gateway leading to knowledge, good and bad. I needed his vision. But he's gone."

Charlotte had no idea how to reach Violette or console her. She barely understood her passions and griefs. How could she, or any vampire, cope with the wild spirit of Lilith?

"Do you need his approval to be what you are?"

"No, but I need guidance!" Violette said fiercely. "They call Lilith child-killer, but I must tell you this. An odd thing happened after I left you. I was compelled to find Benedict's wife Holly. I didn't even know where they lived, but something led me to her. I nearly killed her; she made me so angry in her submissive devotion to him! But when I drank from her, she neither died nor went mad. Yet *part* of her died... I believe it was her childlike dependency. I changed her. She sees more clearly, no longer cares blindly for men who have used her."

"And that includes her husband?" Charlotte was faintly shocked, out of her depth.

"I set her free. At what price I don't know. That's the point, the price may have been terrible. I'm not even sure why I had to do it. It was repulsive and painful for us both… but it had to be. I can only let Lilith guide me, you see. Right or wrong, she is all I have."

Tilting her head, she placed her hand along Charlotte's cheek and paused as if wanting to ask a question.

"What is it?" Charlotte said.

"You drank my blood, darling. Now I want to drink yours. It's only fair."

Charlotte saw malevolent sweetness in Violette's eyes. Apprehension filled her. *God, how do I cope with this monster I've made! How bizarre, to love her and yet fear her so deeply.* Out of love she wanted to say yes – but a deeper instinct said, *No. Don't let her.*

"Does it happen to vampires too?" said Charlotte.

"What?"

"You suggest you killed the infantile aspect of her, the part that needs reassurance and love. What would it do to me?"

"Perhaps it would make you stronger."

"Would it stop me loving Karl?"

"If that love makes you his prisoner – yes, it might."

Charlotte pulled away. "No. I don't want it to change."

"Do you enjoy the fear of losing him, the pain? Wouldn't you like to look at him and not care? All the pain, gone."

"No, never. The pleasure's worth the pain, Violette. It's all I live for."

"That is pathetic! It's woman's downfall, this idiocy! Why do you let him have this power over you, just because he has a beautiful face?"

"You don't understand! You've never known what passion is. I have the same hold over him! It's called love, Violette."

"Then you are both fools. I won't be a slave to anyone. To be free of such feelings is true freedom. How can you know unless you experience it?" More gently she went on, "I want to do this for you,

Charlotte. How strong is your love, if it can't survive my bite?"

"I'd rather not put it to the test."

Violette's face became cool, unreadable. "Well you'd better be careful, then. I'll come back for you and Karl."

"For heaven's sake, stop." Charlotte was scared now, trying not to show it. "I don't know you when you're like this. Why are you threatening us? Are you jealous?"

"Not at all. This torture you call passion isn't necessary."

"Ah. For my own good, is it?" Charlotte turned away, wanting to close herself away from Violette. "My family, friends, even Karl tried to do what they thought was 'best' for me, never understanding that what I needed was the worst."

"Lilith isn't good or kind," said Violette. "I might do it anyway, simply because your stubbornness infuriates me."

"The only advantage I ever had over you was that you were mortal and I was a vampire," Charlotte said, impassioned. "Now that's gone. You've become a goddess and I'm still just me. I want to say, 'Don't talk nonsense.' I want to hold you and tell you I love you; but all you would say is, 'You cannot patronise Lilith.' And you'd be right."

Without warning, Violette put her arms around Charlotte's neck. Charlotte felt her lips on her neck, shiveringly delicate; she waited for the eyeteeth to pierce her skin. *I won't pull away or let her see I'm afraid.*

"I will come back, Charlotte, because I love you. I'll take you away from Karl and you won't care, because you won't need him. One day. And you'll never see me coming."

The feel of Violette's lips remained on Charlotte's throat, metal-cool and sweet; but the dancer had gone.

She leaned on the balcony rail and dropped her head onto her arms.

Some time later – perhaps half an hour – Charlotte sensed Karl's presence in the house. She opened the doors and went in to him.

He read her expression. "*Liebling*, what's wrong?"

"Violette was here. She was so strange." She recounted their conversation. Karl listened gravely, stroking her face, his hand warm with his victim's blood.

When she finished, he said, "It probably pleases her to leave you in dread of some vague threat that means nothing. I refuse to live in fear of her, or anyone. Let her be; it's all we can do."

She sighed, releasing all her tension, leaning into his slender, familiar body. "Your tranquillity drives me mad sometimes, but I'm glad of it now. You've been so philosophical about Violette and Katerina. Your strength amazes me every time."

"I'm not that strong, beloved."

"You are. You seem calm, but I know how much it hurt you, Karl. Don't ever think I don't know."

"I lost Katerina before. It is harder the second time, because I thought it couldn't happen again. But what can I say? Katerina tried to kill you. Violette killed Katti, but she saved you. How can I hate Violette for that? Katti caused me the greatest grief, because I thought she had the grace to accept you – and she hadn't."

"But if I'd been in the *Weisskalt* for forty years, and come back to find you with someone else, I'd be tempted to kill them too."

"It's not the same. Katti and I were never lovers as you and I are."

"But still lovers," said Charlotte. "And this is the love of vampires, isn't it? Fierce, intolerant and possessive."

"When it should be the opposite," Karl said sadly. "Are you defending her now?"

"She can't defend herself."

He smiled at that. "You are more tolerant than ever she was."

"I can afford to be, now. Will you ever forgive me?"

"For what?"

"Violette."

"Dear heart. Do you need me to say yes, before you can forgive yourself? You were never unforgiven. I never dreamed you would meet someone like her, just as you never foresaw Katti's return... But there's no law to govern your behaviour as a vampire. Every transformation is different. I couldn't expect you to stay placidly at my side, a pliant *hausfrau* in an earthly marriage. I wouldn't want you to. No, our union was the exact opposite of a Christian wedding, was it not? So I hardly have any right to complain."

"But I wish you would!" Charlotte exclaimed. "I want you to be possessive; I'd die if you weren't! How badly must I behave before you say 'enough'?"

Karl slid his hand around the back of her neck, his fingertips hard. "I still think what you did to Violette was wrong. But why should I reject you for doing wrong? *Liebe Gott*, we do worse every day! If Katti's death taught me anything, it is that your life means more to me than the world. Charlotte, you feel far worse about Violette than I do. That is why I tell you to forgive yourself."

She bowed her head under the pressure of his fingers. Neither spoke for a time. The light glimmered on her dress; the colours she loved, plum and bronze and dull rose. She looked into Karl's face, luminous with the otherworld glow that had first drawn her to him. And the feeling between them changed subtly. The thorns of distrust were stripped away and only the rose remained.

"One thing we have both learned," he said, "and that's never to fear that other loves can destroy ours. They cannot."

"Let me explain." Charlotte felt tranquil now. "I never loved Violette as I love you. How could I? But she was everything I wasn't – I think that's what drew me to her. I was brought up to be a good girl." She shrugged, smiling. "So much for that. But until I met you I was passive, obedient, frightened of offending anyone. And I'm still the same in a way; afraid of upsetting you, in case I lost your love. But Violette – Lilith – was everything that I was not; headstrong, contrary, independent. That's why I needed her. Dark and light. Something floods us that makes us vampires, both from inside ourselves, and from the Crystal Ring. There was something more inside Violette that made her Lilith."

"And if that something is God?" Karl said darkly. "You find it easy to accept that Violette can become a figure from a creation myth, that vampires can appear to be angels. But it's a hard concept to grasp... unless Kristian was right and his God is real."

He turned away. His anxiety shocked her. "But Karl, it's perfectly simple," she said. "If the Crystal Ring is the human psyche – what are Lilith and her pursuing angels but extracts from it? What if there are certain humans, like Lancelyn and Violette, who aren't merely 'passengers' of the Crystal Ring, but can actually shape it?"

"In that case, if anything can exist in the Crystal Ring – so can God."

"Or a hundred gods! Does it matter?"

"Yes, if He is going to interfere. Here's another definition of our heightened existence: it is the tearing away of the layers between us and the divine."

"Don't," Charlotte said with feeling. "You sound like Kristian."

"God forbid," he said drily. She moved close to him and he put his arm around her. "Did you think our existence would be simple? That we'd be together and nothing would ever part us?"

"Yes, I fondly imagined it," she said. "And that's why, every time we're apart, I suffer this crucifying fear that I'll never see you again."

"Charlotte," he said softly, kissing her. "Our love burns because it never feels safe. But which do we prefer: the pain and the love, or nothing?"

"Oh, the pain," she said. "Always."

Karl kissed her hair and put her away from him, hands resting lightly on her shoulders. His eyes were grave. "Well, I must cause you a little more. There is something I must do."

"What is it?"

He shook his head, and for some reason she was chilled by thoughts of Kristian. "I won't be long, beloved. Don't worry."

But she was worried. "Don't go, Karl!"

"I must. Wait for me." He kissed her lips, and faded like a ghost, leaving empty air in her embrace. She hugged herself, bereft. And she knew he'd come back, knew it; but until then, she had this cruel emptiness to bear, an inner voice murmuring, *"But what if he doesn't come back? What if…"*

Karl once told me that in our immortality, the sin and the punishment are concurrent. That's why we still need love, to shield us from hell. In entering the Crystal Ring, a layer is torn away; we belong to no race, no family, no nation. This chalet isn't home; my only home is where Karl is, and until we're together I freeze quietly in hell.

One bite from Lilith, she thought, *and this pain would be over. I simply would not care. Is that what I want?*

Charlotte looked out of the window and saw a huge white owl rise up out of the forest and flap slowly towards the moon.

THE WHITE CRYSTAL MIRROR

There is no point in time, Karl thought, *no single action, no revelation that can make life perfect forever after. Destroy Kristian and there will be nothing to fear. Is that what I believed? Take Charlotte with me, and she will never love anyone else. Bring Katti back to life, and she will never die again.*

No.

There is always something else, and something else. It never ends.

He sped through the Crystal Ring, his form a slender black whip against the firmament. He sometimes thought of it as Raqia now. Lovely as a clouded sky at sunset, the realm was full of melting colours, more vivid than the sky of Earth. Almost fluid, almost solid. Always changing, like the flow of the mass psyche from which, perhaps, it emanated.

At this moment, Karl was certain of nothing.

He wanted an answer. But even if he found what he sought, it would be no answer at all.

When he arrived at Grey Crags, the house was deserted. The interior felt colder than winter; even the coloured glass in the windows was flatly gelid. A thin rime of dust lay over everything. Karl descended into the gloom of the gallery.

Nothing had been touched since the confrontation with the angels and Lilith. The automata were motionless, glassy-eyed and empty. The braziers were cold; the air stank of ash and metal. One censer lay askew where Karl had hurled it at Simon – and in the scattered cinders, undamaged by fire, barely even singed, rested the Book. *What would it actually take,* he wondered, *to destroy it?*

In grave contemplation, Karl bent down and picked up the tome, brushing ash from its leathery surface. Grey dust had sunk into the pores.

He was used to its greedy chill now, and could tolerate it. Perhaps he, like Charlotte, was not yet guilty enough to owe the Ledger of Death his life. He pressed his fingers to the cover and murmured, "Rasmila. Semangelof."

He felt the Crystal Ring whisper around him, as it had done when Ben had manipulated its fabric against Katti and the others. *Once the Crystal Ring has touched a place,* he thought, *perhaps it remains bonded there forever, absorbed into the walls... like the tunnel where we buried Kristian...*

He had a flash of memory: digging in darkness with Katerina anxiously watching, of finding bones and clothes but no skull...

Embracing the volume, Karl re-entered Raqia. Immediately, the Book's weight increased, dragging like an anchor. He'd wondered if the capricious Ring would accept the Book at all, yet it did. As he forged his way up the cloudy paths, it remained in his arms, a great layered slab of granite and lead.

Struggling, he climbed higher, letting the currents draw him upwards. The magnetic field of Earth was constant against the ever-swelling mountains, arching in auroral lines against the roiling violet slopes and the deep blue of infinity.

Chill breezes blew through his sable demon-form. He saw the layers of crystal cloud above him growing thinner as they rose towards the *Weisskalt*. It was rash to do this; it might be lethal. The absolute cold turned vampires to stone.

But it was a compulsion he must obey. A pilgrimage.

As he rose through snowy sheets of cloud, a winged form appeared beside him; a flow of deep colour, not quite black but a mingling of umber and ultramarine.

"Where are you going?" said the angel, Rasmila-Semangelof.

Strangely, Karl did not feel surprised to see her. It felt inevitable. "Why do you wish to know?"

"You summoned us, did you not?" Her voice was soothing. "You need our help."

"But where have you been?"

"Existing in the dusk, as vampires do."

Karl studied her. In her serenity and strength, she seemed a Hindu goddess. "Can I make you into an angel again, just by wishing it?"

"Almost anyone can – if they know how," she said, smiling. "We knew you would need us eventually."

"No doubt you know what I intend to do, then," he said aridly.

"Are you so afraid of it? Why not just –" she mimed shredding the Book.

"I'm not sure it can be destroyed, or even that it should be. It is subtle, but dangerous, as Lancelyn said, and I don't want it to fall into the wrong hands. The *Weisskalt* is the appropriate place for it. No one can reach it there. No human, at least."

"Let me take it, then," said the angel. "It can't hurt me." Her dark, cool fingers brushed his, but he didn't relinquish the volume.

"No. I'll carry it."

"Don't you trust us?" she said, amused.

Karl answered her with a candid lift of his eyebrows. "Is there any reason why I should?"

"You shouldn't go into the *Weisskalt* alone, you know; it is extremely dangerous,"

"I know. I've been there before, and survived."

"You may not be so lucky this time. But I'm coming with you to keep you warm."

"I don't want your blood."

"I'm not offering it."

As they ascended, he noticed the Ledger of Death growing lighter in his arms, and no colder now than the frost-clouds around them.

They broke through to the *Weisskalt*, a dazzling polar crust under the heatless platinum furnace of the sun. Semangelof brushed him with her filigreed wings, and he felt a shell of coolness fold round him; not warmth, but enough to protect him from the excoriating cold.

Then Karl saw the other two angels waiting; Fyodor-Sansenoy, shadowy white on whiteness, and Simon-Senoy, a blaze of ruby and gold flame. Rasmila-Semangelof was dark, edged with burning silver, an eclipsed sun.

Magnificent, like the ineffable visions of Michaelangelo. Karl wanted to weep with awe at their beauty – but he would not worship them. He wouldn't beg them for forgiveness or mercy. Never.

He still had a lingering suspicion that Kristian was not quite dead, and that these envoys were some terrifying emanation of his labyrinthine mind. He had not found the skull. The manor house tunnel had disgorged the rest of Kristian's remains, yes – but not his head, the throne of the intellect, the one part that could be revivified.

He said, "I had a feeling that I hadn't seen the last of you."

Senoy inclined his expressionless, beaten-gold face. "We have not finished our business with you, my friend."

"Why didn't you finish it before? And why desert Lancelyn? I thought you would have done your utmost to protect your protégé against Lilith."

"You misunderstand our nature," Senoy replied. "We did not *want* to abandon him, but we had no choice. Our only power was that which Lilith gave us; once she refused to submit, our hold on her was lost."

Karl smiled bitterly. "So, with Lancelyn and Lilith you made another mistake. You are not infallible."

"Only God is infallible," said Semangelof.

"Yet you still want to punish me for Kristian's death – even while admitting that you've made mistakes? Isn't it petty, to want revenge?"

"Not revenge; justice," said the white angel, Sansenoy. "If we peel the skin of warmth from around you, you will petrify in this waste. You will feel nothing as we tear you apart..."

And Karl tried not to care, tried to stare death impartially in the face as he had before... but inside, he was in despair. *I will come back*, he'd told Charlotte. He could not break that promise.

"But we won't," said Semangelof.

A moment of silence, pierced by the eerie moan of the ice-gale.

"Something worse, then?" Karl said quietly. "You could have devised no crueller punishment than turning me against my own friends. The God or Devil who rules you is an evil genius. But I warn you, if you try that again I will find a way to kill myself first." He gripped the Book to himself, as Charlotte had, like a shield. "I'd destroy you if I could; but at what cost? When I slew Kristian, you three came; I dread to think what would come to avenge *you*."

Senoy shook his head, like a patient priest. "My friend, there's no call for these bitter words. The punishment is over. You're right, we can't take revenge for Kristian, because his time is past. Something else is coming... and we have no power over it. None of us has."

"Not even God?" Karl said.

"Answer that question yourself."

"I suggest that God has only the power that men give him."

"But the Goddess, Karl," said Semangelof. "No one can control her."

"Do you mean Violette? Lilith?"

Senoy replied, "We can only command her if she will permit it, and she will not. We did our best, but we can do no more. We are not your enemies, Karl; we change according to what is required, and we're here now simply to warn you. We are no threat to your loved ones – but Lilith is."

"Have you nothing better to do than invent ways to frighten me?"

"This is a sincere warning. She is dangerous, Karl; she will take Charlotte away from you, and she will destroy your daughter if she can."

"Ilona?" Karl said, appalled. "What has she to do with this?"

"Violette believes Ilona was responsible for her father's insanity and death; thus, indirectly responsible for her fate in becoming Lilith. We tried to tame her through Lancelyn and failed. For as long as she roams free, Lilith will cause untold harm and sorrow."

"My God, are you telling me to stop her?"

"You have made it quite obvious that no one tells you what to do, Karl." Senoy gave a sardonic smile. "But one day you will *have* to stop her."

"And if I do, will it restore your power?"

"On the contrary, without Lilith we may cease to exist at all in this form. Don't you understand, we are above the lust for power?" He pointed at the Book. "Why do you clasp it like an instrument of suicide?"

"Because I can do so without dying," Karl said in a low voice. "Because I can stand in the *Weisskalt* and defy death."

And suddenly, quietly, he knew himself to be Simon's equal. The knowledge came without excitement or triumph. It didn't seem to matter greatly.

"But dare you read the Book?" said Simon. "Open it."

Karl tried, only to find that the Book had become a solid, seamless entity – curiously light in the *Weisskalt*, as if made of porous stone. "I cannot," he said thinly. "The Crystal Ring has transmuted it, as it changes us. It's only a concrete symbol of itself. Its words have no power here, nor do its ghosts."

Simon's mouth flickered with surprise. "But it can still reveal the Truth."

"Or a version of it." His tone was rational, but the same pangs of uncertainty kept clawing at him. *Is Kristian dead?*

"So remember where you leave it," said Fyodor-Sansenoy with a mocking edge. "You may need it again."

But Karl kept his gaze fixed on Simon's face as he dropped the Ledger into the snow. It landed without sound, white crystals spilling over its edges.

Simon and Fyodor seemed to be drifting imperceptibly away from him as he watched them. He knew he'd get no more answers from them; perhaps there was nothing more they could tell him.

But Semangelof was still by his shoulder. "You had another reason for coming here, did you not? You were looking for something else," said the slender dark angel who had once lovingly and treacherously given him her blood.

He wanted to say, *Yes, I came here looking for God, or a definite answer. I thought I could live without knowing the truth but it's impossible; you cannot leave without telling me the truth!* He held his tongue. It was useless. Either there was no answer, or the blinding light of truth would kill him... and no one was going to tell him anything.

"There it is," she said, pointing to the heaped snowdrift where the Book had fallen.

Instead his gaze was caught and swept up by sudden movement. The three angels were soaring up into heaven, vermilion-gold, white, velvet black. Leaping the boundary into the jewelled universe that no vampire could reach; soaring upwards until the incandescent heart of the sun swallowed them.

Karl felt the cool protective shield fall away. Merciless cold rushed in and clung to him. He looked across the shimmering white plain of the *Weisskalt*, veiled at its edges with ice-mist. He must leave at once, before glacial torpor overpowered him...

In the gilded whiteness at his feet, beside the Book, lay a skull.

It was in four pieces, a jigsaw waiting to be re-assembled. Gleaming curved bone, delicate fretted joints. He saw the splintered wounds where the axe had cleaved through it. Karl himself had made those wounds. And the huge eye-sockets, staring sightlessly at the cruel sun.

It still looked like Kristian. The blackness of his gaze watched eternally from those empty wells.

Kristian. That was his strength, that even in death he had projected a part of himself into the Crystal Ring, woken his sleeping flock, loosed the final wisp of his consciousness in contemplation of the single blazing eye of his God...

Unleashed Lilith and her angels.

Is there any part of your mind still in existence? Karl wondered. *I never knew anyone cling to life as you did! By God or whatever powers exist, I pray that you have gone at last.*

Or if you have found immortality in some other form... may you gain the wisdom to let go of your powers, and to let us go with them.

The Book had revealed one answer, at least. And the angels, despite everything, had given him that.

He picked up the pieces of the skull and flung them away from him in four directions, in echo of a magus evoking the guardians of north, south, east and west. The bones arced outwards and fell from his sight in soft white-diamond drifts of ice.

We weren't meant to compete with the gods, Kristian, my dear father. We weren't meant to live forever, yet still we try. Still we try.

ACKNOWLEDGEMENTS

As with *A Taste of Blood Wine*, the first in the Blood Wine Sequence, there are many friends old and new whom I'd like to thank for their help and support with this book and my writing in general over the years – too numerous to mention without the risk of leaving someone out!

Thank you in particular to my agents, John R Parker and John Berlyne, and to Cath Trechman, Natalie Laverick, Sophie Calder and all at Titan Books, not least their wonderful design team.

Special thanks are also due to many wonderful writers on female spirituality such as Barbara Black Koltuv, Starhawk, Riane Eisler, Merlin Stone, Barbara G Walker, Monica Sjoo and Barbara Mor, and others, for inspiring me with tales of Lilith... and opening my eyes to hidden worlds that we still rarely see.

And I am very grateful indeed to all the readers who have emailed me longing to know when the Blood Wine books would come back into print. It's been a long wait, so thank you for your patience!

ABOUT THE AUTHOR

Freda Warrington was born in Leicestershire, UK, where she now lives with her husband and mother. She has worked in medical illustration and graphic design, but her first love has always been writing. Her first novel *A Blackbird in Silver* was published in 1986, to be followed by many more, including *A Taste of Blood Wine*, *Dark Cathedral*, *The Amber Citadel*, and *The Court of the Midnight King* – a fantasy based on the life of the controversial King Richard III. As well as the *Blood Wine Sequence* for Titan Books, she writes the *Aetherial Tales* series for Tor. Her novel *Elfland* won a Romantic Times award for Best Fantasy Novel. She can be found at www.fredawarrington.com.

THE DARK BLOOD OF POPPIES
Freda Warrington

The ballerina Violette Lenoir has fallen victim to the bite of the vampire Charlotte. Her fire and energy have fuelled a terrifying change and a dreadful realisation; that Violette has become Lilith, the demon mother of all vampires.

Haunted both by what she has done and by Violette's dark sensuality, Charlotte and her immortal lover Karl are drawn towards the dancer and the terrible destiny that has fallen on her shoulders. But other, far more dangerous shadows are gathering around Violette. She poses a threat to the vampire Sebastian and the heirs of Kristian, and their plans to bring all of mankind under their dark wings.

Innocently embroiled in the endgame, courtesan extraordinaire Robyn Stafford finally meets her match as she is torn between the two ultimate lovers: Sebastian, and Violette...

Available October 2014

For more fantastic fiction, author events, exclusive excerpts,
competitions, limited editions and more

VISIT OUR WEBSITE
titanbooks.com

LIKE US ON FACEBOOK
facebook.com/titanbooks

FOLLOW US ON TWITTER
@TitanBooks

EMAIL US
readerfeedback@titanemail.com